A
STRUGGLE
for FAME

Author's Dedication

Dedicated to
Mrs Skirrow,
20, Sussex Gardens, Hyde Park,
In remembrance of staunch friendship
and tender sympathy.

A
STRUGGLE FOR FAME
A Novel

BY
MRS JH RIDDELL,
AUTHOR OF
'THE MYSTERY IN PALACE GARDENS,'
'GEORGE GEITH OF FEN COURT,' ETC.

IN THREE VOLUMES

A STRUGGLE *for* FAME

CHARLOTTE RIDDELL

With an Introduction by
Emma Dale

TRAMPPRESS

First published by Richard Bentley and Son in 1883

This edition published 2014 by
Tramp Press
www.tramp.ie

Introduction copyright © Emma Dale 2014

A CIP record for this title is
available from The British Library.

1 3 5 7 9 10 8 6 4 2

ISBN 978-0-9928170-4-6

Thank you for supporting independent publishing.

Set in 10.5pt on 13.7pt Minion by Marsha Swan
Printed by GraphyCems in Spain

'Irish stories are quite gone out'

Emma Dale

WHEN *A Struggle for Fame* was first published in 1883, Charlotte Eliza Lawson Cowen (1832–1906) was a widow in her fifties. She had moved from Ireland to England, been poor, rich and poor again. By the time she wrote *A Struggle*, Riddell was a heavily scarred publishing veteran, and this novel, charting the journey of two inexperienced and ambitious young people as they seek their fortunes, is her caustic semi-biographical masterpiece.

A Struggle for Fame is about harvesting wisdom and experience, about ambition born from necessity, and courageous endeavour in the face of extremely low expectations. Riddell's characters, Glenarva Westley and Bernard Kelly, begin this three-volume novel ambitious and wide-eyed, but are sculpted by a world-wise and savvy creator, who had knocked on the same doors and received the same rejections.

By the time of her death, Riddell had written and published more than fifty works of fiction. The majority of these were Victorian triple-deckers, a weighty form which remains the nemesis of many an English undergraduate, but an arrangement that was much loved by the library system and publishers of the nineteenth century. Books were still extremely expensive to print and buy, and splitting the novel in three allowed part one to generate both an audience and, importantly, profits to help pay for the publishing of parts two and three.

A Struggle for Fame came more than a quarter of a century after Riddell's first novel, *Zuriel's Grandchild*, was published by TC Newby, under the pseudonym

RV Sparling. It was a crushing failure. For her second novel, *The Moors and the Fens*, published by Smith and Elder in 1875, Riddell used the pen name FG Trafford, and it was under this moniker she saw her fame flourish. With Charles Skeet, Riddell published four novels, including *The Rich Husband* (1858) and *The World in the Church* (1862). With the Tinsley brothers she published an impressive thirteen novels, including *George Geith of Fen Court* (1864), *Maxwell Drewitt* (1865) and *Phemie Keller* (1866). Now enjoying great commercial success, Riddell was convinced to publish under her own name – in much the same way as our protagonist Glenarva finally publishes under her own married name, Mrs Lacere, at the behest of her publishers Felton and Laplash. Female authors commonly wrote under either male or gender-neutral pseudonyms in order to avoid being treated unfairly by the critics and reading public because of their sex, but Riddell was now prosperous enough to buck this trend. And so it was her married name, Mrs JH Riddell, under which *A Struggle for Fame* was published by Bentley.

Many of Riddell's publishers appear in some form in *A Struggle for Fame*. Vassett, for instance, is Charles Skeet, drawn by Riddell as a moderate man, comforted by small successes. The Tinsley brothers were the inspiration for Felton and Laplash, their dubious business practices and talent for showing-off hemming a genuine passion for literature and art.

Like our protagonist, Glenarva Westley, Riddell also travelled from Ireland to England with a sick parent, her mother. Her father, James Cowen, had been the High Sherriff of Co. Antrim, and four years after his death, in 1855, the impoverished mother and daughter moved to London, with Riddell hoping to earn a living from writing. Just as the character Glenarva's adored father died as she found success, so Riddell's mother passed away the same year her debut was published. Moreover, Glenarva and Riddell shared husbands who were unsuccessful in business, both using the proceeds from their writing to pay debts accrued by their significant others – debts that Riddell would continue to pay after Joseph Riddell's death in 1881. Academic Linda Peterson found that, in 1871, Joseph borrowed £285 using the copyright to a dozen of her works, including *George Geith of Fen Court*, as collateral, effectively mortgaging his wife's success.

When it was first published *A Struggle for Fame* was accused of being low-brow by contemporary reviewers. The three-volume novel was falling out of fashion in favour of shorter works that were less expensive to publish. Riddell also suffered under the weight of the myth of the female author as the homely genius, closeted away from the 'real' world but still able to 'imagine' their characters within it. Victorian society thrived on imagining all its women as placid, pure, devout and forgiving as Joan of Darby and Joan in Henry Woodfall's 1735 poem 'The Joys of Love Never Forgot'; what Glenarva especially dreads: 'a quiet, humdrum' sort of life.

In *A Struggle for Fame,* Riddell places her characters firmly within a realistic milieu, allowing Glenarva just a brush with Bohemianism, while Bernard walks the more shadowy and dangerous streets of London that she, as a respectable woman, cannot access. As the nineteenth century drew to a close, this idea of writing about the real nitty-gritty of life became increasingly popular, with Thomas Hardy's *Jude the Obscure* scandalising critics in 1895. However, Riddell's increasingly outmoded triple-decker form omitted her from this movement, and while she worked in *A Struggle for Fame* to express the changes she experienced in the publishing world, and to go some way to plot the wider changes which industrialisation brought to the social landscape, she herself said she was 'behind the age instead of abreast of it'. She became a victim of market forces, and the form that had brought her success wrought her demise; no one wanted to publish expensive, three-volume novels any more.

A Struggle for Fame excels in its characterisation, offering the reader personalities that are rounded, flawed and, even if not likeable, always knowable. She uses this ability to expose the realities of life in London for those considered to be on the outside of English society, the poor and, in this instance, the Irish immigrant. Riddell challenges how we perceive Ireland and 'Irishness' in *A Struggle for Fame.* She confronts what it means to be 'Irish' in England at a time when Ireland was still in the shadow of the famine and bubbling with the struggle for independence. Because this novel is located in England, Riddell can volley between perspectives, offering English views on Irishness; Irish views on Irishness; and a plurality of diasporic Irishness, where origins are amplified and exaggerated, or muted by distance, time and shame. Bernard, for example, is wont in the early stages of the novel to amplify his Irishness, wearing it like a badge of honour, playing up stereotypes with a sharp wit, which also undermines them. As the novel reaches its conclusion his origins are used to publically embarrass him. Bernard's reluctant patron, Mat Donagh, is unlikeably duplicitous in his negation of his Irishness in favour of a dandyish performance of the English intellectual.

These issues of Irishness are still being fiercely debated in academia, where Irish fiction is scrutinised for its willingness to exploit the drunken, verbose, economically poor but intellectually rich, threadbare and cheap representations of Ireland and Irishness. Riddell offers a still relevant insight into how Ireland is viewed from both the inside and outside, showing how Irishness is constructed, marketed and/or negated for economic or artistic profit. It is not always flattering.

A Struggle for Fame adds to the debate with unusual freshness for a Victorian novel. We see the powerful make judgements based upon race, class and gender in order to protect their positions. We can see that the sneering glances and deriding comments aimed at Glenarva and Bernard are shots not at the individual, but at the body of people they are seen to represent.

In *A Struggle for Fame* Riddell allows her characters to eloquently express the caged freedoms offered by nationality and gender, as well as the strident social conventions and belittling prejudices of the times, allowing us to ask an important question: How much has really changed for the latest generation of young Irish men and women leaving a country that fails to support their personal and economic ambitions? Equality and choice are the real struggles at the centre of this wonderful novel.

VOLUME I

Contents

Chapter I

PILGRIMS

THE 17TH OCTOBER, 1854; a dull, cloudy morning, a mist of rain making every-thing damp and uncomfortable, a raw wind blowing off the Channel, Morecambe Bay looking its dreariest, the Irish steamer, very late, just in, laden with passen-gers and cattle; the former in time to hear the London express had gone, the latter frightened and troublesome, already giving assurance – subsequently, no doubt, amply fulfilled – that the work of debarkation would not be light or easy. A Babel of voices, ropes tripping up unwary passers-by, chains rattling, beasts bellowing, sheep bleating, drovers swearing, sailors shouting, porters shouldering luggage, a good column of black smoke issuing from the funnel, the deck wet and slippery, a smell of fried fish mingling with odours of bilge-water, coffee, and tar, rushing up the cabin stairs, men and women with all the colour washed out of their faces looking mournfully at the weather: altogether a miserable scene, which appeared the more wretched because on the previous afternoon the sun had been shining brightly in Ireland, and it seemed as if in England the sun never meant to shine again.

Standing a little out of the confusion, looking at the spectacle presented with strange and unaccustomed eyes, were two passengers, whose worldly position it would have been difficult at the first glance to decide.

Judging from their features and carriage, they seemed to belong to the better class; but their dress betokened narrow means, and their manner was that of persons who shrank from ordinary contact with their fellows. There was an

3

indescribable air of holding themselves apart, which seemed to proceed more from the fear of being rudely touched or intruded on than from any feeling of pride. They appeared interested, although half frightened, and they cast looks upon the land that lay close beside the steamer, which showed they had not crossed to it for a mere visit, but were anxious to forecast what of evil or of good the country which now held out so chilly a welcome might have in store.

Not belonging to them, but travelling quite alone, was a young man, who scrutinised the strange shore with a keener and more impatient regard. He was better clad than either of his fellow-passengers; he owned an assured self-reliance they apparently lacked; he seemed more fit to engage in the battle of life, and yet he looked restless and anxious, perhaps because he was eager for the fray to begin, or possibly because at heart, so far as his own future was concerned, he felt doubtful of its issue.

At an earlier period of the morning, while the vessel was still creaking and groaning towards her destination, he had exchanged a few words with one of the two persons mentioned, and, having done so, he at all events entertained no doubts concerning the social position of the father and daughter, for in that relation they stood to one another.

Mr Bernard Kelly instantly put them down in his own mind as what he called 'has beens,' and considering the state of popular feeling in Ireland at that time concerning the numerous class thus tersely indicated, he was wonderfully little impressed by his conviction; the fact being that he had decided to 'cut Ireland,' because he was heartily tired of everything in the country – turf, poor gentry, bacon, and the very few chances it offered to a 'clever fellow like himself.' Mr Kelly was a very clever fellow, and he was going to London to see whether the metropolis would greet him with effusion. Morecambe seemed singularly indifferent to his advent, which perhaps damped his expectations a little, and caused him to throw a certain amount of cordiality into the remark he made as he passed Mr and Miss Westley on his way to the narrow gangway which, placed high above the terrified cattle, led to the landing-place.

Mr Westley's answer was courteous, but not familiar. He knew the rank from which Mr Kelly had sprung. He understood it was he, and such as he, who got on, and pushed themselves forward into the front rows of life. He felt content such things should be, but as yet he could not quite fraternise with a person he considered so completely below himself.

Mr Kelly, being unembarrassed by any luggage save a carpet-bag which he carried in his hand, made his way ashore as soon as it was possible for him to do so; but Mr Westley, who could not boast good health, and who dreaded a crush, and who owned, moreover, under the tarpaulins a considerable amount of baggage, the moment he heard the express had gone, drew his daughter to a seat, and taking his place beside her, would have waited there calmly for an hour or two perhaps, had not the mate suggested it might be well for him to 'keep an eye on his boxes.'

Poor Mr Westley, who had never during the whole course of his sixty years of life been able to keep an eye on anything, rose and proceeded limply to act upon this hint, but he was swayed hither and thither by loud-talking men and shrill-voiced women; his mild expostulations were drowned amidst the noise caused by frenzied passengers clamouring for portmanteaus, trunks, hampers, packages, sacks, and he was glad speedily to retreat upon the word of a porter who, in the dear familiar accents of a land left behind for ever, assured him: 'There's no call for ye to stand here to be shoved about, yer honour. Troth and faith, ye may trust me to see to yer boxes myself. You'll find them and me at the station sure enough, if ye walk up there quietly when the throng clears a bit.'

No advice could have been given more in accordance with Mr Westley's own inclinations. There never existed a person who so cordially detested bustle and turmoil as this tall, worn-looking gentleman, upon whose figure his coat hung far too loosely, and who, moving slowly back to the bench where he had left his daughter, sank down beside her as though the slight exertion of moving across the deck was too much for his strength.

'Tired, papa?' asked his daughter. 'No – oh no,' he answered, but his tone belied his words; 'only I shall be glad when we can get out of this smoke, and confusion, and din.'

'We could land now if you like.'

'There is no hurry,' he replied; 'we had better wait till the luggage is out.'

'What a pity the express is gone!'

'Yes. I wonder when there will be another train.'

'There is one going in about three-quarters of an hour,' volunteered the steward, who chanced to be close at hand, 'but you'll be just as soon if you wait till the afternoon. This one stops at all stations, and the next goes right through. They would make you and the young lady comfortable up at the hotel.'

'Thank you,' said Mr Westley, but he did not tell the man he meant to follow his advice.

'Your luggage would be quite safe at the station, sir,' added the steward, 'and then the young lady needn't be hurried over her breakfast.' He knew these passengers had declined to partake of that meal on board the boat.

'And how much later do you say we should be getting into London?'

The steward had not said they would be at all later, and now repeated that statement, with the addition that although he could not speak from his own knowledge, he believed they would reach London sooner. As a rule, he explained, passengers who failed to catch the first express – and from his manner Mr Westley imagined such failure to be generally the case – preferred waiting for the second.

'I think we had better be moving now, dear,' remarked Mr Westley to his daughter, seeing that the way was at length clear.

Civil to the last, the steward followed them with a cloak and umbrella, which Miss Westley took from him when they reached the shore.

'It is only a step to the station,' he explained, 'and after you've seen to your luggage, anyone will tell you which is the hotel. Good morning, sir, and I wish you a pleasant journey.'

'Thank you,' answered Mr Westley, once again. In his best days he had never been a man flush of words, brimming over with talk; and now, when those days were all behind, speech did not flow very readily from his lips.

Nevertheless, indeed all the more perhaps, the steward felt no doubt on his mind as to what he 'had been,' and for a minute he stood looking after father and daughter, with a mingled expression of wonder and compassion in his eyes.

'Lord help them!' he said to the mate, who chanced to come up at the time. 'They're no better than a couple of children.'

'Do you know who that is? asked the captain from the paddlebox. He had lifted his cap as the passengers left the boat.

'No,' answered the mate, 'and yet I think I have seen him before. Who is he?'

'Mr Westley of Glenarva.'

'You don't say so!'

'Yes, I do.'

Meanwhile Mr Westley of Glenarva and his daughter were pacing slowly towards the railway station.

'You must have some breakfast, dear,' he said.

'Oh no, papa; but you –'

'I could not eat anything.'

They had a quantity of luggage, which was, however, all on the platform in charge of the porter who had passed his word for its safety. As the man reckoned up the number of bags, boxes, trunks, and baskets, Mr Westley glanced at the pile and sighed. He was marvelling, not without reason, what in the world they were to do with all their things when they got them to London.

'I think,' observed Mr Westley to his daughter, as they stood surveying their worldly goods, 'we had better go on by the first train. It will save a great deal of trouble.'

'I am sure it will.'

'We may just as well be sitting in the carriage as in the hotel.'

'We shall be far more comfortable.'

'But I do not like the idea of your not having any breakfast.'

'I have plenty of biscuits and apples in my bag; but I wish you would take even a cup of tea.'

'I could not, dear; later on, perhaps.'

And then they walked along the platform, and peered into the different compartments; and at length, having settled upon one near the middle of the train, put in their wraps and small parcels, after which Mr Westley, relieved, went to see their luggage placed in the van.

'You are not going by this train, sir, are you? asked one of the officials, after he had looked at Mr Westley's tickets; 'you'll be just as soon if you wait for the express.'

'We may as well be getting on,' answered Mr Westley.

'That's as you like, of course, sir.'

'Now, papa,' said his daughter, when he returned to their compartment, 'do take a biscuit.'

More to please her, apparently, than from any desire to eat, he took the biscuit, and drank a little wine and water.

'I shan't want anything else till we get to London,' he remarked, with a smile which lit up a face that had once been strikingly handsome.

'I wish we were there,' answered the girl wistfully.

'Upon the whole, Glen,' observed her father, 'I am afraid we have been penny wise and pound foolish. We had better, I fancy, have paid a little more and gone by the usual route.'

'Why, papa!' – Miss Westley's surprise at the proposition advanced was beautiful to behold – 'We shall travel first-class for less than second would have cost the other way.'

'There is something in that,' he agreed, glancing round at the cushioned seats, which to the eye of modern extravagance would have seemed very poor and uncomfortable; 'but only consider the time of night it will be before we get into London.'

'The Fleetwood boat might have been late, too,' she insisted.

'It might,' said Mr Westley; but his tone seemed to imply his convictions were opposed to her surmise.

'I hope we shall have the carriage all to ourselves,' observed his daughter.

'Most likely we shall. The steward said through passengers generally waited for the express.'

'For my part, I feel sure the slow train will be the pleasantest. We shall have time to see more of the country. What do you say, papa?'

'I think I will defer giving my opinion till we arrive at Euston,' answered her father, leaning back in his place.

'I am so glad we decided to come first class,' exclaimed the girl, observing how naturally he laid his head against the well-padded partition, and then she turned and looked out at the station for a minute or two. She was thinking, perhaps, how little of comfort or pleasure or luxury life had held for him for many a year.

7

Mr Westley of Glenarva! Yes, he was that still, and would be nominally till he died; but for all the good Glenarva was doing him, or was ever likely to do him, he might have been Mr Westley of any other place. In the whole of Ulster there were few more beautiful domains than Glenarva. Mr Westley himself believed, and there were others of the same opinion, that no estate of the same size could have been found to equal it. Neither the memory of man nor local history knew of a time when a Westley did not own Glenarva. Its gates had opened wide to receive heirs of all ages and all temperaments. The nondescript animals surmounting the pillars which guarded the entrance to the long, dark avenue, could, had voice been given them, have told of all sorts of funerals that wound slowly up the side of the hill, and then dipped behind its crest and disappeared, as one Westley after another had compulsorily sought a more enduring dwelling than Glenarva. The spendthrift, the miser, the keen politician, the man of pleasure, the recluse, the eager sportsman, the gallant officer, the bronzed sailor, had all in turn entered into their patrimony, and had each, after few years or many, been borne out from it to the family vault in a ruined church, which lay desolate, surrounded by the lonely moors inland. And now there was a Westley of Glenarva who knew the gates of his old home would never, living or dead, swing open again for him. He had possessed, and he had lost; his chance had been given him, and he had misused it. Strangers resided now in the familiar house; their servants brought their horses round for them to mount; for them the gardens yielded their produce; for them the trees produced their fruit, and the crocuses peeped forth in the spring, and the summer roses bloomed, and mignonette and heliotrope mingled with the sad odours of the autumnal days. His heritage was to all intents and purposes gone, not through vice, but folly; when he died another Westley would take possession, one who had sons to inherit, instead of his daughter, the only child ever born to him; the slim, unformed, shabbily dressed girl, whose heart was so full of pity for her father's trouble that it often felt fit to break.

There was something about Mr Westley, indeed, which evoked an extraordinary amount of sympathy even from strangers; how much more, then, of sorrowful devotion from his daughter, whose passionate love for him had been so far the love of her life.

'If no one else comes in,' she said, after that pause, 'you will be able to have a long sleep, papa. I dare say you had none at all on board the steamer.'

'Not much,' he answered.

'Well, you must have some now,' she exclaimed, taking up a plaid and laying it over his knees.

'What, this minute, Glen?' remonstrated her father. 'Give me till the train starts, at any rate. What an impetuous child you are!'

'Glen,' as he called her, smiled, while a little suspicious moisture still hung upon her eyelashes. Whatever her sins in the way of impetuosity, no one would have thought of accusing Mr Westley of a similar error.

'I never was in a hurry but once that I can remember,' he often declared; 'and it proved once too often.'

'Was that to be married?' sometimes ventured a listener.

And then Mr Westley's answer was invariably a severe – 'No, sir, it was not.'

'Now they are shutting the doors,' remarked his daughter; 'so we may consider ourselves safe.'

But no. Just as she spoke, a passenger, carpet-bag in hand, came hurriedly along the platform. The whistle sounded. 'Here you are, sir,' said a porter, reopening a door he had just slammed. The new arrival jumped in, and Mr Westley, unclosing his eyes, which he had shut in horror of the din, recognised his fellow traveller of the steamboat.

'I did not intend to shave it so close,' observed that individual breathlessly.

'You are only just in time,' said Mr Westley

'And had to run sharp for it, too,' was the answer. 'But I saw no fun in waiting for the express.'

If any remark occurred to Mr Westley with reference to this statement he did not make it. He closed his eyes again as if excessively tired, whilst the young man, who was to journey in the same compartment to London, opened his bag, and, as is the fashion of many travellers, began sedulously searching among its contents for something which, again in unconscious emulation of other travellers, he failed to find.

Whilst he was engaged in the prosecution of this ever-hopeless task, Miss Westley looked at him curiously.

She saw a man of four- or five-and-twenty, with dark brown hair, which had probably at some former period been red, as his whiskers were still. He wore no beard or moustache; his eyes were of that yellowish-hazel which so often accompanies hair originally red. His face was rather pallid, and its expression inscrutable. His features were fairly good, though in no way noticeable. His topcoat was of an – it is not going too far to say – offensive shade of brown, and all his garments lacked the stamp of even such fashion as the provincial towns then conferred. They had evidently been made strongly and slowly, out of abundant material, by some too-honest village tailor. His boots were new and clumsy, his hat new also, and he looked, as Miss Westley's dear friends, the vicar's sons, would have said, 'just caught.'

As the idea occurred to her, an irresistible smile wandered, like the rays of a wintry sun, over Miss Westley's face, and she turned it aside.

At that moment the young man, having ended his vain exploration, closed and locked his bag, and looked at her.

He saw what he mentally termed 'a slip of a girl', whose features while in repose all seemed out of proportion. Her mouth was too wide, her eyes too large, her nose too short, her hair too sunny for the dark heavy lashes that lay on her pale cheeks. Her figure was perfectly unformed, and set off to no advantage by her dress – an English poplin of a dark blue colour; an old silk jacket, too thin by far for the time of year; a brown straw bonnet trimmed with brown ribbons and lined with dark blue silk; a pair of old kid gloves, and a pair of new cashmere boots, goloshed round, and laced up the side, as was then universal.

'She's not much to look at,' thought Mr Bernard Kelly, candidly critical; and he was right, though any one of the six sons in whom the Vicar of Ballyshane rejoiced would have said: 'Why, Glen Westley is the prettiest girl I ever saw. I don't believe there is a prettier anywhere.' But they knew a different Glen Westley – a laughing girl, with bright merry eyes, hair tossed by mountain breezes, red parted lips, showing white, even teeth; cheeks rosy with exercise – a girl springing from rock to rock, riding over the hills, bending hither and thither to escape a shower of salt sea-spray. Not this Glen – oh no. That other who had run races with them on the sands, and gathered shells with them on the shore, and galloped with them across the moors, and burnt nuts with them at Hallowe'en, and dyed eggs with them at Easter, and eaten gingerbread nuts purchased at the nearest fair, and gone surreptitiously with them to penny shows, and been for years the companion and delight of their young lives; where was she? Gone, like last spring's flowers. They would never see her again while suns rose and moons waned forever.

Most truly the Miss Westley upon whom Mr Bernard Kelly bent his speculative gaze was not much to look at. She was in a very transition state; further, she felt at the moment most miserable. The wretched weather, the tardy landing, the look of utter weariness on her father's face, the feeling that she was in a totally strange country, to which, perhaps, they ought not to have come; the want of a proper night's rest, the absence of any great store of physical strength on which to fall back when an extra demand was made upon her energies, all conspired, not exactly to make her regret having left Ireland, but to doubt whether she had not proved in this, as in other matters of minor import, too impetuous.

After she had done a thing – but never before – Glen always believed she had been too hasty; she felt sure she was right till a thing was beyond recall; then she began to doubt. She experienced no fear of her own powers while retreat was possible; but when once it was too late to draw back, she was seized with dreadful misgivings, which hiding within her own breast, she had acquired the character of being a most resolute and determined young person, possessed of a courage beyond her years, and an obstinacy which would some day land her in a position of considerable difficulty.

When she was a child it had been freely prophesied she 'would break every bone in her body,' be brought home 'maimed for life,' share the fate the country-side fully believed in store for the Vicar's sons, of being drowned and borne out to sea; and now she had 'done growing' and settled down into a 'young lady,' it did seem hard to those who had loved and trembled for her personal safety, that she should turn so wilful in other ways, and give her poor father no rest till he left a place in which he was at least known and respected, and drag him off to London, where he might as well be nobody. It was not generally known that Mr Westley was as anxious to leave Ireland as his daughter, but those who were acquainted with him thoroughly understood that but for 'Miss Glen' he would never have stirred a step. Of that fact Miss Glen herself was as fully persuaded as any of her Job's comforters could have been; and what she sat considering as the train sped south was, whether it had been really wrong of her to urge him to adopt the course he said he believed was desirable. She had been very earnest in pressing matters on; she had refused to listen to the words of wisdom of the countryside; she had turned a deaf ear to all remonstrance and to all lamentation, and yet when the final parting came, and she realised that she would never look on sea or land, on green hill or kindly face with the same eyes again forever, she fairly broke down, and her last memory of Ballyshane was that she could not see the stumpy church tower, or the grand headlands, or Shane's Bay, or the friends who came to see them off, or the children at the cabin doors, or the pigs grunting on the roadside, or the donkey that at that moment lifted up his voice, or the white goats standing on their hind-legs to nibble the hedges, or the ducks in the stream, by reason of a mist of tears that blurred every familiar object.

And it was of all these things left behind forever, and the unseen, unknown future which now seemed so terrible lying before, Miss Westley chanced to be thinking, while Mr Kelly was mentally deciding, 'Your face will never make your fortune, my dear.'

At that moment the young lady, whose matrimonial charms were thus so summarily disposed of, moved her hands towards a bundle of wraps lying on the opposite seat.

Watchfully gallant, Mr Kelly anticipated her wish, and while he was unfas-tening the straps remarked, in a light and airy manner:

'Old gentleman seems tired!'

Miss Westley stared at the speaker. She had not been accustomed to hear her father alluded to as 'old,' and the word struck her like a blow. It was a question, however, she could not well argue, and so contented herself with answering:

'He is not very strong.'

'He does not look strong, at any rate,' was the too-ready reply. 'Not much used to travelling either, I suppose,' continued Mr Kelly volubly.

Now this was a point on which Miss Westley could have held forth with advantage. 'Not used to travelling!' She felt inclined to explain to this irreverent young man her father had seen more in one month than he probably would ever see in his whole life.

All the recollections of foreign towns and scenery, which had made the romance and pleasure of long winter evenings, while the waves of the Atlantic came thundering in on the coast, and the wind was sweeping across barren moors and lonely hills, recurred in an instant to her memory. She could have told him stories by the hour, the scenes of which were laid in Paris, Rome, Madrid, and other towns, the very names of which he had most likely never heard; but she refrained. She only smiled faintly, and left Mr Bernard Kelly with the impression that even the elder of his fellow-passengers had never been more than a dozen miles from home in his life.

'Going through, miss?' asked Mr Kelly, after a short pause.

'We are going to London,' answered the girl; and there was a little hesitation in her tone, as if she felt reluctant to confess the fact.

'That is what they call "going through" here,' explained Mr Kelly, in kindly consideration for her ignorance. 'Shall you make a long stay?'

'I do not know; it depends upon – that is, most probably we shall stay there altogether.'

'That is what I mean to do,' said her fellow passenger; 'no place like London'; and he drummed an air with his fingers on the arm of his seat, after having fortified his courage with this general declaration, which has probably wrought more disappointment individually to thousands than will ever be known on earth.

'You are fond of London, then?' Miss Westley observed tentatively. It was the first remark she had volunteered.

'Yes, as fond as I can be of any place I have never seen.'

'Oh, you have never been there then?'

'No; but I have an uncle there. He is a Magistrate or something.'

'Is he?'

'Yes. He has done well for himself, I can tell you. He might have stayed in Ireland long enough before he could have got up as high as he has. He lives some place near Cavendish Square, if you know where that is.'

'I have never been to London.'

'No; but you might be acquainted with somebody who has. And so you think you will stop in England altogether?'

'It is most likely.'

'I dare say you were glad enough to leave Ireland?'

'No; I was very, very sorry.'

'Were you, now? That is more than I can say.'

'Perhaps you were not leaving any friends behind?'

'Oh, as for that, I was leaving my father and mother, and sisters, and brothers, and cousins, and aunts, and uncles.'

'I wonder how you could do it.'

'Do you? Now, my wonder is why I stayed among them so long. If he has any stuff in him, a man wants to get on in the world, and what is the use of stopping where there is no opening of any sort, kind, or description?'

This question was so identical with that she had herself propounded to her father, Miss Westley felt she could not possibly negative it.

'We are not having a very fine day for our journey, are we?' said Mr Kelly, after a pause. 'May I look at one of your books? It will serve to pass the time,' he explained, in unconscious derogation of his companion's conversational powers to do so.

'I am afraid you will not find much in them to amuse you,' answered Miss Westley; 'they are only some odd volumes that were forgotten till after our boxes were corded. Falconer's *Shipwreck*, Thomson's *Seasons*, Moore's *Melodies* –'

'You seem to be uncommonly fond of poetry,' observed Mr Kelly.

'I used to be,' answered Miss Westley, speaking as if from the heights of years.

'It is a taste we grow out of as we get old,' remarked her auditor, with a suspicious twinkle in his eyes.

'Yes, I think so,' agreed the young lady simply.

The long journey dragged slowly on. At almost every petty station the train seemed to stop. The travellers stayed a considerable time at Preston; they were shunted at Crewe; they dawdled at the outskirts of towns, and waited where they could contemplate turnip fields at their leisure. Mr Westley slept and woke again to find himself but little nearer London. At Crewe some variety promised to be imparted to the proceedings by the entrance of a lady who was handed into the compartment by a meek-looking clergyman, with whom, through the open window, she remained in earnest conversation till the train again started; but all Mr Kelly's hopes were dashed to the ground when he beheld her produce Berlin wools and an ivory needle, and commence to crochet a shawl.

After she took her seat, that gentleman had no eyes for Miss Westley. The newcomer was about the same age as himself; richly dressed, self-possessed of manner, comely of person; her wavy black hair, her dark eyes, her round cheeks, her regular features, her utter absorption in her work, her indifference to the country they were passing through, the way in which she totally ignored the presence of any other person in the compartment besides herself, produced a deep impression on Mr Kelly.

He imagined she must be some great lady; that she was rich – being English – went, in his idea, without saying. He watched the progress made by those busy white fingers, on which rings glittered, with a fascination which did not fail to produce its effect upon Miss Westley. Upon the whole it was a relief to everyone except the lady, when at Stafford another passenger joined their company: this time a short, thin, active gentleman of about thirty, evidently of an inquiring turn of mind, for even while settling himself in the corner seat Mr Kelly vacated for his benefit, he threw a comprehensive look over the occupants of the compartment, bestowing on each a swift scrutinizing glance, which Mr Westley lazily returned, but that made his daughter feel somewhat abashed.

'Thank you; so much obliged,' he said to Mr Kelly, with an ineffable smile, as that gentleman cleared away Falconer, Thomson, and Moore. 'Do not let me disturb you; it is very good of you, I am sure', and then he dropped down opposite the lady, and picked up her wool, which he had swept down, and bowed and smiled, and received a gracious inclination of the head in acknowledgment.

'Miserable day,' he remarked to the company generally.

'And it gets worse,' answered Mr Kelly, accepting the observation as a delicate personal attention to himself.

'The weather always is bad when one goes to London;' just as if, thought Mr Kelly, he was travelling backwards and forwards three times a week. But he said nothing audibly; and feeling, perhaps, that he had done his duty, and broken the ice in an agreeable manner, the stranger took some papers from his left-hand breast pocket, and began to look them over. He could not make much of them, however, for already darkness was beginning to close in; so, putting each carefully back one by one in his pocket-book, he asked Mr Kelly, in a light and cheerful manner:

'And how did you leave Ireland?'

'By the Belfast boat,' answered Mr Kelly, taking the question literally. He was deeply offended; the stranger's English accent seemed in itself an insult, and that he could possibly from his own speech be known for an Irishman assumed the form of a grievance too great to endure.

'Oh, I did not mean that exactly,' said the other, confident his conversation was proving productive of the most unqualified pleasure. 'What is the position of the country? What is the state of popular feeling?'

'About as usual,' was the reply. 'The people are not satisfied; they never have been, and they never will be.'

'Dear me, that is very serious.'

'I don't see why they should,' went on Mr Kelly argumentatively. 'Perhaps if the English lived on potatoes and salt they might not be satisfied either.'

'But why do the Irish live on potatoes and salt?' inquired the gentleman in search of information. Mr Kelly, looking at him, decided he was a man who would go on asking questions till he dropped down dead.

'Because they can't get anything else; at least, now they can only get meal and salt, since the blight, you know.'

'But surely if they worked –'

'There is no work to be had.'

'Not in tilling the soil?'

'It is of no use tilling the soil; there is no sun in Ireland to ripen crops if they were planted. Nothing does well in the country but grass.'

'Then it ought to be converted into a great dairy farm.'

'That would require money.'

'But that could be got –'

'We'd be very much obliged to you if you'd tell us where.'

'Capitalists are always glad to find a good investment for their money.'

'The last place on earth they will send it to is Ireland.'

'Isn't that the fault of the Irish?'

'Time enough to answer that question when the experiment has been tried.'

'In the north, where capital has been invested, the people are fairly prosperous,' said Mr Westley, who felt it incumbent on him to fire a shot for the honour of his native land.

'But the question of religion does not enter there. I have always understood it is Romanism which makes the difficulty in other parts of the island.'

'It does no such thing,' said Mr Kelly brusquely.

'What do you think, then, keeps the country back?'

'The "three curses" of Ireland – dirt, drink, and tobacco,' was the prompt and decisive answer.

'Dear me, I never heard that before. It is very interesting. Then you think, sir, if the people ceased smoking and drinking and washed themselves, they would be prosperous.'

'They need one other thing – to be thrown over openly by England.'

'I hardly grasp your meaning.'

'I'll make it plain enough. England's the rich relation, who, while professing a great deal, really does nothing for Ireland. Still the Irish are always expecting help from her. That is, the notion keeps them unsettled. Instead of turning to themselves and seeing whether they can't do anything with an undrained island and a wretched climate, they are always waiting for assistance that never has, and that never will come. What can England do for Ireland except pour her millions of money into the country? and she is not such a fool as to do any such thing. If she could pluck up courage enough to say to Ireland in plain words, "Go to the devil!" – which is what she really feels – it would be the best day's work she ever did both for herself and her "sister", as she calls the green isle; – green isle indeed! – green enough in all conscience!'

The gentleman of an inquiring turn of mind looked at the lady with the rings, who slightly raised her eyebrows and shrugged her shoulders.

Observing this, Mr Kelly turned to her and said: 'I meant no offence, ma'am; the remark slipped out before I was aware of it. I have not displeased you, I hope?'

'Displeased! oh no!' she answered suavely; 'you have amused me very much indeed.'

'*Amused!*' thought Mr Kelly, hot with indignation. 'There is scarcely a man you'll meet with in Ireland,' he went on desperately, turning to his male auditor, 'but is waiting for a commission, waiting for an appointment, waiting to get into the constabulary, waiting for an agency, waiting to be made something in the Excise; in England a lad is apprenticed to some trade by the time he is fourteen, but whenever you get across the water the young fellows are doing nothing but trying to kill time till they are made inspectors, or officers, or such like.'

'You do not think that is the fault of the English, I suppose?'

'I do not think it is the fault of the Irish, at any rate,' returned Mr Kelly.

'And what,' asked the gentleman still in search of information, addressing Mr Westley, 'is your opinion about the state of things in Ireland?'

'I am afraid,' said Mr Westley, and the tone of his voice was a positive relief after the uncultured brogue in which Mr Kelly had delivered his sentiments – 'I am afraid I have no opinion to contribute to the general store.'

It was noticeable that after this the Irish and the English passengers divided into two contingents.

The last comer and his *vis-à-vis* drifted into conversation, of which only occasional scraps were caught by Mr Kelly; he on his part devoted himself to the Westleys, suggesting various little expedients calculated to make the journey less wearisome to Mr Westley and Miss Westley, asking her at one stopping-place to allow him to take her to get a cup of tea, which offer, however, she declined.

Father and daughter might not be, and in his opinion were not much, but he considered them infinitely preferable to English 'upstarts', for which reason he did what he could for their comfort; but withal both seemed quite worn out when, at nearly eleven o'clock pm, the train stopped at Camden Town to collect tickets.

'How near are we to London now?' asked Mr Kelly of the guard.

'Next station, sir.'

'Next station,' repeated Miss Westley. 'Do you hear that, papa?'

In a few minutes they were standing on the platform at Euston, dazzled with the bright light of the gas-lamps. They had reached the goal of their hopes at last, cold, tired, and exhausted.

It was too late even to think of trying to find the lodgings they hoped had been secured, so a cab was engaged to take them and their luggage to some quiet and reasonable hotel.

'I am now quite sure,' said Mr Westley wearily, as he stood looking at the porters piling box after box on the roof of the cab, 'we should have done better to come by the dearer route. Penny wise and pound foolish, my child.'

Glen did not answer. She felt too tired and too miserable to speak. Just then, without a hair ruffled, the lady who had travelled with them drove out of the station, looking as prosperous and comfortable as ever. The gentleman who thirsted for knowledge had bidden them good night and was gone too; and the last thing she saw and heard as they also departed was Mr Kelly arguing with an indignant cabman, who refused to take him to Stratford 'getting on for twelve.'

'Why, it's six miles if it's a yard,' said that irate individual.

'Then I'll walk,' decided Mr Kelly; but, influenced by the representations of a porter, he thought better of this project, and, carpet-bag in hand, started for an hotel in the City he had heard favourably mentioned by a certain Timothy Neill, who, travelling for a firm of Irish butter merchants, sometimes used the house.

Chapter II

MR KELLY'S FRIENDS

ESSEX IS a somewhat wide address, yet when anyone of Mr Matthew Donagh's many acquaintances asked him where he lived, it was the nearest they were able to obtain. Mr Donagh had an airy way of answering all such questions, and the manner in which he said, 'Whenever I have leisure to go home I run down to my little place in Essex,' left an impression in the minds of his hearers that their friend's little place was, to use their own simple phraseology, 'a very snug sort of crib, situated probably somewhere near Romford, or Loughton, or Rainham, or perhaps even farther out.' Mr Donagh vouchsafed no more accurate information on the subject of his residence, and those whom he consorted with in the City and at the West End had not the faintest idea that when in London he went home every night of his life to a small house with a large garden he had been fortunate enough to discover in West Ham Lane, within two or three minutes' walk of The Broadway, Stratford.

Incredible as it now sounds, such residences at moderate rents were then to be found within a few miles of the Royal Exchange. Railway accommodation was bad, omnibus not much better, and trams were unknown; but people did not think as much of any distance which could be traversed on foot as they do now, and Mr Donagh often in the cheerful companionship of his home circle declared to sympathetic listeners that Abbey Cottage suited him to a 'T'.

In the county of Essex, where Abbey Cottage was situated, he maintained as masterly a reserve concerning his occupation in London as he did in London about the precise locality of his 'little crib.' All even his female belongings knew about him may be summed up in three words: he was 'connected with literature.'

To his credit be it said, he contrived to do what many persons connected with literature fail to accomplish – viz., make a good thing out of it. He made so good a thing, indeed, he might have been a very prosperous individual if he had taken care of his money, and curbed his liking for his national beverage, the soft dew of the mountains.

Mr Donagh was an Irishman, though indeed few persons grasped the fact. He would much rather not have been, but amongst other mistakes made by Fate regarding him, she had ceded to the Emerald Isle the privilege of being his birth-place. Circumstances, however, causing his removal while still a lad to England, he employed his early energies so diligently in mastering the difficulties of the Saxon tongue, that in the periods which flowed volubly from his mouth it was almost impossible for the uninitiated to detect a trace of his origin. The man who could achieve such a victory as this was capable of great things. In his way, Mr Donagh had done great things, of which he felt deservedly proud.

Personally, he was a remarkable-looking individual. At the first glance anyone might have taken him for a man of some importance. His aquiline nose, his regular features, his slightly arched eyebrows, his ruddy complexion, his hand-some mouth, his white teeth, his closely shaven chin, his light hair, a little curly, clustering around a forehead where high thoughts and aims might well find a home; his keen blue eyes, his upright carriage, his walk, which was firm and self-asserting; his command of language, his manner, which was a good imitation of the manners of society – all seemed to indicate Mr Donagh was no common person. Constant mistakes were made concerning him. He was continually accosted for a dignitary of the Church, believed to be a well-known barrister, again addressed as 'Dr', in lieu of a famous physician of the time, and more than once he had been deferentially spoken to in the City, so great was his resemblance to a celebrated financier of the period.

All these honours he accepted with a gracious dignity all his own, though he was perhaps conscious he owed them to his dress rather than to his actual man. Accident or decision had guided him to a style of costume which was very effec-tive, and which included, amongst other details, a shirt the immaculate whiteness of which was set off by jet studs; a faultless collar, and a cravat like the driven snow. The season might necessitate a change of coat, but nothing else in his attire varied. Black and white like a magpie, he was to be met about London in all parts and in all weathers. He would stand in pouring rain under an umbrella to exchange confidences with a friend, and roll out mellow sentences full of strange words to an acquaintance. He seemed equally at home on the deck of a penny steamer, and in the first-class coupe of an express train. He was willing to go anywhere and talk to anyone. Many considered him a person well worth conciliating. Indeed, those who knew him best deemed the promise of his co-operation on a new journal an augury of success.

As regards temperament, Mr Donagh was easily uplifted, and still more easily depressed. He possessed indomitable perseverance; he had a bad temper; the ability of saying most insolent things in a most offensive manner; a keen sense of humour, so long as the lightenings of wit were not playing around his own person; a fatal tendency to believe good fortune would last for ever; a habit, if he earned a sovereign, of instantly spending ten shillings on something he did not in the least require; a haughty, domineering disposition, which might not have been altogether inappropriate had he been the Emperor of Russia, but which in a person obliged to earn his bread seemed ridiculous in the extreme. He was shallow, affectionate, capable of feeling grateful, apt to take offence, ready to forgive when there was anything to be made by forgiving, economical, extravagant, scrupulously honest in some things, eminently unprincipled in others, honourable in many ways, chivalrous in his sentiments and with a gift for lying that amounted to genius.

What with his fluent tongue, his ready pen, his power of repartee, his overflowing imagination, his faculty for believing anything he wished others to believe in, not merely possible, but accomplished, Mr Donagh was in any literary enterprise a valuable friend and a dangerous foe. He was willing enough to help any lame dog over a stile, to lend the lame dog half a crown or five shillings if he had it to spare – a matter of rare occurrence – and to speak for him when perhaps indeed there was not much that ought to have been said in his favour.

Mr Donagh was not married. 'For obvious reasons,' he once observed to an acquaintance, who ventured an inquiry on the subject, 'I never married.'

The acquaintance lacked presence of mind to ask what the obvious reasons were. Certainly not any real want of means to support a wife who might have helped him to save what he did make. In the absence of a Mrs Donagh, he resided with an aunt and cousin; or, to put the matter on a sounder footing, an aunt and cousin resided with him. They also were unmarried, and nobody could have told which was the elder, had not one worn a cap, and the other gone about what she called 'bare-headed.'

If Mr Donagh had contrived to eliminate from his speech all marks of his Irish extraction, not so his mother's sister, Miss Cavan, and his uncle's daughter, Hester Donagh. They were sweetly, beautifully Hibernian. If they had only just landed at St Katherine's Wharf from the Dublin steamer, they could not have been more un-English – in mind, manner, accent, and mode of expression.

Mr Donagh regarded them with a tolerant sort of pity, accepting their devotion in a lordly spirit, taking all they did for him as a matter of right, which indeed they considered it, and treating them kindly, though not familiarly – permitting no interference with his affairs – and keeping them in utter ignorance of where he went, what he did, the persons he knew, and the amount of money he made.

If they had been serfs and he a king, he could not socially have drawn a wider line of demarcation than he did between his relatives and himself. He attended church in the morning and they in the evening. 'They had their pursuits,' he said, 'and he had his.' Neither of them had ever been asked by Mr Donagh to walk out with him, or to take a day's, or even an evening's, recreation in his company; and it was clearly understood that if by any evil chance they met each other in the City or at the West End, no notice was to be taken by the ladies of their relation.

What had led to this arrangement was a *contretemps* which might, but for Mr Donagh's presence of mind, have resulted in harrowing consequences.

One day he was standing with a number of young fellows, just at that point where Duncannon Street debouches into Charing Cross. They were what Mr Donagh termed 'swells – cigars, rings, chains, canes, and eyeglasses,' and it was all 'Mat, my boy,' and 'Donagh, old fellow,' and the 'rest of it,' when just as 'Mat, my boy' was in the middle of a peal of laughter – and his laugh was something to remember, so hearty, so spontaneous, so infectious – the muscles of his face seemed to petrify into a horrible contortion as he beheld a sight of dread and disgrace.

It assumed the shape of an elderly woman dressed in a rusty black gown, an equally rusty black shawl falling back off her shoulders (for the day was sultry), an old black bonnet that had got knocked to one side, and black cotton gloves out at the fingers. With a fatuous smile on its old face this apparition, on catching sight of the faultlessly equipped Mat, quickened its steps, evidently with the intention of accosting its relative; but 'by the mercy of Providence,' afterwards thought Mr Donagh piously, 'I was equal to the occasion.'

Moving back a pace, he raised his hat with such preternatural courtesy and solemnity that the demon was exorcised. If it did not flee howling, it retreated at all events with an expedition which soon removed its obnoxious habiliments from sight.

'A worthy creature,' remarked Mr Donagh, in answer to earnest inquiries as to whether that was his 'young woman,' 'but ignorant of *les convenances*. Most faithful; attached to my family. Knew my father –' And so in disconnected sentences he diplomatically, to use one of his pet phrases, 'averted a *denouement!*'

To say, however, he did not feel greatly vexed with himself would be to slander his better nature. He was more than vexed. If he could have admitted such a thing, he was ashamed. As he walked home that evening, earlier than usual be it noted, he argued the question out.

'It boots not,' he considered – even in soliloquy he never condescended to the common words affected by an inferior order of mind – 'what matter of urgent importance called the poor old soul from the peaceful seclusion of West Ham to the human vortex whirling and seething in the West Strand. She was not there of her own free will, of deliberate intention. Ought I to have acted differently, and boldly acknowledged our relative positions? I do not conceive so. There are persons capable of such deeds of heroism, it is true, but in destroying themselves they sacrifice others; yet I regret such a catastrophe should have occurred. From all points of view it is to be lamented.'

He was very silent during tea, a fact Miss Cavan attributed to annoyance, for which reason, when 'Hetty' chanced to leave the room, she began: 'I have been thinking I ought not to have thought of stopping today, but I was so taken aback at "lighting" upon you that –'

'Not a word, I beg,' interrupted Mr Donagh. 'It grieved me deeply, I assure you, to have to initiate the part I did; but mine is a most difficult and delicate position. You do not know the world, and therefore you can perhaps scarcely comprehend the ruin it would have wrought had those men, seeing you dressed in the garments of poverty, suspected you were my aunt. They would have thought themselves ever after entitled to treat me like a dog – like a dog,' repeated Mr Donagh, rising from the tea-table, and with heightened colour walking to the window.

'Dear me! I am thankful you put it off as you did,' said poor Miss Cavan. 'I was obliged to go to Piccadilly, and remarked to Hetty as it looked likely to rain I would not chance my silk; and when the sky cleared, as it did about twelve, I thought I would walk from the Bank and take a look at the shops as I went along; and then all in a minute I saw you, and I was so surprised and pleased –'

It was at that juncture Mr Donagh, cutting across the thread of his aunt's discourse, said he thought, 'having a view to the possibilities of what might happen,' it would be well to determine that for the future, no matter when or with whom he might chance to be, his aunt and Hetty had, 'in the interests of prudence,' better affect not to see him.

'You might speak to me at a most *mal à propos* time,' he explained; 'break off an important negotiation, for example, or compel me to introduce you to some one it would be undesirable for you to know. Of course, I am about amongst all sorts and conditions of people, and perforce I have to be civil to them, but with you the case is different; you are in the happy position of being able to choose your acquaintances.'

Though it served its turn, this was a pleasing fiction on the part of Mr Donagh.

What chance had two ladies of uncertain age, whose personal income was under forty pounds a year, generally forestalled; who were neither clever nor beautiful, whose time was principally occupied in ironing Mr Donagh's shirts and hemming Mr Donagh's cravats, and nagging their little maid-of-all-work, and making frantic exertions to keep the house as Mr Donagh considered a house should be kept – hearth-stoned, black-leaded, window-cleaned, scrubbed, polished, and curtained – to make acquaintances in what they liked to term their own rank of life?

Heaven only knew what that rank might be. They certainly did not. Though fond of referring to Castle Donagh, and a certain Daniel Donagh of wild and famous memory, it was quite certain they did not come even within the category which Mr Bernard Kelly indicated as 'has beens.' They at all events had never socially been any better than they were. They had known more prosperous times, when they could have 'sat down to turkey every day,' for the same reason perhaps which Doctor Johnson assigned for eggs being only a penny a dozen in the Highlands; when 'everybody knew who they were,' and they drove to church on their jaunting-car; but even then their acquaintances were not what Mr Donagh would have termed the *crème de la crème*. Far from it, indeed, though it suited them to forget that fact, and talk, even in the 'charmed privacy of domestic life,' as though they had visited with the 'best in the county,' and ruffled it with all the 'quality' of their native land.

Abbey Cottage was a good index to the character of those who inhabited it. The garden in front – both wide and long, for the house stood well back from the road – was always neatly kept; but the garden at the rear could only be considered a howling wilderness, where, amongst weeds, a few superannuated fruit trees fought hard for existence, and the family washing was hung to dry. Inside the cottage one sitting-room was fairly furnished, and another, where Mr Donagh wrote, not totally destitute of comfort; but the parlour – appropriated to meals, needlework, the ladies, a cat, and a canary – was an awful apartment, the untidiness and poverty of which could only have found a counterpart in the person of Miss Bridgetta Cavan.

Towards evening a struggle was made to render this room presentable, in case 'Mat' should return to tea. When he signified his intention of not appearing at that meal, Miss Cavan and her niece 'took a bite' anyhow. They were in the habit of 'taking bites' in very 'anyhow' fashion – in the kitchen, in the washhouse, any place – and they preferred their food when eaten thus in haste and standing. They were most unselfish women, caring little what the 'bite and sup' consisted of, so that 'Mat, poor fellow,' had something nice and hot and appetizing, so that his shirt buttons were all right, and his cravats stiff, and his collar unfrayed, and his pocket handkerchiefs fine and of a lovely colour.

Mat's linen, as Mat liked to wear it, was a very serious trouble and expense; but his willing slaves felt more than repaid for many a small personal deprivation and many an anxiety regarding irons that would not get hot, and starch that would stick, when they saw him depart in all the glory of the 'best Irish,' bleached to a whiteness, and got up with a 'gloss,' they believed and declared could be 'touched' by no English laundress.

The small amount of correspondence in which they indulged was kept up with a few old friends in their native country, one of whom chanced to be Mrs Kelly, mother to that Bernard who was tired of many things in the Isle of Saints. Miss Cavan had always considered Mrs Kelly a more profitable than pleasant acquaintance. She looked down on the worthy matron, in fact, and but for the receipt of occasional hampers, which were acknowledged by Mr Donagh's womankind by such little presents as they could afford, and the execution of trifling commissions in London, it is possible they would have dropped the connection altogether.

As matters stood, however, occasional epistles were exchanged between West Ham and Callinacoan, and this was how it came about that one morning – Miss Bridgetta informed her nephew – that Barney Kelly was coming to London, and wanted to know if they could tell him of a decent lodging.

When Miss Cavan made that remark about Mrs Kelly's son, Mr Donagh looked up from what his aunt pathetically called 'that weary writing,' and inquired with more asperity of tone than the occasion seemed to warrant, what the young man was coming to London for.

'To better himself, I suppose,' answered Miss Bridgetta. 'Ye know Mrs Kelly has a brother here it was always said would one day send for them all. He pushed on beyond the common, got made a Magistrate, and married some rich lady that brought a great fortune in her hand.'

'I remember now, to be sure,' said Mr Donagh, mollified, and thoughtfully biting the top of a quill as he spoke. 'But Bernard cannot be coming over to him, or Mrs Kelly would not ask you to recommend lodgings.'

'It is to Mr Balmoy, for all that, he's coming; not to stay at his house, ye know; but the uncle's going to do something for him. By what Mrs Kelly writes, Barney is just full of genius, and only wants the chance to do as well as anybody. Trust those Balmoys for shoving themselves along. There's another of her brothers in Australia it is reported has made a mint of money; and we know she brought Kelly five hundred pounds, which he ran through before the first child was born; and the old man had only a general shop in Derry! Many's the time Miss Keady told me she had been in it as a child to buy sweets –'

'You can write,' said Mr Donagh, interrupting this harangue with a graceful wave of his pen, 'and ask Bernard Kelly to make our modest abode his home till he has time to look about him.'

'Ask him here! Is it that ye mean?' cried Miss Cavan, bewildered.

'Why not?' inquired her nephew. 'Though Abbey Cottage is not Castle Donagh, and the casualties of generations preclude my entertaining guests with the princely hospitality that characterised the economy of my progenitor Dan, still we can offer this young man a bed and a pitcher of water, and I dare say a morsel of bread. Write, I say; or shall I?'

'If ye will,' hesitated Miss Cavan. 'But before ye put pen to paper, Mat, just think a bit. We know nothing about Barney. I've never set eyes on him since he was in short frocks, and bare legs and red socks, and knitted boots; and the Kellys aren't of any account, and the Balmoys are of less. Ye've but to look at Mrs Kelly to know what she is. Good-hearted enough, and free-handed, I am sure we have a right to say; but still –'

'I suppose,' interposed Mr Donagh, 'that what is exercising a deterrent influence on you is the idea that Abbey Cottage is not grand enough to receive such a guest. Make your mind quite easy on that score. The meanest house in England is, as regards its appointments, a palace – literally a palace – in comparison with mansions in Ireland. Why, when I was there last, a gentleman in a large way of business asked me to dine with him, and we were waited on – you may not believe this, but it is a fact – by a strapping wench in a bedgown, with her sleeves turned up, and showing arms as thick as a navvy's, and as red as fire. Why, the veriest little drab in a lodging-house here would have felt ashamed to be seen in such a plight.'

'Ye told me that before,' said Miss Cavan, who indeed had not been so much impressed by the anecdote as she might. 'But still, Mat –'

'We need not discuss the question any further. I will write the invitation, and do you get a room ready. When is he to arrive?'

'He leaves the latter part of next week. He is coming round by the Dublin boat for cheapness.'

'Then that gives you plenty of time; and see here,' added Mr Donagh, dropping into the vulgar idiom, as he saw his aunt in a somewhat desponding mood about to retire, 'you may require to lay out a few shillings in muslin and so on. Here is a sovereign;' and he presented that sum to Miss Cavan as though the coin in question were possessed of the purchasing power of a Rothschild.

Poor Miss Cavan! There was scarcely a necessary article that guest's chamber contained.

'Mat has forgotten himself this time, I'm thinking,' she remarked to her niece. 'Nothing less will serve him than to ask Barney Kelly to stop here, and you know all the Kellys have eyes like gimlets; and there's not a thing in the spare room but a bedstead and the feather-bed.'

'We'll just have to strip our own,' observed Hester.

'And after we've done that it won't look much,' remarked Miss Cavan dolorously; 'and as for food, why, it is well known the Kellys never were within half a dozen flitches of bacon, and beautiful hams, and the best of poultry; and though Mat talks about a pitcher of water, if the son is like the father he'd drink the Shannon dry, but only if it was whisky. However, there is no use talking; we'll have to get on with the work next week, that we may be clear to see to his room before he comes.'

25

Work with poor Miss Cavan meant seeing to Mat's linen. Seven shirts a week, at least, were required by that gentleman, besides an additional one now and then when he 'dined out,' or went to the theatre. To see 'Mat' of a fine summer evening strolling along in full dress to the 'play,' was better to some people than the play itself.

Somewhat as the troubadour touched his guitar, Mr Donagh lightly and gaily flung off his friendly epistle. He was, as he himself said, 'a master of all styles' – the prosaic, the persuasive, the defiant, the bantering, the sarcastic, the curt, the playful, the scathing. In every one of these he considered himself unique. The graceful way in which he accepted an invitation either to take 'pot-luck' or to go down with a few fellows to an elaborate dinner at the Star and Garter, was 'all his own.' The ease with which be dashed off what any other person might have considered difficult letters was indeed remarkable, and the grace of his note to Mr Bernard Kelly should have charmed that young gentleman, though it failed to do so.

'He writes like a fool,' said Mr Kelly to his mother.

'You're too ready with your tongue, Barney,' observed Mrs Kelly; for at that precise period Barney chanced to be somewhat out of favour.

'Oh, I make no doubt he means to be civil enough,' was the answer, 'but it is ridiculous writing such a parcel of rubbish. Here's a bit from Shakespeare, and a line from Milton, and a quotation from Pope, and –'

'You'll be able to hold your own with the best of them there,' exclaimed his parent proudly; 'why, you might have done nothing else but sit and read all your life!'

'I haven't done much else, but I hope it will come in of use to me now. Don't trouble yourself, mother, about old Donagh; I'll send him a grateful enough reply, never fear.'

'And tell him the day you are leaving, and the time he may be looking out for you;' all of which Mr Bernard Kelly did, and then, changing his mind at the last minute, started for Belfast instead of Dublin, and leaving his heavy luggage to go round by 'long sea,' crossed himself by the 'cheap excursion,' arriving in London quite a week before anyone there expected the pleasure of seeing him.

Mr Donagh was sauntering about his front garden before breakfast (he had a way of doing this without his hat, and of scrutinising the flowers and bushes with apparently the keenest interest, which won for him the approval and admiration of many passers-by), when a young man, putting his arm over the gate, unfastened the latch, and, unmindful of the request plainly painted on the right-hand post, 'Please to ring the bell,' walked straight up the path without 'with your leave,' or 'by it' either.

Mr Donagh advanced a few steps to meet him, and then paused, patiently awaiting the stranger's approach.

'Your business, sir?' he asked, in his best and loftiest manner.

The newcomer burst out laughing.

'My name is Kelly, and you are Mr Donagh, I suppose?'

The words were simple. But oh, oh! as Mr Donagh subsequently explained, if a shell had burst at his feet he would have been less surprised and horrified.

This Bernard Kelly – this the guest he had so rashly invited under his modest roof – this the monster after a fashion created by himself – this the nephew of the great Mr Balmoy – this a young gentleman coming to push his fortunes in London!

'I am delighted to see you,' and Mat's face beamed, literally beamed with the brightness of the smile he wasted on the arid desert of Barney Kelly's gratitude; 'but how does it happen you are here so soon? We did not hope to see you for a week yet.'

'There was a cheap trip, and so I took advantage of it. I trust I am not putting you out. If I am, say the word, and I'll go back to the hotel where I stopped last night.'

'Oh dear, no; put us out, indeed!' and Mr Donagh, placing one hand on Mr Kelly's shoulder, surveyed him affectionately the while he considered how on earth he should manage to give Miss Bridgetta notice of this arrival, and prevent the awful spectacle of that spinster in the undress she wore at breakfast appearing before the eyes of her rough-and-ready compatriot.

'How did you leave them at home?' And something in the tone and the question recalling his friend of the train to recollection, Mr Kelly smiled. Naturally, Mr Donagh could not see what he was smiling at.

'All right. How are the old ladies?'

'My aunt and cousin are quite well, I thank you,' said Mr Donagh stiffly. 'This creature has no reverence,' he considered.

'What an awful prig!' thought Mr Kelly.

'If you will walk into the drawing room for a moment,' suggested Mr Donagh – he had been edging slowly up to the house, trusting they might be observed from the windows – 'I will apprise the ladies of your arrival.'

Too late. The last word was barely uttered before Miss Cavan, in a sketchy but not picturesque costume, wearing a pair of blue worsted stockings, her feet slipping about in a pair of Mat's old carpet-shoes, her hair in curl-papers, her cap awry, her whole aspect that of some anointed witch, appeared in the hall, exclaiming:

'The tea'll be –'

The rest of the sentence froze on her lips. The look of horror on Mat's countenance was reflected on her own, and she stood speechless, staring at Mat's companion, who, with wonderful composure, said:

'I am Barney Kelly, Miss Cavan. I am a good deal earlier than you expected, but I hope I am not too early for you to be glad to see me.'

'It was done wonderfully neatly,' observed Mr Donagh, when talking over the matter at a later period.

The sound of the well-beloved brogue, the touch from a vanished past, instantly broke the spell which had bound Miss Cavan, and in accents which fairly matched his own, she bade Mr Kelly heartily welcome.

'This is Barney himself, Hetty,' she cried, as another lady in an equally unstudied toilette, attracted by the bustle, appeared in the hall, and then there ensued what the maid-of-all-work in the adjacent kitchen called a jabber of Irish.

Ten minutes later Mr Bernard Kelly was sitting in Mr Donagh's parlour, with his back to the wild garden, as much at home as if he had lived at Abbey Cottage all his life. He had a bushel of news to communicate about the people Miss Cavan used to know in the happy past, when the Donaghs drove to church on their own jaunting-car: who was married, who was dead, who had gone to the bad, who had emigrated to America, who was living at Castle Donagh, who was coming to Keady's old place. The ladies might never have seen London, never been privileged to reside in West Ham Lane, so fresh and green did their memory seem concerning a number of persons who ought, Mr Donagh considered, to have been 'beneath their notice.'

For himself, he took refuge in the *Times*, and when breakfast was finished asked Mr Kelly if he meant to go into the City then, or wait till later in the day.

'Faith, I don't mean to go out at all again today, if Miss Cavan will let me stop where I am,' answered Mr Kelly. 'I have scarcely had a wink of sleep the last three nights, and that's a mighty comfortable-looking sofa over there.'

'Yes, and it's as comfortable as it looks, and so ye'll say when ye stretch yourself upon it,' exclaimed Miss Cavan.

'Then if you will excuse me –' observed Mr Donagh.

'Oh, I'll excuse you fast enough,' said Mr Kelly. 'Take yourself off, and don't mind me. The ladies and I will find plenty to talk about, never fear.'

'Plenty to talk about,' thought Mr Donagh, as he went into his own special sanctum preparatory to starting for the 'centre of civilisation', 'but how,' and he placed his hand on his forehead, 'shall I ever be able to endure the crudities of this barely civilised creature?'

Whilst Mr Donagh was absent attending to whatever business might be claiming his attention, the 'creature' he thus disparagingly referred to washed, brushed, slept, dined, had a glass of punch, talked to Miss Cavan, and evinced a laudable amount of curiosity as to what the redoubtable Mat wrote. In Ireland they knew he had done very well, or, as Mr Kelly otherwise expressed it, 'made a great hit'; but nobody there had ever met with any of his books.

'Find me one of them, Miss Cavan,' he entreated, 'and I'll be as quiet all the afternoon as a mouse in a meal-chest.'

'I only wish I could find ye one,' answered Miss Cavan, who, now arrayed in a silk gown, and having her hair dressed in two pensive ringlets, and a cap ornamented with blue ribbons covering her head, looked a very different figure from that she had presented a few hours previously. 'But Mat never tells us what he writes; he might never have appeared in print for all we know about it.'

'What does he contribute to?' asked Mr Kelly, after he had digested this unexpected piece of information.

'Everything, I think,' answered Miss Cavan vaguely. 'Looking over the magazines and journals and papers he brings home, we often come across bits we feel sure are his; but it vexes him so if we put any questions, we have stopped asking them.'

'Well, that's a queer notion, too,' said Mr Kelly, referring to Mat's reticence.

'He says we wouldn't understand,' went on Miss Cavan, between whom and their guest had sprung up one of those sudden friendships which are sure to wither away almost as rapidly as Jonah's gourd; 'but if we can understand other things, what is there to hinder us "making off" his?'

'Nothing, unless he writes in an unknown tongue.'

'It might be Hebrew for all we know,' maundered on poor Miss Cavan. 'Now, there's a new thing come out called the *Galaxy*, and I feel sure he has to do with that; but do you think he will tell us which article is his?' And the lady's voice was uplifted as she spoke, more in sorrow than in anger.

That first day passed off, so far as the ladies were concerned, very well indeed. There was one little cloud, when, Miss Donagh playfully suggesting a love-affair must have been at the bottom of Mr Kelly's sudden determination to come to England, that gentleman blazed up for a moment, and angrily inquired if anybody had been telling anything. The charming Hester's wondering disclaimer, however, instantly calmed down his excitement, and he apologised for his hasty speech by remarking that Callinacoan was such a place for scandal no man could imagine what stories might get about concerning him.

With Mr Donagh, however, things did not go on quite comfortably. That gentleman saw so much about Mr Kelly which in his opinion required 'toning down,' he was unable to refrain from dropping various hints which, though his guest at first wisely ignored, he felt compelled at last to notice.

Mr Balmoy was the peg Mr Donagh chose to hang all his remarks on. He warned Mr Kelly against this, that, and the other, because the society in which the Magistrate had no doubt moved since he crossed the Channel must have given him a distaste for accent, phrases, and manners Hibernian.

He advised his young friend to pay a little more attention to his personal appearance. 'People think so much of dress nowadays,' he was kind enough to explain.

The more he drank, and he drank a good deal, the more he seemed disposed to assume the role of Mentor. It was excessively irritating, but Mr Kelly, though not a good-tempered man, bore all his host's strictures with wonderful patience, till at length it struck him it might be well to nip this sort of impertinence in the bud.

'Look here, Donagh,' he said accordingly, 'I didn't come to England meaning to keep my eyes shut, but for all that I am not going to adopt the speech, ways, and customs of the first fellow who tries to make me believe he knows more of the inner life of what is called good society than I do myself. I have much to learn. I am aware; but, to be quite plain, I don't think you are the man to teach me.'

It is doubtful if Mr Donagh had ever in the whole course of his life before been hit so hard; the blow was given so straight from the shoulder – it was delivered with such force between the eyes – that Miss Cavan's Mat was sobered in a moment.

'If I have been intrusive, pardon me,' he said, with frigid politeness. 'Taking an interest I now perceive to have been foolish in your welfare, I could not refrain from mentioning a few trifles I thought you would do well to attend to. My interference, I see, however, though conceived in a friendly spirit, was officious. I shall not offend again.'

'I shall really be obliged if you refrain from criticism, at all events till I feel somewhat less of a stranger in a strange land,' said Mr Kelly, with that readiness of speech and manner which had already surprised Mr Donagh.

'I shouldn't wonder if he has something in him,' thought that gentleman, with a sort of lofty incredulity. 'At all events, he has quite brains enough for a Government clerk, which is what his uncle seems disposed to make of him.'

The next day was Sunday, during the course of which nothing remarkable occurred; but on Monday matters did not progress very well. Before they started for town, which on this occasion they did together, Mr Donagh made two discoveries – one, that Mr Kelly was not flush of cash; and the other, that he was inclined to be impertinent.

'My dear fellow,' cried Mat, rushing in his shirt-sleeves into his young friend's bedroom, 'do you happen to have change for a twenty-pound note?'

'Do I happen to be Governor of the Bank of England?' retorted Mr Kelly.

'Well, have you got a couple of sovereigns?'

'Yes. Do you want them?'

'If you would be so kind, just till I can get change.'

It was when Mr Kelly was 'so kind' his host saw the whole of his worldly wealth did not appear to exceed ten pounds.

'Humph!' considered Mr Donagh, who felt this amount was scarcely sufficient to start on in London. However, the uncle, of course, might come down handsomely, and no doubt in the home stocking, knitted and filled by Mrs Kelly without her husband's knowledge, there were many pound notes.

The other matter seemed more serious.

As they passed to the hall-door. Miss Cavan and Miss Donagh, both wearing stays, and having their hair out of paper, detained their beloved Mat for the tender embrace and rapturous kiss without which he was never permitted to cross the threshold.

From the step outside Mr Kelly viewed this performance, and Mr Donagh heard him mutter quite audibly:

'Well, I'm – !'

They argued the question out going up West Ham Lane, Mr Donagh asserting this 'osculatory farewell gratified two most faithful and loving creatures,' and Mr Kelly saying 'he didn't care who got the kiss so long as it wasn't himself.'

His tone implied such an amount of thankfulness on this score, Mr Donagh felt quite down-hearted, and began to realise he had taken an Old Man of the Sea on his back, whose powers of observation were far too acute to prove agreeable.

'I wish I had taken my aunt's advice, and never asked him to the house,' thought poor Mat. 'However, if the uncle is civil, that will pay for all.'

Mr Kelly could not imagine why his friend should ask so many questions and appear so anxious concerning the Magistrate.

'He is out of town at present,' explained this candidate for an appointment. 'He has not been well. I will call early next week.'

'It was a wonder he didn't ask you to stop at his house,' said Mr Donagh.

'Oh, they are grand people – too grand by far to have a wild fellow from Callinacoan quartered on them,' said Mr Kelly slily.

The time wore by slowly. There was a nameless something about his guest Mr Donagh could not fraternise with. He was a 'strange specimen,' he decided.

The specimen annoyed Mr Donagh greatly with trying to discover what he wrote.

'That is my Blue Beard's chamber,' said the master of Abbey Cottage. 'Everything else about me is free to you, but respect the one locked door.'

'It is mighty odd,' answered Mr Kelly. 'Why can't you tell us what you do?'

'Because I love Truth,' was the reply. 'I revere, I worship her. I could easily tell you I write leaders in the *Times*; but I do not, because that would not be fact – it would be fiction.'

'I shouldn't believe you if you said you wrote for the *Times*,' remarked Mr Kelly, with disconcerting frankness.

'No, and I never will tell you anything of the sort. If you must know, I am a disappointed man. I have not made my mark as I expected, and so, instead of grumbling, I maintain a discreet silence.'

'I suppose it is very difficult to make a mark.'

'The experience of the ages would seem to imply as much.'

'Do you know, I have tried my hand at authorship myself,' and Mr Kelly laughed and coloured.

'Have you?' Mr Donagh's tone was the reverse of encouraging. 'In some "Poet's Corner," no doubt.'

'Yes, there and elsewhere. I used to think I could turn out something worth reading, but now I have given up the notion.'

'Wisely, I should say.'

'Judging from the results even you have achieved, I should say so.'

It was this sort of thing which Mr Donagh called 'banter,' but felt really like a swordthrust, which caused him to long for Mr Kelly's departure.

To do Mr Kelly justice, he troubled the Abbey Cottage with very little of his society. He went out directly after breakfast, and scarcely ever returned till tea-time; so that as far as food was concerned the cost of his maintenance could not be regarded as excessive.

'But he takes it out in the drink,' whimpered Miss Bridgetta. 'There's a gallon gone already, and it makes no more impression on him than if it was pure spring water.'

Which was perhaps the less extraordinary as his share of the gallon, which could only be regarded as the lion's, produced a considerable effect on Mat.

That gentleman, however, by confining his libations to the City and West End, had earned for himself a character for sobriety in his domestic circle a teetotaler might have envied. Even Miss Bridgetta often urged him to take 'just a thimbleful' when he was prostrate with one of his 'dreadful headaches' and almost weeping told Hetty how, almost with loathing, he refused to try a prescription she knew would 'give him a lift.'

At a very early period of his visit Mr Kelly perceived Mr Donagh had no inten-tion of taking him about London – that is to say, about any part of London where they were likely to meet many of Mat's numerous acquaintances.

'He's ashamed of me,' thought Mr Kelly bitterly; but as it suited him to take no notice of this feeling on his friend's part, he went his way and Mat went his. During the course of the week which seemed so long to the dwellers at Abbey Cottage, he contrived to see a great deal of London, and found many opportunities of comparing his own personal appearance with that of other young men of a like grade in life. As he truly said, he had not come to England to keep his eyes shut, and for this reason he astonished Miss Donagh by appearing one evening at tea with his hair cut in the latest style and his whiskers trimmed 'just elegant,' as the lady expressed the fact in her simple vernacular.

More wonders, however, were in store. On the Saturday week following Mr Kelly's appearance at West Ham, a letter arrived from his uncle, to say he had now returned to Upper Wimpole Street, and would be glad to see Bernard if he called between three and four o'clock on the Monday following. This epistle, which, indeed, he had not expected, put Mr Kelly into the highest spirits, and possibly induced him the next morning to electrify his host by descending to breakfast 'decently dressed.'

When or how he had procured the new suit of well-made clothes, which made him 'look another person,' he did not inform Mr Donagh; but there they were, and there was he in them.

'Come, there is hope,' thought Mat, with a gratified smile: 'after all, my words have borne fruit;' while Miss Donagh openly expressed her admiration, and assured Mr Kelly in an easy and friendly manner, 'There was money bid for him.'

As a man gets uneasy the day before his execution, it was noticeable that Mr Balmoy's nephew lost some portion of courage as the time for the momentous interview drew nigh. It is not too much to say he grew nervous; and finally, during the progress of that friendly tumbler which wound up the evening, asked Mr Donagh if he would mind accompanying him to Upper Wimpole Street on the morrow.

Mat snapped at the proposal, and declared that in the cause of friendship he was willing to forego appointments, invitations, everything.

'I'll see you through it, my boy,' he said, clapping Mr Kelly on the shoulder with an air of patronage which made the young man almost repent his invitation.

'However,' he thought, 'anything is better than going alone, and the fellow is presentable enough.'

'Presentable enough!' Heaven and earth must have come together had Mat heard him.

In the cause of friendship Mat the next day 'stood' a luncheon at a well-known City tavern, after which meal the pair started, both in the best of spirits, for Upper Wimpole Street.

Mr Bernard was indeed in the wildest humour. He talked and rattled on as they walked up Chancery Lane to meet a West End omnibus, and proved that he could be what Mr Donagh had much doubted – a pleasant and witty companion.

'He has a great deal in him which only wants bringing out,' decided that gentleman, as with neatly furled umbrella he signalled a passing 'bus.

Mr Kelly got in first. Mr Donagh following, took a seat beside him next the door. Opposite Mr Donagh a gentleman was already seated, most elaborately got up – a regular buck of the old school – with frilled shirt, diamond brooch, tremendous cravat, long waistcoat, high coat-collar, best superfine hat, kid gloves, gold-headed cane, highly polished boots, and gold watch-chain, from which depended a bunch of seals and charms.

His head, long and narrow, was surmounted by beautiful white curls, his whiskers, nicely curled also, were white as snow. He looked some superannuated leader of fashion – some one who might have been a contemporary of Brummel, but had survived to a more prosperous old age.

To Mr Donagh's amazement, the moment Mr Kelly caught sight of this old 'swell' he greeted him with a friendly –

'Ah! how d'ye do?' The gentleman looked as much astonished as Mr Donagh felt.

'I – aw – really, sir, have not the pleasure of your acquaintance,' he said.

Mr Kelly looked at him and nodded. 'How's Maria?' he asked, smiling pleasantly.

By this time the attention of the other passengers began to be aroused.

'Sir – I repeat, sir – I do not know who you are, sir,' spluttered out the gentleman, purple with indignation.

'Where is Tom now?' went on Mr Kelly, after he had apparently received and digested a satisfactory answer concerning Maria.

'The man's mad!' cried his victim, looking helplessly round on the occupants of the omnibus, who by this time were laughing outright. 'Sir, I have to tell you I never saw you, sir, in my life before, and I trust I shall never see you again.'

'I always told you he was the flower of the flock,' said Mr Kelly.

It was too much. The passengers screamed; the omnibus was full, and nine persons roared in concert as the poor old gentleman yelled:

'Conductor! Conductor! I say, conductor, let me out; you have got a lunatic inside. I shall summon you and him. And –'

'I'll come round and see you one of these days,' were Mr Kelly's last words, as the gentleman was set down in the very muddiest portion of the road, where they left him shaking his stick after the retreating vehicle.

'What on earth possessed you to do such a thing?' asked Mr Donagh.

'I don't know. There was something in the look of the old fellow I couldn't resist.'

Mr Donagh shook his head gravely, but made no further remark; and shortly afterwards they got out, and proceeded on foot towards Wimpole Street. Arrived there, the butler, who opened the door, said Mr Balmoy was not at home, but asked them to walk in, as that gentleman would return almost directly.

With a feeling amounting to reverence, Mr Donagh trod the thick carpets, and surveyed the wealth and luxury which was presented at every step.

'This is something like,' said Mr Kelly, flinging himself into an easy-chair. 'He seems better off even than I expected.'

'I wonder if we shall be asked to dinner,' marvelled Mr Donagh to himself. They waited patiently five minutes, ten minutes, fifteen minutes, half an hour; at the end of that time a step was heard, the door opened, a gentleman entered, and in his uncle Mr Kelly recognised their companion of the omnibus!

Mr Donagh never could accurately recall what happened after that. He had a confused memory of angry words, of an attempted apology, of a bell being rung violently, of hearing himself and his friend ordered out of the house, of seeing the butler glide before and quietly and deferentially fling wide the door for them to depart, of feeling that Mr Balmoy stood in the hall to see them actually off the premises, and of finding himself in Wimpole Street, ready to sink under the pavement with mortification and shame.

Chapter III

MR P VASSETT, PUBLISHER

LONG BEFORE the Thames Embankment was thought of, save as a scheme of Sir Christopher Wren's – which it was a pity had not been carried out by him, but that never in the later times could by anybody be made a reality – Craven Street, Strand, was as quiet, respectable, and central a position for a residence as could have been desired by a person whose ideas were moderate and tastes urban.

Mr Vassett had no extravagant notions, and he dearly loved a town, more especially he affected London, in particular those small portions of it described in legal documents as 'The Cities of London and Westminster'; and though, to a certain extent, it might be true that chance first led him to take up his abode in Craven Street, there can be no question but that choice induced him to continue living there.

As a boy he had often been in the then no-thoroughfare, one end of which was close by Charing Cross and the other abutting on the river, and he used to think, looking at the staid, comfortable residences, that men and women who dwelt in them ought to be very happy; while as a man he considered, when, having secured a long lease of one of the houses situated on the east side, he took possession, that he would never leave Craven Street till – he could not help it.

His mind was deeply imbued with that taste for antiquity which enables an individual familiar with the history of former days to make companions of the very stones of the street.

To outward view a lonely man, Mr Vassett, in reality, never felt solitary. He had his business to interest him by day, and when, in the evenings, he took a stroll round the neighbourhood, there came to him from out the past – on the one hand, lords and ladies, kings, courtiers, statesmen, who had lived and loved, sinned and suffered, and rejoiced and made merry, and died and been buried within the Liberties of Westminster; and on the other, trooping through Temple Bar and over Ivy Bridge, grave citizens, turbulent apprentices, rebels, traitors, the martyrs of Smithfield, authors from Grub Street, Milton from under the shadow of All Hallows; Shakespeare, straight from Golden Lane or Playhouse Yard; Johnson, from Gough Square; and Goldsmith, on his way to clothe himself with confusion at Northumberland House.

Standing just within hearing of the din of the Strand, there was nothing which pleased Mr Vassett better at times than to picture the period when that thoroughfare, where now all is 'crowding and bustle,' and 'continual hurrying to and fro,' was 'a bare and marshy shore,' where, doubtless, the 'hollow-sounding' cry of the bittern from its reedy nest has often broke upon the ear of the half-naked, but gaily ornamented, human wanderer from the neighbouring 'City of Mists.'

Nature had made Mr Vassett an antiquarian – necessity, a publisher. It is not often that nature and necessity, hand locked in hand, manage to tread the road of life together.

There was no violent antipathy between his tastes and his business; though had Heaven seen fit to place him in a connection where amongst the accumulated dust of centuries he could have been perpetually unearthing some treasure of the past, he would have preferred it undoubtedly to considering manuscripts, possibly more legible, but certainly much less interesting than black-letter. Dead authors never could have given the trouble and annoyance living writers contrived to do; but still, neither in the world we live in nor in any other, so far as we know, can people have everything their own way. Mr Vassett was a philosopher, and recognised this fact; moreover, out of living writers he had done very well indeed, which perhaps did more to reconcile him to their existence than even philosophy.

He was a prosperous man; his lot chanced to be cast at a time when, to quote the words of those who recently have not been so prosperous, 'Some money *could* be made out of publishing.' Owing to circumstances or himself, Mr Vassett had achieved this feat, and another equally important, viz., keeping his money when he had got it. From the agreeable seclusion of Craven Street he was able, at the period when this story opens, to contemplate coming years without any terror of poverty; on the contrary, he had thousands well invested, and was able to think of both his printers and the firm that supplied him with paper without any fear of that day of reckoning which, though deferred, looms darkly and certainly before the mind's eye of many a modern publisher in an apparently large and prosperous way of business.

As has been intimated, Mr Vassett's ideas were modest, his notions perhaps a little old-fashioned, his views somewhat circumscribed. He was doing a very safe trade, and stood very well. If he could not claim to be a Murray, no one could speak of him as a disciple of the Minerva Press.

No one knew better than he did that the works he published were not likely to live, but in their generation they were good, useful, amusing. That they were not likely to go down through the ages did not much trouble the gentleman who had assisted at their birth. He felt they would live long enough; they had served their purpose, and could die when they pleased. He felt no such frantic desire for posthumous fame as rendered him unhappy because he could not compass it. If Shakespeare had come back to earth, Mr Vassett would not have risked anything he considered very valuable – say, for instance, the lease of his house in Craven Street – for the honour of standing godfather even to a second Shylock. The world's applause he did not consider worth the loss of one night's sleep: further, he had a notion not uncommon amongst those who prefer to seek their mental food among the past of literature, rather than browse on the light productions of the present, that no more great books would ever be written. Mr Vassett was no optimist concerning the books of the future. Looking around, he saw what he considered almost a dead level of mediocrity. Whether the few who struggled out of the mass and achieved distinction, who were run after by readers, and run down by the critics, would be thought much of in succeeding generations, was a question he professed himself glad he had not to decide. He admitted they had many merits; but when asked if he considered they would stand the test of time, he returned the safe answer that he did not know.

There was another thing also he did not know, as he sat at breakfast one November morning in the same year when Mr Bernard Kelly, and Mr and Miss Westley, and the gentleman of an inquiring turn of mind, and the lady with the wavy hair, all travelled together in the same compartment to Euston – viz., anything about the sword which was impending over his devoted head. Mr Vassett entertained an antipathy towards new authors which must be indigenous in the publishing bosom, since it obtains to the present day, unless indeed in those cases where one of the 'new school' spreads wide his arms to welcome some pigeon with sheeny plumage who professes his desire to be plucked forthwith.

Publishing, he felt, might not prove an unpleasant business if tyros would but refrain from bringing manuscripts: poor Mr Vassett had seen so much of 'inglorious Miltons,' of would-be Sheridans, of young persons who believed they had the 'gift 'of historical romance, of poets, novelists, essayists, and travellers, that could he only have conceived the possibility of four would-be authors entering London on the same day, and the same hour, and by the same line of rail, he must have been reduced to despair. All unconscious of what fate held in store for him, he was on that November morning wrestling in imagination with one author, a letter from whom lay open before him. He felt firmly determined to oust her out, but he gave no thought to the other four demons waiting to enter in.

His correspondent was a lady of title, who, having married a wealthy City man and then separated from him, had decided to take the public fully into her confidence, and state in several three-volume novels the causes, the many causes of complaint she considered she had against the gentleman whose name she still bore.

That sort of thing was not so common in those days as it has since become, and Lady Hilda Hicks's books sold remarkably well: not so much on account of any great intrinsic merit they possessed – though Lady Hilda was in her way clever – as of the amount of ill-nature and scandal and misrepresentation she managed to put into them.

Lady Hilda was extremely inconsistent. She had married Mr Hicks for his money, she never pretended she had married him for anything else, and then she turned round and abused her husband for possessing money. No Billingsgate fish-wife could have bespattered a man with fouler insinuations and accusations than this daughter of an earl, who had sold herself willingly for the 'almighty dollar.'

There was scarcely a crime in the Decalogue she failed to lay – by implication – to his charge. Under the poor disguise of Bicks, Cricks, Fricks, Licks, and Picks, she held up his honoured name to scorn and ridicule. Hicks had been a power in the City; now, unless it was on a cheque or a bill, the words served as a mere peg on which to hang irreverent jokes and scurrilous jests.

Lady Hilda ridiculed her husband's friends, ideas, house, business, manners, with an utter absence of shame, reticence, or the most ordinary womanly feeling, which might have put to the rout even some later writers upon the subject of matrimonial grievances. People were always wondering what she would say next. She had her party of sympathisers, and a large following of readers, and, as has been before said, her books sold remarkably well.

Nevertheless, Mr Vassett was beginning to feel he had brought out enough of them. Naturally he was loath to refuse novels written by a woman of fashion as well as of talent, but, as he said very truly, 'there is a limit to all things;' and in his opinion Lady Hilda, rendered daring by success, was passing the limit within which he cared to have anything to do with her. So far Mr Hicks's lawyer had not written to him, but if he went on publishing all the lady indited he knew that any morning he might expect to see an ominous legal-looking envelope lying on his breakfast-table. Annoyance Mr Vassett was well aware fell to the lot of everyone in business; but this special annoyance he was determined should not disturb his peace, even though Lady Hilda left him, as she often threatened, to go to one of what she insultingly called the 'good houses.' Having ventured to remonstrate with her ladyship on some passages in her latest manuscript, to which his reader had not without reason called his attention, her ladyship replied in a letter which brought the blood to Mr Vassett's cheeks, and took the flavour out of his coffee and the freshness from his roll.

'Pretty well – pretty well – vastly well, Lady Hilda Hicks!' he exclaimed, with a spiteful accent on the last word. 'No, I won't publish another of your novels, let the consequences be what they may. Take them where you like. Take them to the – !' and here Mr Vassett became exceedingly emphatic, 'but don't bring them to me. If your husband is a fiend, I pity him, earl's daughter or no earl's daughter. If you were my wife I'd – I'd –' but when Mr Vassett tried to imagine what he would do were Lady Hilda his wife, he was obliged to relinquish the attempt. He really failed utterly to conceive what he would do with that awful woman, who could – crowning horror! – write, tied to him for life.

'Thank Heaven!' piously exclaimed Mr Vassett; 'things are bad enough, but they are not so bad as that. I can get rid of her, and Hicks can't. I have made money out of her, and he has to find her even the money that pays the printer who sets up the type in which he is abused. Unhappy man! what could have induced him to marry such a virago?' And with equanimity quite restored by these agreeable considerations Mr Vassett resumed his breakfast, finding his appetite had returned – that flavour was restored to the coffee and freshness to the roll.

A good-looking man, though not handsome; good-looking in all senses. Honest, wholesome, truthful, kindly, despite a certain sternness of expression which had come with the lonely years, just like the grey hairs that, so far as the man's age was concerned, should not yet have been sprinkled among the black.

There was a little romance, a little sad plaintive story in his life with which few were acquainted, and of which he never spoke. When he was quite young, a mere lad, in the employment of a bookseller in Soho, he lodged with some people who had known his father, and were kind to the boy on that account.

They had one little daughter, a fair flaxen-haired child, between whom and himself there sprang up one of those attachments which seem so unintelligible, and yet which sometimes prove so enduring.

In this case, at all events, it endured. When the lad was grown to manhood, when the child's flaxen curls were smoothed in sunny braids from the maiden's brow, they remained just as fond and foolish, as simply, innocently devoted to each other as had been the case in the early days of their acquaintance.

Then her family was in a worldly point of view above him, but things were more equal now. He had climbed up many rungs of the social ladder, and they were coming down.

Maggie's father was something in the City, and as time went on it needed no gift of second sight to prophesy he would have eventually to make his way into the Bankruptcy Court. A series of misfortunes overtook him. The posts, like the messengers who came to Job, brought nothing save tidings of some fresh disaster. Duly and truly he ran the allotted course of trouble, anxiety, despair. He went through 'the court,' and then he died.

After that Maggie and her mother left London and removed to Halliford, near which hamlet a relative farmed some sixty acres.

It was not then Mr Vassett conceived that aversion to the country which remained with him through life. Quite the contrary. On the Sundays and holidays, 'when the relaxation of the claims of literature,' as Mr Mat Donagh would have said, left him at leisure to visit his former playmate and present sweetheart, the embryo publisher thought nothing could be fairer than all that pensive valley of the Thames – the river, the swans, the cygnets, the aits, the bulrushes, the water lilies, the blue expanse of heaven, the low-lying fields where the cows looked at him with mild, wondering eyes, the hawthorn trees white with bloom, the wealth of wild-flowers, the tall poplars, the quivering aspens, the lonely houses, the quaint little towns.

He was young then – young and soft, and in love, and the best of life lay, as he fancied, before him, and there was a glamour over the landscape – that glamour which sheds its rainbow hues over any earthly landscape but once in our short existence, – and all things seemed fair to him, and all the future full of happiness!

Well, he had his innings, and it is not every man who can say that. He and Maggie were married, and for fourteen months not even a cloudlet obscured the brightness of their sunny home. Then, unaccountably, the young wife began to droop. It was in the early part of September, when all that part of the country is aglow with ripening crops and ruddy cheeked apples, that the doctor sent Mrs Vassett back to Halliford to try whether the fresh sweet air would chase the pallor from her face, and restore strength to her slight frame. Had they told the husband then her case was hopeless, he might have borne the blow that came so soon better; but as matters stood he kept believing she would ere long be restored to health – that when their child was born he should see her well and strong again.

All in the dull winter months, the worst which could happen happened. He was sent for in haste, and though he did not lose an hour or second was too late. When he arrived there were no loving tones to greet him, no sweet eyes to smile their welcome. Instead of greeting or smile there was only that which had been his wife, lying white and still, with her dead baby by her side.

So it ended. The dream of springtime, the summer's idyll, the fruition of autumn: the human harvest was ripe, and the dread reaper had put in his sickle and garnered the grain. It was all over – the love, the hope, the anxiety; nothing remained save the certainty of loss. It was then the blue in the sky, and the green of the trees, and the scents, and songs, and rustle, and silence of nature grew distasteful to Mr Vassett.

It was a dull, grey, chilly afternoon when they laid the young wife down to rest in Shepperton Churchyard. Once he had thought that a sweet and lovely place, but as he wandered miserably about alone whilst the short winter day darkened down, it seemed to him the most mournful spot on the whole of God's wide earth. He went sadly to the swollen Thames, where the discoloured waters were rushing by with a threatening yet sullen fury; he looked across at the fields they had paced many and many a time hand in hand together; he stood beneath the trees where they had waited side by side for the boat into which she stepped so lightly; he saw one lonely swan trying to stem the current – and then he burst into a passion of tears and wept as if his heart would break.

What were success, money, position, to him then? What were happiness, prosperity, worldly consideration? Words, mere words that might to others bear some signification, but to his mind seemed unintelligible sounds.

He returned to town a changed man. The blessed necessity for work after a time brought some mitigation to his grief. Once more he took up the burden of life, to find that there was even for him a meaning in the words that seemed, standing beside the Thames on that desolate winter's day when he left his wife in Shepperton Churchyard, to be but bitter mockery. Business went well with him; he possessed everything he would have liked to own when she walked with him. His love and his loss had grown such an old, old story that when he thought over it all he felt sometimes as if the boy and girl who wandered about Soho, or the pretty green at Halliford, and that quaintest of quaint villages Littleton, who had plucked the wild-flowers, and walked across the meadows, were some creatures who had never really been part and parcel of his later most prosaic life.

Yet it was the memory of what they had done and said, and hoped and fancied, which brought that occasional softness into his face, and tender light into his eyes, many an author, discouraged by his words and manner, took heart of grace again at sight of.

He had a weak spot in his nature, and Lady Hilda Hicks knew it. He was not so hard as he looked, or so resolute as he wished people to think him.

He could not bear to say 'No' to a woman, and he disliked refusing help to a man. Fortunate Mr Vassett, whose lot was cast in days when women as a rule were not pushing, and men had not grown quite so hopelessly impecunious as they have since become; when, in a word, in the literary world females still retained some reticence, and males the traditions at least of self-respect; when the world was nearly thirty years younger, and authors were about three hundred times more modest, retiring, and simple than they are now; when Lady Hilda Hicks was an exception to all known rules, and old-fashioned people felt doubtful as to whether a young person who wrote novels could be 'quite proper.'

If Mr Vassett had only realised the fact, it was in Arcadia and not Craven Street

41

he was deliberately finishing his breakfast, when a lean, clean-shaven, closely buttoned-up, ascetic-looking individual, after having knocked gently at the door, turned the handle and entered the room.

'Well, Pierson, what is it?' asked Mr Vassett, without going through the ceremony of good-morning, which after years is somewhat apt to pall.

'An elderly gentleman and a young lady want to see you.'

'Well, they can wait, I suppose?'

'They have been waiting.'

'Give him the *Times*, and –'

'He has read the *Times*, and she does not seem to care for a book,' interrupted Mr Pierson.

'What is their business?'

'Won't confide it to me; the usual thing, however, I suppose – for he carries the inevitable roll of paper.'

'What does he mean by coming here at such an unearthly hour? Can't you ask him to call again later in the day?'

'No, I think not.'

'Why not?'

'He looks ill; and – and – they are not the usual run.'

'Perhaps he is a prince in disguise.'

'No, he is not that; but he has travelled and read, and he can talk, and there is a something about him I fancy you would rather not send away.'

'Pierson, you are a fool.'

'Well, that's not my fault, is it?'

'When you know that, although you are not worth your salt as a reader, I keep you on out of –'

'Charity,' supplied Mr Pierson, with unmoved countenance.

'No; out of a mistaken notion you will stand between me and the incursions of people who fancy they can write. I would not give ten shillings – not five shillings – a week for your opinion on manuscripts, but you could, if you liked, prevent my being worried to death with incompetent authors, and you won't. I do call it too bad of you, Pierson.'

'I am of some use to you, though, I suppose,' suggested Mr Pierson.

'I do not know in what way.'

'Why, to speak of nothing else – I introduced Lady Hilda –'

'Lady Hilda!' exclaimed Mr Vassett. 'I wish I had never heard of or seen her. I wish I had never published a book for her. I wish she was at Peru or anywhere else I should never set eyes on her again.'

'Dear me,' said Mr Pierson mildly, 'what has her ladyship done? What is the cause of this outburst?'

'Read that, and you will know,' answered Mr Vassett, throwing her ladyship's letter across to his factotum. 'I suppose I had better go down and get rid of this gentleman you seem somewhat afraid of.'

'Oh dear, no! I am not afraid of him,' remarked Mr Pierson, looking up from the perusal of Lady Hilda's epistle.

'I thought you observed you would rather not send him away.'

'I did make some remark of the kind; but that is a horse of quite another colour to being afraid of the man.'

'Though he does come armed with a manuscript.'

'I fancy the manuscript is his daughter's.'

'Worse and worse!' ejaculated Mr Vassett.

'Poor wretches! they are not very formidable,' said Mr Pierson, 'but they are quite new; we have not had anything like them in Craven Street before. Don't go down with a prepossession against them. Hear what they have got to say, at any rate.'

'I suppose I shall be forced to do so, whether I like it or not.'

'I should say in this case you will find that perfectly optional;' and Mr Pierson returned to his perusal of Lady Hilda Hicks's letter with the most exemplary composure.

Chapter IV

AN ASPIRANT FOR FAME

TIME AND CIRCUMSTANCES had imparted to Mr Vassett's face and demeanour a stern gravity, which stood him frequently in better stead even than the discouraging words he so often believed it his duty to utter.

The author did not live who could with any truth say that on the occasion of his first interview Mr Vassett had seemed glad to see him. Quite the contrary. The publisher received all new writers with a manner which implied that, as there were already far too many candidates for literary honours, it was ridiculous to expect any help from him to introduce another.

He was weary of persons 'possessed of genius', of persons who brought manuscripts, of men and women who, regarding him as a mere porter at the gates of the temple of Fame, came clamorously demanding admission into the sacred precincts.

With known authors he could fill his lists as full as he cared to do any day, and it was therefore with the most prudential motives he steeled his heart against the prayers of young beginners, and set his face to repel the attacks of 'rising talent.'

Poetry in especial was his abhorrence. He would almost as soon have seen a serpent enter his office as an 'attempt in blank verse,' or 'a few trifles thrown off in moments of inspiration,' by ladies who believed nothing so charming, so touching, so truly beautiful, had ever been published.

He had laid down a hard-and-fast rule about poetry, however, which, precluding all fear of pecuniary loss, reduced his interviews with poets and poetesses into mere dialogues, more or less disagreeable, according as the 'he' or 'she' were pertinacious and conceited, or modest, and willing to take 'No' for an answer.

Tales and sketches were not so easily managed, for although writers of prose proved generally more amenable to reason than producers of verse, he could not say he never undertook to publish such things at his own proper cost, and he was therefore frequently forced to retain manuscripts for perusal, and to write notes declining them, and, in fact, to 'consider the matter' – a process he found, as a rule, very unpleasant.

Whenever he could get Mr Pierson to take his place, and dismiss the intruders graciously – send them off, for instance, with some cock-and-bull story, to Murray, or Hurst and Blackett, or Saunders and Ottley, or anybody else of note – he felt infinite satisfaction in being well out of a troublesome business. But occasionally Mr Pierson played him false, and then he was placed on the horns of a dilemma; he had either to be determined in his own proper person, and send 'rising talent' about its business, or to promise that some hundreds of pages of manuscript should be read, and the propriety of accepting the production entertained.

What he had said was perfectly true: he did not consider Mr Pierson's opinion of a manuscript – ie, in favour of a manuscript – worth the paper it was written on, and therefore when that gentleman observed, 'I think there is some stuff in this,' Mr Vassett had to read it all himself, in order to make sure he was not either sending away a second Bulwer, or committing himself to a dead loss. Mr Pierson knew very well what was good; but Mr Pierson did not know what would 'take.'

Mr Vassett, on the contrary, had felt the public pulse so long, he could say with a sort of unerring certainty, 'This will never sell'; 'Yes, I have no doubt it is very admirable, and so forth, but I should prefer that some other person lost money over it.'

In selecting his authors, he possessed exactly the same gift successful masters possess in choosing their servants: individual merit and personal liking had no more share in influencing his decisions than such things have in determining the engagement of a clerk or the hiring of an errand boy. He could not have explained the process by which he arrived at his conclusions, and certainly neither could a wealthy merchant communicate the intuitions which enable him to select fitting instruments to carry out his wishes. No doubt it had occasionally happened that Mr Vassett closed his doors upon authors who made their mark elsewhere, but success in these cases was often more the result of chance than anything else; and, on the other hand, it may be certainly averred Mr Vassett never made an author free of Craven Street whose advent subsequently entailed pecuniary loss. It was not by one great *coup*, outweighing a series of annoying failures, Mr Vassett had made his money; so if his authors were none of them stars, they were at all events eminently safe. He knew about what they would sell, about what they would cost to advertise, about what the reviewers would say concerning their works. No need to lose a night's rest wondering how the subscription would go off, or whether he should see his money back again. He had no faith in 'firework' publishing, and, truth to tell, he had very little faith in genius either. He believed, if he believed in anything as regards authors, in plodding. Compilations, reminiscences, biographies, travels, historical romances, and such like, he looked upon with a certain favour; he could understand how they were done, and why; he was able to trace the method by which such webs of literary industry were woven; he could mark the progress of the busy shuttle, and predicate the result which would be produced by any practised hand. But to make something out of nothing, to write a book, not from observation, but from pure imagination, to create characters, and then make them move and speak and act like men and women; – it was 'very odd,' Mr Vassett considered, 'very odd' indeed!

He felt it indeed so odd, and so very little of this sort of writing worth publishing had come his way, he did not care to trouble himself much with fiction of any sort. It was out of his line, he said, though recently he had published one or two novels which had not done badly.

Would his early visitors prove poetical or 'three volume' or practical, he marvelled, as he wended his way downstairs. Under any circumstances he decided to get rid of them civilly. He had enough authors, he did not want any more; and having quite made up his mind on this point he opened the door of his private office, bowed gravely to the two persons he found there, and then, walking round the table to his own peculiar chair, seated himself and waited to hear what the gentleman opposite might have to say.

The gentleman began by remarking upon the weather. It is not a subject that seems remarkable for novelty. Most things which can be said about it have been said. But it forms a good sort of preliminary course in the way of conversation.

'Yes, it was dull,' Mr Vassett agreed. 'But at that precise season of the year we could not expect much sunshine.'

'Well, I suppose not in London?' said the gentleman.

Mr Vassett intimated it was not to be expected anywhere.

The gentleman thought in the open country the sky might be a little brighter.

Mr Vassett did not know in what part of the country.

The gentleman ventured to hint he had seen fine sunshiny winter mornings in various places, and something in the way he spoke, and the allusions he made to towns in England and towns abroad, induced Mr Vassett to imagine the roll of manuscript he saw darkly looming in the future of their interview might take a shape which would enable him courteously to get rid of his visitors by the simple process of stating there was no portion of the civilised or uncivilised earth he was open at that precise time to accept any account of.

He knew perfectly well his man was not an experienced hand – that he was not a 'writer,' that he was too old to begin, that he would never do any good, that all he had seen had been seen before, that all he had to say had been printed before, that probably the manuscript was some old diary, or journal made up from letters written home from Rome, or Constantinople, or Palestine, and –

'We have taken the liberty of calling upon you about a tale,' remarked the gentleman, suddenly snapping the thread of Mr Vassett's reflections. 'We saw one of your advertisements in the Morning Post, and we thought –'

'I publish very little,' interposed Mr Vassett, 'and I fear –'

'We know how full the literary market is,' went on the gentleman; 'but everything must have a beginning. My daughter is very young yet; still, I fancy what she has written possesses some merit, and if you would be so kind as to glance over one short story and give your opinion on it, I should really feel very grateful.'

'It is the daughter, then,' thought Mr Vassett; and he turned his eyes upon this fresh troubler of his peace with an expression which held no welcome in them.

Yet as Mr Vassett looked his expression changed. She was a child – bah! the notion of that young thing writing! It was too absurd. But the glint of the golden hair, the soft curves of the girlish face, the half-eager, half-bashful glance she cast appealingly at him, the shy gesture with which, taking the roll of paper out of her father's hands, she rose and placed it in his own, the scarcely audible 'I only brought the first two chapters,' reminded him of a past long gone, brought for a moment far-away springs and summers out of their distant graves, and filled his office with the perfume of the hawthorn of May, and the odour of June roses, dead years and years before.

He took the manuscript, untied the ribbon which confined it, opened the sheets out flat, and then laid them face downward on his blotting-pad.

'You have begun very early,' he remarked.

'I have been writing for years,' she answered.

He smiled and turned towards her father, who, replying to the look, said simply:

'I fancy she has something in her.'

Mr Vassett shook his head in mournful deprecation of this opinion; then regarding the manuscript as if it were some very nauseous draught which must be swallowed, he took up the written matter, and looking at the title, read:

'*The Hanes of* – of what – of where?' he asked.

'*Of Carrigohane,*' supplied the author.

'Oh!' said Mr Vassett, and thus enlightened he read on. He read to the bottom of the first side of copy, and then he re-read it.

'Humph!' he remarked.

He was surprised – no use in disguising that fact; he had not expected what he found.

'The writing will do,' he said, 'but the title won't.'

She was such a simpleton still, in all save the genius God had given her, she did not know what he meant, but thought he was referring to her handwriting, of which in those days she felt proud.

'I could alter the title,' she suggested, 'if – if –'

'I see it is an Irish story,' said Mr Vassett, eagerly availing himself of this loophole of escape.

'Yes. I don't know anything about England yet,' murmured the girl, in a manner which suggested in a week or two she hoped to supply the deficiency.

'And Irish stories are quite gone out.'

'I could try something else,' she answered feebly.

'Whether the world is right or wrong, I do not pretend to say,' observed Mr Vassett, addressing his observations to the gentleman, and blandly ignoring the authoress altogether; 'but it has an idea that young ladies cannot possess the amount of experience necessary to produce a readable book. For her age your daughter's style is good, very good indeed; it is, therefore, not impossible in the course of a few years –'

He paused suddenly, stopped by an exclamation which was quite involuntary from the girl.

Years! and she had thought to commence making money that week, that day, that hour!

At sound of her little cry of despair, for it almost amounted to that, Mr Vassett turned towards where she sat, and said:

'I am afraid my words seem hard to you, but indeed it would be madness for you to think of publishing anything at present. You are far too young. What can you know about the world or its troubles?' And he smiled upon her benignantly, as though she were a mere child, who had just left off dressing her dolls in order to play at authorship.

'I am not so young as you think,' she answered, somewhat pettishly, 'and I do know something of the world.'

Both men laughed – one a little cynically, the other sadly.

'Your daughter will not resent the imputation of youth so bitterly a few years hence as she does now,' suggested Mr Vassett.

'And till we came to London her sole lookout over the world was from windows that only commanded a view of the Atlantic,' supplemented the girl's father.

'Oh, papa! How can you say so?' she remonstrated.

'Well, my dear, it matters very little what I say or think; the question is what others believe. How are we to get to know,' he went on, addressing Mr Vassett, 'whether she has any talent or not; whether it is worth her while to go on writing or –'

'What is the alternative?' asked Mr Vassett.

'I *must* go on writing!' interposed the girl, before her father could answer.

'Whether you fail or succeed?'

'*Till* I succeed or fail.'

And the publisher and the author looked each other straight in the face.

'In that case there is no more to be said,' observed Mr Vassett, after a second's pause.

He spoke coldly, for there was no quality he disliked more in a woman than pertinacity.

She saw he was vexed, and yet to leave without receiving some word of counsel from this oracle seemed to her like letting a rope slip which might bring her to land.

'If you only could tell me what I must do – how I ought to set to work – I should be so grateful. I do not mind about waiting,' she added valiantly.

He opened the manuscript again, which he had rolled up to return at the first favourable opportunity, glanced down once more upon that awful title, and then looked across at the girl he would have liked to send back to the schoolroom or the nursery, or the Atlantic, or wherever she might have come from.

'My dear young lady,' he said, in his best manner, 'how can I tell you what I do not know myself? There is no Royal road to fame. Those who have achieved it tell me the path is rough, and hard to find; that it is lonely, often dark, always toilsome; while for those who never reach the goal –'

'They have attempted, at any rate,' she finished, as he paused, and there ensued a dead silence.

It was Mr Vassett who broke it.

'Literature,' he began, speaking in a general and didactic manner, 'is, so far as I am aware, the only profession in which persons imagine they can embark without the smallest training or preparation, or the remotest idea of the labour involved in producing an even moderately successful work.'

'I am not at all afraid of any trouble,' came from the special 'person' for whom this rebuke was intended. 'If you only tell me what I ought to do I will try to set about it at once.'

But this was precisely what neither Mr Vassett nor any other human being, author, publisher, or critic, could have told her. It is a question which has been asked hundreds of times. It is one which will be asked hundreds of times in days to come. When beginners beg for advice their real meaning is: 'How shall I compass success?'

At the first blush it seems a reasonable enough inquiry to put to an individual who has travelled the highways of literature; but it is one perfectly incapable of reply, and for this reason Mr Vassett answered:

'If I could publish a key to the problem you want to solve it would sell so well, I should never need to bring out another book. The land you want to enter has no itinerary – no finger posts – no guides. It is a lone, map-less country, and if you take my advice you will keep out of it. The pleasures even of successful literature are few and the pains many.'

'But if there were no authors there would be no publishers,' said the girl, smiting Mr Vassett under the fifth rib.

'I think, dear,' interposed her father, 'we must not intrude any longer. This gentleman has already given us a great deal of time, and –'

'I wish I could do something really to help you,' observed Mr Vassett. 'Under no circumstances could this,' and he lightly struck *The Hanes* of that place with an unpronounceable name as he spoke, 'be of the slightest use to me; but if you like I will have the manuscript read, and get an opinion upon it for you.'

'Oh, *if* you would!' cried its authoress rapturously.

'But should the opinion be adverse?' he suggested.

'I will try not to be disappointed.'

'Very well, then. I will write to you in a few days. Kindly favour me with your address,' he said to the tall, delicate-looking gentleman, who, taking out a card, presented it to Mr Vassett, after erasing one address and pencilling in another.

'Mr Westley,' read out the publisher. 'In a week's time, then, say.'

'Thank you; we are exceedingly obliged for the trouble you have taken.'

'Not at all; do not mention it,' and Mr Vassett, opening the door of his private room, walked with them across the outer office.

If father and daughter had understood they would have regarded this proceeding in the light of a most delicate attention; but they did not know, and did not therefore feel so much impressed as they might have been.

Just as they were about once again to thank Mr Vassett and depart, the door of the outer office swung open, and an apparition appeared on the threshold which fairly amazed the young person who thought she could write something worth reading. It took the form of a lady, fashionably and expensively dressed. Her silks were of the thickest, her velvets of the richest, her furs of the most expensive, her manner assured, her movements graceful. She looked at Mr Vassett with a comical smile, and giving him a familiar nod, stared hard at Mr Westley and his daughter.

Something in the languid indolence of the former, and the timid, innocent look of the latter, arrested her attention, and she scarcely heeded Mr Vassett's annoyed apology:

'Pardon me for one moment, Lady Hilda. Perhaps you will kindly walk into my room; I will be with you directly.'

Having satisfied her curiosity, she swept across the outer office into the inner sanctum, where, throwing herself into Mr Vassett's chair, she utilised the interval in examining the manuscript he had left lying on the table.

She was quietly perusing *The Hanes of Carrigohane* when Mr Vassett returned.

'Who is that girl?' she asked, looking up with the most perfectly unembarrassed expression of countenance.

'I am afraid I can scarcely answer your ladyship's question without giving offence,' he replied stiffly.

'Nonsense about offence!' she retorted. 'My ladyship does not take offence very easily. Who is she?'

'A young girl who has, I fancy, almost as much to learn, as you. Lady Hilda, have to unlearn.'

For a moment Lady Hilda looked at the speaker in undisguised astonishment. Then, breaking into a peal of hearty laughter, she exclaimed:

'You dear old thing! I do believe I have at last succeeded in making you angry. But we must not quarrel. We have known each other far too long for that. *Let us kiss and be friends.*'

Chapter V

LADY HILDA HICKS

THE EXPRESSION OF COUNTENANCE with which Mr Vassett received Lady Hilda's monstrous and impossible suggestion is simply indescribable. Accustomed though he was to her ladyship's random remarks, this latest utterance shocked him beyond measure. When subsequently he told Mr Pierson what she had said, they both laughed at the *façon de parler* as a good joke, but at the time Mr Vassett failed to see any jest in it.

Beyond everything he was 'proper.' Even from a forward young person in his own rank of life such a proposal would have struck him as indecorous in the extreme, while on the part of Mr Hicks's titled wife it seemed too terrible for belief.

If this was to be the end of ladies writing novels, if they meant to indulge in such dreadful and embarrassing speeches, the sooner a stop was put to the whole business the better for society. 'How much more suitable the spinning wheel and the working of tapestry,' he thought, forgetting, no doubt, that there were as 'fast' wives and maidens mewed up within convent and castle walls as ever drove in the Park.

Lady Hilda looked in his perplexed face and laughed again.

'I was *dreadfully* angry when I wrote to you,' she said. 'Why *will* you persist in vexing me? You know I would never say a disagreeable thing to you if you did not provoke me.'

They were happily drifting away from that dangerous phrase, which Mr Vassett knew she was quite capable of following up with even worse if the humour seized her, and he felt consequently able to answer with severe composure, 'he feared her ladyship was somewhat easily provoked.'

'No, I am not,' she retorted, 'not in the least. I have the sweetest and most forgiving temper possible if people only take it in the right way; but of course you cannot expect an author to be pleased when you write and say all the finest passages and most telling dialogues in a book must be cut out.'

'In my letter mention was made only of certain sentences which must be struck out or altered before the book can be published by anyone.'

'Why must they be struck out or altered?'

'For one reason, because no publisher wishes to have an action for libel brought against him.'

'I won't trouble you for the others,' she said, 'but now just let us talk that question of libel coolly over.'

'You must excuse me, Lady Hilda. It would be mere waste of time discussing the matter. I have quite made up my mind –'

'Set your foot down,' amended the fair authoress.

'Set my foot down, if the expression seems preferable,' proceeded Mr Vassett, 'that unless the whole of the libellous portions of the book are expunged, I will have nothing whatever to do with it; and in fact, to be quite frank, I wish to have nothing to do with it even if it were altered to the extent indicated in my letter.'

'Dear me!' exclaimed Lady Hilda.

'I do not wish to say anything rude,' proceeded Mr Vassett, warming to his work, and nettled by his visitor's tone and manner, 'but in justice to myself I cannot refrain from remarking that your ladyship allows yourself a latitude of expression which causes an amount of annoyance to which I feel it would be incompatible with other business arrangements for me to continue to subject myself. Even if I had nothing else to attend to, the mockery and – and the abuse –'

She had commenced checking off his observations on her fingers, but when he stopped, really too angry to proceed with whatever he may have intended to say, her whole manner changed in an instant.

'I am sorry,' she cried, if not repentantly, at any rate with an admirable counterfeit of repentance. 'I can't make any fuller apology, can I? You must forgive and forget. Remember what an impetuous mortal I am. I know I do get into passions; I have never laid that good old creature Watts' caution sufficiently to heart, I suppose; but they are over in a moment – a mere flash in the pan. You could never be so cruel as to think of sending me among those dreadful bears the other publishers, I, who am your own, your very own, who made my success with you, and who have also brought you into note.'

'Lady Hilda,' began Mr Vassett solemnly – her impetuous ladyship's sentences had a beautiful knack of carrying a sting in their tail – 'you have made that assertion before, and I have not thought it necessary to contradict it –'

'No, I shouldn't, if I were you,' interrupted Lady Hilda carelessly. 'Oh, here's Mr Pierson,' she went on with joyous eagerness, as that gentleman, not knowing who was there, looked into the room. 'Come in; we are just wanting you,' she said, for he was about to withdraw. 'Mr Vassett and I have had our little quarrel out, and are now the dearest of dear friends again; only he wants some little things altered in my new book, and I am not very willing to alter them. What do you say? Now, you shall be umpire, and give the decision on my side, of course.'

Anyone seeing Mr Pierson as he stood listening to Lady Hilda, and not knowing who he was, might have taken him for a strict ecclesiastic of the Romish Church. Lean almost to emaciation, pale, clean-shaven, dressed in a closely buttoned-up loose black coat, the end of his thin nose just touched with a delicate red which might have been painted in with cold or severe fasting, a look of deep thought in his brownish grey eyes, his long wasted hand laid flat on the rich morocco binding of an old edition, he was as unlike the popular ideal of a 'reader' as can well be imagined. He had always believed in the earl's daughter, even when Mr Vassett was most inclined to 'pooh-pooh' her, and she had never scrupled to use him as a weapon against her 'dearest of dear friends.'

'You think Mr Vassett is dreadfully unreasonable, now don't you?' she asked with a winning smile, intended to captivate both men.

Lady Hilda was still a very pretty woman, considerably under forty; perfect in her dress, redolent of perfume, powdered, gloved, booted for conquest. It were idle to deny these things, added to her rank, her worldly position, and her talents had their effect, nevertheless –

'I really do not see,' began Mr Pierson, and in a certain clear, metallic coldness the reader's voice matched his features, 'how Mr Vassett could, without considerable alteration, possibly publish the new novel.'

'And even if you were able to see,' interposed Mr Vassett, taking refuge in very decided language, a sure sign of weakness, 'it would make no difference to my view of the question. The novel is one I should much prefer not to publish at all, and I certainly shall not publish it unless the objectionable paragraphs to which I have directed the author's attention are altered most materially.'

He spoke to Mr Pierson as if the author were twenty miles distant. Lady Hilda looked at the reader, smiled, shrugged her shoulders, and made a *moue*.

'You won't desert me, Mr Pierson, will you?' she said, almost tenderly.

Considering it was that gentleman who had pointed out the objectionable passages to his employer, he found it impossible to do otherwise than assert that he really could not take the responsibility upon him of advising Mr Vassett to bring out the book without considerable pruning and softening.

'Hacking and ruining, you mean,' amended the authoress.

'No; I think all the changes Mr Vassett wishes made will improve the story. It is so clever, that it would be a pity to mar the whole by leaving in paragraphs which certainly detract both from its interest and its merits. You would be the first, Lady Hilda, to blame Mr Vassett if he allowed a novel to appear with the blemishes which at present obscure this work.'

'Should I?' said Lady Hilda derisively. 'Words, words, words, Mr Pierson; and it is not right of you both to take this tone with me because I am a woman. If I were a man, Mr Vassett wouldn't dare to dictate which passages should be retained and which expunged. Supposing he ventured to do anything of the sort, a man would say, "It is my business to write, and yours to publish. I don't presume to meddle with your trade, and you shouldn't pretend to meddle with mine." That is what a man would say. But as it is only poor little me, without even a husband who will stand up for the wife he vowed to cherish, I must submit, I suppose. I give you leave to alter the expressions Mr Vassett's superior wisdom considers unfit to print. I bow to his imagined knowledge of the usages of good society, and to his intimate acquaintance with the manners and customs of the Upper Ten. Only, for heaven's sake, Mr Pierson, do your spiriting gently. Don't make me very ridiculous in the eyes of those who do know something of the sort of life I have attempted to describe.'

Mr Vassett turned red, and made a gulp, as if he had suddenly swallowed a very nasty pill, and then he began –

'I should much prefer, Lady Hilda, that you took your novel somewhere else. The trouble I have –'

'Now, now, now,' she interrupted sweetly, 'do not let us go over all that old ground again. Like a dear, kind soul, make up your mind not to try to quarrel with me. It is of no use, I assure you. Two people are required to make a quarrel, and I will not be one of them. You have got me for better or worse. I'll be as good as I can, and you must be good too. Be kind to him, Mr Pierson. Something has annoyed him this morning. Oh, I know. He is thinking too much about a very bread-and-buttery young lady he says has a great deal to learn. Don't have anything to do with teaching her, Mr Vassett. Take my advice; very young ladies are dangerous. I know. I was, little as you may imagine such a thing, bread-and-buttery once myself!'

Whether it was the way she made this assertion, or the contrast suggested by it, who can say? The two men could not, though they laughed outright.

'That is better,' exclaimed the lady who had left her bread-and-buttery days behind. 'I love to see you laugh. It is a thing you both seem so unused to. Now, while you are in a good temper, I will run away.'

And suiting her action to her word, Lady Hilda tripped out into the passage by what she called the 'near way', and was in her brougham before Mr Pierson, hurrying after, could open the door for her.

55

'No, I don't want to say a word more to you,' she exclaimed, letting down the window and instantly shutting it up again.

And then she smiled sweetly and waved her little hand, and departed – a vision of loveliness, so the passers-by considered.

Mr Pierson went back into the calm silence of Mr Vassett's private room.

'I wonder what devilment she is up to now?' he said, addressing Mr Vassett in a tranquil tone, which formed a curious contrast to his words.

'I feel greatly inclined to send her manuscript after her,' observed the publisher valiantly.

'Don't, unless you want her here again tomorrow.'

'What an extraordinary being she is!' remarked Mr Vassett. And then he told his reader about that dreadful proposition. 'Some men would have taken her at her word,' remarked Mr Pierson. 'I wonder if that is the way she brought Hicks to the "scratch"?'

Mr Vassett considered in familiar conversation Mr Pierson had a knack of occasionally making use of expressions almost as vulgar as Lady Hilda's were objectionable, but he found it extremely difficult to insinuate such an idea, and so allowed the phrase concerning Hicks to pass.

'You were not equal to the occasion,' went on Mr Pierson, referring to Lady Hilda's suggestion. 'You missed a chance, Vassett.'

Now the danger was over, something in the suggestion seemed to Mr Vassett infinitely amusing. Perhaps on the whole he was not sorry the interview had gone off well.

He knew other publishers envied him the possession of such a treasure. He was well aware he should feel vexed to see the book announced in any other list save his own. He could afford to laugh, having won, and he was particularly gracious to Mr Pierson, who had, he felt, helped him over a somewhat difficult stile.

Chapter VI

'HOW'S MARIA?'

IN VERY BAD SPIRITS Mr Bernard Kelly stood looking at the ornamental water in St James's Park.

It was a dull, mournful afternoon. At about ten minutes to twelve the sun had made a sudden appearance, but not finding the aspect of things in London to his mind, retired for the day before the clock struck. Never, even in his native land, had Mr Kelly been out in more depressing weather. A good steady deluge of rain, a look-out across a wide morass, with a semi-circle of grey lonely hills bounding the horizon, and a sorrowful weeping sky brooding over the whole dreary landscape, would have seemed a relief in contrast to the brown, leafless trees, the wretched grass, the disconsolate water-fowl, and the mimic lake rippling darkly in the gathering gloom of that miserable afternoon in late November.

Bad as the day was, it did not outdo the aspect of Bernard Kelly's fortunes. As yet he did not look like a hopeless man, but for the first time in his life he was beginning to understand what 'despair' meant. His coat was not shabby, but the wearer felt out at elbows as regards 'luck.' Since his arrival in London, nothing had gone well with him. That unfortunate escapade of his in the omnibus had not merely deprived him of patronage in the only quarter where he could apply, but affected the home supplies. 'Madam,' wrote Mr Balmoy to his sister – whom he had hitherto always addressed as 'My dear Lucretia' –

When I promised to use my influence to advance the fortunes of your son, I thought you were sending to England a gentleman. I find instead – a Boor and a Buffoon. The sooner he returns to the low associations of his native land the better. If he remains in London, I greatly fear the next occasion on which we meet I shall be on the Bench and he in the Dock. Spare me and yourself this crowning humiliation.

Your obedient Servant,
R Balmoy.

When she received this communication, Mrs Kelly, though no rapid scribe, instantly despatched two letters to London; they were carried into Callinacoan by a bare-footed and bare-legged boy-child clad in ragged petticoats, who was told to 'run for his life,' so as to get them into the box before the mail went out.

The epistles were extremely brief, but to the point. That to Wimpole Street ran thus:

My Dear Brother,
In the name of all that's wonderful, what has Barney been up to now?
(a phrase which seemed to the magisterial mind to contain within itself a whole indictment).

Your loving Sister,
L Kelly.

While the missive which went out with the mail to West Ham proved even shorter. Mrs Kelly enclosed Mr Balmoy's letter inquiring, on a piece of coarse paper which had contained brown sugar, 'What have you been doing on your uncle, Barney?'

Delaying his reply to this maternal question, Mr Kelly found his uncle had answered it for him at great length.

Distracted by no sense of humour, Mr Balmoy gave the facts in a strictly judicial manner. Divested of every particle of the ludicrous, Barney's sin seemed not merely great but senseless. In Mr Balmoy's account the intended joke fell so utterly flat, was made to appear so childish a performance altogether, that Mrs Kelly's pathetic –

'You're done for now, Barney; what possessed you?' found an echo in her son's inmost soul.

The Kellys were a family destitute of the elegant graces which distinguished the Donaghs, and therefore when Barney wrote back that the 'devil had possessed him,' Mrs Kelly did not accept the phrase as unfitting or disrespectful. She merely intimated, in reply, that 'it was no good talking that sort of nonsense; anyone could resist the devil if he chose. There was Scripture for it, though she did not exactly know where, but no doubt Mat Donagh, who was so clever, could lay his hand on that text. Barney would have to resist the devil and other things if he ever meant to get up in the world like his uncle. He'd have to learn to keep a quiet tongue in his head. He had better look into the Bible she had packed among his summer shirts, and see what was said there about the tongue. It was a burning shame for him to try to play his fool's pranks on an old man, and one,' went on Mrs Kelly, 'more especially, that could never from a child bear to be laughed at. You had best go to him again and say you are sorry; maybe he would get you something to do in the Customs. I am told there's a heap to be made in the Customs just by holding your tongue; but oh, Barney, that's a thing I am afraid is a bit beyond you!'

If the exchequer had been full, Mr Kelly would have treated these maternal utterances with the indifference he had been wont to accord his mother's words of wisdom in the days which now seemed so far behind; but with funds gradually sinking, with no employment or chance of employment, without friends willing to help, or acquaintances of any sort in London, it cannot be considered wonderful that Mr Balmoy's nephew found it impossible to look cheerfully at his position.

He had written to his mother for money, and that morning received her answer, which certainly was not one likely to raise his spirits.

My dear Barney,

I enclose a pound, which is all I have and all I can get. You'll have to turn to and do something for yourself, for as far as I can see there'll not be much help to be had from here for some time to come. Your father has been on the drink, steady, since Callinacoan fair-day, and he lost or was robbed of the price of a heifer and the old black horse, on the road home. Larry was thrown trying to put a new hunter Captain Desmond brought back with him from Donegal, over the stone wall at the foot of the Duke's field at Castle Donagh, and got his leg broken in two places. Doctor Kane says it will be a six months' job; and the Captain's so wild because that contrary brute of his went off by himself across the moor and sprained his shoulder leaping the boulders for his own diversion, he won't allow Larry a farthing of compensation, though everybody knows Larry couldn't be blamed for what was the horse's fault. The agent is talking of raising the rent on us. They say Mr Fortescue has put him up to it, but now you are gone I don't think much of that myself. Tom Kelly from Galway came here the other day. He is going to try to establish an agency in Belfast for 'pure peat whisky,' but your cousin John thinks the Excise'll never let him do it. His opinion is you did wrong about Miss Fortescue. He believes you would have done better to run off with her, because then, for very decency, the family must have made her a good allowance. As he observes, 'they couldn't let the old woman starve' and you might have got a fine farm or a post in Dublin if you had held out. However, there's no good talking about last year's snow. Hoping you will soon be able to tell me you have got to work,

Your loving Mother.

'They are all turning against me,' thought Bernard as he stood on the bridge, with arms resting on the rail, looking down into the water. 'What to be at I'm sure I don't know. I can't walk into a strange office, and bid a man I never saw before give me something to do, and I see plainly enough Donagh does not mean to lend me a helping hand. He was talking about the Colonies last night, but I am not gone there yet, Mr Mat. You are sick of me, but not more sick than I am of you. Still, what can a fellow do? What the deuce am I to do?'

He pulled a few shillings out of his pocket, and looked at them mournfully. Then he replaced the amount, and was about to resume his study of natural history, when a cheery voice amazed him by saying in his very ear:

'Ha! Good afternoon. Well met!'

Turning to the side whence this address proceeded, Mr Kelly beheld a total stranger, well buttoned up in a topcoat with fur collar, and wearing a hat perched so much on one side, he immediately began to speculate how soon it would be gambolling among the swans sailing about below.

'I have never seen you before, sir,' he answered. 'You are labouring under some mistake.'

'Oh no, I am not,' was the answer; 'I remember you very well.'

'You have the advantage of me, then,' retorted Mr Kelly.

'Now you are natural,' cried the other; 'and nature does not sit half so well upon you as art. Strange, a man's own part never seems to fit him so well as that he assumes. There, don't look so savage, my friend. "*How's Maria?*"'

The expression of Mr Kelly's countenance was murderous.

'I can't tell what the devil you mean,' he said. 'I don't know you, sir, and I don't want to know you.'

'By heavens!' interrupted the other, 'this is too magnificent. He's the other man. "*Where is Tom now?*"' and he laughed till he choked himself.

'Sir, you are either mad or drunk, or both!' exclaimed Bernard Kelly. 'I never saw you before, and I never want to see you again', and he was turning on his heel when the stranger, laying a persuasive hand on the sleeve of his coat, murmured blandly:

'"*I have always said he was the flower of the flock!*" Don't go off in a rage. Lord, this is splendid! I didn't mean to offend you. I have hoped and longed we might meet again some day. I never saw anything better done – never. Why, man, you ought to make your fortune. Shall I ever forget – shall I ever – the face of your ancient friend as he stood in the mud shaking his stick after us? I have told the

60

story over and over and over again. But I couldn't do the thing as you did it. Where in the world did you acquire the trick of that excruciatingly bland and fatuous look the amiable deaf assume? On no stage did I ever behold a better presentment! I would not for five pounds have missed the little interlude.'

'You were in the omnibus that day, then?' conjectured Mr Kelly, somewhat mollified. 'I did not notice you.'

'Ah! my friend, you were too well employed on the stage to observe the audience,' said the other. 'As I before remarked, it was in its way the best bit of acting I ever beheld.'

'If you knew what it cost me, you might think as I do – that the game was hardly worth the candle.'

'Indeed! The matter did not end there, then?'

'No; faith, it only began. Who do you suppose the old swell was?'

'Can't form even a wide conjecture.'

'Balmoy, the Leather Lane Magistrate –'

'Bless and save us! Well –'

'And my uncle.'

'I can't stand this; you will kill me!' cried Mr Kelly's admirer, breaking into peal after peal of laughter. 'Oh! if you could only have seen your own face – if you could only have heard your own voice, as you made that statement – you'd never have forgotten either. And so that was old Balmoy, and Balmoy is your uncle? He had not you up for brawling, had he? How did it happen you were unacquainted with his appearance?'

'I had never seen him in my life. He came to London before I was born. I was on my way to his house when, as ill-luck would have it, I got into that confounded omnibus. He was to have put me in the way of earning my living, but instead of doing anything of the kind he has turned all my own people at home against me. So you see, sir, whoever you are,' finished Mr Kelly, 'that when I thought I was taking off the old swell I was really cutting my own throat.'

'I don't know that,' said the other, 'my experience goes to prove that the little apparent accidents, which turn a man off one set of rails and shunt him on to another, are really merciful interpositions – providences, if you prefer that expression. In what way did your uncle suggest you should earn your living? Remember I am quoting your own words.'

'He would have got me into some Government office, I imagine,' said Mr Kelly.

'You are old for that; but of course influence can override a baptismal certificate. It would have been a crying sin, however, to bury such talents as yours in a napkin, tied up with red tape. Might as well be a clerk in the City.'

'I wish to Heaven I was anything – anywhere! When you spoke to me I was just considering what the deuce to be at.'

'Till getting low?' suggested the stranger.

Mr Kelly stared at him. Similes drawn from trade were not common in Ireland at that time.

'Devil in your pocket?' amended the other, seeing the young man's lack of comprehension.

'Well, I can't say I am particularly flush of cash.'

'And what do your friends advise you to do now?'

'Get to work. Very good counsel, no doubt, if they would only tell me how to follow it.'

'You are not alone in London, are you?'

'I am stopping with some people I know; but for all the use they are to me I might as well be alone.'

'Business people?'

'No; Irish,' answered Mr Kelly, quite unconscious of the absurdity of his reply. 'He is a literary man.'

The stranger pricked up his ears. 'What is his name? I know every literary man in London, I believe.'

'Donagh.'

'Donagh! Never heard of him. A new hand, perhaps?'

'No. He has been connected with the press for years.'

'Writes under a *nom de plume*, then. Well, can't he put you in the way of getting some cash? A clever fellow like you ought to be able to handle the pen.'

'I have knocked off some little things,' confessed Mr Kelly. He did not feel one-half so shy with this free-and-easy stranger as he had done with the master of Abbey Cottage.

'I knew it – I could have sworn it,' exclaimed the other; 'we shall hear of you yet! Such talent was never born to waste its sweetness on the desert air of a Government office. Where were you going when I intruded my company?'

'I was not going anywhere.'

'Which way do you intend to bend your steps now?'

'I have not decided.'

'Let me decide for you, then. Come home with me. I want to know more of you. Besides, as two heads are, it is said, better than one – a proverb the truth of which I beg leave to doubt; for I am sure I know some heads no dozen of which would be equal to one such as yours, for example; still, let that pass. To revert to what I intended to remark: between us, we ought to be able to set you going in something.'

'You are extremely kind, I am sure,' answered Mr Kelly, with a little coy hesitation.

'Kind – not a bit of it. If you consent to waive ceremony and partake of such poor hospitality as I can offer, all the kindness will be on your side, all the pleasure on mine. Stay; you don't know who I am. I think I have a card. No; well, this will serve as well;' and with an air he handed Mr Kelly an envelope addressed to 'S Dawton, Esq., The Wigwam, South Lambeth.'

'That is my name, sir – Dawton.'

'Indeed,' said Mr Kelly, who did not seem so much astonished by the information as S Dawton, Esq., evidently expected.

'You have heard it before, do doubt, often?' cunningly suggested Mr Dawton.

'I can't remember that I have,' answered Mr Kelly, who thought his new friend meant to imply the name was a common one in England, like Smith. Mr Dawton looked at him in surprise, then gravely shaking his head, remarked:

'Such is Fame.'

'Is the name of Dawton famous, then?' inquired Mr Kelly, who felt he had, as he mentally told himself, 'put his foot in it.' 'You must excuse my ignorance; I have been so short a time in London –'

'It is a name known not in London merely,' observed Mr Dawton. 'The provinces Dublin – Edinburgh – America – Australia – wherever the English language is spoken, wherever the Union Jack floats in the breeze; – but never mind that. If you think you have sufficiently studied the appearance and manners of those arch-impostors below us, come along. We shall find some dinner ready. You have not dined, I hope?'

If Mr Kelly had, like his friend Mr Mat Donagh, been 'knocking about London' for even a short time, he would have felt at no loss to determine the profession of Mr Dawton, who believed his reputation to be as wide as the world is round. He had noted that clean-shaved face, the wig, which, though well-made, could have deceived no human being possessed of ordinary powers of observation; the peculiar mode of address, and the more than singular method of standing: but all these things, whether taken singly or collectively, failed to give him a cue to the man's real calling.

Subsequently, when 'behind the scenes' seemed as familiar ground to him as the stable-yard of 'The White Goat' at Callinacoan had ever done, when he was able to exchange as smart repartee with actors and actresses as he had 'cut his teeth on' in the bar of the hostelry aforementioned, he wondered at his own stupidity. Just as an experienced eye can detect a moulder by the knees of his trousers, so in the after-time he could have told a gentleman accustomed to tread the boards by twenty little signs unintelligible to the outside multitude; but when, after a little hesitation, he intimated his willingness to proceed to The Wigwam with Mr Dawton as guide, Bernard Kelly, though he devoutly believed he 'had seen a thing or two,' knew really as much about life as the barefooted 'gossoon' Mrs Kelly had hurriedly summoned from herding the geese to carry her despatches to Callinacoan post-office.

'You won't object to frugal fare, I hope,' said Mr Dawton, as they walked to 'take boat at Westminster.' So strong is the force of imagination that it is possible Mr Dawton, when he used the phrase in vogue when there were 'jolly young watermen' and cavaliers with plumes and doublets, felt himself for the moment a contemporary of Buckingham. 'I leave all the details of housekeeping to my better-half, who, I can assure you, is emphatically the better-half of my fortunes, and therefore it is a simple fact that I never know what she intends to appear smoking on the board. There will be something of the nature of fish, flesh, or fowl, and perchance a tart or pudding, but what I cannot say. Pot-luck, you know. Will you, if the luck of the pot is not overgood today, forgive all shortcomings for the sake of a welcome which is very hearty and true?'

Mr Kelly professed himself quite ready to be satisfied with anything that might be going.

'I should be a churl,' he said, 'not to relish bread and cheese in such good company'; a speech which pleased Mr Dawton mightily, and elicited the consolatory information that Mrs D might be trusted to have something better than bread and cheese awaiting them.

'Not, mind you,' proceeded Mr Dawton, 'that I hold such fare to be despised. I never enjoyed anything in my life more than I did once, in the Midlands at midnight, a few slices from a home-made loaf, and a wedge cut out of a cheese sixty pounds weight, the repast washed down with the best homebrewed ale I ever tasted – ale brewed from Worcester hops, my boy!'

Mr Kelly, who was almost as tired of cheese as of bacon and poor gentry, who had never tasted home-made bread except bannocks baked on the paternal griddle, and who disliked ale rather than otherwise, remarked diplomatically that he thought the relish with which a man ate his food all depended on the appetite he brought to it.

'When I have been out shooting,' he observed, 'I have thought a raw turnip an aldermanic feast.'

'I don't doubt it,' agreed Mr Dawton. 'Only, as the alderman said about the leg of mutton, "it was a pity to waste a fine appetite on a turnip." That's Lambeth Palace, the Archbishop of Canterbury's place, and there to the left stands the Lollards' Tower.'

'I know,' replied Mr Kelly; 'I have been up this way before.' And he might have added that he was better acquainted with the history of Lambeth than Mr Dawton, who lived in the parish, and had read as much about the Lollards as any Archbishop of Canterbury, if indeed the reading of archbishops ever takes a turn in that direction.

But he was wondering at the moment what sort of a place The Wigwam would prove to be.

'The first thing you have to do in England,' said Mr Matthew Donagh to him, with sublime impressiveness, 'is to get rid of every Irish notion you failed to leave behind you on the other side of the Channel.'

Mr Kelly considered this speech great nonsense at the time, but he was gradually coming round to the opinion that there might be something in it. His 'notions' had already prepared so many disappointments for him that he began to wish he could have commenced his London experiences with his mind in the state of that celebrated white sheet of paper mentioned by Mr Locke, and referred to by many persons since the days of that writer.

'The Wigwam' in Ireland would have meant a lovely cottage – large or small, according to the means of the owner, but still lovely – beautifully situated, probably on the bank of some clear stream or tranquil lake, hemmed in with trees among which copperbeech and mountain-ash and delicate birch appeared conspicuous, the rough-cast walls covered with roses and passion-flowers and jessamine, the roof of thatch, and furnished with deep eaves, where thousands of sparrows held carnival; a rustic porch; a cottage – simple in its appearance, yet so comprehensive in its capabilities that, according to the means of the occupier, the meal to which a guest was bidden might mean ham and eggs and potatoes piping hot, or the best effort of a French cook brought over by some gentleman to Ireland for 'the shooting.'

Already Mr Kelly knew he could not expect meandering trout streams or glassy lakes or fine sea views, or coppice and brake in the purlieus of London; but he thought his new friend's house would prove some rural crib, left behind by mistake when the country moved farther from town. In his walks to and from the City he had come across many odd places of this sort about Stratford and Bow, and even nearer Mile End, for the East End was not then such a nest of workmen's dwellings as it has since become. Access was somewhat difficult, and the cost of transit to any one of these suburbs by no means small.

Mr Dawton nimbly and with short active steps – talking volubly all the way – conducted Mr Kelly from the Nine Elms pier through a neighbourhood that gentleman was totally unacquainted with, along Nine Elms Lane and across the Wandsworth Road, up Mile Street, and so into the South Lambeth Road, out of which, after a little time, they turned sharply to the left, and proceeded along a lane bearing evidences of not so very long ago having been quite in the country, that would, had they pursued it to the other end, have led them speedily into the direct highway to Clapham. But they were now at their journey's end. Stopping before a dull-looking dwelling, and pushing open one of the gates, for there were two opening upon a small sweep of gravelled drive overgrown with grass and moss, Mr Dawton bade his companion welcome to The Wigwam.

'A poor place,' he said, 'but retired; within a walk of the City, yet as secluded as though we were fifty miles from the busy haunts of men. The name was a happy inspiration of my own. Observing the house advertised, I came to see it. The agent gave me an order of admission, which ran thus:

"Admit – Dawton, Esq., and friends, to view Buhl House."

'I declare I felt paralyzed, and if the rent had not been very low I should never have troubled myself further about the matter. The house was built by some City man for his own occupation, a cordwainer or something of the kind, who, having made a pot of money, built himself a big mansion out Streatham way, and wanted to find a tenant for his former abode.

'It wasn't everybody's money, but it was mine; so I took the place, and without by your leave or anything else rechristened it The Wigwam, sending a printed notice of the change effected to the tradespeople, post-office authorities, and police inspector. Bless you, in a week every soul in the parish knew where The Wigwam was situated. Those who had never before heard of Buhl House heard of it then. We had the bars of the gates painted to represent arrows tipped and feathered, and my son carried out a beautiful design on the posts, embodying every sort of amusement in which the Ked Indian indulges – canoeing, hunting, swimming, dancing, fighting, scalping. Till the weather spoiled the effect those symbolical posts were the talk and admiration of the neighbourhood. People used to walk out on Sundays to see them. The Wigwam was as good as an exhibition of pictures to the populace. That is the way to get a place known, eh?'

Inwardly wondering why any man should wish to attract such publicity to his private residence, Mr Kelly agreed that it was. In one respect he resembled the children of nature still represented, though very, very dimly, on the gateposts. He evinced no surprise at anything. If his new friend had taken him to Buckingham Palace, and stating the Queen might be expected to appear presently, asked him to take a seat meanwhile. Miss Westley's travelling companion would have died rather than evince the least sign of astonishment. He was not going to let the Saxon imagine he had seen nothing but bogs. He would, if he could help it, give the English no opportunity of laughing at his ignorance.

Many matters he might forget or overlook, but he never forgot or overlooked Bernard Kelly. This young man had every element in his nature for compassing success – a cool head, a cold heart, a selfishness which was as instinctive as his love of ease and money, his dislike of those who were badly off, and his jealousy of those who had the world's ball at their feet.

If he could only have looked forward a little he need not have felt uneasy about his own literary success up to a certain point. Supposing he failed to succeed beyond that point, it would only be because he was not half so clever as he thought, and as his friends believed.

To Mr Kelly the appearance of The Wigwam was much less suggestive of Red Indians in the untrammelled freedom of virgin forests than of rent, rates, and taxes, water laid on by the company, gas supplied by meter, and the other appliances and drawbacks of civilization; but it was evidently with the keenest sense of bivouacking out in the wilds that his host cordially bade him enter the hall, the walls of which were painted in a like eccentric fashion to the gates and posts, and throwing open a door, ushered the unexpected guest into the presence of his squaw, as in moments of exuberant abandon Mr Dawton was wont to call the comfortable-looking, comely, sensible lady who had 'kept things together 'when, if left to Mr Dawton's own management, the household must have dropped to pieces altogether.

'My dear,' said her husband, as Mrs Dawton rose at their entrance, and though apparently somewhat surprised at the appearance of a stranger, extended her hand in ready greeting. 'Congratulate me. Quite by accident I came upon the gentleman whose acquaintance I have been so desirous of making. He has kindly consented to take share of whatever may be going for dinner. I don't know his name, and if I did you wouldn't be much wiser; but you will at once recognise him if I mention the password, "*How's Maria?*"'

'Oh, really,' exclaimed Mrs Dawton, and her voice was as pleasant as her face, 'I am delighted to see you; and my sons will be delighted also, I know. We all feel as if we had known you for years.'

'"*What is Tom doing now?*"' asked Mr Dawton, laughing. 'I introduced myself in that way – upon my soul I did, Bessy! You never saw a fellow look so savage in your life. He couldn't, just for the minute, make out what the dickens I was at.'

'Well, you will allow I have fulfilled one part of the programme, which you did not expect that day we met in the omnibus,' said Mr Kelly. '*I have come round to see you soon!*'

'Neat, neat, confoundedly neat and ready!' cried Mr Dawton, whose pleasant flattery was as balm to the wounds Mr Donagh's too friendly candour had inflicted. 'The idea of a man of your abilities contemplating the swans in a desponding mood! We'll strike out something, never fear. Where are the boys, Bessie?'

'Ted and Jim will be here presently; but Will and Ben are out, and said we were not to wait for them.'

'Then you had better order up dinner at once. If Tom's friend – but there, I really must, even as a mere matter of convenience, ask you to give me a name.'

'Kelly,' said Tom's friend, a little confused at his omission. 'Bernard Kelly.'

'Thank you. I was going to remark if you were half as hungry as I am, something to eat would not be unwelcome.'

Chapter VII

THE DAWTONS AT HOME

MR KELLY, in the solitude of The Wigwam's best bed-chamber, when he had accepted his host's offer of warm water and a 'brush up', felt himself at last in very comfortable quarters.

The house was a far better house than Abbey Cottage; the furniture was far better furniture than any in which Mr Donagh's female belongings took pride; an indescribable look of plenty pervaded the establishment, a good savour floated up the staircase and hung about the landings; the servant who answered Mr Dawton's summons was neat, and young, and pretty; his welcome had been cordial as cordial could be. Out of the cold and dreariness of St James's Park into the heat and comfort of a well-built, well-aired, well-furnished house, with the prospect of an excellent dinner, was a change for the better Mr Kelly felt able to appreciate as much as any man that ever lived. He had come to England for the flesh-pots which he had been told were common in that country; but so far his fare proved no better – nay, far worse, indeed – than at home. The style of housekeeping at Abbey Cottage combined with wonderful completeness every fault to be found in Erin and in Albion, while Mr Donagh's cordiality he found gradually cooling down from boiling to freezing point. As he stood looking at the swans, Mr Kelly was speculating amongst other things as to the number of degrees Mat's first genial hospitality could still fall.

When he once again entered the drawing room, which apartment was at The Wigwam converted into a pleasant and common parlour, where all the furniture was good and nice looking, but kept for use rather than show, he found two of 'the boys' added to the party.

One of them had reached the mature age of thirty, and the other was fast travelling to the same milestone. The eldest, Mr Dawton introduced as 'my son Ted, who is clever with his brush'; the next, Jim, being mentioned carelessly as 'a fellow managers and editors were rather sweet on.' Both of these gentlemen hailed Mr Kelly as a brother.

'How's Maria?' had passed into a household word amongst the Wigwamites, and while soup was still in progress, Jim, to whom his father explained their new friend's position in a slang which would not have disgraced Newgate, observed that he was sure something might be made of the incident which had procured them the pleasure of Mr Kelly's acquaintance.

'I'll think the matter over,' promised Jim, finishing a glass of sherry as he spoke.

Whereupon Mr Dawton nodded his head confidentially to their guest, and intimated in a stage whisper that 'if Jim took it up he could knock a good thing off in a day.'

Mr Kelly had not the faintest notion what Jim proposed to 'knock off' but as he inferred beneficial results were to accrue from the process for himself, he received the information vouchsafed in wise and thankful silence.

Before the pudding, which in Mr Dawton's invitation hung tremblingly in the balance of possibilities, had made its appearance, Bernard Kelly heard more 'shop' talked than during the whole term of his residence under Mr Donagh's roof. Actors, musicians, artists, authors – these people had them all at their fingers'-ends; not speaking about literature, and art, and music, and acting from any external point of view, but familiarly, as men do who, making their living by writing, singing, painting, or acting, talk concerning the things, persons, and surroundings amongst which they pass their lives.

No reticence at The Wigwam about the names of magazines, editors, contributors, plays, dramatists, tenors, sopranos, altos.

Ted, Mr Kelly to his intense astonishment gathered, was a scene-painter; a branch of art he had hitherto somewhat confused with house decoration of an ordinary and humble character. In the family councils, however, Ted was evidently a person of weight, differing in this respect from Jim, who, though appealed to when matters of imagination and invention came on the *tapis*, was clearly not considered either by himself or anybody else so useful and practical a fellow as Ted. While cheese was in progress the party was reinforced by Will and Ben, for whose benefit the joint was brought back; and while they ate they unfolded a perfect budget of news, to which their father and brothers listened eagerly, and Mr Kelly with an amazement he could scarcely conceal. They had been among the editors, and heard and seen everything apparently which was to be heard or seen in London. Names he had read of, but never hoped to become familiar with, were bandied about the table like shuttlecocks. The writers of anonymous articles were declared, the reasons for bad or good reviews given, the machinery which kept the literary world going was exposed, the motives influencing proprietors and publishers revealed, the latest gossip repeated, the most recent jokes laughed at, the row between rival houses or jealous authors fully explained.

'This is living,' thought Mr Kelly, as he sat drinking in those refreshing waters, drawn from the very fountain-head of the wells and springs into which he too desired to dip his pitcher. 'These fellows evidently enjoy existence; why does not Donagh, I wonder?' And then he determined he would not mention Donagh to them at all.

But Mr Dawton mentioned that gentleman for him, asking Will, who seemed the chief authority in matters connected with the magazines and newspapers, if he knew anyone so called.

'No,' he said, 'but yet I fancy the name has, somehow, a familiar sound. What is he on?'

Thus directly appealed to, Mr Kelly answered, vaguely, he believed he was 'on' several 'things.' Already he had learned some of the tricks of their language.

'He is very reticent about what he does,' proceeded Mr Donagh's friend; 'but I heard his aunt speak concerning a new venture, *The Galaxy*.'

As with one accord, when Mr Kelly pronounced this word every man looked up. 'Why, that's our mag,' exclaimed Jim, 'our own particular: we all write for it.'

'And no one of the name of Donagh does, of that I am very sure,' added Will; 'I know every man on it.'

'Except –' suggested the scene-painter significantly.

'Ay, by Jove, perhaps we have now unearthed a mystery! Do you think,' he added, addressing Mr Kelly, 'your friend could write a slap-up prospectus, pictur-esque, alluring, attractive, original, calculated to catch fathers as well as daughters, to strike the fancy of husbands and wives, of the babe in arms and the octoge-narian with senile smile tottering to the grave?'

'Yes, I think he could,' answered Mr Kelly; 'more particularly if it read all the better for not having a word of truth in any sentence it contained. I do not imagine Donagh would allow truth to prove a drag on his wheel.'

'Then we have found our man,' exclaimed Will solemnly; 'let us drink his health. What fun it will be to tell old Hodger we know who his genius is! He twitted me with him the other day. "Ah! Will, my boy," he said, "when you can turn out anything half so clever we'll raise your screw." He spoke of him as some great swell, and now only to think – ahem –' And Mr William Dawton, stopped in the middle of his sentence by a vigorous kick dealt him by his brother under the table, poured out another glass of wine, which he hastily drank to cover his confusion.

Dessert being laid in the drawing room on a table pulled close up before a blazing fire, they all adjourned to that apartment, where the young men of the family at once bethought themselves how they could amuse their guest. Ted brought forth a portfolio of drawings and caricatures; Jim, who could, so his father averred, 'make the piano speak,' played and sang, and gave his famous imitation of a night passed in the quiet country by a gentleman unable to sleep in town because of the noise. During the whole time he spent in bed, whither he repaired early to avail himself of this opportunity of making up his arrears of broken rest, there was not one minute of silence. The dogs in the farmyard baying the moon, the clatter of the horses' hoofs as they moved in their stalls, the peculiarly irritating and constantly recurring bang of the iron ball coming up against the ring to which their halters were attached, the cooing of the pigeons whenever they turned in their nests, the mad and emulous crowing of cocks, who, wakened up out of their first sleep to let the stranger know what was in store, the moaning of a cow for her calf, with a battle of tomcats as an interlude, and the clatter of the morning milking-pails for a finish, constituted the salient points in an entertainment which did not occupy more than fifteen minutes.

Mr Kelly, who, as the reader may have already conjectured, was not easily moved to mirth, laughed till he cried. Like most people, he was pleased with what he could perfectly understand; and with every sound young Dawton mimicked, from the 'Come back, come back,' of the guinea-fowl to the sharpening of the mowers' scythes in the first faint light of day, he had been acquainted since his childhood.

'That always brings down the house, sir,' said Mr Dawton speaking professionally and metaphorically. While his son was giving this recital, he had been standing in a 'waiting to come on' attitude, between the old square piano, a veteran in the Dawton service, and the easy-chair in which Mr Kelly lay back, listening with the keenest enjoyment. 'Jim has given "The Quiet Country" before Royalty. You may look astonished,' which indeed the listener did, for as yet he had scarcely grasped the fact that these men were one and all professionals, either in fact or in intention. 'What do you think of him? I do not pretend myself to be an impartial judge, but competent critics predict he has a great future before him. I am told that a certain Prince who shall be nameless, but whose opinion in such matters carries great weight with it – a word to the wise you know, *verbum sap.*, eh? – remarked, "I consider him better than John."'

Mr Bernard Kelly was so utterly unacquainted with the manners and habits of Royalty that if Mr Dawton had affirmed a certain Prince declared Jim cleverer than Jack, he would have been in no position to contradict the statement.

He had not the faintest notion what his host was talking about; as to who the 'John' thus airily referred to might be, he felt it impossible to form an idea.

'When in doubt,' says the old authority on whist, 'play trumps,' and Mr Bernard Kelly was beginning to understand that amongst strangers it is an equally good rule for a man when in doubt to hold his tongue.

He kept silence then, and was immediately rewarded for his abstinence.

Mr Dawton, who, never feeling in doubt, never refrained his tongue if he could help it, finding Mr Kelly made no comment after that astonishing utterance concerning 'John,' and determined to elicit some expression of opinion on the subject, proceeded to remark:

'Not but that I always myself considered Parry a good deal overrated.'

At length Mr Kelly understood what his host had been driving at. When first he came to London, in those desirable days ere the foul fiend tempted him to make a butt of his own uncle, turn the wealthy and respectable Mr Balmoy into ridicule, and bring the worthy Leather Lane Magistrate into contempt, Mr Donagh was in the habit of talking to his compatriot about the sights of London, and over a friendly tumbler saying, 'I must take you one night to see this or hear that,' as if, felt Bernard Kelly, he were a good little boy just put into all-round jackets, home for the holidays, and Mat his guardian, guide, philosopher, friend.

He would not have cared much about the manner of the promise so given had Mr Donagh only fulfilled it in the letter; but that gentleman had never taken him anywhere, except once to St Paul's on a Sunday afternoon, when they heard some good chanting and a very poor sermon.

Amongst Mat's many excellent intentions, with which Mr Kelly reckoned a large portion of the lower regions was already substantially paved, that of treating his friend to one of John Parry's musical entertainments chanced to be included. Mat had spoken eloquently on the subject. He gushed and wept and laughed, as he talked of all that 'wonderful genius' could do. The more he drank the more he praised; the stronger he mixed his punch, the louder were his encomiums concerning what Parry, 'sitting quietly as I am now,' would compass with a piano, which Mr Donagh usually referred to as 'an instrument,' and himself.

Nothing had ever grown out of these conversations; the suggested 'orders,' the numbered seats, the reserved sofas confidently promised and grandly indicated, had followed the same process as that of other things, smaller and greater, Mat was too ready to speak concerning, with lofty assurance; but his remarks now served a purpose little anticipated by the speaker. In addition to the other elements of success before honourably mentioned as likely to serve Mr Kelly well in his metropolitan experience, that gentleman was possessed of a most retentive and unscrupulous memory. Not a word Mat ever uttered had fallen on deaf ears. The grain he scattered with so liberal a hand was carefully garnered by his friend, who now, in answer to Mr Dawton's disparaging remark concerning Parry, said, with the air of a man having authority:

'And yet how good he is!'

'Certainly. No one can deny that,' agreed Mr Dawton, a little taken aback by the decision of Mr Kelly's tone. 'But he lacks variety. When you have seen him once you have seen him always.'

'Well, there's that, to be sure,' observed Mr Kelly, who made up his mind to go and see Parry once, at all events, as soon as he possibly could.

'We are going to do "Jinks v. Binks," father,' interposed Will at this juncture. The three brothers had been speaking apart while the Parry controversy was on the carpet. 'That is, if you think Mr Kelly would care to be troubled with any more of our nonsense.'

'I do not know when I have been so much amused,' answered Mr Kelly for himself; and there was a great deal more truth in his complimentary utterance than any one of the Dawtons could have supposed possible. Their guest's previous life had flowed rather over a dead level of dullness.

'We shall be back in a minute,' said Ted, as the three left the room, while Mr Dawton remarked, either as a general and dispassionate statement, or with a laudable view to keep up the dignity of the family, which he might have felt was likely to suffer through his sons' accomplishments being displayed too lavishly:

'This sort of thing keeps them in practice, you know. It answers to a morning gallop on the turf.'

The great case of 'Jinks v. Binks' had been conceived and written by Will, simply to exhibit the humours and peculiarities of two well-known barristers of the period. Ted sat as judge, presiding with an owl-like gravity and a countenance of unwinking non-comprehension of what was going on, which seemed to Mr Kelly, who had in the course of his aimless rambles about London seen the legal luminary in question, more perfect even than the raging, declaiming, sneering, bantering, interrupting, contradicting of the two legal gentlemen, who, the more fiercely they quarrelled, the more determinedly referred each to the other as 'my learned friend.'

It may be that he was getting a little tired, for mental excitement had not been a form of fatigue often presented to any human being in Callinacoan – or the brothers may have flagged a little for lack of the 'footlights and the clapping' – one thing is certain, 'Jinks v. Binks' did not prove quite such a success as the farmyard serenade.

'You are a bit done up, boys,' observed Mr Dawton, gazing with parental solicitude at the three young faces under three barristers' wigs. 'We'll have a glass of grog all round. What do you say, Mr Kelly? Are you willing to second my motion? Mother, may we have in the kettle?'

Mother's consent was taken as much for granted as the Royal signature. Still, like obtaining the Royal signature, Mr Dawton considered the form essential to be gone through.

During the varied performances Mrs Dawton had sat beside the hearth, smiling pleasantly and crocheting diligently. Now, directly appealed to in that matter of the kettle – which involved many items beside boiling water – she rang the bell, and quickly as a stage banquet appeared a tray on which was a stand containing three bottles, accompanied by tumblers, spoons, lemons, sugar, and what Mr Mat Donagh, in the redundancy of his ordinary language, would have styled 'The impedimenta and all appliances to boot of a splendid conviviality.'

'Now, Mr Kelly,' exclaimed the host, with somewhat watery eyes surveying the bottles, over the distribution of the contents of which he had presided perhaps too often in the course of his life; 'what's your particular? – whisky, I'll be bound.'

Perhaps it was because of this very confidence that Mr Kelly selected brandy. Mr Dawton, saying he was ordered gin by his doctor, who presumably could have been little acquainted with the condition of his patient's interior, seized upon the decanter filled with that insidious liquor; the three elder brothers mixed whisky for themselves, but Ben, who was, as his father represented, going in for teetotalism, took nothing but a glass of wine.

'Mother' being asked by the head of the family if she would have her potation then or 'later on', laughed, and selected the latter alternative.

If her conscience had not been very clear of offence she might scarcely have liked the jests and covert joking Mr Dawton indulged himself in concerning her abstinence; but as matters were, she went on placidly with her work, only looking up a little anxiously when her husband replenished his tumbler. His glass had a nasty knack of running dry long before its proper time, and poor Mr Dawton could not bear to see it empty. Perhaps it was for this reason, and to provide against possible contingencies, he put in almost a double quantity of gin. Unfortunately, however, for the sake of his good intentions, he forgot to 'fill up' afterwards with a corresponding addition of water.

All this Mr Kelly, who was an adept in the ways and signs and tokens of drinking, noted; from his youth upwards he had lived amongst those in whose homes the green bottle or the square decanter was regarded as an indispensable article of furniture, and consequently his studies in the various modes different men took their liquor might be considered exhaustive.

Spite of Miss Cavan's animadversions, he had no inclination towards becoming a drunkard himself. He could perhaps 'carry', as his friends at Callinacoan worded the matter, more whisky than was altogether good for him; but he knew when to stop, which Mat Donagh did not, and he could have 'pulled up' at any minute, a feat quite beyond the master of Abbey Cottage, whose moral breaks, naturally of the feeblest and most theoretical description, were now completely out of working order.

In common with many another importation from the Green Isle, Mr Kelly had arrived in London with a preconceived idea that the English, being unblest with cheap whisky, did not drink, and it was therefore with a good deal of interest he watched Mr Dawton, wondering what quantity 'the old boy,' as he mentally termed him, 'could stand', and speculating on the particular form into which the evil genius of gin would metamorphose him.

During a momentary silence, made eloquent by the fumes of the various liquors which had completely filled the room, aided by the smoke of four cigars – Mr Dawton alone declining to take anything out of Ted's offered case – there came twanging, first at some remote distance, and then nearer and nearer still, the sounds of a banjo, and next instant the door was opened cautiously, and a black face, surmounted by a comical hat of striped red and white calico, peeped into the room.

'Come in, come in; you are welcome,' cried Mr Dawton a little unsteadily. 'Give us a stave! Minstrels, a friendly tumbler – why, the Queen herself could desire no better entertainment!'

Mr Kelly burst out laughing, he could not help it, and the young Dawtons followed suit.

'Doesn't he make up?' said Ted, referring to his brother, who certainly did look a veritable minstrel, and who now struck up one of the melodies not so common in England then as they have since become, which he sung with a verve and a wild enthusiasm that threw Jim's farmyard imitations into the shade.

Here in its way was genius, and Mr Kelly instinctively recognised the difference between this youngster and his brothers.

'Capital!' he exclaimed; 'splendid!' And involuntarily he clapped his hands, and then they all clapped and shouted 'Encore!' and tears of pleasure filled the fond mother's kindly eyes; and Mr Dawton, on the strength of Ben's performance, mixed himself yet another tumbler, and quoted huskily, with a sly leer at their guest, 'I always said he was the flower of the flock.'

Thus encouraged, Ben once again 'touched his guitar,' and commenced another song, the chief feature in which was a sudden 'Yah,' which came in the middle of every verse, and was delivered by the young fellow with startling effect.

He had not, however, got quite to the end of the second stanza, when once again the door opened, this time to admit the trim parlour-maid, who, coolly advancing to the table, the personification of order and composure amidst riot and confusion, said:

'Mr McCrea, sir, has called, and wishes to speak to you.'

With a theatrical gesture Mr Dawton dashed the palm of his open hand against his forehead and looked wildly at his wife, who had risen from her seat, and was regarding him with an expression of reproachful regret.

'I called as I went into town, Bessie, I did, upon my word,' declared poor Mr Dawton, answering the unspoken accusation he knew was in Bessie's heart. 'He was not in, and I did not care to pay that slip of a girl; and when I got up to Glasshouse Street I forgot all about him, and having the money in my pocket I settled with –'

'Never mind that now, father,' interposed Ted, with a certain rough tenderness; 'tell Mr McCrea to come again tomorrow, or say I will look in as I am passing.'

'It is of no use, sir,' answered the servant; 'I told him master was engaged, but he said he would wait till he was disengaged.'

'The ruffian!' exclaimed Mr Dawton, starting up; 'let me deal with him.'

'No, pray, father,' entreated Ted, pushing him back into his chair. 'I have a fiver; give the fellow this, Mary, and say that his account shall be settled within twenty-four hours.'

'And say also, Mary, if ever I catch him inside these gates again, his vile carcase shall pay the penalty,' added the head of the household.

There was no countermand of this message; all present understood apparently Mary might safely be trusted not to deliver it.

The girl went out of the room, closing the door behind her; there was a moment's lull, then, just as Mr Dawton, recovering his equanimity, bethought him of hospitably passing the brandy towards his guest, the handle of the lock was blunderingly turned, and a terrible apparition appeared upon the threshold and came heavily across the carpet.

It was Mr McCrea, the family baker, who, having the same evening been craftily told by the journeyman of a speculative and hated rival that 'them Dawtons were going to make a bolt of it,' had come round armed with his bill, and thirsting for vengeance. He brought up to the table with him a smell of rum, which seemed to overpower the odours of all the other liquors, rum – 'cold without' – which he had liberally partaken of at home, and rum in its integrity which he had called for at a public house in passing, to strengthen his resolution and increase his indignation against 'swindlers', who, though they really had paid him considerable amounts of money, never reached the British tradesman's notion of good customers, viz., weekly settlements, and no question raised as to the quantity or quality of the articles supplied.

'What good's this to me?' asked Mr McCrea, a red-faced, bloated-looking fellow, who certainly merited the name Mr Dawton had bestowed upon him. He held the five-pound note given him by Mary lying open in his left hand, and with his right stubby forefinger he stood beating a tattoo upon it – a tattoo tremulous by reason both of rum and rage.

'What'll I do with this?' and he glared around the group while waiting for an answer.

It was Will who replied for the family:

'As to what you will do with it, Mr McCrea,' he said, 'we cannot really be so impertinent as to suggest; but as to your first question, I have always imagined a five-pound note must be of good to anyone.'

Mr McCrea was so totally unused to 'chaff' of any kind that for a moment Will's words and Will's manner staggered him; but he was not a person to be easily repulsed, and therefore ignoring the 'impertinent puppy', as he for ever after styled Mr Dawton's third born, by the simple process of turning one broad shoulder towards him, the baker, whom the momentary check had rendered still more irate, proceeded:

'I'd like to know which on you, coming to my shop, which shop is kept' by an honest man as pays his way honest, and a man as is respected, though he may not be able to drink his brandy, *and* his whisky, *and* his gin, *and* his sherry wine at other folkses' expense –which on you, I say, would be satisfied when you wanted a half-quartern if I put you off with a third of a half-quartern? How 'm I to pay my miller with this?' – and the tattoo on poor Ted's hard-earned five-pound note recommenced with greater energy than ever. 'He's coming tomorrow, and if I tell him it's all I could get from them as has eat his flour made into loaves, he'd say, "More fool you to give trust." My bill's a matter of sixteen pounds seven shillings and fourpence three-farthings, and sixteen pounds seven shillings and fourpence three-farthings I mean to have if I stop here all night.'

Indignation, and a consciousness, perhaps, that the evening's potations might have somewhat interfered with his powers of oratory, had hitherto kept Mr Dawton silent; but when The McCrea – who was not a Scotchman born, though at times, when he relaxed from the cares of business, he boasted of a genealogy North o' Tweed which conducted the hearers into shadowy mists 'abune' Ben Nevis – paused, Mr Kelly's host burst out with 'Insolent varlet!' and would have proceeded to even wilder flights of eloquence had not Ted cut across the thread of his discourse:

'Much as we appreciate the pleasure of your company, Mr McCrea,' he began with cutting politeness, 'we should be loth to put you to the inconvenience of remaining away from your home till morning; so if you will kindly step back into the hall, from which I am not aware that anyone invited you, we will look up sixteen pounds seven shillings and fourpence three-farthings, which you say we owe you.'

'It's a cursed imposition!' remarked Mr Dawton, with a loftiness of tone and manner which would have seemed more impressive if his wig had not got a good deal to one side.

What Mr McCrea might have answered to this sweeping condemnation can only be imagined, for at this juncture the imperturbable Mary laid her hand on his arm, and simply remarking: 'There's a chair in the hall, sir, if you like to sit', led him like a tipsy lamb out of the room. When the door was shut behind him, the whole family looked at each other for a moment in silence, which Jim was the first to break. Bursting into a peal of laughter, he cried: 'It is too ridiculous. This is quite a new experience. Father, did you ever come across an infuriated baker before?'

'No, dear, and I hope your father never will again,' said Mrs Dawton softly, with a little unconscious emphasis upon the word 'father,' which may have implied she herself scarcely expected such an exemption. 'Don't laugh, Jim; at least, not till the man is out of the house. What are we to do with him, Ted?'

'First let us see how the finances stand,' was Ted's stout and cheery answer.

'Give the brute a cheque, and get rid of him,' suggested Will.

'I don't think in his present mood he would take a cheque,' said Ted; and, indeed, there was nothing surer than that Mr McCrea could not then have been pacified with what he was sometimes wont to designate as a 'bit of worthless paper.' 'Besides, my account was drawn nearly dry last week. No, let us see what we can make up. How much have you, Will?'

They all turned out the contents of their pockets and purses – halfpennies, pennies, sixpences, shillings, half-crowns; a poor show. Ted began gloomily to sort the money into little heaps.

'I am afraid the silver I have about me won't be much help,' said Mr Kelly, discreetly omitting all mention of the one-pound Bank of Ireland note snugly lying inside the folds of his mother's letter; 'but still –'

'We won't rob you, Mr Kelly – thank you all the same,' answered Ted, looking up from his task. 'Where's Ben? Ben is never within a sovereign –'

As he spoke, Ben, who had left the apartment, now re-entered it, and from a wash-leather bag poured out his contribution to the general fund. 'Three pounds eight and sixpence!' exclaimed his brother. 'Bravo, Ben!'

'If you please, Mr Edward,' said Mary, who had followed the youngest Dawton into the room, 'cook has three-and-twenty shillings.'

'It is not every cook who could send up a dish like that,' observed Jim, as Mary laid the amount mentioned on the table. 'It is not every cook who would,' amended Mr Bernard Kelly, which remark elicited from Mr Dawton a husky 'Good, good – deuced good!'

'But still, with all,' said Ted, surveying his collection of coins, 'we only make up twelve pounds five, and in his present condition it would take Mr McCrea till morning to count over the small silver and halfpence. No; I had better go out and borrow. Dulce will lend me five pounds, I am sure.'

'I should not ask him, if I were you,' advised Ben, whose black face and costume made the aspect of the Dawton family in serious conclave utterly ridiculous. 'There's Arty's money-box.'

'To be sure there is; I never thought of that.'

Just for a moment Mrs Dawton looked uneasy; then, apparently satisfied there was no help for the matter, she said:

'You must keep an exact account of what you borrow, Ted.'

'Oh, I'll see to that,' answered the prop of the household, taking the box, which was curiously carved, and had evidently been perverted from its original uses to serving the mean purpose of a mere receptacle for money.

'Have you got the key, mother?'

For once mother was at fault; she had not got what was required.

'Trust Arty for not letting it out of her own keeping,' remarked Ben.

'I don't want to break the thing open,' said Ted, turning the delicate toy round, 'for I might damage it. Who has some small keys?'

No one seemed to have any possession of the sort, till at last on Mr Kelly's bunch there was discovered a small and, to look at, apparently perfectly useless little key, which belonged to an old blotting-case his mother had packed amongst his linen.

'That's done the business!' exclaimed Will, as his brother shot back the worthless lock and emptied the money the box contained into his left hand. 'By Jove, here's a mine of wealth; I wish I had thought of its existence yesterday.'

'Here's Arty herself,' said Mrs Dawton, as a young girl in mantle and bonnet now appeared on the scene. 'We have been obliged to open your box, Arty love, to get rid of Mr McCrea.'

'Very well,' answered Arty, reconciling herself to the inevitable; 'but you must pay it all back again, remember,' she added, addressing Ted.

'Oh, I say!' from Ben.

'I like the idea!' from Will.

'I am sure it is being put to the purpose intended by the donors,' from Jim. 'It was meant to clothe the naked heathen, and we are only using it to pay the man who fed the hungry Christian. Your friend Mr Jenkins must not depend upon receiving one farthing of this money about quarter-day. He will have to fall back on somebody else's box to satisfy his landlord. Speak, Ted! Have you got enough gold at last to mollify the evil spirit of the McCrea? If so, let me pay the fellow, and kick him to the gate.'

'Just stay where you are,' said his brother, a little sternly. 'The man has a right to his money; and though he was rude, that is the more reason why we should behave better.'

'Oh dear!' exclaimed Ben, 'how high and moral we are all of a sudden, after robbing Arty's heathen! What a difference a few pounds makes! You would not have felt so truly virtuous, Ted, if you had been forced to go to the bar of the Blue Tiger, and, cap in hand, ask old Dulce to lend you five pounds.'

'Hold your tongue,' said Ted sharply.

'That's all the thanks a fellow gets,' grumbled Ben.

The change which came over Mr McCrea when he was asked to give a receipt for sixteen pounds seven shillings and four pence three farthings, duly counted over, was little short of marvellous. He would have apologised elaborately, but that Ted cut short his maunderings with an imperative mandate to sign his name and conclude the interview.

'I am afraid I have not a farthing about me,' he said, after feeling in every pocket for this amount of change. 'We'll trust you that,' said the irrepressible Jim, who had opened the drawing-room door about a couple of inches, and was peering through the gap thus made; 'in fact, we'll *give* you the farthing.'

Mr McCrea, turning in the direction whence this generous proposition emanated, beheld Jim's mischievous face surveying him.

'Ah!' he remarked to Ted, who had reddened with annoyance, 'it's well to be young and have no weight of care to carry on the shoulders. When it comes to having to get both ends to meet, and both always a bit too short, a man finds he has something else to do than making fun and diversion.'

'Very true, Mr McCrea. You find the money right, I think?'

'Quite right, thank you, sir,' said Mr McCrea, turning his hat round and round in his two fat hands, and looking steadily into it, apparently searching for some suitable observation at parting.

Mr Edward Dawton found one for him.

'I will wish you good night, then,' he said.

Taking the hint thus broadly given, the baker, executing a courtly wave of his shabby hat, remarked:

'Servant, sir; much obliged, I am sure.'

'Open the door for Mr McCrea, Mary,' said Ted, with cruel and elaborate civility.

Mr McCrea edged himself out of the door Mary held wide, as though he had but about three inches of space through which to squeeze his burly figure.

'Goodnight, my dear,' he said to the trim young handmaiden.

'Goodnight, sir,' she answered demurely; and then the door was closed again, and Mr McCrea found himself sixteen pounds odd the richer, and in the way of becoming a good deal wiser.

'You understand, Mary,' remarked Mr Ted significantly – meaning no loaf from the McCrea bakehouse was ever again to find its way inside The Wigwam.

'Oh yes, sir.'

When Ted rejoined the social circle he found order once more calmly reigning in the drawing room. Arty, who had been introduced to Mr Kelly, was carefully examining her box to see if it had been in any way damaged. Jim was seated at the piano, and he struck a note now and then, humming softly to himself. Mr Dawton had 'mixed' again, and was urgently entreating Mr Kelly to follow his example.

Shortly he grew a little maudlin, and began to bemoan his fate, and whimper over the 'base ingratitude which left a son of Vincent Dawton's to be the sport and insult of a scoundrel who sold hot rolls.'

The best of the evening was clearly over. Mr McCrea, like a desolating whirlwind, had swept over The Wigwam, and nothing anyone could do or think of was likely to restore matters to the footing on which he had found them.

Even the fire seemed to burn less cheerily and Mr Kelly began to wonder how he was to get back to Stratford.

'Which will be my best way from here to the City?' he asked; and then he was told to take train at Vauxhall for Waterloo, from whence he could get anywhere.

'Look up any manuscripts you have by you,' said Will, 'and we'll see what can be done with them', while Mr Dawton offered, as well as he was able, a 'shakedown', 'sofa', 'rug on the hearth', 'just another thimbleful to keep out the night air', and then fell to weeping and bemoaning himself once more.

'Never mind my father,' said Ted, as he stood at the gate of The Wigwam, showing their new friend the direct way to Vauxhall, 'he is always like that when he has an extra glass.'

With great sincerity Mr Bernard Kelly answered that 'he did not think anything of it,' and, after a cordial 'Good night,' strode off, unconscious of all the changes that day's experience was to affect in his life.

As belated travellers step inside fairy rings, or cross enchanted thresholds, so in his aimless wanderings Bernard Kelly had, without being in the slightest degree cognisant of the fact, strolled into the realms of Bohemia.

Time had passed quickly within those charmed precincts, and it was so late when he reached the City, the last Stratford 'bus had gone.

When in the small hours he arrived at Abbey Cottage, the door, after a long delay, was opened by Miss Bridgetta in an indescribable state of *déshabille*. Her stockingless feet were encased in a pair of Mat's old slippers; she had evidently only huddled on a thick petticoat over her night-garments; an ancient shawl was wrapped round her shoulders; and her grey hair peeped out from under the flapping borders of her cap.

'In the name of wonder,' she asked, 'what has kept you till this time of the morning? We gave you up long and long ago. Step easy. Ah, do,' she added. 'If Mat gets a broken night he's never worth a farthing the next morning.'

What Mr Kelly muttered under his breath about Mat and his night's rest, as he paused at the foot of the stairs and pulled off his boots, was not pleasant; but Miss Bridgetta did not hear his remark. She was engaged at the moment in a futile attempt to snuff the guttering dip she carried with a hair-pin, which for this purpose she took out of the little wisp of grey hair twisted up under her remarkable night-cap.

If Mat had been there he would have asked her 'why the – the proper imple-ment for such uses was never by any chance in its correct place?' But Mat did not happen to be there, and Mr Kelly felt utterly indifferent as to how Miss Bridgetta snuffed her candle, or whether she ever snuffed it at all.

At the moment he was wishing with his whole heart he could leave Abbey Cottage, and afford to pay for lodgings. He was thinking what a wide, desolate place London is for a man with only a one-pound note and a few shillings in his pocket. He was considering the difference of the welcome which would have been accorded to Mr Donagh had he claimed the hospitalities of Moss Moor Farm, from that Mr Donagh extended to him; and as he 'stepped easy' up the narrow staircase, and trod gingerly past Mat's sleeping apartment, he felt very bitter when he thought of the scant courtesy extended to him at Abbey Cottage, and the bare meals now furnished by those who had, as he well remembered, received hamper after hamper of the best his mother 'could pack tight in them.'

When he left The Wigwam it was with the first feeling of real hope that had come to cheer the blackness of his night since the unfortunate episode which offended all his relatives. Spite of the McCrea interlude, the evening proved to him as refreshing and exhilarating as a glass of champagne, or a whiff of pure mountain air, and as he paced the fastnesses of South Lambeth and took train for Waterloo at Vauxhall, he half believed Mr Dawton's assertion that it was well he had quarrelled with his uncle; that fate held something far better than a post in a Government office in store for a clever fellow like himself.

As he neared the City, however, his mood became less jocund. He remembered, as he passed the closed and silent offices of great firms, how he had wondered if amid all the life and bustle and business of Cockaigne at mid-day, there was no vacant place he could fill – no master who would give him a chance of honestly earning his bread.

Even in the semi-darkness of a town, illumined only by its glimmering street-lamps, he seemed to see again the figures he had looked at in broad day, and longed earnestly to address – great merchants, well-known financiers, men, some of them, who, having come to the great metropolis with no possessions save youth and industry, might presumably feel a kind of sympathy for one well-nigh as poor as was their own case formerly. Then his mood changed and grew fiercer, and the smile with which he bethought him of what Mr Balmoy might have to say if a delinquent were brought before him charged with pinning Rothschild to the wall in Swithin's Lane, and shouting 'Employment, or your life,' was more cynical than mirthful.

Along every step of the way that conducted him eastward to Abbey Cottage he dragged a lengthening chain of care. The farther he left South Lambeth behind, the greater became his sadness of spirit. It was as though there he had left the sun shining, while at Whitechapel he was plunging into the accustomed fog. If a man finds a house, or the people with whom he is domesticated, producing an enervating and depressing effect upon his nature, let him get out of the one and cut his lot adrift from the others as quickly as may be.

There are conditions of life which paralyse the best powers of a person's mind, against which it is as vain to struggle, as impossible to make head, as for the body to keep itself active amid ague swamps. There are dwellings and families who constitute what is ironically termed 'a home circle,' capable of transforming the strength of Samson into the weakness of the blind and feeble man the Philistines laughed to scorn, the generous courage of David into the mean treachery of him who caused Uriah to be set in the forefront of the battle.

Intuitively Bernard Kelly felt the Donagh *ménage*, and the Donagh style of life, were dragging all activity and spirit out of his brain and body.

'If I could only see my way to earning ten shillings a week, I'd be out of this tomorrow,' he thought, as he tossed through the hours of the sleepless night. 'London is an awful place for a stranger who knows nobody worth knowing. De Quincey might well speak of the streets as stony-hearted. Blow high, blow low, however, I'll try to put matters here on a different footing. My friend Mat shan't have it all his own way. Confound his smug face and his white shirt, and his stiff choker, and his long words, and his sanctimonious secrecy! Wait a bit, my friend – wait a bit, Mr Matthew Donagh! perhaps some day you will wish you had not shown Barney Kelly quite so plainly you would prefer his room to his company.'

Chapter VIII

GLENARVA

IT WOULD NOT HAVE PROVED the slightest comfort to Mr Kelly, while engaged in those exercises of self-pity and Donagh-commination just recorded, to know that the opinion of another person as regarded the helpless feeling of being stranded in a vast city was identical with his own.

The joys and the sorrows, the hopes, the cares, the disappointments, the successes of other people, were matter which affected that gentleman but little, save so far as they influenced, or were likely to influence, his personal career.

From the moment he alighted at Euston, he had never given a thought to the companions who journeyed from Ireland with him. It would not have vexed him to know they were all begging their bread – it would not have pleased him to know they were doing well – unless he was likely to gain out of their prosperity. It would not have strengthened his own heart to feel others were marching along the same road, bravely setting their faces to meet difficulties and conquer obstacles, hiding sad fears under the cover of ready smiles, and turning cheerful countenances which concealed grave anxieties to a world which, though not a hard, or an unfeeling, or an ungenerous world, is ever – and rightly, perhaps – impatient of outward manifestations of woe. In their different ways and degrees the four persons who travelled with Mr Kelly were nervously considering what the result of that day's journeying would prove. Least, perhaps, of all, Mr Westley; most, no doubt, his daughter, both because her temperament was impulsive, and the weight of responsibility she had incurred seemed to her youth overwhelming.

As to her father, he had come to London filled with a hope which, though destined never to be realised, buoyed him over the first and worst portion of the metropolitan campaign.

Looking back over his life – a survey which it may well be doubted whether he ever undertook – he might have seen enough to warn him of the fallacy of entertaining great expectations on any subject; but Mr Westley was a man who had never learned much from experience in the past, and who it seemed very certain would never learn much from it in the future.

Yet upon the whole, till in one of her crazy moods Fortune smiled upon him, if he had not done well, he had at least not done ill. His father said he was too lazy to work – his mother that he was too delicate to study. There might be truth in both statements – anyhow, while still quite a young man, he abandoned the medical profession, which it had been his own election to pursue, and went abroad with a certain nobleman whose acquaintance he had made at college, and who really entertained what might be termed an attachment for the gentle, dreamy Irishman.

'Desmond will never do anything in the world,' remarked his father – 'he has no backbone; lucky he is not the eldest son.'

If he had been, Glenarva must have come to him on the death of the speaker; but he was the youngest of three, and the property then seemed as far from him as the crown of England.

In due time it devolved upon Captain Westley, E.N., to whom his father left a fine fortune with which to keep up the old place. If he had willed the fortune to go with the place it would have been all right enough; but, as matters stood, Captain Westley settled every penny he was possessed of upon his wife, a certain Lady Emily Wingstone, and dying without children, was succeeded by Major Westley, who, having contracted an unfortunate liking towards a person he could not marry, for the sufficient reason she was already provided with a husband, lived with her and a numerous family at Glenarva in a strict retirement, which none of his neighbours strove to induce him to leave.

For over ten years visitors did not pass through the gates guarded by the stone animals, who sat resolutely on their haunches and lolled out their carved tongues at all who went that way. It was known Major Westley only waited the death of the obdurate husband to make the lady whose presence scandalised the countryside Mrs Westley; and his brother was expecting every day to hear of both events, when quite different tidings reached him. The Major it was who died, leaving no child capable of inheriting Glenarva; and the place, therefore, descended to Desmond – the man with no backbone, and no money independent of the estate, except a hundred and fifty pounds a year, in which, in accordance with his father's ridiculous testamentary disposition, he had only a life-interest;

at his death it descended to whomsoever might at the time be the owner of Glenarva.

It is unnecessary to say the first thing this fortunate younger son did was to take a wife. Needless to add she had no fortune, and that she came of people who were not well off. It was an old attachment – she and Desmond had been engaged for years, and but for the chance of the Major's horse throwing him while leaping a stream he had often jumped across as a boy, the engagement might have gone on forever, since certainly Mr Westley was most unlikely to make enough to support a second self.

As matters stood he was close on forty, and the lady over thirty, when they vowed to take each other for better or worse. Two years later a daughter was born, whom, in the delight of his heart, the proud father decided to call Glenarva.

'She never can be Westley of Glenarva,' he said to his wife, 'so she shall be Glenarva Westley.' More adaptable than many an absurd name, when the evil days fell upon her father this baptismal appellation was capable of judicious abbreviation. 'Glen' did not sound ridiculous, even when the young lady so styled was shorn of wealth and rank, and had sunk into a comparatively humble station.

'And it was for my sake he lost everything,' the girl considered mournfully. 'It was in trying to make a fortune for me he spent his own.'

She could not have explained the matter in fewer words. Knowing he would be unable to leave his daughter Glenarva or any part of it, and disdaining the simple expedient of laying a certain sum aside for her dot, Mr Westley, with that infatuation which may indeed be regarded as a sort of madness, took shares in a venture which was to make him a millionaire, and Glen an heiress.

In vain, people who knew something of business implored him not to be rash, to count the possible cost before he embarked in so hazardous an undertaking. The man never yet lived who did not believe himself wiser than his counsellors. Mr Westley would listen to no warning or remonstrance, and it was only when he saw grass growing in the courtyard of what had been opened with a great flourish of trumpets as the Monster Bank for the North of Ireland, and received an intimation of the first call, that he began to doubt his own prudence, and rushed off to consult the family lawyer.

The tale of the years that followed may be guessed. First one luxury and then another was dispensed with; the establishment was curtailed, grooms were sent about their business, horses and carriages were sold, company given up, gardeners discharged. Glen's English governess dismissed, every expense cut down, a wild attempt made to remain on in the old house, though the very lawn was let out for grazing. But no retrenchment could meet the drain of those perpetually recurring calls. At last it became necessary to find a tenant for the house and pleasure-grounds, and it was then the whole county beheld the unexampled sight of a living

Westley having to abandon Glenarva to strangers and go forth, his daughter by his side, into the wilderness of the world – into the land called Poverty.

If there was comfort to be found in anything at that time, Mr Westley probably extracted it from the fact of his wife having died and been buried before this crowning humiliation came upon him. Her funeral train wound up the long dark avenue where the trees interlaced their branches overhead, and the evergreens grew so tall and thick. Over the crest of the hill her coffin had been borne with all fitting woe and pomp to the family vault in the ruined church, amid the desolate moors that stretched in all directions far as the eye could discern. Not for her the poor cottage and the rough service and the cruel pinching economy; she at least died at Glenarva, in a noble room, the windows of which looked down upon a green sea of waving boughs and leaves that danced and glittered in the sunshine, and on the day of her funeral the roads all around were alive with carriages, and persons who followed the hearse, anxious to show the last tribute of respect to a very good lady, whose married life had been but one long anxiety.

Glen was still a child when her mother died, and nearly two years elapsed after that event before the final crash which necessitated removal from the old home. Though old for her age, she failed to understand all that leaving Glenarva would afterwards mean to her. In early life egotism is so strong, it seems to the young they must remain persons of importance, no matter where they chance to be. Moreover, women rarely feel the deep attachment for place men entertain; they do not know the world, and they are far too prone to believe a change of any kind must be a change for the better.

Considering the life which lay before her, it was well for Mr Westley's daughter that he had to leave Glenarva before the terrible monotony, the enforced isolation, the utter absence of everything bright, cheerful, and hopeful, stamped itself upon her nature. They went to a small house many miles distant which belonged to Mr Westley, and which, chancing to be vacant at the time, seemed to offer a harbour of refuge to the ill-fated gentleman. It stood bare, without even a tree to shelter it, halfway up a hill fronting the sea. No grander situation could well be imagined, and to Glen the transition from her old home – shut in and smothered by greenery – to the wide expanse of land and water, was like passing from darkness to light – from gloom to sunshine.

She, at all events, was happier by far in that whitewashed cottage, where the roses climbed over the windows and a thatched roof defied the violence of the gales which so often tore round the building, than she had ever been in the grand house, with its long avenue and stately portico and imposing front. For the first time in her existence she found companions of her own age – six turbulent lads – with whom she played at ball, ran races, rode shaggy ponies unshod, ungroomed, half-wild, and wholly untrained, like themselves. They galloped them along the sands and over the hills; they had a boat, in which a man would have thought himself mad to peril his existence, but that always brought the young scapegraces safe back to shore, though they had to bale out the water almost incessantly; there was no game those lads played in which they failed to instruct Miss Westley, no place they went to that they did not desire her company. Before six months were over she looked and was a different creature. If Mr Westley had only known a tenth part of the perils she ran, of the hairbreadth escapes she could have told him about, of the chances of drowning she gave herself, of the headlong rides across country, of the steep cliffs climbed, of the caverns explored, of the rapid streams traversed by means of slippery stepping-stones, of the treacherous rocks visited at low water in search of dulse – he could never have endured the anxiety; but, absorbed in the contemplation of his misfortunes, utterly broken and wretched, he saw nothing of what was really going on, and felt glad his daughter could find some amusement which brought a colour to her cheeks and a light to her eyes, and made her happy and cheerful at home – merry she could not be in his presence. When out with the boys she laughed as loud and as long as they; but all idea of laughter died within her when she looked at her father's sad face and drooping figure.

To him the mean cottage, the desolate landscape, the raging sea, the howling tempests, were constant reminders of a state and a place to which he could return no more for ever. For his daughter the breezy walk, the narrow path on the very verge of some tremendous precipice, the exhilarating canter, the dangerous sail with far too much canvas crowded, and one gunwale generally under water. For him only an armchair by the turf fire, or a saunter in the sun, with the memory of trouble behind and the expectation of trouble in store.

It is not too much to say he hated his new home – that when in the morning he looked out over that expanse of desolate sea or still more desolate land, his heart sank within him at the idea of having to pass another long idle day amid such surroundings.

But when Glen was about fifteen there came on her suddenly a mighty change. It was wrought almost in a day, and it was caused by a perfect comprehension of her father's position. Some one said he was breaking his heart; another hinted things were not yet at the worst with him. Then the girl asked in a few minutes more questions about their reverse of fortune than she had put in her life before. Nor were they at the worst, she found. At some not remote period they might not even have money enough to buy the little they required; further, it was quite certain that sooner or later she would have to earn her bread.

For hours after she went to bed on the night when her eyes had been opened, Glenarva Westley lay in the moonlight wide awake. What could she do? If she had been a man there were fifty things to which she might have turned her attention; but being only a woman, which way would it be best, or indeed possible, for her to face the world?

At length she rose, and, crossing to the window, looked out. Beneath her lay the ocean, calm as a sleeping child; in the offing one white-sailed vessel appeared sleeping too.

The moon shone calmly down upon the water and traced a bright pathway, as it seemed to her fancy, across the tide. All thought is but the offspring of some previous thought; all invention only the outcome of a former plan. As the flower is contained in the seed, an apparently sudden project has been growing in silence to maturity; as the infant lying in his cradle will one day be represented by a stalwart man, so every purpose and execution of our lives has had its hour of unconscious babyhood. When we see the result we are apt to forget there must of necessity have been a long time of growth. For a year the whole forces of nature are at work to perfect a single leaf, and which amongst us can tell the length of time even one solitary idea has been germinating before it takes definite form and substance before our eyes?

For many a long day Glenarva Westley thought the idea which sprang into birth as she looked out on the quiet sea and that broad track caused by the glittering moonbeams was one conceived under the spur of the moment; but in after years she comprehended how differently the matter actually stood. During the whole of her young life there had never been a time when to every look and tone of nature she failed to respond with the deep sympathy of an imaginative and poetical temperament. The waving of the branches, the moaning of the wind, the long dark avenue at Glenarva, the rich hues of the summer flowers, the sound of flowing water, the sweet scents that came borne on the breath of gentle June – each one of these things and a thousand more filled her with an exquisite delight, just as the sight of a desolate graveyard touched some deep note of sadness, and a long stretch of wintry shore with grey waves breaking sullenly on the beach awoke thoughts she could not have communicated to anyone.

In fancy she had peopled each lonely scene her eyes rested on. She dreamed of heroes and heroines, of great deeds of courage, endurance, devotion. Whilst at Glenarva she did not live in the monotonous world by which she was surrounded. Down the long corridors of the past walked the men and women of other days to greet the lonely girl, and accompany her with their phantom presence. Amid portraits limned by poets and artists long mouldered into dust she wandered in imagination. Fair women and gallant gentlemen smiled sadly down upon her as she passed. Music, painting, romance – all had been training her for this end; that she herself should begin to struggle and labour, to see whether she was really fit for any work, and if so, for what.

'I will write,' she said, standing in a flood of moonlight; and, opening her little desk there and then, she began.

Years and years afterwards she chanced to come across two or three sheets of letter paper, on which were sentences traced in a girl's unformed hand – only a few sheets, yellow with time, and yet as she looked at the few sentences traced in ink faded with age, an epitome of her life seemed evolved out of them.

What had she not hoped and believed then, what had she not experienced and suffered since? Reversing the experience of Moses, it was on the Promised Land of Morning she gazed back, and the Wilderness of Evening she saw stretching at her feet.

Nowadays, the smallest child has some idea of 'how books are made,' but the schoolmaster had not taken so many walks abroad at the time when Glenarva Westley conceived the idea that she would add one to the already lengthy list of authors, and she knew as little about the ordinary details of the literary profession as any young lady even at that time well could. It was fiction, of course, on which she concentrated the powers of her mind; not a tale or a story, or a modest narrative on an unpretending scale, but fiction in three-volume form and constructed after an ambitious pattern. As day succeeded to day, she piled sheet on the top of sheet, and when recalled from the ideal world to the workaday reality surrounding her, did what she had to do, said what she had to say, with a smile on her lips which perplexed many persons who saw nothing to cause such continuous evidences of cheerfulness, but that really owed its origin to a settled conviction she was getting on admirably, and would ere long be able to restore the shattered fortunes of the then Westley of Glenarva.

The fact may seem mournful, but it is true: the girl knew no more really about the difficulty of earning money in those blessed blissful summer days when she took to writing as a profession, than she did about authorship. To her inexperience anything and everything seemed possible now she had found out her talent, and meant to put it to usury. Amongst the few plans she proposed to execute when she had made her fortune and reinstated her father in the house of his ancestors may be mentioned rebuilding the Vicarage at Ballyshane; purchasing an organ for the church, paying dear old Miss Grunley a salary for playing it; allowing ten pounds a year to each poor family in the village – a sum she believed would raise their condition from abject poverty to luxurious affluence; laying out a carriage drive to the cottage, and planting – climate and Atlantic blasts notwithstanding – shrubberies around it; installing the old servant who attended to their few wants as housekeeper, and leaving her in charge to keep all in readiness for the return of 'the family,' when wearied of the pomp and formality at Glenarva. Further, in her mind's eye she saw the very boat she meant to give to the boys; the gold watch Ned should receive on his birthday; the presents she would purchase for the Vicar and his wife when she went to Dublin to lay out her money to the best advantage; while she never beheld the fishermen's nets hanging out to dry, but she mentally ordered the material to keep their shuttles busy through every idle hour of the hard, honest life they led.

No achievement seemed to her impossible. Had anyone suggested she might by way of a finish clear off the National Debt, she would secretly have considered that more wonderful results had been achieved. But what she thought at that period nor man nor woman knew. Not even to the boys – her friends, her comrades – to no human being did she confide her secret. If the world of letters had been a hitherto undiscovered continent, and she the Columbus to whose longing eyes its trees hung with rarest fruits, its paths strewn with precious stones, were alone revealed, she could not have maintained a straighter and stricter reserve as to the treasures she had found in the fairy-land her feet were traversing.

The Vicar's sons could not think what had come to Glen. In her eyes was the reflection of a sun the very existence of which was unknown to them – from mines they did not wot of the girl was digging of the fabled gold that, though at first it seemed so precious, turns to ashes when required for use.

As a child she had been fond of planting her own little garden with full-blown flowers which drooped and withered within the hour; and through all that early time of literary effort and non-success she was but repeating the old experiment – setting out rootless hopes and fancies, the glories of which dazzled her imagination and gilded with unnatural brightness the waves of the deep dark ocean she had set out to traverse, unwitting that from the unknown shore for which she was blindly steering there is no return.

She began her life-task in utter ignorance of how to set about it. She did not know how books were printed or published. She had never met an author; more, she was not acquainted with any person who ever had met one. The dim ideas she entertained on the subject were gathered from seeing at various times some sermons yellow with age which the Vicar laid aside after service, in a cupboard in his study. Battered and illegible enough were those ancient finger-posts; still, they seemed better to Glen's mind than a road without any finger-posts at all. She wished she could have talked to him on the subject which lay so near her heart, but she felt as shy of speaking about her writing as she might about a lover if she had got one.

During the months which followed that moonlight night, when in the travail of her soul she brought forth the resolve which changed the whole of a life which otherwise might have been passed as governess, or companion, or wife to some poor curate or struggling country practitioner, she wrote enough to have filled, had it ever been printed, several volumes. She wore herself out, she fell ill, she got better again. She gave up scribbling for a little while; but the madness was on her, and she had soon to return to her little desk and the welcome solitude of her low wide bed chamber overlooking the sea.

For ever after there were scents, and sights, and sounds, which affected Glenarva Westley with a strange, sad, faint sense of sickness which caused her heart to die away within her; which brought, with the wash of the glittering waves, with the wild rain pelting against the windows, with wind-tossed white-crested billows madly racing to find their death on a storm-beaten shore, with the heavy perfume of jasmine and the sweet breath of pallid roses subtly stealing through the open casement, a memory of what she had lost in the struggle, and a total, though it may be only temporary, forgetfulness of all she had gained.

Ah me! How little she prized the wild flowers of her sweet free youth, while they were still springing and blooming beside her path! and yet how fair they seemed when remembered amid gardens brilliant with the gay colours in which Summer decked herself, or fields where golden grain was ripening under cloudless skies, or woods already – spite of the glory of their autumnal tints – foretelling the swift approach of the drear dark winter which follows the brightest season man's life on earth can know!

Chapter IX

MR DUFFORD

ALTHOUGH NO ONE in Miss Westley's small world could be considered gifted with any extraordinary powers of perception, still, those about the girl must have been stone-blind had they failed to notice the change which had come over her. Save at the Vicarage, public opinion was almost unanimous in considering the transformation an improvement. Long previously every woman in Ballyshane had, standing over their turf fires while they turned their bannocks on the scorching griddles, or, seated on great stones in front of their doors in the fine summer weather, knitted stockings and patched their husbands' heavy coats, arrived at the conclusion that the only thing for Miss Glen to do was to get married. 'And then the master God bless him! – could live with her.'

A belief was entertained in the village that eventually the Captain's widow – now remarried and known as Lady Emily Wildersly – would adopt Miss Glenarva. It was known her ladyship had twice sent for the girl to stop with her – once at Portrush and once in Dublin – from both of which visits Teenie, servant at the cottage, declared the young mistress returned home 'just loaden with presents.'

When the Vicar's wife saw those presents she said nothing, but she thought a great deal. To her mind at all events it was clear Lady Emily had no intention of acting the part of fairy godmother to the Ballyshane Cinderella.

But other people were not so wise, and it was considered a great gain when Miss Glen, of her own accord, began to turn up her back hair, and 'take kindly to her book.'

'The quality thinks a great deal of reading,' remarked Miss Bella Neill, the village dressmaker, 'and Teenie says Miss Glen is always studying.'

'She's losing her colour a bit,' one of the fishermen was rash enough to observe, thoughtfully.

'Why, that's all the better,' cried Miss Neill, whose own complexion was somewhat muddy; 'the gentlefolks don't like much red in their cheeks. Lady Emily herself is more like a marble statue than flesh and blood. She is just a picture to look at.'

'And it's time Miss Glen was taking thought to herself,' capped another crony; 'she must be getting on for sixteen now –'

'Turned sixteen,' said Miss Neill, rapidly 'basting' a seam as she spoke.

'Turned sixteen!' repeated the other. 'Well! Oh, then she is getting on – it's a mercy she has taken up with her book at last.'

If the speaker, who, being unable either to read or write herself, could scarcely be considered a competent authority on the vexed subject of education, had only imagined the sort and description of book with which Miss Westley occupied her abundant leisure, she, in common with every other human being round and about Ballyshane, would have thought the young lady 'off her head.'

Those were not the days when, in remote districts at all events, embryo authors were patted on the back and taught to consider themselves marvels of genius; and perfectly aware that even her most modest aspirations would meet with no favour, the young author kept her secret, and in the solitude of her own mind dreamed her fancies, perfected her stories, indulged her hopes, and bore her disappointments.

For already she had adventured many doves out over the world's waste of waters, and though they almost all returned to her with terrible promptitude, not one bore an olive-leaf of promise back with it. The agreement which prevailed amongst editors and publishers as to the worthlessness of what she sent them was perhaps on the whole not remarkable, though it seemed so to Glenarva Westley.

When her manuscripts were acknowledged, it was ever in a note that contained a rejection. The notes were differently worded, but the sense was the same. Afterwards she marvelled at the faith which, spite of these constant rejections, caused her to persevere; but the fact was that, having built up her great dream castle, she dared not of her own will sweep down turret and battlement, flying buttress and stately keep, and return to the narrow limits of a home which had once contented her.

She carried her manuscripts to the nearest town, where she posted them to London, and Dublin, and Edinburgh, and to every other likely address she saw advertised in the four days'-old *Times* newspaper the Vicar's brother sent him, and which he immediately lent to Mr Westley. Trudging along the Queen's highway with her parcels made up into one good-sized package, enveloped in brown paper to defy the curiosity of any eyes she happened to encounter, Miss Westley might have been regarded as typifying 'Hope.' Returning to Ballyshane with quite as large a package, she might have sat for 'Despair'; but this feeling did not continue.

Disappointment obscured the cloud-palace for a time, but the cloud-palace was there notwithstanding; ere long the sun of imagination dispelled the mist wherewith some cruel correspondent had encircled it, and then once more pinnacles shone and vanes glittered; across the lowered drawbridge she walked into a spacious courtyard, whence, as fancy suggested, she wandered into room after room furnished with more than Oriental magnificence, and without the slightest regard to cost.

Notwithstanding, it all told on her. The fisherman was right; she had 'lost her colour a bit,' and with her colour had gone something of her old high spirits. Still upon occasions she went on mad expeditions with the boys. Still half-wild ponies were ridden across the moors. Still in the crazy old boat Glen periled her own life, and those as yet unwritten works for which the world did not seem impatient; still dizzy heights did not appal or breakneck paths deter her. But she had changed – the boys were never weary of telling her so.

'What's on your mind, Glen?' they would inquire. 'Has Lady Emily asked you to go and stay with he again? Pluck up courage, and say you won't stir a step. What has she ever done for you that you should do anything for her?'

'There is nothing on my mind,' the girl answered one summer's day, a year after she had taken to writing, 'and we haven't heard from Lady Emily for ages. Even papa thinks she means really to cut us at last.'

'And you are fretting about that, I suppose?' said Ned, the eldest, scornfully.

'I am not fretting at all,' protested Glen.

'I know what's the matter with you,' broke in one of the younger fry.

'What is?' demanded his five brothers and Glen, in chorus.

'She is in love with old Dufford.'

'Oh, what a story, Hal!' expostulated the young lady thus libelled.

'It's not; look at her – look how red she is! She could not be any redder if she had just said to him, "Ausk pawpaw"', and Hal struck a lackadaisical attitude as he imitated not so badly Mr Dufford's ultra-elegant mode of pronunciation.

'I have a great mind to box your ears, Master Hal,' observed Glen, still covered with confusion.

'I do not care whether you do or not, if you will only send me a good wedge of the wedding-cake. His mawmaw will be able to get it at trade-price, no doubt. I hope it may have plenty of almond stuff on the top.'

After this, Glen's love for Mr Dufford, or Mr Dufford's love for Glen, or the mutual affection the pair entertained for each other, grew to be a standing joke with the young savages, as Mr Dufford, in correspondence with his mother, called the

Vicar's sons. A relative had offered the Ballyshane clergyman a wonderful chance of seeing 'foreign parts' without expense; and whilst he was availing himself of an opportunity which, as his wife said, might never occur again, Mr Dufford, who at the time happened to be looking out for a curacy where there was little to do, plenty of good society and a fair salary, kindly consented to 'lie on his oars' at Ballyshane.

'He was the son,' so said the boys, 'of a rich *but* honest tradesman of Cork.' He had been to school in England, and taken his degree at Trin. Col., Dublin. He thought himself extremely handsome. He believed his manners would have graced the Court of St James. He had plenty of money, and was 'old enough,' as Ned once expressed the matter, 'to be a great fool.' And to Ned's irreverent eyes no doubt he seemed so. His calm life had hitherto been passed amongst people as proper and commonplace as himself. His talk was of fashion and the grand persons he knew. To those jibing young sinners at the Vicarage his conversation proved an inexhaustible fund of amusement. His ideas were reproduced for Glen's gratification amid peals of laughter.

He could ride, but only the conventional and regulation horse; he could swim, he averred, but declined to bathe off the rocks, to which six grinning lads joyously conducted him; he would not put his foot in the boat; he would not be coaxed to climb the cliffs, stating that a 'man who had passed his life in study would turn dizzy where a goat or a mere mountaineer might tread secure.' He was extremely particular about his food, and he turned up his nose at the clerical jaunting-car which had done duty at Ballyshane as long as the Vicar himself.

For the rest, he sang when he could get anyone to accompany him; and he felt no hesitation in confessing he believed the way in which he took off his hat to ladies was the very acme of chivalry and breeding.

When first made acquainted with Miss Westley he treated her in a lordly and distant manner which delighted both Glen and the boys. But when he grew more at home at Ballyshane, and learned who Mr Westley really was, and understood a certain Lady Emily was included amongst the Glenarva gods, he unbent, and actually volunteered to take the *Times* up to the cottage with his own white hands, which looked as if they had never done anything useful in their lives; and their looks did not greatly belie them.

'I'd be ashamed to own such hands,' Ned said hotly.

Glen laughed, and cast a quizzical glance at Ned's, which certainly did not err on the side of being too white, too soft, or too small.

'I like a hand which has some work in it,' went on Ned, in clumsy explanation; 'but there, all women are alike: they're fond of dandies'; and Ned turned away, his honest eyes full of tears, and his boyish heart full of vexation.

At times he really thought Glenarva felt a partiality for the newcomer, to whom, sad to say, he habitually referred as 'a whelp,' which was not a respectful way of speaking concerning a man on the wrong side of thirty, 'accustomed to society,' and standing very high indeed in his own opinion.

Fact was, that when Mr Dufford so far condescended as to 'take up the Westleys,' he chanced one day in the course of conversation, or rather of the monologue which usually obtained during his visits at the cottage, to mention, amongst other things true and false, that he had met an authoress who had achieved a considerable reputation. At the word, Glen, roused from the apathy into which Mr Dufford's descriptions of town life and 'the best society' generally plunged her, plied him with questions not merely concerning the lady in question in particular, but authors and literature in general; and then it transpired that to his other attractions the clergyman added the ability to 'throw off a few little things,' which had actually appeared in print, and which he promised to send for from Dublin, if Miss Westley would care to see them.

Bearing in mind that Miss Westley was an author herself – and an amateur author besides – it will not seem surprising that the impression left on her mind when she did see Mr Dufford's effusions was how very much better she could write herself; but as this feeling in nowise checked the interest she took in his efforts, the curate naturally thought her interest in his stories meant an interest in himself, and while he talked learnedly about printers and publishers and authors, concerning all of whom he knew literally nothing, he watched Glen's rapt expression of countenance, and decided that if Miss Westley were well dressed, and debarred from association with those dreadful boys, and placed where she would have the advantage of mixing in polite society, and refined by contact with his own superior mind, she would not, on the whole, be so much amiss.

He had seen worse girls, much worse girls, who, though they had been to boarding schools, and instructed by the best masters, and appeared at parties and balls, were not one half so appreciative as Lady Emily's niece.

It was in this conjunction he spoke of Miss Westley when he wrote his 'mawmaw' a description of the girl he had found 'running wild by the seashore at Ballyshane.' He knew the pleasant weakness of Dufford senior, and that any title could withdraw him in a moment from the contemplation of his butter firkins.

Meantime Glen, utterly ignorant of the honour Mr Dufford had some idea of conferring on her, appeared to the Vicar's sons somewhat inconsistent; for though she seemed to esteem the clergyman's various talents as little as they did, still there was no denying the fact that she listened eagerly to his conversation.

'I believe you are in love with the fellow,' said Ned sharply. 'How you can read that stuff of his puzzles me.'

'Well, if it's any comfort to you, I don't think much of it,' answered Glen, secretly wondering what Ned's opinion would be of her 'stuff.'

And so the summer glided on – days of brightness, days of blue skies, days of cloud and rain; days, as seemed afterwards to the girl, full of the purest happiness; days, had she known it, which should have been very precious to Glenarva, for they were the last she was to spend in that golden time of the year and her own life at Ballyshane.

'GLEN' – it was Ned who spoke; Ned, lying at the foot of a great rock, with his head resting on the girl's lap, and his face a little pallid and twisted with pain – 'tell me something honestly now. You do not care for Dufford, do you?'

'No,' she answered – her own face was a good deal whiter and more drawn than Ned's – 'I do not like him at all.'

'And you won't marry him, will you?'

'He does not want me to marry him,' she said lightly.

'That's all you know about it. Glen, I'm afraid I am a great nuisance to you; put my head down on the stone; I shall do very well, and you are only cramping yourself.'

'I am not cramped at all, but you must be in agony. I wish Hal would come. Oh, Ned! what will your mamma say?'

'Why, that it serves me right, to be sure. What else would you have her say? However, it is better for me to be taken home ill with a broken leg than Hal with a broken neck. I wonder if I shall be lame for life.'

'Do you really think your leg is broken, Ned?'

'Sure of it. Well, it will give old Grunley something to do.'

Ned's statement was quite true; the catastrophe so long prophesied had come to pass at last. In rushing over the Lonely Reef – as a jutting and dangerous promontory was locally termed – to cuff Hal, who more persistently than usual was seeking the nearest way to destruction, Ned had slipped on some seaweed and came down with such a crash, Glen felt assured he would never move again. She flew rather than ran to the spot, to find him vainly trying to rise, and striving to smile up in her face, though his own was covered with blood.

'A near touch this time, Glen,' he said.

'Oh! don't do that, Hal,' as the boy strove to lift him; 'my leg is broken, I think. Run as fast as you can and get help; tell them to bring a gate or something. Run now, and if you see my mother, be sure to say I am not much hurt.'

'Oh, Ned, Ned!' cried Glen; and then she sat down on the sand, and lifted his head gently into her lap, and with her handkerchief stanched the blood which trickled from a cut in his head.

'It might have been worse,' observed the lad; 'it might have been you;' and then he lay still, bearing his pain silently, and speaking a little at intervals, and at last relieving his mind by putting that home-question concerning Dufford the detested.

As a matter of course, Glen went every day to the Vicarage to see how Ned was getting on, and, perhaps equally as a matter of course, Mr Dufford seized every opportunity of walking back with her to the cottage.

For a short time Glen made no objection to this arrangement; but at last, when her companion commenced to pay her small compliments, and make little tender speeches, she thought it well to slip quietly out by the back way, and so avoid the *tête-à-têtes* she began to find embarrassing.

'He will soon be going now,' she thought one evening, as she opened the yard gate and tripped across the field beyond; 'only two Sundays more, and I can go which way I choose. Good gracious! there he is. He must have watched me as I left;' and Glen, with her cheeks aflame, stood at one side of the dry ditch she was about to cross, looking blankly at Mr Dufford, who, standing on the other, and extending one of those faultlessly white hands which stirred poor Ned's wrath, said, with the smile of a seraph:

'*Allow* me to assist you.'

'Oh, thank you,' answered Glen, 'but I can get over quite well myself.'

Which indeed, as a rule, she could do; dry ditches or ditches full of water, or 'gaps' filled up with rough stones, or openings roughly made through thorn hedges, or brambles, never having presented any insuperable difficulty in the way of Miss Westley's pedestrian progress across country; but on the present occasion she was destined not to fare so well.

Usually Glen wore dresses, as regards length, better adapted for getting in and out of boats, climbing headlands, and skipping over rocks, than for what Mr Dufford would have called drawing-room costume; but ere she left home on that sunshiny afternoon she had donned a muslin robe taken from among the olio of oddities wherewith Lady Emily was good enough to endow her, which, at the critical moment, when in the act of springing up the opposite bank, tripped her up so ignominiously that if Mr Dufford had not caught the wilful young lady, she would have measured her full length in the sandy, crumbly soil that slipped away from under her as she stumbled.

'It is a very awkward place to get over,' remarked Mr Dufford, in bland apology for her misadventure. 'You had better have let me help you at first; but you are so independent, Miss Glen.'

Glen made no reply; she was too angry and too much ashamed even to attempt a defence. She only looked down ruefully at the skirt of the large-patterned, washed-out, and hideously ugly muslin dress, which, in addition to its former attractions, now boasted a rent as long and wide – so it seemed to the girl – as the ditch that lay behind.

'Take my arm – pray do,' entreated Mr Dufford, in his most winning tone and best English accent.

'Oh! I could not possibly, thank you,' said Glen, unceremoniously repossessing herself of the hand he had taken in his own. 'I must hold up my dress, you know,' she added hastily, and with a good deal of confusion.

Mr Dufford looked at the garment in question, as if he did not see the necessity.

'There is no dust in the fields,' he observed, as a general sort of proposition, applicable, however, to the present case.

'You would not believe, though, how grass ruins muslin,' said Glen, desirous, doubtless, of imparting useful information.

'Does it really? I shall remember that;' and Mr Dufford smiled as he spoke, for he had known ladies quite willing, more than willing, to run the chance of so ruining even costly dresses, for the sake of perambulating with a delicate pearl-grey glove laid daintily, yet tenderly, on the black sleeve of his own clerical coat.

Quizzically he looked down at the rag – thus he mentally styled poor Glen's borrowed plumes – the girl was holding with both hands out of harm's way; then his glance wandered to the young face, framed in a shabby bonnet which had suffered many things both by sea and land, and then he said in a soft caressing voice:

'Do you know, Miss Glen, if the idea were not too preposterous, I should almost be tempted to imagine you had been avoiding me lately.'

'Should you?' answered Glen faintly.

'Yes, indeed,' he went on, delighted with her manifest uneasiness, which he attributed to anything rather than its true cause – a fear of meeting one of the boys.

'Several evenings lately I had planned to myself the great pleasure of walking home with you – always, until now, to be disappointed.'

As this was a statement which did not seem to require an answer, Glen kept silence, involuntarily, however, quickening her pace. 'Don't walk so fast, Miss Glen,' entreated her companion. 'Surely there is no such great need for haste; *pray take my arm.*'

'I couldn't possibly,' repeated Glenarva, appalled by the honour he desired to thrust upon her; 'you see I *must* hold up my dress;' and she clutched her gown as if the rag of muslin was the only thing left between her and perdition.

Mr Dufford glanced at the girl benignantly. If her clothes were torn, if her bonnet were battered, if her boots were thick, and her hands encased in old thread gloves, such defects could be easily remedied when he translated her to that superior state of life in which he himself moved and had his being.

And she was really very nice, he decided, watching the blushes coming and going on her sunburnt face. Her voice sounded sweet in his ears: the wild, free life had made her upright as a dart; her carriage was easy; her movements, on the whole, save when she tripped over Lady Emily's cast-off finery, were not awkward. There was something to be made of her. She had read; she had thought. Yes; he could mould, and train, and fashion her. It would be a gracious task, a work of love, to cut Glen into the conventional pattern, and make her a town young lady, who might never have seen a pony, steered a boat, or swung in the old swing with the half-rotten rope; or shaken down plums, or eaten apples by the bushel!

'The sea looks very lovely this evening,' at last observed Mr Dufford in his best manner, waving with an air of lofty condescension his white hand, on which a ring glittered, towards the scene spread below.

'Yes,' agreed Glen, stealing, as she answered, a sidelong glance at Mr Dufford's well-brushed hat, superfine coat, trousers to match, spotless boots, snowy shirt, and enamelled studs.

Not one of these items, harmless as doubtless they were singly and collectively, had escaped the criticism and censure of the boys, and it certainly occurred to Miss Westley, as she took in the clergyman's whole appearance, that however admirably adapted he might be to grace a town promenade, say to improve the general aspect of Sackville Street, he was not, artistically speaking, the right thing in the right place as a central figure in the landscape he was good enough to admire.

Old Jim Bishop, for example, unwashed and unshaven, in his long red cap, with his coat off, his trousers tucked up, and his feet and legs bare, going over the wet sands, carrying a net over his arm, would have come out much better in a picture than Mr Dufford, with his black wavy hair and trim whiskers and general air of conventional prosperity and orthodox respectability.

Glen, however, could imagine a man accustomed both to courts and camps, who might not have seemed so utterly out of keeping – nay, she had actually beheld such a one, who, calling at Ballyshane on a spring morning, as he came from the Giant's Causeway, was escorted by the Vicar to various points of interest in the neighbourhood.

He had afterwards lunched in the wainscotted parlour she loved so much, and she and the boys, unseen themselves, peeped through the privet hedge at the tall commanding figure which strode down the drive; and talked for many a long day after about the general's military bearing and warlike moustache, and the scar that disfigured his face, and the battles he had seen, and the fields he had fought on, and the victories he had won, and the courage he had never lacked.

No thought of joking or jeering amongst those young sinners as they recounted the veteran's deeds of daring. With bright eyes and flushed cheeks they repeated their stories o'er and o'er again, and, gathered together on the rocks in a picturesque group, or squatted around a bonfire fed with potato-haulms, told how the man who had been at college with their father, and sat under their roof and broke bread at their table, rose from lieutenant to captain and captain to major, and fought his way upwards in lands beyond the sea, which seemed to them in those days unreal and beautiful as places in an Eastern legend.

All this, suggested by that one swift look at her companion, had passed through Glen Westley's mind before Mr Dufford spoke again.

'And I shall soon be leaving all this beauty and peace behind,' he said sentimentally, as though he did not in his heart detest the country and all its ways, and love better the rattle of one Dublin jaunting-car than the many-toned music of the Atlantic waves.

'Shall you?' observed Glen.

She knew to an hour when he was going, but did not feel herself equal to any other original remark on the subject.

'On next Friday week,' he explained. 'Alas!' and he sighed in a manner which might have brought tears to the eyes of any properly educated young woman, 'I shall carry many sweet and happy memories away with me from Ballyshane.'

'Dear me!' thought Glen, with a tinge of regret; 'where can he have found them?'

'And I want dreadfully to carry something else away with me also,' he proceeded.

His tone was peculiar, and Glen looked up at him in surprise.

'What is it?' she asked.

'Cannot you guess?' he said softly.

'No;' and Glen's thoughts took a rapid and comprehensive summary of the few articles of rarity or value possessed by the Vicar and her father.

'It's not the Chinese box, is it? – or perhaps you mean the petrified dog's head papa showed you the other day?'

'It is something belonging to your papa, but not the dog's head,' answered Mr Dufford. 'What can it be?' puzzled Glen; 'we have so little.' And then a look in Mr Dufford's face stopped her wonder short, and all the blood in her body, as it seemed to the girl, came rushing and tingling into her cheeks.

'Yes,' said the clergyman benignantly, and as he spoke he took one of her hands, muslin dress and all, between his own, and held it tight; 'it is that I want to carry away with me; a kind thought from your papa's daughter.'

'I am sure we should not think unkindly of you, Mr Dufford.'

Was it really she who had uttered these words, or another? The voice sounded to Glen afar off. The sea was glittering and dancing up and down before her eyes, the headlands were spinning round; she could not see the grass under her feet or her companion; she felt a hot scorching sense of shame and misery. Was she vexing herself about nothing, or had Mr Dufford in a second taken leave of his senses? What had she ever done that a man should talk nonsense to her, and hold her hand so close she could not release it?

'Ah I but I want more than that – far more,' said he, almost in a whisper, bending down till his whiskers actually brushed her cheek. A moment more and he would have kissed her; but in that moment Glen snatched her hand away, and put a good space between them, and so averted the catastrophe impending.

'I really must get home, Mr Dufford,' she panted out, as calmly as agitation and amazement would let her speak; 'papa will be wanting his tea.'

'I am very sorry,' answered Mr Dufford, 'but I cannot let you go till I have said what I want to say.'

She stood there, with the sea rippling in on the shore below with the shabby bonnet standing out in full relief against the soft evening sky, with Lady Emily's old washed-out muslin, still in its last moments retaining some pretensions to fashion, trailing on the short grass behind her, and yet with a dignity in her girlhood and a reproachful expression in her face which compelled Mr Dufford to keep to the distance she had set between them, while she exclaimed:

'I do not know what it is you want to say, but, whatever it is, I wish you would leave it unsaid.'

'Matters have gone too far for me to do that, Miss Westley,' he replied. 'In justice both to you and myself, having said so much, I must say more. No, please don't go away; I am not coming near you. The dearest wish – of my heart – Glen –' He broke off suddenly, descending from his stilts, as he saw by her eyes she was meditating flight. 'I love you – I want to marry you – will you marry me?'

She looked at him with absolute incredulity. It could not be real. She must be dreaming.

'Marry you!' she repeated in her bewilderment – 'marry you!'

The honour was too great, the boon he proposed to confer too vast for her to instantly grasp the glory and beauty of the lot offered. She could not realise the seriousness of his proposal, could not take in the length and depth and breadth and height of such condescension on the part of a man over whom 'ladies had quarrelled' ere then.

Well, he could not be vexed with feelings so proper and so natural. He would be very gentle with her; he would give her time to recover her scattered senses, to comprehend he meant every word he said. He did love her: though she had been a tomboy she was not unfeminine; though she conformed to no canon of beauty she was not bad-looking; she was spirited and cheerful and good company, and came of an old stock, and had both connections and friends possessed of influence they would no doubt use for his advantage. Money he knew he should have, position was what he wanted, and –

'Mr Dufford,' said Glen, who was by this time pale enough and calm enough to satisfy any social requirements, 'don't you think you had better forget what you said just now, and go back to the Vicarage?'

How charming it was! She would not take an ungenerous advantage of words perhaps hastily spoken. In her modesty she felt he could do far, far better than marry an ignorant young girl, destitute of fortune, whose father, having played at ducks and drakes with a fine estate and handsome fortune, was forced to hide his diminished head in a cottage little more pretentious than those inhabited by the Ballyshane fishermen. He had never liked Glen so much before; he had never previously imagined she fully appreciated the wide difference in their positions. After all, she was young and inexperienced, and though she could ride wild horses she was not accustomed to lovemaking, and his abrupt proposal had frightened and astonished her.

'My dear child' – beautifully Mr Dufford considered he managed to blend in his manner the dual character of pastor and lover – 'I do not want to forget. I wish to go forward. I desire, when I return to the Vicarage, to carry thither with me the memory of sweet looks of encouragement, of kind words of hope,' and he moved close to where she stood, and would again have taken her hand; but Glen, without really changing her position, though in shrinking from him she seemed to draw back a little, said, in a tone and with a manner which surprised the curate as much as he had surprised her:

'Do not do that, please, Mr Dufford; and I am very sorry to vex you, but I shall never marry anybody.'

Mr Dufford tried to laugh, but the effort did not prove very successful.

'All young ladies say they will never marry,' he remarked.

'I mean, however, what I say,' answered Glen.

'That is nonsense,' expostulated Mr Dufford. 'You must marry, you know; and I am sure I could make you happy. You need not give me an answer now – not even before I leave Ballyshane. I am quite content to wait, to go away without another word, if you only say you do not quite hate me.'

'I hate no one, I hope,' answered Glen, 'but I cannot marry you.'

'Why not?'

'I have told you before – I shall never marry anyone.'

'But what are you going to do?' he asked, almost involuntarily. 'If anything should happen to your papa … ' Then, feeling he was treading on dangerous ground, he hesitated and stopped.

'You mean, I suppose, I should have no money?' supplied Glen.

'Well, I confess that thought did cross my mind,' answered Mr Dufford; 'and it would comfort me – oh, so inexpressibly! – if you would let me place you beyond the reach of pecuniary anxiety.'

Glen shook her head. 'I shall never marry at all,' she said, 'and I should certainly not marry for money.'

'Or for love?' supplied Mr Dufford.

'I am not likely to fall in love' – which the curate felt to be a plain way of stating she had not fallen in love with him.

Matters were looking anything but pleasant. The turn affairs had so unexpectedly taken was one for which Mr Dufford was in no respect prepared. It began to dawn upon him this girl, this chit of a girl, who had seen nothing of life or society, or men or women, or the world, and possessed no money or position, actually meant to refuse him.

Her words were nothing, but her manner was serious. He knew Glen's manner, and he could not doubt but that she really intended to decline the hand he offered.

'Let us walk on,' he said, awaking to the consciousness that, being set upon a hill, their figures must be visible from the beach were anyone there to see. 'I spoke too suddenly,' he proceeded, with a look in his face which touched Glen, in spite of her own vexation. 'I took you by surprise.'

'Yes, I was surprised,' she answered.

'But when you have had time to think quietly over what I have said –'

'Time cannot make any difference to me, Mr Dufford. I shall never marry.'

'The English of which is, I suppose, you will not marry me?'

'Or anyone else,' added Glen; quite sure in her own mind she was speaking the truth, and laudably anxious to make her positive refusal of Mr Dufford's proposal less ungracious by generalising it.

'May I without offence inquire your reason for saying this – that is, always supposing you have a reason?'

Glen looked at him askance, but she was not offended – quite the contrary; the slight tone of sarcasm in his question gave her assurance that though this lover's temper might be ruffled, his heart was not broken. No girl can associate constantly and intimately with a man for months, and fail at the end of them to understand some of his peculiarities; and even had this young lady been willing to remain blind to Mr Dufford's weak points, the Vicar's boys were not likely to leave her in ignorance of the fact that he was, as Ned concisely worded his statement, 'brimming over with conceit and folly.'

Instinctively she felt it was something not much worth fretting herself about she had wounded; and accordingly, with more composure than he anticipated, she answered Mr Dufford's question by explaining that for one reason she never intended to leave her father.

'And *could* you suppose,' said Mr Dufford, with a tender reproach in his fine eyes which he brought to bear full upon Glen's sunburnt face, 'that *I* should ever ask you to do such a thing? No; I trust he would always make *our* home his. In my estimation it would be a high privilege to minister to his declining years, to surround him with comforts, to provide him with congenial and suitable society, to regard him as my father as well as yours, to study his tastes and feelings to the utmost of my ability.'

Mr Dufford intended this for a very telling speech; but it failed to touch Glen, who only murmured something about his being very kind, but she did not think her papa would like to live with anyone. 'And I know,' added the girl hastily, seeing her admirer about to speak, 'that I should not. Papa and I are going to stay alone together always,' she finished decidedly.

'Oh!' said Mr Dufford, and there was a world of meaning in this monosyllable as he uttered it, but Glen failed to read what he was thinking of; indeed, she did not try. Her only desire was to hurry on, and terminate the interview as speedily as possible.

Mr Dufford did not, however, intend to let the matter drop thus. When Glen thought he was vanquished, he was really collecting his forces for a fresh attack.

They were now descending to the shore road Miss Westley had so imprudently abandoned when she skulked out of the Vicarage by a back way, only to be ignominiously trapped by the enemy she sought to avoid, and Mr Dufford felt no time should be lost in trying to make another effective movement.

'Surely,' he began in his suavest accents, 'we need not walk as though we were training for a match. You will not be tried by my companionship much longer, if it is so disagreeable to you. Share me a few minutes, therefore, of your time, which I do not imagine is *very* valuable.'

She made no reply except that involved in slackening a pace which had, indeed, downhill been almost breakneck.

'I need not ask if you are fond of your father, Miss Glen,' began the curate.

'I would not marry for his sake, Mr Dufford, if that is what you mean,' said Glen, who really now felt herself at bay.

'Well, you certainly are one of the oddest girls I ever met,' exclaimed Mr Dufford. (Glen's decided opinions on many subjects which seemed quite out of the natural range of thought for so young a person had ere now amazed and amused him, but he was not prepared for such a prompt expression of her sentiments.) 'Why you should imagine my harmless words held any hidden meaning of the sort you impute to them I am quite at a loss to imagine. You speak as if you had spent your life in considering the question of self-sacrifice in daughters – a question I imagine, perhaps erroneously, can not possibly hitherto have come within the scope of your observation.'

Had Glen spoken out, she could have told Mr Dufford this matter of marrying for the sake of somebody else was one that in her capacity as author she had considered fully and exhaustively.

She had weighed it in the balance and found it wanting. Love, also, she had put into her mental crucible, and though she felt satisfied this absorbing madness could never disarrange the even tenor of her thoughts, she had arrived at the conclusion nothing but love – and that of the most vehement and enduring description – could justify marriage.

She believed there was a limit even to what daughters ought to do for their parents, and had long been satisfied that limit was passed when, for the sake of providing food and shelter, or even screening a father from disgrace, a girl was asked to wed a man she detested.

This formerly merely abstract idea being, at a moment's notice, presented to her in the concrete, she had not the least difficulty in making up her mind, and in showing she had made up her mind, that for the pleasure or advantage of no human being would she become the wife of the gentleman who, for some to her unaccountable reason, had taken a fancy to her.

But Glen was not going to tell Mr Dufford the way she had arrived at this conclusion, and merely answered that, having read about such things, she felt it would be very wrong to marry merely to provide a home for some one who wanted it.

In those days the wording of Glen's sentences sounded to herself quite unworthy of a writer; but this much at least could be said in their favour, they did not as a rule err on the side of ambiguity.

'I quite agree with you,' answered Mr Dufford, 'but I suppose you will concede there is no reason why, because a suitor brings good gifts in his hand, he is *therefore* to be sent empty away. Come, dear,' he added, suddenly getting off his high horse and altering his tone, 'let us be reasonable. I do not ask you for an answer now; so on your side do not refuse my offer without at least thinking about me a little. I want to be your friend and helper as well as your lover, Glen. I would be a son to your father. No one can look upon him and fail to lament he should be so utterly out of his sphere as he is at present. It seems to me his affairs must have been dreadfully mismanaged for such a total collapse to have ensued. Now, my father, though he did not rise from the ranks or commence life with the few pence English people are so fond of talking about, is a thoroughly business-like and practical man. Give me the right to interfere in your affairs. Say no more even than this, "I will give you an answer to what you have asked me at Christmas," and I can truthfully say, that if money, or time, or energy can restore Glenarva to Mr Westley, he shall be back in the old place when next summer's roses are in bloom.'

The girl was crying; he had touched her at last – touched the vein in her heart which bled on the slightest provocation.

'You will not be cruel,' went on Mr Dufford, who lacked wisdom and feeling to let well alone; 'you will give me the right to look after your father's interests – darling!'

At this term of endearment Glen stopped suddenly, and, with the fire of a sudden indignation drying up her tears, turned upon her lover, and interrupted the flow of further eloquence.

'Mr Dufford,' she said, 'I could never care for you in that – that way; and so please do not think of trying to help papa. He – he wouldn't like it. He may go back to Glenarva yet. I hope he will. I sometimes think he may; but if he does, it won't be by my marrying – anybody. Besides,' she added, thinking to clench the nail she had driven home, 'there is nothing in the whole world could induce me to marry a clergyman. I should be miserable as a clergyman's wife – utterly wretched.'

'You would rather, I suppose, be running wild about the country with a clergyman's six unruly, ill-mannered sons,' observed Mr Dufford, whom she had at last stung in his tenderest part.

'Yes, I would far rather,' retorted Glen, getting up speed again, and walking along the splendid high-road – which, by reason of the limestone underlying it, shone before them like a white, glittering thread of light – at a pace which did much more credit to her pedestrian powers than to that feminine weakness and yielding softness of character which Mr Dufford considered the crowning graces of a woman's nature. There had been such irritation in her tone that the clergyman thus disparaged felt it would be useless to imperil his prospects by further remark, and accordingly they walked rapidly on, side by side, till they reached the rude gate, made of unbarked fir, which gave admission to Mr Westley's present home. Mr Dufford had not again spoken, and it is almost unnecessary to add that Glen had maintained a discreet silence.

Now, however, standing against the closed gate, which was only fastened by the primitive expedient of passing a noose of rope over one of the fir rails and the post, she said, extending her hand in token at once of amity and farewell: 'I am sorry you have come so much out of your way.'

'Not at all,' he answered, 'not at all'; but he did not take her offered hand or make any movement as if to part.

Glen looked surprised, and stood embarrassed: she thought she had told him to go as plainly as she well could, and as he did not take the hint, she was at a loss how to act.

There ensued an awkward silence. Glen would not ask him in, yet she felt unequal to passing through the gate and leaving him outside. Alexander-like, Mr Dufford cut the knot of this difficulty. Lifting the loop, he said, as he thus enabled her to enter the rough cart road leading up to the cottage: 'I will trouble you with my company for a few minutes longer, Miss Westley; I should like to pay my respects to your father.'

It was the last thing Glen at that moment wished him to do, but she could not well make any objection to so moderate a desire. Accordingly they picked their way over the coarse black and white gravel as they followed the course of the path which ascended to the cottage.

Chapter X

FATHER AND DAUGHTER

IT DID NOT TAKE Miss Westley long to pull off her bonnet and dress, fill a huge basin full of cold water, and – in defiance of repeated warnings from Miss Neill that 'she would ruin her complexion', 'bring out a rash', 'destroy her skin', and so forth – bury her face in its depths.

Then she brushed and smoothed her ruffled hair, slipped on a cotton gown Teenie had not ten minutes previously laid over the back of a chair – clean, stiff, freshly ironed – fastened a snowy collar with the one article of jewellery she possessed, a small gold brooch; and thus 'prepared to meet anyone', ran downstairs, into the parlour, where the tea equipage was already set out, and everything ready for Glen to take her place as mistress of the ceremonies.

As a matter of course, Mr Westley had immediately invited the curate to share their meal, and when the daughter of the house entered the room, she found the pair conversing as easily and pleasantly as though no question of marriage had been raised concerning herself by anyone.

'If *he* says nothing about it to papa, I am very sure *I* shan't', considered Miss Westley, taking her seat and looking prim enough to suggest to Mr Dufford's mind the idea that after all his lady-love was somewhat of a humbug.

The correct thing, he felt, would have been for her to remain in the solitude of her chamber, and send down a message to the effect she had a bad headache and begged to be excused.

To take an offer of marriage, and such an offer, as coolly as she might the suggestion of a second helping of pudding, was, Mr Dufford felt, only to be accounted for on the ground that Glen was not merely a little savage, ignorant of *les convenances*, but that the girl really could not grasp the extent of the honour and advantages he proposed to confer upon her.

She was young, of course, and many allowances must be made! Further, he felt he had committed a mistake in addressing her first. He should previously have spoken to her papa, but then it had never occurred to him Glen would be other than delighted with his offer. He had felt confident for him to ask was to have. Truly a man never can tell what is in store when a woman is concerned. Instead of kisses, for instance, Mr Dufford got, figuratively speaking, a slap in the face. Glen's words, it is true, were not many; but containing as they did a rejection, by no means hesitating or half-hearted, they stung like the lash of a whip. Well, all he could do now was to strive to repair his error, get the father on his side, and then, backed by the paternal approval and authority, take an opportunity of again attacking the daughter's heart.

Glen very speedily gave the chance he wanted for an uninterrupted *tète-á-tète* with Mr Westley. The moment tea was over, and Teenie – clad in a stuff gown, with a small plaid shawl pinned decently across her shoulders, a fair white apron, and a snowy cap with picturesque borders carefully goffered encircling her sad but contented old face – had removed the tray. Miss Westley, without a word of apology, left her admirer to do his best or his worst in the way of reconciling Mr Westley to him as a suitor.

The girl knew perfectly well what he wanted, and felt if she did not voluntarily quit the room, Mr Dufford in dulcet accents would beg her to do so.

'I am not at all afraid of what papa will say,' thought Glen; but she was a little nervous for all that, and she grew more nervous as time went by, and the even murmur of earnest and continuous conversation ascended from below.

'I wonder what they can be finding to talk about all this while,' she considered. 'Now, whatever he says to papa will make no difference to me. I don't like him, and I never shall; and I don't trust him, and – oh dear, I wish he would go!'

She had opened her desk and tried to write, but for once that solace failed her. She reread a note which in the morning seemed intensely laudatory and gratifying, but even words of praise penned by a gentleman who spelled 'excellent' with one 'l' failed to comfort her. She paced her room restlessly; she stood with her arms resting on the window – sash thrown wide, and looked, while the roses softly touched her face, over the sea and the land – both of which, as they lay spread out before her eyes, were soon to become memories to Glenarva Westley.

'If I am to do anything, I must do it soon,' she thought, with the impatience of youth, which thinks every minute spent in waiting is a year lost. 'I wonder – I wonder – I wonder what is the way to get into print; if I could once have anything published, I am sure I could make money – heaps of it;' and then the dear delightful dreams of all she would do when very, very rich came again to enchant her imagination. Glenarva! Wealth! Consideration! There was not a cloud in the azure of the heaven she looked on with the eyes of her mind – though over the real world lying at that minute around, twilight was creeping down, and sea and land, bay and headland, were fading softly and gradually from her sight.

At last the sound of movement in the room below! The door opened – she heard her father's voice in the hall – he was speaking to Mr Dufford in the porch covered with creepers; she drew back from the window, still however watching and listening eagerly. Mr Dufford was saying something, then a step crunched over the gravel, and the curate went out into the gathering darkness – alone.

Her father did not accompany this visitor to the outer gate, as was his pleasant wont. Even by so slight a token she knew the interview had ended as she could wish, but still she did not go down immediately. She drew a chair to the window, and sat down for a little while. Had Mr Dufford really spoken? Yes, of that she felt sure; would her father name the matter to her? Glen could not tell. They had ever been parent and child rather than friend and friend – even concerning his troubles he had been reticent towards her; it was from others Glen knew the full extent of their misfortunes, and understood she would some day, if she lived, have to support herself.

The moon had risen ere the girl gathered courage sufficient to enter the quiet parlour where her father had, since Mr Dufford's departure, remained sunk in reverie.

'All in the dark, papa!' Glen exclaimed, as she entered.

'No, dear; there is the moonlight,' he answered, pointing to the cold silvery beams, that seemed to thrust the roses aside to fall clear and unearthly upon the floor. 'Come here, my child,' he went on, as she lingered in the shadows, 'and let me look at you. I am told,' he went on, as he took her face and held it framed in both his hands, 'that my little girl is almost a woman, old enough to be asked in marriage.'

'Papa, papa!' and the girl clung to him passionately.

'It is now,' he said, tenderly touching the head laid on his bosom, 'that you miss your mother, my darling.'

'No, no!'

'You want someone to talk to fully – to speak all your thoughts to.'

'You – you, papa,' she cried, 'if you will only let me.'

'Let you? oh, my dearest Glen!'

There ensued a minute's silence while they stood clasped in each other's arms. Then Mr Westley, gently disengaging himself from his daughter's embrace, said interrogatively:

'Now, Glen –'

'Yes, papa dear.'

'What have you to tell me?'

'What do you want to hear?'

'I scarcely know, my child. I am told you are possessed of will sufficient to say "No" to a man who, I believe, means very fairly by you. Is that so. Glen?'

'Yes, papa – you are not vexed with me, are you?'

'My love, it is your own future you have to give or withhold. You are sure you could not marry Mr Dufford, dear – sure and certain?'

'Most sure and most certain,' answered the girl. 'What did he say to you, papa?'

'He said a great deal,' answered Mr Westley thoughtfully, 'which had little or nothing to do with the real matter in hand. Because the real matter is, Glen, whether you like him or could like him. If you do not and could not, there is no more to be said.'

'Do you wish me to marry him, papa?'

'I will answer your question, dear, when you tell me if you wish to do so.'

'No – papa – no – I don't like him. I never shall like him!'

'Then there is no more to be said.'

'Oh, papa, if you really wanted me to marry him, there might be ever so much to be said!'

'But I don't. Glen. Good heavens, no! Only –'

'Only what?' she questioned.

'I was wondering,' he said sadly, 'what my darling's future would be.'

Then in a moment the girl's carefully guarded secret escaped her.

'I think I can make a future for myself,' she cried, with a trembling exultation in her voice, and then she told him all.

In the after-days neither could have indicated the form or mode in which the knowledge was given and received; but Glen's explanation, though hurried and excited, was clear, and Mr Westley's intelligence acute.

'Write!' he repeated. 'Is it possible?'

To Glen it was so possible as to be quite certain. Had not she proof positive upstairs in piles of rejected manuscripts? Had not she letters from editors and publishers by the score, politely regretting their inability to avail themselves of the tales she offered?

Had she not also that precious note saying her story was very *excelent*; and adding the honest but, under the circumstances, perfectly unnecessary caution, 'but if you decide to publish at your own expense, you must not do so on my judgment alone'?

This advice, which in Glen's judgment was superfluous, tried the girl's faith a little, though Ned would have explained her correspondent was in his orthography merely following a good Biblical example.

The boys were in those days far ahead of Miss Westley in all Scriptural knowledge.

In Chronicles, and indeed in all other portions, they could, so Ned declared, 'beat her in a canter;' and therefore Glen really did not know the gentleman who professed such admiration for her talents was merely in the one case following old fashions, and in the other forestalling the modern innovation of dispensing with doubles.

Still the praise, however spelt, was grateful; and the authoress felt delighted to place this testimony of what others thought of the productions she deemed exquisite in her father's hands.

'You see, papa,' she said, 'not one of them says I have no ability.'

'But, my dear, not one of them says he will take your manuscript.'

'That is true,' she sighed, 'but' – unconsciously paraphrasing Disraeli's famous utterance – 'they will be glad some day to take anything I offer.'

'There is nothing like hope,' remarked Mr Westley, in the tone of one who had never hoped in all his life.

'There is nothing like perseverance, papa,' amended Glen, 'and I have made up my mind to succeed. Oh! if I could but once see a publisher, I think I might get him to print something; and a start is all I want – I feel it is all.'

Her father smiled. 'As a rule, dear, a start is what most people require. You are but expressing the old idea of "*le premier pas*" in another form.'

Mr Westley said this pleasantly, yet with a certain doubtfulness of manner which Glen fancied, and truly, was caused by his strong impression there were several other small items needful for his daughter's success besides a start.

'Should you like me to read you some of the things I have written?' she asked eagerly, anxious at once to commence the task of conversion.

'Not tonight, my love,' answered Mr Westley, meanly deferring the evil day, and perfectly unconscious he was in so doing only following the lead of all friends and relations happily able to follow the bent of their own inclinations. 'I must leave a letter out before I go to bed for Teenie to send to the Vicarage in the morning.'

'To Mr Dufford?'

'Yes, Glen.'

'To tell him –'

'That, as he wished, I have talked the matter over with you, and find you are not disposed to alter your decision.'

'Did he mention anything to you, papa, about his father being able to get you back Glenarva?'

'Yes; amongst other subjects he touched on that.'

'And what did he mean?'

'I don't know, my dear; and I am inclined to think he did not know himself.'

'He said your affairs must have been mismanaged.'

'It is a natural idea. Lookers-on always fancy they see more of the game than the players.'

'Then you do not think anything that could have been done was left undone?'

'For my benefit – no. The ruin affected has been tolerably complete; but if my lawyer had chanced to be dishonest, we should have found ourselves a good deal worse off even than we are. Mr Dufford, senior, may be a very wise man – judging by the money he has made, I am sure he must be – but Solomon himself could not undo the evil wrought by my own folly, and under no circumstances should I feel inclined to "lay the state of affairs," to quote our friend the curate, before his father. It is one thing to be beggared, and another to flaunt one's rags and tatters in the public street.'

'Mr Dufford must have put papa out dreadfully,' Glen decided as she went up to her room that night, leaving Mr Westley in a solitude which the unwonted exertion involved in writing one important letter seemed to require, and in this surmise she chanced to be quite correct.

Mr Westley had been greatly 'put out.' After all, it is not pleasant for a shy, sensitive nature to hear hard truths hurled at it even by a good-looking curate. Mr Dufford determined not to jeopardise his chances by over delicacy, and failing to impress upon his lady-love's father the full extent of the Westley impetuosity, dealt some very telling blows as he proceeded with his arguments.

Not a shilling owned by the elder Dufford, not an acre of land or house he possessed, was forgotten. Mr Westley was literally pelted with sovereigns; he felt during the interview, indeed, smothered in bank notes. He was not even left the slight satisfaction of believing himself better born than this clerical aspirant for his daughter's hand. When Mr Dufford began to 'get up in the world,' he felt it incumbent to look out for a decent family-tree, which he easily got by paying for it; and as this tree had grown and ramified with the growth of his riches, it was now of such goodly size it could bid the Westleys and half a dozen other of such unillustrious families come and roost on its branches.

Mr Westley had not enjoyed the acquaintance of Mr Dufford, junior, for so long a time without hearing frequent reference made to his descent; but matters having now arrived at a point when the curate felt it necessary to marshal all the family forces and pass them in review before the eyes of Glen's father, he raised every apocryphal ancestor out of his or her grave, and paraded the whole host for the benefit of a most patient listener.

In reply, Mr Westley said nothing – indeed, what could he say? His guest's glib tongue confused rather than enlightened him; and at the end of over an hour's diligent attention, the only three facts he felt thoroughly able to grasp were that his unobtrusive poverty had been intruded on and insulted – that opposite to him sat a man whose heart was set on marrying his daughter, and that Glen had with rare good sense refused to have anything to do with him.

But yet, what was to become of the girl if, or rather when anything – as Mr Dufford expressed the contingency 'happened to her father'?

For the first time he saw her – as the curate was good enough to draw a vigorous sketch of the future orphan – penniless, forlorn, ignorant of the world, unfitted both by education and temperament to battle with it – his poor, dear Glen! his child, he had lost his all in hoping to make an heiress.

He was cut to the very heart. Though he did not know it, Mr Dufford had drawn a knife across veins that throbbed with deep absorbing love for his daughter.

The sun which illumined for Glen the gloom of Mr Dufford's proposals had not yet arisen on her father's horizon; and even now when he stood in the full blaze of this new knowledge, it failed to show him a way out of the incertitude of his position.

He was not stricken dumb with delight at the prospect of his daughter entering herself in the race for fame. Things which of late had vaguely puzzled him about her were now clear; but he felt doubtful whether the fancy she had taken might not, instead of mending matters, make them worse.

However, let what would come, he could not regret that she had refused Mr Dufford. The double character in which that gentleman offered himself, as son and son-in-law, fairly appalled Mr Westley. 'Yes, it is better Glen can't fancy him,' he decided; and finally, taking pen in hand, he wrote a few courteous lines to the rejected suitor, who, when he read them, felt as he had never done before in the whole course of his life.

To remain at Ballyshane after what had occurred was impossible. He did not in the least degree understand the Westleys, and thought his offer and Glen's refusal would soon be common property. Only one other Sunday intervened before the time appointed for Mr Beattie's return, but when the post brought him several letters he feigned to have received a missive urgently requesting his immediate presence in Dublin.

Diplomatically he put the question to Mrs Beattie.

'Did she think it would be possible for him to leave at once? Could a substitute be procured? Was it likely one of the clergymen in the neighbourhood would take the duty on the following Sunday? Any expense which might be incurred he should, of course, be most happy to meet, but the business which recalled him was of vital importance. Would dear Mrs Beattie set her woman's wits to work and see if she could help him out of the dilemma?'

Dear Mrs Beattie, who was at that moment darning stockings – a necessary work Mr Dufford, as a rule, regarded with much disfavour – threaded a coarse needle with blue worsted, and commenced operations upon a large hole before she answered.

The prospect of getting rid of the curate filled her with such delight, she could not for a moment trust herself to speak. Then she said, with praiseworthy composure, that she had no doubt, under the circumstances, the Rector of Artinglass would either come over himself or send one of his curates.

'And so you really believe I may leave with an easy mind?' remarked Mr Dufford.

'I am sure you may,' she answered. 'Even if we had to close the church for one Sunday, I don't suppose it would do the people much harm to go to Meeting.'*

Mr Dufford looked at the lady with severe incredulity.

'I never thought,' he said, in a tone of lofty rebuke, 'to hear such a sentiment from the lips of a Christian woman!'

---

* Dissenting places of worship are in Ireland called meeting-houses – not chapels. [Author's note.]

Chapter XI

STONY-HEARTED LONDON

SAVE TO THE INITIATED – nay, it will be better to amend the phrase, and say even to the initiated – a manuscript is a very fearful and terrible thing to contemplate. Within its folds lurk unknown horrors, and the thought either of reading the scroll, or hearing it read, fills the stoutest heart with dread.

It is better, however, to read for one's self than let the author read. Probably there is no infliction, save the rack, equal to that, and yet it was an ordeal through which poor Mr Westley had, after the night when Mr Dufford drank tea at the cottage for the last time, very frequently to pass.

His daughter felt no more pity for him than she might have done for a lay figure. She tried her productions upon him, but was not particularly delighted to find he built his hopes of success less upon her great merits than upon the exceeding feebleness of some other writers whom he named. Glen's heart did not swell with pride at this sort of encouragement.

'I have read much worse, my dear,' or, 'If Mr and Miss Blank can get their stories published, I really do not see why yours should not be accepted.'

It was very faint praise, but still Glen's courage did not fail her. In her own opinion, the tales she read to her father were perfect; they had not a spot or blemish; they were amusing, pathetic, dramatic, but she could not blind herself to the fact that for some reason they did not touch the listener as they did the reader; that there was something lacking. What was it? the girl wondered. She had put her own whole heart into the work, but she could see plainly the heart of another was not moved by it. She understood this perfectly, because she remembered the first time any music she made ever found its way to a human soul.

It was a little air she heard when staying with Lady Emily Wildersly, an air the whole beauty and effect of which lay with the player. But the lady under whose fingers the piano seemed to sob out the plaintive melody was a mistress of her craft; and Glen, catching the trick from her, so reproduced the effect one evening at the Vicarage that Mrs Beattie, her eyes full of tears, kissed the girl tenderly, and Mr Beattie turned away to the window, and looked wistfully over the sea, and the boys spoke no word, good or bad, and days passed away before Ned remarked:

'I say. Glen, how stunningly you played that new thing you learnt in Dublin.'

It was a cruel disappointment to the author to find her words of beauty and of wisdom fall flat, as, indeed, they did. And what made the matter worse was that she knew very well the fault must lie in her writing; it did not originate in any want of appreciation on the part of her father. No; though undoubtedly it is, as a rule, true that a prophet is not without honour save in his own country and amongst his own people, in this instance Mr Westley would only too thankfully have recognised and acknowledged the existence of inspiration in his daughter. He was willing to believe, but faith wanted some stone on which to build. Of course he did not possess the feeling of power which was driving her along a road the end of which was hidden from mortal eyes. All he understood at the time was that Glen seemed able to spin little stories he fancied ought some day to find a purchaser.

Suddenly, however, the genius the girl had in her quickened into life. So far there was nothing in her writings which shadowed forth, even dimly, any promise of a great future. But all at once there came a mighty change; and one evening, after her return from a long lonely walk over the headlands, the while a wild sad sea tossed its billows towards a gloomy sky, Glen somehow managed to produce a few pages which made Mr Westley remark, after a few minutes' amazed silence:

'I really do believe, dear, you have it in you to do something; but I am afraid you will find the way long and very steep.'

While he believed her safe in the plains of mediocrity, he had not foretold the weary path and the steep hillside; but now – now – the whole prospect of her future life seemed to get lost in the mists of possibility. She had touched his heart, and he felt it might be she should touch the heart of others.

'Oh, papa! – dear papa!' – she cried, feeling the impression she had made at last, and as she spoke she could not see sky, or angry billows, or stretching moorland, for happy tears.

From one point of view, how marvellous seems that general prejudice in favour of the commonplace; and yet when we come to think the matter over calmly, it is utterly impossible to say there is not a great amount of reason in the idea that safety is only to be compassed by confining ourselves to the customary.

Where one person stands in need of the services of the extraordinary, a thousand are willing to pay for the help of the ordinary. For example, paint a child's head just as its mother is accustomed to see it, and ten million mothers will buy the worst lithograph of the drawing which can be produced for sixpence; *but* – and oh! my friends, the virtue of a 'but' in such a case – from the very travail of your soul produce a picture that cannot fail to live through the ages, and each person you know will stand appalled, doubtful whether to praise or blame, but certain in either case to say you have chosen the road which leads to sure and fell destruction.

So long as he felt his daughter was treading the safe path of mediocrity, Mr Westley had only regarded her writings as something which might bring her a living; but now – but now – with all his heart and soul the poor father – who could see so short a way ahead – hoped and trusted Glen might never need fully to use such talents as she possessed.

For God Almighty had given her both strength and genius – the brain to conceive, the courage to develop. Circumstances had not forced the one, or cowed the other – yet.

So far the girl was mistress of her own position, and she utilised this fact characteristically, and in a mode auguring well for her future success. Save a few of her very earliest productions – which she laid aside tenderly, as a mother might the outgrown dress of her first baby – after that last achievement she gathered together all her old manuscripts, and one day, when Teenie was engrossed in ironing, and feeling Mr Westley's shirts and Miss Glen's dresses the only things much worth being anxious about on earth, carried the papers down to a remote part of the garden, where she watched them consume till no scrap remained of that mound of rejected addresses.

Then, with a lightened heart, she betook herself to a different sort of writing – bolder, more ambitious, and indeed, considering her youth and inexperience, extraordinary.

'Where does she get her ideas?' thought Mr Westley, whom the change almost frightened. Where? If you put the question to Glenarva now, she would ask you in return: 'Whence does the dove get the glinting colours that shimmer and glitter and keep continually changing in the light?' And for me, I can tell you no more.

Still, though her work held the promise of better things than the manuscripts she had destroyed, acceptance of her efforts seemed far off as ever, and she began at length almost to sicken of rejection. The returned manuscripts appeared to lie like a load on her heart.

'It is because I have to tell papa,' she thought, and there was a good deal of truth in this idea. The girl did not find pain lightened when shared; on the contrary, it seemed doubled.

What a weary road that grew to be at length between Ballyshane and Artinglass! And yet not so long ago she could remember treading it with feet that felt winged by Hope.

Months ran on in this state, when one day Mr Westley's lawyer, returning from Londonderry to Belfast, broke his journey at Ballymoney, and drove across country to see the ruined gentleman. He wanted to confer with him about a little matter which he thought ought to return some money.

The tenant at Glenarva wished a few trees cut down, and it occurred to Mr Merritt that a considerable amount of judicious thinning might be effected in the autumn.

To Mr Westley the felling of timber seemed little short of desecration, but in the Glenarva woods chestnuts were now smothering oaks; willows, elms, and pines hopelessly jostling each other.

If the best trees were to live, it was high time some one set the axe to work; and as at that period there chanced to be a further demand on Mr Westley's purse, the opportunity appeared favourable for suggesting a means of replenishing it.

Mr Merritt stayed over the night, and of course saw a good deal of Glen, who had, somewhat to his surprise – for people are apt to forget the passage of years – shot up since last they met from a child into 'quite a young lady,' as the lawyer remarked.

He thought her, on the whole, rather good-looking, and a quiet, well-behaved girl; and he might not then have given another minute to the consideration of her future but for the chance of his mentioning over the breakfast table that he had lately been to London.

'Oh!' cried Glen impulsively, 'what would I not give to be able to go to London!'

'I hope you will go some day,' said Mr Merritt vaguely and politely, and he said no more at the moment; but subsequently, when he and Mr Westley were slowly pacing the cliffs, he astonished his client by asking:

'Why don't you go to London? You could live almost as cheaply there as here, and your daughter might have a chance then' – he did not say of what, but Mr Westley understood, and winced. 'Consider the matter,' went on Mr Merritt; 'I think the idea is one well worth turning over in your mind.'

The lawyer did not know it was one Mr Westley had already been turning over in his vague, hesitating, irresolute fashion.

'Glen,' he answered, 'I know, would like to go.'

'Of course; she said so,' returned Mr Merritt briskly, 'and it is quite natural – she must be moped to death in this place.'

'Moped to death!' That might be the lawyer's idea; but when she had achieved her wish, and the London she so ardently desired to visit was reached, and Ballyshane lay as far behind as childhood, Glen's pillow was wet with tears, shed because of the terrible homesickness some natures never experience, but which to those that do seems as bad as death – indeed, is no poor type of the last parting.

By the agony the girl endured for nearly two months after her arrival in England it was easy to foresee what the actual loss of those she loved would prove in the sorrowful hereafter – the donkey, the ponies, the cats, the dogs, the boys, Mr and Mrs Beattie, Teenie, Doctor and Miss Grunley, recurred severally and collectively to Glenarva Westley as she lay awake at night or paced the London streets. She sickened for the roar of the waves, for the taste of the salt brine, for the sweeping wind straight off the Atlantic, for the sight of the turf fire, for the smell of the familiar griddle-bread.

She could not eat; food, even such as their landlady considered necessary for her own physical support, was quite beyond their means; and she had thus no equivalent for the milk new and pure, the butter straight from the churn, the eggs that had 'seen no sorrow,' and the fish fresh from the sea – unaccounted luxuries when capable of being procured for a few pence, but things to be wished for when no longer to be had.

Only a great courage and a persistent will kept the girl up during many trying awful weeks.

At first her father seemed cheerful and in good spirits. London, though unvisited for years, was not strange ground to him, and it somewhat comforted Glen to see his quiet, and to her unintelligible, enjoyment of streets, which appeared to her but one long weary maze, filled with people they did not know, and who knew nothing of them, and with whom the girl felt satisfied they never for ever could have anything in common.

But even this source of consolation soon failed, and Mr Westley sank for a time into a state of deep depression, which Glen, who was totally ignorant of the hope that had arisen in his mind, could only attribute to disappointment at the chilling reception her best writing met with, and regret for having left the sure safe haven of a place where, though poor, they were loved and respected.

One day, when she felt terribly low herself, she ventured to suggest the question to her father whether he thought they had done a foolish thing in coming to London.

'No, my dear, certainly not,' he answered. 'I think in time you may be able to get something to do here, which I am very sure you never could at Ballyshane. Why do you ask, Glen?'

'Because I thought you were dull and out of sorts, papa.'

'I have been a little vexed because of the non-success of a little scheme of my own, that is all – and another thing, I do not like lodgings. When the spring comes I think we had better look out for a cottage somewhere.'

'Very well, papa,' answered Glen, though her heart sank within her at his words. If they found it hard to make both ends meet in lodgings, how were they to accomplish the feat in a house of their own? She knew the amount of their income only too well; and at last she had well-nigh lost hope concerning her writing. A dreadful experience had come upon the girl. She could produce nothing; the trees were not more bare of leaf or bud than Miss Westley's once active mind of an idea. To pen an original line was a matter quite beyond her ability. She had lost even physical energy, and weary in body and sick at heart, with a dreary persistency carried a bundle of manuscript from publisher to publisher, only to meet with 'No,' worded in a hundred different ways, but still pronounced with unmistakable decision.

Father and daughter had indeed, without knowing it, settled themselves in as unfavourable a neighbourhood for persons fresh from a wild seashore as can well be conceived; and Glen did not possess sufficient wisdom and self-pity to under-stand that starting upon a long day's march with nothing to sustain her strength save a cup of weak tea was almost a sure method of compassing failure.

She went now with her manuscripts alone. She found she must do this or abandon the attempt altogether, and after a few feeble protests Mr Westley let his daughter do as she liked. To watch the faces of publishers and editors, to wait for the inevitable refusal he had learnt to expect, was, he felt, beyond his ability.

At first it seemed to him a dreadful thing for Glen to go out alone through the crowded streets and walks into strange offices and ask to see unknown gentlemen, unchaperoned; but he soon saw that a girl in narrow lodgings in an unfashionable part of London, plainly dressed, and only adventuring into the main thoroughfares upon business, is, however bred or born, quite a different creature from a young lady residing at the West End who has never in all her life crossed the threshold of her house without an escort.

Glen was safe enough, he felt that, and so he swallowed this pill as he had gulped down many another affront to his pride; and in quite a regular and system-atic way she made a round of the trade, who one and all were perfectly agreed upon one point, namely, that even if Lady Morgan or Miss Edgeworth, or Banim, or Carleton, were to return to life and offer an Irish story for their acceptance, they would have nothing to do with it.

Ireland at that period had dropped to a tremendous discount. Fashionable novels, Glenarva was told, were the rage – tales of high life – chronicles of the doings and sayings of the Upper Ten in London – nothing else, one gentleman was good enough to tell her, would go down. Several names of successful writers were cited for her benefit – novels shown her which had achieved notoriety.

In those days Glen did not in the least doubt her own ability to produce a most interesting narrative relating to wicked lords and fine ladies; but, unfortunately, when she approached the task she found she could not write at all.

Matters were in this state when, one dull, damp, miserable afternoon, the girl, after a longer round even than usual, during the course of which she had seen and talked with the editors of several new magazines destined to an early death, found herself towards the close of the short day standing on the steps of their lodging-house, which to her mind seemed almost like a mean prison.

The street lamps were lighted, and within doors the hall as she entered was almost dark.

Wearily she turned the handle of the sitting room, where her father was leaning back in an armchair, talking to a gentleman who sat at the opposite side of the hearth.

As she paused on the threshold surprised, for no visitor had hitherto appeared to brighten their solitude, Mr Westley said:

'Oh! here is my daughter; Glen – Mr Lacere.'

Chapter XII

EVERY DOG HAS HIS DAY

ALTHOUGH MR BERNARD KELLY was not suffering from home-sickness or experiencing any wild longing for the sight of his relations, still about the same time as Miss Westley thought she had well-nigh sounded the depths of despair, her fellow-pilgrim, with hands plunged into empty pockets, where a whole legion of devils seemed to be holding high carnival, gloomily decided he had somehow 'got to the back of his luck.'

It was very low water with him. Things indeed had got so bad, he more than once found himself pulling out his watch and contemplatively regarding its merits, not as a chronometer, but as an article upon which he might raise money. His training had caused him, however, to regard a visit to the relative sportively referred to by the young Dawtons as the 'gentleman with three balls for crest' in the light of a crowning humiliation, and he felt almost that when reduced to such a strait he would retire from the sight of men; for which reason he still could tell Mat and his female belongings the 'right time,' a matter which seemed at West Ham wrapped eternally in mystery.

As for Mr Donagh's watch, it appeared never to be right for a week together. Either the spring got broken, or some misfortune happened to the glass, or the hands failed to move properly, or the works wanted cleaning.

Before he had been many weeks at Abbey Cottage Mr Kelly became quite accustomed to disappearances which at first struck him as most remarkable.

Nothing Mat and his belongings now did or left undone interested him in the least. He saw very clearly the Donaghs were not likely to prove the slightest help on his way, and that, even so far as the mere matter of shelter was concerned, all they desired was to get rid of him.

Mr Donagh actually went so far as to ask Miss Cavan one Sunday morning at breakfast if 'the Videlles, from Saffron Walden, were coming at Christmas'; but the poor lady proved herself so unequal to carry on the ingenious stratagem for which Mat had forgotten to prepare her mind, that Mr Kelly heard him afterwards, in softly modulated but intelligible terms, reproaching his relative for being 'destitute of the first rudiments of sense,' because if we do not 'take Basan by the horns, he will inflict his incubus upon us till we succumb from sheer exhaustion.'

That same afternoon Mr Kelly boldly took Mr Donagh by the horns, and asked whether he might for a time remain at Abbey Cottage as a lodger – paying for his 'shot.'

'I know I shall be having money ere very long,' he explained, 'and I will then settle up honestly. Meantime, you could put that two pounds you borrowed as a trifle to my credit. It would be a great convenience to me to stop here for a little longer,' he added, 'but I do not like encroaching on your hospitality.'

'My good friend,' returned Mat, with a benign air of pity and forgiveness which might have seemed effective to anyone but the unimpressionable mortal he addressed, 'we don't profess to keep a lodging-house!'

'I did not mean any offence, Donagh,' explained Mr Kelly. 'I only wanted to know if you would let me share the expenses.'

'Couldn't think of such a thing,' answered Mat wisely. 'Fallen I know we are – every dog has his day, and the Donaghs have had theirs, and it is past and gone – but still while I am able to keep a roof over my head, I trust I shall never have to descend so low as to take pecuniary acknowledgment for extending its humble shelter to a friend.'

'Then I am very sorry to say you will have to keep him as your guest till the state of the exchequer improves,' said Mr Kelly, who did not mean to move till it suited him to go.

'You are very welcome to such poor hospitality as I am able to offer,' returned Mat; but his tone was far from cordial, and his manner lofty and dignified in the extreme.

From that day Mr Kelly, who was by no means deficient in shrewdness, could not avoid noticing the ridiculous suggestions his host was always throwing out on the subject of employment.

Apparently, in Mr Donagh's opinion no field of labour was too distant, no post too obscure, for his friend. He had arrived at the conclusion he declared, after a long experience, that any place on the face of the wide earth presented a better opening for a man than London.

'Look at me,' he said, 'after all these years, known as I am, respected as it is only right and fair I should be, a power, though I say it myself of myself – I repeat, a *power* – still just from hand to mouth, nothing tangible, nothing certain. Why, I declare to you there was one week, shortly before you came to us, I earned close upon a hundred pounds in two days, while during the whole of this last month I have not received a fifth part of that amount.'

'I wish I was in the way of getting even a tenth every month,' returned Mr Kelly.

'I dare say you do,' said Mr Donagh patronisingly.

'And I must remark,' proceeded Mr Kelly, a little nettled by his host's tone, 'that it seems to me, judging from the small quantity of writing I see you turn out, twenty pounds a month, if you never made another sixpence, is a very good screw.'

'And permit me to remark,' retorted Mr Donagh, 'that, primarily, you know nothing about what I do, and therefore are not in a position to form any opinion whatever about my concerns; and, secondarily, that since you came to London you have grafted upon your Irish solecisms the most extraordinary amount of slang I ever heard accumulated in so short a space of time, even by those whose circle of undesirable acquaintants was much more extensive than I can imagine even yours to be.'

'My acquaintances do not as a rule talk on stilts, if that is what you mean,' answered Mr Kelly, as he went off laughing, to indict a letter to one of his mother's brothers who had succeeded to the paternal shop in Derry.

The burden of this epistle was, 'Send me ten pounds, for I am regularly stranded. Once Christmas is turned, I have good hopes of getting on; but till then, without help from some one, I scarcely know how I can manage.'

A week elapsed, but brought no answer. At the end of three more weary days, however. Miss Cavan handed their visitor a letter with the Callinacoan post-mark.

It was from Mr Marcus Balmoyle, and stated that his nephew's letter had to be forwarded on to him from Derry, or he would have answered it sooner.

I have come here at your mother's request [he went on in very crabbed characters to explain] *to see what's to be done at all with your father, for he'll neither kill himself with drink nor keep from it; and now I am here, I feel I might just as well have stayed away. It was an evil day for the whole of us when she set eyes on Daniel Kelly. And then there's you, as might have been a comfort and a credit, making your family a laughing-stock both here and there, setting the one of our name we were so proud of, and who would have made your fortune, against the whole of his relations. It's a burning shame for an able-bodied man to be writing home for money like a helpless child. Here's five pounds, in a bank draft at seven days (which saves the commission), and I tell you plainly this is the last farthing you need expect from any of us. Barney, Barney! you'll just have to set to and do what I know you abhor from your very soul – work. You must try and make an honest living, 'if it is only by picking pockets,' as the Quaker said.*

I was talking to the priest about you this morning, and he remarked what a pity it is you have not been brought up in the true faith, because then some of the good fathers in London might have been able to give you a hand. I told him I didn't think it mattered a pinch of snuff, for I believed you had not a bit of religion about you.

Tell Miss Bridgetta, with your mother's respects, I am going to ship off a hamper as I go home for her. She may find it useful about Christmas-time, particularly with you in the house. If you play as good a knife and fork across the Channel as you did at home, I know it is not sixpence a day would find your breakfast, to say nothing of other meals; and, indeed, I wonder to myself you haven't more spirit than to be troubling the Donaghs as you are doing, and running the chance of wearing out your welcome into the bargain.

Your mother bids me let you know Miss Fortescue and the new pad-groom from England were married three days ago on the sly. Mr Fortescue is willing to give two hundred pounds down if they'll sail for America, but the husband wants double that and leave the old woman behind. It's a pity, when you had got things so far on, you took fear. You might have made yourself for life; and if she wasn't young, she had genteel ways with her, and any amount of good clothes.

We shall all be glad to hear you have got some work, and mean sticking to it.

Your loving uncle,
Marcus Balmoyle.

Whatever Mr Bernard Kelly's feelings might be on reading this epistle, there was no alloy in the pleasure Miss Cavan experienced at the prospect of the coming hamper; and she rushed off with the news to her nephew, who, on hearing that good Mrs Kelly was forwarding another 'crate of edibles,' commented 'on the principle of sending coals to Newcastle' with that princely manner of his which ignored such vulgar creatures as the butcher and the baker. Indeed, Mr Donagh seemed to think all food came into the house spontaneously, and was supplied gratis.

'Oh! you wouldn't find such butter as hers if you searched London through,' answered Miss Cavan, whom the certainty of a well-stocked larder filled with unselfish delight. 'We'll not need now to buy anything for our Christmas dinner; and the eggs'll see us well into the New Year. And I'll hang the bacon, and –'

'Pray, spare me these distressing details,' interposed Mat, waving his hand as a signal that he 'would be alone.' At the time he was in an exceedingly impecunious condition, and consequently more than usually inclined to lordly silencing of his womankind.

He had spent his hundred pounds, and a good many other pounds to the back of that.

Christmas, with its bills, its duns, its many requirements, and its accustomed difficulty of providing money, was what Mr Donagh, in his simple language, described as 'imminent.' Further, he had saddled himself with an old man of the sea, whose presence would, he felt, render a six-months-old hen turkey tough, and make butter fresh from Mrs Kelly's churn ranker than anything Miss Cavan, in the exercise of an economy laudable in intention, though unwise in fact, sometimes procured from 'that thief of the world,' as Mr Madlow, a local grocer, was usually styled by the ladies at Abbey Cottage.

But Fate and Mr Kelly decreed otherwise.

When that five-pound Bank of Ireland draft arrived, Mr Kelly said to himself:

'If I'm ever to get out of this hole, where, as my uncle implies, I have worn out my welcome, if I ever had one, I must make a try for it now.'

A few days previously he had seen the advertisement of a lodging to let in Bermondsey, which he thought would suit both his convenience and his purse; and he went to look at it with a trembling determination to cut himself adrift from West Ham, and sink or swim, unaided and unimpeded by his own countryfolks. Cautious, however, in all things, he did not close with the landlady on the spot. He told her he would think the matter over, and while he was doing so he bent his steps towards a tavern much frequented by the younger Dawtons, where, indeed, already he had met one or other of them frequently.

As it happened, just as he was walking up the court, at the top of which the familiar portals stood invitingly half open. Will Dawton overtook him.

'I am so glad to have chanced on you today,' said the young fellow cheerily, clapping him on the shoulder, 'for at last I am the bearer of good news. Our editor has read your story, and accepts it, and says you may send in another as soon as you like.'

Mr Kelly made no answer, for the simple reason that he could not. The revulsion of feeling was too sudden, the relief too great. He stood still and silent for a few seconds, like one dazed. Then Will Dawton took his arm, and led him into the dingy tavern, remarking the while:

'Never mind, old boy. I know what it is. The first time I saw my name in print I had to walk for half an hour about the Temple before I dare venture into Fleet Street; and as for Jim, he disgraced the family by throwing up his tile in the Strand and kicking it across Wellington Street. He narrowly escaped being taken in charge.' And thus talking, he conducted Bernard Kelly to a box in a quiet corner, and whispering a command to the waiter, he hung up his hat, and after performing the same office for the man who had at last got his start, proceeded:

'Let me see, this is Thursday. Well, it would be no use trying to see the editor this week; but you had better come about Monday or Tuesday and be introduced. You must not mind his finding fault. He is always finding fault. He was chosen for his present post solely, I believe, on account of his disagreeable manner; but he is all right when you get below the surface. Now have some wine to pick you up.'

Though he had not a penny in his pocket, Mr Kelly drank and was comforted. Hope was now in residence instead of the legion of devils. A day – an hour – a minute had sufficed to change the whole aspect of his life. He felt a man, not a beggar; he would be able to leave Abbey Cottage – to tell his uncle luck had turned, to make a joke about Miss Fortescue; he could laugh at the humours of his friend, and say what he had never dared to say before when the reckoning came.

'I must ask you to lend me half a sovereign, for I have no money about me except a bank post bill, which has still a week to run, and be hanged to it.'

'You are not going to be paymaster, though,' answered Will, who when he had money flung it about right royally; 'but if you want anything changed, I'll get it cashed for you. What are you going to do this afternoon? Come home with me and have some dinner; the old folks will be delighted to hear you are accepted.'

But Mr Kelly declined to avail himself of this invitation. There was, he told young Dawton, something he wished particularly to attend to that very day, and accordingly after he had got his five pounds duly counted out by the obliging waiter, and drunk some more wine and eaten a few biscuits, and made an appointment to meet his friend at the same place on the following Tuesday at one o'clock, he wended his way back to Bermondsey and closed with the widow, who promised to have a couple of rooms ready for him to take possession within a week.

That night he gladdened Mr Donagh's heart by mentioning three facts – namely, that he had at last got something to do; that he was going to dinner with some friends on Christmas Day; and that he had found lodgings, into which he proposed to move very shortly.

'Indeed!' exclaimed Mat. 'May I inquire the name of the locality in which you intend to bivouac?'

'Bermondsey,' was the explicit answer.

'You have probably selected that neighbourhood as being near the scene of your future labours.'

'I think I shall find it convenient for my work,' returned Bernard Kelly; and, declining Mat's offer of a second tumbler of punch, which was made with a cordiality to which that gentleman's manner had for a long time been a stranger, he lit his candle, and marched off to bed.

For some reason best known to himself, Mr Donagh evolved out of his internal consciousness a conviction that his 'uncivilised compatriot' had, through the 'medium of some other savage from the wilds of the sister island,' procured a situation at one of the many wharfs in Rotherhithe. Mr Kelly had said nothing calculated to lead to such an idea; but, upon the other hand, when he found the nature of Mat's surmises he took no step to dispel the illusion. He never mentioned the Dawtons; he refrained from uttering the name of the *Galaxy*; he said not a word about his literary efforts; he remained silent while Mat, overflowing with good spirits which the prospect of Mr Kelly's speedy departure induced, made many jests and remarks he afterwards wished he had kept to himself, and reassumed all the old lordly airs that for a time he doffed only in order to don a robe composed of general sulkiness and irritability.

He gave the departing guest many raps about his accent, his manners, and his deportment, by inference suggesting there was only one model of a perfect demeanour in London. He revelled amongst long words, he held himself up as an example, he bounced and bragged about what he had done and what he should do till his listener could have kicked him. He rolled French and Latin phrases through his mouth as if he were gargling with foreign languages, and he 'mixed' lunch in a manner which next morning made poor Miss Cavan hold up her hands in horror at sight of the depleted contents of the decanter, and observe to Miss Donagh that if Barney did not 'mind himself', he would soon be 'a worse drinker than his father.'

Bernard Kelly knew pretty well what they were all thinking – but he said nothing.

He only vowed that if ever the chance came his way, he would not spare Mat.

There are men who, though ready enough to register such vows in the time of adversity, speedily forget them when the sun of prosperity appears above the horizon; but Mr Kelly had no weakness of this sort – quite the contrary.

Mat failed to understand this, however. In his egotism and conceit he persisted in considering 'Young Kelly' a poor insignificant creature; and even had he been told that Mr Barney was an edged weapon with which it was extremely dangerous to play, he would not have believed the story.

Somehow or other, nevertheless, the pair got through four days of the time intervening between the guest's departure without any open rupture, and they might have bade each other farewell tolerably civilly had not the week opened for Mr Donagh with some stroke of good fortune which immediately threw that gentleman's extremely ill-balanced mind off its equilibrium.

At his best it was hard to get on with Mat, whose conversation was an even mixture, according to Mr Kelly's mental summing up, of 'uninteresting reminiscences and lies' but when luck befriended him, the master of Abbey Cottage grew simply unendurable.

Then he ascended the throne, assumed the crown, seized the sceptre, folded the ermine majestically around his form, and held forth.

Heavens! How he did hold forth! If he had been the father of railways, if he had invented balloons, if he had owned the *Times* newspaper, if he had paid off the

National Debt, if he had won the battle of Waterloo, he could not have rated his achievements higher.

And the worst of the matter was, he never said what those achievements were, and so gave his companion no chance of disputing their value. Instead of doing this, he adopted the safe plan of criticising Mr Kelly's failures, and extolling his own success by the mere force of contrast.

Now, this is an extremely irritating process to the individual who has failed, or who is supposed to have failed. It is one under which the best-tempered man might be excused for losing his patience, and Bernard Kelly was not good-tempered. He had suffered many things at Mat's hands, and that night he found the temptation to hit back and hit hard more than he could withstand. In the course of his 'connection with literature,' Mat seemed to find drink as necessary as ink, and even before he began to 'mix' that initial tumbler for which Mr Kelly's presence gave him so plausible and fatal a pretext, anyone, except his female belongings, must have perceived he was in that state Jim Dawton figuratively indicated as 'Pretty well, I thank you!'

Very shortly he grew hypercritical, and spoke with a candour which, unhappily, is not confined to gentlemen in his then condition, of the many shortcomings of his fellow-creatures in general, and the scapegoat Bernard in particular. The supposititious wharf came in for a large share of his animadversion. He could not understand anyone 'voluntarily, or even under compulsion, sinking his identity amongst tar and bargees.' 'No doubt he was peculiarly constituted, but rather than chain himself like a galley-slave to the desk, at the beck and call of some coarse and uneducated master, wallowing in the mire of his ill-gotten riches, he would turn peripatetic tinker, and mend the domestic kettle.'

'There is one advantage, and only one, I can perceive in the nature of the appointment you have accepted,' he went on. 'Your Irishisms will pass unnoticed amongst a class whose native English is a libel on language. Where you are going you will not find your accent an insurmountable drawback, as it might be elsewhere.'

'I don't think I will,' answered Barney.

'One of the accidents of my life, for which, though it was brought about by misfortunes almost unparalleled, I can never feel sufficiently thankful,' pursued Mat, 'is that fate willed I should be brought up on the right side of St George's Channel. To have found it indispensable in the first flush of early manhood to unlearn the habits of the most impressionable years of life would have been well-nigh unendurable. Some one says the perfection of language is so to speak that no man could declare the country of the speaker.' And having thus modestly placed this keystone in position, Mr Donagh complacently took a long pull at his tumbler and waited to hear Mr Kelly's remarks upon what Mat was in the habit of calling his *ipse dixit*.

All Mr Kelly elected to observe was this: 'If there be any truth in the extremely foolish statement you have just repeated, you fail to reach the ridiculous standard indicated, for no human being could imagine for a moment you were anything but an Irishman.'

'I confess I don't understand what you mean,' said Mr Donagh, turning red and looking very angry.

'I mean exactly what I say. Though you have been so many years out of Ireland, anyone who wasn't an absolute fool could tell in a moment the place you hail from.'

'Do you wish to insult me?' asked Mr Donagh.

'No, indeed. Why should you be ashamed of the country of your birth? I would rather be thought to have been born in Ireland than any other place. Indeed, I never knew any fellow who tried to cut his native land except yourself, and it really is great nonsense on your part, Donagh, because, as I said before, you can't disguise the matter – your tongue betrayeth you. If only, to go no further, I never heard you pronounce anything but the word "boy," I should know on which side the Channel you had spent your calf days.'

'Here is a second Daniel come to judgment!' exclaimed Mat, addressing vacancy, his lips trembling with rage, the while he tried to speak with composure.

'I am not a Daniel at all, first, or second, or third,' answered Mr Kelly. 'I only say if I were in your place, I would not try to talk as the English do. It comes natural to them, but it is not natural to you, and your accent does not sound natural. Besides, you use phrases no one but an Irishman ever employs, and not even an Irishman who had been taught better.'

'You really are extremely good,' said Mat. 'Will it be troubling you too much to ask you to instance one of the phrases you are so kind as to indicate? That is, if you are able.'

'Oh, I am able enough,' answered Barney. 'Do you remember this evening telling your aunt about one of your acquaintances who would not step off the boat?'

'Certainly. And what then?'

'You said: "So, *if you please*, the gangway had to be shoved ashore for him." Now, that is an Irish vulgarism, not an English.'

To state that Mat was stricken dumb would be an exaggeration, because he still retained the power of speech; but he felt like a boy who, after having stood at the top of his class in one school, suddenly finds himself shifted to the bottom and called dunce in another. He was so angry and amazed, his indignation could not find vent all in a moment, and he was obliged to take refuge in what he considered the cutting sarcasm:

'And where, may I venture to inquire, did Mr Bernard Kelly acquire his marvellous knowledge of the signs and tokens which distinguish an Irish gentleman from an English? I should have considered such lore quite out of the beaten track of his former life. Who was the teacher, where the college? He never, I am satisfied, studied the niceties of language amongst the porcine animals on his father's farm!'

Mr Kelly coloured. 'Never mind,' he said, 'who was my teacher, or where the college; but take my advice, and don't be ashamed of your country. Amongst people who know what is what, your affectation of superior pronunciation must render you a complete laughing-stock.'

The string of Mr Donagh's tongue was at length loosed.

'This comes well,' he observed, with a withering glance directed to the corner of the room, 'from the guest seated on my own hearthstone.'

'Hang it, Donagh!' retorted the guest referred to, 'am I always to take and never to give? Am I to keep silent for ever while you go on taunting me and extolling yourself?'

'I have never taunted you!' thundered Mat, striking the table with his clenched fist.

'What have you been doing, then, the whole of this evening till I broke cover? I am as good a man, and as clever a man, and a precious deal more sensible man than you; and yet if you were Solomon and I Phil Adrain, the town fool at Callinacoan, you could not evince greater contempt for my understanding. I would never have said anything about your accent had you only let mine alone. As you are fond of criticising, consider a little what you are yourself. Look at home before you begin to look about you out of doors.'

'This is the viper,' began Mat, in a dull sort of recitative – 'this is the viper I nursed in my bosom, the ingrate I welcomed to my humble home.'

'Now stop that, Donagh, do,' broke in Mr Kelly; 'in the first place, you never welcomed me; and in the second –'

'He has shared what we had to offer him,' pursued the irrepressible Mat, 'he has been treated as a son of the house, he has eaten of the best we could procure, and drunk of the same liquor as myself. I deemed him harmless if dull, grateful if deficient in the higher qualities; but now I see the true nature – the cloven hoof begins to show itself, the Kelly taint becomes apparent, the –'

The true nature of Mat's peroration was never revealed, for at this juncture Mr Kelly rose, and, taking his tumbler, still half full of punch, flung the contents under the grate, and saying, 'It is so late I am obliged perforce to avail myself of the shelter you think so much of for the night, but I will never again take bite or sup under your roof,' walked out of the room, leaving Mat alone with the decanter and his own wise thoughts.

'I'll just have a thimbleful more to compose myself,' he decided, after he had recovered from the first astonishment caused by Mr Kelly's words and Mr Kelly's exit; but so many thimblefuls were required for the purpose, that when he at length essayed to go to bed he experienced great difficulty in finding the whereabouts of the friendly baluster.

It was not very late, however, next morning when he descended to the parlour, where he was anxiously greeted by Miss Cavan with the inquiry:

'What have you been doing on Barney, Mat? Mary says he started off at screech of day without any breakfast, or waiting even to have his boots cleaned. I don't wonder at his wanting nothing to eat, considering what he drank overnight. There's not a tablespoonful of whisky left; but it's strange he should go out with dirty boots, and him so particular.'

Mr Donagh closed his eyes and groaned in spirit. Never, never before had his aunt's 'figures of speech' seemed to him so abhorrent. 'Pray moderate the rancour of your tongue,' he entreated; and from these few words Miss Cavan understood he and Barney must have had a 'fall-out.'

'And it was a pity, too,' she said afterwards to her niece, 'when the time was so short they had to put in together.'

'I am glad,' thought Mr Donagh, 'he is going to that wharf in Rotherhithe; such a ruffian is not to be encountered with impunity in civilised society.'

END OF VOLUME I

VOLUME II

Contents

Chapter I

MR KELLY'S DAY

AS BEST HE COULD Mr Kelly whiled away the hours till one o'clock, when, according to agreement, he met Mr Dawton, and was by him introduced to the editor of the *Galaxy*, a periodical which not long before had been started under good auspices. Amongst its contributors were numbered the best men of the period. On every page sparkled wit, talent, high spirits, high thought – now dead, or grown old and very feeble. It was a most excellent magazine; stories, poetry, articles, were all admirable.

Bernard Kelly, who would have been glad to procure insertion anywhere, felt proud beyond description to think he should appear before the public in such capital company. 'How's Maria?' had indeed done something for him.

'What about the Government office now, eh?' the head of the Dawton family had said one day when he encountered his new friend in the street; and Mr Kelly answered only with a smile which told he accounted the loss of his uncle's patronage a gain.

As it was the fortunate author's intention to return to West Ham to remove his effects from beneath Mr Donagh's roof that same afternoon, he declined all young Dawton's blandishments and invitations; but while they stood together in Fleet Street arguing out the question whether or not Mr Kelly should regard The Wigwam in the light of a short cut back to Stratford, they were joined by three other congenial spirits, all of whom likewise were what they called 'members of the same gang.'

Just at the same time, Mat, after a most satisfactory interview with the manager of the *Galaxy*, which had resulted in the transfer of a goodly amount of current coin of the realm into his pockets, emerged from the office, an air of holy calm pervading his countenance, a saintly smile flickering about his lips, and his whole deportment that of a man at peace with himself and the world at large.

As he passed the group Will Dawton and one of his friends spoke and nodded to him, while Mr Donagh returned their salutations with befitting dignity. Had the matter ended there, all would have been well; but one of the others, turning his head to see who was thus greeted, recognised a familiar presence, and called after the retreating figure:

'Well, old fellow! And how goes it?'

At the words Mat looked back, and saw not merely the man who uttered them, but Barney Kelly – Barney evidently hand and glove with these gay 'swells' – Barney, with a laugh frozen in his throat at sight of the man he had parted with on such bad terms some fifteen hours previously.

Here was in visible presence the haunting terror which had made Mat's life of late a weariness to him. Here he met that 'ruffian' in the last place he desired to see him, and amongst the very set of people he most dreaded his knowing. He had presence enough of mind for most accidents, but it failed him now. There were few things he could not face, but he felt it impossible to make the best of this encounter. With a smothered reply and an almost involuntary wave of his hand, he turned on his heel, and diving down one of the narrow streets leading southward, was immediately lost to view.

'I did not think you knew him!' exclaimed Mr Kelly.

'Know him!' repeated Will Dawton, to whom the remark was addressed. 'Of course we do. Everybody knows him.'

'But you told me you did not.'

'Nonsense! You are dreaming, man. When did I ever say anything so ridiculous?'

'The night I asked you about him you said you knew no one of the name.'

'What name?'

'His name – Donagh.'

'But that's Mat – majestic Mat, marvellous Mat, miraculous Mat, mendacious Mat.'

'Of course, Mat Donagh.'

Young Dawton took the speaker by the shoulders, and looked him straight in the face.

'Is that your friend?' he asked.

'Yes. That is he – what does he write? Oh! for heaven's sake, Dawton, satisfy my curiosity.'

'I really don't know,' answered Will Dawton, with a pleasing reticence.

'I don't think he writes anything,' interposed one of the others; 'he touts for advertisements.'

'What is that?' asked Kelly.

There was a roar of laughter at this question, and then young Dawton said: 'Pray treat Mr Donagh's name with due respect, Myers. He is a most important factor in the success of the *Galaxy*. Truth is –' he went on, speaking to Bernard Kelly – 'your friend is the best advertisement canvasser in London.'

'What is an advertisement canvasser?' inquired Mr Kelly, whose ignorance on most subjects connected with literary matters was almost as great as his curiosity.

Will Dawton answered the question. In a few telling sentences he explained, adding, that though possibly the *Galaxy* might exist without its 'crack' novelist or sledge-hammer leader-writer, or sportive essayist, or tender poet, or cynical reviewer, it could not live without Mat. Understanding the cause of the gloom which overshadowed Mr Kelly's countenance, he good-naturedly went even further, and implied that while it might be practicable, though difficult, for the *Galaxy* to secure such another editor as it happily possessed; though a double to the present efficient publisher probably existed in London, yet a second Mat could never be found, so bland, so winning, so persuasive, such a favourite, even with the roughest of advertisers; such a treasure, in fact; such a very mine of wealth, indeed, to the journal which had been fortunate enough to secure his services. All these utterances Mr Kelly received with a show of satisfaction he was far from feeling. The assurance that Mat could net his five hundred a year 'without turning a hair,' capped by a further hint from one of the company that he might easily double the amount named if 'he chose to stick to it,' scarcely filled his heart with that pleasure the statement ought to have aroused.

'Mat came to London, I have heard, meaning to make a great splash in literature,' proceeded the last speaker; 'tried prose and poetry both, hacked about for a while on the *Somers Town Sentinel*, and did slating notices for the *Peckham Pioneer*, but he could not get on as he expected, and therefore adopted what he calls his present profession. He says it was quite by accident he took to it; but, however that may be, he makes a deuced good thing out of the work. And he is so high and mighty into the bargain. He won't do this, and he can't accept that, and his peculiarities have to be humoured, or off he goes. We poor devils of authors are forced to study the fads and whims of publishers and editors. In our case the boot is quite on the other leg. What do you say, Dawton?'

Will Dawton laughed.

'I don't think you study anybody's whims,' he answered; then, turning to Bernard Kelly, added, 'I suppose your friend has a snug crib down at – what is the name of the place – West Ham?'

'He lives in a good house,' replied Mr Kelly. He was not going to disparage

Mat's habitation to these lively young men, or correct them as to the amount of that gentleman's income, which indeed, for all he knew to the contrary, might have been princely.

'And where did you get to know him, Kelly?'

'He comes from my part of the country. His ancestors were great folks once upon a time. There is a place not far from Callinacoan that goes still by the name of "Donagh's Leap"; no man and horse, before or since, could take it. They were a rare wild lot, the Donaghs of Castle Donagh – went through their money and their acres at the same rattling pace they followed the hounds.'

'Anyone could tell at a glance Mat had come of a good stock,' observed one youth who wore a glass screwed into his right eye. 'There is a sort of "keep your distance" about his manner which I confess always impresses me. Well, I suppose some must go up and some come down. It's only fair, old families should have their noses brought to the grindstone, in order to let the newest snob have his turn. Every dog has his day, and I dare say Mat's forbears had theirs.'

'Yes; he was saying just the same thing no later than last night,' answered Mr Kelly, privately reflecting that his day was come. He could meet Mat now on his native heath. He knew, if nobody else did, that his host was groaning in spirit, weeping and wailing and gnashing his teeth at the idea of that 'uncultivated boor Barney' having at length come to the comprehension of what he did – the kind of literature to which he devoted most of his shining hours.

In good truth, Mr Donagh was more annoyed than words could express; not even the money in his pocket reconciled him to the notion of Barney knowing how he got it. There did not exist a human being he less desired to become intimately acquainted with his affairs than the guest he had persisted in inviting to Abbey Cottage, whom he had not treated civilly, and who was now in a position to smite him hip and thigh with a weapon snatched from Mat's own special armoury.

'What a cursed casualty!' he considered, as he wended his way to a tavern he wot of in the heart of the City, where the steak was of the juiciest, the ale mellow, the cheese ripe, and the port unexceptionable.

In such modest haunts he managed to get rid of a good deal of superfluous cash, but on the occasion in question no appetite appeared with the viands. Barney Kelly had destroyed his relish for food – Barney, who with one slight kick could destroy the lordly castle Mr Donagh was supposed, by those who knew no better, to inhabit – Barney, who at last understood exactly 'what he wrote,' the true nature of the manuscripts which, figuratively thrust under the domestic pot, kept that utensil boiling.

Contrary to his usual habit, it was scarcely five o'clock when he put his latch-key in the lock and let himself into Abbey Cottage. Miss Cavan had 'just closed her eyes between the lights, and was taking a bit of a nap.' Miss Hester did not chance

to be in, having 'stepped across to the Broadway for a pen'orth of tape', but the maid
-of-all-work, hearing the master's step, looked out into the hall, and, in answer to
a question concerning Mr Kelly, said:

'No, sir, he has not gone yet – he is up in his own room.'

Mat, full of the purpose which had brought him home so early, straightway
ascended the stairs and knocked at the door of his unwelcome guest's bedchamber.

'Come in!' cried Mr Kelly lustily, with a dreadful cheerfulness in his tone. Mr
Donagh went in, and found the objectionable Barney in his shirt-sleeves, kneeling
before a portmanteau he had filled to overflowing and was struggling to lock. A
solitary dip illumined the apartment. Amongst the many things which had not
been done at Abbey Cottage was laying the gas upstairs; and in the exercise of that
economy which was evinced by saving at the spigot and spilling at the bung, the
Donaghs had got into the habit of considering one candle enough in all conscience
for any man, and more than enough for any single woman.

As Mat entered, Mr Kelly looked up.

'You are back early,' he remarked.

'Yes,' agreed Mr Donagh, as he closed the door.

He paused for a few moments before he spoke again – moments Mr Kelly
utilised in forcing the portmanteau to fasten. He was busy with the straps when
his host said:

'I conclude you now know the secret of my life.'

'I am sure I cannot tell,' answered Barney carelessly; 'I know how you earn
your bread, if that is what you mean.'

'Yes, that is what I mean – you have learnt how, in order to supply the most
vulgar and ordinary wants of existence, a Donagh has been compelled to forget
the traditions of his family, and descend so far in the social scale as to accept a
commission for the orders he is able to wring from reluctant and paltry trades
people – men the very fact of whose existence his ancestors would scarcely have
deigned to recognise.'

'There is not much use in talking about your ancestors,' replied Mr Kelly, rising
and planting one foot on the portmanteau, so as to get a better purchase of the
strap he was wrestling with. 'I think you ought to consider yourself a deucedly
lucky fellow, Donagh, though your only "connection with the Press" is through the
medium of the advertisement columns.'

Mat waved his hand with a deprecating gesture, and shook his head mournfully, the while he said:

'The heart knoweth its own bitterness, and with the gall and wormwood of
mine no stranger may intermeddle. I had my aspirations, I had my day of proud
hope, my conviction of eventual success in the highest walks of literature, but
between promise and fulfilment intervened the cursed necessity money – money

to provide food and raiment to satisfy grasping landlords and impracticable collectors of rates and taxes. But why prolong this agonised explanation? I beheld all my soul had longed for – all my higher nature had panted to reach and possess – engulfed in the vortex of carking household cares – of common domestic wants in which ere now many a nobler ship than mine has foundered.'

'Well, it can't be helped,' observed Mr Kelly indifferently, looking round the room to see which of his belongings he had best begin cording next. 'What's the good of crying over spilt milk? And you have been very fortunate, Donagh; it is not everyone who fails in literature that has the luck to find such easy and profitable work as you have taken to.'

'Easy!' repeated Mat scornfully. 'Profitable! yes, truly, I do make a sufficient yearly income; but I did not come to you intending to complain of my lot, or to ask sympathy for blighted hopes which once blossomed fair and gay – no! My object now is to entreat your forbearance – your chivalry. Those poor women below still believe in me. They know nothing of the horrible depths to which I have descended. Let them remain happy in their childlike ignorance – let them in their innocence cull the flowers which have sprung from the grave where my genius lies buried, and sport with the blooms which have their roots in my broken heart.'

Mr Bernard Kelly, accustomed as he was to Mat's figures of speech, stood transfixed during the delivery of this final sentence, which was uttered in a subdued voice, and with a touching humility. When Mr Donagh paused a spell seemed broken, however, and he answered: 'It is too late; I have told your aunt what you do.'

'Miscreant!' exclaimed Mat passionately; 'ingrate, to rush home and sting the bosom that warmed you!'

'There was no particular reason why I should keep your counsel,' said Mr Kelly carelessly. 'You had it in your power to help me, and you took very good care not to do so. You might have got me on the *Galaxy* long ago, and now I am writing for it; no thanks to you.'

'Writing for the *Galaxy!*' echoed Mr Donagh. Amidst all his trouble he had never dreamt of this additional misfortune.

'Yes, my friend, "tis e'en so",' answered Mr Kelly. 'I assure you I haven't found my accent or nationality the slightest hindrance to me in literature; quite the contrary.'

Having received which fresh arrow in his broken heart, Mat turned slowly, and without uttering another word left the room.

It was three hours later. Mr Kelly had taken his departure – or, as Miss Cavan tersely observed, 'the house was shut of him' – and the ladies were seated at needlework when the master of Abbey Cottage, who had declined to partake of tea with his relations, or to allow a cup to be sent in to him, suddenly abandoning the seclusion of his sanctum, appeared in the parlour.

Walking up to the chimney-piece, he took a commanding position, with his back resting against the marble slab. Neither Miss Cavan nor Miss Donagh spoke. They saw that in his face which held their kindly tongues silent.

'Girls,' began Mat, and his features twitched a little as he uttered this inappropriate word. 'You know the worst now. Do you despise me?'

'Despise you?' repeated both in a breath; and next instant two fond, foolish, faithful women were clinging round his neck, sobbing out endearing phrases, and conducting themselves altogether in a most idiotic manner.

'Ah! you poor souls!' exclaimed Mat, wiping his eyes – for he was really deeply touched – 'Why did I leave it to Barney Kelly or Barney anybody to tell you the story of my lost life and marred career? Why didn't I trust you from the first?'

'Ay, why didn't ye?' asked Miss Cavan, and then they all fell to weeping again. But after a time the luxury of sorrow began to assert itself, and they settled down to the enjoyment of their misery in the most comfortable manner possible.

The ladies felt that it was their own Mat they had got back at last, while Mat, 'now that the felon irons of silence and dissimulation were struck off his spirit,' revelled in telling the story of how he had 'conquered fate.' With bated breath and eyes fastened eagerly on his face, Miss Cavan and her niece hung enraptured on his accents, and listened entranced as he spoke of the 'lions' he had found lurking in his path, of the difficulties he, a second David, had taken by the throat and killed.

'And indeed it's yourself could make your way, if it was even through stone walls,' exclaimed Miss Hetty admiringly, while her aunt opined Mat's energy was so tremendous that a 'dungeon could not contain, or fetters bind it.'

Never, perhaps, had the household at Abbey Cottage spent so pleasant an evening. Mat off his stilts seemed quite a different person from Mat up in the air. He was quite 'affable and familiar.'

'Though Barney let out what he did for nothing but spite,' said Miss Cavan, with that quick perception of motives which, as Mr Donagh was good enough to declare, 'distinguishes the feminine mind,' 'he did us a good turn. If he knew how comfortable and cosy we all are he'd be ready to bite off the end of his tongue for envy. Ye'll never keep anything from us again, Mat, no matter how bad it is, will ye?'

Mat declared he would not, which was a very large and a very unwise promise; but at the moment he had no mental reservations – his heart was full of gratitude and compunction.

'How could I ever have been ashamed,' so ran his thoughts, 'of these admirable creatures, who combine in their own persons every virtue of their sex? Why did I sacrifice to society that which should have been offered on the altar of home?'

Possibly it was with some idea of even at the eleventh hour repairing this error that Mr Donagh presently suggested they should have a 'morsel of supper together in peace and comfort.'

Suppers did not much obtain in that house, and were rarely of an impromptu character, being, as a rule, confined to Sundays, Easter, and Christmas.

Mat partook of so very few meals at home that the ladies seized upon his idea and adopted it with the delight of children bidden to a feast.

'Thanks to Mrs Kelly, there's plenty and to spare!' exclaimed Miss Cavan; and proceeding to the kitchen, which was vacant, the servant having retired to bed, she soon 'tossed up a little repast' her nephew assured her was a *chef-d'oeuvre*.

Very merry were they all, and very happy, and in such unwonted spirits that when Mr Donagh, who was told by Miss Cavan, 'You must have a glass of punch tonight, Mat, though Barney is not here to take one with you,' said he should not touch a drop unless she and Hetty partook of some also, the poor lady, who scarcely ever drank anything stronger than tea which had stood brewing till it was bitter, answered he might, if he pleased, mix her and Hetty a very very little, only he must be sure to make it 'as weak as weak.'

Which was accordingly done, after an appropriate remark from Mat concerning the time honoured joke 'Hot, strong, and sweet,' and then, to the end that aunt and niece might not seem to be 'sitting down to punch regularly,' they drank the seductive beverage out of one tumbler, which gave rise to a running fire of –

'I've had as much as I need, Hetty.'

'Nonsense, aunt.'

'Well, I'll just put my lips to it.'

'Go on.'

'If I take any more I shan't find my way to my bed.'

'Mat, you've put twice too much whisky in.'

'Have a teaspoonful.'

'Not a drop.'

'Wet your lips.'

'I'll have half if you will,' and so forth, till it was all gone, and Miss Cavan had washed and polished the tumbler and 'put it past' carefully, so that Mary's weak morals might not be destroyed by such an awful example on the part of her mistresses.

Poor simple women – dear, honest, kindly souls – what a trial you must have proved to any man save the one for whom you would cheerfully have laid down your lives; and yet how exactly you suited him and adapted yourselves to the many angles and twists of his complex character!

Chapter II

LADY HILDA'S HUSBAND

MEANTIME MR VASSETT'S PATH could hardly have been considered one strewn with roses.

He had got into the thick of a difficulty, and did not exactly see his way out of it.

'The next time,' he said to Mr Pierson, 'the next time I have anything to do with a lady, and that lady a lady of title, you may write me down anything you please.'

'One swallow does not make a summer,' returned the reader, who, having given it as his deliberate opinion that 'some day' the 'Irish girl would make her mark,' did not mean to eat his words or retract his advice, 'to encourage her.'

But Mr Vassett was adamant. 'Have we not had enough of petticoats?' he asked. 'Men can't deal with women in business matters. If her ladyship were of the other sex I'd know what to say to her, but as it is –' and a gloomy silence enfolded the conclusion of Mr Vassett's sentence in mystery.

'She is a slippery customer, as I always thought,' observed Mr Pierson, speaking as if he had prophesied the exact trouble which had occurred.

'You never thought she would serve us the scurvy trick she has done.'

'Why don't you go and see Hicks?' asked the reader. Mr Vassett shrugged his shoulders with a gesture of distaste.

'What's the good of writing about such a matter? You could tell him more in five minutes by word of mouth than it would be possible to explain by letter in five months.'

'I do not feel disposed to seek an interview with Mr Hicks. As a business man, there can be no question he will consider I have acted with culpable carelessness.'

'Pooh!' exclaimed Mr Pierson. 'As the happy husband of his wife, he must understand the nature of the lady who has let us into this hole better than we could be supposed to do.'

'I am inclined to imagine his intimate acquaintance with her peculiarities will not make him look more favourably upon my part in the transaction.'

'Shall I go and beard the citizen in his den?' asked Mr Pierson. 'He can't put me in the Tower, or take me before the Lord Mayor, and I don't care what he says. Hard words, you know, break no bones.'

Mr Vassett remained silent for a minute, casting this suggestion about in his mind; then he said:

'No, I shall first write. A letter will serve to open the ground, at any rate.'

'And when shall you open the ground?' inquired Mr Pierson, with the suspicion of a sneer.

'This day,' answered Mr Vassett, speaking determinedly.

'And what do you intend to say? Shall you tell him the high jinks her ladyship has been playing?' Mr Vassett winced visibly under this dreadful expression.

'I wish, Pierson, I really do wish –' he was beginning, when the other cut him short.

'Yes, I know you do; but never mind that now. Are you going to say exactly what has happened, or is it your intention to lead him gently on till you consider he is prepared to hear he will have to fork out –'

'Pierson! Pierson!'

'Nearly double the amount he was led to expect,' finished Mr Pierson, resolute not to amend his expression, but to complete the sentence in its integrity.

'All I mean to indicate in the first instance,' replied Mr Vassett, with as much dignity and precision as a severe cold in his head would allow, 'is that I find it will be necessary to lay before him a difficulty which has arisen in connection with the novel placed by Lady Hilda in my hands for publication. We shall then hear what he says in answer, and my future course will be to a great extent guided by the terms of his communication.'

'I can't see the use of all this diplomacy,' remarked Mr Pierson, in that disparaging tone which never failed to rouse his chief's temper. 'Why not go to the man at once, and explain the trick his wife has played you? Bless you, he won't be astonished! He must know her. He is perfectly well aware there is no sort of cheating she is not up to. Better take a 'bus into the City tomorrow, and get the matter of your mind at once. That's what I should do.'

'Is it?' said Mr Vassett. 'Then it is what I should *not* do.'

'Oh, of course you know best.'

'Yes, I imagine I do. Rapid and violent measures are always, in my opinion, to be deprecated.'

Mr Pierson looked at the speaker and smiled, as he said suggestively;

'If much time is expended on this interesting correspondence you will have Lady Hilda coming here to know why she has not received the remainder of the proofs.'

'Should her ladyship come, I shall know what to say to her,' observed Mr Vassett.

'All right; only don't ask me to help you out of that scrape.'

'I am not aware I am in the habit of either getting into scrapes or of asking you to help me out of them.'

Once again Mr Pierson smiled. There are times when a smile is more irritating than a blow, and Mr Vassett felt at that moment as if he could not endure his reader's impertinence much longer.

'You allow yourself too much license of speech, Pierson,' he said coldly.

'Do not confound me with Lady Hilda, pray,' entreated Mr Pierson. 'When she swoops down here for proofs, you will know more about license of speech than you do now. However, it is not my business, thank goodness! What have we got here?' he added, thinking it prudent to change the subject, and turning over some newly arrived manuscripts Mr Vassett had brought downstairs and laid on his table. '*Three Years in the Southern States of North America*, by Sir Richard Draper, MP. What is that about?'

'You had better see,' answered Mr Vassett, with less urbanity than usual.

'*From Mexico to Moscow, by an ex-Diplomatist*,' proceeded Mr Pierson; 'who on earth wants to know anything about either Mexico or Moscow?'

'A considerable number of persons, I should say,' observed Mr Vassett loftily.

Mr Pierson glanced up for a moment with a very good semblance of surprise, and then continued: '*Sitella: a Life Study*, by Gregory Bacon. Why, I returned that a week ago.'

'So the author writes. He says he knows you did not read it, and that he returns the MS to enable you to do so.'

'Set a trap, I suppose?' remarked Mr Pierson, with unmoved composure; 'turned a leaf upside down, or left a scrap of silk between two pages. I did look at the opening and the wind-up; it is rubbish. *Reminiscences of the Footlights*, by S Dawton. You will look them over yourself, I suppose. *Six French Actresses*, by C Cheshire – Cheshire Cheese.'

'I think that may be worth attention,' remarked Mr Vassett, ignoring the attempt at wit involved in this transposition.

'It is clean, clear copy, at any rate,' commented Mr Pierson, reconciling himself to the inevitable. 'And here is another "specimen," I declare, from our young Irish friend – *The Next Heir* – not a bad title,'

'Send it back at once,' interposed Mr Vassett, with a firmness worthy of St Senanus, 'as well as the other manuscripts of hers you were speaking of. We'll have no more women here.'

'Lady Hilda! Lady Hilda! What have you not to answer for!' said Mr Pierson, shaking his provoking head with solemn waggishness, as he gathered up the bundles of manuscript, and retired with them to his sanctum – a little room built out at the back of the premises and lighted from the roof, and which had possibly been a tool-house in the days when gardens, but no publishers, were to be found in the select seclusion of Craven Street.

Rid of his reader, Mr Vassett began to indite his letter to Mr Hicks. Though he said little more than he had indicated when speaking to Mr Pierson, the epistle occupied some time in the composition, for not merely was the theme one on which it seemed to the publisher inexpedient to commit himself, but in addressing a citizen – a man who was 'merely wealthy,' or as Lady Hilda expressed herself, 'disgustingly rich' – Mr Vassett's pen assumed almost unconsciously an elegance of diction, a choice of phraseology, and an ambiguity of style intended to produce an impression on Mr Hicks, who went as straight to the point as a bull at a red rag, and who had about as much talent or taste for diplomacy as, once again to quote from his wife's forcible vocabulary, 'a mad dog.'

The situation was indeed painful to the publisher 'in his capacity both as a man of sense and a man of business.'

Very early in their acquaintance with Lady Hilda he had so far gauged the character of that fascinating individual as to induce him, in order 'that subsequent complications and misunderstandings might be avoided,' to obtain from Mr Hicks an authority to expend a certain agreed sum which might fairly be presumed to cover all expenses connected with and attendant on the publication of a three-volume novel.

Her ladyship's idea of the nature of the partnership of matrimony may be gathered from the fact that she stipulated all profits arising from the sale of her books were to be paid over to her without deduction of any kind – not the net profits, be it understood, but the gross – and even when this was done faithfully, not merely for love of honesty, but for fear of the authoress, she grumbled and scolded, and accused Mr Vassett in very plain and vigorous English of cheating her. She tried hard to make him pay for the press copies, while as for allowing the publisher to keep a copy for his own reading, and in pleasant memory of their agreeable relations, as he courteously suggested, Lady Hilda would not hear of it. She said she could never understand why she was defrauded out of the retail price. The novel was advertised at thirty-one and sixpence, therefore why did she not receive a guinea and a half? Pitched battles had she and Mr Vassett over this question, and also the 'thirteen as twelve' which figured in his accounts.

'It is all nonsense,' said Mr Vassett, 'talking to me about a woman not comprehending business. What she cannot see is justice, so long as half-a-crown is to be made by remaining blind.'

Nevertheless, as has been said before, he was proud of having Lady Hilda's name in his list, and if he did not get meal out of the wife he got malt out of the husband; therefore, though he and her ladyship were always quarrelling, they had rubbed on together 'fairly well,' as the Scotch say, till she took it into her head to write a book he could not publish without the certainty of being dragged into several actions for libel.

Even one action for libel being a possibility too terrible to contemplate, he set his foot down, and compelled Lady Hilda for once to yield her point and allow the obnoxious paragraphs to be expunged.

Duly and truly Mr Pierson, who in common with his principal entertained, not without reason, the gravest doubts of her ladyship's good faith, toiled again through the manuscript, erasing all personal and questionable suggestions, and reducing the novel to a level of dull propriety which might have satisfied the requirements of a bench of bishops.

At this point, considering he had seen enough of the book to satisfy his curiosity for the present, he relinquished all responsibility. Where the works of authors he deemed important were concerned, it was Mr Vassett's practice to run through the proofs himself, only referring to Mr Pierson when he thought some change might be effected with advantage.

The reader, however, prepared manuscript for the press with such care and judgment that, as a rule, no corrections had to be made in Craven Street. The author saw to all those which were necessary, and it need scarcely be added that whatever other mistakes the printer might fall into, he was never guilty of the omission of not charging for even the slightest alteration in the text.

For a time, then, Lady Hilda's latest novel had proceeded joyously through the press.

No matter how long a publisher may have elected to keep a book back, there always comes a period when he wishes to get it out without delay. This is the case at the present moment, and this was the case in the very different era when Lady Hilda had the field of fiction, comparatively speaking, to herself. Mr Vassett having heard of an important work being 'in preparation' by a rival house, desired to get the start with Lady Hilda's novel. Then, as now, the librarians had only a certain amount of money to spend; and then, as now, they did not like spending that certain amount if they could avoid doing so.

Quite aware of this, it seemed good in Mr Vassett's eyes to hurry on the printers; and, accordingly, proofs came fast and thick to Craven Street, and were posted every day to Lady Hilda.

The proofs were not returned for press from Craven Street, but they were from Lady Hilda's residence; and as fast as she returned the sheets her corrections were attended to, and the book printed off.

The first volume was completed, the second also, and the third was half-way through, when, at the printing-office, the attention of one of the principals was drawn to the enormous number of author's corrections in the novel – corrections which not merely involved the alteration of sentences and the necessity for revises, but the re-imposing of pages, and in some cases the almost entire resetting of chapters.

Taking up one of the proofs, black and almost illegible by reason of her lady-ship's emendations, in order to satisfy himself there was reason in the complaints made on this subject, he saw enough to induce him even at the eleventh hour to inform Mr Vassett of the increase in expense he might confidently look forward to.

'Lady Hilda has almost rewritten the novel,' he said.

Mr Pierson did not happen to be in the way when this communication reached Craven Street, but within five minutes of its receipt Mr Vassett was en route to Soho – and for a quarter of an hour after he arrived at the printing-office it might have been thought the end of the world had come. Everyone was talking at once – explaining, recriminating, remonstrating; men in paper caps were running hither and thither, clasping soiled revises in their blackened hands. All the compositors seemed wanted in a hurry; the manager displayed corrected proofs; boys scurried about after perfect copies – there was such a to-do it might have been thought the Father of Mischief himself had got loose among the type and was setting up broadsheets by the score.

'There is one comfort, Mr Vassett,' said the head partner at length, meaning to be consolatory, 'we discovered the matter in time to prevent publication.' Mr Vassett could bear no more. He was known as a publisher of mild and courteous manners, not given to strong language or many words; but on the occasion in question, though he did not say much, what he did say was to the purpose, and there was an energy in his diction and a concentration in the one sentence with which he flung himself out of the office never to be forgotten by those privileged to hear.

All those goodly reams of double crown wasted, all that composing, and re-imposing, and re-setting, and revising, and re-reading, and printing off, worse than useless! All the advertisements thrown away! Mr Vassett felt as if he should go mad.

And then arose the extremely interesting question: 'Who was going to pay for this?'

The printers had given him clearly to understand they did not mean to lose their money; from Mr Hicks Mr Vassett only held a guarantee for a certain fixed amount; from Lady Hilda it was vain to expect anything except gibes and insolence; and there was one thing quite positive, Mr Vassett did not intend to pay the bill himself.

Under the circumstances, therefore, it will be seen some necessity for diplomacy existed.

'You are fond of exercising a little strategy,' Mr Pierson was ill-natured enough to say. 'Here is a capital opportunity:' and then ensued the conversation recorded at the beginning of this chapter. Poor Mr Vassett! Well might he declare the next time he had anything to do with a woman's book the sky would fall. No wonder he told Mr Pierson peremptorily to return Miss Westley's manuscripts.

'I call it a piece of great impertinence on her part,' he remarked later in the same day, 'to continue sending me a chapter or two as a "specimen." As I have told her, no one can form an opinion unless a whole book is submitted for perusal. Authors nowadays seem to think publishers exist simply for their convenience.'

'As far as the rejection of manuscripts is concerned,' said Mr Pierson, ignoring Mr Vassett's general statement, and confining himself to the special iniquity of which Miss Westley had been guilty, 'I can form an opinion as well from reading one side of copy as a whole book. The acceptance is quite a different matter.'

'Pierson, you are talking nonsense,' said Mr Vassett, not, perhaps, without reason.

'At any rate,' replied Mr Pierson, 'I shall not tell the girl she must send in a three-volume novel before I express an opinion on her work.'

'Tell her to send nothing' answered Mr Vassett. 'If I cannot get manuscripts I care to publish from men, I will cease to publish.' But Mr Pierson did not obey this command. He returned Miss Westley's 'specimen' with a little kindly word of encouragement.

'She'll do something yet,' he considered; 'but she may wait a little – waiting does not hurt them.'

By 'them' he meant authors, and more especially lady authors. He had never tried authorship himself, and he knew nothing of the long-drawn-out sickness of hope deferred, which though it may harden the tree – takes the bloom off the fruit, and renders success when it comes quite a different thing to what youth believed it would prove.

When we grow tall enough to gather the grapes that once hung high above our reach, the taste is not what we imagined we should delight in; but, after all, is not this the case with all the grapes of life – wealth, love, fame, happiness? If we could only realise at the beginning what poor things in reality the clustering bunches we spend our strength striving to grasp, are in fact, what a vast amount of trouble we should save ourselves long before we arrived at the end! Only in that case we might probably do nothing; and so it is best for men and women to go on hoping and believing, even though the close of their day should find the sun setting amid clouds of disappointment.

Even a publisher has disappointments. Remember that, discouraged authors! and take heart again. If the children of this world, in the shape of hard and stern capitalists, have their losses and crosses, how can writers, over-apt to consider themselves children of light, expect to find the literary road easy under foot, bordered with shady trees, and fragrant with sweet-scented flowers?

The next day Mr Vassett received Mr Hicks's answer to his diplomatic mission. The happy husband's reply ran as follows:

> *Dear Sir,*
>
> *I must ask you to explain the nature of the difficulty you mention to my solicitor, Mr Daunt, Crosby Square, who, I trust, will be able to arrange matters with you satisfactorily.*
>
> *Yours faithfully,*
> *T Hicks.*

'This is dreadful,' thought Mr Vassett. To explain the matter to Mr Hicks had seemed bad enough, but to explain it to a vague solicitor, one of a class he regarded with laudable misgivings, seemed impossible.

'Now you see you ought to have taken my advice, and gone in person to the fountainhead,' observed Mr Pierson, when he was told what Mr Hicks said.

'I had better write and explain the state of the case,' suggested Mr Vassett feebly.

'You had better do no such thing,' retorted Mr Pierson; 'see this Daunt man at once, and get the thing off your mind. For my own part, I think you ought to feel thankful a solicitor has been imported into the question, for he may perhaps stand between you and Lady Hilda.'

'I can't go anywhere with this dreadful cold,' said Mr Vassett, coughing as much as he could, and striking his chest pathetically.

It was deferring the evil day, and Mr Pierson knew this, but he only answered:

'There is no time to be lost. Shall I go?

'No; it will be better for me to write,' coquetted Mr Vassett.

'For heaven's sake don't commence a correspondence which may continue for a year,' entreated Mr Pierson. 'Let me go and try the ground. I promise you I won't say a word that can implicate you.'

It was some time before Mr Vassett would listen to this suggestion; and if he had not dreaded receiving a visit from Lady Hilda before he knew in what way to deal with her, the reader would probably never have carried his point. Mr Pierson was extremely fond of meddling in matters which one would have thought in no way concerned him, and on a few occasions he had consequently proved really of use to his chief.

'After all,' considered Mr Vassett, 'he can speak about what I have done for Lady Hilda, and all I have suffered at her hands, as I could not possibly speak myself. His brusqueness will probably not offend a lawyer as it might a husband; and, on the whole, it is perhaps prudent to put the affair in train as soon as possible.'

For these reasons, and for another much more cogent than any of them, viz., that he did not want to go himself, Mr Vassett at length graciously yielded an apparently reluctant consent to the course proposed.

Fearful of any change of mind if he allowed time for the publisher's mental thermometer to vary, Mr Vassett, though the rain was coming down in torrents, set off at once, poohpoohing all suggestions as to the advisability of delay, and saying for his part he would rather catch a cold than that Lady Hilda should catch them unprepared.

'For she will insist on the book being published, you may depend on that,' said the reader, buttoning up his overcoat preparatory to leaving Mr Vassett to consider at his leisure the extreme likelihood of these words proving prophetic.

Several hours elapsed before Mr Pierson returned – he had waited to see Mr Daunt, he had also lingered to dine, and loitered to partake of something hot to keep out the cold.

He was dripping with wet – he looked spare and hungry as ever – and his appearance would have done credit to a man who had been fasting for a long time and did not exactly know where his next meal was to come from; but there was a buoyancy in his step and a twinkle in his eyes, and a self-satisfied expression on his face which assured Mr Vassett he had to some extent, at all events, succeeded in his mission.

'Well' said the publisher.

'Well!' answered Mr Pierson, provokingly reticent.

'Did you see Mr Daunt?'

'Yes, and had a long talk with him. By Jove! it was lucky I went.'

'Will they pay the money?' asked Mr Vassett, anxious to hear Mr Pierson's 'luck' had assumed some tangible and desirable shape.

'Oh yes, that will be all right,' said Mr Pierson carelessly. 'Daunt is going to advise Hicks to make no fuss about it – but what do you think? *Hicks wants her ladyship to go back to him!*'

'You don't mean that?'

'Yes, I do; and I have undertaken to get her to go back.'

'You will never induce her to do anything of the kind.'

'Shan't I? We shall see.'

Chapter III

MR PIERSON 'RECEIVES'

IT WAS A MOST MISERABLE DAY in the miserable February of 1855. The snow which had fallen previously lay still on the horse-roads. A way had been cleared through it on the side-paths, but only in a perfunctory manner, and pedestrians were compelled in many thoroughfares to walk single file between frozen banks of mud. The sky looked black and heavy, as if laden with more snow. Sleet and rain drifted in the faces of the passers-by, while a damp cutting wind, swirling round corners, and rushing down cross-streets, and raking the main arteries of the metropolis, bade defiance to topcoats, and at times rendered umbrellas worse than useless.

A most miserable day, indeed, to be abroad; but then what day during the early part of that year proved otherwise? and it was with a pleasurable glow of satisfaction that Mr Pierson, ensconced in Mr Vassett's own office, looked at the fire he had just stirred up to a blaze, which went flaring up the chimney, and glanced around the comfortable room where for the time being he was monarch of all he surveyed.

Mr Vassett was upstairs with a cold, the newspaper, and his correspondence; and during his compulsory absence from business Mr Pierson occupied his office, sat in his especial chair, piled coals on his grate, stood on his hearth, and warmed himself, and, looking out at the wretched weather, reflected gladly he was not as those poor sinners who were forced to trudge the streets and get soaked with mire and rain, but snugly housed in a room which was well furnished, and cosy, and free from draughts, and which, moreover, he was paid for sitting in, and doing very little while he sat.

Ostensibly he was reading manuscripts, several of which lay on the table; really he was looking about him in a listless, idle, contented sort of mood.

The bookcase with its glass doors and well-filled shelves; the thick carpet, worn a little round the table and where the feet of anxious and hopeful, and despairing and successful, and well-to-do and impecunious authors had trodden; the bust of Socrates, mellowed by time and smoke; the picture, hanging in a bad light, which Mr Vassett had picked up a bargain in Drury Lane, and still believed to be an old master and priceless, though he could find no one else to share his opinion; the quaint chimney-piece and the round mirror above it – placed, fortunately, too high to reflect the distorted face of any human being; the library-table, on which so many letters had been written and cheques signed; the small cabinet, where were dozens of manuscripts kept till the proper time came for returning them to their owners; the window, the lower panes of which were cunningly ornamented with various curious designs intended to prevent a too-close scrutiny of the back regions – all these things and many more had been familiar to Mr Pierson for years, yet they now seemed to strike him with a quite fresh sense of pleasure and novelty, and to inspire the feeling that in so comfortable and home-like a room it would be a pity to exhaust his mind by doing anything.

'Bad as the weather is,' considered Mr Pierson, 'they'll be coming in after a while. It is of no use beginning anything. I'll just lie on my oars for a little;' and, having so decided, he threw himself into Mr Vassett's easy-chair, stretched his legs out over the hearthrug, and, basking in the heat of an immense fire, began to think, amongst other things and people, about Lady Hilda Hicks.

'I wonder she doesn't come. I made quite sure we should have seen her ere now,' he thought. 'What can she be doing? We may be certain of one thing, at any rate, namely, that wherever she is she is up to no good;' and he gazed into the fire dreamily as his thoughts wandered off to the affairs of Mr Hicks and his wife, and his hopes that he should make something out of the settlement of the matrimonial squabble.

There are things understood which are never exactly spoken, and Mr Pierson knew Mr Daunt would write him a cheque if he was able to carry out what he had promised to undertake.

'He will "recognise" my part in the transaction, to adopt Vassett's favourite expression,' thought the reader, 'and I certainly do not consider he can do that properly under twenty pounds. How shall I spend twenty pounds when I get the cheque? It is a long time since I had twenty pounds of my own in my hand at once.'

There were persons who pitied Mr Pierson, who thought what a sad thing it was for a man possessed of his intellect – so well educated, so clever, so industrious, so honest, so assiduous – to be forced by cruel circumstances to fill a subordinate position. Mr Vassett himself had once been of this opinion, and really hesitated about offering him the vacant post in Craven Street; but he knew Mr Pierson better now, and if he did not exactly comprehend why he had never got on, he grasped the fact that his reader never would get on.

There were two qualities, amongst many, Mr Pierson lacked – ambition and self-denial. If he desired a thing today, and found himself possessed of enough money to purchase it, he would purchase, no matter what he went without tomorrow: and as he loved his ease more than power, or position, or social standing, the prize could not have been offered which would have induced steady application on his part.

By starts he was industrious and energetic; but as a rule he had to be driven to read manuscripts and answer letters and return proofs.

Had it not been for this quality he might have risen high in a good house – eventually, perhaps, become partner in it to a small extent; but there came a time when even his abilities could not counterbalance his sins of dilatoriness and omission, and he and the great publishing firm referred to parted company not on the best of terms.

It was then Mr Vassett, who had been acquainted with Mr Pierson slightly for years, met him lounging aimlessly along Piccadilly, and stopped to speak.

Mr Pierson was full of his wrongs – and, as the other side of the case did not chance to be represented, he made out a very full bill of complaint.

He rehearsed all he had done for the firm and did not hide his own light under a bushel. He mentioned all the many great writers who, coming to his principals poor and unknown, would have been sent empty away but for his prescience. He dwelt upon the manner he had 'worked up' a certain magazine when the editor walked off in a huff, taking his staff with him. He declared he had been treated with the vilest ingratitude. He expressed his belief that the elder partners, though they had got of late 'mighty uppish' and hard to endure would never have parted in the manner they did with so old and faithful a servant, but for the machinations of a certain 'young puppy' lately admitted into the business.

'And what are you doing now?' asked Mr Vassett, with a sincere feeling of sympathy; for, as was natural, he did not love the great firm with that affection brother publishers should entertain for each other. 'What are you doing now?'

'Starving,' answered Mr Pierson.

It was not quite true, but it served. Mr Vassett knew that it was easy for a man who has not saved, soon to feel the iron grip of actual want. He felt very sorry indeed for Mr Pierson, whom hitherto he had always seen well dressed and apparently well cared for. He knew large houses are not, as a rule, too considerate. He was aware that the ways and manners and habits of 'young puppies' are often trying to those over whom they chance to be placed in authority; it hurt him to see a 'man like Pierson' with a frayed shirt-collar and a coat very white at the seams; so he said:

'Mine is a small business after that you have been accustomed to; but still it has grown a little too large for me; therefore, if you care to come to Craven Street till something more suitable offers, I dare say we can agree about terms.'

Mr Pierson jumped at the proposal, and declaring that he had no doubt they could, volunteered to 'look in' the next afternoon.

Thus he came, and thus he stayed. The business exactly suited him; if he liked to absent himself for a day, or even two, Mr Vassett made no complaint; if he chose to let the manuscripts accumulate for a week, the publisher was not – to quote his own expression – 'after him tooth and nail.' So far as he could like anyone – which was not far – he liked his employer; he would have felt extremely sorry had Mr Vassett failed or died, for he knew he would not drop into such another berth; he had as little to do as the heart of man could desire, and that little he did at his own time and in his own way. Mr Vassett treated him not only as an equal, but as a friend. He was not kept at arm's length in Craven Street, as he had been in Golden Square. He knew all the ins and outs of every transaction; he was shown the letters; he was consulted in difficulties; he was remembered in success; and, in a word, Mr Vassett, without making any fuss or display about the matter, did to Mr Pierson as he would that others should have done by him had he been in a similar worldly position, and if an attached and devoted adherence did not improve the result, it was merely because Mr Pierson was utterly deficient both in attachment and devotion. He had not cared for father or mother, brother or sister – he did not care for wife or children; and, therefore, it is not to be wondered at that he did not spend his days thinking how he might best exhibit deep gratitude for all Mr Vassett's kindness to him.

He was faithful to the best of his ability, and if that ability was not of the most trustworthy order, Mr Vassett did not expect to find perfection even in the person of a reader; so the two got on together very well indeed.

At an early stage of their business connection an arrangement had, with the concurrence of Mr Pierson, been entered into between Mr Vassett and Mrs Pierson – namely, that a certain sum was to be 'kept back' each week in order that the rent might be duly provided for as each quarter came round.

'That's all I wants from him,' exclaimed Mrs Pierson, who, as Mr Vassett mildly put it, 'was not a highly educated person.'

At that period he pitied Mr Pierson most heartily for having so thrown himself away, but he learned in the course of time the pity was due to the wife.

'It is a very strange world,' Mr Vassett was wont to remark, and in this conclusion no doubt Mrs Pierson would have agreed with the publisher most fully.

That Mr Pierson much preferred Mr Vassett's house to his own is as little doubtful as that Mrs Pierson always felt thankful when her husband was out of the way. For this reason it was Mr Pierson made long hours at Craven Street; often stopping to take tea with his employer, and not slipping on his out-of-door coat so as to be ready to start when the first stroke of the clock indicated that the time for leaving business had come, as is too much the habit with old and young gentlemen on salaries at the present day.

The reader was still exercising the powers of his mind, not in deciding upon the merits of any particular manuscript, but in speculating concerning the probable amount of the cheque he saw, in anticipation, signed and cashed, when the clerk who reigned supreme in the outer office – who attended to the book-keeping, kept bores civilly at bay, supplied the wants of collectors who then, as now, went about with heavy loads on their shoulders, and grumbled a good deal when they could not instantly get what they wanted, and always seemed to be sent out in the worst weather possible, and were afflicted with chronic coughs, and indulged in a good deal of 'chaff' – opened the door and announced that a lady wanted to see Mr Vassett.

'Well, he's ill, you know,' answered Mr Pierson.

'Will you see her then?' asked the other with a sad want of respect, born perhaps of knowing more of Mr Pierson even than his master did. 'She has never been here before,' he added in explanation.

'What is she like?' inquired the reader.

'She is just like the rest of them,' returned the clerk, in whose breast familiarity with the aspect of 'rising talent' had bred something very near akin to contempt.

'Show her in, then,' said Mr Pierson, resignedly murmuring as he turned to the table and began turning over the manuscripts. 'I must some day get Muggins to tell me "what they are all like."'

The lady entered. Though she had just come in from the wet street she looked trim and spruce enough to have stepped that moment out of a band-box.

Her hair was not dishevelled; her bonnet was straight, the strings tied in an admirable bow. On her skirts there was no speck of mud; her boots were not splashed; her manner was calm and self-possessed. It might have been quite a beautiful day in summer for all the signs of distress she exhibited.

'What a dreadful person to live with!' thought Mr Pierson; but he only remarked audibly, whilst with a solemn dignity worthy of Mr Vassett himself he indicated a chair, 'that the weather was most unpleasant.'

'It is not very agreeable, certainly,' said the lady, with admirable composure; 'but at least it has this advantage – one finds every person is at home.' Mr Pierson did not compromise himself by making any reply, and his visitor proceeded: 'It is such an absolute waste of time calling at different places and finding no one within able to give a definite answer on any subject.'

Still Mr Pierson did not speak; there were times when he was fond of thus playing a waiting game, and on such occasions he proved himself an absolute master of the art of silence. By experience he knew nothing brings a woman so soon to the point as making no comment on what she says; and having taken a dislike to his visitor, he thought he would get her to the point as soon as possible.

The result proved his wisdom, for in her very next sentence she broke ground.

'I sent a manuscript to you a fortnight ago,' she said, 'with a note requesting you to give me a speedy answer. As yet I have received no reply.'

'I am sorry for that,' observed Mr Pierson, in a manner that might have been taken either as ironical or sympathetic, as his auditor chose to interpret his tone.

'Oh, I did not much expect an answer,' she proceeded. 'I am told that you never take the slightest notice of letters.'

'Your informant must have some curious ideas as to the mode in which we conduct our business,' remarked Mr Pierson, with unruffled serenity.

'I did not mean you in particular. I mean all publishers.'

'I assure you, madam, we reply to letters,' protested Mr Pierson.

'Then why did you not reply to mine?'

'That I am quite unable to inform you,' he answered. 'A fortnight, however, is not a long time to give. If you only saw the number of manuscripts which arrive each morning, instead of wondering at a slight delay, you would marvel they so soon receive consideration.'

'I do not think I should,' she retorted. 'But however, to leave the general and come to the particular question, have you looked at the papers I sent you?'

'If you will kindly tell me what they were, I may be able to say. I am still, remember, ignorant even of your name.'

'My name is Yarlow – *Miss* Yarlow,' she added, with emphasis – ('As if,' thought Mr Pierson, 'any human being could imagine you were a married woman!') – 'but as I do not wish it to be published, I attached a *nom de plume* to the manuscript.'

'And what was the nature of the manuscript?' asked Mr Pierson.

'Well, it was an attempt to reproduce in popular and attractive form the life stories of six French actresses. Such subjects, even when treated in a more prolix style, have generally been found to possess a great interest for the mass of readers, and I am assured by good judges that these biographies, dealt with as I have done, only require to be well placed before the public to secure a wide audience. My knowledge of French literature is quite exceptional, and my information has been drawn from sources, I have reason to believe, inaccessible to any other author.'

'I fear, however,' ventured Mr Pierson, 'that the time for these sort of compilations has rather gone by.'

'Compilations!' repeated the lady; 'my manuscript is original – every word of it.'

'Then it can't contain the biographies of six French actresses, or even one of them,' objected the reader.

'It is perfectly evident you have not read a line it contains,' said the author.

'I have not, certainly; but I do not see how that fact can alter my contention.'

'Has anyone looked through the work?' asked Miss Yarlow indignantly.

'That is a question you ought to be able to answer much better than I,' replied Mr Pierson. 'You alone can tell how many publishers have seen the manuscript, and you alone can judge, from the nature of their comments, how many have read it through.'

Miss Yarlow, though not much given to blushing, coloured up to her eyes. He had struck her in a vital part at last. There was not a publisher in London of any standing to whom she had not offered those memoirs, and there was not a publisher of any standing in London who had not refused to have anything to do with them. Quite unconsciously, she and Miss Westley had been traversing the same round, with the same result. Glenarva happened to have 'worked the trade' more exhaustively; but that only chanced because she was younger, ignorant of many conventionalities which bound and fettered Miss Yarlow, and less careful of herself altogether than that personally considerate lady.

'I wonder of what use publishers really are!' said Miss Yarlow, at last recovering from the cruel blow Mr Pierson had dealt her. She did not address this pleasing remark to him, but uttered it in a sort of involuntary soliloquy, the expression of feeling being wrung from her by actual stress of despair.

'I really cannot inform you,' answered Mr Pierson, though he knew she had not spoken to him. 'Probably, however, they are intended to serve some purpose – whether good or evil it is not for me to say – in the scheme of creation.'

Miss Yarlow looked at him. She looked for a moment as if she were at bay – as if she would have liked to cross over to where he sat and box his ears or pull his hair; then, apparently feeling how useless it was to fight against a power such as that he possessed, she said, in a more humble and conciliatory manner than she had yet employed:

'And you – you, I suppose, like the rest, have not deigned to cast a glance on my poor attempt?

'I have seen the manuscript – that is about all; but if it is likely to prove any satisfaction to you, I will have it read now. I fear, however, whatever its merits may be, you would stand no chance of persuading Mr Vassett to undertake the publication at present. His lists are quite full for the season.'

'And when do you suppose –' faltered Miss Yarlow.

'Next year, perhaps, he might be open to consider a work of the kind you indicate. I beg your pardon, did you speak –'

'No, I did not speak,' answered Miss Yarlow; and she sat and looked in dumb misery at the leaping firelight. Next year! Gracious heavens! Were years, she thought, so plentiful in a human life that any person could afford to waste one in waiting?

'A year is a long time,' she said at last.

'To look forward to,' suggested Mr Pierson.

'And you really will not help me?'

'I really cannot help you,' he amended.

'And I heard Mr Vassett was so exceptionally kind and courteous.'

'He is exceptionally kind and courteous,' argued Mr Pierson, taking no notice of the suggested comparison implied as regarded himself; 'but though he might frame his refusal more pleasantly than I have done, he would refuse all the same.'

'I wish I could have seen him,' she said.

'If he gets better you will, no doubt, be able to see him some time during the course of the spring.'

Miss Yarlow looked at the speaker as he unfolded this hopeful prospect in such a way that he felt compelled to add, 'But when you have seen him, I do not think you will find yourself much further forward.'

She did not reply. She only turned her eyes again towards the fire.

'Does she mean to stop till we accept her manuscript?' marvelled Mr Pierson. He had seen a great many authors and a great many women, but he had never before come across any author or any woman exactly resembling Miss Yarlow. He was beginning to wonder when she would go – what he should be obliged to do to get rid of her – when the door opened, and Muggins appeared to say: 'Mr Dawton has been waiting for some time. He wishes to know if he shall call as he returns from Fleet Street.'

'No, no,' interrupted Mr Pierson hurriedly; 'ask him to stop a few moments longer. I want to see him particularly. Give him the *Morning Post* to look at.'

'He has read it through, sir,' explained Muggins, who took in the position at a glance.

'Well, say I shall be disengaged directly. Have you tried any of the magazines?' asked Mr Pierson, turning to Miss Yarlow as Muggins withdrew.

'No,' she answered, still looking intently at the fire.

'I think you might find it worth your while to do so.'

'Probably their lists would be full also,' remarked Miss Yarlow, with a fine irony.

There ensued a dead silence, which Mr Pierson at length essayed to break by rising from his chair and making a feint of arranging the papers scattered on the table; but Miss Yarlow took not the slightest notice of this movement.

Was she going to beat him with his own weapons? Was he at last to find that saying nothing may, on the part of a woman, be even more of a vice than a virtue?

'The best counsel I can offer you,' he began, when he felt he could endure her rapt contemplation of the fire no longer, 'is to try the magazines. Even if editors should consider your articles unsuitable, you would be in no worse position than you are now; while if by any good chance you did secure acceptance, papers of the description you indicate would be just as available for publication after they had appeared in a periodical as they are now.'

Miss Yarlow removed her eyes from the leaping flames, and looked at Mr Pierson with considerable interest. Clearly here was a lady who, though she could be dumb, did not happen to be deaf.

'I think you really will find that your best plan,' went on Mr Pierson, anxious to follow up the impression he had made. 'If you do not know where the offices of the leading magazines are situated, I will write you down the addresses with pleasure.'

Coming from the source it did, this offer should have been regarded as extremely courteous; but Miss Yarlow did not seem much impressed by it.

'Was there ever such a woman?' thought Mr Pierson impatiently. Instead of taking the blessings that the gods sent her, and going out into the rain rejoicing, with a few useless names and addresses written on them in a hand so clear as to convey a tacit reproof to careless calligraphers. Miss Yarlow simply took no notice whatever of the civility proffered, but, seizing upon the one point in Mr Pierson's previous sentence which had seemed to her worthy of attention, asked:

'Do I understand you to mean that hereafter, whether these memoirs have appeared in print or not, Mr Vassett will entertain the idea of publishing them?'

'I scarcely intended to say he would "entertain the idea of publishing them,"' amended Mr Pierson, who felt he had to do with a lady whom it might be inexpedient to mislead even in the way of kindness, 'because so many extraneous circumstances, entirely independent of the merits of your productions, have to be considered before a work by an as yet unknown author can be produced with satisfaction to all parties concerned.'

'What did you intend to say, then?' inquired the lady, with a directness which might have elicited some tangible statement even from Mr Vassett, who had a peculiarly happy knack of combining ambiguity with courtesy.

'That after your *Six French Actresses* have appeared in a magazine we shall be as happy to read and consider them as at the present moment,' answered Mr Pierson, driven to bay, and not perceiving the mistake he had made till reminded by a contemptuous exclamation from Miss Yarlow of how very little satisfaction his assurance was calculated to give.

'Well, you are a Jesuit!' remarked Miss Yarlow, irritation tempered by admiration struggling together in her tone for mastery. 'Why can't you tell me at once you never mean to read the manuscript? What is the good of all this beating about the bush?

'You *will* misconceive me,' said Mr Pierson desperately. 'If it is likely to prove any satisfaction to you, the manuscript shall be read immediately; but I tell you candidly, that let the report turn out as favourable as report possibly can, there is not the slightest likelihood of Mr Vassett accepting the work at present. He does not care to bring out many books; and his arrangements are made for some time to come. If the author of *Nine Poems by V*, or Charlotte Brontë, or even Miss

Martineau herself, were to offer him a manuscript at the present moment, I know perfectly well he would say its appearance must be deferred, otherwise he should reluctantly be obliged to decline it.'

Oh, days that seem gone so long! When *Jane Eyre* and *Paul Ferroll* were titles as familiar in men's mouths as *Lady Audley's Secret* and the *Woman in White* have been since; when Miss Martineau was still living, and the *Scenes of Clerical Life* were not thought of; when no one had heard of George Eliot, and publishers were still plodding slowly and safely along familiar roads; when all the world had not begun to write, and there were still left a small number of persons who read!

On that particularly wet morning those days now departed were present with Mr Pierson, and the names he invoked to convince his visitor of the thorough honesty of his assertions stood high on the glory-roll of fame.

'Perhaps,' suggested Miss Yarlow, 'Mr Vassett is waiting for the reappearance of the Queen of Sheba carrying a roll of manuscript in her hand containing an account of her visit to the court of King Solomon.'

'He may be,' answered Mr Pierson coolly; 'but he has not mentioned the fact to me. And now, Miss Yarlow, to revert to your matter. Will you leave your *Six Actresses* to be read, or will you adopt my advice, and first submit them to one or other of the magazines?'

'I think,' said the lady, 'as you are so evidently anxious to get rid of my manuscript and myself, I had better take it with me. The next time I come I hope Mr Vassett will be well enough to attend to his business for himself.'

'It is gratifying to find there is at least one point on which we are agreed,' answered Mr Pierson, as he opened the cabinet and took out the despised *Actresses*.

'Mr Dawton, sir,' here interrupted Muggins, opening the door – and never surely was the sight of Muggins's face more welcome – 'wishes to know if you could speak to him for one minute. He says he need not now detain you longer, but he has an appointment –'

'Ask Mr Dawton to walk in,' said Mr Pierson; 'and, see. Muggins, put up this manuscript. Can we send it anywhere for you?' he asked, turning to Miss Yarlow.

'No, thank you,' answered that lady.

'We will with pleasure,' urged Mr Pierson; 'it is a bulky parcel for you to take.'

'A workman should not be above carrying his tools,' said Miss Yarlow, with a beautiful humility.

'Good! Excellent!' exclaimed a voice behind her; and, turning, she beheld a most singular-looking person, who bowed and smiled, and hoped she would 'excuse an old man's appreciation of her ready wit.'

It was Mr Dawton. Mr Dawton dressed as if it were a hot July afternoon – in grey trousers, a white waistcoat, a swallow-tailed coat, a washing necktie. The only item inconsistent, perhaps, with the idea of sultry weather was a pair of Hessian boots; but the boots were beautifully made and highly polished, and detracted in no way from the astounding effect of the general get-up.

'Why, Dawton!' exclaimed Mr Pierson, 'where are you going? What have you been doing? Getting married this fine sunshiny morning, eh?'

'No, my friend; I married once – more years ago than I can remember.'

'And found it once too often, eh?'

'Not so. My draw in the matrimonial lottery proved singularly fortunate. Let who else will – but we must not talk treason in the presence of so fair a representative of her sex,' Mr Dawton broke off to say, with a winning smile, and his hand laid on his heart: '*Are* you going, madam? I trust my appearance was not inopportune?'

'You had better put that question to Mr Pierson,' answered Miss Yarlow, with a Parthian glance shot at that gentleman; and then, announcing her intention of waiting in the outer office till Muggins had finished tying up her manuscript, she bade her late adversary good morning, and walked out of the inner room, followed by a look of profound admiration from Mr Dawton, to whom she bowed stiffly, and who held the door wide and watched her retreating figure as he might have done had she been retiring down one of the 'wings' from the gaze of thousands.

'Ah!' he exclaimed, as he reluctantly closed the portal between him and this vision of loveliness, 'there's nothing like woman.'

'That depends a good deal, I should say, on what the woman is,' returned Mr Pierson, drawing a deep sigh of relief. 'Well, and what can I do for you?' he added, motioning to the chair Miss Yarlow had just vacated, and flinging himself into the depths of the sacred armchair.

'Vassett's laid up, your clerk tells me,' observed Mr Dawton, sitting well on the edge of his seat, and holding his hat in his hand, after the most approved traditions of how a gentleman (on the stage) comports himself when paying a morning visit.

Mr Pierson inclined his head in indolent acquiescence.

'Nothing serious the matter, I trust?'

'No – a cold – this beastly weather has been too much for him; for beastly weather it is, though you are arrayed as if the young lambs were frisking about in the green meadows, and you were intending to join their gambols.'

'You think I really look the character, then?

'What character, in the name of Heaven?' asked Mr Pierson.

'The country squire – the good old country gentleman of ancient lineage, and possessed of broad acres, antiquated and prejudiced it may be, but true to his principles. Conservative even in his dress – up in town to see a friend at court, with a view of obtaining a lucrative appointment abroad for his prodigal son. His appearance tells its own story. If you were to meet him in an omnibus now –'

'I should think, if I met you in an omnibus, dressed as you are now, you had either escaped from Bedlam, or were a fit candidate for it.'

'Ah! I see you don't understand –'

'The fun of a man at your time of life turning out on such a morning in a white waistcoat and a frilled shirt – no, faith, I can't understand that. However, if the costume pleases you, I am sure it may please me.'

'Wait a bit, my boy – fair and softly wins the day – wait till I send you tickets.'

'Oh, it is a play, then? I thought as much! But you are not going to perform in Craven Street? Why the deuce do you choose to roam about the town with no clothing on your back to speak of?'

'I attribute most of the success I have achieved in my life – and mine, Pierson, has been an eventful life – By-the-bye,' Mr Dawton broke off to say, 'I suppose you have read the manuscript I sent here some short time since, containing just a few jottings of an experience which has not been unexciting'?

'I only looked at a page or two; Mr Vassett read it.'

'And what did you think of it – now, candidly?'

'I thought it very poor stuff indeed,' answered Mr Pierson, with a frankness which could be considered as nothing less than appalling, 'but Vassett imagines something can be done with it.'

'You see, you are scarcely a judge of matters connected with the noble profession,' said Mr Dawton, much as if he merely substituted this sentence for – 'You see, you are only an ignorant fool.'

'No; I do not profess to know much about the stage, but I fancy I comprehend something about literature.'

'Ah! I sent the sheets to you in the rough; they require a little correction, I am aware – a mere matter of detail,' said Mr Dawton.

'And who is going to undertake that correction?' asked Mr Pierson, who certainly did not desire to undertake it himself.

'Well, as you know, I have sons – all capable, all good men and true. The mere preparation for press need present no difficulty. I should have liked to see Mr Vassett,' proceeded Mr Dawton, with a wandering expression in his eyes and a furtive glance, the meaning of which Mr Pierson could read perfectly, 'because I want the work brought out soon – now, in fact, when all London will be ringing with my name – and you and I could not settle terms, I suppose?

'No, certainly not,' answered Mr Pierson, with a prompt acquiescence which proved anything but gratifying to Mr Dawton.

'I wish I could have seen Mr Vassett,' he said, as if he had not made the same statement before.

'Well, I have little doubt he will be able to attend to business in a few days.'

'Ah! but I wanted to see him this day' – which fact he need not indeed have told Mr Pierson, who comprehended thoroughly not merely that he wanted to see Mr Vassett, but also why he wanted to see him.

There was a pause. Mr Pierson stirred the fire, and Mr Dawton looked at the blaze almost as intently as Miss Yarlow had done.

'Well, they *are* a queer set!' considered Mr Pierson, referring, like Mr Muggins, to authors in general, and forgetting how extremely odd he himself could be on occasion. 'I wonder how long it will be before *he* speaks?'

It was not long – silence could not be reckoned amongst Mr Dawton's failings.

'Do you think,' he began in a subdued and confidential tone, 'Mr Vassett is so ill that reading a note – a very short note – would hurt him?'

'I don't suppose it would,' answered Mr Pierson; but he spoke doubtfully, and not at all as a man might have been expected to speak who knew perfectly well his principal was able to come downstairs to attend to his business had it pleased him to do so. 'Should you like to write him a note?'

'Thank you. Yes, I should;' and Mr Dawton laid his hat down carefully, drew his chair to the table, accepted with a bland inclination of his head the paper Mr Pierson placed before him, and took pen in hand, as he might have done had the eyes of pit, stalls, boxes, and gallery been concentrated upon his act.

Never a man existed so utterly permeated by his profession as poor Mr Dawton. When he laid him down to sleep and drew the sheets up under his elderly chin, there can be no question he felt still before the footlights, and in his last conscious waking moments posed for the 'gods.'

Though he dipped the pen in the ink he did not write, however. He sat considering what he wanted to say, and how he had best say it; then, probably finding the task more difficult than he expected, he said to Mr Pierson:

'I do not think I need trouble Mr Vassett with a note at all, if you would only be so kind as to take a message to him. Could you do this for me?

Mr Pierson thought he could, but before fully committing himself, intimated it might be as well for him to know what the message was.

'Well, the fact is,' said Mr Dawton, 'I have most unexpectedly and unaccountably forgotten to bring any money out with me, and there is something I wish particularly to pay this morning. If you explain the difficulty in which I am placed to Mr Vassett, perhaps he would be so good as to advance me a nominal sum, say five pounds. I should feel infinitely obliged to him; I really should – and to you also,' added Mr Dawton as an afterthought.

'I will ask him with pleasure,' replied Mr Pierson; 'but of course I can't say whether he has any five-pound notes lying about,' with which depressing observation the reader disappeared, leaving Mr Dawton to go through the charm, 'He will, he will not' – minus the 'property' flower.

Mr Pierson was not long absent. He came back almost directly, and saying, 'Yes, you can have five pounds,' opened a drawer, from which he took Mr Vassett's cheque-book.

Mr Dawton tried hard to hide the relief he felt under the words,

'I am infinitely obliged to him,' uttered in a majestic tone and with a dignified composure; but Mr Pierson saw his whole face change its fashion for a moment with delight, and laughed to himself as he went up the stairs with the cheque-book.

He had not reached the first landing, however, before his name was pronounced, and looking back, he beheld Mr Dawton making mystical signs for him to return.

Mr Pierson was the last man on earth to do anything of the sort unless he knew exactly what he was wanted for.

'One moment!' exclaimed Mr Dawton.

'Yes,' said the reader, standing still.

'Not crossed,' entreated Mr Dawton in a stage-whisper, putting his hand to the side of his mouth, so that no breath of his utterance might be wafted along the passage. 'Open.'

'All right,' answered Mr Pierson; and then Mr Dawton walked back into the office on tiptoe, and as if there were mortal sickness in the house, to be suddenly confronted with an unexpected apparition, which addressed him sharply and imperatively with the words:

'Where's Mr Pierson?'

'Madam,' said Mr Dawton, backing a step or two, for he felt really frightened, 'the gentleman will wait upon you directly.'

'He had better!' exclaimed the lady, walking round the table; and flinging herself into Mr Vassett's armchair, she commenced beating a tattoo on the floor with her little feet, which she made no scruple of freely exhibiting to Mr Dawton.

'Will you – may I offer you the newspaper pending Mr Pierson's return?' he asked, timidly (extending the *Morning Post*, which he had brought in from the outer office).

'No,' she snapped, and beat a louder tattoo than before.

Mr Dawton retreated as if he had got a slap in the face, and stood looking in surprise, not unmixed with terror, at this last specimen of 'angelic woman.'

'Now, is that man ever coming?' she cried, suddenly turning sharply round, and catching Mr Dawton staring at her with more curiosity than good-breeding.

'I assure you, madam, he will be back almost immediately,' he stammered.

'Go and fetch him at once.'

If she had told him in that tone to take off his head, Mr Dawton would have tried to obey her; and accordingly he again went out into the passage, where he ran up against Mr Pierson, who had paused for a moment at sound of the well-known voice.

'Stormy weather impending,' he thought; and then Mr Dawton appeared as if he had been blown out of the room, and said, with a scared face and in a tremulous voice – 'A lady – a – a lady –'

'I know,' interrupted Mr Pierson. 'Here's your cheque – put it up. You did not let out I was with Vassett, I hope, did you?'

'N – n – no,' answered Mr Dawton, who at the moment had not the slightest recollection of anything he might have 'let out.'

'I have left my hat in the room.'

'Come and get it then,' advised Mr Pierson. 'Bless my soul, she won't eat you.'

'Take her for all in all –!' began Mr Dawton, but Mr Pierson was by this time in the room, and the storm had burst.

Chapter IV

MR PIERSON 'EXPRESSES HIS SUPRISE'

A QUARTER OF AN HOUR PASSED; comparative calm had succeeded to tempest, and Mr Pierson was still alive. There were times during that exceedingly bad fifteen minutes when he held his head in both hands to make sure it was still on his body. Like a hurricane, Lady Hilda's passion threatened to carry everything away before it. For once Mr Dawton was stricken dumb; in the outer office the usually phlegmatic Muggins stood listening, ready, as he afterwards stated, to 'make a clean bolt of it,' should flight become necessary. On the first floor, with door ajar, Mr Vassett hearkened, appalled by her ladyship's torrent of indignation, doubtful whether, in spite of anything Mr Pierson might have said on the subject of his ailments, he ought not to descend to his reader's assistance. Prudence, however, overcame valour, and Mr Vassett decided that upon the whole he had better let Pierson fight out the battle alone.

Bravely enough Mr Pierson stood his ground; though her ladyship's balls were whistling round him, though he had to bear the brunt of a hot and heavy cannonade, his courage never really failed.

'It was bad while it lasted,' he remarked afterwards, 'and it lasted a long time.'

Nevertheless, spite of the fury and violence of the storm, he managed now and then to edge in a word. Notwithstanding the enemy's fire, he stood firm to his own guns.

'As Lady Hilda had altered her book, she need never expect to find any good publisher to stand godfather to it.' 'Her ladyship could, of course, if she doubted the fact, take it the round of the trade – to Longman, Chapman and Hall, Bentley, Hurst and Blackett, or any other firm she could think of.' 'He felt as satisfied as he could feel on any subject that she would not get a respectable house to put their imprint upon it.'

'Then I will get a house that is not respectable,' retorted her ladyship.

'I don't think you will,' answered Mr Pierson, 'unless your husband proves willing to give a guarantee for damages.'

'Don't talk to me about my husband!' cried Lady Hilda, and then the storm, which had lulled for a moment, burst forth again.

But at last it really seemed as if the worst were over, as if her irate ladyship had exhausted her almost inexhaustible powers of speech. She saw, in fact, there was nothing to be done with Mr Pierson; and so, now flinging herself once again into Mr Vassett's chair – she had stood during the controversy so as to give greater effort to her threats and denunciations – she said she meant to remain there till Mr Vassett was produced.

'He undertook to bring out my novel,' she said, 'and I must hear from his own lips why he refuses to do so.'

'I am afraid your ladyship will have to wait some time, then,' said Mr Pierson. 'Vassett is very ill indeed. I fear he will not be able to come downstairs for some weeks.'

'If that is all,' answered Lady Hilda, 'I am quite able to go upstairs this minute;' and she started from her seat, as if to carry her suggestion into immediate effect.

'Mr Vassett is in bed,' explained Mr Pierson, with reckless mendacity. 'You would not go to him there!'

'I would go to him if he were in his coffin, sir,' said Lady Hilda.

'Ah, that would be quite another affair!' remarked the reader, who could not have withheld his tongue from an observation of this sort if life itself had depended upon his silence.

Lady Hilda looked at him. Could a glance have killed, Mr Pierson had never again returned home to his wife and family. Her eyes literally seemed to flash fire; and as she stood there, erect and indignant, waiting, apparently, to swoop down and destroy her quarry, Mr Dawton thought he beheld before him the very incarnation of a handsome virago.

The storm, which had seemed passing away, now gave signs of working round again. The sky grew black, the atmosphere thick and heavy, and there appeared no likelihood of another thunderclap being averted, when, 'for the first time on any stage,' Mr Dawton quite unconsciously played the part of 'special Providence.'

Hitherto he had failed to get his hat. Fearing to venture out into the open, and so draw Lady Hilda's attention to himself, he remained behind Mr Pierson, and, under cover of that gentleman's body, made several futile attempts to secure his head-covering. Now, however, feeling satisfied another tempest was impending, which might prove even worse than any of its predecessors, he 'dodged' from side to side of Mr Pierson in a manner which must have won the approval of his particular friends, the gods; and all his eyes fastened on his hat, and his whole energies devoted to securing it, forgot for a moment the awful presence in which he stood.

Lady Hilda's attention was at last arrested by his gestures. 'What does that creature want?' she asked Mr Pierson sharply. 'Is he mad?'

'No – your ladyship – no,' stammered out Mr Dawton. 'I – I do not want to interrupt – I am sure – and I beg a thousand pardons – but –'

'What is it?' said Mr Pierson, who had for some time been oblivious of his presence.

'He wants his hat. Can't you see?'

And snatching up the extremely shiny article in question, Lady Hilda was 'graciously' pleased to thrust it towards Mr Dawton in the most rude and ungracious manner possible.

'I beg your pardon, I am sure,' apologised Mr Pierson. 'I had quite forgotten. This is a gentleman, Lady Hilda,' he added, thankful for even a moment's diversion, 'with whose name I have no doubt you are well acquainted –'

Lady Hilda looked at the actor curiously, as she might at a chameleon, or a prairie dog, or a kangaroo, or any other animal she did not know familiarly.

He now came forward a step, as if to the footlights, and, laying his hand on his white waistcoat, and bowing profoundly, murmured:

'Dawton – Dawton, at your ladyship's service.'

'What's his name?' demanded Lady Hilda, turning to Mr Pierson.

'Dawton,' said the reader.

'Never heard it before,' observed her ladyship, with contemptuous brevity.

'A mere tyro in the arena where your ladyship has won renown,' explained Mr Dawton, who had not the faintest idea even of her ladyship's lawful name. 'The few laurel leaves I have been permitted to gather,' he added, touching his forehead, which was adorned at that moment by a perfectly new wig, 'have been culled by me in Thespian groves. On the mimic stage the name of Dawton has achieved distinction – three generations have trodden the boards, and left, if I may so express myself, an imprint on the sands behind them. I have sons who will, I think – in literature, in art, in the drama – keep up the old traditions; and, for myself, I am your ladyship's most humble and admiring servant.'

Lady Hilda laughed – actually laughed. Like Mr Donagh, she had a keen sense of humour when the joke was not at her own expense; and the spectacle of Mr Dawton, dressed as he was and acting for the benefit of herself and Mr Pierson, might indeed have moved the mirth of Muggins, who in the outer office heard Lady

Hilda's laugh, and wondered 'how Pierson had managed to bring her to at last.'

'This is delicious,' she remarked, turning to Mr Pierson as the only appreciative individual within reach; and then she smiled sweetly on Mr Dawton, who, thawing under the influence of this unlooked-for condescension, proceeded:

'It is in the field of fiction, as I understand, your ladyship's proudest triumphs have been achieved; and yet, if without impertinence I – who do possess some knowledge of that which is, after all, the noblest profession of all, the living, breathing, moving presentment of our actual existence – may venture such an observation, I feel confident that could your ladyship only be induced to repre-sent before an audience the indignation – righteous indignation, I doubt not – it has been my privilege to hear you enunciate in this room, you would bring down the house. No, I never in all my long experience heard anything so magnificent. Siddons herself could not have done it, madam.'

'Because Siddons had never such cause for righteous anger,' answered Lady Hilda. 'I don't know, Mr Dawton – that is your name, is it not? – what sort of treat-ment you may meet with here, but I can only say Mr Vassett treats me shamefully. He keeps me without money, and he desires also to prevent my becoming famous. I have written a novel – oh, such a novel! – one that must cause a perfect furore, and now he says quite coolly – or rather, Mr Pierson says so for him – he won't publish the book unless I cut out all the finest passages, and reduce it to the dull level of propriety and stupidity old ladies of both sexes have set up as the standard of literary perfection.'

Poor Mr Dawton! With Mr Vassett's cheque in his pocket, with the hope of more cheques from Mr Vassett in his heart, he felt the publisher's side of the question was that he ought to espouse; the cause of propriety, even if propriety involved stupidity, the safest for him to champion. But, upon the other hand, he was at close quarters with a beautiful termagant, with 'angelic woman' in one of her most stormy moods, with a lady (of title) who seemed capable of doing anything if crossed, and yet who, in Mr Dawton's then opinion, only required, like all the rest of her charming sex, a little discreet management to be delightful.

For the latter reason, and also because Mr Vassett was absent and Lady Hilda present, with a deprecating glance towards Mr Pierson, and feeling, as he patheti-cally put the matter subsequently, as Naaman after he was cured of his leprosy must when he bowed himself in the house of Rimmon, Mr Dawton declared her ladyship had good reason for complaint; that if any passages were excised from his poor book, he should feel the operation acutely. But he was certain there must be some mistake. The matter only required explanation, and Mr Vassett would see it was put right at once.

'I have had the pleasure of Mr Vassett's acquaintance for over twenty years,' he said, 'and during the whole of that time I have never known him to do an ungentlemanly or ungenerous action. Besides, he could not treat your ladyship's slightest wish with discourtesy; he is kindness itself, most gallant –'

At this point Mr Pierson interrupted the proceedings.

'Dawton,' he suggested, 'don't you want to go to Fleet Street?'

'Yes, certainly. I have an appointment there.'

'Then hadn't you better keep it?'

Mr Dawton coloured up to the roots of his wig; but he had not lived his life, even such as it was, for nothing. Though Mr Pierson's lack of politeness, as he told the reader afterwards, 'entered into his very soul,' he turned with a very good affectation of indifference to Lady Hilda, observing, 'There is scant ceremony amongst friends, your ladyship will perceive,' bowed profoundly to her, and saying, 'Good morning, Pierson,' in a tone of hurt dignity to that gentleman, retired from the scene.

'Thank heaven,' observed Lady Hilda piously, as the door closed behind him, 'one bore is disposed of! Well, Mr Pierson?'

'Well, Lady Hilda?'

'Is it to be peace or war?'

'So far as I am concerned, peace always towards your ladyship; but you are aware I have a duty towards my employer also.'

'Fiddle-de-de!'

'And he has a duty to discharge towards himself.'

'Meaning he won't publish my book?'

'Meaning he cannot publish your book as it stands.'

'Then I must take it elsewhere; and I have been so ill, Mr Pierson. I went to stay with a friend in the country for a few days, and got laid up there, and it was such a horrid house! And then, when I came back to town, expecting to find the book finished – no proofs, no letters, no anything! I wrote to the printers at once; they referred me to Mr Vassett. I went to the printers; they referred me once again to Mr Vassett. Now I come here, and I can't see Mr Vassett, who I believe is keeping out of the way. I feel quite satisfied he is afraid or ashamed to meet me.'

'Whatever shame there may be in the matter,' said Mr Pierson boldly, 'certainly does not attach itself to Mr Vassett. To be quite plain, Lady Hilda, you tried to play him a most shabby trick, and one which, had it succeeded, might have proved his ruin as a publisher.'

'But why? Everyone would have read the book!'

'And said any man capable of sending out such a work was not fit to remain in the trade.'

'Oh! Of course it is your interest to take his part.'

'There is such a thing in the world as honesty, though you, Lady Hilda, do not seem to believe in its existence,' remarked Mr Pierson in a tone of conscious virtue.

'I do not think there is any audience,' suggested her sceptical ladyship, 'and moral sentiments of all kinds are quite thrown away upon me.'

'Indeed, I should imagine so,' replied the reader with disconcerting readiness.

'I wish I had never heard the name of Vassett!' exclaimed Lady Hilda. 'If I had only in the first instance gone to some good publisher, I might have been a rich woman by this time.'

'It is not too late for you to take this book to a good publisher.'

'And how in the world could I account for the novel being in print?'

Mr Pierson laughed outright as he answered: 'I should not presume to suggest to Lady Hilda Hicks the particular excuse it might seem most expedient to make use of. Your ladyship's vivid imagination may be trusted to find some way out of the difficulty.'

She did not speak for a moment; but then she broke out again with this plaint:

'And I never in all my life wanted money so much – wanted it so cruelly.'

'If you had dealt fairly by Mr Vassett, you need not have wanted money,' returned Mr Pierson, who was getting too tired of the discussion to waste his breath in what he called 'figures of speech.'

'And till I can find an accommodating and sensible publisher, I shall not be able to get a penny, I suppose?'

'I really do not know. Mr Vassett will not advance even that small sum, I am very sure.'

'Come now, Mr Pierson, could you not persuade him to bring out my book as it stands?

'I could not if I would, and I would not if I could,' answered Mr Pierson, who was becoming quite disagreeable in the strength of his rectitude.

'There is really not an atom of harm in anything I have written,' she persisted.

'We will not travel over all that ground again, if you please, Lady Hilda.'

'All I wanted was to shame my husband into making me some decent allowance.'

Mr Pierson maintained a discreet silence.

'I am quite sure you could not guess the pittance he has the conscience, or rather the want of conscience, to dole out to his wife.'

'Your ladyship mentioned the amount when you first came here,' answered Mr Pierson. 'Six hundred per annum. I remember at the time thinking it was not actual starvation.'

'Perhaps it might not be to you.'

'Perhaps it might not be to a great many people,' answered the reader.

'But to me such a sum means absolute penury. And what makes the matter all the worse is the knowledge that twelve hundred a year would be no more to Mr Hicks than – than what shall I say?'

'Twelve pence to me,' supplied Mr Pierson.

'Thank you; I do not know that I could find a better simile.'

And Lady Hilda smiled sweetly, as if she had paid Mr Pierson's pecuniary position some delicate compliment.

'Yes, I believe he is enormously rich,' said the reader, twisting and untwisting a piece of paper as he spoke. 'I wonder how people get to be so rich. Somebody was saying the other day Mr Hicks had bought an estate, and paid – how much down for it? – a quarter of a million, I fancy – yes, I think it was a quarter of a million.'

Lady Hilda leaned forward and listened with parted lips and eager eyes. He had interested her at last.

'Where is the estate?' she asked.

'Let me see, did I hear? – I must have done – Stifford? Enfield? Dulwich? – no; where on earth was it? What's the place out somewhere to the north of London – not Hornsey, or Highgate; Southgate – that's it, Southgate.'

'The property that belonged to the Dundas family – do you mean that?'

Mr Pierson shook his head, and contrived to look as if the subject had not contained the smallest interest for him.

'Some big man owned the place,' he said; 'that is about all I know, except – yes, by-the-bye, I was nearly forgetting the most important part of the business – the person who told Mr Vassett said it was currently reported Mr Hicks meant to entertain Royalty this summer.'

Lady Hilda jumped straight off her chair, and then sat down again.

'And pray,' she asked, 'who is going to do the honours of this new house for Mr Hicks when he receives Royalty?'

'I can't say, I am sure. He has a sister, hasn't he? I feel almost positive I heard something about a sister in connection with the matter.'

If Mr Dawton had seen her ladyship then, he might have found something to say about 'bringing down the house.' A look which contained volumes swept over her expressive face. She did not speak, but Mr Pierson understood. There was no need of words to tell him the strife which had raged between husband and wife was as nothing in comparison to the war Lady Hilda felt she could undertake against her sister-in-law.

At last Mr Hicks's better-half broke the silence.

'That book *must* be published,' was her remark. '*She* is in it.'

Mr Pierson raised his eyebrows and shrugged his shoulders.

'I really do not think,' he said, 'a publisher of any standing could be found to bring out your novel; and this I know, that nothing would induce Mr Vassett to do so.'

'Oh! that I clearly understand,' snapped back Lady Hilda.

There ensued another pause, which Mr Pierson suddenly ended by unexpectedly throwing out this remark: 'I suppose your settlements are all right?'

Lady Hilda looked at him in amazement.

'What do you mean?' she asked.

'But of course they are,' continued Mr Pierson, as if answering some doubt raised by himself, 'considering the nature of the policy which has been pursued.'

'I do not understand. What are you talking about!' cried Lady Hilda. 'Of course he is bound to pay me six hundred a year.'

'I was not thinking of that,' answered Mr Pierson; but he refrained from saying what he was thinking of.

'I wish you would explain!' exclaimed Lady Hilda irritably. 'You and Mr Vassett are both so extremely fond of dark utterances.'

'I am not fond of dark utterances,' said Mr Pierson deprecatingly, 'but I am equally averse to giving unnecessary offence. It was foolish of me to speak; only, as the idea crossed my mind, I gave expression to it without due consideration.'

'Evidently you wish to drive me mad,' she returned. 'Tell me instantly what your idea was. I insist upon knowing.'

'You must not be angry with me, then,' he pleaded; 'I admit it was a very silly notion, but it came into my head without rhyme or reason. What I thought of was this: I wondered if you were quite independent of Mr Hicks, and then I knew of course you must be, or you would try to conciliate him a little.'

'I am independent of him so far as that wretched six hundred a year goes.'

'But was no other settlement made than that?'

'I don't know what you mean.'

'Was no settlement made before your marriage?'

'No; there ought to have been, of course, but there was not. I was dreadfully taken in, Mr Pierson.'

Mr Pierson thought she was not the only person taken in, but he refrained from saying so.

'Then,' he went on, 'if anything were to happen to Mr Hicks – supposing he died, in a word – is that six hundred a year so settled that you would continue to enjoy it as a widow?

'Certainly I should – I suppose –'

'You ought to be *sure*, Lady Hilda,' said Mr Pierson impressively.

'Why, the man couldn't let me starve.'

'Men have left their widows to starve; but you can't be serious, Lady Hilda. If the whole of your future had really been in Mr Hicks's power to make or mar, you would never have so mercilessly ridiculed him and his friends and relations.'

'I only wish I had the chance of getting what I have said about them all in this last book published.'

'Unless you are very certain as to your position I do not think you are wise, Lady Hilda. But, I beg your ladyship's pardon, I have no right to interfere in an affair which is certainly no business of mine.'

'It is only I who have to suffer,' she answered, in accents of the deepest sincerity; and then, like Miss Yarlow, she sat for a moment looking earnestly at the fire.

With at least equal earnestness Mr Pierson looked at her. 'The spell is working,' he thought.

'Heigho!' said her ladyship, at last rising and gathering her shawl in graceful folds round her still beautiful figure. 'Heigho! You men are all alike – you think of nothing except yourselves. Well, I have not done much good by coming out this wretched day.'

'It is a wretched day,' agreed Mr Pierson.

'Tell Mr Vassett I consider he has treated me shamefully, and that I shall advise every person I know never to have anything to do with him.'

'I am very sorry to hear you say so.'

'I do say so. Some day, perhaps, he will regret having let me slip out of his hands; but that will not do me much good.'

She lingered a little longer, only in order apparently to express the same idea again in different words, but at last she took her departure, and Mr Pierson rushed upstairs to give Mr Vassett a full account of the interview – full, that is to say, so far as the novel was concerned.

When Mr Vassett dined at five o'clock, he invited his reader to partake of that meal with him, and during its progress they talked a good deal about Lady Hilda and her book, and the pity it seemed so good a selling author should be lost to Craven Street.

Mr Vassett was in the act of asking Mr Pierson if he would take a little more beef, when Muggins appeared with a note, which he said a special messenger had brought from Lady Hilda Hicks. It was directed to the reader, and ran as follows:

I want to see you at once. Come without a moment's delay.

Mr Pierson did not wait for that second helping of meat.

'Finish your dinner,' remonstrated Mr Vassett; but Mr Pierson, with a queer smile, said Lady Hilda was of a great deal more importance than dinner.

'Now,' he went on, 'if I can get that book on your own terms, have I *carte blanche* to deal with her?

Mr Vassett did not like to be hurried, but he answered 'Yes,' only adding, 'don't compromise me.'

'You may be sure I shall not do that,' answered Mr Pierson, and went off joyously.

Before he parted from her ladyship that evening he had promised to get Mr Vassett to publish what Lady Hilda called 'a mutilated edition' of her novel, to effect a reconciliation with Mr Hicks, to so arrange matters that Royalty should be entertained by her ladyship instead of Miss Hicks, and to endeavour to procure a sum of money to rid the fair authoress of some pressing duns.

They separated on the best of terms.

'By-the-bye,' said her ladyship, after bidding Mr Pierson 'good night,' detaining him for a moment, 'what has become of that girl I saw at Craven Street one day?'

'I have not seen her for some time,' he answered.

'She has not set the Thames on fire, then?'

'Not yet,' amended Mr Pierson; 'not yet.'

Chapter V

MR LACERE

That was all. Glen bowed, and they became acquainted.

A minute previously and she had been unaware such a person existed; and now, quietly, and as a mere matter of course, he walked into her life to fashion and change the whole of it.

Looking at the stranger by the leaping firelight, she saw a tall, grave man, clad in deep mourning, who to her young eyes seemed quite elderly, and who, in fact, was nearly double her own age.

Certainly not the ideal of male beauty, as that beauty appears to a Miss in her teens; certainly not the hero of Glen's imagination, if an imagination constantly engaged in casting about for heroes of all sorts and aspects and degrees could be supposed to hold one especial image in its innermost recesses.

Like no man, however, she had ever seen before – and at that time Glen considered her experience almost exhaustive, for since the wide field of London was opened to view she had kept an attentive watch both on her own sex and the other, with the view of completely furnishing a gallery of types of character for future use or reference.

A pair of brown eyes glanced down on her with a kindly yet quizzical expression – an expression she learned later on indicated the tenderest heart that ever throbbed, joined to a sense of humour as subtle as it was quiet. Glen was deadly tired, but she did not appear to be so then. On the contrary, coming into the warm room out of the cold evening air, and meeting a visitor when she did not expect to find anyone except her father – the ready blood had rushed to her face – and at the moment she might have stood for a picture of girlish health and strength.

Such beauty as God had given her – and it was not much – happened at the moment to be well in evidence, but Mr Lacere's calm and inscrutable countenance expressed no admiration as he looked at Mr Westley's daughter. She did not know then, and she never knew afterwards, what his first impression of her was. Perhaps he could not have told himself, save that he saw the mould she was cast in differed from the pattern of the conventional young women he had hitherto been privileged to meet.

'Glen,' said Mr Westley, 'Mr Lacere will have some tea. I had a fall today when I was out, and he not merely assisted me to my feet again, but insisted I should sit for a while in his office, and actually accompanied me here. He did not wish to stop, but I told him you would not be long, and –'

'You had a fall, papa?' interrupted Glen a little anxiously, but less anxiously than Mr Lacere had expected. 'How did it happen? – where did you fall?'

'I do not know how it happened in the least,' answered Mr Westley. 'I found myself down and I found myself up, thanks to Mr Lacere's strong arm and ready help. As to the where, it was fortunately for me in Sise Lane, otherwise I might not have met with so good an example of a modern Samaritan.'

'I am very glad to have been of the slightest use,' said Mr Lacere. He had not spoken since Glen came into the room, and involuntarily she glanced at him once again.

A pleasant voice, but not the voice belonging to that of any hero in Glen's mental collection. A slight lisp, which, arising more from shyness than any natural impediment, disappeared as he grew more at home with his company; a smile not exactly sad, yet that had a look akin to sadness underlying it; something about the face, something in the tone, something in the expression, an indefinable something pervading the whole man which arrested Glen's attention and puzzled her!

But she had no prevision that the time would ever come, when even in memory's glass she should be unable to see that face because of a mist of blinding tears; that the days were to dawn when, in the morning and at noon and at evening, she could not speak aloud his name; when to hear that voice once more it would have seemed little to relinquish fame which had grown valueless, life which had lost its savour: no, she had no thought or knowledge or fear of the trouble she was going on to meet, and yet already she was standing in the shadows cast by that so far-distant future, then apparently as remote as the great dim awful eternity itself.

Meanwhile Mr Lacere was surprised she did not evince more concern about her father's fall. All his life he had lived amongst people who attached a considerable amount of importance to slight accidents and small ailments, who were extremely fond of the pastime which is well known as making mountains out of molehills, who bemoaned themselves over cut fingers and burnt hands, and treasured such accidents as things of great interest and value in the family archives, and he could not consequently understand an affection which was not fussy, and fidgety, and foolish. Any one of these three words he would have repudiated as utterly inapplicable to the tender feminine solicitude he had been accustomed to witness; but no other could express the useless and maudlin sympathy some persons are fond of showing on occasions of no importance, while they regard with non-comprehending wonder the wreck of a life – ruined hopes – a broken heart.

As for Glen, truth to tell, she did not attach much importance to the accident. When once her father said nothing was broken or dislocated or sprained, and that he felt no ill-effects from his fall, she dismissed the matter from her mind. In her own London experience – short though that experience might be considered by some – she had herself made personal trial of the hardness of the pavements too often to regard a tumble – many tumbles, indeed – as anything abnormal.

So far she had found the thoroughfares so slippery that to keep up – not to go down – seemed to her by far the most extraordinary achievement.

She was now getting a little accustomed to the 'greasy' stones and the coal-gratings, and the slippery basement lights; and the boys' slides and the orange peel, and the many other traps which make London to a newcomer a terror and a snare; but in her early days of metropolitan peregrination she had over and over again measured her length on the side paths, and come down on her knees ignominiously, and been greatly indebted for help to chance passers-by, and become an object of derision to the street Arabs, and been laughed at, and been forced to laugh at herself, till it had become an actual impossibility for her to conceive of anyone walking day after day and not at least occasionally 'coming to grief.'

'Let us have tea, dear, soon, will you?' said Mr Westley, who, being by this time pretty well accustomed to the usual lodging house delay in the apparently simple matter of boiling a kettle, felt it necessary to remind Glen they were not now at Ballyshane, where no one need ever have waited two minutes for hot water, where fires had no unhappy way of 'getting black,' and servants were not in the habit of turning sulky.

'Yes, papa, I will take off my bonnet at once,' and Glen turned and left the room and ran upstairs, just pausing in the passage to ask the small maid-of-all-work, who always looked as if she had been blackleading her face instead of the grate, if she could bring up the kettle.

'Yes, miss; I'll make it boil,' was the encouraging answer, an answer the exact meaning of which Glen knew so well, that meeting the landlady's daughter, who had just been bedizening herself, on the first landing, she said persuasively:

'Papa wants his tea so much. Miss Dingwell. *Do* you think we could have it soon?

'Law, yes!' replied Miss Dingwell, who 'bore no malice' to Glen, though that young person had refused many well-meant offers to 'take her about a bit.' 'I'll help to get it ready myself; and you'll like some sort of cake, won't you? And if I was you I'd send for a jar of marmalade and potted beef. Nothing but bread-and-butter does look so mean; and now your beau has come we must make as much as we can of him.'

Glen turned almost rigid with indignation.

'What are you talking about. Miss Dingwell?' she exclaimed. 'I never saw the gentleman before in my life; and if he does not like to eat bread-and-butter he must do without food, for I shall get nothing else for him' – after which ultimatum, and giving Miss Dingwell's too-ready tongue no time for retort, Glen entered her own room and banged the door.

'Well, I'm sure!' exclaimed Miss Dingwell, surveying her own person over her left shoulder with considerable approval; 'I dare say she won't change her dress, or smooth her hair, or anything,' in which surmise Miss Dingwell proved to be both right and wrong.

Glen did smooth her hair, but she did not change her dress. Her heart was very hot within her, for she did not find it easy to forgive or forget such a speech as that made by the fascinating young person who to the country girl's mind seemed the embodiment of everything most hateful and offensive in woman. She had heard of Miss Dingwell's lovers *ad nauseam* – in that house she had grown weary of the word 'man.' It was one of the trials of her then life that their landlady's daughter would persist in thinking she was even such a one as herself. Hitherto Glen had been happily exempt from experiences of this sort. But for this fact her mind might not have been left so free for the 'great work' with which it was occupied; still, just then, even as regarded her mighty enterprise of getting her writings placed before the British public, Glen felt singularly disheartened, and perhaps for this reason Miss Dingwell's blow struck home with double force. At that moment she felt as if doomed to those lodgings for life, as though she would never again be able to get a kettle boiled when she wanted it, or take herself and her belongings beyond reach of people who could scarcely speak, even with the best intentions, without rubbing her sensitive fur the wrong way.

If Miss Dingwell had simpered complacently at her own reflection in the glass, not so Glenarva Westley. Fagged and worn, and pale and haggard was the face presented for her consideration by a most unflattering mirror, and she went down into the parlour feeling as satisfied as Mr Kelly had done 'she was not much to look at.'

Mr Lacere and her father seemed getting on exceedingly well together, and as the tea-tray, on which Miss Dingwell had considerately placed the second best 'set,' generously adding 'ma's electro pot,' very shortly made its appearance, and the brass kettle followed in its wake with marvellous and unprecedented speed, the awkward pause which ensued upon Glen's appearance proved of short duration.

Mr Lacere ate bread-and-butter as if he liked it, and the three, who were soon talking, might have known each other for years, so frank and unembarrassed was their conversation.

Just at first Glen felt the unwonted splendour of Mrs Dingwell's second-best set and the glitter of that electro-plated teapot weigh down her soul; but she soon took comfort from the reflection that Mr Lacere could not possibly be acquainted with the pattern of the delft deemed good enough for the everyday use of Mrs Dingwell's 'parlours,' while his intimacy with the battered Britannia-metal pot was of a similarly negative description; and her mind being set at rest on these points, she was able to lend an attentive ear to what her father and his visitor were saying – nay, even after a time to join in the talk herself.

'Mr Lacere tells me, Glen,' observed Mr Westley, after he had asked his daughter for another cup of tea, 'that we are unwise to remain here – that it is not at all a healthy neighbourhood.'

'Quite the contrary,' said Mr Lacere.

'Why, I thought,' exclaimed Glen simply, 'that all parts of London were alike. I don't mean as regards fashion, of course,' she went on, as both gentlemen laughed a little at the innocence of her remark.

'Where you are living now,' explained Mr Lacere, 'was once all a swamp, or rather a lake. You might as well be at the bottom of a well.'

'Oh!' said Glen, not exactly understanding all the pains and penalties attaching to such a position. At Ballyshane people had never thought about healthy or unhealthy localities. Their greatest anxiety was to keep themselves from being blown away by the wild gales which swept down upon them from the Atlantic. A house in a hollow was considered a residence to be desired; and those few trees, which Londoners seem never happy save when they are lopping or grubbing up, were esteemed, in a neighbourhood where it was difficult to get anything except grass as hard as wire to grow, possessions as precious as springs in the desert.

Not all the refuse fish left on the beach to rot, not all the dirt and squalor of some of the poor homes, was able to breed a pestilence. The kindly sea flowed over the sands, and deodorised them twice a day; and the keen salt breezes carried the poisonous smells far inland from the wretched huts down by the Shane, which were the despair of Mr Beattie, and a matter of shame to many a sturdy fisherman and his cleanly decent wife.

At that time of the world's history, on the iron-bound, wave-beaten, tempest-tossed coast, so far remote from England and 'civilisation,' sanitary arrangements did not possess much interest for a thin, widely scattered population, who had enough to do to earn their daily bread without troubling themselves concerning devices that might add a few years to the length of lives passed in looking death straight in the face – in wresting food for wives and children, indeed, out of its very jaws. No latter-day Solomon had then propounded the theory that by a judicious attention to natural laws people might be enabled to live almost for ever, and for this and other reasons it had not occurred either to Mr Westley or his daughter that the lodgings they had found were not quite as good as any lodgings they were likely to find at the price they could afford to pay for them.

But now Mr Lacere told them of localities far pleasanter and no dearer. He seemed to know London by heart – indeed, he seemed to understand something about every subject Mr Westley touched on.

Looking at their visitor while he was answering a question addressed to him by her father, Glen wondered vaguely, first, whether he was in mourning for his wife; and second, if just by chance he knew anything concerning the highways and byways of literature.

A few minutes later she was enlightened, not indeed concerning his supposed widowhood, but as regarded authorship. Mr Westley, it appeared, had mentioned to him before she came in that 'his daughter wrote a little and wished to get into print.' Now Mr Lacere reverted to this matter, and said he was afraid she must find 'going about among the publishers very discouraging work.'

Glen could have discoursed to some purpose on this text, but she forebore. She was getting to feel very doubtful as to whether she ought ever to have intruded into a publisher's office. She was losing, she had lost heart altogether. She did not now believe in herself or her fitness to become an author. She had that day been on the pleasing errand of recovering her 'rejected addresses' from the hands of various most unlikely persons, with whom, in her determination to try 'every-body,' it seemed to the girl in her young wisdom well to leave them.

From place to place she trudged valiantly; taking the familiar 'No' with appar-ently stoical indifference, till at last across one counter a manuscript on which many bright hopes had once been built was handed back to her without a word. Her heart was full, and the trouble may have been evident in her face. At all events she fancied the man looked sorry, and that he did not speak because he knew of no word likely to prove of comfort.

Afterwards Glen never could exactly remember how she got out of the office, which was situated on the first floor of a great building in a back lane. She had reached it by means of a wide staircase and a wide landing, and now there was not a creature coming up or going down, and she felt so fairly 'beaten' – no other word in the language fully expresses the utter weariness which seemed to oppress both soul and body – that, cowering on one of the broad easy steps, she covered her face with her hands, and cried as if her heart would break, after which exercise she arose refreshed, and went once more out into the street to pursue her dreary task.

But Glen said nothing about this experience then or for many a year afterwards, and in answer to Mr Lacere's remark, only replied:

'It does seem very difficult to get a manuscript accepted, but I suppose all authors have to go through the same ordeal.'

Had Mr Lacere spoken his mind at that moment, there can be little doubt he would have said Miss Westley had better dismiss all thoughts of authorship from her mind. The girl did not look as if the making of a writer was in her – no fire of genius burnt in her eyes – her expression was not that of a person so full of imagination that Nature had deemed well to set her lot apart from the realities of life. In no solitary respect did Glenarva Westley fulfil any of the traditional ideas people have agreed to accept as typifying the possession of talent – manner, voice, appearance seemed more fitted to the quiet arena of home existence than the mad fight and the fierce Struggle for Fame. It was hard upon Glenarva that no human being ever believed she was the right person in the right place. Not when she was plodding amongst the London publishers – not when she was making a little money – not when she had gained a great reputation – not when the time came no one could deny she had achieved more than nine hundred and ninety-nine women out of a thousand ever do achieve – no, not even then did any friend, or relation, or stranger realise it was really Glenarva who had won success, and not some quite independent power associated with her in an unaccountable and uncanny sort of alliance.

Mr Kelly had thought nothing of her personal appearance. Mr Lacere, certainly, did not regard Glenarva as a shrine in which it seemed particularly probable genius had chosen to take up an abode. He saw before him a slight, young, underfed-looking girl, who appeared to him deficient in physique, and still more deficient in will. No two more incompetent individuals, he conceived, had ever come to London on a wild-goose chase than Miss Westley and her father. Had he heard the words uttered by the steward of the Morecambe steamer, 'God help them; they are no better nor a couple of children,' he would have echoed them cordially.

But he felt heartily sorry for the poor gentleman and his daughter. He knew what a lonely wilderness London must seem to them, and he did not believe it would be a true kindness to disillusion the girl at once.

She would find in time she had no true mission to become a writer; he would not cross her whim, he would not say what he thought about the absurdity of her writing. He would do what he could to help her.

'Yes,' he said, 'all young authors find publishers a little impracticable at first, but it is a mere question of time. Sooner or later genius must obtain a hearing.'

'Ah! but it is such a long time,' exclaimed Glen, with involuntary sadness, 'and it is generally so much later than sooner.'

'Why,' exclaimed Mr Lacere, 'you are surely not beginning to despair yet! You have not, I think, been in London six months!'

'No,' said Mr Westley, answering for his daughter, who did not seem inclined to do so for herself; 'we only left Ireland in October, and of course, as you observe, she has all her life before her in which to make her mark.'

Mr Lacere had not adventured on any observation of the sort, but, understanding perfectly that Glenarva's father was merely putting into his visitor's mouth the idea with which he sought to comfort and reassure himself, he allowed the utterance to pass unnoticed, and said to the girl, kindly:

'Very probably that time seems like six years to you.'

'It seems a long time,' agreed Glenarva, but she added no other syllable of explanation; she did not speak of the events, persons, disappointments, bodily weariness, actual physical hardships, which had caused the period of their residence in London to lengthen itself out so unduly.

Looks, however, occasionally can talk more eloquently than tongues; and Mr Lacere gathered from the expression of Glenarva's face at that moment some knowledge of what the girl never could have spoken in words.

It then occurred to him to ask her if she had seen all the sights, and which of them impressed her most.

'I have not seen any of them,' she answered, 'except Westminster Abbey and St Paul's. We generally go to service at the Abbey on Sunday afternoons.'

'But do you not think it would prove an agreeable change if you were to visit a few, at all events, of the places strangers generally go to see?'

Glen did not seem to know. She said sightseeing would take up a great deal of time, and, she might have added, money also, only she was not likely to bring that question on the *tapis*.

'Have you been to any of the theatres?' persisted Mr Lacere, talking to these people as he would have talked to those amongst whom his previous lot had chanced to be cast.

'No,' answered the girl; 'papa does not care for places of amusement, and neither do I.'

And Glen looked as if she and her father were persons who, having run the whole round of innocent dissipation and exhausted its pleasures, had resolved to settle down for ever to a quiet, humdrum, Darby and Joan sort of life.

In spite of himself, Mr Lacere smiled. He could not help it.

'And so,' he went on, 'since your arrival in London you have done nothing except try to make an impression upon the publishers, who are so stony-hearted and so difficult to impress?

'I think I have been to them all,' answered Glenarva, 'and it has taken me a long time, because,' she added apologetically, 'places are so far apart in London.'

'They are, but you find the omnibuses very convenient.'

'I scarcely ever go in one,' said the girl. 'I always walk.'

'Always walk! Why, you must get very tired.'

'I should not get tired if the streets were not so slippery,' she replied.

'My daughter is a capital walker,' explained Mr Westley.

'Yes. We hadn't many omnibuses at Ballyshane,' Glen said, with a touch of merriment Mr Lacere had not heard in her voice previously; and then she went on to tell him about Ballyshane – about its cliffs and its bogs, and its magnificent views, and its loneliness, and the wild tempests that washed the salt spray so far inland, and the waves rippling in on the shore when the weather was fine and calm, and the crested billows that came thundering in from the Atlantic in the stormy winter-time, billows pursued by other billows that raced over the sunken rocks, and beat themselves madly to death against the great headlands that frowned above the ocean; and Mr Lacere said he should like to see that grand desolate coast, and Glenarva thought she would too – but she did not say so. She sat silent while Mr Westley, taking up her parable, spoke of the geological formation of that part of Ireland, and told Mr Lacere many things concerning the Giants' Causeway, Fairhead, and Carrick-a-rede, and the Cushendall Caves, and the Salmon Leaps at Coleraine, which were strange to that gentleman, and impressed him with the same sense of unreality as a fairy-tale might have done.

And all the time Glenarva was recalling sadly the dream she had dreamed – looking out over the sea, and wandering across the cliffs, and traversing the road leading to Artinglass, and writing in her bedroom, with the roses peeping in at the window to see what she was doing, or tapping against the glass to win her out into the sunshine flooding the whole landscape with a glamour of golden light.

Then suddenly the past faded away utterly, and she was back in dreary, shabby London lodgings: all her hopes as dead as last year's roses, the sunshine gone, stern reality around instead of a golden glamour, and Mr Lacere looking at her intently.

'I think,' he said gently, reverting to the one subject which at that time was of paramount interest to Glenarva, 'you are expending your strength uselessly in going about among all the publishers. A vast number of them can never be of the slightest benefit to you. Why not confine yourself to a few good houses?'

'What is the use,' asked the girl, 'when they will not read what I take them?'

'Why not try to write something they will read?'

'I do not exactly understand what you mean,' said Glen.

'What I mean is this,' answered her new friend, 'that writing, like everything else in the world, requires pains and practice. I see you have been at work at some pretty embroidery –' he suddenly added, with all a man's deep appreciation of that purely feminine art.

'Glen is very fond of work,' said Glen's father; and, indeed, this statement was true in its widest sense.

At that time, whatever her hands found to do the girl did with all her might. Idleness seemed to her then an impossible condition of existence. She would rather have hemmed dusters for Mrs Dingwell than done nothing; and as she found the small amount of mending required by her own and her father's wardrobe insufficient to occupy her leisure-time, now she found writing so difficult as to be impossible, she had bought some designs stamped in blue outlines on white muslin, and was embroidering herself a pair of cuffs and a collar.

'Well, go back to the time when you first began to learn to sew,' said Mr Lacere, with that look in his eyes that had already become familiar to Glen. 'You could not have filled in all this delicate tracery of leaf, and stem, and flower then;' and he took the fragile scrap of work in his hand almost tenderly as he spoke, and looked at it as he was never likely to look at any manuscript with which she might present him.

'No, indeed,' said Glen, laughing in spite of herself. 'I remember quite well my first essay in that line. It was made with a pin, to which my nurse securely tied a piece of strong thread; and I had for material a strip of flannel, and each time I dragged the pin through the flannel I made a hole as large as that,' and she touched one in the collar – called, as Mr Lacere heard from her subsequently, a 'wheel.'

'Yet now see what you can do,' he remarked, looking at the elaborate pattern worked in by Glen's fine needle. 'And as regards your writing,' he went on, 'it may be that some day hereafter you will think of your present efforts as you do of the strip of flannel disfigured with holes. I have known many beginners, and the mistake they seem to make is that they imagine writing comes by inspiration. Of course, unless a person has a certain aptitude – or genius, if you prefer the word – no amount of time and patience can enable him to produce a book worth reading; but I do not believe any genius, however great it may be, will ever carry a man to success without the help of dogged perseverance and determined plodding on his own part.'

'But I have plodded, and have persevered,' pleaded Glen, with almost tearful earnestness.

'For how long? For a few weeks?' suggested Mr Lacere.

'No; for years, and years, and years.'

'You must have begun, then, before you could walk, I should think.'

'She did begin very early,' interposed Mr Westley; 'and I do not see at all, Glen, why you should feel so dissatisfied with your success. I am sure since you came to London you have had a vast amount of encouragement.'

'In words, papa.'

'What do the publishers say to you, Miss Westley?' inquired Mr Lacere, determined to obtain some explicit answer.

'Well, a few of them say I can write,' answered Glenarva, maintaining a wise silence concerning the many who said nothing at all; 'but no one I have met with as yet will really read a manuscript. I have only written Irish stories, and they want English.'

'Then why do you not write English stories for them?' naturally inquired Mr Lacere.

Glen did not reply, so her father said:

'I fancy she has not felt much inclined for writing lately.'

'No?' interrogated Mr Lacere, with a sympathetic expression of countenance, but in reality pleased to hear this. There never yet lived a wise man who wished women to turn artists, or actresses, or authors; and Mr Lacere, theoretically at least, was a wise man. By some subtle intuition he knew Glen would be far happier if she never gained a hearing – if she laid aside her manuscripts as a child lays aside its toys which have pleased it for a while, and betook herself to the business of life, as such business usually presents itself to her sex – taking her pleasure while she could, mixing with other young people, going to places of amusement; then being loved and loving; then marrying and ruling her husband's household.

Mentally he went through all this catalogue of recreations and duties while Mr Westley was saying:

'She has not been quite well lately. I am beginning to think, with you, this neighbourhood does not suit either of us.'

'It is most depressing,' observed Mr Lacere. 'I am sure you ought not to remain in it,' and he made this remark with such thorough conviction, that when shortly afterwards he rose to go Mr Westley said:

'We will take your advice and look out for other lodgings at once.'

'But you will let me know where you decide to settle,' answered Mr Lacere quickly. 'I may be able to prove of some assistance to your daughter.'

'I shall certainly keep you informed of our address, since you are so good as to wish to have it;' and then the three shook hands cordially, and quite like old acquaintances, and when the door closed behind their visitor Mr Westley said:

'What a kind man, Glen! I really shall begin to consider that a most fortunate fall of mine which brought me into contact with him,' but Glenarva did not answer. She was thinking at that moment of Mr Lacere less as a pleasant acquaintance than as a person who might be able to help forward her great work.

'We will at once, dear, begin looking out for different lodgings,' went on Mr Westley, not noticing his daughter's silence. She woke up as though out of a dream. 'If you remember, papa, I told you a little time ago there were some rooms advertised near Russell Square I thought seemed cheap; but you fancied nothing we could live in was likely to be had in that neighbourhood at a moderate price.'

'But I find London has changed since I knew anything about it,' he answered. 'What a pity we did not inquire concerning them at the time.'

'I kept the address,' she said.

'Then, Glen, you had better go and see what the rooms are like tomorrow.'

'Very well, papa,' she answered, more than willing to take all the trouble she could off his hands, and quite unconscious of what her father's growing disposition to leave such burdens for her to carry really meant. Looking back afterwards she understood, and thanked God earnestly her strength had been great and her spirit willing; that wind or weather, fog, frost, or snow never kept her within doors when there existed any need for her to be out; that it was she who usually faced the stinging cold of that cruel winter, and who saw to everything a girl might, and to many things most girls never do.

Next day she came back radiant, looking as Mr Westley had not seen her look since they left Ballyshane. The rooms were still vacant, and they were such pleasant, cosy rooms, but very high up – two on the second floor and one on the third. The people wanted to let them to persons who would not require much attendance, 'so if we go there,' proceeded Glen, 'we shall not have another Miss Dingwell dancing in and out all day long.' For indeed that young lady was somewhat apt to introduce her presence uninvited and unwished-for, and she had a knack of making a fresh scuttleful of coals an excuse for a long conversation, and the removal of the tea-tray an opportunity for gossip, which wore the thread of Glen's patience almost to its last strand.

After some hesitation Mr Westley decided to take the rooms of which his daughter spoke so highly, and though the ground was covered with snow and the sky was black and lowering with the promise of more, they very shortly transported themselves and their belongings to that part of London called the Bloomsbury district, where for the first time Glen began really to enjoy her metropolitan experiences, and to think some pleasure might be extracted from life, even in a great town 'where one knew nobody.'

Ere long she commenced writing again with something of the frenzy and fervour of old. She got through an enormous amount of work – such as it was – in the dull, dark days of that most dreary winter. Her spirits revived. She could still imagine and record her imaginings. She had a story which was perfectly true to tell, and she told it on page after page of blotted foolscap. It was a story of sin and sorrow and injustice, or what seemed to her injustice. There had been a time when she would have hesitated to present it in any form to the public, but she had left Ballyshane now far behind her on the road of life; no one there knew she wrote; she could utilise her experiences without the fear of giving offence.

She brought all her Irish characters over to England, and planted them on a wild portion of the Yorkshire coast. She knew nothing in the world about the coast she described, but that was a matter of detail which troubled Glen as little in those days as it seems to trouble many authors in these. Had anyone hinted that her English peasants were not true to Nature, and her lords and ladies creations almost as impossible, she would not have believed the statement; but no one did hint anything of the sort, for which reason Glen's latest barque glided swiftly over the sea of fiction, leaving a trail of inky paper behind it, and the girl pressed hopefully onward, feeling quite satisfied she was at length producing something the world would not willingly let die.

Poor Glen! In the whole of London I doubt if there was then a happier girl than she who from that second floor beheld in fancy the golden gates of Fame opening to admit her.

She had secured a publisher – found a man at last who said if she liked to write him a good novel of English life he would be at the expense of bringing it out; and he said more also, namely, that he would give her thirty pounds for another if her first book succeeded as he believed it would.

He was a gentleman who seemed to have less to do than any person she had yet come across in London; but he had published a great many books, and known a great many authors, and over the fire in his inner office the pair held many long and delightful conversations.

He told her the amount he had paid this person and that; what a *Times* review was worth; how novel-publishing was going to the dogs; wondered what the end of it all would prove; waxed confidential concerning his own domestic affairs; and one day when Glen, having contrived to cut her hand badly, appeared with it bandaged and in a sling, advised her as to her treatment of the wound with an earnestness he could scarcely have surpassed had her management of an intricate and exciting plot been the theme.

But, notwithstanding the friendly relations thus established between them, the ungrateful young author decided she would not give him that wonderful book with which she meant to astonish the British public.

In the course of her peregrinations amongst all sorts and conditions of men engaged in the book trade, she found out that though the individual in question was supposed to have 'made a lot of money' by 'working the libraries' – an utterance which seemed Delphic in its obscurity to the girl's then unenlightened mind – he was not by any means at the 'top of the tree.'

'Pedland is well enough in his way, but he does not stand like Hurst and Blackett, or Chapman and Hall, or the other great guns,' explained one uncommonly common publisher in the Row, while the next time she saw her new friend she was privileged to hear from him what he thought of the 'great guns.' Had Glen only availed herself fully of the educational advantages offered to her at that time concerning the ways of publishers, she might have been qualified to write an exhaustive treatise on the race; but the girl was too much taken up with her own doings to pay the attention she ought to have done to the doings of other people.

A confused notion that she was 'getting on' somehow; that by some unintelligible means she was pushing herself to the front, was all she seemed thoroughly to grasp. Mr Lacere told her she was doing too much, but his words of wisdom fell on heedless ears.

In those days Glen thought nothing of writing a novel. She turned one out in a month for the gentleman who 'worked the libraries.' She herself thought of it as 'quite good enough,' and really it was not so bad.

But, good or bad, Mr Pedland seemed no more ready to read her manuscript when completed than anybody else. He said he 'had not time; that the season was past; that he would attend to her presently; that she would have to take her turn; that really the number of authors who wrote remarkably well was getting so great he could not imagine how their books were ever to be published; that the libraries were overstocked; that he could get novels with well-known names on the title page for a song, a mere song; that he could remember the time when he was glad to pay so-and-so a hundred pounds down for any manuscript he liked to bring, and now,' finished this modern Jeremiah, 'I should think twice before I gave him a hundred shillings.'

He told her rival houses were ruining the trade, 'cutting each other's throats,' and then, having depressed her spirits to zero, he said if she looked in again in a few weeks' time he might be able to talk to her.

But Glen was not exactly made of the stuff to bear this sort of thing with equanimity.

She said she would not look in again in a few weeks' time, and that if he had not time to read her manuscript she should like to take it back with her.

Then he promised to look at it, and failed to do so. He always found some good reason for escaping from his duties – his wife had been ill, or he had been ill himself; or he was called suddenly out of town; or a man who owed him a heavy account had gone into the *Gazette*, and he was forced to rush off to the Land's End in order to see if a dividend of a penny in the pound could be rescued out of the wreck.

He provoked Glen, and amused her too. In the after-times she always retained a certain grateful memory of that snug old publishing establishment, where the office was so quiet, and the fire so large, and the easy-chairs so comfortable, and where she heard so much, true and false, concerning the inner life of literature, and the dealings of printers, and publishers, and authors, and editors. In spite even of herself she was learning a great deal, and she never returned to those second-floor lodgings without a budget of news ready to be unfolded for her father's benefit.

One afternoon in the early spring, when barrows filled with flowers were just beginning to appear in the streets, when the winter weather seemed gone, and the snow had at last disappeared, and a blue sky stretched overhead, and the sun shone occasionally for half an hour or so at a time, Glen was making her way back from the west when she ran up against Mr Pierson, who, greeting her with the greatest cordiality, remarked she was quite a stranger in Craven Street.

'You have deserted us totally,' he said. 'Why don't you come and see Mr Vassett?

'Mr Vassett does not want to see me,' Glen answered, a little saucily.

'Oh! but he does,' declared Mr Pierson, with that utter disregard of truth which was one of his distinguishing qualities. 'We were talking about you only the other day, and wondering what had become of you. Now that the fine weather is here, it is a thousand pities you should not call and have a talk with Vassett. You had better look in as soon as you can; tomorrow if you like. He is in very good twist now, though I suppose you don't know what I mean by that.'

'Oh yes, I do,' said Glen, who had not grown up on terms of familiar intimacy with six graceless boys for nothing.

'Well, then, step round tomorrow, and tell us what you have been about for so long.'

Glen laughed, and said she would, and as she pursued her onward way felt more and more satisfied she was getting 'well to the front.'

Chapter VI

STRANDED

IT HAS BEEN PREVIOUSLY HINTED that when Mr Westley arrived in England he brought with him across the Channel a project for improving his worldly condition, but with the reticence which was so marked a feature in his character he did not consider it necessary to communicate his idea to Glen.

Of himself he never would have summoned up enough energy to travel to London with it; but as his daughter wished to put her fortunes to the test at the headquarters of literature, and as Mr Merritt urged him strongly to leave Ireland, and advanced enough money for the purpose, Mr Westley arrived in Babylon as has been chronicled; and, stimulated perhaps by the rush and movement all around, and by a host of olden memories associated with his pleasant youth, the poor gentleman donned the best suit he had in his possession, and started off one day to Bolton Row, Mayfair, where resided the former friend to whom he had once been mentor and companion, and who had since those days become Marquis of Thanet.

It was not till he stood on the very doorstep that a doubt of how he might be received crossed Mr Westley's mind, but even this passing cloud soon disappeared from his sky; he had been only after a fashion a dependent then, and he was going to ask for nothing save employment now. He had been rich and considered since he parted with Lord Charles; but all the prosperity, and the greatness, and the ruin wrought by his own folly, and the gradual descent into the valley of poverty, were matters quite independent of the life which had been his when he mixed intimately with lords and ladies, and the door of the house before which he now stood was opened wide for him to enter as a matter of course.

He had a tale to tell, a petition to prefer. He did not much doubt the result. Too many kindnesses had been showered upon him in the past to permit him to fear repulse or coldness now. All he regretted was not having sooner thought of so excellent a plan for improving his prospects. He had mooned away years in idleness and vain regrets when he might have been making money for his child. Well, it was late in the day, certainly, but better late than never; and so with a courage which had in it no trace of assurance, Mr Westley knocked at the once familiar door.

His knock was answered by a servant out of livery, who said his lordship was not in, and he did not exactly know any hour when he could certainly be found. His lordship was merely in town for a few days, en route from Rome to Brushwood, and was very rarely to be found at Bolton Row. No, he did not think he could be met with at his club; but 'if you will leave your name, sir,' he added, with a certain amount of doubt and hesitation Mr Westley did not at the moment understand, and which vexed him unreasonably in consequence.

'I will write to his lordship,' he said, taking out his card and giving it to the man, who exclaimed with a certain bewildered wonderment, 'Mr Westley! It is not, surely – and yet I thought, sir, there was something about you I remembered.'

'Why, are you Harling?' asked Mr Westley. 'How you are changed! You were but a mere stripling when I saw you last.'

'Yes, sir; won't you walk in? Pray do. His lordship may return presently, though we never know when to expect him. He would be sorry, I am sure, to miss seeing you. Yes, sir, as you observe, it is many years since that day at Nice when the news came for you to go to Ireland.'

Many years indeed, yet as he looked once more round the well-remembered room, they seemed to Mr Westley but as few and evil as those of his pilgrimage appeared to the patriarch of old.

'The late Marquis often talked about you, sir, and said over and over again if ever he went to Dublin he would try and get up to your place in the north.'

'Which I have lost and left for ever, Harling,' answered Mr Westley. It was not his nature to trade upon the feelings of his fellows and seek for sympathy in his misfortunes; but neither could he pose as a man still possessed of fortune before this servant, who knew that when they last parted he left a life of obscurity in order to take up a position amongst those who, by virtue both of birth and wealth, rank amongst the Upper Ten.

'Indeed, sir; I am very sorry to hear you say so. I do not think the late Marquis knew anything about that, or he would have mentioned it to me; for he often spoke about you, he did indeed.'

'Harling,' said Mr Westley, looking at the man with sudden anxiety, 'whom do you mean when you talk about the "late" Marquis? surely not –'

'Lord Charles? Yes, indeed, sir; he died quite suddenly. Is it possible you have not heard?'

Mr Westley stopped the speaker with a gesture of grief and dismay. Dead! Then all his hopes were dead too, and yet at that moment it was not of himself he was thinking; it was of the frank, generous nobleman stricken down in his prime, of the face he remembered flushed with boyish health, and the frame full of youthful strength now cold and quiet in death.

'You did not notice the hatchment, then, sir?' asked Harling, after a pause.

'No; I walked on this side of the way. And the present Marquis is?'

'His brother – Lord Louis, sir, you remember. The late Marquis left no children. But you will wait a few minutes longer, Mr Westley, will you not? I am sure his lordship would like to see you.'

'No, oh no, thank you. I did not know, or I should not have intruded. Tell the Marquis how grieved I am to hear of his loss, and –'

'Here is his lordship,' interrupted Harling, and he hurried away to inform the new Marquis that Mr Westley was in the library, while Mr Westley himself stood in the middle of the room irresolute, not liking to go into the hall for fear of encountering a person who perhaps might not wish to see him, and liking almost less to remain, lest it should seem as though he did not mean to leave without compelling an interview.

But his doubts were next moment laid at rest by the Marquis himself, who, dressed in the deepest mourning, entered the apartment, and, addressing him most cordially, said how heartily sorry he was his brother was not alive to greet his old friend.

They had always loved each other tenderly, those two sons of the old Marquis, and it seemed a comfort to the one that was left to talk about the dead man to a person who had formerly been in daily and familiar companionship with him.

'Will you come and dine here quietly?' asked the Marquis. 'I am only in town on my way to Brushwood, and everything is in confusion – it was so sudden, so unexpected, poor fellow; but still, if you can spare an hour or two –'

Mr Westley hastened to excuse himself as the other paused, and then in a few sentences he told why he had come, and what he had wanted to ask.

'Perhaps,' he added hesitatingly, 'you might hear of something, and –'

'You may feel quite sure I shall do all that lies in my power to forward your wishes,' said the Marquis. 'Leave me your address, and should any idea occur to my mind before I see you again I will write at once. Come to dinner, though. We shall be quite alone. No? Well, then, if it must be so, goodbye for the present. I shall think over what you have told me, and consider the best way to serve your interests.'

Time is one quantity to those who wait, and quite another to those who are not waiting. The days and the weeks and the months which slipped by after Mr Westley's visit to Bolton Row may not have seemed long in passing to the new Marquis, who had just succeeded to a great property, who had to see lawyers and stewards and friends and relations, and whose time was occupied from morning till night by the claims of Society and the thousand details to which he was forced to give his attention; but to the ruined gentleman in narrow lodgings, with most limited means, with poor health, without society or occupation, or anything pleasant to reflect upon in the present or to look forward to in the future – how did that period appear?

Ah! not Glen herself waiting for the 'No' she said certainly must come, but which for all that she did not expect, experienced a greater trouble and sickness at her heart than her father, who kept his disappointment to himself, and felt he was forgotten by fortune and forsaken by man.

It was the last straw his feeble hand strove to clutch. He knew he could do nothing more. He could not write and remind Lord Thanet of his promise; it was impossible for him to go and knock again at the once familiar door, and ask if the Marquis had heard of anything to suit him.

There are persons who can lie down and die and utter no complaint, or, sitting alone beside a fireless hearth, will starve and make no sign. Mr Westley was one of these. For his daughter's sake he, a shipwrecked castaway on the world's wide ocean, hoisted that one feeble signal of distress; but he could not continue holding out the flag. As help failed to come to him he let this last hope drop from his nerveless fingers, and resigned himself to the conviction that if anything were to be done for Glen, it must be done by Glen herself.

The girl could not imagine why her father was so anxious she should punctually fulfil the promise she had made Mr Pierson.

Somehow she was not very desirous of keeping her appointment in Craven Street, and said that after all she did not think it was worthwhile wasting the time it would take to walk there.

'I am quite certain Mr Vassett will not look at any one of my manuscripts,' she declared; but Mr Westley told her she could not tell what the publisher might do unless she asked him.

'I thought him most kind and courteous,' said Mr Westley, hearing which, Glen laughingly suggested he should go in her place.

'You can go and talk to him, papa,' she observed, but her father did not see the beauty of this proposition.

He had never been able to understand how Glen could walk into shops and offices and ask to see editors and publishers. He supposed, as she did not seem to suffer either anguish or shame, there was nothing wrong in her going about as she did; but he felt she must possess or lack some quality which in his own nature was either non-existent or else developed to an undue excess.

Poor Mr Westley! He had never attempted to analyse any character; not even his own. And yet sometimes, as he noted his daughter's tireless energy and her dogged industry, the idea occurred to him that, regarded as a soldier in the battle of life, he was but a poor feeble creature, and that the sensitiveness which made him shrink from the noise and the bustle, the clang of tongues and the call to arms, was less a virtue than a vice.

What had his pride – which after all was not an unworthy or an ignoble or a sinful pride – done for him? Now he was beginning dimly to comprehend that even when the worst came – when he lost money and lands and home he might to a certain extent have retrieved his error had he, instead of avoiding his fellows and sinking into a melancholy recluse, turned a brave face to the world, tried if there was not something still left his hand could find to do, and determined, in the face of blackest fortune, to 'quit himself like a man.'

He could not understand his daughter, but dimly he was coming to the comprehension, that what she found possible he ought to have found possible also.

There is nothing much more sad or pitiful than this awakening in age to the knowledge of a defect possible only for youth to remedy. When the blood is growing cold and the pulse slow, and the limbs feeble, and the heart weary, how shall we take up a burden we thought too heavy to carry in the noontide of our strength, and bear it triumphantly home? At the eleventh hour it is possible for a man to repent, but it is as a rule impossible for him to repair the evil he has wrought.

The day of work is behind him – the night of death, when no man can work, before; and what shall he who has permitted all the long hours of light to glide away unimproved do in those brief minutes when the evening gloom is darkening down apace, and the long shadows cast from that land which to us is all mystery, are lying athwart the path his laggard feet must tread? God! If it might only be as some modern divines tell us, that in the world where we are lonely journeying 'we may undo much that we have done here wrongly; do again with perfect grace that which we have done imperfectly; become what we have aimed and wished to be; achieve what we have longed to achieve; attain the wisdom, the gifts, and powers to which we have aspired;' who is there that would not long to leave the old and begin the new, and to enter on that life which, as Dickens, apparently inspired by the same idea, says, 'sets this one right'!

As is not unusual in cases where men have left their own noontide hours unimproved, Mr Westley grew day by day more anxious that his daughter, on whom the hopeful glory of morning still shone in all its brightness, should make the most of her opportunities.

He did not talk to her of fame. Indeed, the idea of Glen, his Glen, ever making for herself a name and a position seemed to him inconceivable. As we know, 'a man is not without honour save in his own country and amongst his own people,' and there are very good reasons for this. It is hard to realise that which has been with us in common achieving something uncommon; the child we have taught to walk, climbing to heights our feet cannot scale; the girl we have hushed to rest wandering out of the sweet home life to be greeted by the world's applause! After all, it is only what we see we really believe, and therefore when before our eyes the boy stands on the dizzy height and the girl smiles back to us through happy tears, with the laurel crown resting on the sunny tresses of yore, we come dimly to understand there was something in them we wot not of. We cannot begin our day with a forecast of its end; and if we were wise – which we are not, any one of us – we should be able to comprehend that, though we may bend over a child in its cradle, it is not given to us to know the bed in which it will lie when life's long dream is over. It may be Westminster Abbey, a felon's grave, a hundred fathoms of water, or the shallow hole hurriedly dug on the field of battle where he gave up his life for duty and his country!

So to come back. Though Mr Westley hoped and believed Glen would make a few pounds a year by her pen – which implement he spoke of as he might her needle – he never really thought, save for a few wild moments, his daughter had it in her to do great things.

He saw her writing, about which she set in a prosaic, domestic sort of way that perplexed him exceedingly. If Mr Westley wished to write an important letter, the decks had to be cleared for the purpose. It was while Glen was out of the way he indited those epistles to his lawyer which that gentleman regarded, and not without reason, as the embodiments of so much time and labour lost. If, on the contrary, Glen decided to commence a quite new novel, which perhaps she did after five minutes' consideration, she put on her bonnet, went out and bought a few quires of foolscap, set to work stitching the pages together into dozens, and began.

Yes, then and there, with an old pen, the top of which she had bitten almost through when struggling with the intricacies of an involved sentence, or the difficulties of a farfetched comparison. Writing seemed no trouble to her at that period, and an outsider might well be excused the argument that what cost so little could not be worth much.

Ah! the day of her travail was then afar off – the hour when, in sorrow and in agony, she produced a living, breathing book; something with the imprint of God upon it, a coin stamped with the superscription of that mint which sends nothing into circulation except the gold of genius.

Nevertheless, Mr Westley believed she would get on; perhaps he was afraid to think of the depths of poverty she might have to sound otherwise – but that is beside the question.

'Take that last tale of yours, dear, down with you to Mr Vassett,' he said. 'Who knows what may happen?'

'I know, papa,' she answered. 'He will not look at it.'

'Still, I would take it, dear. You believe yourself it is very good, don't you?'

'What do you believe, papa?' she asked, with a smile which told her own opinion of the work.

'Well, Glen, I can't say I profess to be a judge, yet I think it ought to be liked. To tell the truth, however, it seems to me you never have surpassed, and you never will surpass, that chapter you wrote at Ballyshane the evening you had been out on the cliffs.'

'But that is so dreadfully Irish!' objected Glen, quoting some of her critics.

And, in good earnest, this was a difficulty the girl happened then to be contending against. She did not know enough of England to write about it – no, not even the aspect of nature in England. How could one accustomed to that wild sea, to those tossing billows, to the lonely rocks where the seagulls built, the stretching moorlands, the desolate bogs, and the sullen headlands frowning darkly on the Atlantic – write of gliding streams and flower-decked meadows, of the great, open, red-tiled barns she had not yet seen, or straw-yards, or cowslips, or any one of the thousand sights which render an English landscape so pre-eminently dear to all who love the English word 'home'?

She knew nothing about the homestead as it appears to the eyes of the youngest English child; she was still an alien, though learning to love and admire the country of her adoption. She regarded everything as an Englishman might the sights and sounds and customs of a foreign city. So far, the land and the people and the customs of the nation lay outside her; and it was not till they became soul of her soul, and heart of her heart, Glen moved the souls and hearts of those she wrote for. Till there were tears in the music she made, till she sobbed out the words of her lay, and felt the warmth herself of the sunshine she bade others bask in, success did not come to Glenarva Westley, in spite of the fact that she followed her father's advice, and took with her to Craven Street the Benjamin of her life, the 'last, best, sweetest, strongest book,' according to her own estimate, she had as yet written to astonish an ungrateful world.

When she arrived at the publishers, Muggins, who seemed plunged into a depth of gloom which nothing save impending bankruptcy on the part of his employer and an execution in his own home could possibly have justified, informed her Mr Vassett was out, and Mr Pierson engaged three deep.

'You can wait if you like, you know,' he said; but something in his tone induced Glen, whose temper was rather of the hottest, to say she should like to do nothing of the kind, and she was turning to leave the outer office when Mr Vassett himself entered.

'Oh! and how do you do?' he exclaimed, not seeming, however, in the least degree glad to see her, which fact Glen felt acutely as she answered:

'I am very well, thank you. No, I did not want anything – only I told Mr Pierson I should call today.'

'As you are here, come in,' suggested Mr Vassett. 'Eh, what did you say?' – this to Muggins, who was making various telegraphic signs to his employer.

'Lady Hilda's there, and Mr Pierson, and the actor gentleman, and some one he has brought with him.'

'Well, just come in then, will you?' said Mr Vassett, with a certain irritation in his tone Glen did not fail to notice.

By this time she knew all about Lady Hilda. Mr Pedland had given her the full story of the Hicks alliance, had told the girl every scandal there was to tell on the subject – true and false. Miss Westley's six months' term of study in the Metropolitan Academy had taught her many things about authors and authoresses Mr Vassett did not know. Flitting about from place to place, she heard every piece of gossip worth hearing; she was a good listener, and often when pacing the back streets homewards – for Glen's knowledge of London within a certain radius was even then almost exhaustive – she laughed softly to herself over the stories she was carrying back to that cheap second floor in Bloomsbury, while the passers-by turned with a quick, sympathetic look in their faces, wondering who the girl could be, and what she was smiling at with such thorough, though quiet, enjoyment while she passed swiftly along.

Lady Hilda was more radiant than ever. She was in the highest spirits, and greeted Mr Vassett with effusion. She playfully called him a 'grumpy old dear,' and said, after the success of her book, she expected to see his face bright with smiles instead of gloomy as a November day.

'If you take my advice,' she said to Glen, 'you won't have anything to do with him. I never mean him to publish another book of mine.'

'One side of a story is good till another is told,' remarked Mr Pierson.

'Now, don't *you* begin to be disagreeable,' exclaimed the lady. 'Mr Vassett, I wish you had stayed away. We were all as comfortable and pleasant as possible till you came in. You might serve for the skeleton at a feast – and that reminds me I want you to come to *my* feast. The great day is at hand. Blow the trumpets, sound the drums! The noble building for Decayed Fishwives is to be opened on the 20th by one of the Blood Royal, whom we are afterwards to have the honour to receive at luncheon, and all the county people are expected in force, and everybody in the City who has a million of money and upwards; and I shall not be happy unless you witness my triumph. You won't refuse. Now do – *do* – DO say I may count on seeing you!'

But Mr Vassett utterly refused to say anything of the kind. She could not cajole or scold him into compliance, so at last, saying 'he was a horrid creature,' she turned in despair to Mr Pierson, and entreated that he at least would not desert her.

For a time she went on in this way, dealing out invitations like a pack of cards, and receiving for answer only murmured apologies or amused smiles, till it occurred to her the 'bread-and-butter' girl, who was sitting a little in the background, had not been included in the game.

'You can come too, if you like,' she said, nodding to her over the barricade formed by Mr Dawton's right shoulder.

Glen was not stricken dumb with indignation at this cavalier address, because she answered it, but her voice sounded to herself strange and unfamiliar as she said:

'Thank you. You are very kind.'

'Then you will come?' observed Lady Hilda, who did not really want her to be one of the party.

'No, thank you,' replied Glen, beautifully concise, for fear of being once more misunderstood.

'Why not? Probably you may never have the chance of seeing a thing of the sort again.'

This time Glen, who was getting up to boiling-point, did not vouchsafe a word.

'Say you will come, there's a good girl;' and Lady Hilda smiled across Mr Dawton in a manner which might, as that gentleman observed subsequently, have vanquished a 'monarch of the forest.'

'Thank you, no!' persisted Glen.

'But why won't you be good-natured?'

'We don't visit,' answered the girl, whose cheeks were literally aflame with anger. It was too much for Lady Hilda. She burst into a peal of laughter, the sound of which dried the tears that filled Glen's eyes.

'Oh, Mr Dawton! Oh, Mr Dawton and Mr What-ever-is-your-name – Kelly – can't you make something of this, "*We don't visit!*" Sweet seventeen, with the dignity of a dowager and the pride of a queen. What a funny child you are! Have I offended you? I did not mean to do so. I am sorry! Shake hands and be friends.'

But Glen did not shake hands; she only let her hand lie passive, while Lady Hilda, who had come round to where she sat, took the girl's worn glove in her own dainty fingers, and went through that ceremony of reconciliation which probably meant as little on her side as on Miss Westley's.

There was a raging fury in Glen's heart that had never stirred it before – beyond speech, beyond sign. She had but one thought – how she should get out of the office – away – any place where she should never meet this odious, ill-bred woman again.

It was when the flood was at its highest that Mr Pierson, with the best intentions, remarked:

'Mr Kelly is a compatriot of yours, Miss Westley, who has already won great distinction in the character of the deaf gentleman in *How's Maria?*'

Mr Kelly, thus honourably mentioned, bowed, and so did Glen. Then, as their eyes met, she remembered his face, and where she had seen it last.

As two strange cats might, the 'compatriots' stared at each other.

There had been but one drop wanting to fill Glen's cup of mortification to overflowing, and now that drop was supplied; whilst on his side Mr Kelly – who, happening to have 'got on' a good deal since that drizzling October day, had hoped never again to behold any one of his fellow-passengers on the journey to London – felt when he recognised the girl, who was not, even after so many months of metropolitan experience, much 'to look at,' as if he had suddenly gone back in the world – as though he had sunk from the heights of the *Galaxy* back into gauche, untrained, untravelled Barney Kelly, fresh from Callinacoan, who had 'amused' – forsooth! – his English audience by using that remarkably strong expression which in his belief embodied the feeling of the Saxon towards his native land.

'I have seen you before, I think,' said Glen, steadying her voice as well as she could.

'We crossed in the same boat together, I believe, to Morecambe,' he answered, speaking as unconcernedly as annoyance would let him. 'I did not know,' he added, 'you were travelling to London to try your fortune as an author.'

'She has come to set the Thames on fire,' observed Lady Hilda; 'at least, so I gather from her admirer, Mr Pierson.'

'I trust,' added Mr Dawton, always restlessly anxious to put an unnecessary oar in the conversation, 'she will give us due notice when the conflagration is likely to come off.'

'I will,' said Mr Vassett, with a decision which took his hearers by surprise, while Glen contented herself by hoping mentally Lady Hilda might then be out on the river in a boat, and determinedly rose to go.

Mr Pierson walked by her side as far as the street door.

'You have got a manuscript for us, I see?' he remarked.

'No,' said Glen, whose feathers were still ruffled.

'Yes,' persisted the reader, laying hold of the end of the roll.

'I won't leave it,' declared Glen; 'nothing shall induce me. You would let Lady Hilda Hicks see it!'

'On my honour I will not! Muggins shall take charge of it till they are all gone. Can't you trust me, Miss Westley?'

If Miss Westley had spoken out her mind she would have answered that she could not; but to this point of candour Glen's courage refused to carry her.

'Well,' she said reluctantly, 'as you promise so faithfully' – and she gave him the manuscript as if it were some rare and precious treasure – 'it is my best, Mr Pierson,' she added, forgetting her anger for a moment, as she remembered all the merits and all the beauties and all the originality, all the fire and passion and pathos of this her youngest born, her Benjamin; 'it is far and away stronger than anything I have done yet. You won't let that hateful Lady Hilda laugh over it, will you?'

'No; nobody shall see it but myself. Do not be downhearted, Miss Westley. We will see your name printed in big capitals yet.'

Spite, however, of which hopeful assurance, before she was a fortnight older there came a letter from Mr Vassett, saying that, although 'the report on the manuscript she had been good enough to leave for consideration was in many respects favourable, he did not feel disposed to undertake its publication.'

'I still adhere,' finished Mr Vassett, 'to the opinion I first expressed – namely, that you cannot yet have had sufficient experience of life to enable you to produce a satisfactory work. To write well, an author must have thought much. Pardon me if my remarks seem obtrusive. I trust you will believe they are prompted solely by my interest in your welfare and success.'

'What is it, Glen?' said Mr Westley to his daughter, as she let her hand holding the open letter drop with a despairing gesture to her side. 'Another refusal?'

'Yes, papa, as I expected.'

'Where does the refusal come from?' asked Mr Lacere, who had called, as he explained, 'in passing,' to see if Mr Westley continued to like the Bloomsbury lodgings. 'Do you mind telling me?' he went on, speaking in a tone of kind sympathy.

For answer, Glen gave him Mr Vassett's letter to read.

'I think all these people give you great encouragement, Miss Westley,' he said.

'And I think,' observed Glen, 'that they all consider time to be of as little importance now as it must have been in the days of the patriarchs, when a few years less or more of waiting could make but little difference.'

With which petulant retort she was turning to leave the room, when Mr Lacere noticed an expression on her father's face he had seen there and wondered at more than once before.

Doubt, anxiety, trouble, were all written on that melancholy, pensive countenance, and something beyond – something Mr Lacere could not analyse or understand, but which filled him with a pity, the cause of which he would have felt puzzled to define.

It was then he took the first decided step along a road the end of which he could not see.

'Miss Westley,' he said, almost involuntarily, 'give me your manuscript. Let me try if I cannot find a purchaser for it.'

Chapter VII

A STRANGE ENCOUNTER

A HOT, CLOSE EVENING in the summer of 1855. A thunderstorm brooding over London. The streets dusty and stifling; scarce a breath of air stirring: what Mr Dawton, surveying the aspect of the heavens from one of the front gates of The Wigwam, described as 'a portentous stillness' pervading the atmosphere.

'You had far better stop at home, Will,' he expostulated. 'Kelly, do not go yet; do stay and have a morsel of supper – the crisp lettuce and the cool lobster – and we'll ice a bottle of champagne – what say you?

'That I must go home,' said Mr Kelly. 'I have copy to finish that can't be put off even for lettuce and lobster.'

'And I promised to turn up at Cayford's, and I shall turn up,' added Will.

'Well, young blood, young blood – it will have its way, sirs,' commented Mr Dawton. 'Don't forget Friday, Kelly – just a friendly party, you know – only a few old acquaintances – a carpet-dance – sandwiches and a glass of wine. Arty will never forgive you if you slight her birthday – a spoiled child – a spoiled child – sole daughter of my house and name.'

'Who rules the whole establishment,' said Will, holding the gate open for his companion. 'Now, Kelly, if you are ready,' and the pair strode off, walking together to Westminster Bridge, where young Dawton hailed an Atlas 'bus to convey him to Paddington, while Mr Kelly thoughtfully wended his way along the Belvidere Road towards Bermondsey. It was his invariable practice when alone to select all the narrower and meaner thoroughfares. He got a great deal of his 'copy' out of the less frequented streets; some papers he had written concerning Rotherhithe and Bermondsey were about that period attracting a good deal of attention. 'Studies from Life in Pen and Ink,' he called them; and the editor of the *Galaxy* having intimated he preferred these sketches to stories, Mr Kelly was considering whether he could not take a few more in other parts of the town.

It is an important element in worldly success when a man proves capable of learning from experience, and is not afraid to ask himself, 'What am I best fitted to do?'

So far Mr Kelly had not been able to settle this last point to his satisfaction, but he was coming to understand the conditions under which he displayed such talents as he possessed to the least advantage.

For example, he found his genius did not lie in the direction of story-telling – he was destitute of some faculty without which he felt he could never really take what Mr Dawton described as 'a grip' of the public. The best tale he could write would not, he felt, 'bring down the house.' He had been rejected by every magazine in London except the *Galaxy*, and he knew the only reason why his stories found admittance there was because Jim Dawton polished them up. The younger Dawtons all possessed the knack of turning out a readable tale. In most of them there was not, as a candid friend kindly told Will, 'a mortal thing.' Nevertheless, they were airy, sparkling, and vivacious, and 'took' with the public. Just as one woman out of the costliest materials finds herself unable to construct a bonnet 'fit to be seen,' while another, the rich possessor of a scrap of silk, a bit of net, a morsel of ribbon, a few stray leaves and flowers, will manufacture as coquettish and ravishing a headgear as lover need desire to see, so not all the narrative 'stock' Mr Kelly undoubtedly possessed could be metamorphosed by him into palatable literary soup.

'I can't tell what the deuce it is the fellow wants,' said the editor of the *Galaxy* one day to Jim Dawton, when that young gentleman, thinking, as he expressed the matter, 'Kelly could surely now be trusted to walk alone,' had handed two of Barney's tales in without 'running his eye over them.'

It was quite by chance the editor glanced at the manuscript, but when he had done so, he sent for Dawton, and taxed him with having on previous occasions retouched and almost rewritten 'that Irishman's copy.'

'And I am sure I can't imagine why you bother yourself about him,' finished the great man, 'for he'll throw you over when you have served his turn, see if he don't.'

'I think he will,' answered Jim; 'but, bless you, we never expected he'd pay us in meal or in malt for any little thing we were able to do for him. It's a poor sort of way that, according to my fancy, some folks have of giving with one hand and holding out the other to take.'

'You will never learn sense, Dawton, I am afraid,' observed the editor gravely, at which remark Jim laughed, and said he did not know who was to teach him; and then he took Mr Kelly's rejected manuscripts and 'polished them up a bit,' and subsequently remarked to that individual:

'I say, old boy, don't you think it is almost time you learnt to pepper and salt your stories for yourself? I'm about tired of having all the work while you get the halfpence.'

Very innocently, Mr Kelly inquired what his friend meant, though he knew perfectly well. After he first began to write for the *Galaxy*, a letter was directed to him at the office of that paper, which proved to be from the editor of the new opposition magazine, started by an enterprising firm immediately after the 'tremendous hit' made by the *Galaxy* with the benevolent intention of knocking that journal 'into a cocked hat.' In this epistle the editor presented his compliments to Mr Kelly, and intimated that in case the author of 'Tidford's Pet' were disposed to contribute some short tales to the *Sceptre*, he would be glad, if possible, to meet Mr Kelly's terms. Now, as the price Mr Kelly received from the *Galaxy*, though about six times as much as that brilliant writer would have felt thankful to receive when he began to turn out copy for his daily bread, was so much less than he heard other men boasting they were paid, he thought he would see whether he could not do as well as they; and accordingly, without committing himself about terms, he dropped a couple of manuscripts into the editorial box, together with a note, signifying he would do himself the honour to call on that gentleman during the course of the ensuing week, when, he felt no doubt, they would be able to come to some satisfactory arrangement.

He refrained from saying a word to Mr Dawton about this letter and his own answer, being well aware that between the *Galaxy* and the *Sceptre* a feud was raging like unto the Montague and Capulet business of old, and spite of all his lately acquired experience of literary moods and morals, he did not yet quite understand that so far from holding him back from spoiling the Egyptians, the Dawtons would simply have patted him on the back and said, 'Go in and win,' or given him, in even more forcible words, the advice vouchsafed by the parish priest of Callinacoan, who, after stating from the altar steps it had come to his knowledge that gifts of food and clothing and money were being distributed amongst his flock by those who, like the Pharisees, hesitated not 'to compass sea and land to make one proselyte, and when he is become so, make him twofold more a child of hell than themselves,' went on to say, 'Take what ye can get from the heretics, my poor people – everything they are willing to give, for God knows ye have need of it all.'

Mr Kelly was unable to quite realise that though honour among thieves may be possible, chivalry as regards editors and publishers is usually accounted among authors as worse than folly, and for this reason he said nothing concerning the *Sceptre*, a reticence he felt indeed very thankful subsequently to remember he had maintained.

All in due time he 'did himself the honour' of calling on the editor, who was out; but the sub, who was in, sent a message that he should like to speak to him.

Nothing doubting, Mr Kelly entered the editor's room – a well-furnished, well-carpeted, well-appointed apartment, very different from the den at the *Galaxy*.

'Money no object,' thought Mr Kelly complacently. Afterwards he learned that it is not from the best-looking offices the largest cheques issue.

From out of the depths of a great office chair, placed at the side of the table farthest from the door, rose a small man with the palest face and the darkest eyes and the blackest hair Mr Kelly had ever seen.

'I sent some manuscripts here last week at Mr Hetley's request,' said the fortunate author, after the exchange of a few words of ordinary courtesy, with the assured smile and manner of a man accustomed to acceptance; 'I hoped to have been fortunate enough to see him.'

'He has gone away for a few days,' answered the other, 'but I know all about the matter. Pray be seated,' and with a wave of his hand he indicated a chair.

Why, he never could tell afterwards, but at that point Mr Kelly began to feel vaguely uncomfortable. This was his first interview with an editor unblessed by the genial introduction and cheerful presence of one or other of the Dawtons.

'Your manuscripts have been carefully considered, Mr Kelly,' said the sub, laying one out quite flat on the table as he spoke, and smoothing it gently over with the palm of his hand, an action which somehow gave the author the impression of erasing all the words, 'but I regret to say –'

'Oh! if you do not want them I can place them elsewhere,' interposed Mr Kelly, speaking in such a hurry that his words almost tripped each other up. 'I shouldn't have sent you anything of mine if you had not asked me to do so.'

'Mr Hetley was aware of that,' answered the second in command, with unruffled composure, 'and begged me to offer his apologies for the trouble he has given you. He regrets very much indeed that he cannot make use of either of your stories.'

'Of course I bow to his decision,' observed Mr Kelly, with a fine irony perfectly thrown away on the man he addressed – a man who understood his business thoroughly, the best 'sub' perhaps in London, 'but as a matter of curiosity I should like to be informed of the grounds on which you reject my work after having requested me to submit it.'

'Yes, Mr Hetley felt that even for his own sake some explanation should be given. When he wrote to you he had only read "Tidford's Pet," and concluded the rest of your work would be up to the same mark. Now, Mr Kelly, if I may say so without offence, these stories are *not* up to the same mark.'

Mr Kelly answered, with a beautiful humility, that he was sorry his poor stories did not meet with approval. He confessed they had not seemed to him so inferior, but then no author could be considered a fair judge of his own work; and, warming to his subject, Barney threw out a general statement to the effect that he presumed there were few writers able uniformly to keep to the same standard of excellence.

Mr Kelly had advanced a good deal in his ideas and manners since he came to London. He now talked as one having authority; who had been nursed on printer's ink and weaned on small pica; who knew all about editors, and authors, and copy, and 'trade' jealousies and old-fashioned officialism; for whom the 'profession' held no secret, and who knew his way blindfold through all the ins and outs of journalism.

But he was speaking to a man who for twenty years had been walking the highways and by-ways of literary life; who, though he might be little better than a machine, still, like a machine, had come in contact with the productions of some splendid workers; who understood his business if he understood little else; and who was not to be diverted from his argument by the great and mighty airs of even a much more important person than the author of 'Tidford's Pet.'

'No writer can make a greater mistake than to play tricks with his reputation,' he remarked sententiously, 'and upon the strength of a later success to try to float the immature productions of an earlier period of his life. That is what you have tried to do with us, Mr Kelly, and even in your own interest I am bound to say I think you have committed an error of judgment.'

In a moment Barney grasped the state of the case. This man thought he had been trying to foist off on the *Sceptre* some of the crudest of his manuscripts – the very refuse of his labours. It was gall and wormwood to the author to find that, wanting the Dawton light touch, minus the few bold strokes which gave a finish to his work, stories which had cost him labour enough, which were indeed the very best he had ever produced, should be accounted unfit for anything save swift burial without funeral honours in the nearest waste-paper basket. He had cleverness enough to conceal the cause of his chagrin, and answered, with a sudden change of manner which a good deal surprised Mr Hetley's sub:

'I dare say you are right; and at any rate I feel obliged for your candour. I did not really think the tales bad myself; but, as I said before, authors are not always the best judges of their own work. Just at the present time I am exceedingly busy; but after a while I hope to be able to bring you something you will consider more satisfactory,' and then they had a little conversation on general subjects, and Mr Kelly smilingly took his manuscripts, and they parted very good friends.

That evening was spent by Bernard Kelly in comparing his original manuscripts with those manuscripts as they read in print, after one of the Dawtons had 'run them through.'

'I can't make it out,' he at last exclaimed. 'I can't tell how the deuce they do it,' for the fact was, Barney had hitherto considered his brain-children marred and deformed by the Dawton hacking, and dressing, and shortening and altering. He thought his finest passages were ruthlessly deleted – that for all the beauty and pathos he had read and re-read to himself with never-failing delight to be cut out by Dawton's remorseless pen, was an indignity he could scarcely endure. Even his amusing scenes were curtailed; and what he considered his finest efforts of humour sometimes expunged altogether, and the author had only held his peace concerning these mutilations from prudence.

Now, however, he began to see it was to this chopping and changing process he owed such success as he had secured. He did not really think his compositions improved by the merciless action of the Dawton pruning-knife – quite the contrary; but Barney was not bigoted. His firstborn in literature was dear to him, no doubt; but he would have sacrificed it or anything else for bread-and-cheese.

'I wish I could learn the knack of how they do it,' he reflected, referring to the ease with which any one of the Dawtons could 'touch up,' or 'knock off,' or 'boil down' an article. 'I know twice as much as any one of them. I have read ten times as many books – and good books too. What on earth can it be they have that I want?'

It was while this question still burned in his mind he happened one Saturday night to be passing through Hoxton while the usual market was in full swing in Pitfield Street. The sight was new to him. He went home with a vivid picture of the stalls, the flaring naphtha, the eager sellers, the anxious buyers in his mind's eye, with the quaint expressions, the curious retorts, the elbowing, the jostling, the badinage, the persuading, the huckstering, fresh in his memory; and before he lay down to sleep he produced a graphic and taking pen-and-ink sketch of the scene.

'It is capital!' said Will Dawton. 'It only needs a dash of colour here and there. Hand it over, Kelly; that's precisely the sort of thing the *Galaxy* wants.'

In the pursuit, therefore, of that 'sort of thing,' Mr Kelly wandered south and east through all sorts of disagreeable neighbourhoods, but he liked them. Quite honestly he said he preferred Whitechapel to Belgravia, and Ratcliff Highway to Pall Mall.

There came a time when he tired of those neighbourhoods, and, indeed, sometimes to hear him talk now, anyone might imagine he had spent his whole life amongst the Upper Ten. For Mr Bernard Kelly has done remarkably well for himself, and if you, reader, chance to be of those who go visiting at great houses, you will certainly some evening have the pleasure of meeting a gentleman who, from the first hour of his literary life, laid himself out to 'please the public'.

After parting from his friend he strolled idly along Belvidere Road and Upper Ground Street, got on to Bankside, and so, just as the threatened thunderstorm began, found himself in that exceedingly old-world part of London which is still existing, though probably it will not exist much longer – Clink Street. It was a place he often chose to pass through; he liked the passage round St Saviour's Church, and the queer little bit of covered way leading from Clink Street to St Mary's Overy Dock.

A genuine corner of ancient London it all seemed to him as he often paused at the top of the steps to look on the one hand down on the water, and on the other to take a backward and comprehensive view of Clink Street however, as heavy drops of rain began to fall on the stones, he thought only of getting into shelter, and hurried up the steps and under the covered passage that to this day seems so quaint a relic of times long gone by.

There were other persons there before him, as others came after; but not very many, for Clink Street cannot be considered a leading thoroughfare, and is certainly not largely affected, save by those pedestrians who either reside or have business in the neighbourhood.

Mr Kelly, who had a long distance still to traverse before he reached his lodgings, and who did not feel the slightest desire to get wet through, managed, after a few minutes, to secure for himself a very comfortable corner, in which he stood warm and dry, while the rain poured down in torrents and the thunder pealed and the lightning played about the river and round the tower of St Saviour's Church, and women with their dresses tucked up and shawls drawn over their bonnets took advantage of any lull in the tempest to scuttle off through the passage, and men who had waited till the worst of the storm was over buttoned their coats close, turned up their collars and the bottoms of their trousers, and set out, to be driven again to shelter when they reached the other side of the market.

It was getting late; the shades of evening were closing down, and still there appeared little chance of a storm which seemed always 'working round,' 'blowing over,' when Mr Kelly's attention was excited by the appearance of two men, who, in one of the short lulls of the rain and thunder, came running up the steps, and took advantage of the best position they found vacant at the top.

'By George!' exclaimed the shorter of the two, who took off his hat and mopped his forehead, and wiped the perspiration from his face, 'we are just in time, Noll. How it comes down! My luck all over! Thin boots – no overcoat, no umbrella!'

'Well, you are no worse off than I am,' replied the other, in an oily, unctuous, persuasive voice, 'and we are in very good quarters here; and the rain, doubtless, will soon give over.'

'And we'll see a rainbow in the sky, and an angel will bring us changes of raiment, and perhaps a carriage to convey us to our destination – that's the sort of thing, ain't it? – your sort of thing, I mean.'

'I wouldn't, you know – I wouldn't, really, if I was you.'

'Wouldn't you? If you were me, you don't know what you might do,' and then, in a lilting sort of monotone, the first speaker went on, 'Suppose that you were

I – suppose that you were me – suppose we both were somebody else – I wonder who it would be? Riddle me, riddle me ree, Noll, can you tell me that?'

The rain was now falling fast and furious, and the thunder making such a din, Mr Kelly could not have heard any more of the conversation for some time, even if his attention had not been distracted by the flashing of the lightning and the noise made by the rain as it plashed heavily into the dock below.

For the time the corner was full, and even the passage beyond, only partially protected from the storm, held a fair number of people who did not care to expose themselves to the full violence of the tempest; but whenever the rain abated even a little, most of the persons sheltering repeated the experiment of venturing forth, and once again the place became comparatively empty, though the drops still pattered down and the thunder continued to mutter angry threats from the distance, whither it had temporarily departed.

That the talk had never really ceased between the two men Mr Kelly was aware, and now, as they drew a little nearer to him, the younger said, evidently in answer to some previous remark of his more self-possessed and decorous companion:

'I suppose you have heard, however, that at the corner of every street in London there is a capitalist waiting to be taken in?

'I have heard,' replied the other, 'what comes much to the same thing – namely, that every half-hour in the day a fool crosses London Bridge with a rogue following him.'

'Well, and what do you make of that?' asked the younger man triumphantly.

'Surely there is not much to make of anything of the sort. We know there have been rogues and fools, and dupes and knaves since the beginning of time, and till our poor, imperfect human nature is different from what it is –'

'Now, drop that,' interrupted the serious man's companion; 'you know I can't stand preaching.'

'It was you began it –'

'Preaching! I'll swear it wasn't,' cried the other, in such an excited tone that those persons who were still 'standing up' involuntarily turned and looked at the pair.

Mr Kelly found it impossible to catch the remonstrance addressed to the younger man by the elder; but his words produced an effect for a short time – not for long, though; every woman who furled or unfurled her umbrella was addressed with jocular familiarity; every man had a remark of some sort addressed to him. There were a few who, being wet and sulky, did not take kindly to this chaff; but upon the whole, pater and mater familias and the younger lads and lasses only laughed at the outpouring of spirit of the 'funny chap,' as Mr Kelly mentally called him; and when Barney himself was addressed as an 'old cock,' and asked whether 'the missus would give him a wigging when he got home for stopping out without leave,' the merriment of the audience culminated in shouts of laughter.

Stimulated by these marks of approval, the young man, with his hat pushed to the back of his head, his hands deep in his pockets, his back up against the woodwork, and his feet a little inclined to slip away from under him on their own account, proceeded to improve the occasion still further by asking whether he should 'go home first to make peace and tuck up the young ones,' a question which so delighted many ladies present that they were fain to bury their faces in their handkerchiefs, and put their hands to their sides, cast sidelong glances of amusement at each other, and giggle and otherwise encourage 'the gentleman' to proceed to greater lengths.

Which indeed he did. He found many things to say, and he said them; he seemed in the highest, maddest mood, and treated the perpetually recurring 'I wouldn't if I was you – I wouldn't indeed,' of his mentor as a capital joke. He even attacked one staid and starched spinster with the question whether she wanted a 'nice good little boy to bring up,' because personally he felt he had 'great need of a mother's care.'

'You have great need of something, sir, I think,' she retorted, and walked away with great dignity, a handkerchief tied over her bonnet and her silk dress uplifted sufficiently to show a very neat foot and ankle, followed by such a pantomime from the young fellow of kisses wafted after her retreating form, and heart-pressing and deep sighing, and a stave of a song in admiration of 'charms he might ne'er see again,' that even Bernard Kelly, who was not easily moved to laughter, had to join the chorus of merriment which rang out from that harbour of refuge perched above the dock of St Mary Overy.

One thing, however, Mr Kelly noticed – that through all his folly the young man, who was called by his grave companion Lance, never seemed to lose hold of a certain thread of dialogue, to which at intervals he returned again and again. When he thus took up the original subject – whatever it might be – his face was serious enough; then people might come or people might go without eliciting any remark save the most cursory and trivial. At such times he forgot to look about him either, though his companion did, as though uneasy lest what he said might be overheard, or anxious to get away and so end the discussion.

The author stole a glance at them both now and then, and utterly failed to arrive at any conclusion as to what they might be, till he chanced to hear the elder say:

'I can't – I assure you what you ask is not within my power to do. I am only temporarily associated with a religious society, and –'

'O Lord!' broke in the other, 'talk about Saul among the prophets – what's that to Noll Butterby?

'Hold your tongue, do!' remonstrated Noll angrily. 'Why will you talk so loud? People can hear all you say, and –'

Here he dropped his voice so low that even Bernard Kelly, who was standing near, could not catch the remainder of the sentence, to which Lance replied in a much less exalted tone than that he usually employed.

He was but little over twenty, Mr Kelly decided; so thin that he really looked as if he had not an ounce of flesh on his bones – a restless, electrical sort of being, who could not have kept still or silent had he been paid for doing so, possessed of a temperament that would never let him get even moderately fat. He was wiry, but not muscular; certainly no athlete, Barney – who knew a good deal about men who hunted, and boated, and walked, and jumped, and fought, and played at cricket – felt very sure. His thin, straight hair, which he was constantly pushing upwards with nervous, bony fingers, hovered between the confines of bright yellow and dark red; his complexion was muddy, his expression anxious; his eyes were small, and of a greyish-blue, and as a rule ranged from object to object with the same quick, jerky uncertainty that characterised all his movements.

'Mad,' thought Mr Kelly; and then he amended his phrase, 'drunk.' Yet for a man not sober he was wonderfully fluent; he never stopped for a word; he went right on with a flow of language Barney had seldom heard equalled except by a 'Cheap Jack.'

On the whole, he more resembled a 'Cheap Jack' with a slight knowledge of literature added to his other stock-in-trade than anything else; and as the rain, though still coming down pretty steadily, was not nearly so heavy as it had been, Mr Kelly might have gone away to Bermondsey satisfied the young fellow followed the occupation in question, or at all events one analogous to it, had he not, to his astonishment, suddenly heard him break out with this:

'How did I first get to know the Dawtons? and why did I break with them? I don't mind telling you or any man. I have nothing to be ashamed of in the matter, have I?'

And he turned on Barney, who, in the excess of his astonishment, was staring at him with all his might.

'Unless I knew what you were talking about, I really could not venture to give an opinion,' answered Mr Kelly, with diplomatic reticence.

'You're Scotch, ain't you?' cried out the other. 'I am sure you are. You are Scotch!'

'Something of that sort,' agreed Barney carelessly.

'I could have taken my affidavit of it. You see, Noll, he won't reply straight-forwardly even to the simplest question. Never mind, I like the look of you. Jew or Gentile, I can always tell when a man is a good sort by one glance in his face. My friend here wants to hear how I fell in with a certain family, and why I fell out with them. I don't mind telling him, or you, or anybody. When a man hasn't done anything wrong, though he is a bit down on his luck –'

'I wouldn't, Lance – I wouldn't indeed, if I were you.'

'If you don't quit that parrot-cry I'll wring your neck for you,' interposed Lance, with an expression of the most perfect amiability, 'or chuck you into the sewer there – our noble Thames is nothing but a common sewer. Here, you, sir, why have you shrunk back into your corner? Come here; or, better still, I'll edge up to you.'

And, suiting his action to his word, he moved close beside Mr Kelly, and laid one hand on that gentleman's shoulder, while with the other he drew the reluctant Butterby into conclave while he said:

'Oh! you need not be making signs and tokens to him about me. I know very well what I am doing and saying. If you keep as cool a head among your religious folks as I have now, you'll get on, never fear. Do you happen to know,' he added, addressing Bernard Kelly, '*who stole the squire's apples?*'

'No, I don't,' answered Barney, laughing; 'do you?'

'Yes, I know, bless you! but never mind that now; we were not talking about apples or the squire, but about me and the Dawtons. Did you ever meet any of them?' he stopped to inquire.

'I have heard of a Mr Dawton, an actor, if that's the man you mean.'

'That's the man – does old fathers and heavy swells; awful muff on the stage, I think, and a far greater bore in private life. But that's nothing. You are not a friend of his, are you?'

'I? How should I be a friend of his?'

'I didn't think you were; you are out of that sort of beat altogether; but still, it is as well to be careful. No, I am not going to hold my tongue, Noll. However, as I was saying, Dawton's an awful bore, but he did not behave half badly to me. He was good to me – I'll say that for him; and so was his wife, so were the sons, and so was everybody – only – well, I was a fool; you are not surprised to hear that, are you?'

'Of course he is not,' remarked Mr Butterby. 'Why should anybody be who hears you talking about your private affairs in this way?'

'I did not ask your opinion, and I am not such a fool as I look, as some persons may find out before they are much older. I do not say I have done as well as you, Mr Noll; but the end is not yet, and while you are still plodding through the highways and byways, distributing tracts, you need not be surprised to see me driving past in my carriage. Should you like to hear how I came to London without a shoe to my foot?'

'Well, I don't know,' answered Mr Kelly, thus once more appealed to; 'this is scarcely a place to pass the night, and –'

'Ah, you are laughing at me! You mean I'd keep you talking till morning. No, I wouldn't. I wonder somebody doesn't start a bar in this corner. What I'd give now just for the least taste of Scotch whisky! We'd have that in compliment to you. Dawton was the fellow to lap; that's how he got himself out of all his engagements. Couldn't keep his nerves steady; got maudlin, too, at times. If drink hurts a man, he ought to take the pledge – "Taste not, touch not." What are you grinning at?' he asked suddenly. 'I suppose you are thinking, "Physician, heal thyself;" but you are out – quite wrong. Bless you, I don't drink! I haven't the chance. I only wish I had! You can't get drunk unless you have money, or tick, or friends; and I have neither money, nor tick, nor friends, and all because of a young woman – such a trim little craft, such a pretty, clever creature! She might have made a man of me; but never mind, when I am riding in that carriage I was telling you about,' and he nodded to Mr Butterby, 'she'll be sorry she's not sitting at my side!'

'Perhaps you may make up your quarrel,' suggested Mr Kelly.

'Oh no! I am not one of your forgiving sort. I have no notion of huffing today and kissing tomorrow. So far as I am concerned, Miss Arty will have all her life to repent in.'

'Who is Miss Arty?' asked Mr Kelly, as innocently as though he had not seen a young lady of that name a couple of hours previously.

'Old Dawton's daughter. She does not take after him, though.'

'And she wouldn't have anything to do with, you, Lance?' said Mr Butterby.

'It was this way, you see. She did not seem able to forget how poor I was when she first set eyes on me – *they* had the bailiffs in at the time for that matter, and so I reminded her. I told her I meant to be a big fellow yet, that I knew I had it in me to 'make a splash,' that all I wanted was a wife to keep me steady, that I would win a fortune for her; but she didn't see it, or she wouldn't see it. She said she thought we had better wait till I had got part of the fortune, at any rate. I declared I would do nothing of the kind, that if she liked she could have me then, but that if she did not choose to take me as I was, she might do the other thing.'

'And so?' ventured Mr Kelly, as the rejected suitor paused.

'She did the other thing,' explained Lance. 'I put it quite plainly to her. I said, "Remember, I am not going to come begging and praying to you to reconsider your decision. I have made you a fair offer, but I will not make it to you again. It must be now or never."

'"Then I am afraid it must be never," she answered, as coolly as you please. That was a way to treat a fellow who worshipped the ground she walked on, who would have dressed her in satins and velvets if he could, who thought there was nobody like her in the world. It's no matter, though; I am not going to break my heart because a woman's false. When I think of the walks we used to take over Battersea Fields, I – But she'll be sorry some day, won't she?'

'I dare say she is sorry now,' observed Mr Kelly soothingly.

'No, she's not. She won't feel much sorrow till she hears a great talk about me, and people saying: "What a clever fellow that Lance Felton must be! Why, he came to London with scarcely a shoe to his foot, and look at him now – he's rolling in wealth!"'

'There's some work cut out for you before anybody can say that about Lance Felton with any truth,' remarked Mr Butterby, with a saintly sneer.

'And to enable him to do the work cut out,' exclaimed Mr Kelly, 'I propose, now the rain is abating a little, that we adjourn to the nearest tavern and drink to his success in the best "Scotch" we can get.'

'I knew you were the right sort,' cried Lance with enthusiasm. 'Oh yes, I can always tell with the most cursory –'

'Never mind that now,' interrupted Bernard Kelly. 'Come along!' and, thus exhorted, Mr Felton, as he expressed the matter, 'toddled.'

The tide of improvement which has for the last fifteen years been setting steadily through modern Babylon and converting London from the ugliest and most interesting city in the world, into the handsomest and most hopelessly commonplace, could not, of course, when it was sweeping better things into the limbo of forgetfulness, be expected to spare so insignificant a tavern as the old-fashioned public house to which Mr Kelly and his companions repaired for that modicum of Scotch whisky which was, so said Mr Felton, to be ordered in honour of his new acquaintance's nationality. To Bernard Kelly his nationality had become a matter of the most supreme indifference. He was not a man likely to gush about 'old Ireland' and Brian Boroihme. Erin's harp, and Erin's shamrock, and Erin's wrongs, were mere phrases which conveyed even less meaning to his mind than they could possibly have done to the 'falsest' Saxon in the whole of England. If anyone had asked him then his views on the vexed question of Irish policy, he would have confessed to entertaining none. He was not eager to flourish his native land in the face of the tyrant. He had found a country full of leeks and cucumbers, and fleshpots and money, and he meant to adapt himself to its manners and customs, as far as possible.

Supposing it pleased people to take him for a Scotchman, well and good – he would not undeceive them. He had learnt at a very early period of his metropolitan experiences that the native of any other land – Jew, Greek, Pole – was more acceptable to the English mind than an Irishman, and consequently he did not now go about the world proclaiming that he claimed Callinacoan as his birthplace, as he might once have done. He had heard quite enough of that sort of thing from Miss Bridgetta Cavan to warn him off the subject forever. Beggars in rags and tatters Mr Donagh's aunt was wont to greet with delight as having been, like herself, born in the Emerald Isle, and accustomed to potatoes boiled in their jackets. Not a man, woman, or child with whom she came in contact round and about West Ham and Stratford did she suffer to remain in ignorance of her Irish extraction.

When she haggled over the price of a fowl, she told the dealer she could have got a 'far better one' for sixpence at Callinacoan; and the same information was vouchsafed concerning every other necessary of life, were the matter in hand a 'hank' of worsted or the 'smoothing' of Mat's immaculate shirt-fronts.

With a considerable amount of ostentation Mr Lance Felton, producing a crown-piece, which he loudly declared he would tell no man how he became possessed of, insisted on 'standing treat.'

Closely watching him, Mr Kelly could see that crown-pieces had not been plentiful in the young man's pocket. From the way he flung the coin down on the counter it almost seemed as though he were challenging the resources of the house to produce sufficient change.

'H'm,' thought Mr Kelly; and when the whisky was brought in a measure instead of in the fair and simple shape of 'outs,' to which the liberal-minded youth had evidently been most accustomed, Barney – the liquor having been first passed to him 'out of compliment' – poured into his glass a quantity which made both his companions stare.

'Come, I say – you know,' expostulated Mr Felton; 'leave other fellows a chance, do. I did not mean you to take *quite* all.'

'Oh! there's enough left for you,' answered Barney carelessly. 'English heads are more easily upset than ours. However, let us have another measure. I don't care to drink my grog as weak as tea.'

'Well, you must be a seasoned vessel,' exclaimed Mr Felton, as, not without admiration, he noted the exceedingly moderate quantity of water Mr Kelly mixed with his potations.

'Why, if I was to take that –'

Mr Kelly smiled meaningly. He knew very well why this youngster's hand was unsteady, and his talk rambling, and his eye unsettled, and his tongue indiscreet.

'Yes,' he decided; 'my lad, you began with the bottle betimes. You have had a touch of DT already, or I am much mistaken. Unless you mind what you are about, things won't go well with you.' But he spoke no word of this aloud; he only sipped his own fiery draught, and laughed inwardly to see how young Felton was all unconsciously following Mat Donagh's lead, and adopting the course people learned in the ways and customs of drunkenness assert conducts to swift and sure destruction, viz., adding spirit to the top of the tumbler, instead of conscientiously depositing it in the bottom.

Few men living probably knew more about the vice of intemperance than Bernard Kelly. He had seen every form, he thought, of intoxication before he set foot in England; but once in London, he found he had still a great deal to learn.

He felt quite interested in watching his two companions: Noll, who it seemed to him could himself have drunk a quart and walked away as steadily afterwards as if he had never tasted a drop; and Felton, who was, he felt convinced, already a confirmed tippler, and to whose nervous and excitable nature stimulants were evidently a swift and sure poison.

Strange to say, Kelly had, since he quitted Abbey Cottage, well-nigh become a practical, though not professed teetotaler.

It needed no prophet to foretell the probable result likely to ensue from the habits into which Mat Donagh and Mr Dawton had fallen.

Nothing except a miracle, thought Barney, could save either from eventual bankruptcy and degradation. He knew what his father had sunk into; he had seen others well-off, lose lands, and houses, and character, simply because they lacked self-control, because the demon of drink took possession of them and turned every good angel that had hitherto dwelt in their bosoms adrift. This was not a form of temptation he had expected to find waiting for him in London; but as he did meet it, he determined it should not ruin his future.

He drank nothing at home, and no more out than seemed to his mind necessary, unless he had a purpose to serve in assuming the semblance of good-fellowship. If Mr Bernard Kelly liked he could tell today of many a noble craft, laden with the treasures of genius, he has seen go down engulfed in seas of champagne and burgundy – to say nothing of those more prosaic destroyers, brandy, and rum, and gin – but he would not. Mr Kelly is now above all things respectable, no man better understands the wisdom of silence – the beauty of accepting things as they seem to be rather than as they are.

He would not amend the doctor's certificate for any consideration – conventional phrases are eternally on his lips. He has never written a line posterity need desire to read, yet he sits high above the clamour of struggling authorship a successful man!

Standing in front of the bar of the old public house, Mr Felton was kind enough to enlighten all within hearing as to his own opinions, talents, and antecedents. From the period when he went to a dame school to have the alphabet beaten into him, to that present hour in which he had made the acquaintance of his new friend, he spared no incident which seemed for the moment important to his wandering brain. He was as discursive as Barnaby Rudge, and to Mr Kelly he did not seem much wiser. True, his folly was dashed with a vein of shrewdness, which shone occasionally across his discourse like the flash of a lantern through the darkness of night. But Barney had grown very weary of him, utterly tired of his awful egotism, and was just considering how he could manage to slip him off, when Noll, whose eyes were no brighter, and face no ruddier, and tongue no looser for all the whisky he had swallowed, said in that aggravatingly slow voice of his:

'Now, Lance, if I'm to see you home it is time we were moving.'

'I don't want you to see me home,' cried Lance indignantly. 'I can see myself home without any help.'

'No, you can't,' was the calm reply; 'you'll get locked up, or you'll lie down on some doorstep and catch your death of cold; or –'

'You go home yourself; go to Jericho, if you like. You'll come with me to my crib, won't you?' went on Lance, appealing to Barney Kelly.

'Well, I don't know,' answered the latter; 'it all depends upon where your crib may be. For instance, I won't go back with you to Hammersmith, or Tottenham, or –'

'Oh! I'm not particular,' interposed the other; 'I'll take a shakedown wherever you live, and welcome.'

'Couldn't possibly oblige you in that way,' said Mr Kelly; 'I reside with my grandmamma, a most particular old lady – bedroom candlesticks brought in at half-past ten, all lights out at eleven. She would disinherit me on the spot if I introduced such a wild spirit as you to her.'

'What's the matter with me?' asked Mr Lance Felton, a little thickly.

'A good deal, I think. You had better take your friend's advice, and get home as soon as you can. I'll set you a good example, and be off.'

But Lance would not have the knot thus cut; he bade Noll take a Brixton 'bus, and said plainly:

'It is no use your waiting for me.'

A very demon of contradiction seemed raised within him, and while with one hand he persistently pointed Noll to the door, with the other he clung to Mr Kelly, who at length, in order to pacify his excitement and avoid a scene the landlord's looks seemed in anticipation to deprecate, promised to take care of him.

It was quite fine when they all left the tavern; a delightful coolness had succeeded to the heat of the earlier part of the evening; the stars were shining overhead; and though the pavement under foot was wet, the heavy rain had so completely washed the thoroughfares, that walking seemed what it rarely is in London – an absolute pleasure.

'Which way?' asked Bernard Kelly, as they stood waiting to know what it might please Mr Felton to do next.

'Wait a minute,' answered the younger man. 'We'll see Noll into a 'bus first. I'm not going to have you prowling after us,' he added, rudely addressing his friend.

'I wouldn't speak in that way if I were you,' said Noll, resorting to his accustomed formula.

'I'll speak any way I like, without asking your leave; you may depend upon that,' retorted Lance.

'Then I may as well cross over,' remarked his friend, with unruffled composure; and suiting the action to the word, he picked his way deliberately to the other side, where he took up his position, waiting for the Brixton omnibus to make its appearance.

'We won't go till we see him fairly off,' said Lance, who still, perhaps for prudential reasons, kept a firm hold of Bernard Kelly's arm. 'He is as deep as a draw-well; he would follow us in a minute.'

'What would it matter if he did?' asked Barney, who was beginning to wish himself well rid of his companion.

'It mightn't matter to you,' answered Lance, 'but I don't choose him to know anything about me. He is a mean, close, dangerous, double-faced cur, that is what he is, if you want to know, and he did steal the squire's apples!'

'Well, suppose he did? There was no great sin in that, was there? Most boys steal squires' apples when they can get a chance.'

'Ay! but he wasn't a boy, and he let somebody else get the blame of it.'

'Oh!' said Mr Kelly, beginning to see light.

'He's a cad! that's what he is; now, when he could make a bit of amends, he won't. His old aunt died a while ago, and left him £600. A clever fellow might make his fortune with a quarter of that. There's the 'bus – full inside – oh! he's getting up on the knifeboard – see him? Now we may get along.'

'I hope we haven't very far to go,' remarked Barney, who felt his companion leant far too heavily on his arm, and heard with dismay his speech becoming thicker and less articulate.

'Not far – don't be afraid, I know my way – stop a minute, and let's look at the lights in the water.'

'No, no; come on, do!' entreated Mr Kelly. 'It is getting late, and I want to get home. You can look at the lights any other night.'

Never before had London Bridge seemed so long to him; never before did the City, to his eye, wear so deserted and dreary an aspect.

'If I only knew where the drunken idiot lived,' he considered, 'I should not so much care; but I doubt very much if he is in a state to get safe there.'

He did not overrate the point of inebriation at which Lance had arrived, but he greatly underrated the clearness of that young gentleman's mind, even at times when his limbs were particularly unsteady. Though his talk was rambling, a thread of connected sense ran through it. The main facts Mr Kelly gathered from his desultory conversation were that he had a special spite against 'Noll'; that, indeed, he had a spite against most people; that he felt a fervent admiration for, and envy of, a large number of persons whom he vaguely designated as 'swells'; that he had the greatest desire possible to 'ride in his carriage' and 'splash' those who had shown him 'the cold shoulder'; that he entertained unlimited confidence in his own abilities; that he had very little belief in the cleverness of anybody else; that he hoped Miss Arty would live to regret having turned up her nose at him; that he meant to marry very soon, if only to show he had no notion of wearing the willow; that he knew a girl who worshipped the ground he walked on, and was worth a thousand – aye, a hundred thousand – of Dawton's daughter. He was not always perfectly audible, and he was very often wholly unintelligible, but the impression he left on Bernard Kelly's mind was that Miss Arty might consider herself well rid of her lover, for that no weaker, vainer, more vindictive, less reliable young fellow ever reeled home to bed.

It may be said at once that the sight of this extraordinary suitor – who, even according to his own account, had sprung from the people – increased the determination Mr Kelly formed at a very early stage of their acquaintance of getting out of the Dawton set as soon as he felt strong enough to do without their assistance.

He was fast getting into a maze of speculations concerning the Dawtons' antecedents and his own chances of success in the future, when he felt himself suddenly pulled up, and Lance came to a full stop at the door of an old house in a narrow and dirty City lane.

'Here we are,' said the young man, lurching heavily against his companion as he began searching for the latch-key.

'What do you mean? Is this where you live?

'It is where I lodge. Come in, and you'll see how I'm treated – worse than any dog; enough to make a fellow with brains shoot himself – or somebody else.'

Seeing that the shaking fingers could not succeed in their search, Mr Kelly coolly put his own hand in Lance's pocket and extracted the key. Throwing open the door, they stepped into a wide hall, where a gas-jet was burning.

'Now, where are we to go?' asked Barney, who felt a weight lifted off his mind. 'Upstairs?'

For answer Lance only shook his head.

'It's in here I stop,' he said, indicating a room on the left hand, in which also there seemed a light.

'Well, this is a queer adventure, too,' decided Mr Kelly, as he stood inside a bare, meagrely furnished office, which contained little beyond two counters running at right angles, a stool, a desk, and a chair.

Some maps were hanging on the walls, which were likewise embellished with shipping bills representing imposing-looking vessels in full sail.

'I may leave you now, I suppose,' said Mr Kelly, drawing a deep breath of relief.

'What's the hurry? Wait a minute, and then you can turn out the gas for me.'

'But you don't sleep here?' looking round in search of any possible couch and perceiving none.

'Don't I! You'll soon see. I told you I was treated worse than a dog, and I am. And he makes a great merit of what he does for me, too; thinks, I suppose, I ought to be grateful to him for his charity. Well, time, they say, proves all things. Here's a nice, comfortable bed for a man to turn into;' and, suiting the action to the word, Mr Lance Felton with much difficulty got down on his knees, and then, without the ceremony of dismantling himself of any article of dress – not even his hat, which, however, tumbled off, apparently of its own accord, he rolled under the counter and disappeared from Mr Kelly's sight.

In astonishment too great for words Barney surveyed this proceeding; then, peeping over the counter, he beheld the youth's prostrate figure extended on some sacks, over which was laid a piece of baize.

'By-by,' murmured Lance. 'I'm dead beat, I think. You'll come and look me up soon, won't you?

'Oh yes,' answered Bernard Kelly, who, however, had not the faintest intention of doing anything of the kind.

'And turn down the gas, will you, and shut the door, to keep out that old housekeeper!'

'All right,' replied Mr Kelly. 'Good night, and pleasant dreams.'

Then he closed the door, as requested, but paused for a moment in the hall to read the names which were painted on the wall.

Second floor – Duncombe and Co.

First floor – M Logan Lacere.

Ground floor – Lacere Bros., Shipping Agents.

'It's a strange world,' thought Mr Bernard Kelly, as he retraced his steps across London Bridge, and thence wended his way to Bermondsey; and indeed it is, the strangest thing about it being that, wide as the world seems, we find it practically so small we are always jostling and running up against each other.

Chapter VIII

NED'S LETTER

DOWN IN THE VALLEY OF THE THAMES, on the Middlesex side of the river, but quite away from the water – among the moors that give a character of such peculiar loneliness to that little-known part of the country – the Westleys had found for themselves a small cottage; and, remote from London, Glenarva, in a silence that after the hum of the busy streets made her ears ache, and in a solitude by comparison with which Ballyshane might have been accounted a populous city, was trying to write another novel.

At first she did not find it easy work; the absence of all mental excitement, the utter stillness, broken only by the songs of the birds and the bleating of sheep, the flat and to her most uninteresting landscape, the lack of young companionship, depressed her for a time beyond measure – bowed her spirit down to the very earth. But this did not last for long. After a few weeks her imagination took root in this fresh soil, and wound itself round desolate tracts of stretching moorland intersected by sluggish streams, and twined fanciful wreaths about domains where the grounds were wild and neglected, and startled deer bounded across parks that there seemed no owner to enjoy. Had she known all about these places, the explanation of their unregarded appearance might have proved prosaic enough, but as matters stood she found abundant scope for fancy, and ignorant of everything connected with the men and women who some day meant to return and live in those great deserted mansions, she made up stories for herself of wrong and sorrow and sin and suffering. It was about that time Glen began to find writing harder work than she had ever previously conceived it could become. She did not suffer now from that trouble which had startled and perplexed her when she first arrived in London – the absence of ideas. Plots and characters she soon found came almost unbidden; but her difficulty was to mould them into shape, to fit the different pieces of her puzzle together, so as to form an intelligible whole, to make her people lifelike, to show them doing simple things in a simple manner, and talking as men and women do talk in real life, and not as they so often talk in books.

Sometimes the girl lost heart altogether; her thoughts were so vast, her power of expressing them so small! It cost her more trouble to write a single chapter of that book than it had done previously to produce a whole volume. Quite unconsciously to herself she was passing out of the mere rudimentary stage of authorship into its higher branches, and no one stood beside her desk to explain she was not retrograding but progressing, that the reason she found writing now so hard was not because any virtue of genius had departed from her, but because the discipline which alone could make her writings worth reading had begun.

The sadness of the landscape also sometimes oppressed her very soul. It lacked all life and animation and cheerfulness – flat fields, stretching commons destitute of gorse and heather, slowly flowing water, more like dykes than rivulets, bordered by mournful pollards, and only enlivened by the occasional presence of a party of ducks; farmhouses at distant intervals, a few cottages scattered here and there, wide roads where once coaches passed constantly, now totally deserted; no station within three miles, and only about four trains a day to town; few inhabitants above the rank of labourers, and those there were perfectly unable to comprehend why Mr Westley and his daughter should have selected such an out-of the-way corner of the world to live in – a non-resident rector, a curate and his wife, who were very kind and friendly, but who evidently could not quite understand the position of these new parishioners – altogether a strange experience for Glenarva, who did not perhaps take very kindly to the place or the people, and who was regarded by them as a perfect enigma, keeping herself to herself as she did, taking long solitary walks, and generally maintaining a dignified seclusion from which she never willingly emerged.

For some reason best known to the local wisdom of the village, popular opinion soon decided that Mr Westley was engaged in a lawsuit which had brought him over from Ireland, and kept him till it was settled chained near London. The many letters and the large packets of papers were thus satisfactorily accounted for, and even the few journeys Glen took to town were assigned to the same cause 'Mr Westley, poor gentleman! Being in weak health, of course his daughter had to see to the business for him.'

Mr Westley was in weak health, and his daughter, as is usual in such cases, seemed the only person who failed to realise the fact; indeed, it might have been hard enough for a much older individual who had always lived with the once owner of Glenarva to comprehend he was less strong than usual.

Always delicate, always, save by fits and starts, limp mentally, from the day he saw his grand castle begin to totter, Mr Westley sank into the condition of an invalid. He had at first nothing whatever in a physical sense wrong with him. The mournful tone of his voice, the languor of his movements, his dislike to anything which brought him into contact with his fellows, arose not from illness, but the utter collapse of hope. Had he been a stronger man, he must either have died or gone out and fought fortune again – again, perhaps, to lose; but in any case he would have made another bid for success.

As matters were, he simply sank without a struggle – unless, indeed, the feeble effort he made on first returning to London to recall the fact of his existence to one former friend could be termed a struggle. His worldly affairs got gradually worse and worse, while he himself, with, as has been said, nothing really wrong as regarded his health, sank into the condition of a confirmed invalid.

He did not walk, or work, or ride, or boat, or visit. People accepted the fact of his illness and incapacity without troubling themselves to consider what was the matter with him.

He had no intention of posing for a martyr, or crying 'Wolf'; and yet in effect it was owing to his constant depression and gentle inactivity that Glen, when disease really laid its hand upon him, failed utterly to see what was happening.

Mr Westley knew, however. With the silence of love, he kept his knowledge to himself, but he was perfectly well aware that at last a mortal ailment had fastened upon him, and that though the course it pursued might be slow, the end would prove fatally sure.

Then it was at the eleventh hour he began to reproach himself, to consider what he might have done, if he had but possessed sufficient energy. During the long summer days, when Glen was writing or out walking, when she was thinking, planning, hoping for the future, he sat, with the scent of the simple flowers growing about their little dwelling filling the humble sitting-room, anxiously considering his daughter's life, which ere many years he knew would have to be lived without him, and reproaching himself for not having in the past done something which it was absolutely impossible a person of his temperament ever could at any time have accomplished.

To say that a man might have done this or that had he been more energetic seems about as sensible as to suggest he might have written an opera or an epic poem, or painted a picture, or built St Paul's, or tunnelled the Alps, without the genius for compassing any one of these feats being conferred upon him by nature.

To have asked Mr Westley to go out into the world and fight among the rank-and-file was like asking a lame man to run, or a deaf man to hear, or a blind man to see! After he first left Glenarva he had thought to insure his life, but, perhaps without any sufficient reason, the doctor gave so doubtful a report of his constitution that the money asked in the way of premium could not be considered other than prohibitory.

Then he strove to put by a little, and in effect did manage, by dint of the most painful economy and beautiful self-denial, to fill a small purse for a rainy day – or for Glen, when days with him were past forever.

On this amount he had tried not to encroach, keeping it in a bank where he got low interest, but felt his small store safe. The money Mr Merritt had contrived to get him before he left Ballyshane was pretty well expended.

He and Glen had lived close – painfully close – but as it was impossible for them to limit their expenses to the trifling sum which sufficed at Ballyshane, somehow pence had gone, and then shillings, and then pounds, and the sovereigns laid aside for 'extras' dwindled down, till at length but few remained to give a sense of strength and security to the regular income, which was far – far too limited.

Nevertheless, Mr Westley was not uneasy – not very uneasy, that is to say. As the guineas went, his conviction on the subject of Glen's ability to earn money grew. He had substantial reasons for this belief. Mr Pedland's mind was at length made up to bring out Miss Westley's novel in the autumn, while through Mr Lacere's intervention one of the best publishing houses had been induced to accept the great work Mr Vassett felt it 'would be inexpedient for him to produce,' and Mr Lacere believed she was to receive some small sum for the copyright.

If these good things had come to Glenarva at Ballyshane, if a five-pound note had dropped out of a publisher's letter while she was within sound of the wash of the Atlantic waves, the girl would have gone mad with joy; but now, though she was glad and thankful, she did not feel elated, as might once have been the case. The first meagre course of success was announced, but its advent had been so long delayed the girl's eager appetite was gone. She had been trying to reach the grapes for such a time that she felt too weary and jaded to eat now she was assured they were within her grasp. She was strangely quiet about the matter, her father considered. Even Mr Lacere, who did not know her nature so well, felt surprised she failed to evince more pleasure when he cautiously broke the news of victory to her.

He and she talked about it all one evening as they paced slowly back from evening service at an old-world church to which Mr Westley had said his daughter would accompany Mr Lacere if that gentlemen wished to see a quaint building. The Westleys' new friend found his way sometimes down to the remote corner of the world where they were living; he discovered charms in the neighbourhood and beauties in the cottage Glen had never done; he partook of the tea she poured out as though it were some rare and expensive beverage the like of which he had never tasted except under Mr Westley's roof; he watched Glen as she flitted about the room, and listened to her father's conversation as if the whole world could hold for him no higher delight than the society of a young girl and a man whose name was writ large in the black books of Fortune.

Mr Westley liked him greatly; he looked forward to his visits with as much pleasure as anything in those summer days could afford him; he had a vague intention of sooner or later taking Mr Lacere into his confidence, telling him how utterly alone Glen must stand when she lost her father, and entreating on her behalf the good offices of this grave, shy man, who under an apparently stern manner hid a warm heart, for the daughter he would, ere she was very much older, have to leave.

But precipitancy, except when he ought to have been cautious, had never proved one of Mr Westley's besetting sins, and so he deferred and deferred the confidence till there was no necessity to make it.

All this time Glenarva herself was not very well, while Mr Westley had often of late caught what he called a chill. If he had styled these attacks by any other name, his daughter might have felt more uneasy than she did, but an illness which can be attributed to cold, and yields apparently to a day's rest in bed and a few simple remedies, is not one calculated to arouse keen apprehension.

It never certainly occurred to Glen to feel uneasy, though she was often depressed.

Even when Death knocks at the door, there is nothing much more difficult to realise than that one who has been with us always will talk with us no more; that we shall never again – never till we ourselves have passed to that land which is to us now all silence and all mystery – hear the familiar voice, see the familiar face, touch the familiar hand; that solitary and desolate, we, who never thought the word 'loneliness' could for us have a practical meaning, must labour till the evening, work till the gathering shadows tell us the day is well nigh spent and the night close at hand.

And Glenarva Westley found it just as difficult then to conceive of mortal sickness crossing their threshold as she did afterwards to realise the coming of that one visitor who may not be denied admittance.

Once, indeed, when she had sat up very late beside the fire which that 'chill' necessitated being lighted in her father's room, a terror for which she could in nowise account seized her; and moved by some secret instinct, she crossed the room softly, and stood beside the bedside, listening to the regular breathing which told that sleep had at last come brooding gently down on Mr Westley's eyelids. She looked at him as he lay, his features in utter repose, his arm thrown out over the coverlet, his hand half closed and still as possible. Unbidden tears rolled down her cheeks as she gazed; the whole of his wrecked life, the sadness and pathos and misery of it all, seemed for a moment more than she could endure, and when she went back to her seat and watched the leaping firelight, she wondered, with no triumphant feeling of success, but a trembling marvel, whether such blessing might be hers, she should indeed be able to make his future better than his past had been, to get all those good things for him in the days to come he had been forced to do without through the many long days that were past.

Upon another night, too, when she could not get to sleep till the early dawn of the summer's morning stole into her room, the same unreasoning terror shook the girl's very soul: it was no tangible fear which came and laid its cold hand upon her heart, which drew her out of bed and caused her to throw wide her window, and, leaning over the sash, try to find solace in the voices of the night.

How weird, and solemn, and strange they sounded as she stood in the silence and the semi-darkness all alone. If there be any truth in the idea that the trouble we shall have to pass through is faintly indicated in our imaginations, as it is said the shape of the fern is seen in miniature if we cut across its stem, Glen then beheld as in a glass darkly the form of the spectre she was going forward to meet. But with the sun and the morning light, and the thousand happy sounds of day, the horror faded away, and Glen did not think much more of it than she might of a bad dream.

Nevertheless she sometimes marvelled, 'Why is it I do not feel more elated at my success? Why do I not dance and sing with delight? Why am I not inclined to ask all the world to share my joy?'

The reason, if she could have known it, perhaps was that she did not herself believe in the success which had come. Like David when he told Ahimaaz to 'turn aside,' and waited for the tidings Cushi was bearing to him, she had a trembling presentiment that there was news to follow the announcement of her victory which should quench the shout of exultation with the bitter cry of mourning.

And for her, then, there was not even to be more than that gleam of hope which her own hand darkened. As a rule, when youth sees, or thinks it sees, the winning-post just ahead, some friend or foe walking across the course destroys the chances of success that had seemed absolute certainties. Later on, circumstances often perform this act of fouling; but in the outset of life it is generally a human being who, from a love of marring and meddling and proffering unasked-for advice, and gossiping about matters which concern no person save the racer pushing onward to the goal, affects the results of the struggle, and sometimes changes the whole course of existence.

It was an apparently slight cause that prevented the great house bringing out Glen's novel; the check came suddenly, and in the form of a letter from Ned Beattie.

As was her usual practice, the girl, always an early riser, had walked across the fields to meet the postman. No more lovely morning ever dawned. In the woods the doves were cooing, high above head the larks sang loud and clear; over the distant moor hung a purple haze – a sure sign of heat; down by the watercourses the cattle were standing knee-deep in the stream, or lying amongst the rich rank grass luxuriously chewing the cud; on all sides arose the bleating of sheep; the fields were dotted with snow-white lambs; from the farmhouses came the occasional bark of a dog, the quacking of ducks, the clucking of fussy hens escorting their active broods to favourite corners where insects were to be found in plenty; there was a great peace about the landscape, and standing still in the midst of waving grass and growing corn, Glen, looking to right and left, felt satisfied there was something in all this rich and bounteous country she did not thoroughly understand or appreciate; but which, if things continued to go well with her, she might learn to value, as wiser and older and cleverer people than herself had done before she was thought of.

She waited for the post at a point where the man made a detour ere coming straight on to their cottage, which cottage lay indeed at the extreme limit of his beat.

She expected – what? A letter from Mr Vassett, or Mr Pedland, or one of the many editors she had written to, or Mr Lacere, or perhaps even proof. If once she could see anything of hers in proof, she felt she should take fresh heart, and go on with a braver spirit. Afar off she could hear the rush of one of the early morning trains as it swept through the tranquil valley to London. A collie with whom she was on intimate terms came and licked her hand. The air was full of pleasant sounds and grateful scents, and there was the postman, who, seeing her, paused and took out a letter.

'Only one this morning, miss,' he said; and then, turning down the lane, went to deliver his good and evil tidings to farmhouse and hall and rectory and hovel.

'Only one – from Ned.' Glen sat down on the lowest step of the stile and opened the envelope. As she did this, there came wafted in imagination the familiar sound of the waves – the glitter of the sun upon the sea – the smell of the iodine – the smoke of the kelp fire – the plash of oars – and even the taste of the salt brine upon her lips.

That had been her past – the wild, grand coast – the raving billows – the strip of yellow sand – the frowning headlands – the screaming gulls – the stretching bogs and the treeless expanse of desolate country – and now she looked around and smiled half sadly, and drew out Ned's letter.

Ned's letters were of the nature of manuscripts. They were the produce of many hours, in many weeks. They proposed to convey an epitome of the news of the district, and it may at once be said they fulfilled their promise.

There was nothing too great or too little for Ned's pen to exercise itself upon, and Glen's conscience had often reproached her when she remembered how scanty were the tidings she returned in exchange – how closely she kept the secret of what she was doing, hoping, expecting, from this friend of the dear old happy careless days gone by.

As she pulled the enclosure out of the envelope these were the words on which her eyes fell:

> *It was mean of you, Glen; I could not have believed it. All the same, though, we wish you success – every one of us. Write soon. – Ned.*

What did this astounding conclusion mean? She turned the letter over, and found the gist of the whole lay in a postscript hurriedly added, much smeared and blotted, and written evidently in much perturbation of mind. The cat was out of the bag at last. Every soul in Ballyshane, every inhabitant of Artinglass, knew now why Mr and Miss Westley had gone off in such a hurry to London. Her old admirer, Mr Dufford, had come down to take the duty at Artinglass while the Rector was ill, and, as chance would have it, he lodged at the Berlin-wool and fancy shop, the owner of which likewise kept the local post-office.

To him came one day a book parcel of manuscript, which, happening to elicit from the postmistress a remark to the effect that 'few of such things came now to Artinglass since Miss Westley was gone from Ballyshane,' led to further inquiries, and to a perfect conviction on the part of the whole countryside that the girl was making her fortune.

Miss Grumley had brought the news to the Vicarage, believing Glen's old friends would be only too delighted to hear she was doing so well. 'They say you are writing for the *Penny Rambler*,' added Ned, mentioning a publication which in those days was relegated to the kitchen, and deemed too poor and silly to find favour in the eyes of mothers of families, 'whatever that may be. Miss Grumley has heard the people who own it pay well. I am sure I hope they do. But, oh, Glen! why could you not have told us? Mother is quite hurt. You know if you had been her own daughter she could not have loved you more. No wonder your letters were short, and had nothing in them worth reading. It is only surprising you could write to us at all, knowing what you were keeping back;' and then he added the words previously quoted.

The letter dropped from Glen's fingers. She had not read, she never did read the first part of it; she sat for a little while stunned; she did not feel the sunshine, or hear the birds, or smell the meadowsweet, or see the stretching fields dotted with sheep and lambs. The first thing that roused her attention was the collie licking her hand.

'Oh, Nell!' she exclaimed. 'Oh, Nell, I am miserable!' and laying her cheek on the dog's grizzled head, she cried as if her heart would break.

She was not crying because Ned called her mean and close, though that hurt her sorely, but because her secret had become known to those she wished to keep it from; and all comfort and security and freedom in writing was over.

The very book Mr Lacere had sold for her could not now be published; it told a story she never would have ventured to have put on paper had she not felt secure under the shelter of the assumed name selected after much thought and mature deliberation. In the work she had introduced her own relations, Lady Emily and others, who seemed to Glen equally objectionable. Her pen had run freely, unrestrained by the slightest fear of consequences while she was writing. It never once occurred to her anyone would ever know who was the author of this remarkable novel; but now in a moment the whole position was changed, and in despair Glen dried her eyes and tried to consider what she had better do.

Before she reached home her mind was made up. She must get back the manuscript; no matter what the consequence, that novel must not appear. It was dreadful, it was heart-rending; but still she could think of no other course. Naturally, Mr Lacere would be deeply offended; well, even the forfeiture of his friendship was a result which must be risked. She talked the matter over with her father, who, though more doubtful than his daughter as to the course which ought to be adopted, still did not think it would do to publish the book.

'You had better go to town, Glen,' he said, 'and explain the whole matter to Mr Lacere. To a certain extent you might be guided by his advice,' added Mr Westley, who most earnestly desired to shift the burden of this new and sudden responsibility on to the shoulders of some other person.

'I am afraid,' answered Glen, 'there is nothing to be done, except get back the manuscript. Mr Lacere will be terribly annoyed. After all his kindness and the trouble he took, too –'

It was mid-day before the girl got into London, and hot, tired, and dusty, reached the welcome shade of the City lanes. To turn into Mr Lacere's office after the stifling heat of the carriages on the South-Western line, and the glare of the streets that led from the terminus into the heart of the Lord Mayor's kingdom, was like entering some cool grot in the midst of a parched and sandy desert. For a moment she paused in the hall to read the names painted there. Mr Logan Lacere was the person she wanted, and she wended her way slowly upstairs, thinking as she went how she should begin to say what was in her mind.

She knocked at the panel of the first door she came to, turned the handle, and went in. A gentleman stood behind a desk, and looked across it at her as she walked shyly forward.

He was not her friend; she had never seen him before, and he seemed perfectly amazed at sight of her.

'Is Mr Lacere within?' she asked, feeling as she put the question strangely flurried and uncomfortable.

'*I* am Mr Lacere,' was the unexpected reply.

Glen stared at the speaker for a moment, and then made this extraordinary statement, 'But you are not *my* Mr Lacere!'

The stranger smiled. His smile was what most persons would have considered mild, tolerant, reassuring, and benignant, yet in the midst of all her hurry and confusion Glen found time to feel she neither liked it nor him.

She could not have told what the something was which repelled her. She only knew she wished she had not come into the office, and that she was well out of it again and walking back to the station.

Yet the gentleman was well favoured, his manner courteous, and the voice in which he said, 'It is Mr Logan Lacere you wish to see, I presume?' gentle and by no means unpleasant.

'Yes,' said Glen; 'I did not know – that is, I mean –'

Probably it would have been extremely difficult for her to explain what she did mean – at all events she did not try, but stopped at this point.

'He is out at present,' remarked the other Mr Lacere, coming to her assistance, 'but I do not think it will be long before he returns. If you would like to wait,' and he pulled forward a chair, and with a polite gesture of his hand invited her to be seated.

Glen hesitated – perhaps in all the few years of her life she had never before so hesitated. She glanced round the office, she looked for one swift second in the face of the man who was looking at her: she thought of the hot dusty pavements; that she was very tired; that she had no other place to call at unless she turned back to the west and paid Mr Vassett or Mr Pedland a visit – for which, perhaps, neither gentleman would be especially grateful; that she must see Mr Logan Lacere or else return home with her mission unfulfilled; that the room was cool and pleasant after the glare of the streets. Nevertheless –

'He is almost certain to be back shortly,' said this strange Mr Lacere, noticing her hesitation and understanding the cause of it as little as she did.

'If I shall not be intruding –' Glen murmured.

'Not in the least,' was the reply. 'You will have the office to yourself, for I am going out. Should you like to look at the newspaper?' and he handed her the *Times*, which she took mechanically.

There was a clock on the mantelshelf; after Mr Lacere's departure, it seemed to Glen that she and the timepiece were alone in the world together. She might have been in a far-off desert for any sound of human life which reached her. How silent the whole house seemed – how loud the clock ticked! Glen's heart and the pendulum appeared racing together, but her heart won. Its throbbing distanced the regular beat of the clock, till growing weary of the conflict, the girl rose, and began pacing the limits of the narrow room. Her life since she came to London had told upon a nervous system never before really put upon its trial; and Glen, who in the days not yet a whole year gone by rode shaggy ponies, and climbed dizzy cliffs, and walked at the very edge of precipices that looked sheer down into three hundred fathoms of water, and stepped without a thought of fear into a crazy old boat, now found danger in the sudden stoppage of a train, almost dreaded to cross a crowded thoroughfare, could not bear the sound of a clock ticking, and was unable to possess her soul in patience for half an hour, even with an office quite to herself, and a whole copy of the *Times*, advertisement sheet included, for companionship!

Suddenly, as in her restless walk she had reached a row of bookshelves that lined a recess opposite the window, and was trying for the twentieth time to fix her attention upon the volumes and read their odd-looking titles, a step sounded on the stairs, and before she could regain her seat the door of the office opened, and Mr Lacere entered.

At sight of the girl, his face, which had previously worn a look of heavy care, lighted up and brightened instantly.

'Why!' he said, and held out one hand, while he took off his hat with the other. 'Why!' and for a moment it seemed as if that were the only word in the whole of his vocabulary.

'I have come about that book, Mr Lacere,' Glen explained. She did not feel afraid now of his being vexed; she only felt a great trouble because of what she had to say.

'You got my letter, I hope? This was interrogative.

'Oh yes, and I was so happy and thankful; but now that is all over; it can't be published.'

'Indeed! why not? Sit down and tell me what you mean;' and thus entreated, Glen resumed her chair, while Mr Lacere stood leaning against his desk, and with one foot resting on the rail of an office stool, waited to hear her explanation.

There was a rest and a strength about the man, in his voice, his look, his manner, which soothed Glen's unquiet spirit – as a mother's cool hand laid on a child's feverish brow seems to ease the pain in the throbbing temples. At last the ticking of the clock did not distress her. Now her heart beat calmly and evenly as was its wont. Almost before she knew she had begun her story, it was half told. Mr Lacere did not move or speak or interrupt her till she had quite finished. Even then he remained silent for a moment ere he said:

'It seems a great pity.'

Pity! Glen knew more about that than he did, or at least she thought so; but she held her peace while he proceeded:

'It is such an opportunity as may not occur again for some time.'

'Never,' agreed Glen vehemently; 'such a chance is not likely to come to anybody twice in a lifetime.'

'I would not go quite so far as that,' said Mr Lacere, with a smile – oh! so unlike the smile of that other Mr Lacere Glen felt she mistrusted – 'but still, I think you ought to consider the matter well before you finally decide on adopting any course. You must recollect how difficult it is to get publishers to accept a manuscript at all.'

Yes, Glen was aware of the fact; but still this manuscript must not be printed. She went over the ground once more, explaining with greater emphasis than before how dreadful a thing it would be if, now it was known she wrote, the book were read by any of the persons who had all unconsciously sat for their portraits in it.

'But why should anyone imagine you to be the author of this particular work?' asked Mr Lacere.

Glen thought him dense for patting such a question. She did not say so, but feeling, since Ned's letter, as if she went about with the word 'Author' branded on her forehead, her manner implied that secrecy now was out of the question; besides, the work itself bore internal evidence she had produced it.

'People would know,' she declared, 'and besides – Have you read the story, Mr Lacere?' she inquired abruptly.

Mr Lacere confessed he had not – he had glanced at the first page; but 'I have not much leisure,' he explained, 'and a manuscript is really a formidable affair.'

Glen sighed, but could not controvert a statement which she had heard too often rejected to feel any doubt concerning its accuracy. Experience – even her experience – had taught the truth that a manuscript is the point where humanity draws the line. A man might risk his life for a friend; but where, oh! where is the person to be found who would, unless compelled, plunge into the depths of inky 'copy' to please or benefit the nearest and dearest belonging to him? Glenarva had still to meet that Curtius upon the summer's afternoon when she sat in Mr Lacere's office, and it may be added she has not met him yet.

As she remembered how hard she had found it to get anyone to read through even the shortest tale, she happened to look up, and found Mr Lacere's eyes fixed on her with an expression which showed he knew of what she was thinking.

'And as we have got a book accepted,' he said, as if in amplification of the idea that had been passing through her mind, 'I do not want you to lose the advantage gained without weighing carefully the probable consequences.'

For answer, Glen assured her adviser she had weighed everything – thought of everything – considered all consequences – and forgotten no possible contingency.

'It is already partly set up,' urged Mr Lacere.

The author was willing to pay for any loss that might have been incurred.

'And I had great hopes of being able to get you twenty pounds,' he said, playing the court card he had kept back for the last trick.

Glen drew a long gasping breath – twenty pounds! What a fortune it seemed to reject – then she answered valiantly.

'I must give up even that, Mr Lacere;' and he understood the case seemed urgent to her, whether it was urgent in reality or not.

Nevertheless, he asked her to think the matter over for a few days, which suggestion the girl negatived, stating, as neither days nor years could make any difference in her sentiments, it would only prolong her misery to defer deciding the affair at once.

'Well, if you think it best,' he remarked, at last, 'I will write to my friend. Yet still –'

Perhaps he was all the more pertinacious in entreating delay, because in his heart he wished she would abandon authorship altogether. He did not feel so sure now as had once been the case that Glen would never make her mark. Some words the reader in that great publishing firm dropped when speaking of the novel impressed him with the idea there might be more in this young person than appeared on the surface.

But she did not look like an author! Like many another, Mr Lacere possibly associated authorship in ladies with middle age and spectacles.

That he certainly could have understood, but Glen with her young face and the soft curves of her girlish figure, and her hair which glistened in the sunlight, and her eyes that then held no shadow of the sorrow they were to look on, and her voice with the sound of no tears as yet prisoned in its cadences – was quite another matter.

Here seemed a life to be lived, an existence to be enjoyed, not a battle to be waged or struggle won. Deep within him lay the almost forlorn hope that she would turn back ere it was too late, and abandon a strife he did not believe could conduce to her happiness.

And possibly he was right. It might have been better for Glen and those nearest and dearest to her if she had never written another line.

There are some women for whom even one leaf of the laurel crown proves too heavy a burden, even the faint echo of the world's applause too loud a sound, to whom genius seems but a demon driving its possessor out into dry and stony places, where is no tender grass for the weary feet to tread, and no trickling rills to refresh the tired and parched heart, nay, to whom fame itself becomes a mere mockery to the spirit searching vainly for something it shall never attain on earth.

'Yet still –' that was what he said; but he said no more, for Glen stopped him.

'I must begin all over again, I suppose, but it cannot be helped. I will never write another book founded on fact, so long as I live – never.'

Hearing which statement, Mr Lacere only looked at the girl more dreamily and speculatively than ever, and hoped with silent earnestness she might never write another book at all.

'I am ashamed,' said Glen, rising, 'to have taken up so much of your time.'

As she spoke she glanced at the clock, and felt really shocked to see how long the interview had lasted; and then she added some words about feeling grateful for all his kindness, which indeed she found hard to utter, not because her heart was empty, but because it was at that moment too full.

He did not answer directly; he only observed, a little coldly as it seemed to Glen, he wished he could have been of more use; and she was going to take her leave, with the consciousness of feeling rebuffed and chilled, when he said he meant to see her to the station.

'Oh, I could not think of giving you so much trouble!' exclaimed Glen.

'And I could not think of allowing you to walk back there alone,' he declared decisively.

So through the long, busy streets, where the westering sun was streaming, they paced slowly side by side. It was a happy walk for one of them – perhaps the happiest walk he ever had in all his life. On his arm rested the hand he would have liked to take and hold for ever in his own; the voice he had learned to love best in all the world murmured in his ear; the glamour he had escaped hitherto held him captive then. It was an enchanted river that glided away that evening beneath the bridges to the far away ocean he could not see. Vane and dome and pinnacle were lit with the glory which streams upon every earthly landscape but once in a human life, and then – then it was all over, and she did not know that he had been walking through a Paradise, the gates of which closed behind him as the train glided out of the station.

No, she did not know; and he strode back along streets whence sunshine seemed to have departed, to his office, where he worked hard and late, perhaps to finish some allotted task, perhaps to drown thought.

A man Hope had ever hitherto kept even step with in his darkest hours, but who for once heard only the rustle of her trailing garments, as slowly and reluctantly the angel that had upheld him in the worst troubles he was ever yet called upon to encounter left him at this crisis alone, and with uplifted hands covering the radiance of her face departed through the night, which was but little blacker than his worldly prospects.

Chapter IX

YES

A YEAR HAD COME AND GONE since that October morning when the Irish steamer entered Morecambe Bay. The summer, which always, no matter how long and how fine it may be, seems so short a space, was over. London was looking its worst and dullest in damp autumnal weather, and Mr Westley and his daughter were back in town, having decided their country cottage was too far from everywhere, and that the great literary battle could only be properly fought out within the metropolitan bills of mortality.

It was a wretched season – worse, far worse, Glen decided, than that which inaugurated her search for a publisher. A green winter, which always and ever makes such fat churchyards; dull, damp, warm, depressing; terribly trying to a girl accustomed to Atlantic breezes, to pure mountain air, to a climate which, though often mild through the worst months of the year, was never enervating.

The weather, however, in London, or the medicine he was taking, seemed to suit Mr Westley better than the lonely moors in Middlesex, the glorious summer sunshine, the simple remedies he had before experimented with. Apparently the course of his malady was stayed; those cruel 'chills' ceased to shake his frame; his appetite, which had in the country rebelled against the simple food they were there at least able to obtain fresh and pure, accepted in town anything provided for it. So far as her father was concerned, Glen felt happier; but her own prospects were far from bright.

'I am going back,' she thought – 'back – back – back.'

In the lives of most authors there occurs, I imagine, a crisis when they stop disgusted, or else go on in sheer despair. They either turn to something else, or otherwise persevere not from any real hope they feel of ultimate success, but because they know they must 'see the thing out.'

Such a crisis had come to Glenarva Westley. If at that juncture she could have seen her way to adding twenty or five-and-twenty pounds a year to their income, she would have put the cover on her ink-bottle, laid her pen in the stand, and said, 'Well, I have tried that, and it has failed. I was mistaken in thinking I could write.'

As matters stood, she did rack her brain considering whether she could not make money by any means; but, alas! save for needlework the girl seemed then to have no gift.

She was fairly educated, but she did not know enough to teach; and if she had, would rather have swept a crossing. She played well, but was nothing of a musician; her drawing was of the usual commonplace character; for languages she had no more aptitude than for arithmetic. No one could have affirmed with truth that Glenarva Westley was a dunce, yet in most branches of learning a schoolmistress would have said she was 'singularly backward.' She had not even a speaking acquaintance with any 'ology. Such gifts as she possessed – and they were not many – did not lie in the direction of money-making.

'I am fit for nothing,' she thought one night in a frenzy of self-depreciation, and sobbed herself to sleep.

Things were not going well with her. The novel Mr Pedland published turned out, so far as she was concerned, a hopeless failure. The papers had not a good word to say for it; the critics were beautifully unanimous in making merry over her finest passages – in exposing the absurdity of her plot, the faults in her grammar, the solecisms of which she was guilty, the meagreness of her ideas, the poverty of her invention, the tallness of her talk, and the impossibility of many things which were literal facts ever having happened.

The very fierceness of the attack caused Glen to gird on her armour. She was disappointed, but not beaten; disheartened, but not driven back.

The non-success of *Tyrrel's Son*, by GBW Shane, did not send her crying to bed; it was the weary, weary waiting of the days and weeks and months which came after. Though even *Tyrrel's Son* held a cruel and terrible disappointment for the girl – the particulars of which it may not be totally unprofitable to summarise here for the benefit of those young authors who think the way to fame lies along a well-turfed alley bordered with flowers and shaded by trees, in which the nightingale jug-jugs ceaselessly.

Amongst many other things not so nice as herself, Mrs Beattie possessed a maiden aunt who, having as great a craze for travel as Madame Pfeiffer, spent all her small fortune in marching from pillar to post, from city to city, and from land to land.

As good or evil fortune would have it, just about the time Glen's novel was published, this lady arrived in London from some twentieth-rate spa in Germany; whither she had repaired to test the virtues of the waters and the merits of a certain local physician concerning an 'affection of the ear' she had contracted while residing, for economy's sake, in uncomfortable lodgings where she was obliged to sleep exposed to the draughts from window, chimney, and door.

Her first act was to look up the Westleys – her next to merge her very identity in Glen's novel.

Knocking about the world as she had done, it was her fortune to have come in contact with all sorts and conditions of authors – except good. She had met and discoursed with Miss This and Mrs That and Mr The Other, who each and all vied in telling 'travellers' tales' concerning that land, the mysteries of which can never be fully known, save to those who have carried the burden and passed through the trouble, and felt the heat and the cold of the long, long years filled with disappointment, and trial, and success.

All enthusiasm, she carried off Miss Glen's first venture. She read it – she approved. She said the girl had a 'great future' before her. She wrote that by the most curious coincidence she had formed an acquaintance in her then lodgings with a gentleman who could, she found, influence the young author's future most materially.

'He is on the *Times*,' she explained. 'He can get you a review. The moment you receive this letter, send me another copy of *Tyrrel's Son*, or, if you have not one, go to your publisher and procure the novel without delay. If Mr Elphin has it at once he will put you a good notice in the *Times*, which *ought* to be worth ever so much money to you.'

On the strength of this letter Glen repaired to Mr Pedland, who smiled and said he had heard so much of 'that sort of thing' he did not attach the slightest importance to it; which observation rather nettled Miss Westley, for, as she told him, her friend would not have promised her a review unless she felt certain of being able to get it.

Word led to word, and answer to answer, till at length Mr Pedland 'backed his opinion', as the lower orders are so fond of phrasing the matter, with a memorandum to the effect that if a review of *Tyrrel's Son* appeared in the *Times* – not as an advertisement (those were the days when advertisements in extremely small type, and the charge for which was very high, were inserted in the body of the paper) – within a month, he would give her seventy pounds.

Placing this document, about which she had happily sufficient common-sense to keep silence during the impending interview, securely in her pocket, Glen, with the three volumes filled by the doings of *Tyrrel's Son*, and other people, tied up in a neat brown-paper parcel, and wended her way to Miss Stanuel's lodgings, where that lady, who if not saving was nothing, received her in a dingy bedchamber, having only, as she explained, the occasional use of a sitting-room for which she did not pay.

'It is fortunate,' she exclaimed, 'that you happened to come at this particular time, for Mr Elphin has not gone out yet. I will introduce you to him; and mind, you must be on your best and prettiest behaviour, for he is a person who can either make or mar you.' Having finished which sentence, so admirably calculated to set the young author at her ease and render her manners natural and pleasing, Miss Stanuel left her visitor alone for a moment, while she herself went and apprised the great man of the impending interview.

Glen had already passed through some curious experiences, and seen some strange sights in the course of her London life; but she certainly considered this 'power on the *Times*' not the least singular person who had come across her path. He was a short, dark, dirty-looking individual, who rose and bowed as she entered, and then sat down again beside a table strewed with papers. He had been writing, and, for greater convenience, doing it with coat sleeves pulled up, and wristbands – not over-clean – turned back. He did not look as if he had washed himself for a long time, or as if the *Times* paid handsomely for the work he did. His manner was curt, not to say rude, but Miss Stanuel followed his utterances with the rapt and earnest gaze of admiring belief.

'Are you paying attention, young lady?' she would say to Glen, after the delivery of some truism as old and hackneyed as that water finds its level. 'Now, don't forget this – be sure you remember every word Mr Elphin speaks. It is not often it falls to the lot of beginners, more especially to a chit like you, to get advice from the fountain-head.' To an outsider the whole affair would have seemed inexpressibly ludicrous. The brazen self-assurance of the gentleman without whom the *Times* must have sunk into oblivion; Glen's amazed contemplation of the celebrated writer; and Miss Stanuel's almost worshipping regard, composed a spectacle which indeed it seemed a pity should have been so entirely destitute of an audience. Afterwards Glen felt too much provoked to laugh about the matter. It was the first time she had been made a fool of, though it may here be remarked it was not the last.

'Now, shall I cut this book for you?' suggested Miss Stanuel, when the distinguished writer seemed inclined to intimate that the interview had lasted quite long enough.

'No, thank you,' said Mr Elphin loftily; 'I always like to cut for myself as I go on.'

Miss Stanuel looked triumphantly at Glen as he made this statement.

'Well, we will not take up any more of your valuable time,' she remarked.

'I am going out,' he answered – as one who should say, 'I'll take very good care you don't.'

'And I am sure Miss Westley can never feel sufficiently grateful to you.'

'Oh! that's nothing,' exclaimed Mr Elphin, but whether his words referred to Miss Westley's gratitude or his own good offices it was difficult to conjecture.

The days went by – the weeks – a month – and still no review appeared; instead there came a note from Miss Stanuel, saying she felt dreadfully angry with Glen.

'Mr Elphin tells me *Tyrrel's Son* is *very poor indeed*, that you could not have taken any pains with it, and that you never will succeed unless you produce something a great deal better than that. Of course, even in your own interests, it was impossible for him to insert a review of such a book. He assures me he has done the very kindest thing possible in taking no notice whatever of it.'

'I am not surprised,' observed Mr Pedland, when Glen repeated some of these encouraging remarks to him. 'I have seen and heard too much of that sort of thing to believe it. If your friend had been as good as his word, I should have felt very much surprised indeed.'

Had the author of *Tyrrel's Son* thought of telling Mr Pedland of Miss Stanuel's obliging offer to cut the pages, and Mr Elphin's refusal, he could have formed a shrewd conjecture as to what the gentleman on the *Times* had done with her book, and how he spent the few shillings he got for it!

This was all bad and disappointing, but it did not seem to Glen so bad and utterly disheartening as the fact that when Mr Lacere took her latest manuscript to the great publishing house from which she felt obliged to withdraw her former book, it was 'declined with thanks,' the reader telling him afterwards he did not consider it nearly so good as the first.

Mr Vassett also made no sign of entertaining any mad desire to secure a book by the 'gifted young author.' He was very kind and very friendly, but he did not seem to 'see his way' any more clearly than had been the case the first day he saw her. Glen felt that 'getting into print,' on which she had so pinned her faith, was a mere mockery and delusion – more particularly after one of the partners in a very well-known firm told her kindly she had better for the future not mention the fact of Mr Pedland having published anything of hers.

'His works do not stand well,' explained this gentleman; 'they are regarded in the same light as the "Minerva Press" novels were formerly.'

Mr Vassett laughed when Glen told him this. She went to him for comfort, but he could not deny the soft impeachment brought against poor Mr Pedland.

'I dare say he does a business which he makes satisfactory to himself,' he said; 'but he has not brought out anything remarkable.'

'Except in the way of badness, I am told,' added Glen. 'I hear if his name is on a book it is at once stamped as feeble, poor, and trashy.'

'Well,' answered Mr Vassett, 'he has not the monopoly of dull novels; the fact is, there are very few written worth publishing at all.'

'I wonder – I wonder,' cried Glen, 'if ever I shall write anything worth publishing.'

She would have felt immensely obliged to Mr Vassett had he replied he was certain of it; but he made no reply of the kind.

He only hazarded a vague statement to the effect that out of all the authors he had known, scarcely one had achieved what he should call a great success; but at the same time he implied he thought it not totally impossible that after a few years, when his visitor had seen more, and thought more, and read more, she might be able to produce a book he would feel justified in considering.

Meantime, however, as Glen had no intention of waiting a moment longer than she could help, she went occasionally to one or other of the new publishers, who then, as now, were constantly springing up like mushrooms.

If they did not determine, however, to have nothing to do with Miss Westley within the first five minutes, they were sure to want a portion of the expenses paid, or a certain number of subscribers guaranteed, or a known name on the titlepage as editor.

It was weary work, more especially as Glen often took a most intense dislike to some of these gentry. She said something about this one day to Mr Vassett when Mr Pierson was present, and the latter made a laughing remark, to the effect that her instinctive aversions seemed to be wonderfully accurate.

'Why do you dislike Mr Blank so much?' he asked.

'I am sure I can't tell,' answered Glen; 'I always either like or do not like people at once.'

'And do you never find occasion to change your opinion, Miss Westley?' asked Mr Vassett.

'I have not yet,' she said.

'Instinct,' suggested Mr Pierson.

'I suppose,' observed Mr Vassett didactically, 'that Providence, having denied women reason, gives them instinct as a compensation,' And then they all laughed, and Glen declared she thought a little reason had been given to her, and Mr Vassett answered, 'No, it had not; why should she be an exception to the rest of her sex?"

'You trust to your instinct,' he advised; 'that won't deceive you.'

There came a time in Glenarva's life when in anguish and bitterness she remembered those lightly spoken words, when she understood from sad experience a woman's best reason is but a will-o'-the-wisp, leading her on over marsh and brake and quagmire; while one swift intuition will, if followed in dumb, unquestioning faith, take her safely to the end of whatever road – darksome or light – she may be travelling.

During all that period of doubt and gloom, the Westleys were cheered on their way by the kindly advice and the staunch friendship of Glen's Mr Lacere. Like Glen herself, he had his troubles, which assumed the prosaic form of pecuniary losses. He talked a good deal to Mr Westley on the subject of his own reverses and disappointments, and for so reserved a man was extraordinarily frank in stating the extent to which he found himself embarrassed. Mr Westley, who had forgotten the few days of his own experience during which he was not harassed, listened to these revelations with sympathy, but without alarm. Mr Lacere had a business of some sort – a profitable business; he would soon be able to make more money. Anyone almost ought to be able to make money in London. What opportunities there were in the modern Babylon; what riches, what marvellous chances – ah! if he had come to London when first he left Glenarva, they would never have been poor. He was strong then, comparatively, and younger, and more active; but now he lay back in his chair and thought of his wasted life, and the hill he was descending, and listened while Mr Lacere talked about his own prospects, and trials, and hopes; and what he trusted to do, and what he expected to achieve, with the small amount of attention he was able to spare from the contemplation of his personal affairs. Mr Westley marvelled a little at these confidences till one evening, when a glimmer of the state of the case dawned upon his mind.

He shrank back involuntarily from the light, and closed his eyes against it; but when he looked again the light was still there, growing clearer and clearer as he gazed.

Mr Lacere was in love with Glen – his Glen – he did not feel a doubt on the subject; he could not be mistaken. He would ask him for her; and when this request came, what answer should be given?

For hours that night he lay wide awake thinking, considering, doubting, deciding. Glen, his motherless daughter; Glen, who would be left all alone in the world if, or rather when, Death should call for him, and say, 'Now I want you; come;' Glen, who on the face of the wide earth did not possess a relation for whom she cared or that would be likely to care for her; Glen, who would have little or no money; Glen, who could never, he felt, return to the old life she had, drowned in tears, left that October day which seemed to her so far back in the mystic past; Glen, who had never been, so far as he knew, in love with anybody, and to whom he believed it would be a terrible surprise and shock to find that Mr Lacere was in love with her.

'*She* must decide,' thought Mr Westley ere he fell into a troubled sleep, from which he awoke with a start and that sense of impending trouble which it is so hard to exorcise. And 'Glen must decide for herself' was the answer he gave Mr Lacere when that gentleman asked if he would trust the girl's happiness to him.

With the memory of Mr Dufford's rejection in his recollection, Mr Westley felt doubtful as to what Glen might say, and his manner indicated this doubt so strongly that Mr Lacere would have deferred the evil hour had Glen's father not remarked:

'If she says "Yes" I shall not make any objection. I wish, of course, your means had been better; but money, though much, is not everything, and I believe you would try to make her happy.'

Glen did not, however, say 'Yes' – she said 'No' – not as she had spoken the word to Mr Dufford, but rather after the manner of one on whom the proposal came too suddenly, and who did not exactly know her own mind. 'She had not thought about marriage.' 'She was not disposed to marry anyone.' 'She was very sorry – she liked Mr Lacere very much – she liked him better than anyone she had ever seen, except her father and the boys.' No; she liked him 'better than the boys, because he was older and wiser,' and knew 'more about everything.' 'Still, she could not marry him.' She 'hoped they would remain good friends.' 'It would grieve her greatly if he ceased to come and talk with her papa,' and she felt 'very grateful,' and 'truly grieved;' and Mr Lacere, who was not a bold wooer, and had not frittered away his affections on a dozen pretty women, quitted the house a good deal disheartened, and Glen went to her own room and had a little cry, after which she sat gravely and quietly down to needlework, and did not speak till Mr Westley broke the ice, and asked her plainly what answer she had given a very honest gentleman.

Then Glen told him her mind so far as she knew it herself, and Mr Westley saw clearly enough that there stood in Mr Lacere's way no real obstacle.

Glen had her own notions about love and lovers, gathered from hearsay, gleaned from books, evolved, perhaps, out of her internal consciousness; and it is only fair to say that neither Mr Lacere's love-making nor Mr Lacere himself realised even the poorest of her ideals on the subject. For one thing, the affair was to her feeling all far too serious and commonplace. The glamour of wooing should preface a proposal. She wished she could have known what was in his heart during those long walks and talks which took place among the Middlesex moors.

Vaguely she understood she had lost something that could never be given to her again. She was not old enough, or wise enough, though she had written books, and thought the whole experience of life was plain reading before her eyes, to put in words to herself the truth that the lover should always precede the possible husband, that the two characters should not come suddenly on the stage of a girl's life together; the prosaicism of marriage, the thought of ways and means, the fifty practical considerations which must obtrude themselves when the whole future of existence is concerned, are matters that ought to be led up to gradually – wandered into through fanciful alleys carpeted with moss, bordered with flowers, arched over with roses, within sight and sound of sparkling foun- tains – alleys where it is always summer, where the birds never cease singing, and to which, amid the thousand sordid cares and petty troubles of dull wedded experience, memory can revert as to a bright holiday – so bright, so beautiful, that even the bare recollection of its sunshine, its birds, its songs, can light up the whole of the dull after-days of existence with gleams of that golden glory.

Years afterwards Glen knew this was what she had missed, but it took years and years and years for her to understand it was the accursed money-troubles which dogged every step of his way – that tied the man's tongue, and froze the words trembling on his lips, and kept him silent when speech had been the truest wisdom, and made him, when he did make up his mind, taking his future in his hand, to ask her to share it, receive her doubtful 'No' almost as a final answer, and say to his own soul, 'It is best so. What right have I, with my poor fortunes, to "expect" any woman to marry me?'

And yet – he did not know; he could not receive his rejection as absolute; he would try again, and, if her answer was still the same, never see her more. There were other places on earth besides London. He would go abroad.

He had thought of leaving England when he sustained the loss that had during the course of the previous summer thrown him so far back in the world, and now he decided, that in case Glen refused him a second time, he would bid her and all his friends goodbye, and try whether in another country fate might hold a better fortune for him than had been the case hitherto.

But when he repeated his question Glen did not say 'No.' She had thought the matter out by herself. She talked a little to her father.

'My dear,' said Mr Westley, 'you have drawn many a hero after your own pattern out of your own fancy; but you will never, so long as you live, meet with a better man or truer gentleman than Mr Lacere.'

'I believe that, papa,' she answered, and yet still she hesitated.

She did not tell her father why – perhaps she could not have told herself. Some of those heroes of romance were, it might be, stopping the way, or, as is more than probable, Glen felt there were greater practical objections in the way of marrying Mr Lacere than Mr Westley seemed to realise.

One thing, however, was quite certain – she must now either say 'Yes,' or 'No,' without any future possibility of reconsidering her decision. When this calm, quiet, earnest suitor came for the second time, she understood he would not ask her again if she refused him. They would part, and part for ever. Could she let him go? She felt it would be impossible. Very patiently – far too patiently to accord with any romantic ideas – he waited for her answer. Glen looked about the room, at the worn carpet, at the old-fashioned chairs, the pembroke table, the glass over the mantelpiece – everywhere, anywhere save at those wistful brown eyes, at the yearning expression on that grave, worn face.

'Will you not speak?' he said at last. 'Tell me, if you can, the best – or – the – worst.'

Then she did look at him with the anxious, questioning look a child's face wears when it trustfully turns to its mother for a solution of all perplexing doubts and difficulties.

'I don't want to say "Yes," and I don't want to say "No,"' she explained.

His heart gave a wild leap, but he asked quietly, '*Can't* you say "Yes"?'

'Yes, then,' she answered. The words were spoken almost in a whisper, yet they sounded to his ears like the crash of joy-bells smiting the stillness of a summer's noon.

'Oh, my darling!' and for a moment she felt frightened at the vehemence of his tone; the revulsion of feeling – the knowledge that doubt was ended and security begun was almost more than he could bear; then: 'May God do so to me, and more, if ever I give you cause to repent your consent!'

It was but a young thing – a young, slight thing, though possessed of a grand courage and a big soul – he gathered to his heart and kissed as he had never kissed woman born of woman before.

If she had known, if she had only known that in the whole of his life she was the first creature he felt he could take in his arms and call wholly his own – something to care for; something to live for; something to work for; something to die for!

Is it well or ill, I wonder, that we, each and all of us, have so little real comprehension of past, present, and future? Well, possibly – or we should for ever in our uncertainty stand shivering on the brink of life's wide tideless river. As for Glen, just as she was wont at Ballyshane to step into the old crazy boat that generally scudded to its destination with one gunwale under water – so she now tripped into her place in the barque which was to convey her across life's heaviest seas. Whilst, as regards Mr Lacere, he had but the faintest notion of the sort of passenger he was taking on board.

He loved her – that was enough for him. He did not think then or afterwards how perilous an experiment it is for experience to undertake the guidance of ignorance; for Middle Age to say, 'I will pilot Youth, and Enthusiasm, and Impatience, and Hope "to the harbour where it would be."'

Chapter X

SUCCESS

FOR ONCE FATHER AND LOVER were of the same mind. Mr Lacere wished for a speedy marriage. Mr Westley raised no objection. He did not see the good, he said, of long engagements. 'After a short time,' he added, 'when I have got accustomed to the idea of Glen being your wife, as well as my daughter, I will give her to you with a feeling of perfect reliance.' And so it came to be understood that during the course of the autumn Miss Westley was to be transformed into Mrs Lacere.

So far, diplomatic arrangements between the two families had been friendly. Their limited intercourse partook of the nature of state visits. Mr Westley, always somewhat of a recluse, showed, Glen could not but observe, even less than his usual disposition to cultivate close and intimate social relations with the members comprising Mr Lacere's household. He said little about them, and the little he did say was in their praise; but Glen knew perfectly well her father did not take to the ladies of the Lacere family, and that, as if, by common consent, the fact of their existence was usually ignored.

'I hope, Glen,' he remarked on one occasion, 'you will always be good friends with your husband's family.'

'I hope so too,' answered Glen, stitching at a piece of work she held in her hand. When not writing she was generally sewing.

'He has no idea of our living with them, I trust?'

'Good gracious, no, papa!'

'Because, dear, I should not like to give you up altogether; and I do not think – indeed I am sure it would not be desirable for what one may describe as three families to reside under one roof.'

'You may be very sure, papa, I am going to live with you, and not with Miss Humphries.'

Now Miss Humphries was the name of the lady who was supposed to preside over the domestic arrangements at Kentish Town, where the Laceres resided, and Glen managed to impart such an amount of decision into the manner of her reply that Mr Westley paused and looked at her for a moment in doubt before he made any further observation. He had often before wondered whether it would not be wise for him to draw out some charts for his daughter's future guidance through the Lacere country, as, for instance, 'I should not be too intimate with them, Glen;' 'It is always competent to increase the amount of intimacy, but ungracious to lessen it;' 'Their ideas may not be yours, still, that is no reason why you and they should not remain excellent friends.' But he never expressed one of these axioms in words, and now all he said was:

'So long as that is clearly understood, my dear –'

'Oh, there shan't be any misconception on that point!' Glen assured him; and once again Mr Westley took refuge in silence, feeling that, while he could not define where it was, a hitch had arisen in some place, and that, although no one gave open expression to the fact, things were not going quite so smoothly as they ought.

He entertained no doubt matters would right themselves after a little time. Meanwhile he and Glen seemed tacitly to have arrived at the conclusion that 'least said,' even between themselves, 'would be the soonest mended.'

The consciousness that his daughter had not a sixpence to her fortune, that she was indeed a beggar maid, tied his tongue. A not unnatural reticence about expressing her sentiments concerning the family she was about to enter kept Glenarva herself silent, whilst Mr Lacere, who would only have felt too thankful had anyone planned his future course for him, held his peace, because, although he was aware the Westleys were poor, he did not in the least know how modest and moderate were the expectations of both father and child; that they would have been perfectly content to set up house on the most humble scale, and confine the domestic expenditure to a point far below any on which he had hitherto supposed respectable establishments could be kept going.

As for Glen herself, her first introduction to the ladies of Mr Lacere's family had proved a most bitter disappointment. She was privileged to make their acquaintance before any question arose of lovers and marriage, and she brought accordingly a perfectly unprejudiced mind to bear upon the subject. With that fatal desire to bespeak a favourable judgment which generally impresses the hearer falsely, Mr Lacere had spoken in such terms of his womenkind as had led Glen to believe they must indeed be little, if at all, lower than the angels. They were possessed of every possible virtue. They were unselfish, devoted, amiable, clever, industrious, forbearing, charitable in word and deed, thoughtful for others and forgetful of themselves. Like Lady O'Loony, in a word, they were 'bland, passionate, religious.' One of them painted in watercolours with delicacy, fancy, and skill; another understood everything in music there was to understand; while a third was a poetess of no mean order; and Miss Humphries posed alternately as a house brownie and an excellent cook, a sick nurse without compeer, and a manager such as is not often met in this wasteful, ill-regulated world.

Unhappily for herself, instead of following Charles Lamb's admirable example, Glen idealised all the persons thus presented for her admiration. Mr Lacere believed he was giving her merely rough outlines of forms he had from childhood been accustomed to admire, and the girl set herself at work to finish each portrait off with a delicacy the lady who painted miniatures most exquisitely on ivory might have tried to emulate in vain.

If they had been saints, and heroines, and martyrs, they could not have realised her fancy sketch, and as they were nothing of the sort, the disappointment she experienced proved proportionately severe.

Poor Glen! With all the will in the world she could not rush into friendship with any one of the four. She was quite content to believe they were most admirable people – possessed of every quality with which she had heard them credited, but at the same time she felt very sure – she never felt more sure of anything – she never could have much to do with them; that her way and their way lay in quite opposite directions, and that while Mr Lacere seemed everything that was pleasant, she could not really like any one of the ladies, who, according to his account, had a monopoly of earthly virtues.

And if this were the case before she was engaged, it grew to be ten times more the case afterwards.

All in vain the Misses Lacere embraced and welcomed her 'as a sister.' In vain Miss Humphries said, 'Now you will have *all* of us to love you, darling!' In vain they repeated singly and in chorus that 'though they had never thought a wife could be found good enough for the best man that ever lived, they were more than satisfied with his choice.'

Glen could not get up any enthusiasm on her own side. She could not adopt as sisters women old enough to be her mother, but who were far more gushing than she had ever been even at five years of age. She could not say she loved one of them, for she did not. She failed to feel that the fact of meeting with their approval filled her with the delight and astonishment it perhaps ought to have done; and lastly, there is little doubt that even then she believed in her heart every word they spoke lacked the ring of truth.

When a man has kept unmarried till middle life, his womankind must indeed be more than human to look upon the designing person who has ensnared him with approval, more especially when that person presents herself in the guise of a 'chit of a girl,' a 'tocherless lass,' a stranger, an author, and, worse than all, a native of Ireland.

The Misses Lacere were narrow-minded, prejudiced, selfish. They had lived in themselves and among themselves, till they lost all knowledge, if they ever possessed any, of a world outside their own petty aims, hopes, fears, interests. Instead of being glad the man was at last going to try to make a little happiness for himself in life, they were heartily sorry. They talked the matter over with bated breath, with solemn shakes of the head, with many 'Ahs!' and 'Yes, indeeds!' and 'We never thoughts,' and 'It is to be hoped it will turn out better than we expects;' and all the time Mr Lacere believed they were perfectly sincere in their praise of Glen; and Glen, though she felt they did not like her, and knew she did not like them, hoped she would outgrow her prejudices in time, and that, after all, if Mr Lacere was pleased and satisfied, and her father felt content and happy, it did not much matter what anybody else thought on the subject.

Mr Lacere and the Misses Lacere and Miss Humphries were especially careful at a very early period of the engagement to tell Glen the exact state of their pecuniary relations.

The ladies of the family were utterly without fortune.

'Well, so am I,' said Glen, which fact, if she could only have realised the truth, did not tend to render the position easier.

She was only laudably anxious to make her relations who were to be, feel that as she was in precisely the same condition as themselves, they need not be uncomfortable about their own impecuniosity.

The wisdom of adding 'another pauper to the domestic difficulty,' to quote the Mr Lacere who was not hers, might be questionable; but this view of things had not then occurred to Glenarva Westley. She did not come of a stock remarkable for worldly prudence. The drain thus indicated upon a man's income failed to strike even Mr Westley with dismay. He regarded it as he might a jointure, a settlement, or a mortgage on an estate; that it was optional with Mr Lacere to continue or discontinue it, was an idea which failed to strike either father or daughter. Neither was made of the material which would take from another what he had. None of the Laceres need have felt any uneasiness on that score. Poor though they were, the Westleys had not, to quote an Irish phrase, 'a mean drop of blood in their bodies.'

No fear of the young wife in this case coming in and sweeping the decks clean for her own benefit, her father aiding and abetting. Glen was prepared to do with limited means married, as she had done with limited means single; only she would have preferred to make the trial without the gushing endearments of her future relations. Words cannot express the disfavour with which Glen beheld middle-aged women comporting themselves as if in their first teens; heard her future husband called, 'Mordy, my treasure!' or, 'My precious Mordy!' or, 'Mordy, dearest darling!' when not addressed by some ridiculous pet name, which it is not too much to say made the girl – who was somewhat disposed to exalt her future husband into a hero, and worship him accordingly – shiver.

It was over this matter Glen became possessed of a curious involvement of family history.

Said Mr Lacere:

'I have never yet, dear, heard you speak my Christian name;' and he looked at her a little anxiously.

Glen fidgeted with the object nearest her ere she answered:

'Your first name is long, and I do not like to hear it shortened. May I call you by your second – Logan? I think that is so beautiful.'

'It is a surname. Glen,' he explained; 'my father's people were Logans, till one of them intermarried with a Miss Lacere, an heiress. He took her name and got her money, and that was the beginning of all our misfortunes.'

Glen thought this over at great length, and took an early opportunity of referring the question to Miss Lacere.

'You don't sign yourself Logan-Lacere?' she suggested.

'Oh dear no! *We* are not Logan-Laceres, I am happy to say – *we* have nothing to do with the Logans.'

'How does that happen?' asked Glen, mystified.

'Don't you know? Why, when Mordy's father died, after a time his mother married our dear papa, Owen Lacere.'

'But you are older than he is,' interrupted Glen, thoroughly mystified.

'Of course we are; we had lost our darling mamma three years when papa married again.'

'Wait a moment, wait a moment,' entreated Glen; 'then what relation are you to – to – Logan?'

'What do you mean? We are his sisters, of course.'

'That's impossible,' said Glen, with an energy which proved how exceedingly anxious she was to sever the Logan-Lacere connection.

'My dear, we have been always just the same in love as though we were the closest blood relations. Poor papa always said, "Whatever you do, never forsake Mordy," and we haven't. We have from the first felt the same to him as if he had been our own, own brother, and I am sure when darling Claudine died, if she had been aunt's very own niece she couldn't have fretted more about her.'

'I am getting lost,' observed Glen. 'Where does Claudine come?'

'Claudine was dear Philip's wife.'

'I give it up,' cried the future Mrs Logan-Lacere. 'I can't follow the matter at all.'

'And yet it is as simple as ABC. Our dear papa was Owen Lacere, who married for his second wife the widow of Logan-Lacere – the father of our precious Mordy and his sister Claudine. Claudine married our darling papa's nephew, and so –'

'You are not one of you a drop's blood, as we say in Ireland, to Logan?'

'If you like to put it that way, of course;' and Miss Lacere drew herself up offended. 'Though as for what you call a "drop's blood", we were all cousins, and we all love one another, oh, so dearly! and this question of relationship never was raised till –'

'Till somebody cared to raise it, I suppose,' said Glen wearily.

She thought during those days she should have lost her senses. What with trying to unravel the mystery of the Lacere connection; with holding her tongue concerning them to her father; with practising reticence about his relations to a man she felt she could not bear to wound; with her own non-success; with something about her father she could not understand; and with an attack of neuralgia which for months never left her, which drove her out of bed at four o'clock in the morning, and kept her pacing her room till after twelve at night; which seemed as if, like a dog, it took her in its teeth and worried her; which starved her almost, because the moment a meal was spread the inexorable pain came to table also and prevented her eating. She went and had a tooth out, and as she returned from the doctor's, met with that dreadful sympathy which was the curse of her new life.

'That poor little girl has got the face-ache,' said one City 'swell' to another as she passed the pair, holding a handkerchief to her mouth, suffering literally agonies.

Yet upon the whole, if she could have known it, both the City and the West End swell was very good to her in those days, very good indeed. He troubled her a little, as was only to be expected considering how fresh she was from the wild seashore, and the solitary moor, and the lonely hillside; but he certainly did, upon the whole, respect her ignorance and her innocence, and left her as free to traverse the London streets as though her unaccustomed feet were traversing some lonely path in the domain which might still have been her father's, had she never been.

That awful pain – that maddening, racking pain, which through the whole of the long summer never completely left Glen an hour's physical ease, rendered her almost indifferent to the shortcomings of the Lacere family, and blinded her – oh, poor Glen! – to a mysterious change in her father.

Other people saw he was getting to look very old and frail; but Glen though it was only the hot weather that tried him, and went out on wonderful quests after new-laid eggs and milk fresh from the cow, the only procurable luxuries that his fitful appetite affected.

'My darling, when are we to be married?' asked Mr Lacere, in the beginning of that brilliant August.

'Oh! any time,' she answered indifferently. 'Next month, if papa and I are both better.'

'Both better,' he thought. 'Oh, Glen – my Glen!'

The first hint of the tempest came shortly after. Glen and her father had been out together, and as, on their return, he went up the stairs, he staggered, and would have fallen but for her swift protecting hand.

'I think I have over-tired myself,' he said; and still Glen looked forward to a future when, in the pretty house at Sydenham which her husband who was to be talked of taking, she would be able to surround her father with every comfort, perhaps hire a phaeton occasionally to drive him out; get him soup, wine, grapes, something in addition to the milk and eggs and their ordinary bare diet.

But the next morning he did not seem inclined to get up, and when Mr Lacere came he went for a doctor.

The doctor asked a few questions, which Glen answered, though she did not exactly understand, and went away, saying he would send something round.

After that the girl never could exactly remember the sequence of events. Her whole time was taken up in nursing, and in learning how to cook for the sick. The hours passed, the days, the weeks, the months. It was the dead of winter. To herself she never seemed to have slept, or eaten, or rested during all that period. She was fighting death; but death wins in the long run, do what we will.

Mr Lacere looked on the struggle appalled. This was a catastrophe the near probability of which had never occurred to him.

'Glen, dear,' he entreated, 'marry me now. Give me the right to be near you, no matter what happens.'

But Glen laughed him to scorn. Nothing should happen. She would save her father. How could he ask her to leave that sickroom to go and be married to him?

'My love, my darling, I only want to be able to call you my wife. I won't ask you to steal even one second from him to give to me.'

But she would not listen to his pleading. She was fighting – fighting every step of the way to the grave – and she could spare no time or thought for anything save that terrible campaign.

For which, as is the case in most campaigns, money was absolutely necessary, and her store was getting very low. She went down to Mr Vassett and offered him the book written amongst the Middlesex moors for the modest sum of fifty pounds. She was quite in earnest, she explained – and indeed the publisher, looking at her, could not doubt that fact – she wanted fifty pounds for it.

As might have been expected, Mr Vassett did not see his way to complying with her request; so then and there she took the manuscript on to a great house, where she managed to obtain an interview with the reader. He was very courteous, and, though he did not hold out much hope of acceptance under any circumstances

– for he knew Miss Westley's writings of old – still he promised to look at the book; and having done all she could for that day, Glen went back to her post.

Miss Lacere was with her, and shared some of those awful vigils the girl must otherwise have passed alone. Most of them she did so pass; God only knew – God and herself – the misery of those nights when she watched beside one who scarcely recognised her; when she moistened the lips that had forgotten to smile on her; when she raised the head that had grown a dead-weight; when she replenished the fire which was burning low, and watched for the grey light of morning and prayed for dawn, and wrestled with the mystery of existence as Jacob did with his Maker.

But through all she failed to understand what the end must be. She never believed she was merely tending the slow flicker of an expiring lamp; hour by hour she clung to the hope the feeble flame would grow stronger, and that her father would come back out of the depths of that terrible illness to life, strength, and his daughter. Even the doctors had not the heart to tell her there was no hope whatever; if they had, she would not have believed them. They warned her of danger, but they never spoke of death. She was the only person that entered the sickroom who failed to realise there was but one change possible. And so the days went by, and the weeks, and Glen afterwards wondered – as we all do mercifully, only afterwards – how she found strength to pass through such an ordeal.

There came at last one evening a change which made her fear he was worse, and in hot haste she despatched a messenger for a great physician who had been a friend of her father's in the days before he was Westley of Glenarva, or married or ruined, or thought he should die in London lodgings with a daughter beside him almost distraught by grief.

This doctor had come to see him more than once, and in this crisis Glen felt sure the wisdom of the faculty was centred in him, and that he alone could tell her what she ought to do, and how her father was to be restored to health. She wrote a note, and bade the servant take a cab and tell the man to drive fast.

While she waited the post brought a letter, and mechanically almost – for she was in the state of mind when it seems as though nothing in the world could prove of interest save one absorbing subject – she tore open the envelope and carelessly took out the enclosure.

It was from the reader of the great publishing firm where she had left her manuscript – and contained an acceptance of the novel!

For a minute she could not exactly understand this – the words seemed blurred, and the letters danced before her eyes – but at last she made out her book was thought highly of; and that if she would call and sign an agreement a cheque for twenty pounds would be handed to her in exchange.

Great heaven! She had waited all these years for this – and it came *then*!

She crossed the room, and kneeling down beside her father, said, 'Papa, can you understand me? They have taken my book, and are to give me twenty pounds for it.'

She fancied – but it could only have been fancy – that his eyes turned towards her for a moment with a gleam of pleasure in them. 'Oh!' she cried passionately, 'if you would only get well now, papa – only get strong and well – how happy we might be!' And then her thoughts reverted to the great physician, and she marvelled how much more time would elapse before he came.

There was a dinner-party at his house, so the servant said when she returned, 'but the butler took the note to him, and he sent out word he would be round early tomorrow morning.'

'Go for another doctor,' that was all Glen said; '*any* doctor, only don't come back without one.'

Meanwhile at that dinner table, of which the servant's eyes had caught through the open door one bewildering glance, the celebrated physician had remarked to a gentleman who sat near him:

'I don't know whether you remember Westley, who was with Lord Thanet's cousin at Rome. That note was from his daughter. Poor fellow! The sands of his life are almost run out.'

'Westley!' repeated the other; 'why, Lord Thanet tried to find him everywhere more than a year ago. He got him an appointment, and I wrote myself saying how glad the Earl felt. The letter was returned by the post-office people, and we have never heard a word from him since.'

'Well, it is quite certain you will never hear from him now. He consulted me some months ago, and I then saw the case was hopeless. Still, I did not expect he would go off quite so soon. He is dying; there can't be a doubt of that.'

This was how it happened, that next morning, when the physician drove up to the house where Mr Westley lodged, he found Lord Thanet turning away from the door.

'It is all over,' said the Earl.

'Ah! I thought the end could not be far off. I'll just go in and speak to the daughter.'

'I asked for her, but she cannot see anyone. A gentleman came down and told me so.'

Chapter XI

MARRIED

A BRIGHT SUMMER'S DAY in the August following Mr Westley's death; high water in the river; the Thames looking its very best – no sign of mud-banks or bleak black shore – white sails dotting the wide expanse of rippling blue, a pleasant breeze blowing off the German Ocean, and on the rising ground above Leigh, at the foot of which that village nestles, Glenarva Westley and Ned Beattie seated on the grass, their eyes idly wandering over the landscape, and their hearts almost too full for words, busy with the past which had been theirs once – but which could belong to them again no more for ever.

Glen was visiting the curate and his wife, whose acquaintance she had made amongst the Middlesex moors. He was now rector of a scattered parish lying back in the lonely country, away from the river; and it was a pleasure in that desolate place to receive even so quiet a guest as the girl who, dressed in her deep mourning, sat often on Sundays in the great square pew belonging to the rector, looking with eyes that seemed drawn to it by some sort of fascination at the east window, which was the glory of the church, which people came from far and near to see, and which was, in its way, at once a triumph of art and a specimen of splendid colouring, such as modern mediocrity contemplated with despairing envy. The subject was the woman washing our Lord's feet with her tears, and often, as she gazed upon it, Glen found her own starting in sorrow for the sinner who, more than eighteen centuries before, stood in an agony behind her Saviour – weeping.

In the fine summer weather, Ned, coming from London to see his old companion, was invited to remain for a day or two; and thus it came to pass Glen had walked across country to show him the river and the ruins of Hadleigh Castle, and now they were resting on the heights above Leigh, and thinking of other days and far different scenes.

It was Ned who broke the silence. Stretching himself at full length on the grass, putting his hands under his head, and tilting his straw hat a little over his eyes, he said, evidently in resumption of some previous conversation:

'Glen, do you really mean to tell me none of your people ever did a single thing for you after your father's death?'

Glen turned a thoughtful face in his direction as she answered:

'Lady Emily wrote me word she had some black things, "almost as good as new," she could have packed up for me if I knew anyone who would bring them over; and Mrs Westley –'

'Stop a minute,' entreated Ned, raising his head a little and bursting into a hearty fit of laughter. 'Kindly repeat that sentence; it sounds almost too funny to be true.'

'It is perfectly true,' answered Glen; 'and Mrs Westley sent me a letter stating she supposed I had long before given up the disreputable idea of earning my living by writing mischievous and frivolous books, and that if I thought of qualifying myself to be a governess she was willing to let me try and teach her two little girls, and as I was a relative, would make me a present of ten pounds. I had committed a great sin, it seemed, in wanting to have my father buried at home, but she would "overlook my folly," she said, "knowing how badly I was brought up."'

'You must be inventing this, Glen, as you go on.'

'I should invent something pleasanter if I was inventing at all, you may be very sure of that. I'd say, for example, Lady Emily enclosed a cheque for a hundred pounds, and that my cousins asked me to pay a visit to Glenarva, and stay as long as I liked – as your mother invited me, Ned, to Ballyshane.'

'And why did you not come to us?'

'For several reasons – one because I thought it would break my heart; another that I could not spare the money; and the third that I found I must stop near London. The publishers are worse than any *leprechaun*, Ned. If you take your eyes off them for a minute they are lost.'

'Or, rather, the author is, I suppose,' answered Ned. 'And so it is a fact accomplished that you are an author, my dear.'

'Even so, Ned.'

'And is the game worth the candle?'

'It is generally admitted that one must live, and I have made enough to live on this year.'

'Have you really? Well, I suppose that is better than governessing, even at Glenarva?

'A good deal, I should say.'

'They have cut the trees down in front of the house to open up a view of the Bay, and thinned the branches so as to let daylight in along the avenue. It is an improvement, I dare say, but I liked the look of the old place as it was best.'

'I never talk nor think about Glenarva, Ned, now, if I can help it.'

And silence reigned once more.

'I read that book of yours, Glen, *Tyrrel's Son.*' It was again young Beattie who broke the stillness. 'Aunt Stanuel brought it over with her. I did not think it so bad, at all.'

'Did you not? That's consolatory,' observed the author.

'No; I considered it good on the whole – good, that is, for a girl. Of course, women can't be expected ever to know anything of life.'

For a second Glen remained speechless with indignation; then she retorted:

'If you mean the very disreputable sort of life you are best acquainted with, I am thankful to say I do not; but of a better kind I know far more than Mr Edward Beattie.'

Mr Edward Beattie raised himself lazily on one elbow, and looked at her in amazement.

'Why, Glen,' he exclaimed, 'do you imagine I am leading a disreputable life? It strikes me, young lady, your temper has got shorter even than it used to be at Ballyshane; but don't let us quarrel, and for mercy's sake don't imply things you know are untrue.'

'Well, Ned, you *must* confess it is not true to say I know less of life than you.'

'I shall confess nothing of the sort. What *can* a woman know of life? How is she to get to know it? I'll be bound I have seen more of London since I came over last month than you during all the time you have lived in it.'

'Perhaps so,' answered Glen, with a smile of contempt.

'What are you writing now?'

'A little story suited to the comprehension of children about five years of age,' with withering irony.

'Ah, then, it won't suit me,' said Ned resignedly, and he laid his head down again.

Glen contemplated her old companion stretched thus at his ease on the grass. He was not much changed, yet he had changed. It seemed to her he had grown strangely tall and manly since they were boy and girl together. There was a down on his upper lip, which she remembered smooth as her own. He had developed physically in a way which she thought little less than extraordinary, whilst his manner, never lacking in force and decision, had now a something of masculine strength and power added that struck Glen as almost unpleasant in its careless determination.

Nevertheless, young or old, tall or short, masterful or standing on an equality with herself, he was the dear Ned of the happy, vanished long ago, the Ned she had ridden with, walked with, climbed with, boated with, read with, quarrelled with, faced danger with, nursed, tended, loved.

As she looked, as fond memory laid its gentle hand on her heart, which had been so cruelly torn by time and circumstance, Glen's thoughts softened, and she felt sorry for having spoken even one sharp word to Ned, who she knew quite well never could mean to vex her. Already, as was usual with Glenarva Westley, the process of repentance had begun immediately. In the years then stretching before her, when Ned had forgotten all about her little temper, she knew she would suddenly remember that on the heights above Leigh she had been cross with her earliest friend.

Surreptitiously Ned, from under the sheltering brim of his straw hat, was out of the corner of one shrewd blue eye watching her. He knew – none better – Glen's every mood and tense; he understood her, not with a comprehension born of any great power of mental analysis, but with a lore caused by a power of perception in which few Irish men and women are deficient he was perfectly aware that, sooner even than usual, she was ready figuratively to kiss and be friends; that was all right – but he could not fail to see something else about Glenarva which puzzled and perplexed him. She had no down on her upper lip; she was not a bit taller or fatter or older-looking than of yore; her manner had not changed in the least; her little trumpery success had not made or marred her, and yet –

'Glen,' he said at last, 'is it at all likely you will be in London before I leave?'

With a start Glen returned to the questions of everyday life, and answered, 'Certain.'

'Where shall I be able to find you?

'At the Laceres'.'

'Oh! you've spent a good deal of time with them since – since last winter.'

'Yes, Ned.'

'Are they a pleasant family?

'They are exceedingly good-natured.'

'It seems to me you have formed a great many acquaintances since you came to London.'

'I have met with a great deal of kindness, if that is what you mean,' answered Glenarva gravely. Often in London she had not felt very grateful for the exceptional kindness which had been extended to her; but now, when she was well out of the toil and turmoil of the gigantic city – the noise and bustle of the busy streets – and found time to think, she could not help but be thankful for the genial words which had been spoken, and the kindly hands held out in greeting. Youth is all too apt to take such words and help for granted, but Glen, who was getting old – quite old – though still not out of her teens, could, when she found adequate leisure, afford to consider them.

For Glenarva came of a grateful stock. It was not in the nature of those from whom she drew life to forget the gift even of a cup of cold water, or a morsel of bread.

'Glen! did my mother tell you Aunt Louisa had left me a thousand pounds?' It was Ned who, from under cover of his straw-brimmed hat, put this question.

In reply Glen shook her head; though she gazed with quite a new and wondering interest at her old playfellow.

'Why don't you ask me what I am going to do with it?'

'What *are* you going to do with it?'

'I think of emigrating, or of taking a farm at home. Which course should you recommend?'

'If I were you, I should emigrate.'

Ned paused and considered this reply ere he remarked:

'I should want a wife to take out with me.'

'A wife!' screamed Glen. 'A boy like you with a wife!'

'Do you think I am too young to be married, then?' asked Ned. 'I am fourteen months older than you.'

'Of course you are.'

'And do you imagine you are too young to be married?'

'No. If you remember I told you once I met at Lady Emily's a Mrs Betheling, who was a wife, a mother, and a widow before her seventeenth birthday.'

'She married again, I suppose, immediately.'

'No, she did not marry again at all.'

'Had enough, even in so short a time, of the holy state,' suggested Ned.

'I know nothing about that.'

'At all events you think a girl may marry before she is out of her teens?'

'Of course I do; don't you?'

'The sooner a girl marries the better, I should say.'

'I feel very glad to hear that is your opinion, Ned, because I am going to be married.'

'You are going to be what?' He was sitting bolt upright now, his hat lying on the grass beside him – the wind tossing his hair – looking straight at Glen.

'Married next month.'

'Oh! Indeed!'

'I should have been married nearly a year ago – only –'

'Is it indiscreet to ask the name of the happy man?'

'No, Ned; he is called Mordaunt Logan-Lacere.'

'Lacere! By Jove! I thought there must be something in it. And ink and paper were so scarce, I suppose, and postage so dear, you could not have told us this sooner.'

'I do not know why I have told you now.'

'It has slipped out just by accident! But for a mere chance we should have heard nothing about it till we read the announcement in the *Times* of Mordaunt Logan-Lacere being united in the bonds of matrimony to Glenarva, only daughter, etc., etc.!'

'I don't see,' retorted "Glenarva, only daughter, etc", 'what there is in being married to make a song about, as old Betty used to say.'

'Faith, in some cases a dirge might be more fitting,' returned Ned, as he gathered his long length up from the turf and walked away from Glen to a distant point, where he stood for a while, his hands deep in the pockets of his loose grey suit, apparently contemplating the view.

Stretching out her arm, Glen took up Ned's hat, which he had left unheeded on the grass, and began to smooth out the dark blue ribbon which encircled it, the time her thoughts went back to the many, many days she had seen just such another hat encircled by just such another ribbon shading a boy's honest sunburnt face as he shouted out her name on shore, on sea, on cliff, on bog, at Ballyshane.

As she passed her fingers over and over the narrow silken band, tears rose unbidden to her eyes, and coursed one by one slowly down her cheeks. Had she been looking at the river she could not have seen it for that mist of inexplicable trouble. She had gone a long, long journey back into what seemed to her a far-distant past, and in spirit she was travelling the well-remembered paths once more, when a tall figure threw its shadow on the sward, and Ned again stood beside her.

'Glen,' he said, and all bitterness had died out of his voice, in which, however, there was a ring of pain, 'what is there in this marriage that you never told your best friends a word about it?'

'My best friend knew all about it,' she answered.

'You mean your father. Did he then approve the match?'

'Fully.'

'And how long have you known – a – Mr Lacere?'

'Ever since the first winter we were in London.'

'So that all the time we were pitying "poor Glen," and thinking how lonely she must be, Glen had got plenty of friends, and was enjoying herself very much indeed?'

Glen sat silent. The false indictment was nothing, but had she opened her lips in defence, the memory of all she passed through during the period Ned thus lightly described as one of unalloyed enjoyment must have broken her down.

'I suppose he is disgustingly rich,' went on her tormentor, after he had for a moment waited in vain for a reply.

'No, he is not rich.'

'That is, not rich for England, but still what we in Ireland should account a sort of millionaire?'

'Have it your way, Ned,' answered Glen quietly.

'How old is he?'

'I don't exactly know.'

'Oh! come, Glen – that is too good. Give me an idea – is he older than I am?'

'Yes; he is older than you.'

'How much?'

'Ever so much.'

'Do you remember telling us all how you never would marry anybody?'

'Yes; but it's a free country, and besides, one knows what one is – but –'

'You certainly did not know what you might be,' finished Ned, with relentless decision. 'I told you once, if you recollect, you would marry your grandfather.'

Yes, Glen recollected, though she did not say so. Across the years there came to her a whiff of sweetbriar, and the scent of a lavender-bush growing within the Vicarage garden, where she and the boys stood talking about the grey-haired hero who had lunched that day with Mr Beattie.

'We ought to be thinking about going home,' she said, after a pause.

'Not just yet,' he objected. 'When did you tell me the great event was to come off?'

'Next month. I don't exactly yet know which day.'

'Is our friend of the parsonage to act as chaplain at the gallows?'

'No.'

'Who is to tie the knot, then?'

'I haven't an idea – anybody.'

'Well, you are a funny girl – I don't believe you care a bit for the man you are going to marry.'

'Don't you, Ned?' There was something unutterably sad and weary in her voice as she spoke.

'See, Glen' – he had thrown himself once more on the grass, and was now leaning towards his companion – 'give me your hand, and say this after me, then I won't trouble you any more: "I'm so fond of the person I have chosen, I would take him if he had not a penny, and I feel I can trust the whole of my future life to his keeping."'

'God knows I can!' she added, when she had repeated this strange formula; and then, as Ned slowly released her hand, she covered her face for a minute ere, rising, she said: 'Now we had better go home.'

'Come down to the river,' he amended, 'and let us see if we can get a boat. It may be many a long day before I shall have a chance of rowing you again.'

Along the grass and down the steep hill they went, silently, side-by-side, together, and it was not till they were standing at a little shelving landing-place, waiting for a boat to be brought round, that Ned spoke again.

'Wouldn't it be better, Glen, for you to come back with me to Ballyshane, and let my father do all that is necessary under the circumstances?'

She shook her head, and answered, 'I would rather be married in London.'

A minute more and they were on the river – water all around them – the outward-bound ships making their way slowly against wind and tide, the Thames like a sheet of molten gold – the August sun westering over London, where the man Ned imagined to be 'disgustingly rich' was sitting in his quiet office, pondering 'ways and means.'

'Do you remember, Glen, the time I fell and broke my leg?' asked Ned, holding his sculls suspended for the moment as he asked the question.

'Of course I do,' she answered, watching the pearly drops falling like summer rain into the water.

'And that afternoon I bade you goodbye on board the Morecambe steamer?'

'Yes, Ned.'

'And when the years have come and gone, you will not forget today, and how everything looked from the heights yonder, and the way the sun shone on the water, and the shadows stealing round the church tower?'

'I shall not forget,' and she turned her head aside while he rowed steadily on.

'If I call I suppose I may be allowed to see you in London?' he said, as an hour and more later they walked in the evening light across the lonely wolds almost in utter silence.

'Of course! They will make any friend of mine welcome.'

'Where did you say Mr Lacere has his office, Glen?'

'In Sise Lane.'

August was past, and September had come ere Ned, still wearing that unconventional straw hat and loose grey suit, on both of which Miss Humphries looked with distinct disfavour, paid his promised visit to the future Mrs Lacere. When he called it was afternoon, and all the existing ladies of the Lacere family were in evidence. Glen had long ceased to count how many were dead as a vain and profitless calculation.

Looking round the quartet – to each one of whom he was duly and specially introduced – Ned irreverently summed them up in the same terms as a deceased Lord Abercorn is stated to have stigmatised two distinguished authoresses of his period, while it is only fair to say that the impression produced by Mr Beattie was as little favourable as that made on him by Mr Lacere's female relations.

He was asked to partake of tea, and, accepting the invitation, endeavoured to talk on such subjects as he supposed might prove agreeable to ladies, all of whom were old enough to be his mother, while one of them might, as he subsequently expressed the matter, 'have counted years, and won, with Miss Stanuel herself.'

It was after Miss Humphries had said solemnly, 'Will you allow me to give you another cup of tea, Mr Beattie?' and Mr Beattie, who was accustomed to take a great many cups of tea, had answered, 'Yes, thank you,' that he proceeded to scandalise all the ideas of the Lacere connection by remarking across the table:

'Well, Glen, I took Sise Lane on my way here, and saw your man.'

Glen felt the startled chill which for a moment froze the blood of her relatives who were to be, at Ned's free-and-easy designation of Mordaunt Logan-Lacere, but she answered:

'Did you? I hope you were pleased with each other.'

'I was pleased with him,' said Ned, taking no notice of the stony looks of disapproval with which his utterances were received; 'we had a long talk. I dare say I stopped there an hour. I told him I hoped he would not let you get your head.'

Glen smiled.

'And what is his notion on the subject?'

'The usual thing, of course,' replied Ned.

'Thinks you would be sure to go right – without bit, bridle, or curb. "Very well," I said, "do as you like; but remember I knew her before ever you did, and the very best thing for both of you will be to keep her well in hand."'

'It seems to me, Mr Beattie, your advice, however admirable, has the great drawback of being somewhat obscure,' remarked Miss Lacere, with great dignity.

'Oh! he knew well enough what I meant, and so does Glen,' returned Ned, as if it were of no consequence whatever whether Miss Lacere were similarly fortunate or not.

'I suppose the old girls will be kind to you,' he said, as he and Glen strolled together towards the Regent's Park. He had suggested she should put on her bonnet and walk part of the way back with him.

'They seem inclined to make a great fuss over their new sister-in-law.'

'Yes, they have been very kind to me,' answered Glen.

'That other Lacere is a very velvety-spoken sort of individual. He thinks, I fancy, he has got a monopoly of all the virtues, as well as all the talents.'

'I can't tell, I am sure.'

Meantime there was quite a flutter going on in the Lacere dovecote.

'I don't approve of that young man's manners at all, Glen,' observed Miss Lacere when Glen, looking a little pale, returned home and took a seat as far distant from the chandelier as possible.

'Don't you?' asked the girl.

'No, indeed! Fancy him talking of our precious blessing as "your man" and hoping he would not let you "get your head!"'

'Poor Ned!'

Already Glen had a feeling no friend of hers would meet with much favour in that household. 'But it does not much matter,' she thought. She felt strangely tired and peaceably minded.

'I wish I had married a year ago,' she decided; and undoubtedly it would have been much better, as no one knew more certainly than Mr Logan-Lacere himself.

Though late, however, the wedding-day dawned at last, a dull morning, obscured by a damp mist which resolved itself before the appointed hour into a wretched drizzling rain.

Unless they had walked into church alone together, no pair could have been married more quietly.

One of the Misses Lacere for bridesmaid, Mr Lacere for best-man, a gentleman who was a stranger to Ned for father – that was all the wedding-party.

In a half-hearted sort of way Glen had asked young Mr Beattie to be present, but he refused on the ground that he was leaving London.

Nevertheless, though she did not see him, her old friend was there, and as he walked from the church to Euston Square Station he shook his head once or twice mournfully.

'It was as sad a ceremony as I ever need desire to witness,' he thought; 'yet if they are unhappy I am sure the fault will not be his.'

END OF VOLUME II

VOLUME III

Contents

Chapter I

ONE ROAD TO SUCCESS

HOW'S MARIA? had long been played out; 'less,' observed Mr Dawton, 'from any want of life or animation in the fair Maria herself, than in consequence of a curious and to him (Mr Dawton) inexplicable lack of enthusiasm on the part of the principal performer.'

'If I may be allowed the expression,' proceeded Mr Dawton, 'he always acted the part under protest. Give you my honour, sir, he seemed as if he took it only out of compliment to *me*, and during the whole time he had his full share of the profits. Full share, ay, and more.'

'From the first I told you he was a "cad," father,' said Ted, which opinion, indeed, the elder son of the house had freely expressed soon after forming the acquaintance of Mr Bernard Kelly. 'He only went into the matter with you because he was short of cash. He was deadly ashamed of the whole business, and took the earliest possible opportunity of getting out of it.'

Incredible as this statement sounded to Mr Dawton, it happened to be perfectly true. For anyone to be 'ashamed' of the stage, and despise the 'noblest profession man ever entered,' seemed to the poor old actor a theory too wild for acceptance. But Ted had read his man accurately. If he had descended into the pit of Mr Kelly's mind, and gone with a light through all the workings of that intricate mine, he could not have arrived at a more correct conclusion than was the case.

Mr Kelly had loathed *How's Maria?* and felt each time the name of that mythical female was placarded about the towns in the Home Counties, beyond which distance Mr Dawton did not think it prudent to travel, as if a date were fixed for his own execution.

'You see, he never forgets Bernard Kelly,' explained Ted to his brother; 'and for this reason, if for no other, he will never, let my father say what he likes, do a bit of good as an actor.'

'And I'm very sure he won't as an author,' capped Will. 'From the minute I stopped touching up his stories, not an editor would take one of them.'

But Mr William Dawton proved to be wrong in his idea that the Irishman would fail to make his way as a writer.

He lacked genius, it is true; but he made up for the want of a gift which does not always enable its possessor to compass worldly success, by indomitable perseverance and a determination to try all the gates of fortune till he found one that yielded to his hand. Nothing except that shortness of cash mentioned – a not uncommon want among all sorts and conditions of men – could ever have induced Mr Kelly to appear in the little play Mr William Dawton had 'knocked up' out of the omnibus incident which introduced Bernard to his uncle; but he was so poor at the time, he agreed to whatever Mr Dawton proposed; and, as a natural consequence, found himself carried, much against his own goodwill, to Croydon, Kingston, Hertford, and such-like towns, as well as to places more properly to be regarded as outlying suburbs of London.

Amongst others to Stratford, where, although he saw them not, Miss Bridgetta and her niece saw him.

'I don't know what you'll think about Barney going the round of the country with a parcel of strolling players,' wrote Miss Cavan to Mrs Kelly. 'It seems a great come-down for a man reared in decency – and I am truly sorry for you – respected and respectable as you always were and kept yourself. Me and Hetty paid our shilling apiece, and went into the back seats to get a look at him; and we felt it was money wasted. It was a pity you could not keep him at home, or get him off to America. Maybe your brother in Derry could give a helping hand to get him out there yet. He's in the middle of a gang of actors, Mat says; and, indeed, I think it's only my duty and a kindness to write and let you know how he's going on.'

Which was a very weak, foolish letter for poor Miss Cavan to indict, though she sent it to Callinacoan only with the laudable idea of taking the sting out of whatever Barney might have said about Mat.

Now, Barney had hitherto said nothing to the good people at home on the subject, and might possibly have held his peace forever, if Miss Bridgetta had refrained her pen. As matters stood, however, he returned a short but incisive epistle to the letter of maternal lamentation which arrived in due course at Bermondsey.

He told his mother not to be fretting about him – that he was doing very well, and meant to do better; that Miss Cavan was an old idiot; that Mat was only a common tout for advertisements; and that if he made five hundred a year, he was drinking six; that it was a pure waste of Irish produce to send hampers to West Ham; and that, if she found she had at any time more than she knew what to do with, she had better send it to him than to a house where there were two slanderous old maids, and a man who had grudged him even the poor shelter their contemptible cottage afforded. Bernard was very angry indeed, and when he was angry, he knew, as his mother said, 'where to lay on the whip.'

Nevertheless, this little incident confirmed his previous resolution of severing his slight connection with the stage.

'It does not matter,' he considered, 'what a man does or leaves undone, so long as he can *keep it quiet*; but you can't keep things quiet if you give any fool able to pay twelvepence leave to learn to know all you are about.'

So Mr Kelly, looking around, saw there was a great field in London open for any man who liked to push his way steadily and unpretentiously.

'It's the horse that steals along wins the race,' he thought; 'that makes no great show, but just creeps on, and on, and was never thought of perhaps at all in the betting. So far as I have seen, it's the talk and the drink spoils a man's chances here.' And he vowed to himself that neither drink nor talk should destroy the chance of Mr Bernard Kelly.

Brought up as he had been, the amount of money which sifted through the fingers of the people he came in contact with literally appalled him. Snow in June could not have disappeared quicker than sovereigns did out of the possession of Will and Jim Dawton. No one ever seemed to him to put by a halfpenny. What his friends got they spent, and then they were short till they got more. It was either 'a feast or a famine' – either debt or profusion.

'It is a sort of life that would not suit me,' Mr Kelly said in after-years, referring to life in Bohemia – but what perhaps he really meant was, it would not have suited him to pay for it. So long as somebody else found what the young Dawtons called 'the shot,' he said nothing in dispraise of Bohemian practices. Nay, most undoubtedly he liked them, always at another person's expense *bien entendu* – the snug supper-parties – the Blackwall dinners – the trips up the river – the picnics – the dances – the play-goings – the luncheons – he took them all just as he took good wine, when he could get that good thing: but they did not turn his head any more than wine. After the pleasantest party he could go home and instantly buckle to his work. So far from unfitting him for his daily labour, society only seemed to supply some stimulus his nature needed.

'He never forgot Bernard Kelly,' to quote Ted Dawton's words; and for that very reason, the life which might have over-excited and undermined a more sensitive and sympathetic nature really only proved a favouring wind which blew him onward to success.

Ere he had been eighteen months in London the Dawtons felt that though he was among, he was not of them. He had got a literary connection quite outside their own, and a visiting acquaintance into which his literary position never entered. How he had managed this was a question frequently mooted amongst the first friends whose kindness helped him over the difficulties of his earlier metropolitan experience. Mr Bernard Kelly knew, but he did not mean to enlighten them, parrying all inquisitive inquiries with, to quote Jim Dawton, 'a wisdom beyond his years.'

The Dawtons could not make the matter out. Mr Donagh had darkly hinted to them that 'Kelly was a low fellow,' 'born in the ranks;' that 'Mr Balmoy himself came from the dregs of the people.' 'Fellows,' proceeded Mat loftily, 'my grandfather would not have spoken to, except from the back of his thoroughbred, while they were running barefoot through the bogs;' and, indeed, when he first arrived in London, there was nothing so particularly refined or aristocratic about Mr Kelly's appearance, manners, and modes of thought as to induce a belief that he had been what Mr Donagh called 'cradled amid the purple.' They knew that when Mr Dawton, senior, first beheld him gazing darkly down into the water in St James's Park, he was as destitute of friends as of money; and now, behold, he had the *entrée* to good houses; 'and by Jove, sir,' added Will, 'he can plant a book with a publisher almost when and where he likes.'

All of which was true, but the apparent miracle of Bernard Kelly's success had its origin in two extremely simple causes. First, he started in the race unweighted. He had no wife, father, or child to consider; it was not necessary for him to keep up appearances beyond dressing fairly well; he could lodge where he pleased, live as cheaply as he liked: put the width of London between himself and those who might have intruded upon his time and distracted him from his work; what he made he could keep, he might save or spend, whichever pleased him best. In the second place, circumstances before he came to London so placed his lot, that he had splendid opportunity for reading books not generally resorted to for purposes of study. As a pigeon wheels round in the air, uncertain apparently at first in what direction to bend its flight – as a dog often first scents three roads out of four where that number meet, ere certainly electing to choose the last – so Mr Kelly tried his hand at many things before he finally found out what he was best fitted for, and stuck to it.

Almost by accident – at least, if a conversation with Mr Vassett could be deemed accident – he found he could utilise his almost exhaustive acquaintance with the works of those dramatists the present age has decided to shelve. Bernard Kelly knew them by heart. He read them at a time when he had no thought of coming to London and only the vaguest idea of ever publishing anything had entered his mind, and therefore started with the enormous advantage of not having to go to the British Museum to 'read up' his subject. When he did enter that building, it was merely to verify a quotation or refer to some work the gist of which was already known to him. At that time he chanced to be earning enough by those London sketches – to which allusion has already been made – to keep his modest pot boiling, and he could therefore write the book he had in his mind at leisure, and afford to spend time in giving it an amount of local colour which delighted Mr Vassett, himself an antiquarian and a lover of the study of that long-ago time, when gallants ruffled it in doublets and plumed hats, when 'prentice boys fought, when grave citizens had to keep strict watch over fair wives and pretty daughters, when the Fleet afforded splendid opportunities for romance and scoundrelism and comedy and tragedy, when jolly young watermen pulled gay cavaliers to London Bridge, and down the stairs at York Gate – then lapped at high tide by the water, and not lying stranded back in a garden as it does now – ladies with hoops, and fans, and patches, and powdered hair, and looped-up dresses, and high-heeled shoes, were handed by lords wearing swords at their sides in order to take an airing on the river.

It was concerning the dramatists of this time Mr Kelly wrote what Mr Vassett termed 'an important work.' He went into it with love, and he finished it with honour. He knew what he was about; knew the plays the authors he spoke of had written, not merely by name, but line by line and sentence by sentence; he under-stood their spirit; he saw the tendency of their times reflected in the loose morality of their plots and characters: but beneath the grossness and the levity and the scoffs at decency and dullness and religion, he found a wealth of genius which surprised and delighted the Craven Street publisher.

More than this, he haunted the localities described, the places where these men had lived, made his way into wretched tenements where genius and wit and beauty had once held high court, and weaving into his narrative the very stones of the street, and the aspect of the rooms, and the carving of the mantelpieces, and the paintings on the ceilings, and the pattern of the balustrades, produced a series of pictures, so said the reviewers, as well as a brilliant and accurate history of the period he described.

The book stamped Mr Kelly as a man worth cultivating; but even before it appeared, he had made his way into houses where people are not usually asked merely because they have written a book or flashed some artistic fireworks in the face of the multitude. He achieved this social feat by the kindness of a friend at whose hands he scarcely deserved such consideration.

Not then, but years after, he stated, in what reviewers termed a singularly graceful dedication, that to this lady – for his friend was of the better sex – he owed every good thing he possessed in life. And yet before he left Ireland he served her what a less forgiving and confiding nature might have regarded as a scurvy trick. He had professed to be deeply in love with her; he had given her to understand that life destitute of her presence would be valueless; he had been on the very eve of marrying her – indeed, without doubt he would have married her, but that at the eleventh hour her brother, getting wind of the matter, sent for Barney, as he was called in the easy vernacular of the neighbourhood, and said:

'Now, look here! you think my sister has three hundred a year?'

'And hasn't she?' asked Barney, 'simple as a baby,' to quote his mother's somewhat incorrect statement.

'*As long as she remains single!*' answered Mr Fortescue, for the gentleman's name was Fortescue, and the lady was Miss Fortescue – generally referred to among the Kelly connection as the 'old woman.'

'How's that?' inquired Barney, naturally anxious to obtain all the information he could on so important a question.

'Well,' said Mr Fortescue in a friendly confidential sort of manner, for at this stage he felt affairs were in his own hand, 'you see – pray take a glass of wine, Mr Kelly' – Barney had been ushered into the dining-room after the departure of youth and beauty as personified by Miss Fortescue, and Mr Fortescue now pushed the decanter over to him. 'You see, my father made his will when my sister was a young girl. He never altered it: there were reasons, as you will allow, why it was wise he never did.'

Mr Kelly sipped his wine and remained silent; there were reasons why he did not wish to answer 'Yes,' and he felt he certainly could not answer 'No' till he knew more.

'So,' proceeded Mr Fortescue, 'to cut a long story short, when my father died and his will was read, we found that everything was left to me except three hundred a year to my sister *so long as she remained single* – the amount to cease totally on her marriage *unless she wedded with my consent.*'

Mr Kelly finished his wine. He felt matters had reached a climax.

'And, Mr Kelly,' proceeded Mr Fortescue – 'pray take some more wine,' which Barney did, fearing he might never get anything else out of the Fortescue connection – 'to be quite plain, I have no intention of giving my consent to her marrying you; still, as I have no desire to act unhandsomely towards a person who I think may have been led very much astray in his ideas –'

He paused, but strong in the virtue of silence, Barney declined to compromise himself with any statement as to whether he had been the deceiver or the deceived.

'I am willing,' said Mr Fortescue, after an almost imperceptible pause, 'to – to – do something for you. If you like to leave the neighbourhood and – go – anywhere – you can have fifty pounds.'

Fifty pounds and no Miss Fortescue! At that moment, if possessed of fifty pounds in hard cash, all things seemed possible to Mr Bernard Kelly; so he closed with the offer on the spot.

'Ye didn't know your own worth, Barney dear,' commented his mother, when she heard of the transaction. 'With your wonderful brown eyes and that soft melting voice of yours, ye might wile a bird off her nest. Ye'd have doubled that fifty if you'd only stuck out a bit. And now where at all d'ye think ye'll go?'

Mr Kelly did not know – he thought of America, and of Australia, and of Africa and New Zealand; and then, feeling he lacked the spirit either of a pioneer or adventurer, said, 'I'll go to London.'

London was not so far off as Mr Fortescue could have desired; still, in those days it was a long way. A man who wished to return might, were he so inclined, get back almost as easily from America as from London; and besides, he well knew that after the first cold plunge into the swift stream of metropolitan life had been taken, men did not often desire to return to the turf and the pigs, and the dead-alive existence of a place like Callinacoan.

Mr Balmoy was communicated with, and expressed his willingness to assist a relative represented as so extremely clever as far as lay in his power; the outfit was procured, and Barney left what Mr Donagh would have called his 'natal bogs.'

The letter in which he bade farewell to Miss Fortescue was a masterpiece of falsehood and diplomacy; but what he said, knowing the writer, may be safely left to the imagination of the reader.

The lady, who, though not young, was tender, wept bitterly over the desertion of her devoted swain: he wanted 'faith', she said sadly – took, indeed, to her bed when her brother told her how he and Kelly had talked the matter over, and decided it was better for Barney to go to London; but after a time she tired of tears and solitude – got up, went downstairs, and in pursuance of her domestic avocations discovered the new pad-groom was an extremely handsome young man, and decided that he must be a hero in disguise.

The end of that romance is written in the chronicles of the house of Fortescue.

Wiser than his predecessor, the handsome young man wasted no time over his wooing or his wedding either: and on this occasion the first hint Mr Fortescue received of what had been going on, arrived in the form of an intimation that Mr Robert Underwood had that day wedded Dorothea, only daughter of the late Thomas Fortescue, of Manchester Square, London. If a shell had exploded at Sulby Park it would have caused less confusion.

'Married – and to a groom!' gasped Mr Fortescue. 'Why, Kelly was nothing to this!'

'Serve him right,' thought Mrs Kelly, 'turning up his impudent English nose at my Barney.'

'Something might have been made of Kelly,' considered Mr Fortescue, which judgment Barney, as soon as he heard the news, immediately justified by despatching a letter to the bride full of earnest hopes for her happiness, touching expressions of gratitude for her kindness to himself in the days gone by, and assurances that almost every hour he found occasion to recall some of her excellent advice and necessity to use the information she had given him.

It was a sprat thrown to catch a very vague herring, but still Mr Kelly decided the chance must be worth the postage-stamp and the time which it cost. By return of mail came an answer from Mrs Underwood. She did not say much about her husband, but she said a great deal concerning Barney – remarked how thankful she felt to know her poor advice had proved of the slightest service; begged him to tell her if she could not be of some real use to him in London; entreated that he would confide all his hopes and fears to her as of old. She had always prophesied he would rise, and rise high, and as a true, though *humble* friend, she desired from the remote spot where her lot was cast to be able to follow the course of his upward progress.

It is almost unnecessary to say Mr Bernard Kelly was not at all backward in availing himself of the chance thus offered. He told her he was writing – getting on in the world wonderfully, all things considered; that merely to provide the 'sinews of war' he had temporarily joined fortunes with a family named Dawton, well known in the theatrical world, and acted in their, company a little play called *How's Maria?* – founded on the incident which had destroyed his hopes of assistance from Mr Balmoy – at various country towns. Having thus drawn the venom from Miss Donagh's sting, he went on to say that he had met with many curious persons and passed through many strange vicissitudes since they parted, and that he often wished he was near enough to resume the charming companionship he had been privileged to enjoy at Callinacoan.

'Then,' he added, 'it was you who were wont to amuse and instruct me with stories of a world of which I knew nothing. If we met now, I am vain enough to think, short as has been my London experience, I could relate many things which would interest you.'

The correspondence prospered; Mr Underwood, holding out, got his five hundred pounds and went to America, where popular rumour stated he immediately took to himself another and younger wife. He was quite firm in the matter of not subjecting Mrs Underwood to the inconveniences of a sea voyage and uncertain prospects when she got on the other side, so the lady returned to her brother's roof – where, as it was clearly impossible she could marry again, a great peace began to reign. The correspondence with Barney supplied all the elements of romance, lacking which, as Miss Fortescue used to say, life lacked everything. 'Existence,' she wrote plaintively, 'is ended for *me*, but in your success I sometimes feel like one raised again from the dead.' She gave him letters of introduction; she 'worked her friends,' to use a phrase of the Dawtons', for his benefit; she opened doors for him he never could have opened for himself; in a word, Mr Kelly was doing very well indeed, yet he did not feel quite satisfied. He knew now he could make a certain sum per annum for several years – perhaps for life – but he could only do this by continuous work on the literary treadmill. A thousand miles in a thousand hours seems a vast pedestrian feat to those who are little given to such exercise; but the life of an author without private fortune, or the fortune of getting into some good thing, just means what is equivalent to walking a mile every working hour of his life. The task is never done – even when he is lying on his deathbed the hack leaves some 'copy' unfinished. The simile of the crutch and the walking-stick is almost too trite to be repeated here – yet it is so true, use can scarcely render it stale – and Mr Kelly, who, for all his common-sense and industry and patience and perseverance, was thoroughly Irish in his love of pleasure and hatred of routine, felt sometimes he hated authorship, and wished he could get into another groove where at least some little variety might compensate for inadequate remuneration.

Leader-writing had not at that time got to be the money-making business it has since become, and at all events Mr Kelly was not on any newspaper. Literary men would have looked round their fourth-floor chambers in incredulous astonishment had they then been told they need only borrow enough money for the railway fare to some remote borough, in order to write MP after their names. The honours conferred by a seat in the House of Commons were not in those days as easy to be obtained as foreign titles and diplomas; there were fewer prizes in authorship than there are now, but as a balance there were not quite so many blanks. The monotony and the drudgery, however, even of an assured success, appalled Mr Kelly. He felt thankful for what he had been able to do; but he wanted something more – something that would, as he phrased the matter to himself, be going on like rent or interest while a fellow was sleeping. He desired, in brief, a salary – an editorship – anything which would not necessitate the eternal turning out of 'copy.' He even fixed the amount of that salary, if he could get it, at precisely the same annual sum as that maiden lady, whose relations were not as kind as she thought they might have been, prayed for. 'And lest, Lord! Thou shouldest not know what I mean, I mean three hundred a year, paid quarterly.' Three hundred a year would have suited Mr Kelly to a nicety, but though he was a great deal about London, editorships were things he did not seem to hear about, in time at any rate; and the Dawtons, who did hear, were not in any hurry to tell him.

Perhaps they thought, and with good reason, that once this 'chief butler' got comfortably placed himself, he would forget all about the struggling Josephs of his former prison house.

At all events, he was wishing very much for what he did not seem likely soon to get, and was pondering how other people appeared to fall into 'excellent berths,' when one day – the very same day, in fact, when Glen and Ned Beattie sat on the heights above Leigh looking down upon the Thames – he took boat to go to Lambeth. It had dawned upon him it might not have been quite wise on his part to cut the Dawton connection even so far as he had done. True, the Dawtons and the rank to which he wished to belong, and with which he was in fact privileged to associate, were social ingredients so different as to be well-nigh incompatible. But bankers and clergymen, and old dowagers with assured positions, and prim maiden ladies distantly related to the nobility, put nothing tangible in his pocket: while the pleasant Bohemians, whose ways and doings and conversation seemed to him so pleasant, but whom latterly he had grown somewhat to look down upon, could tell when and where every new venture on which for a time money would be spent freely was to be started. He could not afford, he decided, to get 'out of the swim;' not at all events till he met with a rich wife to be had for the asking. Mr Kelly's preferences certainly lay in the direction of a rich wife rather than that of any magazine, new or old; but spite of his brown eyes and melting voice, no lady with a handsome fortune had, as yet, shown him the slightest favour.

'Faith, there are more after them here even than in Ireland,' thought Mr Kelly. 'Lords, and baronets, and parsons, and barristers, and judges, and princes too, for aught I know.' Fact is, 'Barney dear' had been much against his will forced to the conclusion that there is no spot on earth where a rich woman, no matter how old she may be, is not worth more than an impecunious young man.

'Talk about Miss Fortescue!' soliloquised Mr Kelly. 'Why, she was a mere girl in comparison to some I have seen married to fellows no older than myself. There could not have been more than two or three and twenty years between us: and I am sure that old woman Greeson went to church with last week was seventy if she was a day.'

From all of which it will be seen, Mr Kelly, spite of the success he had won, was still feeling his way after further fortune. It is impossible for a man to live for nearly three years in a great city and feel the same modest sum he then considered absolute wealth, satisfy his desires. Money in a large town goes literally no way. The bare necessaries of existence may certainly be procured at as cheap a rate, if not at a cheaper, than in the country; but Mr Kelly soon found 'the minute you set your foot over the doorstep you've to put your hand in your pocket.' A satisfactory income is a point upon which no human being was ever able to come to an exact conclusion. It always means more than a person possesses. As a rule, wants grow in precise proportion to the means of gratifying them; and though Mr Kelly was far too astute and careful to outrun the constable or even spend anything like the whole amount he was making, still he could not avoid casting anxious glances ahead, and wondering if he ever should be rich enough to take a house and keep servants, and 'live like anybody else.' He was extremely fond of riding, and when he went into the Park his very soul grew sick with envy at the sight of the splendid animals bestridden for the most part by grooms. At Callinacoan a capital horse could have been bought for about the sixth part of his price in London, while his feed scarcely needed to be reckoned; and here, once again to quote Mr Kelly, 'his keep costs as much as a man's.' Musing on these things and many others of a like nature, wondering more particularly if the Dawtons knew any of the staff on a newly started paper which had taken a higher literary position sooner than paper was ever known to have done before in so short a time, Mr Kelly stepped on board the steamer on the Surrey side. He had prefaced his intended visit with a present of a two-gallon jar of Bushmills, procured for and sent to him by his uncle at Derry – who wrote, between jest and earnest:

'I only hope, Barney, you don't drink all I get for you without help.'

In those days the duty was not equalised, and how his uncle managed to smuggle over so much whisky puzzled his nephew a good deal. As for the young Dawtons, when the present arrived they only laughed and wondered 'What Kelly wants now?'

'Don't let us look a gift-horse in the mouth,' entreated Mr Dawton, whose love for good liquor was undiminished, though every day that had gone by since Barney first met him decreased his ability to indulge in it with impunity. 'Upon the whole, he is not a bad fellow, Kelly. I have known worse – far worse.'

'So have I,' said Ted: 'but I have also known better.'

'Well, you never tasted finer whisky, at any rate,' answered his father, who had been testing the quality of the Bushmills by pouring small quantities into a wine-glass, and taking them off at a gulp as he might medicine. All unconscious of the criticisms passed on himself and his national beverage, Mr Kelly, smoking a cigar, left the Surrey-side boat at St Paul's pier, and walking across the gangway of the Chelsea vessel, made his way forward. As he did so he caught sight of a face which seemed familiar to him, and on which impulse, for it certainly was not at the moment memory, at once induced him to turn his back. Where had he seen that face before? He stood looking down into the water asking himself that question; and then he suddenly remembered he had seen it first in the little covered passage overlooking St Mary Overy's Dock, and that he had beheld it last as it sank away from sight under a counter in Sise Lane. That was more than two years ago, and his eyes had never rested on it since; but the face was not one to be easily forgotten. Its owner did not look a day older – or very much soberer. He was a man who possessed the doubtful advantage of always appearing to be the worse, or the better – precisely as an observer might choose to consider – for drink. Yes, Mr Kelly remembered him perfectly – remembered the light wiry frame without an ounce of superfluous flesh upon it; the hat pushed as far back from the forehead as was compatible with keeping it on at all; the hands plunged deep in the pockets; the nervous, fidgety, excitable manner; the shrewd yet wandering eye; the sharp expression of the countenance; the curiously, muddily pale complexion – that certainly was not an acquaintance he desired to renew, so he kept his back steadily to the passengers, and endeavoured to look with an air of attention and interest at the various wharves, and warehouses, and coal-sheds, and ale-stores, and stranded barges, and black mud, which at that time fringed the Middlesex side of the river, where the Embankment now runs.

'How d'ye do?' said a voice at his elbow. Mr Kelly turned at the words, and saw his questionable friend smiling up at him in the most affectionate manner possible.

'I am very well, thank you,' he answered, with an excellent assumption of surprise, and utter want of recognition.

'You don't seem to remember me,' remarked the other, in a tone of disappointment.

'Now I look at you more closely, your face does appear familiar,' observed Mr Kelly, who saw it was of no use fencing any longer with the difficulty: 'but –'

'You can't exactly call to mind where last you had the pleasure of seeing it,' supplied Lance quickly. 'Now that's odd. I knew you again in a minute, and I wasn't quite as sober as you – but I never forget. I am never so far gone that I can't recollect distinctly next morning what happened overnight. My memory never gets drunk; let me help yours a bit. One confoundedly wet evening in the summer of 1855, three persons – and a good many more – might have been seen sheltering in an alcove at the eastern extremity of Clink Street, Southwark. There, I see you know now where we met, and how tenderly we parted: good commencement that, by the way, for a novel after the style of "George Prince Regent James, Esq."'

'Well, and how have you been getting on since that wet evening in 1855?' asked Mr Kelly, with an agreeable affability, making a virtue of necessity now that he found his assumed want of recollection could serve him no further.

'Oh! middling; slouching along.'

'Still sleeping in the queer bedstead where I left you tucking yourself up?'

'No! had to turn out. The choice was given to me whether I'd walk out or be kicked out, so I elected to walk. I shan't forget it, to my gentleman. Only let me have the chance, and he'll wish, perhaps, he had kept a civiller tongue in his head. It was nothing to him – it was not his office – there was no harm that I know of in sitting on the stairs for a few minutes after business hours, considering how soon I'd turn in. Should you say there was?'

'Well, you see, that depends on a good many things – on the time you had been sitting upon the stairs deciding upon your future movements – the state you were in while you were so sitting – also whether anyone wanted to go upstairs. I confess I think if you had drunk as much as on the night when I escorted you home, your better course would have been to retire at once under the counter; but of course, that is only my opinion.'

'Look here,' answered Lance, 'I like you – there's a good lot of fun in you, I'll swear – and if it had been you told me to clear off the steps, I shouldn't have taken it so much amiss – but as for that Logan-Lacere, blank him – a proud, stuck-up, *noli me tangere*' (which phrase Mr Lance gave as '*nolly me tangier*') 'sort of fellow, I wouldn't walk on the same side of the road if I could help it.'

'It is a pity, then, you sat on his stairs.'

'Pity for him, you mean, I suppose – none for me. I was glad we came to high words. I had long been trying to make up my mind to cut myself clear of his precious brother-in-law, but I'd never have done it but for his impudence. However, we won't talk any more about that lot. Where are you bound for?'

'I am going to Chelsea,' answered Mr Kelly, in whom the instinct of self-preservation was strong.

'I'm bound for Lambeth,' explained the other. 'Old Dawton has not been well, and I thought I'd just go and have a squint at him. He drinks too much – can't stand it – it is a bad habit for anyone to get into.'

Mr Kelly looked at the speaker in amazement, as he remarked:

'Well, really, I should scarcely have thought you were the fittest person in the world to throw stones.'

'Oh! I know what's what, though I mayn't always do or care to do the right thing. Besides, there's a great difference in our ages; a young fellow can drink, when an old fellow gets knocked over. Drink is cumulative, you know, like most poisons.'

'That is a theory I *never* heard advanced before,' observed Barney, looking with a certain curiosity at an Englishman younger than himself whose knowledge of the great liquor question seemed even more exhaustive than his own.

'It is not a theory, it is a fact; and many a man pulls up when he gets to fifty or thereabouts just because he can't go on.'

'Is that about the age you intend to turn over a new leaf?' asked Mr Kelly, striving vainly to make a hurried calculation as to the amount of sterling coin of the realm his wise friend would have consumed at the expiration of five-and-twenty years or thereabouts.

'I!' said Lance. 'Oh! I shall be dead long before that.'

'You'll be what!' exclaimed Mr Kelly, amazed – for indeed, the matter-of-fact way in which the words were spoken was enough to astound any one.

'Dead!' repeated Mr Felton, as though he had lightly mentioned the possibility of being bankrupt, or the certainty of succeeding to some good reversion.

'Why, have you any disease? Do you come of a short-lived family?' asked Mr Kelly, for the moment feeling his sympathy aroused and his interest excited.

'Lord, no,' answered Lance Felton. 'My people have a bad habit of living to ninety or a hundred, emulating the example set by Adam, Noah, and the rest of that old-world lot. And I have nothing killing the matter with me that I know of – indeed, I have nothing at all – only I shan't live, and that's enough; and I've a deal of work to get through first, and I'm just about starting on it.'

'Going to ask that fair damsel you spoke about two years ago to reconsider her refusal,' suggested Mr Kelly, relieved to know his companion's pessimist views as regarded his own length of days had no better foundation than a cracked and wandering brain.

'No, indeed. What the deuce does a man who intends to get on in the world want with a wife? Besides, I am married.'

'Oh! you are.'

'Yes, worse luck: not, mind you, that I've a word to say against my wife. She is as good a soul as ever drew breath. Managing – contriving – all that. Bless you, there is nothing pleases her better than to consider how she can re-trim an old dress or jacket, and make it look as good as new. But that is a sort of thing I can't stand: and besides, it's hard enough work for a fellow to pull himself uphill, without having to drag a wife and child after him.'

'So I should say, indeed.'

'I'd bet something you are not married.'

'No: as I told you, I live with my grandmother.'

'That you told me two years ago – you might have married a couple or three wives in the time.'

'I might, but I have not: the same arrangement still continues,' said Mr Kelly: who afterwards, thinking the conversation over, could not imagine what made him tell so many falsehoods to his companion.

If he had exhausted the matter, he would have found it was because he was afraid of speaking the truth.

'Your grandmother can't be a chicken now,' remarked Mr Felton.

'She is eighty-three,' answered Barney, on the principle of 'in for a penny, in for a pound.'

'And warm, doubtless.'

'She has enough to live on.'

'Which will come to you, I dare say?'

'That depends on how I behave myself, and other things.'

'And what are you doing till the dear old lady retires to the family vault?'

'Eating my dinners,' said Mr Kelly mendaciously.

'What! Are you a barrister?'

'Something of the sort.'

'Well, I'm –'

'What did you think I was, then?'

'I don't know. I was divided between something in the brewery line, and Guy's. Butterby thought you travelled for lead pencils.'

'Evidently I carry letters of credit in my face,' said Mr Kelly bitterly.

'Don't be huffed, old fellow,' entreated Mr Felton. 'We don't pretend to be judges – we can't be. We know a swell when we see him – and we can tell a potboy; but we've a lot to learn as regards the intermediate stages.'

'Lambeth,' said Mr Kelly with a great sense of relief, echoing the word which rang out from the gangway. 'This is your pier, I think, is it not?'

'Yes, I shall get out here. Won't you come along too? I can take anybody I like to Dawtons', and there's always something going. They'll be delighted to see any friend of mine. Say yes – like a good fellow, do!'

'Couldn't possibly, thank you,' answered Mr Kelly with the gravest composure – 'mustn't throw my people at Chelsea over for anybody.'

'Goodbye, then, till our next merry meeting.' And after a shake of the hand which made every bone in Barney's fingers tingle, Mr Felton betook himself amidships and leapt ashore, scorning the aid of the gangway, and exchanging as he passed light pleasantries with the piermen and the takers of the tickets.

So extremely anxious did Mr Bernard Kelly feel to defer the date of that next merry meeting indicated by his festive friend that on stepping ashore at Millbank Pier, which he did, he immediately took 'bus for the City, where, going to a modest tavern in the very heart of Stock Exchange land, he ordered a chop and modest potation of bitter, after which he betook himself by means of that cheerful Thames Tunnel Route which will never more be explored by any adventurous pedestrian, back to his lodgings in Bermondsey, where he at once penned an extremely neat and telling little paper, entitled 'Undesirable Acquaintances,' for which he received the sum of two guineas.

Chapter II

THE NEW STORY

IN THOSE LONELY WOLDS where since her father's death Glenarva Westley spent a good deal of time, an idea had taken root in her mind which shortly after she was married began to grow rapidly. She had wandered over the sparsely inhabited country, which for all signs of life and activity it presented might have been thousands of miles from London, till its desolation entered into her spirit, became a part and parcel of her very soul. There was one especially solitary farmhouse lying in a hollow surrounded by some elder-bushes and ash-trees which Glen never wearied of contemplating. From a little knoll on the side of the low hill beneath which this house nestled she could see the almost empty farmyard, the horsepond shaded by a great weeping willow, the neglected orchard, the plot of ground that had once been a garden, but was now a mere mass of tangled weeds; the house with its small windows and steep red-tiled roof, the walnut-tree shading the front door, and the tiny stream which ran so slowly it scarcely seemed to flow at all.

In this spot dwelt a mother and son. She was a widow. The son was reported to be studious, or in the words of the neighbourhood, 'over-fond of his book;' he was a tall, earnest-looking fellow, with deep-set eyes and overhanging brows; a stern mouth which could, Glen knew, relax into a beautiful smile; a sad expression of countenance, and the voice of a man who thought many times before he spoke once. The mother was a small, thin woman, who had apparently seen better days. The aspect of the farm itself was starved, and people said it was a shame to serve good land as that was served, and that young Blandford either ought to put his shoulder to the wheel, or give up the place, and let somebody take it who could get something out of the ground.

'Ashtrees,' which was the name of the farm, lay in another parish to that of which Glen's friend was rector. So the widow and her son did not attend the church which boasted the beautiful painted window, and there was no further acquaintance between the parsonage and the lonely house in the hollow than a mere greeting in passing, or the exchange of a few words, if the dwellers chanced to meet at the railway-station, or in the High Street of the nearest town.

It was, perhaps, because she knew so very little of the pair that Glen's fancy never wearied in imagining what their inner life must be. She pictured to herself the long winter nights in the quaint old house; the glorious summer days, when the fruit ripened in the orchard almost unheeded, and a few flowers struggled into bloom beside the moss-covered walks in the weed-grown garden – she thought of the mother not perhaps understanding her son, and wishing him more practical and commonplace – the son struggling with a sense of undeveloped genius and sickening of the monotonous life – the dreary round of common duties – eager to leave the place, and yet tied to it by tender memories, and by the affection he bore the woman who loved him more than all the world.

Possibly Glen was quite wrong in all her ideas concerning both Mrs Blandford and her son; but if she were she never knew the fact, and long before the story of which the seed was sown one stormy day in early spring, had grown to its full stature, the personnel of mother and son had utterly changed in her mind. She imagined a youth looking at the painted window Sunday after Sunday, till it became a part and parcel of his nature. She thought of him wandering over the bare, unbeautiful country dreaming of sculpture and painting – living mentally with the monks of old, and returning ever unwillingly to the constant routine, to the common drudgery of his daily life.

So far she had got when she married, but no further – and as two of her books were then about to appear almost immediately, both under assumed names, the idea seemed to drift away and become lost amongst the practical matters with which she was at the time occupied. Since her father's death she had written a new novel, which Mr Vassett published almost before the ink was dry, and sold another to one of the great West End houses; this latter work, indeed, being no other than the manuscript she formerly besought Mr Lacere to take out of the hands of the firm that had bought it. When she told him of this proceeding he smiled quietly, but he spoke no word of comment on her inconsistency. 'I told you so,' or 'I am not surprised,' or 'I thought you would do it,' were words she never heard from his lips.

'If Lady Emily were to know I had written every line of the book, I should not care now,' she said, in feeble explanation. 'I only wish I had taken the same view of matters two years ago that I do now, and I might have been doing well by this time.' The fact being that Glen by sheer force of audacity had got fifty pounds for a novel which would have been dear at five. She wanted money so badly and she was so determined to have it, that she extracted an acceptance of the work and cheque in payment from a publisher who otherwise might have coquetted with the matter for a long time, and then 'declined the story with thanks.' Till the last day of her life Glenarva will always remember two cheques she received; and that fifty pounds was one of them.

'I had not the least idea I should get it,' she added – 'in fact, till I went to the bank and received the notes over the counter I did not believe the transaction real.' Later on she had another cheque and another transaction she did not at the time believe real either. History repeats itself, even in the lives of human beings.

And now she was married – the mistress of a house – the wife of a man who thought she was without spot or blemish; who did not want her to write; who knew perhaps it would be better for her and happier for him if she never wrote another line; who really had not the faintest idea of the power she possessed; who said to her:

'Remember, dear, that I never wish you to think of publishing except for your own pleasure. Do not trouble yourself now about money or money-making; leave all that to me' – an injunction it is only fair to add Glen obeyed most literally for a time. Her life had been hard and anxious ever since she came to London – she had done a great deal of work; the trouble of her father's death was as yet scarcely dulled. Her bodily health was not good – her mind was weary – her energy seemed to have departed; and it is just possible if she had not happened about this time to make the acquaintance of a man who saw more clearly than anyone had yet done what was in the girl, she might have laid aside her pen and never written the book which made her name. As for her new friend, he treated her fancies and prejudices with even less ceremony than Ned Beattie. He laughed at her whims and tempers, at her 'tall' writing, at her little displays of knowledge, was severe on her sins of omission and commission, but still said, 'I know I am not mistaken: you have a great gift, but you must learn to use it properly.' He reviewed her books, or got them reviewed, in a manner which made Glen sometimes feel that she wished she had never written a line. She was lashed, she was ridiculed, she was accused of plagiarism, but then there came some word of praise which atoned for all that had gone before. Upon the whole, she wondered at the amount of commendation bestowed. Already she was beginning to show one sign of improvement; she now understood how extremely bad her best efforts really were. Her grandest passages no longer filled her with delight; faintly the beauty of simplicity was dawning upon her. She could at last see serious faults in her books, and certainly the quality of modesty appeared in her estimate of them.

'If I cannot do any better work than I have done,' she considered, 'I may as well cease writing altogether.' Not a happy mood for an author, perhaps; but a most fortunate one for the reader! Meantime the reviews had actually stimulated Mr Vassett's appreciation to such an extent, that he sent to know if Mrs Lacere felt disposed to enter into an engagement to let him have another book.

Glen said 'Yes;' but she failed to add when he might expect to receive the manuscript. She thought she had no plot on which to found a story. Vaguely the lonely wolds, the solitary farmhouse, kept recurring to her memory; but she did not see her way to raise any superstructure upon such meagre foundations, till one evening, when her husband and a friend of his were talking about the rich deep permanent colours to be seen in old church windows, which modern art sought in vain to reproduce, she looked across the table to her husband, and said: 'I shall write a novel about stained glass.'

They all laughed at the idea. 'Not a very likely subject,' remarked the visitor; while Mr Logan-Lacere's brother-in-law smiled the quiet, tolerant smile Glenarva had long learnt to detest.

'We shall see,' answered Mrs Lacere determinedly, and though she did not, like Charlotte, 'go on cutting more bread and butter,' she proceeded to pour out more tea, while the talk she had interrupted flowed back into its former channel, and Glen took refuge in silence – an asylum she latterly somewhat affected.

Day by day the story grew in her mind. She never perhaps afterwards wrote a book which through so many months was such a companion. Busy with various other matters, she could not write much at a time, and, as a consequence perhaps, what she did write, read very close. No human being who glanced at a work the reviewers criticised not only mercifully but most favourably, imagined the clear, nervous sentences born of sorrow, experience, love, disappointment, were penned by the same author who had given to the world a novel it did not in the least want, called *Tyrrel's Son*.

It was a curious book to take the fancy of the public. Often during its progress, Mr Vassett, after reading some of the chapters which set utterly at naught all established precedents, all foregone traditions, felt it his duty to write and remonstrate with the author on the failure she was about to achieve for herself, and the loss such a novel must ensure to him.

Actually he read the manuscript as it proceeded – Glen gave him abundant leisure for doing so – and differences of opinion were of such constant occurrence between the two, that at length the publisher, resigning himself to making the best of a bad business, determined to print as small an edition as possible, and decided, if ever he accepted another book from Mrs Lacere, to stipulate the whole of it should be placed in his hands before any definite arrangement was arrived at.

The book experienced many difficulties ere it was bound. In the first place, Glen did not find it easy to write, and she kept it 'dawdling about,' as Mr Pierson said, for eighteen months; in the second, Mr Vassett insisted on one chapter being expunged altogether. Mrs Lacere naturally objected to Mr Vassett's dictum. The incident described, she insisted, happened to be absolutely necessary to the plot, and she could not expunge it. Mr Vassett thereupon said he would prefer not publishing the book. He had already paid for it, and he therefore must have been very much in earnest. Glen felt this, though not so acutely as she might have done subsequently; and after a long and friendly interview, a compromise was effected. Mrs Lacere, whom Mr Vassett declared to be 'for a woman and an author most reasonable,' agreed to find some other road by which the desired end could be reached; while the publisher, on his side, stated that though he thought the whole book a complete mistake, he would do his best with it.

The 'mistake' was finished – the book was complete – the 'hand that had written it laid it aside;' and Glen for a time went lonely and desolate about the duties of her daily life.

The people she described had grown to be heart of her heart; they had walked with her in hope, and joy, and sorrow; their interests had been hers – their fears hers. She had turned to them for companionship when she felt sad and low-spirited – their troubles had beguiled her from the contemplation of her own. And now they were dead and gone – they could never walk the City streets with her again – she should never cross the Essex wolds in the wild March weather, or February sleet, or summer's sunshine with them any more – she should not see them sitting in church or listen to their sobs or behold their smiles ever, ever in the future. The manuscript was 'set up' – the tale told – 'the end' printed on the final page. The world would read – the reviewers blame, perhaps – some readers scoff – a few, a very few possibly, understand; but they, the men and the women who had been more real to her than the men and women she came in bodily contact with, were gone – never to return – never any more, forever!

Then came a lull. The book was advertised, subscribed. The subscription was fairly good – quite as good as Mr Vassett expected; for he still anticipated loss.

'Ah!' he said to Mr Pierson, 'if she had only taken my advice and followed beaten paths, something might now have been done with a book of hers.'

'Why did you not advise her to try strange roads?' suggested Mr Pierson; 'then she might have gone the way you wished – women and pigs, you know.'

'True,' answered Mr Vassett, 'if scarcely polite. It is too late, however,' he added.

'I have a notion myself the novel will go,' said Mr Pierson. 'Somebody must sometimes strike out a new line.'

Mr Vassett smiled a smile which meant Glen had much better have abided by the wisdom of her elders.

'I think there is stuff in the book,' repeated Mr Pierson doggedly, varying his words but not his meaning.

'I think there might have been,' amended Mr Vassett.

'It strikes me, you know, people must tire occasionally of the love and twaddle business.'

'Not so long as love and twaddle form the principal business and conversation of so many persons' lives.'

'But do they? Candidly now, doesn't there come a time when a man gets tired of all that sort of thing?'

'Not till he has done with everything, I imagine,' answered Mr Vassett, under all whose hope of profit, and dread of loss, and caution and worldly prudence, and desire to make money, and wish to stand as a publisher, and delight in the old streets, and interest in the houses where noted men had lived, a little sweet, sad, tender romantic strain was ever wailing, which bore for its burden some words about a time of roses and a day of pain, of some never-to-be-forgotten love-passages in the fair, fresh springtime of existence, and hours and hours of agony ere its autumn, when all things worth having or thinking about in life were hid away forever, so far as this world is concerned, in Shepperton Churchyard, hard by which the Thames flows calmly, past dipping willow and fairy ait, mansion and church and hamlet, beside green pastures, bordered by reeds and rushes, decked with water-lilies, onward to the great unknown city, and beyond it to the unseen mysterious sea.

And in truth at that time Glen had done a very daring thing – taken a very doubtful course in making love merely occupy the same position in her story that it does apparently in the lives of most of those with whom we come in contact.

It was an innovation sure to be unpopular with her own sex, who are, after all, the public for whom a novelist has to cater. Ladies and boys were then the audience to whom all authors, who wished either for 'praise or pudding,' or both, felt it wise to appeal. Times in that respect are not much changed; even to this present day the novelist who rings but the changes of one eternal song – the loves of lovely woman – the beauty of lovely woman – the unselfishness of lovely woman – the dress of lovely woman – the lovers of lovely woman – will be the most popular. Where, for example, George Eliot counted her thousands, the *Family Herald* counts its tens of thousands!

Thus Mr Vassett was, in one sense, quite right when he accounted Glen's book a mistake; but the greed for gain or applause was not on her when she began her task, and she finished it, not for the sake of writing, but because she had something to say, and could know no real rest till it was said.

As has been stated, the desolation of the part of Essex where she had been staying entered into her very soul, and the vision she conjured up was that of a young man looking Sunday after Sunday on the painted window, which was at once so sad, so solemn, and so beautiful, till an overmastering ambition seized him to discover the secret of colour, which seemed to have died out with the monks of old. Though not an artist, he was possessed of keen artistic tastes, and the walls of that wainscoted parlour in the farmhouse which he owned were decorated with weird drawings faithfully representing the wild, lonely country amid which he lived, as seen under summer's suns and winter's snows – fast bound with frost, and smiling when the golden grain was cut and gathered into bundles, ready for carrying under the glorious autumn skies. And amid and through all these land-scapes one fair form constantly reappeared – now standing beside a stream – now mingling with the reapers – now tossing the newly-mown grass – again tripping across the lea – and anon, 'through buds and branches peeping.'

She was his love, his life, his inspiration; for her he told himself he desired wealth and fame – for her sake he desired to emulate the blues, and the yellows, and the greens, and the reds, which, all exquisitely softened and blended together, made up the perfect whole of that picture, even to see which, told the soul a little of the lesson our Saviour came to teach.

She was fair, young, merry. All the gloom of that gloomy house had failed to cast one shadow over her. She loved everything about the farm – the pigeons, the cats, the horses, the grim old grumbling bailiff, every tile on its roof, every single brick in its walls, but for the sake of the man she loved beyond all men, she was willing – more than willing – to leave the pleasantness of the only home she had ever known, and go away with him to London, where he felt certain he should be able to reduce many theories to practice, and find the colours modern humanity had so long wished for, and wished in vain.

It is not necessary to tell how the story ended – how the author worked it out is all which concerns this tale. Painfully, surely, slowly, she gathered all her parts together, wove into the narrative the trials, the sorrows, the self-denials, the successes of trade – explained processes of manufacture unknown utterly to the reading public – took the outside world due east in London, and asked it to walk into dreadful little manufactories, and listen to 'shop' talk, and take an interest in the doings and sayings of men who had probably never been to a dinner-party in their lives, and knew nothing of Sir Bernard Burke, and were not acquainted with lords or baronets: but who were yet some of them gentlemen and some of them cads, following the nature of their kind.

A book certain never to be popular amongst the many, that goes without saying; a book, nevertheless, which was talked about, and made a mark.

'Who is the author?' everyone asked, and many people answered, 'Oh! I know him very well indeed;' and then he was drawn respectively as a barrister, a gambler, a man who had neglected his wife, a man whose wife had run away from him, a man who was about town, a man who had been about town, but who now represented her Majesty as consul somewhere at the world's end; and, lastly, he was represented to Glen's husband, by a chatty individual who professed to know everyone, as 'a devilish good fellow, sir – and clever too!'

It may have been about this time some doubts entered Mr Lacere's mind as to *what* he had married, while for eighteen months a dreadful question had been agitating Glen:

'There must be some mistake,' she thought. 'It is not Mordaunt Logan-Lacere I have taken for better or worse, but *the whole family*, and I am a nobody in it.'

Which was all quite true; she and Mordaunt Logan-Lacere were now one, and as he certainly had ever been a mere cipher among his relations, it followed as a matter of course that the woman who was supposed to be in subjection to him counted as nothing. From the first good care was taken to teach Glen her proper position, and since she promised to be a somewhat difficult subject, Mr Lacere, the cousin-brother-in-law, adopted the admirable course of ignoring her. He had always led Mr Logan-Lacere by the nose, and he did not mean any wife on earth to weaken his influence in that quarter.

Almost unconsciously he had read that Glen was not to be humbugged, but he felt, with her hot, impulsive temper, she might be driven off the field; and finding, much to his dissatisfaction, that, spite of many delays, the marriage really was a fact accomplished, the moment Glenarva Westley became Mrs Lacere, he commenced his tactics. They were beautifully simple. It was easy to make a girl whose life had been spent amongst loving and frank friends feel she was not wanted in a family sufficient to themselves; and Glen did feel this bitterly. If he wished to tell her husband it was a fine day, for example, he made the communication either with closed doors, or at the other end of the room in a subdued and confidential voice; and finding that this treatment only roused Mrs Logan-Lacere's ire against himself, he began in conversation with her dexterously to exalt his own abilities and good qualities, and try to make her think the man she had married was, after all, a poor sort of creature. But Glen's eyes had long been open to this little failing on the part of her new male relative. She was well aware that not only to herself, but to others, Mr Lacere was in the habit of glorifying himself and depreciating Logan-Lacere. She tried to make her husband understand this, but he resolutely declined to attach the slightest importance to her representations; and Glen, after madly beating her spirit and bruising her heart, and shedding passionate tears of sorrow and anger, battling against the cruelty of circumstances she found herself powerless to alter, suddenly abandoned the hopeless contest.

'If he likes his brother-in-law better than he does me, let him,' she thought, in an access of bitter loneliness. 'I have no father or mother to talk to – I have no home to go to, or I would go. I must bear it just as I can.'

Possibly 'it' was one of the very worst experiences which could have come to such a temperament.

Shortness of money she did not care for – she had served a long apprenticeship to that; but to live amongst people who were reserved, with whom she knew now she never could have any sympathy, who stood perpetually between her husband and herself, who were a burden to him pecuniarily and a drawback socially, were matters Glen felt something too hard to bear and yet, so great was her antagonism to this opponent, that she firmly made up her mind he should never crush her.

Perhaps he knew something of all this. If he did not, it was certainly from no reticence on the part of Glenarva. Fierce passages of arms had occurred between them, in which both sides went so far they found it expedient at length to withdraw their forces by tacit consent. It was a miserable experience, one bad for soul and body, which left ineradicable traces on Glen's face and mind. For ever the calm, peaceful look of youth left her brow, and though her character strengthened, there grew at the same time a mental irritability as well as a weary unrest, foreign to her original nature. To anyone who had known her at Ballyshane, the change would have seemed most marked; indeed, when, after the lapse of two long years, Edward Beattie saw his old friend again, he asked himself in astonishment if this grave, cynical, self-contained woman could ever have been light-hearted, frank-spoken Glen Westley.

For a time he watched her in silence – he was staying at Mr Lacere's – but the third day after his arrival he asked:

'What has altered you so much? You are not in the least like the Glen you used to be.'

'Getting old,' answered Mrs Logan-Lacere laconically.

It was noticeable she did not deny the truth of his remark, or fence with it.

'It is not that,' he said. 'What is it, dear?' he went on; 'won't you tell *me*, Glen?' he said, as she shook her head, 'you must tell me – me, your brother Ned – the Ned of the old days when we didn't think much, either of us, of death, or trouble, or sickness, or anything but amusement. Aren't you happy?'

'*Most* unhappy,' she answered slowly. The words seemed wrung from the very depths of some dark despair, and then she turned aside to hide the tears now coursing down her cheeks.

For a minute Edward Beattie looked at her in utter amazement; then he said, 'Glen, you must be mad: why in the world should you be unhappy, married to a man you love – and who simply adores you?'

'He doesn't do anything of the kind,' she answered, with the manner which was new to her.

Ned laughed, relieved. 'Oh! That's it, is it! and Mrs Glen, for all her strength of mind, finds she is not superior to the little feminine complaint of jealousy! *Who is she*?'

Glen flashed round upon him indignantly.

'It isn't a "she" at all, and I am not jealous.'

'That you are, my dear,' he retorted, 'and now you have taken a notion of that sort it can't be easy lines for your husband. I always was afraid he would let you get your head. Fact is, Glen, you are too well off. As the mothers say to their children in Ireland, you want something to cry for. You have married a man who thinks you perfection; who worships the ground you walk on; who if you expressed a wish to have the top brick of the chimney, would at once send for a ladder to humour your fancy.'

Glen did not answer. Perhaps in her heart she knew every word Ned spoke to be true. But there was something he did not know – something he wanted to find out.

'Yes, it must be hard for your husband,' he went on provokingly; 'but it serves him right for marrying a clever woman, or rather, a woman who is considered clever. When I choose a wife I'll take very good care that if she can read she can't write.'

'Perhaps you may find something at the Asylum for Idiots to suit you,' remarked Glen.

'I think I should like a mute best,' said Mr Edward Beattie. 'By the way, Glen, what induced you to favour the world with that last book? You had much better never have published it. I wonder Lacere allowed you. If you had been my wife I would have made you burn it.'

'What is your particular objection to a work which has not been wholly unsuccessful?' asked Mrs Lacere, with a fine scorn.

'My objection is general as well as particular. It is a morbid, unhealthy book.'

'If you think of any other bad quality the novel possesses, pray do not forget to mention it.'

'Supposing you found you were unable to exist without writing something,' persisted Ned, 'why did you not give us a story calculated to make us all happier and brighter and better – a womanly sort of tale about flowers and children and happy lovers?'

She made no answer; the old pain was tugging at her heart-strings. She could have told him the sweet folly, the hopes and fears, the dreams, the pangs, the trembling doubts of happy lovers had never been for her – might never be for her while the sun rose and set. She understood now what a loss had been hers. Her past lacked one great good, for which no future, however fortunate, could ever atone. Out of her very capability for wretchedness she was beginning to estimate what her capability for happiness might have been. Was the life she had once thought would prove so beautiful, so prosperous, so complete, to be after all but one long series of disasters and disappointments? She had longed for success, and when it came it was with death close following on its heels; her wounded heart craved for an absorbing love, but when it had lavished its full store of warm, passionate affection, found for return it was but one love amongst many. That a man should leave his father and mother and cleave unto his wife was an article of faith which found small favour in the Lacere connection. One of the very few funny things which Miss Lacere ever said, quite unconsciously – for like most persons of the same grim category she was utterly destitute of all sense of humour – chanced to be that we were only told two things about heaven, namely: There was a great deal of love, and *no marriage*!

'A sort of heavenly Agapemone,' observed Glen sarcastically. But that flippant remark did not exactly contain the gist of Miss Lacere's meaning – it was a brotherly and sisterly love she dreamed of, in which the mad craze for a wife should have no place!

'Wives always cause disunion in families,' said another of Mr Logan-Lacere's female relations, from which statement alone, the pleasant and unselfish spirit animating his belongings may be conjectured.

And finally, to put the case in a nutshell, Glen being a woman who had never before in the whole of her short life known what it might be like not to stand first in the love of those by whom she was surrounded – found herself married to a man who conceived it to be his duty as well as his pleasure to let his relations feel wedlock had not made any difference in his sentiments towards them; who refused utterly to hear with Glen's ears – see with Glen's eyes – to notice with Glen's perceptions – to judge with Glen's sense; who let himself be made a mere shuttlecock, for all these battledores to play with; who, although, as Ned would have said with that terrible candour of his, fifty times cleverer than his wife, she knew never had, and never could compass any worldly good for himself, burdened as he was with the opinions, prejudices, and traditions of these terrible Old Men of the Sea.

All these things and fifty more passed through Glen's mind as Ned finished his agreeable sentence, and leaning her head against the lattice-work of the arbour in which they sat, she answered him never a word; then she rose, and would have gone away quietly without letting him guess the anguish she felt, had not one uncontrollable sob broken the spell.

'Glen, sit down,' he said, almost sternly; and after she obeyed there ensued a silence rent by no sound save that of bitter weeping.

At last Ned spoke. 'Look here, Glen,' he began, 'whatever your trouble may be, crying won't mend it. In most lives, I suppose, there is something not quite right; but I am very sure we don't improve our lot by moaning over it. So far as I can see, you ought to be a very happy woman; but if you are not, if you have any real sorrow, don't let it conquer you. If my poor father could speak to you now, he would say, "Glen, take my advice and go and weed in the garden for a couple of hours every morning; or find out someone who has a mangle, and ask them to let

you turn it; do anything rather than sit idle nursing a real or imaginary grievance."
Now,' finished Mr Edward Beattie on his own account, 'put on your bonnet, and come out for a walk.'

It was good, honest, wholesome advice; but he did not know the depressing nature of the influences by which Glen was surrounded. She saw the evil, but she could not alter it; she felt, at last, she could not try to alter it; her health was bad; she had got into a low state of mind; she saw everything through darkened spectacles. Saying no further word to her about the change wrought since her father's death, Ned, keeping his eyes wide open, soon arrived at a pretty accurate idea of the state of affairs.

It was towards the close of his visit he one evening over tea exploded a shell in the midst of the whole Lacere connection.

'Why don't you persuade your husband, Glen, to leave England?' he said. 'I am not particular where I go. Suppose we all start together for Canada. Plenty of shooting, fishing, boating. It would set you both up in health; and I am sure clear blue skies would be an agreeable change after the smoke of London. What do you say, Mr Lacere? Will you consider my proposition?'

To describe the faces of the ladies of the Lacere family as Mr Beattie rattled out these words would be simply impossible.

'Oh! we could not part with either of them,' declared Miss Lacere, as spokeswoman, and a murmur of assent followed from the others.

'The best friends must part sometimes,' answered Ned carelessly; and so the talk went on till a very pretty spirit of hatred and antagonism was established between Glen, Glen's friend, and Glen's relatives.

Possibly it was during Mr Beattie's visit the idea first dawned upon Mr Logan-Lacere that his female relations were not quite perfect.

He was too loyal to admit even to himself they were prejudiced, yet he could not but feel it was a pity they had, for some reason best known to themselves, conceived such a prejudice against everything Irish – 'dear' Glen of course excepted.

Mr Edward Beattie had a store of capital stories, which he told remarkably well, but the Misses Lacere could 'see nothing in them.' Mr Edward Beattie had braced up his old comrade Mrs Lacere, and benefited her mentally, morally, and physically; nevertheless the Lacere connection heard with pursed-up mouths and silent tongues their 'darling Mordaunt's' encomiums on his wife's friend.

'It is all very well,' said Miss Humphries, in the privacy of that awful and secret family inquisition which was forever sitting upon Glen, Glen's ways and waywardness, Glen's antecedents, Glen's former friends, and Glen's present misguided and led-by-the-nose husband – 'but ah! –'

Whereupon 'ah!' was echoed by the whole family with the solemnity of a curse.

Mr Logan-Lacere, however, always retained a pleasant memory of the cheery young fellow, and said most truly he felt very sorry he could not stay longer with them.

'You have done my wife a great deal of good,' he said.

'You ought both to start with me for New Zealand, or Australia, or Canada,' answered Ned; while to Glen he spoke with grave conviction:

'Your husband will never do a day's good while he stays among his own people. Get him away from them; they would sink a man-of-war. And as for you, my dear, spite of all the loves, and darlings, and flattery, and all the rest of it, they only care for what they think they can coax out of you.'

Certainly no one could accuse Mr Edward Beattie of unduly flattering anybody.

Chapter III

BARNEY'S LUCK

TIME WENT ON, and Mr Bernard Kelly was doing remarkably well indeed. He chanced to be the sort of man success makes, but does not mar. With only half-a-crown between himself and nothing, he might have felt inclined to play a reckless game, but possessed of a sovereign, he turned the coin over and over, and decided it was too valuable to risk losing in any mad or careless fashion. He worked hard – he lived frugally – he adventured carefully; his barque carried no passenger save himself, and bore no freight save his own fortunes. Why should he not have got on? Why should a man who regards himself alone, fail to succeed? Fame to Bernard Kelly meant so much hard cash. The reputation of a Shakespeare or a Milton would in his eyes have seemed valueless, unless it had brought for dowry a good house, a possible carriage and pair, and the certainty of never again being short of a ten-pound note.

He had advanced considerably in his ideas since he stood drearily contemplating the swans in St James's Park. No human being ever exactly knew how he had managed to do so remarkably well, and it is quite possible he could not have told himself. The *Galaxy* was dead and buried. Its short and brilliant life may have been a merry one to the contributors, but the proprietors groaned in spirit when they reckoned up the amount they had to pay for its peculiarly unprosperous career. There is always, however – so says the old proverb – one door open when another is shut; and wherever Mr Kelly found a door open he had a knack of walking in, and having obtained a footing, keeping it. Formerly, as has already been mentioned, he was asked to submit some manuscripts to the editor of the opposition magazine, on which occasion he received that figurative slap in the face which caused him very seriously to consider the demerits of his own productions. Months went by, and again he received a polite note, this time begging to know if he was disposed to contribute some short papers to the journal in question. Mr Kelly had, long before this epistle reached him, ceased to be a novice in literary matters; so, without writing, he called to see the editor, who turned out to be the inquisitive gentleman he travelled with up to London when he first came to seek his fortune in the great metropolis.

The recognition was not mutual. Bernard knew him again in a moment, but the confident, well-dressed, easy-spoken author, who talked so glibly about manuscripts, and journals, and publishers, and men on the press, and all the rest of it, bore small resemblance to that gauche, half-civilised Barney who had vexed the pharisaical soul of righteous Mat Donagh and disturbed the whole economy of Abbey Cottage.

The former sub-editor was gone. When Mr Kelly explained how his previous stories had been treated with contumely, the chief expressed his extreme regret, and trusted 'the unhappy accident, which must have arisen through some gross misapprehension, would not deprive thir magazine of services he felt only too anxious to secure.' Barney permitted himself to be appeased; he was willing, he said, to 'contribute,' but he must decline to 'submit.' The editor declared he never should have thought of asking him to do anything of the sort, and begged to know his terms.

It was all very well and all very nice, and Mr Kelly thought he had really no reason to complain; nevertheless, he could not blind himself to the utterly precarious nature of a literary profession. Manuscript did not grow while a man slept; it failed to put fat on his ribs unless the author was always at work. Though he had proved himself capable of hard and prolonged labour, it would be folly to say that to an Irishman the prospect of grinding out 'copy' during the term of his natural life seemed agreeable. He wanted an appointment of some sort – an editorship, if nothing better offered – and at last he managed to, what his mother would have called 'put his foot in the jamb and keep it there.'

His new friend, who said 'he had really conceived a very high opinion of Mr Kelly's abilities,' chanced one day to be expressing his regret at the impossibility of getting out of town even for a week. 'I have not a soul now to help me,' he went on, 'except the clerk, and he really is worse than no one.'

It was then Bernard offered to look in for a few hours each day to correct proofs and look over manuscripts.

'I want something to amuse me and occupy my time,' he explained; speaking like a person who had the wealth of Rothschild at his back, and the length of days of the patriarchs stretching in front; 'and I should really be delighted if you would make use of me – supposing you think me capable,' modestly added Barney, who had taken the measure of his man pretty accurately.

The offer was instantly accepted, and though Mr Kelly received no salary, so many things were 'put in his way,' correcting, re-writing, touching up, and softening down, that this nominally unremunerative post proved really a valuable addition to his income. Further, it brought him in contact with quite a new set of literary people; amongst others he met Miss Yarlow, who often looked at him very curiously and said, 'I can't think where I have seen you before.'

Upon these occasions Mr Kelly was wont to remark he thought he must have met her somewhere, and then the two would go over a list of the houses they had perhaps entered once, and the people who had happened to send them an 'At Home' card; and so, airing their intimate acquaintanceship with and knowledge of the aristocracy and gentry, mutually humbugged each other.

For in truth Miss Yarlow and Mr Kelly had conceived as strong a mutual liking as such natures ever seem capable of developing. They were both selfish, both prudent, both capable, both determined to achieve success if success were to be gained by perseverance and pushing; but Miss Yarlow thought Bernard had means, and he imagined the lady possessed a pretty fortune and was highly connected. When he found out, as he did in some marvellous manner from Mr Pierson, that she had been a 'nursery governess,' or something of the sort, it was wonderful how Mr Kelly's 'warm Irish heart' cooled towards her. His criticism of her next manuscript proved somewhat severe; and when she went again to the office it was only to find he no longer occupied his accustomed chair. Barney had at last got something good. He was editor of a quite new weekly journal, which had for its capitalists one of those fools mentioned by Mr Lance Felton, who stand at the corners of the streets waiting eagerly for some one to take them in.

Mr Kelly did not, however, intend to take his man in, as he honestly meant trying to make a success of an impossible venture, and he certainly felt very well satisfied with himself and his principal when he looked around the newly furnished room sacred to him, and gave audience to authors who hung trembling on his answers – as he even had listened in agony for the inevitable 'No,' which, spoken in all sorts of tones, in all manners of offices, greeted his arrival in London.

One morning, he had just taken possession of his editorial chair, just laid a sheet of headed note-paper on his blotting pad before him, just dipped a new pen in the freshly filled ink-bottle, when the clerk told off for his especial use, entering the room, presented him with a letter. It was from his mother; in the pride of his heart he had been unable to resist the temptation of letting the good folks at Callinacoan know the Barney whom they had regarded as a good deal lower than themselves, was now 'a power' in London; and as he cut open the envelope with the editorial paperknife, he wondered what she would find to say about his rise; while his thoughts flew back to the time when she had told him 'to put his shoulder to the wheel, for it was of no use asking her to send any more money to keep him in idleness.'

But since it is always the unexpected which happens, so, instead of any triumphant rejoicing over her Barney's 'great future,' Mrs Kelly's epistle proved rather to be a Jeremiad over what he had 'let slip past him.' 'Oh! Barney dear, what d'ye think,' were the words with which the letter led off.

> *Mr Fortescue's dead, and hasn't left behind him as much of a will as you could light a candle with. So the old woman, they say, 'll have all the property, or rather Robert Underwood will – ay, that's what they tell me. The whole of Sulby Park, and the grand furniture, and the horses, and the carriages, and the cows, and the pigs, and the gold, and the silver, and all the big houses the Fortescues own in London, and the money in the bank, and the Three per cents, and everything that could be named almost. Barney, Barney, and you let all this slip past you for the sake of a dirty fifty pounds – why, you might have been as big a man as the Duke of Leinster! My heart feels bursting when I remember if you'd had the spirit of a mouse you'd have taken her to church, and then gone up bold like a man and made your terms with the brother. Oh! Barney, you're just another Esau, and all I hope is you won't come to the same bad end. You're mighty set up with that mess of pottage you call an editorship; but only think of the farms and demesnes, the river and the yearly income you've lost! And sure, though she wasn't young, she had the good blood in her veins, and she's not a bad sort, and has lived quietly and respectably since that thief of the world took himself off to America. But there – it's no use lamentin'; a peck of care won't cure an ounce of trouble. I hope you'll let this be a warning to you not to think so much of yourself.*
>
> *Your heart-broken Mother.*

The note which Mr Bernard Kelly had been about to write was not even begun on the morning when he read his 'heart-broken mother's' communication. He sat in the editorial chair for a time like one stupefied; then, taking his hat, he walked round into Essex Street, and sought the office of a solicitor with whom recent circumstances had made him acquainted.

This interview with the lawyer was upon the whole unsatisfactory; nevertheless, that authority conceded there were some points in the Underwood case worth fighting – points Mr Kelly did not believe the ex-groom would care to fight. He felt perfectly satisfied in his own mind that if the whole of the property could not be secured to the wife, a compromise of some sort might be made with Mr Underwood, who would want to finger the money immediately, and prove possibly willing to listen to reason rather than wait the result of a Chancery suit and an application for a divorce. Mr Kelly had asked the solicitor questions that gentleman candidly confessed himself unable to answer off-hand. He said he should like to consult various authorities, and refer the matter to counsel. He fancied something might be done – at all events, he agreed with Bernard Kelly it would be a thousand pities for the lady to let everything go without a struggle.

If there were a single precedent in her favour, or if her case could be made a precedent, he did not believe any judge in the land would hand over an estate to the scoundrel Mr Kelly described. He 'would think the case over and take the opinion of his partner, who was more up in that sort of thing than himself.'

'You might look in the day after tomorrow, Mr Kelly,' he said, and Mr Kelly told him he would do so; but scarcely was he out of the office before a more excellent plan suggested itself. He decided to start for Ireland that night, full of which resolve he turned into the Strand, and was making his way hastily towards Temple Bar, when he ran across Mat Donagh and another congenial spirit standing at the door of the George. The pair had been lunching presumably – drinking certainly. Mat's usual austerity of manner was relaxed; the starch in his immaculate collar and shirtfront did not seem quite so stiff as Barney remembered it; the bow of his white cravat had got somewhat twisted and crumpled. On his waistcoat were vestiges of crumbs; in his cheeks was a pinky colour attributable to wine, sound and old. He had evidently just finished the narration of a good story, for his friend was laughing loudly and, Mat himself did not disdain to evince some signs of merriment.

'By Gad, sir,' he was saying, backing across the pavement as he spoke, when Bernard Kelly, who had tried to avoid the encounter, came into collision with him.

'I beg your pardon,' apologised the new editor Mr Donagh was in the habit of casually referring to as that 'sneaking upstart.'

'*Your servant, sir!*' answered Mat, wheeling round, taking off his hat and making a bow so low, so ironical, it almost collected a crowd. 'There goes the most unmitigated cad in London,' he added, looking after the retreating figure, 'a fellow who came over here from his native bogs with scarcely a shoe to his foot.'

If Mr Kelly had been superstitious, the sight of his old enemy, whom he had not come athwart for months, almost years previously, might have struck him as unlucky, as the sight of a red-haired man, or a hare, or anything else of that sort did in the days when people turned back from a journey if any such evil omen crossed their path; but Bernard was not superstitious, and accordingly, though his chance encounter irritated him a good deal, he went back to his office and got through the day's work well, and arranged everything for the time he must be absent; and feeling a very different person from the stranger who had with dazed and dazzled eyes looked upon the crescent of lamps at Euston long enough agone, crossed the platform rug on arm, followed by a porter carrying a small portmanteau, and took his seat in the 'Wild Irishman,' bound to reach Holyhead about one a.m. or a little after.

'This game is worth the candle,' he thought, as he pushed a five-pound note through the pigeon-hole of the booking-office. Only imagine the change of times and position when the once impecunious Barney could afford and venture to throw sovereigns down in this fashion!

As the train whirled through the night he thought long and anxiously concerning the destiny of Mr Fortescue's estate. If Mrs Underwood could get a divorce; if the lapse of time proved no bar to her ultimate freedom; if an arrange-ment were possible with the former pad-groom; if Mrs Underwood were Miss Fortescue once more, and in possession of, say, a clear ten thousand pounds – what then? Why then Bernard Kelly, Esquire, could lead her to the hymeneal altar, and literature and the Three per Cents, might contract a highly eligible alliance.

Ten thousand pounds was Mr Kelly's figure; he decided the lady would not be too dear or himself too cheap at that sum. Anyone who knew how to manage could do a great deal with ten thousand pounds, and Bernard fancied few were better able to cut his coat according to his cloth than himself. Yes, if ten thousand pounds were forthcoming he would marry her; and accordingly, on the wings of prudence if not of love, Mr Kelly sped across England, and shipping his precious person at Holyhead on board the fine steamship *Munster* next morning about seven, after years of absence, once again set foot on his native soil. No Saxon could have thought less of that native soil than did Bernard Kelly. It was with the most supreme disgust and contempt he surveyed his countrymen and women from the ignoble eminence of a rickety jaunting-car, which conveyed himself and his fortunes from the Westland Road Station to the Imperial Hotel in Sackville Street. At Kingstown, leisure, if not occasion, had been wanting to enable him to study the humours of a land he had forsworn; but as they rattled through the streets of 'dear dirty Dublin,' as he looked at the capital of Ireland in her morning apparel, he felt he could not wonder at anything Englishmen said about that island, from which, about the time he exterminated toads and snakes, St Patrick seems to have banished order and external cleanliness as well. It was not that Barney loved England more, but he liked Ireland less. He felt he had left civilisation behind, and returned to a sort of modified barbarism. He understood now what had once seemed a dark utterance, the remark of a lady, who said she always, on returning from Scotland, thanked Heaven when the name of the first station was called out south of the Border.

'Think,' she said, 'what it is to feel free at one blow – of Scotch coal and the Scottish accent!' Judge what it was to Barney Kelly to plunge back into the abyss from which he had emerged, and consider, 'Such as these barbarians are, I, even I, might have remained!'

He did not remain very long at the Imperial, where he partook of breakfast and consulted a timetable. A long cross-country journey lay before him, and he wanted to time his movements so as to reach Sulby Park in the gloaming. He knew Callinacoan and Mrs Underwood; he desired to elude the curiosity of the one and arouse the interest of the other, and accordingly fixed upon a town a few miles distant from his birthplace, from whence he proposed to drive over to what in the dreadful phraseology – to quote Mat Donagh – of the neighbourhood would have been called 'his calf-ground.'

Arrived at Sulby Park, he delivered a letter to the sedate butler, and said:

'Perhaps Mrs Underwood may wish to send an answer.'

No human being, no detective, not the mother who bore him, could have recognised the 'just-caught' Barney of the commencement of this story, in the fashionably dressed, self-possessed, handsome man who was at once ushered into the library, on the shelves of which were ranged some of those books that had helped to gain him the five pounds wherewith he paid his fare.

Altogether a most curious experience. For my own part, I marvel those who have so wonderfully risen never seem able to reproduce intelligibly the impressions such a total change of circumstances must have produced. Perhaps they do not care to recall even to themselves the past an outsider would imagine must have held some pleasant hours. Yet it all seems such a mistake. Bad as we account the world – I am sure I do not know why – it yet honours a man true and faithful enough to say from what he has risen and how! There seemed a fascination for Bernard Kelly in the brown gilt-letter binding of those old books of plays, for he stood looking at them while his mind took a swift but comprehensive review of the years that had passed since he sat beside the river reading for hours together.

It all came back to him: the rush and hurry of the water flowing over the gravel, fretting against the stones; the dipping branches swaying with the current; the sun streaming through the trees upon his book, casting a tracery of leaves across the page; Miss Fortescue coming to meet him, and –

The door of the library opened at that moment – a soft muffled swish of paramatta and crape sounded in his ear – two white hands were extended towards him, and Mrs Underwood's remembered voice was saying:

'Oh, Mr Kelly! oh, Mr Kelly! – this is kindness and friendship indeed!'

He took both her hands in his; for a moment there was utter silence. She could not see him for the tears which blinded her, but he could see her; and he availed himself of the opportunity to take a comprehensive survey of a lady he meant, if all things worked favourably, should one day be his wife. The result was satisfactory. She did not look much older, and black suited her – yes, she must always wear black. She had never been handsome, but, comparing her with many of her sex, she was really not plain. Her figure, always elegant, struck Barney with quite a new surprise; yes, she would do very well indeed. He could not, it is true, make her younger; but then if she were younger he might have stood a poor chance of marrying her.

'Dear Mrs Underwood,' he said at last, 'I feel truly sorry for you – I thought you might want a friend; and so the moment I heard the sad tidings I decided to come and ask in person if I could be of any assistance. I trust you do not consider this visit an intrusion.'

'No – no – *most* grateful – such kindness is – I shall be more composed presently.'

He led her to a seat, and leaning over the back of the chair, began at once to open the business that had brought him in such a hurry across the Channel. He knew her of old, and was perfectly well aware, although it suited her to seem absorbed in grief, she could listen to what he said, and understand it too. He advised that she should at once travel to London, and obtain the best opinion on her case. If she were not to be left utterly at the mercy of a man who had proved himself undeserving of her generous trust, action of some sort should be taken immediately.

He did not pay much attention to her broken utterances, which told him 'she deserved her fate,' 'it was a fitting punishment,' and so forth; he kept steadily to the main question, and said plainly if she did not wish to be left a pauper, she ought to put her affairs into the hands of some firm of solicitors and do exactly as they advised. As a large part of the Fortescue property was situated in London, he thought she had better direct her attack from that capital. 'Besides which,' added Mr Kelly, 'I shall always be at hand to help and consult. I could not help and direct you here – people will talk, and a woman situated as you are cannot be too careful of appearances.' He had been so careful of appearances, he meant to keep this visit a secret even from his own relations. He told her how he had come and where he was going; he would not partake of any refreshment or make any lengthened stay; he wanted to catch a late train back to Dublin, and must cross to Holyhead en route for London next morning. If she wrote to him he would secure suitable lodgings and meet her at Euston.

Mrs Underwood said she need not write: she would do exactly what he told her. 'It is so sweet,' she went on, 'to feel one has a friend in whom one can trust entirely; I feel that with you, Mr Kelly; I am able to put my hand in yours, and say, "Wherever you lead me I will go, for I know you will find some means of extricating me from this labyrinth of doubt and misery into which I have blindly and foolishly strayed."'

So it was settled that Mrs Underwood should follow Mr Kelly to London, and that no time must be lost in declaring war against the recreant husband. Everything Barney advised was done. Lawyers were found who 'saw no difficulty about the matter.' A divorce was to be sought for, evidence from America procured; Mr

Underwood's hands kept off the property pending the result of whatever suit or suits it might be found expedient to institute; and Mr Kelly was beginning to think he had perhaps underestimated the probable amount the future Mrs Kelly might bring him for dowry, when, one day, calling to know the result of an interview she had been summoned to at her solicitors', Mrs Underwood met him with a radiant countenance and the words:

'Congratulate me!'

'Certainly,' agreed Mr Kelly, surprised. 'What has happened? – have they heard from him?'

'Of him,' amended the lady.

'And does he propose a compromise?'

She shook her head.

'Any fresh evidence?'

'He will never trouble me any more.'

'What do you mean?' asked Mr Kelly, a little impatiently. 'He does not, I suppose, give up *all* claim to the property?'

'He can never make a claim,' she answered. 'He is dead.'

'Dead!' repeated Mr Kelly, really stunned for a moment, not only by the intelligence, but by the way the widow communicated it. Then, as his senses returned to him, he began to consider that so far from cutting the knot of the difficulty, Mr Underwood's decease might actually make it harder to undo. 'When did he die?' he asked.

'*Just ten days before my brother,*' said Mrs Underwood, with an exultation even her training could not enable her to repress.

'Well!' exclaimed Barney, 'well – I am amazed!' but in his heart he did not feel pleased.

Foolish and weak though he knew her to be, he could not think Mrs Underwood would fling herself and her fortune at the head of a man who had nothing to offer save himself and a literary reputation by no means of the highest order.

But he need not have been uneasy. Mrs Underwood was only too glad to give her former admirer to understand she would gladly bestow upon him everything she possessed, and accordingly, in due course of time, Mrs Kelly, making a 'convenient' hamper serve as an excuse, indited the following epistle to Miss Bridgetta Cavan, Abbey Cottage:

As ye, maybe, haven't heard the great news about Barney, I write to tell you he's a made man at last – married to Miss Fortescue that was of Sulby Park. She has thousands a year, besides gold and silver and jewels, and furniture and house linen, and lands and mansions, and I couldn't tell you what all. And he'll be in Parliament soon, and maybe a lord or a marquis, before we know where we are. It's me's the proud woman this day: I don't know how to contain myself for the joy. They've sent fifty pounds a piece to the priest and the Church minister for the poor of Callinacoan, which will buy a mountain of blankets and flannel petticoats: and they do say the minister's own children have new clothes on them already out of it. Barney told the priest if he'd get his father to keep from the drink, he might ask what he liked in reason; but indeed, it's neither priest nor pope either will wean him from the whisky bottle. Sulby Park is to be let, and the happy pair have taken a grand house in London all among the quality. I'm in such a tremble of happiness I can't write more.

'And *I*,' said Mr Donagh, when he heard the news – and in his tone there was the dignity of an anathema on a state of society in which such things could be – 'And *I*, with fifty times his talent, and ten thousand times his heart, am a mere drudge, a hack at the beck and call of any ruffian who cares to secure my services for a paltry twenty per cent. Many a man would turn atheist, but I think and believe there is a world where these things will all be set right;' and then he wept, and Miss Bridgetta wept, and so did her niece: and Miss Cavan murmured something about the 'devil's luck,' and a distinguished character who 'takes care of his own,' and they were all much comforted by the hope that Barney might find a 'thorn in his foot yet.'

If they had only known it, Barney had a thorn there already. He was dissatisfied. Having almost all other good, he desired yet one thing more – to excel as a novelist!

Chapter IV

THE NEW FIRM

HAD ANYONE TOLD Mr Bernard Kelly on that evening when they were storm-stayed together hard by St Saviour's Church that the eccentric Mr Felton, he a few hours later had the privilege of beholding retiring to rest under a counter in Sise Lane, was destined to change the whole aspect of publishing, and to set every Miss throughout the country who had learned to write scribbling stories under the idea there was nothing to do save send in her slipshod manuscript, and receive a handsome cheque in return, it is doubtful, conversant as his metropolitan experiences had rendered him with strange vicissitudes, whether he would not have laughed the idea scornfully aside as preposterous in the extreme.

And yet duly and truly this all came to pass not from the slightest desire on the part of Lance Felton that any but what he would in his simple language have called 'crack authors' should receive due reward for their labour – but owing to the mere force of the machinery he himself set in motion.

Mr Kelly had been nearly eight years in London. The wonder of his marriage was more than a twelvemonth old; he had dropped into a humdrum, wealthy, respectable, wearisome society, which he was wise enough to know meant social and pecuniary safety; after a gallant struggle the impossible venture had gone down in a sea of debt – all hands, however, being saved except the capitalist, printers, and paper-makers, who in such cases, for some inscrutable reason, never seem to count – and the now wealthy author, having nothing at the moment on the stocks specially calculated to feed his own literary ambition and the vanity of a wife whose pride in and greed of praise for him were insatiable, bethought him of collecting his series of street sketches from the various journals and magazines in which they had appeared, and getting Mr Vassett to publish them. Knowing how utterly Mr Kelly's worldly circumstances had altered, Mr Vassett tried hard to induce that worthy to run a portion of the risk; but, as Mrs Kelly never wearied of telling her Callinacoan gossips, 'Barney wasn't born yesterday,' and altogether pooh-poohed the suggestion.

Accordingly the matter ended as might have been expected – the astute Englishman proved no match for the astuter Irishman – more especially when that Irishman appeared in Craven Street with thousands a year at his back.

It was 'take it or leave it;' and little as Mr Vassett felt disposed in those days to take anything, he could not quite reconcile himself to letting a good book on a just then taking subject, written moreover by a man who kept his carriage and pair, and had menservants and maidservants, and visited great people, be brought out by another house, perhaps even by that detested new house in Burleigh Street which was, to quote the exact words concerning the matter generally in use at that period, playing the 'devil with the trade.'

While Mr Kelly's 'gutter fictions' – as one envious critic ill-naturedly re-christened his book – were in the earliest stage of publication, Mr Vassett one day ventured to show him a little of his mind concerning the men who were 'ruining everything, and could not by possibility benefit themselves.'

'I had a novel here,' proceeded Mr Vassett, waxing confidential, for this was a grievance about which he really felt he could not hold his peace any longer, 'that with judicious management I thought might be made to return the author a satisfactory amount – two hundred and fifty pounds; and though I am not in the habit of offering such sums in the first instance – not, in fact, till I see how the subscription goes – still, I did in this case write to say I would pay it. I got no answer for a few days – then down came the author for his MS. He had sold it for five hundred pounds, and was to get more if the sale proved good. I see the work advertised this morning in the *Times*, at the head of the Burleigh Street list – which, by the way, occupies half a column.'

'Who are they?' asked the successful man negligently – authorship and the things appertaining thereto did not seem to him matters of quite such vital importance as they had once done.

'Felton and Laplash – men without a sixpence of their own – they are the talk and wonder of the trade. Surely you must have heard of them.'

'I dare say I have,' answered Barney; 'yes, I'm sure I have. Who is Felton? – that name at all events seems familiar – ah! now I remember.'

'He is a friend of the Dawtons, whom you used to know,' said Mr Vassett, not perhaps sorry to give the prosperous author this sly dig.

'Whom I know still, Mr Vassett,' amended Barney, with a graceful inclination of his head, which caused the publisher to consider what a difference the possession of a large income makes in a man's manner.

'Oh! I beg your pardon, I am sure,' he answered nervously: 'I only thought from something Mr Dawton said you were not exactly –'

Mr Kelly laughed, and asked whether if Mr Vassett were left fifty thousand pounds, he should at once consider it necessary to disembarrass himself of half in order to oblige various persons with whom he might have once dined. 'Honestly,' proceeded Barney, 'I was and am quite willing to help my friends in any moderate way, but unhappily their expectations have grown with my means, which after all are not *my* means; they are my wife's.'

Barney was always very careful to make this point quite clear. He had nothing save what he could earn – the carriage he drove in, the horses that drew it, the coachman on the box, the footman in attendance, were all Mrs Kelly's. *He* had the use of the carriage, he lived in the great West End house on sufferance, he ate and drank of the best on the same terms. Of course, this was the most enormous fiction, for in his marriage, as in everything else, Mr Kelly had taken sufficient care of Number One.

Still this was not sufficient reason why a man who was quite willing to give a five, or ten, or even under extraordinary compulsion a twenty-pound note to Dawton *père* should be branded as ungrateful when he refused him, say, five hundred pounds to spend in some utter foolery.

Mr Vassett was not insensible to the suggested parable. He had never much liked either Mr Dawton or Mr Kelly, and consequently he felt able fairly to judge between them. No doubt old Dawton had thought to swoop down on his prey, and no doubt Mr Kelly had repelled him. No doubt, also, Mr Kelly was quite right; and yet Mr Vassett, a most prudent man himself, felt he would have admired Barney more had that gentleman proved a little less prudent.

These are the troublesome inconsistencies in the world which must forever lead people astray. And yet to anyone acquainted with the ups and downs of life, how far preferable it seems to have to do with the man who is all worldly than with him who has a thousand pleasant impulses leading him, and enticing you to follow where is no fruit (for you) worth gathering – nothing but the deceptive greenness of the barren fig-tree. To Barney's credit be it said, he never led anybody astray; he did not promise great deeds and leave other people to fulfil them. I declare solemnly, when I remember the things I have known done in London, as it might seem in the mere wantonness of sport; the offers of help made – help which was not asked for, and never would have been thought of being asked for, that of course ended in nothing; the cruel stabs of disappointment inflicted quite unnecessarily upon hearts whose only failings were distrust of self and too much trust in others;

the hopes deferred from day to day and week to week, it could not have been intended from the first should result in anything – I feel I like Bernard Kelly, for at least no word of his ever lost a woman an hour of her honest work, or a man his 'bus fare through any even implied promise he failed to keep.

From Mr Vassett's upon the day in question he went straight to his club; and searching the *Times*, soon found Messrs Felton and Laplash's list.

He was amazed – the list comprised the names of authors any of the great houses might have been glad to secure. Could this Felton be identical with the man who wanted to stop and look at the lights in the river? The thing seemed not merely improbable but impossible. 'It must be a brother, or some more distant relative,' he considered. 'No doubt the Dawtons know the whole connection.' Mr Kelly was aware the Dawton circle of acquaintances, though amusing, could scarcely be called select. Yes; no doubt whatever it was quite another Felton, and not Lance and his friend Noll. What had become of them both? he wondered – a singular pair – truly as singular a pair as even he had ever met.

Spite of a few ill-natured criticisms, the sketches proved a great success. In the main they were extremely well reviewed, and Mrs Bernard Kelly went among her friends in jubilant mood – wearying a great many of them, to tell the truth, by the manner in which she sang with different words one eternal tune – 'My husband.'

In society, however, people are so accustomed to be bored, that, providing the operation be performed by someone sufficiently rich and fashionable, complaints are rarely heard. Mr Kelly's acquaintances laughed a little sometimes, it is true – but immediately recollecting what was 'due to their order,' said, 'Her affection is very beautiful,' and 'What a model of a husband he must be!' – with various other original remarks of the same nature, all commendatory of the happy pair. One night, after a more than usually laudatory notice of the sketches had appeared in a morning paper, the last post brought this note to Barney.

Dear Sir,

If you have any MSS by you of which you wish to dispose, we shall be happy to meet you on your own terms.

Yours faithfully,
Felton and Laplash.

Now this was certainly not such a letter as Mr Lance Felton might have been supposed likely to indict; and after thinking the matter over for some time, Mr Kelly decided to answer it in person. Since Mr Vassett had broached the subject of the new firm, many persons had spoken to him about the 'wonderful splash' it was making. Twelve months previously the names of the persons composing it were unknown; now they were the dread and detestation of all the old publishers.

'It can't last, you know,' people said; but still, while it did last, authors naturally thought they might as well have share of whatever was going. Messrs Felton and Co.'s mode of doing business seemed eminently simple – it consisted in looking out for names and trying to bag them. Powder and shot apparently were regarded as merely trifles in the transaction. An author of any celebrity had only to mention his own price, and somehow the money was forthcoming. In the history of literature nothing like the doings of Felton and Laplash had ever been known before, and it is earnestly to be hoped nothing resembling such doings ever may be known again. Had the business been bona fide, a good deal might here be said in its favour, but it was rotten from the first as the South Sea Swindle. If a sufficient number of books could have been sold even to cover the mere outlay, leaving the barest profit to the partners, the house had never come down with the crash it did; but, as a matter of fact, taking the works they brought out as a whole, enough copies never were sold (legitimately) to warrant the prices offered to writers.

When an almost unknown author who had only received twenty pounds for his previous production was run up by Messrs Felton and Laplash to two hundred, the climax of absurdity seemed to be reached. If he had been old china he could scarcely have fetched more, and instead of china of any sort he was often only most inferior clay. His book was frequently not worth even twenty pounds. Talk of Tom Tiddler's Ground, why, here it was in Burleigh Street, the only marvel being that the Duke of Bedford did not put in his claim for treasure-trove and so sweep the literary decks.

Unknown authors had not the faintest chance. Genuine worth was at a greater discount in Burleigh Street than it had ever before sunk to in any publishing office in London.

'We can't be bothered reading manuscripts here,' said the head of the firm: 'but bring us anything with a good name at top, and it goes straight to the printers,' which was indeed literally the case; and at the printers, as everywhere else the house went, expense seemed no object. Sober men of business rubbed their eyes, and, prophesying ruin and disaster, held for a time aloof; but while they were expecting the deluge it did not come, and so, after a short delay, persuading themselves 'times were a good deal changed even within their memory,' and feeling satisfied somebody 'with a lot of money' must be in the 'background,' they approached Burleigh Street with cautious steps, and were soon drawn into that mad current, the strength and velocity of which were becoming famous throughout all England.

The feeling dominant in Barney's mind while wending his way towards Covent Garden was curiosity; and as he walked down Burleigh Street he looked around, almost expecting to see some publishing palace meet his eye. In this he was, however, disappointed; the premises of the great firm consisted simply of two small shops, between which a door of communication had been broken – the walls were of the roughest – the floor of the oldest – the fittings of the rudest and scantiest description.

'Any plank serves,' said the chief one day, when an officious friend suggested the desirability of having things a little more elegant, or even comfortable – 'across which you can sell two thousand pounds' worth of books a day – and that is what I have done over that old counter. No, you won't persuade me into your French polish and your lacquer and all that sort of humbug. I am not going to change my luck for any man living. What d'ye say about ladies? – Lord love you, much you know on that subject. If I liked to set up shop in a cellar I'd soon have enough of them trooping down the steps. They come here in their silks and satins and furs, and trailing dresses and all the rest of it; and you should just have a chance of listening to how they go on. It's "What a quaint, delightful place!" – and "Oh, how charming!" – "So perfectly unconventional" – "So snug and homelike" – and "You'll dine with us, won't you, on Thursday? – just a few friends – Portland Place – eight o'clock." Then I say, "I'll dine with you if you like, but I won't take your manuscript", and then they laugh, and don't believe me. But it is true, for all that – one is obliged to draw the line somewhere.'

From which specimen of the new publisher's style of conversation, the reader will instantly perceive it was Mr Lance Felton, who, having at last achieved greatness, had all unconsciously set himself to work that social revolution, the result of which he could not with all his sharpness foresee – and the end of which it would, even now, be extremely imprudent for any man to predicate.

Yes, it was indeed Mr Lance Felton, and no other man of the same name, who, when Barney entered the shop, chanced to be in evidence on the other side of the 'fortunate plank.'

'Hillo!' cried the great publisher, as he beheld his St Mary Overy acquaintance: 'what wind has blown *you* here?'

'Your letter,' answered Barney.

'I never wrote you any letter, though I should have written to you long ago if I had known your address.'

'Well, somebody, at any rate, sent a letter. Here it is,' and Barney handed the missive over the counter.

'But this is to Mr Kelly – the author of *Street Sketches*.'

'I am Mr Kelly.'

'God bless me! Why, I thought he was some great swell.'

'Did you?' said Barney. He could not have prevented the blood rushing into his face at this unexpected slap if he had died for it.

'Oh! I didn't intend any offence,' exclaimed Mr Felton quickly. 'What I meant was a tip-topper, regular out-and-outer, aw-awing sort of fellow. You understand, don't you?'

'Yes,' agreed Barney, 'I understand.'

'And everybody was in the same story; I can't imagine how they got hold of the idea,' proceeded Mr Felton, with such evident ignorance of there being anything in his words at which Mr Kelly could take offence, that the original sin of his first remark became deadlier with each later utterance. 'The street you live in though, I dare say, may have given rise to the notion. You lodge there, I suppose.'

'Yes, I'm only a lodger,' answered Barney.

'You don't reside with your grandmother, then, now?'

'No, with my wife.'

'Oh! you're booked also, are you? I can't help thinking marrying is a great mistake – at least till a man knows what he is going to be and do. If I had waited now,' and here Mr Felton paused, perhaps in order to give himself an opportunity of considering how many duchesses and marchionesses might have suggested alliances with him in exchange for the publication of books of travels, poems, reminiscences, and so on.

'How's your friend?' asked Barney, anxious to lead the publisher away from purely personal matters – 'Noll, you called him.'

'He's all right; he has got into a first-rate berth now.'

'In the philanthropic line?'

'No; something better by far. He is manager of the Westminster and Pimlico Circulating Library Co., Limited.'

'Stealing the shareholders' apples now perhaps, instead of the squire's,' suggested Barney quietly.

The flush which had a few moments previously overspread his own face was now reflected in a deeper tint on that of Mr Lance Felton.

'Oh, come, I say,' entreated the publisher, 'don't be too hard on a fellow. That was one of my mistakes – unfortunately it always is one of my mistakes when I take half a teaspoonful too much – I must have been awfully drunk that night to mention the matter. Fact is, it was all a bit of fun that I used to delight in repeating to tease poor old Noll. We have now, however, made an agreement, that as amongst strangers such remarks are liable to misconstruction, I am always to choke myself off, or let myself be choked off when I begin. There never was a word of truth in the whole story – there couldn't have been, for the squire had no apples.'

'Perhaps there was not even a squire,' said Barney.

'You are right, there was not,' answered Mr Felton eagerly; 'there was only his widow the squiress, and it was because her children got so many aches and pains in the fruit season she had the orchard cut down.'

'What a very curious thing to do,' remarked Barney: 'I suppose that happened almost before your friend was born.'

'While he was still in arms – and as there was not another orchard to speak of within ten miles, he could not have stolen the apples, could he?'

'It would have been difficult for him, certainly.'

At this juncture the outer door opened again, giving admission to a stiff-built man, who, slouching lazily in, with both hands in his pockets, let the door slam behind him. Lance put both his hands to his ears and ground his teeth at the noise.

'Now, why could you not have shut that door, instead of allowing it to bang?' he asked.

A muttered and wholly unintelligible reply was the only answer vouchsafed, as the indolent gentleman walked round the counter, and took up a position from which he could dissect Barney's features at his leisure.

'What do you think, Zack?' asked Mr Felton, recovering his good-humour as speedily as he had lost it. 'This is the Mr Kelly we all imagined to be such a heavy swell. We have just been laughing over the idea – why, he turns out to be an old friend of mine!'

'O-h!' said Zack, turning away, while he drawled out this monosyllable in a manner which seemed to Barney little less than superhuman, as though the contemplation of Mr Kelly's face had suddenly lost all charm for him.

'Come into my sanctum, won't you?' entreated Mr Felton. 'Now Laplash is here, I can go off duty.'

Judging from appearances, Mr Laplash thought he could go off duty too, for he followed them into the triangle-styled office, where, taking up a position with his back against the wall, he stood silently surveying his partner and the successful author.

'Now we'd better get to business,' suggested Mr Felton; 'what have you to offer us, Kelly?'

Barney winced a little – he had not been prepared for such an amount of familiarity, but, nevertheless, answered the question with tolerable composure.

'Nothing, except what has appeared before?' said Mr Felton. 'That's bad, Zack, eh?'

Zack, replying to this interrogatory with a grunt of acquiescence, Barney ventured to observe Mr Vassett had never found that the fact of previous publication in a magazine interfered with the sale of a volume.

'Oh, Vassett!' exclaimed Mr Felton, with a lofty scorn; 'don't talk to us of Vassett – what he does, or finds, or says, or thinks, is no rule for us;' at which utterance Mr Laplash laughed a dog's laugh – his face remaining all the time perfectly grave in its expression; the right-hand corner of the upper lip alone showing the slightest sign of movement.

'No, no,' went on Mr Felton, encouraged by this sign of approval, almost imperceptible though it was; 'we don't want any Vassetts held up here for our example. We've shown that good gentleman a thing or two already, and before we've done with him we'll show him and others a thing or two more. But now to settle with you. How much do you want for the lot?'

Really Mr Lance Felton's way of putting things was too dreadful! Never since that memorable day when he got his rejection from the sub-editor of the *Galaxy* opposition had Mr Kelly felt himself of so little account. What did he want for the lot, indeed! As though he were selling old clothes or the flotsam and jetsam of rubbish left at the tail end of an auction.

'I have no particular desire to sell,' he said at last, 'but if you wish to buy you had better make me a bid.'

In a minute Mr Felton's pencil went to work; then, pushing the paper across the narrow table, he observed, 'I think that's about all I can do.'

Mr Kelly looked at the figures, returned the paper, smiled, rose, and took his hat.

'As a matter of curiosity,' he began, 'I should like to know what you meant by saying you would meet me on my own terms. Do you suppose for a moment,' Barney went on, waxing virtuously irate, 'I have been accustomed to write for such a pittance as you have the assurance to offer?'

'Don't you think it enough, then?' asked Mr Felton: 'I assure you – Laplash, just look here, will you?' and he thrust the paper towards his partner, who, having altered the figures, and again added up the sum total, returned it to the vivacious Lance with the merest but most significant nod.

'Will that do?' said Mr Felton.

'Yes, that is something nearer the mark,' replied Barney.

'Very well, then, we will send you on the agreement.'

'Thank you.'

'And "rush" one book, at all events, as soon as possible.'

'Will that not be somewhat imprudent, considering how recently a work of mine has been brought out?'

'Exploded nonsense!' commented Mr Felton; 'there are some authors I only wish I could get a book from every week in the year.'

'The wisdom of the ages, then, seems foolishness to you?'

'I should think so, indeed. I am my own wisdom, and my own age, and my own everything; and if you can show me any other man who could have done as much as I have done out of the same material, I'll give you leave to call me what you like.'

'Dear me! I have no desire to call you by any other name than that of Felton,' said Barney deprecatingly. 'I only imagined I might venture to make a suggestion concerning the time of publication of my own work.'

'Then you were mistaken,' retorted the genial publisher. 'No, sir. I allow no interference here. I bring out my books when I think I will, and I don't bring them out when I think I won't. If I once allowed that sort of thing,' he added viciously, 'I might soon give up command of the ship. See who that is, Zack; and mind, unless it's somebody worth seeing, I'm engaged. I have about a hundred letters to write before post.'

'I won't detain you longer, then,' said Barney, taking his hat.

'Oh! I didn't mean that as a hint, believe me. It is only that Zack will not keep out bores. He knows well enough who to let in and who to keep out, but he allows himself to be talked over.'

'Does he never talk himself?' asked Barney demurely.

'Talk? I wish he didn't!' – and Mr Felton tossed some of the papers on the table about angrily, as if unpleasant memories had been aroused by even the mention of his partner's powers of speech. 'There was something I wanted to ask you, I know – you have put it out of my head – oh! I remember; did you ever happen to hear who wrote *Ashtree Manor*?'

'Some one of the name of Lely, wasn't it?'

'That's a mere *nom de guerre*.'

Barney stared a little at the speaker, and then answered, 'I know nothing more about the matter, then.'

'Look here,' went on Mr Felton, 'I wouldn't mind tipping a five-pound note to anyone able to give me the right name and address. Lots of people say they knew who wrote the book, but then it turns out they don't. *Now I want that author*.'

'Why don't you ask Mr Vassett, then?'

'Have – he declines to give the slightest clue.'

'Why not send a letter to the author through him?'

'No; I'll not do that either. You've read the book, I suppose – wonderful. I'd give anything to know who wrote it.'

Barney admitted the work so enthusiastically spoken of was clever; and considering he had at home a novel of his own in manuscript which he thought a great deal more wonderful than *Ashtree Manor*, this modified praise was perhaps quite as much as could be expected from him.

'Clever – I believe you!' cried Mr Felton, 'and then there is another by the same fellow, *Due East*. And to think of Vassett having had two such books! Lacere was in here the other day; you remember him?'

'I remember his office,' said Barney, a place which indeed he was never likely to forget. 'I never saw him.'

'He's not much of a see,' observed Mr Felton: 'came here dunning. What do you think of that?'

'Do you owe him any money?'

'Well, I had some from him in the old days, and he said he called thinking I should like to repay it – as if anybody ever wanted to repay money or to be reminded of a debt; besides, it is not always convenient – but, as I was saying,' Mr Felton added hurriedly, and with some confusion, 'I asked him, as I ask everybody, about the author. "Had he ever heard his name?" "Yes." "What was it?" "Declined to tell me." "Did he know him?" "Very well indeed." "Did he ever see him?"

"Occasionally." "Would he give a message to him?' "Yes." So then I sent word that whatever amount Vassett was giving him, I'd treble; but I've never heard another word on the subject. It was all brag, I've no doubt: he is as much acquainted with him as I am.'

'Don't you think,' suggested Mr Kelly, 'that as a proof of the bona fides of your offer it might have been wise to give your former landlord a cheque for whatever amount you may have owed him?'

'No; and I am not going to pay him – at least, not till I choose. I don't see, because I have got a bit of meat for myself, every vulture in the kingdom is to have a share of it.'

'But really, when you talk so recklessly of doubling and trebling the amount of authors' remuneration –'

'Look here,' interrupted Lance, 'I like you, and I don't want to quarrel with you; but take a bit of advice – let me and my authors alone. I can manage my business without any help of yours. Bring the agreement about those books along with you, and you can have the money – that's all concerns you, isn't it?'

'I am thankful at last to hear you make one remark with which I can perfectly agree,' and lest this happy state of things should come immediately to an end, Mr Kelly took leave of Mr Felton forthwith, and walked out into Burleigh Street literally stupid with surprise.

Spite of the lordly manner in which the versatile Mr Felton referred to pecuniary matters, when Mr Kelly carried his reprints round to Burleigh Street, a difficulty he had certainly not anticipated arose about that trifling matter of payment. The outer shop he found full of people, some of whom he knew, most of whom he did not. Conspicuous amongst the crowd was poor Mr Dawton, with hand more shaky, eye more watery, speech more wearisome than of old. At once he fastened upon Barney, reminding that worthy of the 'pleasant days gone by,' when they were 'young together;' when they travelled the country and 'drew crowded houses' to hear *How's Maria?*

'Lord! Lord! those were times!' cried Mr Dawton, wiping his eyes. 'How the sovereigns used to tumble in! I can hear their musical jingle now.'

'Yes, and you used to pocket them,' thought Barney; which indeed was too truly the case.

Mr Dawton had not dealt quite fairly by his 'young friend' in the matter of that clever entertainment, but his only mistake was in having professed to do so. When beginning his London life, Barney would have been as willing to accept an actual fourth as a nominal half. He could not have made a half or even a fourth for himself, and he knew it, only Mr Dawton need not have lied to him; as a rule, however, people give themselves an enormous amount of unnecessary trouble in inventing falsehoods when the truth would serve much better.

'You know *him*,' said Mr Dawton, turning an uncertain thumb over his left shoulder in the direction of Mr Felton's office.

'Only in the slightest manner.'

'Ah, wonderful! When I first knew him – but 'tis a tale to be whispered in thine ear anon. Hist! – the door opens.'

Which indeed the inner door did, to afford egress to a lady dressed in deep mourning, whom Lance escorted to her carriage bareheaded, with a respect which in so red a Republican could be regarded as nothing short of marvellous.

'Who is she?' ran in a sort of buzz round the shop.

'Don't you know?' said somebody, in an unmistakable Irish accent. 'It's the Hicks derelict.'

'Mr Kelly, please walk this way,' cried Mr Laplash; and Mr Kelly, working his way into the triangular room, found himself alone with the senior partner, who asked him to be seated.

'I've just made a bargain with the lady you may have noticed going out,' said Mr Felton, looking up from his writing. 'She is a great person – a very great person indeed.'

'She's Lady Hilda Hicks, isn't she?'

'Yes, an earl's daughter – and she piles everything of that sort on the top of her book. My word, she does open her mouth, and she won't shut it again till filled. I only hope I'll ever see my money back again. She can't write a bit, in my opinion – but she sells. Here's the manuscript;' and Lance patted a goodly pile of square ruled paper.

'Take care you don't offend her, or she'll put you and your partner in her next book.'

'Let her – I don't care. She has asked me to go and see her one evening next week.'

'And are you going?'

'Don't know, I am sure. The fact is, I'm getting tired of standing about doorways, and ices and negus, and a sandwich perhaps. I'm due tonight at a very swell party at Shepherd's Bush – tip-top – all the ladies velvet and lace, and all the gentlemen with their hair parted down the middle, and eye-glasses, and patent boots. I must rig myself up a little, I suppose;' and here Mr Lance Felton, with a self-satisfied smile which almost upset Mr Kelly's powers of self-control, pulled forward the lapel of his new frock-coat – took a side glance over his left shoulder at the unexceptionable quality of the broadcloth in which he was clad – pulled down his white waistcoat – contemplated his nether garments and natty boots – and then glanced at Barney as one who felt tempted to say, 'See what money and fashion conjoined have achieved for the once unregarded and impecunious Lance!'

He so evidently considered his attire the 'correct thing,' even for evening wear amongst ladies clad in velvet and lace, and 'swells who wore their hair parted down the middle,' that Barney felt it would be most unkind to dissipate his illusion. Had there not been a time when he, Bernard, spite of all his quickness of perception and extraordinary power of adapting himself to circumstances, blossomed out in the matter of fancy vests and cornelian buttons and glittering studs – all of which vanities he soon learnt to eschew, replacing them with a Quakerish simplicity of attire which quite deceived Mr Lance Felton, who, deciding 'Kelly has enough to do to make the two ends meet,' and would be duly impressed with anything in the way of swagger, proceeded – fingering his watch-chain – to remark: 'I'll have to get something different from this, of course – something more up to the mark, eh?'

'I don't think you could buy any guard that would look better,' said Barney, who had indeed been admiring the article in question, and wondering where in the world Mr Felton had picked up a piece of jewellery so quaint and in such excellent taste.

'It does well enough in the office,' answered Lance carelessly, 'but I must wear something more like money when I go among the grandees. They do take such stock of a fellow. But now to get to business. Have you brought the agreement signed? Thanks – that's all right. Here's the duplicate' – and Lance dashed off an impetuous 'Felton and Laplash' – 'and this you'll find quite correct.' Perhaps he expected Barney to pocket both documents without opening them: but if so, he was disappointed. Mr Kelly first read the agreement quite through, and then unfolded the slip of paper Mr Felton had handed him.

At the latter he looked for a moment most curiously; then he said:

'May I ask what this is?'

'Why, our acceptance at three months,' answered Lance glibly. 'The amount is all right, isn't it?'

'Yes,' answered Barney, 'the amount is all right; but I'm not going to take a bill for my work. Don't entertain any delusion on that subject.'

'Why not? Everybody does; usual thing. How do you suppose we are to carry on our business if we pay months and months before we get our returns?'

'I'm sure I don't know, and I'm very sure I don't care; only I'm not going to find you capital either in meal or malt. If at the end of three months you could not or did not meet your bill, where should I be? No; if that's your way of doing business, hand me back my agreement, and we will consider the matter at an end.'

During the course of this agreeable address, Mr Lance Felton's face had changed in colour from red to purple, and from purple to white; till finally, so great was his pallor that his very lips seemed bloodless.

'Well, you must be hard up,' he managed at last to say. 'If you had told me cash was such an object, the money should have been waiting for you. Come back in an hour, and I'll be ready for you. Will that do?'

'Certainly,' agreed Barney, 'and meantime we may as well exchange agreements,' which suggestion was accordingly carried into effect, with a running commentary from Mr Felton, that 'thank God there was no suspicion about him;' 'his fault lay in quite an opposite direction;' 'he believed every man to be honest till he proved himself a rogue, and even then he found it almost impossible to credit any actual cheating had been intended;' 'sooner than imagine everyone he shook hands with to be a liar and a thief, he would hang himself or cut his throat' – with a good deal to the same effect, which was interrupted by the opening of the door and the appearance of Mr Dawton's wig.

'Now, shut that door, will you?' shouted Mr Felton viciously. 'Can't you see I'm engaged? Won't you take no for an answer?' And then, as the poor old actor, appalled by the violence of this address, meekly withdrew his battered and wrinkled face, the publisher stigmatised him as an 'old fool,' and said he 'wouldn't – no, blanked if he would – have a parcel of drivelling antediluvians making a common lounge of his offices.'

Soft-heartedness could certainly not be reckoned amongst the weaknesses of Mrs Kelly's Barney, and he felt no wild desire to make Mr Dawton's cause his own. Nevertheless, when he passed out amongst the crowd waiting for audience, and saw the collapsed figure of the 'world-renowned actor,' he took him by the arm, and leading him down Burleigh Street, pressed a couple of sovereigns into his hand, and bade him forget the roughness with which he had been treated.

'"Sharper than a serpent's tooth,"' sobbed poor Mr Dawton; 'and I made him, sir; when I knew him first he was ragged and hungry, and I may say homeless; and I took him to my house, and fed him, and clothed him; and Ted taught him, and – and you see how he treats me, Mr Kelly – as if I were a dog, sir – a dog.'

'Never mind him,' entreated Barney; 'put a beggar on horseback and you know where he rides to. How is Mrs Dawton?'

Then and there in the Strand Mr Dawton came to a standstill, and poured forth his tale of woe. His wife was ill; Ted had married and gone abroad; Will, having met with an accident, kept his bed; Jim was trying his fiercest to prevent the ship sinking; the youngest son had in despair accepted an engagement with some wandering minstrels.

'A scattered household,' finished Mr Dawton; 'The Wigwam will soon be deserted save by the squaw and the grizzled old Indian. Ah me! who would wish for length of days when he sees how they destroy the noblest trees in the forest? Had anyone told me twenty years back –'

'I must bid you goodbye now, Mr Dawton,' interposed Barney, finding an appreciative crowd was collecting, 'but I'll see you soon again. I will make a point of going to The Wigwam and cutting short Mr Dawton's effusive and maundering farewell, he crossed the street and walked rapidly westward. He could not refrain, however, from once looking back, and beheld, as he expected, Mr Dawton eagerly making his way to the nearest tavern. 'Poor old chap!' thought the well-to-do author, and something very much like an earnest thanksgiving to God for having enabled him to steer clear of the rock on which he had seen so many a gallant barque founder, silently passed his lips.

Ere returning to Burleigh Street he went home, had his luncheon, took a turn in the Park with his wife, and finally got that lady close upon five o'clock to set him down near his destination.

In the outer office he found only Mr Laplash and 'Noll', but the door of the inner apartment stood wide, and, as he appeared, the voice of Mr Lance Felton was heard in greeting.

'Oh! so here you are at last. And now you are here, what have you got to say for yourself?'

'I have come for my money.'

'Good heavens!' shouted Mr Felton, screaming with laughter; 'only hear this, Noll – he has come for his money! and he says it just as if he was a super going up for his screw on a Saturday. Oh! you'll be the death of me,' he went on. 'Poor fellow poor fellow! Now I dare say this amount is all you have between you and Slocum's.'

'I am not quite so badly off as that,' answered Barney, who scarcely understood and utterly failed to appreciate this delicate badinage. 'But still, I have no doubt I shall manage to find a use for your cheque.'

'Here it is, then,' said Mr Felton; 'look that there is no mistake this time – do, pray! And now, sir, just tell me what you mean by coming here with your false pretences and your poverty pleas, and looking as if you had never seen a ten-pound note in your life, and your lodger story, and all the rest of it – you, who have your horses and your carriages, and your livery servants, and your grand acquaintances, and a house in Grosvenor Street, where you can hang up your hat for the rest of your days?'

Thus reproved, Mr Kelly took refuge in his usual formula. Everything belonged to his wife – he had nothing but what he could make. Her friends were good enough to ask him to their houses, but he could never forget he was only a poor author – with many more statements to the same effect, which were received with derision, and various ironical and objectionable remarks which made him wish he had never sold his reprints to the great firm which meant, so Mr Felton explained, to 'lead the trade a dance.'

'We'll waken them up a little,' he said. 'If Vassett and the rest of the slow-coaches never footed it before, they'll have to foot it now, or make up their minds to stay behind for ever. Here's a list,' he added, thrusting the just issued *Athenœum* into Mr Kelly's hand; 'did you ever see anything like that? There's scarcely a known author we haven't bagged. There – leave me all of you for a minute; I must just finish this letter before post. It's to that Lord with the hard name who went to Rome and back again, and wrote his soul's experiences both ways.'

'Oh! then you are going in for theology, are you?'

'I don't care what the ––– I go in for,' retorted Mr Felton, with cheerful profanity, 'so long as it pays; if Tom Paine were only alive again, I'd advertise him and the Archbishop of Canterbury in the same column. But now, clear out, please; time's getting on.'

Thus exhorted, Messrs Zack, Barney, and Noll retreated into the outer office, where they soon fell into easy and confidential chat.

'I am glad to hear you have dropped into a good berth,' observed Mr Kelly to Noll.

'Well, I can't say it's a berth exactly to my mind,' answered that gentleman. 'I'd have liked something where I could feel of use to my fellow-creatures.'

'Yes, that's what he's always on about,' observed Mr Laplash, with admiring appreciation. 'He's just as eager to be doing good as many a one is to be doing harm. If he picked up a half-crown in the gutter he'd know no rest till he had found the poorest and the dirtiest old woman he could benefit with it. That's Noll, Mr Kelly;' and Mr Laplash, humming an unmelodious tune, fell to whittling a bit of stick after this unexpected testimony to Noll's perfections.

Barney looked at Noll and formed his own opinions, which he wisely refrained from expressing.

'You see, Mr Kelly,' said Noll, addressing the rich man, and edging up to him with unctuous perseverance, 'I do feel it on my mind and conscience that light literature is no sort of proper reading for immortal souls destined for heaven, or it may be doomed to hell. The novel mania oppresses me like a nightmare. They come to us hot pressed and gaudily bound. Soul-traps I can't but consider them. But the bulk of our customers won't look at anything else. I'd like to be out of the business, I would indeed. If you should hear of a nice secretaryship now, Mr Kelly, to some Christian association, or even a vacant post as collector to a worthy charity, I feel I could devote my energies to congenial work of that sort.'

No one could accuse Mr Kelly of raising unfounded hopes merely to level them with the ground, wherefore he immediately answered that though Mrs Kelly of course contributed liberally to religious societies and charitable institutions, she had no influence – none whatever.

'And so far as I am concerned I don't even subscribe,' added Barney, with a touching modesty which might have affected anyone susceptible to the softer emotions.

'Indeed I shouldn't mind,' proceeded Mr Noll, in a monotonous sort of whine, serviceable, no doubt, for the purposes of Scripture-reading and street-preaching, 'taking charge of a compact estate composed of weekly tenants. I believe in such a position I might effect much good. I could enclose a tract suitable to the circumstances of each household in the rentbook, and say a word in season to the mothers; don't you agree with me, Mr Kelly?'

322

'I dare say,' answered Barney: 'but my wife has no property of the sort you indicate. If I should hear of anything likely to suit you I will let you know: but it is not at all probable –'

At this juncture the outer door was pushed timidly open, and a bonnet, veil, jacket, and something inside these articles of apparel came slowly up to the counter.

Mr Laplash, leaving his bit of stick, lounged forward to meet the newcomer, who addressed to him some remark which was perfectly inaudible, as at that moment a van came thundering down the street, shaking every pane of glass in the old edifice in which the new firm had established itself.

'What d'ye want?' asked Mr Laplash, as soon as he could make himself heard, addressing the lady with the gruffness that seemed to do duty in Burleigh Street for ordinary civility.

'Can I see either Mr Felton or Mr Laplash?' she inquired nervously.

'My name is Laplash,' returned the second in command, with aggressive distinctness.

'I – I – really don't know that I ought to trouble you, but a long time ago you sent me a message – and – as I – was passing – I thought I might call – but I feel – I –'

'What's your name?' inquired Mr Laplash, as if she were deaf, and he catechising her.

'You would not know my name if I told it you,' she answered, scared apparently out of what few wits she possessed; 'but I once wrote a book called *Ashtree Manor*.'

'Open Sesame' never produced a more magical effect than those two words. The flap on the counter was lifted and banged back on its hinges.

'Come in,' said Mr Laplash, leading the way to the inner apartment, when, saying, 'Lance, here's *Ashtree Manor*,' he stepped aside to let the lady cross the charmed circle. 'God bless me!' cried Lance, looking up from his writing: 'why, I've done everything short of advertising for you in the *Times!*'

'Have you?' she answered, a little faintly.

'Yes: sit down for a minute, will you?' And so she sat and looked at the great publisher finishing his correspondence, and at Zack pasted up against the wall staring at her with all his might, and out into the dim office beyond, where the gas was not yet lighted and two figures stood hazily in the shadows, and she wished she had not turned into Burleigh Street, and longed with all the veins of her heart to be safe at home.

Chapter V

MR LOGAN-LACERE IS AMAZED

THOUGH THE WORLD – their poor little world – remained ignorant of the fact, since the appearance of *Ashtree Manor* things had been going very badly indeed with the Logan-Laceres. Day by day, week by week, month by month, they drifted hopelessly astern. Ostensibly doing a good business – in reality doing a very fair business – Mr Lacere's incomings and outgoings failed utterly to meet. At the end of each halfyear there was an ever-increasing deficit, which one memorable spring arrived at such proportions that Mr Logan-Lacere at last, opening his mind to his wife, said, 'I think, dear, I must stop.'

By this time Glen had learned a great deal about her husband's business and himself. Nevertheless, her knowledge of both was still superficial. Unless a man engaged in commerce is doing extremely well, he rarely cares to examine his debit and credit with the attention his liabilities at all events deserve; while, unless a woman goes down into the thick of the conflict, she is far too apt to take the man's representations as facts.

'I could make at least fifteen hundred a year,' says the struggling merchant, 'if I had only a thousand pounds capital.'

Find me the wife who, when the husband she loves and believes in tells her this pleasant tale, will not eagerly swallow the captivating bait, and I shall say you have discovered a new Eve.

Poor Glen – poor Mordaunt Logan-Lacere! Had the wand of some enchanter gifted you with ten thousand pounds instead of the usual ten hundred everyone wants, you would have found yourselves at the end of twelve months precisely where you were at the beginning.

For the man did not live, or the woman either, who could have made head against the Lacere connection. Ned Beattie was quite right when he said they would sink a man-of-war. Not merely were their pecuniary demands unceasing, but after a time – a short time indeed – Glen found their ideas weighed her down to the earth.

There are some people, perhaps because they do nothing themselves, who exercise a depressing, almost stultifying, effect on workers. It is doubtful whether even Mr Logan-Lacere himself could have resisted the enervating effect of the home atmosphere, had he been exposed to it; but in his bachelor days he adopted the singularly wise course of rarely returning to the domestic hearth except to sleep, and since his marriage, being busier than ever, he seldom saw his female relations except upon those high days and holidays, when Glen usually made herself excessively disagreeable, and by the mere force of contrast must have made her husband consider his own relations paragons of amiability. Glen knew what all this semblance of genial good-humour was worth, but she had crushed and bruised herself so cruelly in trying to make the man they all regarded as a fortress to flee to in time of trouble understand the position, that, abandoning open warfare, she resorted to a provoking sort of antagonism during the time she was forced to listen to reminiscences of the Lacere greatness and disparagement of the Logans, to gush about 'dearest Mordaunt,' to lamentations over a cut finger, to complaints anent the impertinence of her own servants, and general statements that all domestics were 'very different from what they used to be;' that kindness and consideration toward those in an inferior station of life were errors certain eventually to lead to disastrous results; that tradespeople were little, if at all, better than thieves; that the only human beings worth knowing, or considering, or remembering, were the Laceres; that all foreigners were treacherous, Americans detestable, the Irish more treacherous and detestable perhaps than either; that Glen herself was making a woeful mistake in refusing to adopt the Lacere code for her own guidance; that some day she would repent having rejected the love they so earnestly desired to lavish upon her, and find the friends she thought so much of would desert her totally.

To all this, and a great deal of the same interesting and improving sort of conversation, Glen found she could only – successfully – oppose one weapon – sarcasm.

Argument she soon found useless with people destitute of the faculty of reasoning; who were puffed up with exaggerated ideas of their own importance, and who, never having adventured out into general society, which they regarded as a howling wilderness, had not been, and were never likely to be, taught their level. But they had one weak spot in their armour. There existed a vulnerable spot, and Glen knew it. They could not endure ridicule; the barbed arrow of satire penetrated between the joints of their harness and inflicted lacerating wounds. If she were strong, Mrs Logan-Lacere was not merciful, and she knew who came worst off the field after any particularly bitter struggle. About money her tongue was tied, but there remained a wide range of subjects on which to exercise her talents. It is not too much to say she studied and perfected a particularly annoying and incisive style of repartee which rarely missed its mark, and proved almost as fatal to her foes, the Laceres, as did the smooth pebble David selected from the brook and hurled from his sling into the forehead of the braggart Philistine.

One of the opposition ladies, who had for a considerable number of years read her Bible, with the satisfactory result that she felt she at all events need be under no apprehension about her place of abode in the next world, occasionally tried the effect of flinging at Glen one of those texts in general use when family matters come on the carpet, but she had better have left it alone. Ned Beattie's remark that he could in either the Old or New Testament beat Glen in a canter, was quite correct; but Mrs Logan-Lacere's Scriptural knowledge was by no means to be despised. It was general as well as particular, and Miss Lacere, though she never confessed the fact even to herself, found she had made a blunder when she tried a wrestle with one to whom Biblical phrases and Biblical references were familiar as household words.

Glen not merely could correct a misquotation, but she did. She swooped down on an error like an eagle on its prey, and she was able further to prove the strength of her position, not by any reference to Cruden, but by producing straightway chapter and verse. Small marvel she engendered a fine feeling of hatred towards herself! If she could have induced 'the family' to say in so many words they disliked her cordially, she would have felt perfectly happy, and perhaps relaxed some of those acts of annoyance in which she was becoming an adept. But no, they would not quarrel with her: they stated plainly it took two to make a quarrel, and they were determined not to quarrel with her – a remark Glen felt to be maddening, since a sensation of utter helplessness must supervene when you find, if you ask a man to walk out of the front door, that he immediately walks in at the back, smiling as if nothing had happened.

Between her husband's brother-in-law, as Mrs Logan-Lacere always carefully defined the relationship, and herself, she had managed to establish at one time an open feud. If they met, their conversation was one of the most distant; if they wrote, their notes were of the coldest; and their epistolary mode of addressing each other was beautifully dignified and formal. Glen had, opportunity offering, undertaken to teach Mr Lacere what was due to her in the triple character of wife, author, and Irishwoman; and as the gentleman in question did not think much of her in any capacity, he naturally resented the instruction, which was perhaps not very courteously conveyed.

Glen carried her point, however, in so far that he declined to visit the house over which she was nominally mistress; but this victory proved, after all, to be a barren one. Her husband would not make her quarrels his; so far as his relations were concerned, he was in the matter of fighting a very Quaker. He thought his wife wrong, and he told her so as decidedly as the extreme gentleness of his disposition permitted him to say anything disagreeable; while to make up for her shortcomings he showed greater kindness than ever to his brother-in-law, and showered on him those favours which Glen knew would keep them poor for the whole of their lives.

In comparison to the drain Mr Lacere was upon the good business which ought to have prospered, the Misses Lacere could only be regarded as light and agreeable encumbrances; while the faith with which Mr Logan-Lacere continued to believe in his kinsman's rotten ventures, savoured not merely of infatuation, but folly.

There were not wanting those who warned Glen of what the result must prove. If advice could have saved the ship of their fortunes, it would have never gone down; but Glen was not in command, and resolutely refusing to believe the cry of 'breakers ahead', her husband sailed calmly onwards to destruction. He had a good business; but where is the struggling business which does not require careful nursing? What trade could have borne the daily drain demanded by two families and a speculative brother-in-law? Twice already in Glen's married experience had Mr Philip Lacere been compelled to meet his creditors, and on each occasion her husband was 'let in' for an amount which caused wise people to express a not unreasonable astonishment.

During these periods of bitter trial and anxiety, the husband and wife came very near each other; and perhaps Glen was never happier than in those days when doing her poor best to help a sadly overweighted man. She could not do very much, for it took her three hours to add up correctly a column of figures, while her knowledge of arithmetic was of the crudest description; she could somehow work out a sum, but she utterly failed to explain how she did it. Not much of a help certainly – but she could take one trouble off his hands; she could write his letters, she could get through a mass of correspondence that might well have appalled a man: and though occasionally Mr Logan-Lacere received irritable epistles urging him to instruct his clerk to write legibly, still, considering Glen's wretched calligraphy, there were very few complaints, which caused her husband to consider that there must be scattered throughout the country a much larger number of persons capable of deciphering hieroglyphics than he had imagined.

Glen did not care how heartily her husband laughed at her. She was only too delighted to know that he had the keenest sense of humour, and that spite of all his anxieties and troubles he could make merry over some trifle which tickled his fancy or excited his risibility.

He came in contact with so many odd people, he encountered so many strange incidents, that now, when at last he found an intelligent and appreciative auditor, his overtaxed mind sought relief in speaking of things no other human being belonging to him could have understood. Often late in the afternoon Glen repaired to his office, which he had removed from Sise to Creed Lane; and while her husband was busy with journal and ledger and cash book, steadily worked her way through piles of unanswered letters. Bit by bit she had learned enough of his business to know what to say without troubling him on the subject; and then as they walked home together through the silent streets they laughed over the events of the day – though God knows both their hearts were often heavy and anxious enough. As a wife, Glen was greatly improved. She had laid Edward Beattie's advice to heart in many ways: she did not now cry over the irremediable; she did not sit and brood about troubles she was powerless to alter. Gradually she had formed a small but pleasant circle of acquaintances who made home cheerful for her husband, and but for the eternal drag and drain of money, which could not be got in, and money which had very surely to be paid, Logan-Lacere might have been accounted a very happy man. At all events he was a happy man. His was not the temper which goes out to meet trouble half-way – no day's work was too long for him – no toil too hard; and, as Ned Beattie said, he adored his wife.

About this period of her life all matters were going pretty well with Glen, except pecuniary. She felt the shoe pinch very often; literature had not, so far, proved a gold mine to her. When she finished *Due East*, for the first and only time in her life she wrote a preface with which she proposed to enrich that work: but unhappily it never saw the light. In it she stated her determination to retire from the field, since she had found authorship was the only profession in which a labourer was not considered worthy of his hire. She went into figures, a most unwonted mental exercise for her, and stated that in so many years she had only made so much money; from which amount the cost of pens, ink, paper, postage (and she might have added shoe-leather) ought to be deducted. She proceeded also to draw comparisons between the literary and other professions, and wound up with a general sort of commination of an unappreciative world. As has been said, however, this expression of opinions and feelings was never printed, for the sufficient reason that Mr Vassett, when she sent him her manuscript, intimated she might reasonably reckon upon receiving a hundred and fifty pounds for this novel. A hundred and fifty pounds seemed a great deal of money to Glenarva, till she found how very short a way that amount went; but her soul revived within her when the reviewers expressed themselves in terms of such almost unanimous approval that Mr Vassett said if she carefully thought out another work he would give her two hundred and fifty pounds, and if the book went well would deal with her as liberally as possible.

So far as authorship was concerned, Mrs Lacere, since she became a successful author, had become the slowest of slow writers; further, she got into the habit of doing her work by fits and starts; weeks and weeks elapsed without a single line being added to the novel; she allowed every social, domestic, and business matter to take precedence of her own legitimate employment.

To some extent all this arose from the want of ready money, which caused her to spend her strength in affecting petty economies instead of concentrating her energies on the exercise of her profession; but the source of the evil lay deeper than this. Fame had been so long deferred, she wearied of the struggle before she touched the prize. The author of *Amelia Wyndham* has given to the world an excellent piece of advice, namely, 'to beware of the faults of one's own family.' If she had added the caution to 'beware of the faults of one's own nation,' the additional warning would not have been misplaced. The hatred of monotony – the detestation of waiting till the corn ripens – the impatience of watching the slow progress of fruition – the belief that the grapes which cannot be gathered at once will never be worth eating, which are all integral parts of the warp and woof of that strange web the Irish temperament, were at the bottom of Glen's lack of systematic industry.

The opinion of those days also militated against the rapid production of books of any sort. A novel in two years was thought the proper course of procedure; that a time should ever come when a popular author could find a market and an audience for a work of fiction every six months, was an idea which never entered into the mind of man at that period of the world's history to conceive. The insatiable cry for something new, which can now only be gratified by the publication of the veriest trash, had not then arisen. Books brought out in the spring were still being read in the autumn; the novels even of a previous year were asked for at the libraries – in effect, publishers and authors and readers were going on much as they had been doing for a quarter of a century previously, and nobody dreamt a literary revolution was at hand – during the course of which the biggest houses in the trade would come to grief, and great firms as well as mushroom adventurers fall together in one general crash.

It was about the time Mr Vassett proposed those liberal terms named for Glen's third novel – for she now eschewed all mention of her early failures, and dated her career from the publication of *Ashtree Manor* – that Mr Philip Lacere, having for the second time passed through the insolvent court without paying anyone sixpence, thought he ought to embrace this favourable opportunity of again entering into the state of holy matrimony. What had ever happened before to the Misses Lacere in comparison to this? They did not believe it; for a long time they would not believe it – they stood out against conviction till further doubt became impossible – they expected some miracle to intervene to prevent this slight to their darling Claudine's memory – they would have prayed for fire from heaven, or the sun to stand still, or the stars to drop from the firmament, if they had felt in a mental condition to pray for anything – they refused to call on the lady, and declined to allow her to be brought to their house – they were most indignant because Mrs Logan-Lacere paid a visit to the woman happy enough to have won the approval of the pensive and soft-spoken widower, and felt more angry still when poor Claudine's own brother allowed her to be invited to dinner, and said plainly he did not see why his brother-in-law shouldn't marry again if he wished to do so.

It was dreadful. Glen had been bad enough, but Glen was nothing to this. They fought the question as long as fight was possible, and then the moment the marriage became an accomplished fact they all turned round and formed an alliance with the new wife, offensive and defensive, against Mrs Logan-Lacere, whom they spoke of to her face as the 'Commander-in-Chief.'

But it did not then signify to Mrs Logan-Lacere what they called her. The last failure of her husband's brother-in-law had, she fondly hoped, wrought such ruin that no opportunity would again be afforded that ingenious gentleman of entangling their affairs with his own. Mr Logan-Lacere professed, and probably believed, his eyes were at length opened to the perilous consequences of going surety for his relative, getting his bills discounted, and otherwise assisting a man who preferred the road to destruction to all other thoroughfares. When he spoke to Glen about 'stopping,' he was very much in earnest; he did not see, he said, how in the world he was to go on; still, it was a great pity, because with the trade he had worked up he surely could pull through if time were given in which to recover from the losses he had sustained.

Long and anxious were the discussions between husband and wife. If he stopped, Glen did not exactly see how the domestic pot was to be kept boiling – so long as fuel had also to be provided for the due boiling of the Misses Laceres's pot, which would, she knew, have to be kept filled as of yore. It was a curious thing, that in this extremity it never occurred either to Glen or Mr Logan-Lacere that the ladies of his family might with advantage try whether they could not contribute something towards their own support. It was an idea which would have met with a prompt negative from the Misses Lacere, who, if they believed themselves incompetent in no other particular, were beautifully decided that it was quite impossible for them to earn any money. Long previously, Glen, by dint of diligent research, had discovered the portraits on ivory were mere copies touched up by the hand of some forgotten drawing-master, and her own ears told her the songs so belauded lacked the great merit of originality. She knew, if nobody else did, that not one of the family was clever except her husband, and that all these hangers-on lacked the will to exert themselves in any common useful way to earn their bread; but she did not mean to trouble herself on that score.

If only her husband would sever all business connection with his brother-in-law, she believed they might still 'win through'; keep their pretty cottage – their lovely garden – their furniture which had been collected so slowly – and the good business which promised an ever-increasing return. Mr Logan-Lacere was vexed with his brother-in-law, and fully determined that plausible individual should never compromise him again; he decided their intercourse should be confined to the homecircle, and not be permitted to encroach on the precincts sacred to business; a hollow peace was patched up between Glen and her particular aversion, and her husband devoted his attention to considering how that terrible impending evil of bankruptcy might be averted.

He had but one important creditor – the firm for whose specialities he was working up the trade he believed, and rightly, had an enormous future before it. If this firm gave him time, he thought he could retrieve his position; at all events, before taking any decisive step he determined to refer the matter to those most interested in his success or failure. It is not often that the right course seems the pleasantest, but in this case duty and inclination appeared to clasp hands, and Mr Logan-Lacere put the position before his principals. There can be no question, humanly speaking, it was the worst day's work he ever did for himself in his life. When a man feels he has got to the end of his tether, his wisest policy is to break it, and start at once in the direction of new pastures. There are matters one human being is mad to refer to the judgment of any other human being. Mr Logan-Lacere had spent time, money, health, industry, energy, in solidly laying the foundations of a business he hoped would eventually recompense him for his toil and trouble. He had advertised freely and judiciously – his advertisements and circulars, the result of much thought, attracted attention and eventually inspired belief. Except on the subject of quack medicines, the British public is notoriously difficult to persuade; and taking this idiosyncrasy as the basis of her theme, Glen in one happy moment of unamiable inspiration produced a little pamphlet, which, given away by thousands, caused such a division in families as pamphlet probably never did before. Husband ranged himself against wife; sisters refused belief in brothers; servants gave notice; and masters loudly declared their intention of being paramount in their own houses. In omnibuses the oldest travelling companions fell foul of each other, some declaring the pamphlet to be 'a mere bundle of lies.'

When Glen wrote it, which she did more out of despair and annoyance than from actual hope of affecting any good, she had not the slightest idea of creating such a clamour. Never one of her books was read, criticised, praised, and pooh-poohed like that three-page bill. Some persons regarded it as a personal insult; but at any rate the arrow found its mark.

'Who the deuce is Lely?' men who never had read, and never were likely to read a novel, inquired.

'Some impudent scoundrel!' 'A most pestilent ruffian,' old-fashioned gentlemen, well accounted of in the City, with noses artistically tinted with sound port, would indignantly reply. Be sure they were not spared in the Logan-Lacere manifesto, copies of which at last came to be eagerly asked for, and were finally only given away as a favour.

Well, all this had been done for the benefit of the speciality manufactured by the provincial firm to whom a considerable amount was owing.

They had never imagined such a trade could have been worked up, and they were steadily purposed that when it suited their own convenience they would step into Mr Logan-Lacere's shoes and tell him calmly to walk barefoot out of the business he himself had made. They knew perfectly well he was a poor man, also that he was an overweighted man, and that when once they established a London house he would not have a ghost of a chance against their capital and their facilities of production. But they kept their intention within their own heart – they professed a desire to act most liberally towards Mr Logan-Lacere, and accordingly the iron pot and the earthenware continued to keep company apparently on the best terms possible.

At the time Glen's husband felt he could not go on, there was nothing more certain than that it would have proved especially inconvenient for the great firm to let the London business stop, or take it over; and accordingly when the state of the case was laid before them, they professed their willingness to enter into an arrangement which on the face of it seemed actually generous. Cash was to be paid at certain short intervals for all goods supplied, but the payment of the old indebtedness was to be thrown over a period extending beyond two years.

Without another liability, perfectly unencumbered as regarded domestic expenses beyond his own household, the man might have fulfilled the conditions imposed; but as matters stood, he and Glen saw the months glide away without the slightest apparent chance of being able to pay anything off the arrears. The business was still not strong enough to stand alone.

If advertising ceased, trade fell off – yet advertising was an expense which properly ought only to have been taken out of a large capital, and the repayment thrown over many successful years. How her husband worked perhaps no human being but Glen ever knew. He started for his office at seven, and rarely got home before ten. Often Glen bore him company in those long evening vigils after office hours were over. If 'Elia's' real works were, as he said, to be found on the shelves of a certain great building, now demolished, in Leadenhall Street, so the bulk of Mrs Logan-Lacere's manuscripts commencing 'Sir,' and ending 'Your obedient Servant,' were at that time scattered over all lands. She wrote acres of letters – unwitting the seed she planted was destined to be reaped by others – that for herself and husband there should ripen no harvest but disappointment!

She had commenced her new book before the arrangement mentioned was come to, and went on writing by fits and starts till she completed rather more than two-thirds of the novel. Mr Vassett unhappily was not pressing her to complete it. He evinced no undue anxiety to receive the conclusion – quite the contrary. Several things had of late occurred to damp the ardour of a publisher in his most enterprising days somewhat prone to over-caution.

Had Mr Pierson been still in Craven Street the encouraging statement he would certainly have made, that 'though the trade seemed going to the he felt no doubt it would come right in the end,' might have helped to restore Mr Vassett's confidence; but Mr Pierson was not in Craven Street. He had 'departed to that bourne,' as Mat Donagh would have said, 'from whence no traveller (even a publisher's reader or advertisement canvasser) returns.'

He had gone, not in a brisk and businesslike sort of way, but lingeringly, as though loth to leave the greasy London pavements and the familiar fogs and the accustomed small-talk – gone after evoking a great deal of sympathy from, and costing a large sum of money to, Mr Vassett, who took his reader's death seriously to heart – so seriously indeed that he never even tried to replace his loss. The 'circumstance,' as Mr Vassett delicately styled Mr Pierson's reluctant step from this world to the next, undoubtedly preyed on the publisher's mind. When for years one has been accustomed to a familiar voice, the daily routine seems silent and lonely without it.

The long, dreary illness – the dragging journey from life to death – the pinched features – the yellow skin – the wasted hands – the weak accents of the man he had kept so long out of the workhouse, undoubtedly left an impression on Mr Vassett's mind too deep for words.

'You'll miss me, Vassett, more than you think,' said Mr Pierson one afternoon in the mournful winter twilight. That was the last sentence Mr Vassett ever heard him speak, for it was uttered after the accustomed parting. Next morning it was only that which had been Pierson Mr Vassett beheld fantastically arrayed, lying in a shell of the publisher's providing, the while a weeping widow and several children took perfectly practical views of the 'sad event,' and wondered what the dead man's friend would do for them.

Mr Vassett did a great deal – he was practical, but generous; if he did not assist Mrs Pierson to the extent that lady perhaps anticipated, she yet found him in her time of need more liberal than she had the slightest reason to expect. He paid the doctor and the funeral expenses (during the illness his purse was always open); he provided plain though decent mourning: he wrote a cheque for a moderate sum to enable the widow to get her head above water again; and then he figuratively shook hands with the Pierson connection and cut their acquaintance.

In consequence they said many hard things of the Craven Street publisher which were extremely ungrateful, and vexed the soul of that kind-hearted man greatly when repeated to him, as they were duly and truly by some of his various excellent friends.

On the top of Pierson's death came many (and sad) changes in the literary world. For example – the gradual extinction of all small libraries, the birth of monopolies, the growth of great enterprises in connection with railway extension; and last, but by no means least, the sudden upspringing of the Burleigh Street house. Trade is a doctor which needs no minute or second hand in its watch to feel the public pulse. One day when Mr Vassett went out to subscribe a book, he knew some awful change was impending. At Mudie's, he met that engaging young gentleman, Mr Lance Felton. As a rich old dowager, with Heaven only knows how many quarterings, would avoid an introduction to, say, an ex-Lady Mayoress, so Mr Vassett desired to decline the acquaintance of the irrepressible Lance; but Lance refused to be repulsed. That dreadful Bohemian, risen from the people, who, as Mr Vassett knew, owed even his ability to read and write to the (mistaken) kindness of the Dawton family, sidled up to him, and with a terrible impudence, after presenting his own unattractive person by name to the eminently respectable and old-established publisher of Craven Street, showed him the subscription list of a work Mr Vassett had declined to purchase, which turned the elder man green with envy.

'I candidly confess I don't know how you manage,' said Mr Vassett, who, though mortified, was too wise and truthful to deny facts, when thrust in his very face.

'Ah!' answered Lance sententiously, 'there are more ways of killing a dog than hanging him,' which utterance, though undoubtedly true, did not much help Mr Vassett in his endeavour to get the libraries up to the point he wanted to reach in his own subscription lists.

That afternoon a particularly nice turkey, stuffed, boiled, and served with celery sauce, greeted Mr Vassett's return to Craven Street. An apple-tart and custard followed the turkey. Stilton cheese supervened; and then he was finally left to himself and his own reflections, with some sound Madeira which a friend had sent him, and the usual meagre and mortified-looking dessert. To not one of the items composing that dinner could Mr Vassett, as a rule, be considered indifferent; but on the day in question he sent the turkey down almost untasted, refused to cut into the apple tart, said he wanted no cheese, and declining Madeira, rang the bell for hot water, and mixed himself a tumbler of punch.

That apparently was the beginning of his illness, one which for years chronically affected every plan and purpose of his life. Truth is, he had arrived at an age when if a man takes little exercise in London, and goes into the country not at all, and has his meals regularly and the means to provide them without undue anxiety as to the how and the wherewithal, dyspepsia in some one of its many forms is pretty sure to fasten upon him. This proved the case with Mr Vassett – to quote his own phrase, his 'nerves were not what they used to be,' his appetite became capricious, he could not tell 'what the deuce ailed his stomach,' and whenever he called upon his head to make an effort, his head flatly refused to do anything of the sort.

Mr Vassett had never been famous for reading manuscripts, and now he simply declined to read them at all. He felt no desire to enter into competition with men like Felton and Laplash. His business was rapidly becoming distasteful to him. He began to turn his mind to stocks and shares and good investments in freehold land and ground rents rather than to the immature works of rising genius. If a man takes to rather disliking authors, it is not long before he begins to hate them. There is nothing particularly attractive about the appearance of a manuscript, say three volumes long. Mr Vassett found manuscripts so extremely unattractive that he at last said to himself:

'Confound it, why should I peddle away my time reading all this stuff? I can put both time and money to much better use.'

This was the precise state of mind he had arrived at when, one dreary day towards the end of a peculiarly unpleasant November, Glen walked westward, meaning to confer with him on the subject of her new novel.

In the matter of advances Mr Vassett had been very liberal; whenever Glen required a few pounds those pounds had been forthcoming. But now she not merely wanted a good deal of money, but also some positive assurance as to the time when, if she finished her novel immediately, she might expect it to appear. In her own domestic province a deadlock seemed imminent. She had never been one of those persons who could make a single sovereign do the work of two. So far as she was concerned, nothing seemed easier than to forego any luxury or even necessary – but the expenses of a house cease not by day or night. The indebtedness of the most moderate establishment, like the grass, grows in the dark, and as Glen did not mean to trouble her husband about such details, she felt, as she expressed the matter to herself, it was 'time to do something.'

Probably on the face of this earth there never existed a woman who so cordially detested asking for money as Glenarva; and it was for this very reason she always seemed to Mr Vassett to be needing it. She could not bring herself to name a sufficient sum at once, and so the publisher fell into the habit of thinking, 'I wonder what Mrs Lacere can do with all the money she has from me,' forgetting how small an amount the 'all' came to at the end of the year.

However, on this especial afternoon, Glen, as she walked westward, decided that she would say out all that she felt and wanted. She chalked out the plan of her intended campaign – she determined to put her affairs on some tangible footing – she would ask Mr Vassett whether he thought he could publish one novel a year from her pen; in which case she meant to give an amount of time and attention to authorship she had never before attempted.

335

She considered what she would say; she felt very strong in this new determination. If, for example, she could make enough to pay for household expenses – take rent, taxes, tradesmen's bills, servants' wages off her husband's shoulders – what a comfort it would prove. She meant to be confidential with Mr Vassett. He had known her so long, he had always treated her so kindly, he could not think it strange if she did lay bare before him some of her pecuniary anxieties. Glen had quite made up her mind; she would get affairs put upon a more regular and business footing – she would hurry on her work – she would begin to regard authorship really as a profession – she would not for the future attend to her writing last, and to every other little trumpery affair first. She longed for mental rest; to be delivered from the thraldom of considering halfcrowns and sixpences. 'Yes, Mr Vassett was at home,' Muggins told her; Muggins was also good enough to intimate she might seek the publisher in his office.

'He's not engaged,' said Muggins; to whom the author of *Due East* and *Ashtree Manor* did not appear in the slightest degree a more important person than the girl who used to bring her manuscripts in Mr Pierson's time in order to have them rejected.

'There's nobody with him,' added Muggins, thinking Mrs Lacere had not quite grasped his meaning. Truth was, Glen's courage was already oozing out at her fingers' ends. Her well-arranged sentences seemed to be getting a little confused; nevertheless, at Mr Muggins's last intimation, which was conveyed in a somewhat querulous tone, she took her 'heart in her hand' and entered Mr Vassett's private office.

An hour later she emerged from it, having said no single word she intended to utter. If she had spoken out that afternoon, the end of her Struggle for Fame might have been very different; but then that simply means that another than Glenarva must have stood in her shoes, and talked with another tongue and been altogether another person from the woman Glenarva was or ever grew to be.

She lacked a quality.

So did her husband.

Lacking it, neither of them ever achieved success. Lacking it, the man was never born nor the woman ever breathed capable of making any considerable amount of money.

At all events, finding Mr Vassett indisposed to discuss business, in a mood indeed to discuss any other subject in preference to business, Glen sat on, listening to his utterances dismayed. She had not courage to ask for money, and inquire when her book would be published if she finished it at once, or even to say, 'Do you like it?'

The light of the winter day waned – she felt she could stay no longer – she desired to petition for even ten pounds, but she felt she could not do it. The curse of Glen's life was on her in full force that afternoon. She could not bear asking for money. Had her husband, who was unable by any means possible to give her a fixed allowance, failed continually to say, 'My dear, I am sure you cannot have sixpence in the world,' Glen could not have troubled him even for a shilling.

Pity the contrast between his wife and the Misses Lacere never struck the man in those days! They certainly wanted nothing which could be had for the begging!

'Rather than go away empty,' sighed Glen 'they would strip the garden;' and the remark was true. Locusts never left a land barer than the women who, not loving 'dear Mordaunt's wife,' still called her 'darling Glen' and 'our wonderful sister.'

Sick at heart and worn and weary, 'our wonderful sister' said goodbye to Mr Vassett, and passed out into Craven Street. She did not turn in the direction of the Strand; instead, she walked slowly to the bottom of the street. In her soul she felt she was a very coward, and that in the battle of life she never should do much good. She would have made a fine private, if only some different spirit than herself had led. Take comfort, ladies, however; after all, there are not many among you so constituted. Glen was only a poor simpleton, spite her occasional glib tongue and poor power of slowly producing a decent book, and gift of plodding. She divined then what she clearly understood afterwards, that there was not much in her: certainly not enough to do a great deal of good for herself or anyone else.

She walked to the bottom of Craven Street, and stood there for a time, looking at the Thames and reviewing her position. At the time, if Mr Vassett had only known how horribly short of money she was, he would have written out a cheque at once. Then she paced slowly up the street again, and began to make her way eastward via the Adelphi. She had got to Adam Street before she exactly knew what was in her mind; then she stood quite still. Something was urging her on at the moment she never afterwards understood – despair, perhaps.

'I can do nothing with this book,' she thought; 'but as regards the next, I will try to get something more decided.' And so, with that indifference to externals and dress, the darkening twilight, and what may be called the feeble instinct of a feeble sex, which characterised most of her proceedings, Glen, totally unarmed for conquest, turned her weary steps in the direction of Burleigh Street. It was then Lance said:

'God bless me! I have done everything but advertise for you in the *Times*,' and Glen answered:

'Have you?' the while she felt strongly she did not like Mr Felton or Mr Laplash, or the appearance of the place generally.

'Now, what have you got?' asked Lance, when he had despatched Noll to the post office.

Glen replied she had nothing. Mr Vassett was to publish her next book.

'No – it wasn't finished; two volumes were done. But next year, perhaps –'

'Next year? Nonsense!' interrupted Lance. 'Now, look here – what's your name?' He had been critically examining the personnel of the successful author, and felt sure she was no swell – no lace-and-velvet – no diamond-and-ruby young woman.

'Mrs Logan-Lacere,' answered Glen, unwitting that the name stank in Mr Felton's nostrils.

'*Logan-Lacere!*' he repeated in amazement.

'God bless me!' he exclaimed for the second time in their short interview, though, indeed, there was nothing in that establishment less believed in than the Almighty. 'How the ––– did he get hold of you? Oh, I beg your pardon,' he hurriedly added, as she made an almost involuntary movement of disapproval and departure; 'I only meant it seemed so strange. I have been hunting the world over for you, and you were just here to my hand all the while. Besides, you know, we thought you were a man – and that book of yours, *Due East* – by Jove! I read it through three times! And I used to know your husband; but that was long before your time, no doubt. I suppose you never heard him speak of me?'

'Oh yes, I have,' answered Glen promptly; 'since you began to publish, that is, I have often heard him speak of how clever you were, and of how hard you read at the British Museum.'

'Bravo!' thought Lance, looking straight in *Ashtree Manor*'s face, which bore the most truthful expression; as it might well, since, indeed, that was nearly all she had heard her husband say on the Felton question. 'Come, Mordaunt, you are not half such a sneak as I thought you: the minute a fellow gets on a suit of new clothes you don't want to tear them off his back.'

'And I knew his brother, too,' added Mr Felton aloud.

'His brother-in-law,' amended Glen; and in a minute the publisher, to use his own expression, 'knew how the land lay *there*.'

'I sent you a message by him,' Mr Felton said tentatively; 'but I suppose he forgot to deliver it.'

'No,' answered Glen, and she flushed a little. 'He delivered it to my husband, and my husband told me.'

'Then why the deuce – excuse my swearing, but it's enough to make anybody swear – why didn't you come to me months ago?'

Glen looked at Mr Felton, then glanced round the office, then let her eyes rest for a moment on Mr Laplash ere she answered. In her heart she was wondering why she had come there then; but as it would have been scarcely courteous to say so, she contented herself with remarking Mr Vassett had made her name, and she did not care to take her books elsewhere.

'Oh, that sort of thing is all nonsense,' retorted Lance; 'business is business, and sentiment is quite out of place in an office. I am very sure Vassett never gave you anything like the sum I am willing to pay.'

Glen answered she was very well satisfied with the prices Mr Vassett paid. She was thinking as she spoke of what she had heard pass between her husband and brother-in-law on the subject of Mr Felton's worldly position.

'He is a clever fellow,' remarked the first: 'but unless he has some one with a large capital at his back, I do not see how he can stand his ground.'

'Who would have anything to do with him?' returned the other. 'He has no capital except impudence.'

About Mr Felton himself, or his place of business, or his partner, there was certainly nothing to suggest the idea of money; and perhaps for this reason Mrs Lacere did not rise to the bait, as the publisher expected.

'Well,' he exclaimed, 'I have often heard of the difference between authors and their books, but the difference between you and your books is something almost incredible. I said to myself when I read *Ashtree Manor*, "This is written by some fellow who has knocked about the world and knows a thing or two, a sharp hand at a bargain; it wouldn't be easy to take him in." And now it turns out the author is a woman, who talks more foolishly than I ever heard any woman, even my own wife, talk before, and who does not seem to have enough spirit to say "Bo" to a goose.'

Glen laughed out. It is unnecessary to say she did not entirely recognise the truth of Mr Felton's unflattering portrait, but it amused her all the more perhaps for that very reason.

'Come,' cried Lance, 'that's better. And now, to waste no more time – let's get to business. I'll give you eight hundred pounds for your novel. Will you take it? If you won't, what will you take?'

Eight hundred pounds – good heavens! At the words Glen's head seemed to turn round. Eight hundred pounds! Why, the mines of Golconda could yield no more! But she did not feel the whole affair real; she thought she must be dreaming, and that she would waken presently to the reality of a life which lacked many necessaries and possessed no solitary superfluity.

'I am beginning to imagine you must be dumb, Mrs Lacere,' said Mr Felton impatiently.

He was fast working himself up into a rage. He thought she was not satisfied with his offer, and he knew Mr Laplash was most dissatisfied. From his position against the wall that gentleman had been making a series of signs which were perfectly intelligible to Lance, and not wholly mysterious to Glen herself, who, in answer to the publisher's last observation, said:

'I beg your pardon; I was considering. The book I am writing now is sold to Mr Vassett, but I shall be very glad indeed to make an arrangement with you for my next novel. I must not intrude on your time longer now. It will be better for me to call upon you again in the spring,' and Glen was calmly rising to depart when Mr Felton interposed.

'Don't go,' he exclaimed. 'Now I have got you I mean to keep you. I have had trouble enough with you, and intend to advertise you next week in my list.'

'But what are you going to advertise?' inquired Mrs Lacere, with some natural astonishment.

'The book Vassett has got.'

'That is quite impossible,' said Glen.

'What is impossible? All you have to do is, go to Vassett and get to know the sum he wants for his bargain.'

'I am sure Mr Vassett would not stand in my way, but I could not ask him to release me from my engagement.'

'Why couldn't you? Gracious goodness, would anybody believe you wrote your own books? The thing is simple as ABC. In the first place, where is the manuscript?'

'At Craven Street.'

'Well then, you run along to Craven Street and get the first volume, and bring it here. You tell Vassett you can sell it for far more money than he'll ever give you; and just say in so many plain words – "How much will you take to cancel our agreement?"'

It is said that all the events of a lifetime have been known to pass through the mind of a drowning man – that in one supreme moment the whole panorama of existence, from boyhood to age, has flashed across his mental sight; and it certainly is true that as Mr Felton spoke, all the many kindly words Mr Vassett had uttered, all the hopes and fears and despair and rejoicing experienced in the familiar office, recurred to Glenarva's memory, and urged her to refuse this new publisher's suggestion. And yet the money! She did not believe he would or could ever pay her such a sum. Nevertheless, the very dream seemed for the time being pleasant: and besides, she thought Mr Vassett really did not want her book, or to be troubled any more with her. There were two volumes completed, and not a definite word yet said about commencing to print.

'If I go to Mr Vasset –' she began slowly.

'Of course you will go; that is quite settled,' interrupted Lance, with a decision really refreshing.

'I shall want some money,' proceeded Glen; 'I owe him money.'

'Very well; you can have whatever you require.'

'And I should like some for myself,' she added desperately.

'All right; you have only to say what you need. Now go and get the manuscript; we shall soon be closing here.'

'Oh, I could not possibly go back to Craven Street this evening: I have only just come from there. Mr Vassett would think I must have had some idea of this kind while I was in his office, and –'

'Look here,' exclaimed Lance: 'you'll drive me mad. Kelly – I say, Kelly, step this way a minute, will you? Now listen to the position, and as a man of sense and experience give this lady a word of advice.' And then, almost without drawing his breath, Mr Felton explained how matters stood, and asked if Mrs Lacere ought not to go that hour, that instant, and rescue her manuscript from the Parliamentary train, as he called Mr Vassett, and 'shove it into the Burleigh Street express.'

Glen had glanced at Mr Kelly as he entered, and remembered that they had met before, but she made no sign of recognition. She wanted to hear what he had to say. Perhaps she was longing to be urged to adopt a course she knew perfectly well she should afterwards repent. She always did repent every course she adopted, so after all it seemed to signify little which road she selected to travel.

'What is your opinion?' repeated Mr Felton, addressing Mr Kelly, who, hat in hand, stood within the doorway, a contrast to Mr Laplash, who, with his hat on, leaned against the wall, and Noll, who, similarly covered, hovered just outside.

'It all depends,' answered Mr Kelly; and as he spoke, standing where the light of the gas fell full upon him, Glen could but consider how greatly the years had improved him. What! was this the gauche fellow-traveller in the slow and never-to-be-forgotten journey to London? – this the man who had been introduced to Lady Hilda's notice as the clever actor in *How's Maria?* Though the same, he was altogether different. Glen had heard something about his marriage from Mr Vassett, and could not deny matrimony had produced a wonderfully beneficial effect on his outward appearance.

'It all depends,' he said, 'on whether it is of importance to Mrs Lacere to receive the additional sum you offer.'

'I imagine there is not much doubt about that,' answered Mr Felton, quite unconscious that his remark could scarcely be considered agreeable.

For a second Glen only gave consent by silence; at last she said, straightforwardly, 'Mr Felton is quite right. Money is of importance to me.'

'Then I think you would do wisely to go and talk matters over with Mr Vassett,' decided Barney.

The successful author took one reluctant step towards the door, while Lance cried out, 'All I want her to do is to get her manuscript. I entreat of you to go at once. Do, for heaven's sake, put a little of the spirit into yourself you have put into your books. If I could find an old shoe I'd throw it after you, but everything is so confoundedly new here.'

'I am going,' said Glen calmly; 'but remember, I don't like it;' and, with a slight bow to Mr Kelly, she went through the outer office and passed into the street.

'Did you ever see such a duffer?' was Mr Felton's flattering criticism, the moment she disappeared.

'Do you think she is the author?' asked Mr Kelly.

'Certain sure. Now I wonder how long she'll stay discussing the matter with Vassett?'

He need not have troubled himself on that point. Muggins was closing the offices as she got there, and it was almost in the dark she held her brief interview with Mr Vassett. He said he would not stand in her way – perhaps for the reason that it never occurred to him she knew anything of Felton or Laplash, or even the benignant Noll. Nobody was aware who the author of *Ashtree Manor* might be, and he did not feel inclined to go back into his own office and hold another lengthy conversation with her.

He gave her the first volume of the new book, and when she said she would see him the next day, he answered, a little shortly, 'Very well', then Glen bade him good night, and the interview was over, and she was hurrying through the darkness back to Burleigh Street, having taken the first step along a road which led her afterwards into the blackness of a night that seemed at one time without even one star to lighten its terrible gloom.

'So you have come back at last', commented her husband, as she walked into his office and passed round his desk and came and stood silently beside him. He could not bear her being out after dusk, and had passed through every possible phase of anxiety on her account. 'And where do you think you have been?'

'I have been selling a book', she answered. 'Look!' And she took out of her purse – which only held sixpence besides – a cheque for fifty pounds.

'Why, where did you get this?' he asked in utter amazement, looking only at the amount and not at the signature.

'And there is seven hundred and fifty more to follow some time', proceeded Glen, without the slightest elation of tone or manner.

Her husband looked at her. He did not know whether she was in earnest or not, or if she had suddenly taken leave of her senses.

She returned his look very steadily, and then made this remark, which in the often future he recalled with a vague wonder:

'I only hope it may not turn out I have done a bad evening's work.'

'My dear', he said – 'my dear!' for he could not comprehend the presentiment which seemed weighing on her, and the relief to him was something simply beyond the power of expression.

Chapter VI

MR KELLY'S ADVICE

'AND, PRAY, WHO IS Mr Logan-Lacere?' It was at Mr Kelly's hospitable table this question happened to be put. During the course of the six months following Glen's visit to Burleigh Street it had been asked a good many times by various persons in different places.

'Something in the City,' answered a gentleman seated opposite.

'Greengrocer or millionaire?' which of course, as was only right and proper, produced a laugh at the expense of the City.

'I am sure he is not a greengrocer, and I do not think he is a millionaire,' interposed Mr Kelly; while at the other end of the table a little running fire was going on of 'Only to think, after all, of those books being written by a lady;' 'I wonder what she is like;' 'Must be a very masculine sort of person, I should think;' 'It is perfectly dreadful the way she speaks of her sex;' 'The general opinion is, her husband writes her books; I have heard he is very nice;' 'Really! do you know what he is?' and then everyone paused for a moment to listen, as a man very like a sharp, cross terrier – whom, had he been a dog, one would have instantly set down as a 'good ratter,' with a rimless glass well screwed in his right eye – said in the tone of one having authority, 'I can tell you all about Mr Logan-Lacere.'

'Why, you don't mean to say you ever were in the City!' observed the gentleman who had made the hit about greengrocer or millionaire.

'Wasn't I? – went down once among the hosts of the Philistines, and came back sorely wounded.'

'Poor innocent!' murmured his friend.

'However, it wasn't then I knew the fortunate husband of our distinguished author. It was in the happy days of childhood. I have the pleasantest recollections connected with the name of Mordaunt Logan-Lacere. We fought together, robbed orchards together, birds nested, went nutting, rode by turns an old but extremely vicious pony that generally finished by throwing me into the nearest and dirtiest ditch, or what was far worse, the middle of a quickset hedge. Yes, his uncle had a jolly little place down in our part of the world, and till I went to Eton we were close friends. When I returned home the next time his uncle was dead and he gone to London; and except once, I never heard of him since till I saw in the columns of the *Times* – *Heron's Nest* (which I may remark was the name of his uncle's house), "by Mrs B Logan-Lacere."'

'How romantic, how interesting!' sighed a middle-aged spinster sitting by his side; 'and do you know anything of her?'

'No; out of mere curiosity, for I need scarcely tell you I am not a novel-reader, I got the book from Mudie's, and the description of Heron's Nest and the country round about is so accurate, I thought Lacere must have married some girl from the old neighbourhood; but I understand I was mistaken. She is Welsh, or Scotch, or –'

'No – Irish,' interrupted Mr Kelly.

'We shall get at something presently,' said a portly dowager seated beside the host. 'What between Mr Hibbs, who knows all about the husband, and Mr Kelly, who can tell us all about the wife, it will be our own fault if we are not soon the best-informed persons in London concerning this long-vexed question.'

'I fear all I can tell you about the wife will not add greatly to your store of knowledge,' answered Barney, who had made it the rule of his married life to profess total ignorance of the existence of all ladies except those to whom his wife introduced him. 'I certainly have seen her. She came into Mr Felton's office once when I was there.'

'Do satisfy our curiosity about her,' implored a lady who had previously expressed her conviction Mrs Lacere 'must be the sweetest of the sweet – a delightfully melancholy and unhappy sort of creature, you know.'

'I don't think there is much to say about her,' answered Mr Kelly, who would have made the same reply had Glen been beautiful as Venus. 'She certainly doesn't look clever, or like a person capable of writing a successful book, but the race is not always to the swift or the battle to the strong,' added Barney, thinking of his own unappreciated novel, which had gone the round of nearly every London publisher, and been rejected by all.

'Judging from her books I should say they are a miserable pair,' observed a lady, who entertained the conviction that some of Glen's bitterest utterances had been directed against herself personally.

'If they are I am sure it is not Lacere's fault,' spoke up Mr Hibbs briskly; 'but they are poor, I understand, so of course they must be unhappy. He was cruelly imposed upon by his stepfather. He is just the sort of fellow people could not resist cheating. He has got such a lot of brains it seems an equal fight, but it is not; intellect is no match for trade "sharpness."'

'Depend upon it *he* writes the books,' said the dowager, *sotto voce*, to her neighbour. Just then, Mrs Kelly with a gracious smile inclining her head towards the dowager, there ensued a general movement and flutter, and rustling of stiff silks, and sweep of velvets, and frou-frou of trailing skirts; and since, for most of the men present, literature in any shape did not offer the slightest attraction, conversation drifted into other channels, and it was some weeks later ere Mr Kelly, meeting Mr Hibbs at a lawn-party, where they were both bored to death, asked him for some further particulars concerning Glen's husband.

'Yes, it was from the Lacere union all the misfortunes of the Logans began,' explained Mr Hibbs. 'There were two sisters co-heiresses – one died unmarried, and her portion went to some far-away relations in Durham, I think; the other married Logan, who had a small patrimony of his own, and who, so far as birth was concerned, stood far above the Laceres. He was the great-grandfather of our friend; so, you see, it has not taken long for the family to get to the bottom of the hill. The father was a very good, quiet sort of man, I believe, who died when his son was two years of age – and his daughter still unborn. He left a cousin of his own, guardian and executor – a widower with a large family – a needy man, and dishonest into the bargain. The widow seems to have been a poor creature, and soon married him; and the boy, who happened to be delicate, and no doubt in the way to boot, was sent to Heron's Nest. After his uncle's death, it seems, he went back to the step-paternal roof, where he was taught to regard Lacere as his benefactor, his best friend, and so forth.

'Actually, he was twenty-five before it came to his knowledge, quite by accident, that he had not been a pauper living on his stepfather's bounty. That good gentleman had quietly appropriated every sixpence of his money, and, having died in the odour of sanctity, left his whole family to the care of the youth he had defrauded. It is a beautiful connection into which your countrywoman has married. I know a solicitor who is pretty well acquainted with the Laceres, root and branch, and his opinion is that whatever income the lady makes, or her husband earns, will be engulfed in the family quagmire. He has lost a lot of money, I am told, through becoming surety and that sort of ridiculous thing. I believe his business is a good one, but I have reason to know he is *not* in easy circumstances.'

This was the first-fruits of Glen's visit to Burleigh Street. Never saying 'By your leave,' or 'With your leave,' Messrs Felton and Laplash, considering the mystery concerning her had lasted long enough, advertised her name throughout the kingdom, and everyone was consequently free to discuss her husband's affairs, and both their antecedents, to speculate concerning their home-life, to repeat any story, true or false, about what they were and had been.

The charming privacy of anonymous authorship could be Glen's no longer. Thanks to Messrs Felton and Co., she was now common property. Hitherto she had shrunk morbidly from publicity; now she was placed well in a strong light for everyone who pleased to stare at and criticise. Mr Vassett had stood well between her and the world. No one ever elicited a syllable of information concerning the new author from him; but with Mr Felton and his partner the case was widely different, and almost to her terror, and certainly to her annoyance, Mrs Logan-Lacere found people were talking about her by name, and that the still safe haven of a quiet life was exchanged for that wide sea of notoriety where authors make more enemies than friends – where very bad weather has often to be encountered, and where the build of the vessel, and the canvas she carries, and the flag she hoists, are far more considered and discussed than the freight with which she is laden.

Not all the solid benefits she derived from Burleigh Street ever reconciled her to Mr Felton's place of business, which was constantly full of loungers, who called each other by their Christian names (abbreviated), who chaffed and laughed at and about nothing, the while the senior partner discoursed, generally with his hat on and his legs dangling from the counter, concerning the habits of high life and those things which it was correct, as well as those things which it was not correct to do.

Nevertheless, through a period of very hard work, Glen soon began to feel it was a golden stream down which the barque with their fortunes was then smoothly gliding. No shortness of money at that time; no need to consider sixpences or shillings either, to stint in housekeeping, to pause ere buying a dress. So long as she chose to sign an agreement and take bills for the amount, she could have what she wanted in the way of money from Burleigh Street; and the more she spent, so as to 'look as if she was well paid,' to quote Mr Felton's own expression, the better that gentleman was pleased.

He had exactly the same feeling about his authors that some mistresses have about their servants. He wanted the writers on his list to 'cut a greater dash' than the writers on the list of any other publisher.

He desired, in fact, not merely to be a 'swell' himself, but to make 'swells' of others. He would have liked to see a string of carriages in Burleigh Street, and nothing annoyed him more about Mr Kelly than that gentleman's persistent refusal to bring his wife's bays to help advertise the Felton and Laplash establishment, or to grace in his own person, or allow Mrs Kelly to grace, any of the banquets to which the adventurous Lance was in the habit of hospitably bidding all his 'great guns,' and some of his 'little guns' too, if they chanced to be favourites.

For some time Glen and her husband managed to elude these festivities, but at length it seemed to them both that to persist in this refusal would be to vex a man who seemed to mean very kindly towards them, and who, throughout the whole of their business relations, never varied in one respect – namely, his belief in Mrs Logan-Lacere's power as a writer, and his admiration for her books.

He praised her till her very name became abhorrent to the loungers in Burleigh Street, till men longed to pull her work to pieces, and tell Mr Felton how utterly sick and weary they felt of what he called his 'crack author.'

'Felton used to bully us about you,' a well-known essayist, with whom Glen became great friends in after-years, once laughingly told her. 'I believe we all hated you then,' he said; and Glen answered she was not in the least surprised. If it had fallen to her lot to be wise beforehand, and understand how little she was loved by the Burleigh Street fraternity, she would probably have elected at first, as she did at last, to decline meeting any of them under Mr Felton's roof, where that excitable individual almost worked himself into a frenzy, lest each guest should not get what he liked, or be properly attended to.

Poor Lance Felton! Whatever his other faults might be, he was the soul of hospitality, and it hurt Glen to see, what he never saw himself, how little those who came to the feast thought of the giver of it – how much more ready they were to note little solecisms in social etiquette, and to remark on the ignorance evinced in the neglect of small details, than to recognise the generous desire to promote their comfort – the nervously anxious wish that they should all feel thoroughly at home and enjoy themselves.

Yet certainly the host was irresistible; no man or woman, with the slightest sense of humour, could have helped laughing at him, and there was not much harm in that, had the laughter been all good-natured, for he laughed loud and often at himself. He was forever taking the whole company into his confidence about matters concerning which anyone else would have maintained a pleasing reticence. He could not hold his tongue. He preferred to tell the world of his shortcomings. It was extremely funny to hear him talk about what he did not know, but extremely sad to notice the cruel sneers with which many of these utterances were greeted.

Long as Glen had been writing, this was her first experience of social life in Bohemia.

She had seen authors on their best behaviour in Mr Vassett's office, and somewhat inclined to be a little wild in Burleigh Street, but the dinner at Mr Felton's place down Hampton way was quite another matter. The decorous slowness and solemnity with which the evening commenced formed an extraordinary contrast to the frantic hilarity that heralded its close. Curiously enough, there were not many of the guests who knew each other except by name. A few men talked together in the drawing room, and spoke to some of the ladies as though they had met them before, but at first it seemed impossible that from such diverse materials any pleasure could ever be extracted. The best jokes of the best joker fell utterly flat – even Lady Hilda, who was present, failed to strike a spark of fire. The truth is, her ladyship infinitely preferred a small audience, where she could keep attention to herself exclusively. Stage asides, little snatches of conversation – such as, 'So Jennings has gone!' 'Yes; saw him off.' 'What do you think of Carew's comedy?' 'Did you read that savage review of Tomkins's work in the Saturday?' – drove her to the verge of distraction. Glen had recognised her lively ladyship at once, and shrinking from too close a proximity to Hicks's derelict, found herself at Mr Felton's elbow.

'I say,' he whispered eagerly, 'I am going to take you in to dinner.'

'You must not do that,' cried Glen.

'Why not?'

'Because Lady Hilda –'

'Oh Lady Hilda!' retorted Mr Felton, while Glen murmured, 'H – sh! h – sh!' soothingly following up this hint with a series of entreaties, which in due time produced the desired result.

The dinner-hour came, the dinner-hour passed; there were messages from the kitchen, there were hurried retreats of Mr Felton to, as Glen suspected, the dining-room, to fortify his courage – since on each occasion he returned a little more excited and a good deal less inclined to endure contradiction. At last he put the position to the company. Dinner had already been kept waiting half an hour for the great Mr Gossage and the greater Mrs Gossage – ('Who is,' confided the publisher to Glen, 'such a sixty-gunner'). Should they wait any longer for these illustrious personages? Lance only 'wanted to know,' so he proposed that the question should be put to the vote.

Then, as with one voice, every man in the room answered 'No' and the Mercury, who had been waiting at the door for final orders, flew with them to the impatient cook.

'Fact is, you know,' confessed Lance to Mrs Lacere, 'it's deucedly awkward. She promised to come early and put us a bit in the way of things – also to bring some damask and silver we were short of; and now, how we shall manage with such a lot of people I'm sure I can't imagine.'

'I do not fancy anyone will know you are short if you don't tell them,' returned Glen, in the same tone. 'No – no, Mr Felton: I *cannot* go in before Lady Hilda,' she added hurriedly, as 'dinner' was proclaimed from the doorway; and thus compelled. Lance offered his arm to Lady Hicks, as he sometimes called her, taking good care to tell her ladyship, in the short passage across the hall, that he wanted to escort *Heron's Nest*, but she refused to have anything to do with him.

'She is here, then, is she?' said Lady Hilda. 'I looked about, but I could not see her.'

'I don't know where she has got to,' answered Mr Felton, glancing back over his left shoulder – and, indeed, at that moment it would have been hard to tell where anyone had got to – amongst the tightly packed crowd who, at last, having somehow pushed and fought their way into the dining-room, found there were not seats for much more than half their number. It was of no use standing on ceremony in that house, so some of the gentlemen, forming themselves into a volunteer corps, marched backwards and forwards between the rooms, carrying chairs, seats, and every portable article of such-like furniture.

'That's all right!' exclaimed Lance, blandly surveying results, 'sit as close as you can – we'll all shake down presently. Where's Mr Lacere? Thank you, Gervais,' as a meek-looking gentleman in spectacles, who seemed as if he hadn't a joke in his whole body, and yet who was, in Mr Felton's opinion, the greatest humourist that ever lived, landed Glen safely three seats from Mr Felton's right hand, and consequently next but one to Lady Hilda, whom the publisher, in an access of friendliness, had just addressed as 'My dear soul.' He was relating to her the Gossage misadventure – how Mrs Gossage had offered to show them what was what. 'Because, you know,' he added, 'we don't pretend to be up to all the ways of grand society.'

'Why did you not ask me?' remarked Lady Hilda: 'I should have been only too delighted had you deigned to make use of my poor services. But perhaps,' she added, with an engaging modesty, 'you thought I might not be exactly – capable?'

Greatly shocked at this suggestion, Mr Felton assured her he could not have dreamed of taking such a liberty. 'And besides, there was the plate – and the damask –'

'I fancy I could have managed even that,' said her ladyship; and then, as the work of dinner began, she leaned a little towards Mr Felton, and inquired in a low voice, 'Now, tell me which is Mrs Lacere.'

'Next but one – Mrs –' he was proceeding to call out, when Lady Hilda, laying her hand firmly on his, stopped the words in mid air.

'I want to see her, that's all,' she explained, and leaning a little forward, so as to get the humourist's person out of the way, she stared hard at Glen, who at length, as if subtly conscious of this scrutiny, turned her head to the foot of the table.

Lady Hilda nodded pleasantly.

'How d'ye do?' she said. 'So you *have* set the Thames on fire.'

Mrs Lacere was about to answer, when the noise of a fresh arrival caused Mr Felton to spring from his chair, and, exclaiming 'It's the Gossages!' rush excitedly from the room. There was a pause, during the continuance of which the company looked at each other, and listened to the sound of eager talking in the hall; then the door was flung wide, and Lady Hilda, looking calmly up from her plate, which she had been regarding with a good deal of interest, beheld a figure in trailing black velvet sweep into the room. She had so little clothing on the upper part of her person, and there lay such a mass of wasted material on the carpet, that Lady Hilda might almost be excused her astonished exclamation of 'Good heavens!'

This was Mrs Gossage, who had promised to come and do the prunes and prism business for the hostess, who did not sit at the head of her own table, and whom nobody but Lady Hilda seemed to know. This was Mrs Gossage, whose face was of an unearthly pallor, and whose neck, against the deep black of her bodice, appeared the colour of driven snow. She came in coughing plaintively, and she sank, with a faint, thankful smile, into a seat vacated for her benefit, leaving about half a dozen yards of velvet on the floor for the servants to trip over, which they did, till one man, possessed of considerable presence of mind, tucked the bundle under the lady's chair.

'She's a stunner, isn't she?' said Mr Felton to Lady Hilda, proud to think here at length was something worthy the attention even of an earl's daughter.

'She has stunned me,' answered Lady Hilda demurely. The soup, of which she partook of one spoonful, was brought back for Mrs Gossage; then she had fish, eating about as much as would have covered a shilling; at intervals she coughed and was very languishing, and people paid court to her for her husband's sake, and a general frost seemed to set in over the whole of the company, that had been about to thaw before the arrival of the Gossages, till champagne appeared, which Mr Felton told his guests he hoped they would find good – for that his wine merchant had assured him it was the very vintage for literary men.

Whatever the merits of the wine might be, it unloosened the tongues of some of the talkers present – Babel itself could not have been noisier than that dining-room. Mr Felton laughed and applauded to the echo. There were good things said, had anyone across the table been able to hear them. The heat grew oppressive – the din more furious and Glen was wondering how much longer the ladies would be expected to sit at table, when Mr Felton's right-hand neighbour, after looking vainly at the hostess for the usual signal, and seeing Mrs Felton did not seem to have the faintest idea of giving it, took the initiative upon herself, and, glancing at Mrs Lacere, said, 'Had we not better go?' and rising as she spoke, walked out of the room, greatly to the relief of the males, who had been inwardly wondering when on earth 'those women meant to move!'

'Dear me!' exclaimed Lady Hilda, standing in the middle of the drawing room, and fetching a deep breath; 'Dear me!' and then she crossed over to the mantel-piece and looked at herself in the mirror, and afterwards strolled leisurely round the apartment, examining everything in it – undeterred by any supervision on the part of Mrs Felton, who had gone, as one lady suggested, to the nursery to see her dear children.

'Kitchen most likely,' amended Lady Hilda, with calm insolence; then, turning her attention to Glen, she observed, 'You are rather bread-and-buttery still. Oh!

I see you do not understand – that dear, delightful Vassett never told tales out of school. Never, never, never, so long as I live, shall I forget the solemn face with which he told me the first time we met, "You had as much to learn as I to unlearn." You don't look as if you had learnt much, but "still water runs deep," et cetera: I suppose you know the end of the proverb.'

Yes, Glen confessed she did; and as Lady Hilda spoke Mrs Lacere's memory took a long flight backward to that breezy hillside, where she had first heard one of the 'boys' delivering himself of the objectionable sentence in its entirety.

'I thought so,' commented her ladyship. 'Ah! I see we shall suit each other admirably. Well, and how is our old friend in Craven Street?' and marching Glen slowly about the room, perfectly regardless of and indifferent to the looks of surprise and indignation which followed them, Lady Hilda found herself once more on the hearthrug, and again gazing in the mirror.

'Won't your ladyship sit down?' asked an elderly dame, who had prayed to be allowed to come in just for an hour – that she might say she had seen all 'those wonderful writers' – rising and offering Lady Hilda a corner of a sofa, otherwise well filled by the wives of two men great in the opinion of Lance Felton.

'Her ladyship' surveyed the speaker for a moment in amazement; then, 'I never sit down,' she answered.

'Lor'!' exclaimed the other.

'I never voluntarily doom myself to the chance of being bored,' kindly explained Lady Hilda. And then she would have swept on her travels round the room for the second time, had a low, tremulous voice, murmuring, 'Oh, Mrs Lacere!' not arrested her progress. 'I have so longed to make your acquaintance,' proceeded Mrs Gossage – for it was she. 'I hope you will allow me to introduce myself – my name is Gossage. Of course you have heard Mr Felton speak of my husband? We are both enthusiastic admirers of your books; indeed, I may say it was only the hope of meeting you brought me here this evening. It was madness, I know, to venture; but I told my husband, whatever the consequences, I could not miss the chance of seeing you.'

And she smiled sweetly up at Lady Hilda, who was staring stonily at her, while Glen stammered out some reply to the barefaced compliment, looking as she spoke certainly as though she had never written a line of manuscript in her life.

'I ought not to have come,' continued Mrs Gossage. 'My doctor said if I did it would be simple suicide, and that he could not answer for the consequences. I have been very ill with inflammation of the lungs, and my chest is naturally delicate –'

'Then why in the world, if you have been so ill, and are so delicate, did you not put on some clothes before undertaking such a journey? Here,' and at this juncture Lady Hilda pulled a striped woollen antimacassar from behind the highly proper dame who had offered her a seat – threw it over Mrs Gossage's white shoulders

– wrapped it round her neck – drew it tight up under her chin, where she fastened it close with a hairpin extracted from her ladyship's chignon – and then, remarking 'That's better,' took Glen by the hand and led her away, unmindful of the extraordinary figure she left standing on the hearthrug, and the looks of blank dismay with which all the ladies present regarded her proceedings.

'Let's go into the conservatory,' suggested Lady Hilda, 'and get a breath of air. Funny sort of place this, isn't it? By-the-bye, don't you have anything to do with that woman – Mrs Gossage, I mean.'

'Why not?' asked Glen.

'Never you mind – be a good child, and do as you are told. Well, and what do you think of the Felton *ménage*? Dear me, you need not be so cautious,' she went on, when Glen said she had not seen much of it as yet. 'I never told you my first experience of the establishment, did I?'

It would have been difficult for her to have done so, as she had not exchanged a dozen words with Mrs Lacere before in her life; but, speaking as if Glen were an old acquaintance, she added:

'When our publisher asked me to come down and stay at his "place in the country," and I accepted his invitation, I thought I should see some great mansion; so to do honour to Mr and Mrs Felton – who I felt sure would have heaps of servants and were living in grand style – I borrowed a friend's carriage, and drove down one afternoon with my maid. It was dark when we arrived. The gas was lighted in the hall, and, as no one appeared in answer to my summons, I walked straight in through the door, which usually stands wide open.

'At that moment Mrs Felton, whom I had never seen, was coming out of the dining-room, arrayed in a black skirt and a white garibaldi. I mistook her for a servant, and asked her to send some one to carry in my boxes, which she did; never telling me who she was, or enlightening me when I begged her to show my maid my rooms.

'Meantime, seeing a fire in the apartment we have just left, I thought I would warm myself a little till somebody came to me, and was about stirring the coals into a good blaze, when Parkins – that's my maid – rushed downstairs, at a pace quite unprecedented.

'"If you please, m'lady," she began, quite in a temper, "where am I to sleep?"

'"How, in Heaven's name, should I know, Parkins!" I answered.

'"Because Mrs Felton – *that*, if you please, m'lady, was the mistress of the house you saw in the hall – says if I don't sleep in your apartment, she doesn't know where she can possibly put me up, *except in Mr Felton's dressing-room*! And so I've come down, if you please, m' lady, to say –'

'"Don't say it. Parkins!" I entreated. "The best thing you can do is to go straight back to town. The carriage is still here, I think. Tell the coachman to wait for you."

'I dressed myself for dinner that evening by the light of one solitary dip with a long snuff in a flat candlestick, and the children partook of the meal with us, and messed their food about; and Mr Felton was sulky because something had gone wrong in Burleigh Street, and he told me Laplash was a "stupid beast," and that there was not a soul in his office he could trust to make out an invoice – whatever an invoice may be – and –'

"'Oh! see, there is Mrs Felton at last!" interrupted Glen: "I must go and speak to her. I have never been introduced, or – or anything. Pray excuse me,' and, leaving the conservatory, she found the hostess, and sat down beside her, and talked as much as she could; for which heroic effort she was rewarded by Mrs Felton telling Mr Felton next day, for her part she could see nothing in that Mrs Lacere, who talked 'just like anybody else. In her opinion, Lady Hilda Hicks was worth fifty of her.'

The gentlemen by this time were dropping in slowly, and Lady Hilda, having got hold of a great traveller, was gravely asking him what he thought of the British Lion?

"'I prefer the African," he replied, both question and answer being Greek to the old lady who was waiting for pearls and diamonds and emeralds to drop from the mouths of Mr Felton's guests.

It was at this moment Lady Hilda, whose eyes were everywhere and on everyone, saw a glance pass between Glen and her husband, which told her a certain grave-looking individual was Mr Lacere. Leaving the distinguished traveller, of whom she had already wearied, and who felt extremely glad to be rid of her, she sidled round to this new object of her curiosity, to whom, without the slightest preface, she remarked:

'Your wife is a wonderful woman.'

Mr Lacere only bowed in reply, but as he bowed he smiled.

'Humph!' thought Lady Hilda, 'spoony on her still.' And though her own literary career had been one long glorification of women, and a series of essays on the general hatefulness of men, illustrated by examples drawn from personal experience, she yet felt so angry at this unexpected folly on the part of Glen's husband that she would have liked to slap Mr Lacere on the instant.

'For there is something in him,' she decided, 'and there's nothing in his stupid idiot of a wife.'

'You must be very proud,' went on Lady Hilda sweetly, 'of what she has done.'

'I am more proud of what she is,' he answered; and then he let his eyes rove off again in search of Glen, who this time, her attention being otherwise engaged, was not looking at him.

'Good heavens! what a simpleton a wise man may be!' considered Mr Hicks's widow; and she was proceeding to say some pleasant things about Mrs Lacere's 'extraordinary book,' when Mr Felton, making his way across to where she stood, hoped her ladyship would kindly 'sing them a song.'

'One comfort,' answered Lady Hilda, 'if I do, nobody will listen.' And she walked off to the piano, taking Mr Lacere for her escort, and asking him as they went if his wife played and sang, and whether it was true that he wrote many parts of her books, and wondering he had not been afraid to marry such a clever creature, – 'because,' she added, 'I know as a rule men detest clever women' – and begging him to say what he would like her to sing, and stating, *sotto voce*, she felt it would be like lifting up her voice in the Zoological Gardens. And then at last she began a simple little ballad, into which she flung such taste and feeling and soul, a dead silence fell on the room, and there was an involuntary movement towards the vocalist.

'And now I'll sing you something merry after that!' exclaimed her versatile ladyship; and striking a few chords, she broke into a catching, mocking little German song, which made her audience laugh without exactly understanding why, and caused Mr Felton to applaud so loudly, and call for an encore with such vehemence, that, under cover of the noise. Glen managed to get beside her husband and suggest they should steal away as soon as possible. They were in the hall and bidding good night to the hostess, whom they encountered there, ere Mr Felton missed them. When he did, however, he was on their track in a moment.

'You're not going yet!' he exclaimed. 'Why, the evening's scarce begun. Last week there were a lot of fellows here, and when they got down to the station they found there was no train till seven o'clock in the morning. So they came back again, and we sat up all night and had a jolly time of it.'

Mr Lacere, at this juncture, stated very positively he did not intend to miss the next train or to sit up all night and, laughing, Glen shook hands with Mr Felton, who followed her to the door, exclaiming:

'Now, are you sure you have enjoyed yourself? – have you had a good time? – did you have everything you wanted? Lacere, do take a glass of brandy – do, before you go out into the night air! And you'll come again, won't you? We don't profess to know what's what; but if our friends will only say what they would like – Well, if you must go – good night, good night! and thank you for coming.'

Mrs Lacere could not have told anyone what it was about this address that touched and somehow seemed to hurt her; but when she got out under the stars, she could not see them for a mist of tears, and she felt she was very sorry for Lance Felton, and that, so far as she herself was concerned, she wished – ah! most heartily! – she had never turned out of the Strand that evening and walked up Burleigh Street, and passed through the office of Felton and Laplash into a new world!

The next afternoon she had an appointment to see Mr Felton, and discuss some business arrangements. According to custom, the principal in the firm was not alone – Mr Kelly chanced on that occasion to be the welcome visitor, and to him Lance was pouring out an account of the delights of the previous evening – reciting the names of the celebrities that had been present – recounting the episode of Mrs Gossage, who left them in the lurch 'for linen, silver, and manners: not but what we did very well without all!' – and giving Barney a rapid sketch of the doings and sayings of the company.

'That's what she wants, you know,' proceeded Mr Felton, referring to Glen, who did not dare to look at her former travelling-companion, as Lance took up his parable. 'It will do her all the good in the world to see a little of life, and mix in society, and know what's going on amongst her fellow-creatures. We were never intended for hermits; and for a writer in particular to lock the door against everybody is the greatest mistake possible. New ideas – new ideas are the things, Kelly; what do you say?'

'That I hope Mrs Lacere will not abandon her old ideas till she is very sure the new are better. If she takes my advice she will stay quietly at home, and leave general society to those who do not need time for thought, or leisure in which to produce original books.'

'There's a compliment wrapped up somewhere in that sentence, if we could only find it,' observed Mr Felton, a little puzzled.

'There's a warning, at any rate,' said Barney. 'I hope I have not offended you, Mrs Lacere.'

'No – oh no!' she answered; and then their eyes met, and Glen knew she and Mr Kelly did not differ greatly in opinion concerning the demerits of the clique with which, against her better judgment, she had become associated.

And so Time, which never stops, went on very rapidly, and Mrs Logan-Lacere, who had once lived the quietest of lives, got acquainted with many sorts and conditions of men, and found herself, as Mr Lance Felton felicitously expressed the matter, 'before she knew where she was, in the full swing of general Society.'

Chapter VII

MR FELTON CRITICISES

'I CANNOT IMAGINE, Kelly, how it is you get so near nature, and yet never manage to touch it.'

This agreeable speech was, of course, made by Mr Felton, and the matter under criticism chanced, unhappily, to be that novel which Barney had fondly believed would prove, in comparison to all other modern novels, as 'wine unto water.'

He had kept the manuscript by him (compulsorily), if not quite for seven, at least for a good many years; and during the whole of that time his greatest pleasure was to correct and rewrite a work he considered only required a pushing publisher to make a mark in literature not likely soon to be obliterated. It was a book constructed, as he fondly believed, on quite new principles, combining the advantages while avoiding the faults of every style of narrative which had yet appeared.

It possessed all the merits of Godwin's play as slyly enumerated by Charles Lamb, and fell quite as flat. It was 'too clever, too rich, too full of plums, too refined, too epigrammatic; its sarcasm was too delicate – its humour too subtle – to find favour with a public whose taste had been vitiated by a course of modern fiction,' said Mr Kelly's friends.

'It's heavy as lead,' was the shorter commentary passed upon it by the Felton clique; while the 'outside barbarians' – the subscribers to Mudie's – sent the book back as if the plague were in it.

'A dead failure,' was Mr Felton's summing up of the matter. 'Well, there is nobody to blame but myself;' for he had, in spite of Mr Kelly's coy protests, and shy 'I don't really think it will suit you,' insisted on publishing the novel – which certainly did not owe its ill-success to any want of advertising, pushing, or puffing. Preliminary paragraphs in the literary papers hinted that a rich treat was in store for the readers of fiction; that such a book as that advertised by Messrs Felton and Laplash, the work of Mr Kelly, the well-known essayist, had not been produced since the days of Fielding.

Lance himself had blown its trumpet till listeners were almost fain to stop their ears; and now the three volumes were to be had at the libraries for the asking, nobody wanted them. The worst novel of the season went better than Barney's masterpiece, which he had been improving and expanding and curtailing and interleaving for years, which was, in fact, an epitome of his Hibernian and London experiences – a treasury full of all the good stories he had heard – a mine of wisdom – a storehouse of knowledge – dramatic, pathetic, sensational, objective, subjective, and Heaven only knows what besides. Barney had felt going over the proof-sheets a labour of love. The printing, the paper, the binding, were all matters of anxiety and solicitude to him. No title, he fondly believed, ever before looked so well in an advertisement. He read all, and indeed wrote many, of the preliminary puffs, and believed everything they stated; and this was the end – a dead failure and Mr Felton's criticisms!

Ignoring that pleasing remark concerning his inability to draw from life as beneath contempt, Mr Kelly stated his willingness to repay his publishers any loss they might have sustained through the book. It was a proposition with which the junior, or 'silent' partner, as Glen called him, would have closed on the spot, but Mr Felton pooh-poohed the idea, as if he had the Bank of England at his back.

'That's not the way we do things here,' he said. 'If we make a good bargain, we take the profit; if we make a bad one, we put up with the loss. We'll pull through your deficit over Mrs Lacere's book – now, there's nature if you like!'

'We can't all be Mrs Laceres,' remarked Barney, with a fine irony perfectly thrown away upon Mr Felton, who answered:

'No, faith! – I only wish you could. In that case publishing would be more of a moneymaking game than it is. By Jove! I didn't think she could have beaten *Heron's Nest*, but she has. There's go – there's sparkle – there's wit – there's life. I declare, when I was reading over that book in proof I had often to stop and ask myself, "Can a woman have written this? How the deuce does she come to know all about these things?" And such a woman, too – skim-milk and colourless, and still bread-and-buttery, as Lady Hilda says. To quote Hicks, "You would swear she had passed her whole life mending stockings and reading tracts, and cutting out flannel petticoats for Dorcas societies."'

As he paced the London pavements that day after leaving Burleigh Street, Mr Kelly thought more about Mrs Lacere than he had ever done before. Always he felt a certain, though possibly unconscious, antipathy to her. From their first meeting on board the Morecambe boat, she failed utterly to attract him in any way – quite the reverse. 'Has beens,' to repeat a remark made in a very early chapter, possessed no charm for the then unfledged Barney. The class from which he had sprung, and the class to which he aspired, seemed tangible and intelligible; but people who were going down in the world, instead of struggling up the social ladder, seemed to Mr Kelly's common-sense, anomalies that had no business on the earth at all. And now the shabbily-dressed young girl, grown into womanhood, presented herself as a rival in the field of literature – further, it was impossible for him to guess what she might not have said concerning her travelling-companion on that gloomy October day!

He had always entertained his doubts about her. When they met at Mr Vassett's he marvelled whether she would remember and repeat that slip of his concerning the English nation and his Satanic Majesty; but from no sign or word of either the Craven Street publisher or Mr Pierson could he conjecture she ever mentioned him at all. Still, when Mr Felton got hold of her, a deeper anxiety took possession of Barney's mind.

From fifty little trifles he knew, whatever else she lacked – and, according to Mr Felton, outside her books she was deficient in most things – Mrs Lacere did not fail in the faculty of observation. Was it likely, therefore, she had omitted to photograph him in her memory as he once had been – raw, gauche, practically utterly ignorant of the manners and habits of good society, and clad, moreover, in a brown coat made by the Callinacoan tailor – the very memory of which made Mr Kelly's blood tingle as he recalled the figure he must have presented in it.

When he met Glen on that memorable evening at Burleigh Street, something in her weary look, the indecision of her manner, her 'senseless loyalty,' as Mr Felton said, to Mr Vassett, the reluctance with which she went to make hay surely any other woman on earth would have eagerly sprung to stack, inspired him with a certain chivalrous sympathy and conviction she had never confided to anyone the circumstances of their first meeting; but, without knowing Lady Hilda's expressed opinion, he had long been coming round to the idea that still waters do flow deep.

'She's a deuce of a "take off," I'm sure,' confided Mr Laplash once, in a special burst of irritation against the successful authoress. 'She may think I'm blind and deaf, but I can both hear and see. She scarcely ever opens her lips without a sort of sneer.'

'But what is there to sneer at?'

'Ah! you mightn't find anything, because you haven't much sense of humour, as it's called;' Barney stood rigid with indignation – he who believed his own perception of the ridiculous to be the finest and most prominent trait in his literary character! 'but others know what she is after. There's Noll, now, he can't bear her; and for all he is so pious and quiet, he is able to read character well.'

It was of these things and many more Mr Kelly thought as he bent his steps to New Oxford Street. He had declined Mr Felton's eager offer of the Lacere new book, on the ground that he had little time for reading. Nevertheless, he was going straight to Mudie's to get the novel so disgustingly be-praised, and find out if he could what made it sell, while his own much better work hung fire.

That evening, and the next morning, he devoted to Mrs Lacere's lengthy three volumes. When he came to the last page, he smiled – not pleasantly.

Very shortly after, there appeared in a then-noted journal a savage attack on the work of 'a greatly over-rated author.' This review was written by Barney, and many were the guesses – all erroneous – made as to the personality of the reviewer. If Barney's own book had been heavy, the same fault certainly could not be found with his critique. It was airy and amusing. He used the whip judiciously, and touched up every raw nerve to be found in the author's style. He ridiculed the passages other reviewers had praised; he was severe on grammatical mistakes, on erroneous quotations; he extolled the productions of other novelists in order that he might the better contrast their excellences with Mrs Lacere's defects; he said the book lacked consistency, probability, and interest; that her villains were impossible, and her virtuous characters tame and mawkish; that she wrote concerning a state of society of which she knew nothing; and, that in effect, she placed her heroes and heroines in a world the like of which no eye had ever beheld, and no mind would ever be able to understand.

In Burleigh Street this review fell with the force of a thunderbolt. It was the first really bad notice Glen had met with since she 'made her name.' Coming from the source it did, the review made a great impression, and one that was unfavourable to the author. People felt ashamed to have admired passages they were now told were only calculated to cause wonder and mirth in cultivated minds; to have been touched by pathos, they were credibly informed could not be considered other than utter bathos; to have been amused by poor and twaddling anecdotes, and to have considered a story wonderfully original, the plot of which the reviewer conclusively proved had been taken bodily from one of the trashiest novels ever issued by the Minerva Press.

The number of persons who called in at Burleigh Street to ask Mr Felton if he had seen the review in the *Independent* was astonishing.

'You have got a jolly slating at last,' said Lance to Mrs Lacere, who laughed till Mr Laplash observed it was no laughing matter – for them, at least.

'Well, Mrs Lacere,' exclaimed some of the Burleigh Street loungers, 'and what do you say to the notice of your book in the *Independent*?'

'Oh! I don't mind,' she answered. 'I suppose the person who wrote it has to earn his living as I have, and it must be far easier to write a bad notice than a good one.'

'I am so sorry,' said Mrs Kelly to her husband, 'to see that shockingly ill-natured criticism on Mrs Lacere's book in the *Independent*. I consider it absolutely cruel to write about a lady in that bitter way. In my opinion it is most unmanly.'

Barney looked up from the *Times*, which he was reading, and answered, 'I dare say the review will make the book sell all the better; and as to the lack of chivalry about the notice, when women choose to enter the lists with men they must not complain if they occasionally get hurt – sex is neither recognised nor respected in criticism.'

'Well, I do not think the review fair, and Mrs Lacere is really so nice it makes the matter far worse. As I told you, I was introduced to her last night, and when we were talking about your novel, she said, "She thought the heroine the sweetest female character she had ever met with in fiction;" it was such delightful praise.' And Mrs Kelly bridled a little, and toyed with her toast, and looked conscious as sweet seventeen might have done; while Barney, his eyes only that instant opened to the truth, thought, in utter astonishment, 'Why, she imagines she sat for the portrait! Good heavens!'

'Who was with Mrs Lacere?' he asked aloud.

'Her husband; quiet, gentlemanly, but to my fancy somewhat reserved and cold. He took me down to supper, and I happened incidentally to mention Mrs Lacere's pretty compliment to your novel.

'"Yes," he said, "my wife is charmed with the book."

'"Have you read it?" I inquired.

'"No," he replied. "Unfortunately, I have little time to spare now for reading of any kind."

'"But no doubt," I suggested, "you have pored over every line Mrs Lacere has written."

'He actually smiled as he answered, "I am sorry I have not even read all her books."'

'Sensible man,' commented Barney.

'My dear, I call it horrid. Fancy my saying I had not read *your* books – fancy missing a single word you ever wrote! And then, besides, she really is very clever. I assured him she possessed great talent, and he said, "Yes, he thought so too," but quietly, without the slightest enthusiasm, as if he had been remarking that it was a fine night.'

'Really, it is quite a comfort to hear Mr Lacere is so discreet a person. His wife living in such an atmosphere of flattery out of doors, he does right to teach her she is not regarded quite as a prophet at home.'

'But surely you think she is clever – for a woman?' asked Mrs Kelly.

'I think she is clever, decidedly,' he answered, 'and she has made a certain mark in the world; but she is going the fair way to lose all the advantage she has gained. She ought to stop at home and write her books and mind her house, and see her husband's slippers are warmed, instead of going about to parties and listening to foolish compliments, and frittering away such talents as God has given her in small-talk and company babble.'

'How you talk, Bernard! Would you permit a woman to have no mental relaxation in bright society? No –'

'My dear,' he interrupted, 'circumstances alter cases. That which is quite proper for you is improper for Mrs Lacere. Her husband has no private means, and is only in a modest way of business. She had not any fortune, and though she may have made some considerable sum by her writings, you must remember when she ceases to write she will cease to make money. All this modern business of society making lions of authors, and authoresses rushing frantically into society, is a complete mistake. Not so did the great men, whose names will live as long as the English language is spoken, conduct themselves. Routs, and balls, and dinners three hours long, and garden-parties, knew them not. To the outside public they were only known by their works. Now the outside public is so constantly given the opportunity of seeing men who are thought great, at play, that it will soon begin to doubt if they ever do any work at all.'

'That is very true, no doubt,' answered Mrs Kelly; 'but still Mrs Lacere is a woman, and it is only natural, poor thing, she should like to visit, and hear people praising her books, and –'

'Well, all I mean to say,' interrupted Barney, who had no desire for the Lacere question to haunt him even at breakfast, 'is, Mrs Lacere cannot have her cake and eat it too. To turn to another subject. I have determined to start a review of my own, conducted on new and equitable principles. It seems to me there is an opening for a really good critical paper, written by men who have not got into a groove, and do not belong to a clique. I shall call it the *Dragon*, and think it will prove a great success. What do you think?'

'Why, of course, Bernard, if you commence a review it *must* be successful. The idea strikes me as delightful. I wonder it has never occurred to you before.'

'It has often,' replied Barney: 'but I did not see my way till lately.'

'Shall you have Mrs Lacere on the staff?' asked Mrs Kelly; and her tone warned the fortunate husband that if he was not careful fifty little green-eyed monsters might rise to trouble his domestic peace.

'Not a woman,' he answered emphatically – 'maid, wife, or widow – shall write a line for it. As deep-sea fishermen object to push off with a parson on board, so I should feel my venture doomed to shipwreck if a lady were one of the "hands." No,' he added, 'except yourself, no woman shall have a say in the matter. My review will be the sainted isle, and I – Senanus.'

'Ah! but remember,' said Mrs Kelly, 'Moore's song implies that if the lady had waited till there was light enough for the saint to see her, she had never left the isle.'

'I can solemnly assure you no lady shall get the chance of seeing me in my double capacity of proprietor and editor,' observed Barney, smiling.

'To hear you speak about my sex,' exclaimed Mrs Kelly, 'anyone might think you were most unhappy in your matrimonial relations.'

'It is because I am so happy,' returned Barney gallantly; 'I feel I must have made the one lucky draw out of the bag of snakes.'

'Oh! fie, fie!' said Mrs Kelly rebukingly; but she was delighted nevertheless, and would still go on praising Glen for her talent, and the 'delicate compliment' about Barney's heroine, and pitying her concerning that wretched review in the *Independent*, without any stalking figure of jealousy casting its shadow before.

Chapter VIII

A GREAT WINDFALL

IT IS NOT GIVEN to many men to pass one whole year into which no pecuniary trouble enters, and yet it was just such a reprieve Glen had brought her husband.

Never before – never – in all his struggling youth and his hardworked manhood could he remember such a time of blissful ease and prosperity. It was only too good, too free from anxiety; but Mr Lacere's was not a temperament to question concerning the blessings Heaven sent him. He could only thank God, not aloud – not for the world to hear – but silently, sincerely, amazedly, for the relief compassed for him by the only woman he had ever loved.

It astonished him. He felt it was impossible he could sufficiently prove the gratitude he felt to her and his Maker. Prosperity flowed in upon him like a tide. The seed he had sown was bearing fruit; the business he had made and watched and tended had grown big enough to shelter him and his household. Looking back, he could scarcely believe that in so comparatively short a time it had been possible to build up such a trade. Money! it came in that year like water; and though it may have been spent as freely, it was honestly, if not judiciously, spent in paying old debts, in still extending his trade, and in adapting the household to changed conditions and altered circumstances.

For him it was the first year of plenty since he had taken the cares of manhood on his young shoulders, and the Almighty alone knew what the burden of the nearly three times seven barren years preceding must have proved. Years of labour;

years of hope deferred; years during the course of which what he made was wrested from him almost ere he could count his winnings; years the light of love had not brightened or friendship strengthened. The life of a horse in a mill it might have seemed to some, and yet it was a beautiful life in its total self-abnegation, in its utter unselfishness – its toil for those who were most ungrateful, but who seemed to him, viewed through the glamour of a deluded affection, possessed of all virtues.

The pleasure of conferring kindnesses, of being able to feed, clothe, and house the members of his family, had ever seemed to this man worth all the work, anxiety, and toil the burden entailed; and now, when he was easy as regarded money matters – happy in his home and his wife – it seemed to him as though he were floating in a dream down a golden river towards a golden sea.

What a year that was in which every day might have been marked with a white pebble! If only Glen would have liked and understood his relations, he felt life could hold nothing more to ask for; but she never had liked, and he was convinced never understood them, and the change wrought by success in his circumstances of necessity produced an apparent estrangement between him and his family, which he strove by every means in his power to prove was wrought by no alteration in his feeling for them.

To him, success in business meant an increase of work which might well have appalled a different man; but he never complained. The close of the long day never found him fagged, or cross, or weary; no matter how late he went to rest, he was always astir early. What! should he idle now, when, for the first time, fortune seemed tired of persecuting – when everything was going well with him and his?

A whole year without sickness, or sorrow, or loss, or anxiety! A year, during which Time's footsteps, shod with velvet, slipped so swiftly and silently by, it was gone ere half its blessedness was felt or comprehended – gone like a radiant summer, which has scarcely served to warm hearts chilled and numbed by the snows and frosts of winter before the autumn leaves are falling and the moaning wind is singing their requiem. During the year, opportunities such as had never before come in his way presented themselves; offers were made – agencies pressed upon him. But, believing that by entering on any fresh undertaking he would be unable to devote all his energies to the old, he held blindly on, strong in the faith that he had established a trade which would eventually make him practically independent of the world.

His cousin also had ceased to be a drag upon his resources. He was at length established in a business which promised solvency and respectability. Everything was going well. To such a temper happiness can never come 'too late;' indeed, to one who, without any pretence, or ostentation, or outward and visible signs of his inward belief, save what may be gathered from his life, walks silently on earth with God – that phrase, 'Too late,' is one utterly destitute of meaning. Though she had been brought up in the straitest sect of the Pharisees, Glen, by comparison with her husband, was an outer heathen. Her life in those days could be regarded but as a long unrest.

'She does not know what she wants,' said Lady Hilda, freely discussing Mrs Lacere amongst her friends. 'Success has turned her brain; and if Mr Lacere were other than the most devoted of husbands, he would not have patience with her.'

Making all allowance for the fact that Lady Hilda herself was a woman and a novelist, it must be confessed there was too much truth in her summary of Mrs Lacere. The outer world might and did think that lady pleasant and agreeable; but, nevertheless, success had somewhat 'turned her brain,' and she persisted in refusing to listen to the 'still, small voice' of common-sense which kept for ever crying to her in those days: 'You are mad. Glen. Was it for *this* you had such a chance given you as does not fall to the lot of one woman in a million? Look back to the humble home and the modest aspirations of your girlhood, and say whether you believe your present life is fitting or unfitting you for the career in which you have already achieved a success as astonishing to yourself as to those who never thought there was much in you.'

Often in the middle of the whirl of society in which she had no right to live, Ned Beattie's words, long forgotten, recurred to her: 'I only hope he won't let you get your head.' She had 'got her head' now with a vengeance, and was going a pace which could not by any possibility last.

Well, there was this much to be said in her excuse – her early youth had never known gaiety. With her temperament, with her nationality, she must have been more than human to turn her back to the lights and the music and the glamour of Society – to sit apart whilst others were dancing, to seclude herself from praise, which was to her the very breath of life – to decline invitations such as anyone might have felt gratified to receive – to thrust back proffered friendship and pleasant acquaintanceship, and to say in that time of triumphant hope and – fame, shall we call it? – 'All is vanity.'

Still, most undoubtedly she was wrong, and she knew it; as a man cannot serve two masters, so an author cannot work and play.

She was doing herself no good, morally, physically, or intellectually. She took her pleasure then, but she had to pay for it afterwards. She was spending her strength, her time, her substance, for naught. At the end of a year, what was left for all those wasted hours, in which she ought to have been building up and fortifying her literary reputation, save a confused memory of luxury and perfume, and amazing extravagance, and rich dresses and rare wines and costly food, and the recollection of thousands of strange faces and unfamiliar voices, and the knowledge she had brought no single great thought, or original idea, or high aspiration out of the turmoil?

But she did not pause either to reflect or repent while leading a life which left her no time for quiet thought. As she imagined, she had almost touched the highest peak of fame to which she could ever hope to climb. Sought after, flattered, caressed, made much of – ah me! – did there come no moment when she dared to ask herself what the end would prove? Even in dreams was no warning vouchsafed of the hour when for her the lamps would be extinguished and the flowers fade and perish, and the sound of music be heard no more, and the footsteps of the dancers be silent – when she should know in all its bitterness what it is to be forgotten – understand the applause she had delighted in was not Fame, and, proclaiming her name and what she had done, receive for answer, '*We never even heard of you*'?

She had read of such things happening to other people, but for her, of course, they could have no application. When the woods are green and the banks bright with blossoms, who realises the coming time when the trees will stand brown and bare, and not even a daisy appear to gladden the eyes of the weary wayfarer? When the prima donna stands half buried in bouquets, listening to the wild applause of a delighted audience, does it ever occur to her that the fate which has befallen others may yet prove hers, and that she will in the future be hissed off the boards now deemed honoured by her tread? In like manner Glenarva Lacere, then able almost to command her own prices, could not foretell that evil days were coming when she should be able to command no price at all.

Yet she ought to have known. The three warnings given by Death were never plainer than the signs vouchsafed to Mrs Lacere. If no other human being knew Mr Lance Felton's resources were not exhaustless, she did. By a score of tokens she was perfectly well aware the great business in Burleigh Street was not built upon a rock; further, she should have remembered the period of scarcity during which her husband had been barely able to hold his own, and devoted herself to saving what money she could; improving her mind, laying in fresh stores of knowledge, and strengthening her body, which she was doing her very best to enfeeble.

And yet still she would not listen to the evidence of her own eyes and ears. Plainly almost as a man could speak, Mr Felton told her the harvest authors were then gathering could not last.

'So far I have been going in for fame; after a while I mean to go in for money,' he would say. And again, 'You know I can't afford these prices. It's all very fine having a lot of crack authors on my lists, but I want to see some margin for myself.' Or else, 'You mustn't take these bills to my bankers; they have as much paper as they will stand' – a most ominous declaration, and one certainly not to be explained away by the fact that Mr Felton was not quite sober when he made it.

Mrs Lacere had long previously discovered that 'Lance' was very rarely sober; indeed, so rarely as to be never.

It was over 'the bid' he made her for the two books honourably mentioned to Mr Kelly she arrived at this fact, and also at the other fact likewise patent to Barney, that whatever Mr Felton's physical condition might be, his business faculty never got drunk.

For, sitting on one side of the office-table, and Mrs Lacere on the other, he managed on the occasion in question to knock just six hundred pounds off the sum *Heron's Nest* had expected to receive.

He told her all his struggles, or at least as many of them as he thought would serve his purpose; again said how badly he had been treated by some persons, concerning whose identity he was discreetly reticent, but whom he earnestly longed to 'splash' when he drove past them in the carriage he meant hereafter to set up; he explained that he and Mr Laplash did not 'hit it off' – which, indeed, everyone who entered the office could not fail to see. He was very contemptuous in his references to his partner, whom he described as a 'slow-coach', and even dropped various hints disparaging to saintly 'Noll.'

'Neither of them like you,' he said, with unnecessary frankness. 'But never you mind that; I'm the head man, and I mean to keep the lead, but you must help me. You stick to me, and I'll stick to you. I can't give you what I thought I should be able for those two books; but if you don't hold out for terms now – and you won't get such good terms as I offer anywhere else – when things are a little smoother you won't find me forget you. Don't you believe me? Don't you think I have done well by you? Don't you know I'm your friend?'

The end of it all being that Glen consented to the proposed reduction, and that Mr Felton wished to shake hands over the bargain; but, finding himself unequal to the feat of standing on his legs, wisely abandoned the effort and took refuge in tears. He recited his troubles over again, and said most of his authors were an ungrateful set; that all they wanted was to 'suck a man's blood,' after which they would leave him 'as a spider leaves a dead fly.' He declared he meant to do great things, and that with Glen's help he would do them; that she need not trouble herself about money; that Mrs Lacere would never find cause to repent trusting him.

'I've just got into a bit of a corner,' he went on; 'but that will come all right. My bankers would advance me any sum I wanted – thirty thousand, if need be – but I don't like to ask them; it looks bad, you know – deuced bad. And now you'll get on with your work, won't you? and we'll rattle a book out as soon as ever you can let me have it; and put plenty of life and anecdote and "go" in every chapter, and we'll carry the town by storm yet.'

Which was all very well, and very encouraging; but when the time came for Mr Felton to fulfil his part of the bargain, Mrs Lacere found he did not evince the same alacrity in offering to increase her payment as he had in lowering it.

Quite the contrary, indeed. Not merely did the diplomatic Lance volunteer no suggestion of 'sticking to Mrs Lacere as she had stuck to him,' but he actually remarked that he thought it would be good for her to take a holiday, and give her brain a little rest.

'They say, you know,' he proceeded, 'you've been overdoing it; and then that review in the *Independent* – not that I mind reviews; know too much about who writes them, and where they are written, and why they are written. Still, the public believe in them; and, after all, there was a great deal of truth in that notice. You'd better take care what you are about. Suppose you lie by altogether for a few months. There is no reason why you should always have a novel on the stocks. At any rate, I'm not in a position – I have not the time to go into the matter of a new book from you now.'

And so, professing to be in a great bustle and hurry, having to go to the West to see a 'tremendous swell,' who wanted him to bring out a book of travels, son of the Earl of That, and nephew of the Duke of Something Else, and married to a Russian princess – Mr Felton begged Glen to excuse him, and rushed out of the office, leaving her to confide her sorrows and grievances, if she pleased, to Mr Laplash. But Glen did not please to do this. Following Mr Felton's example, she departed from the office, after exchanging a few words with the two men who 'didn't like her,' wondering greatly. This was the first real check she had met with in Burleigh Street, and she did not like it. She felt she had been badly treated. While writing those two books, she had been urged on by both partners. If life and death had hung on her copy, they could not more earnestly have implored her to supply good 'batches' to the printer. She did not spare herself in the matter. It was real honest work she turned out, even at high-pressure speed; and she finished one book, under the compulsion of incessant entreaty, in so short a time that even Mr Laplash was moved to admiration, and wrote, 'I can say nothing but bless you,' from which the intelligent reader will gather there was indeed urgent need the book should be completed.

And now, when *she* wanted money, to be told to take a holiday! Why, for those two books she had not got more than she hoped, after the success of *Heron's Nest*, to receive for one. She felt she had spent herself in vain. She was dreadfully hurt and mortified and disappointed, and returned home so utterly downhearted, that if her husband had then returned from business, he would not have known what to make of her. But before he returned, a wonderful thing happened – Glen got the great pecuniary windfall of her literary career. It came from an editor, and it came in this wise.

When from any cause the circulation of a magazine, which has once been satisfactory, begins to drop, and goes on dropping till it really seems as if it could not drop much more, proprietors instantly begin to look out for 'names.' As a rule, the aid of authors possessed of names is invoked too late. The greatest physician is powerless to save a patient already moribund, and the writer is not in existence who could resuscitate a journal which has been permitted to sink into dotage. However, the persons connected with a then well-known magazine thought the time had come to spend a great deal of money to prevent the total loss of a larger sum still, and, casting about for suitable authors, they selected as likely resurrectionists the author of *Heron's Nest* and a male writer of great eminence, who had 'not produced too many books,' and who, it was well known, 'carried a large portion of the fashionable world with him.' Both authors were on the Burleigh Street list; to Burleigh Street, as if it were some sort of literary agency, application was made, and it occurred to the astute mind of Mr Lancelot Felton that if he could 'place' a book by Lady Hilda Hilton instead of one by Mrs Lacere, he might make a considerable pecuniary profit.

Had the firm owning the magazine alone been to deal with, Mr Felton would have carried his point. He told them Mrs Lacere was 'knocked up;' that she had done 'such a lot of work,' she wanted to 'have her shoes taken off and to be turned out for a while;' that his advice to her was 'not to write another line for a twelvemonth. Besides which,' he added, 'her books require to be read as a whole; the minute you begin to chop them up into portions, they lose all interest. No, take my word for it. Lady Hilda's your best card. She reads; Lord, how she reads! You'll have all the Westenders waiting for your magazine, wondering who her ladyship's going to "pitch into" next. If I had a journal I would secure her at any price.'

'But isn't she a little   doubtful?' modestly suggested one of the firm. 'The press took exception to her last book, if I remember right, on the score of propriety.'

'As for that, she mightn't exactly satisfy the requirements of the Religious Tract Society or the *Saturday Review*,' returned Lance; 'but for all ordinary people and purposes she's right enough. You be advised by me – that is, if you want to send up your circulation. Run the pair I have chosen; they'll go well in harness – both showy, high stepping, credit to any establishment. Come, now, say Lady Hilda for the second novel, and we'll sign the agreement, and I'll send over the manuscripts.'

'I can't say yes off-hand,' answered the gentleman who had on this occasion come to Burleigh Street, 'but I'll talk the matter over with my partners, and you shall hear from us very shortly.'

'Well?' queried Mr Laplash, lounging into the office when the outer door closed after his visitor.

'It's as good as done.'

'Thank God!' murmured Zack piously.

But ere long Lance found experimentally the truth of that time-worn adage which declares 'there's many a slip 'twixt the cup and the lip,' and Zack, spite of the liberal religious education vouchsafed him by Noll, decided he had uttered his thanksgiving prematurely. Indeed, when the news reached Burleigh Street of 'Lacere' having been 'tampered with' by that blank, blanked editor of that blanked magazine, Mr Laplash felt there was very little left in this world to thank God for.

For, so far from saying she was 'knocked up,' Mrs Lacere declared she would be only too glad to contribute the serial asked for; and to keep the matter in his own hands, and prevent a total loss to Burleigh Street as regarded the second novel required, Mr Felton had to come out with the astounding offer of one thousand pounds for a new work from *Heron's Nest*, all rights to remain with him for the space of three years.

The sunshine of such success might well have dazzled the eyes of a man. As for Glen, it simply blinded her. She did not see how nearly she had missed getting sixpence; she failed to understand she had then reached her pecuniary zenith, and that for many a day afterwards her road would be all downhill.

And in actual life the downhill road is not an easy one, especially when the path nears the valley. Patience, reader! the pace quickens then – towards the last the descent is very rapid!

But it has been said the brilliant sunshine of that enormous success utterly blinded Glenarva Lacere. It is not adversity which is the test of character, but prosperity; and in the hour of her prosperity my heroine forgot the bitter past, and fancied of her own strength she had done this great thing – that for ever, hundreds and thousands of pounds would lie at her feet, only waiting her pleasure to stoop and pick them up! Not for her the calculating wisdom which should stop to count sixpences and shillings – grudge pence to ragged lads who opened a carriage-door for her – shillings to cabmen – gratuities to servants.

Ah, Glen! what a sorry fool you were to give so lavishly to those who could never pay you back! And yet I know not – perhaps you had the return somehow – in the friends who stood by you in time of trouble – in the memory that you had in your day helped the poor and needy; that your charity was indeed without stint; in the knowledge that in your darkest hour God did not leave you comfortless, but taught you moreover that while the day lasts there is work to be done in it; that while life endures there is some one, whether sick or well, rich or poor, sorry or glad, to be made the happier because you were born.

For, after all, what is kindness but a coin?

The great mistake some people make is that they regard it as an investment. They expect it back direct from the borrower with interest; and when they fail to get it, talk of ingratitude.

What an error! Speak a kind word, perform a kindly action, out of the abundant goodness of your heart, instead of the cool calculation of your head, and both are returned, not tomorrow by the recipients, but after many many morrows by some once far-away fellow-creature whom the kindly word has travelled on to touch, or the kindly action benefited in a manner you can never trace, and who thus brings you back your own long-forgotten coin – not indeed with fair interest added, but multiplied a thousandfold!

'We'll advertise you on every hoarding in London,' said one of the partners of the great house, meeting Glen in Burleigh Street, when a solemn interview was appointed to arrange about the title of her new book.

Think of it – only think of it!

Let the reader cast a backward glance along the course of this story to the night when Glenarva Westley traced her future career upon the track of the moonbeams she saw reflected in a moonlit sea, and say if this were not success, what should be required to compass it?

In her very early days of authorship – long before she travelled in company with Mr Bernard Kelly to London – writing in that room which overlooked billows tossing down from the wild Atlantic, Glen in an oft-rejected manuscript asked one of these questions at which publishers and editors, when they saw her, were apt to smile irreverently; namely, 'What is Fame?'

An exceedingly difficult question even for maturity to answer; but Glen, rushing in with the fearless and intemperate ardour which characterises young people as well as fools, at once proceeded to solve the problem for herself. Fame, she declared, was a bubble, a breath, and so forth.

Pity she had not in her hour of triumph looked up some of the old-faded writing, and asked herself if she believed there was a word of truth in the lines traced so carefully in the ink that had turned so brown; and if there were, laid it to heart.

It was about this time Mr Kelly, whose review was now an established success, and a great power in literature, stopped to read one of the huge posters on which Mrs Logan-Lacere's name was placarded in the face of London.

'Humph!' thought Barney, and he proceeded thoughtfully on his way. When he returned home, he sat down and wrote a stinging article, entitled 'Fame and Notoriety.' His contention was that the moment an author came prominently before the public he compassed Notoriety – that the author's work alone was capable of securing Fame.

From out of the treasure house of the past he produced name after name to prove his point. The books of men considered great in their day, he said, were forgotten; while the works of men who had been thought of small account, little regarded by their contemporaries, unknown to fashion, disregarded by society, were, though the men themselves had mouldered into dust, quick and living still.

It was an excellent paper, to which Barney brought all the resources of his extraordinary range of reading – his caustic powers of perception – his epigrammatic style.

The week it appeared, everybody went about asking everybody else: 'Have you read "Fame and Notoriety" in the *Dragon*? Capital, isn't it?'

Mrs Lacere read it, of course, and was not much convinced.

'Those that win may laugh,' she said to Mr Edward Beattie, who, having arrived on a visit to England from Canada, was literally stricken dumb to find what Mrs Lacere had done – the strides she had made – how rich, prosperous, almost fashionable, she had grown!

Ned was taken to parties of all sorts, till he craved piteously for rest.

'My dear Glen,' he remarked, 'it has constantly been dinned into me that women are stronger than men; but I never believed that statement till now. There is no man who could do what you do. Let us stop quietly at home, just for variety.'

And again he said before he left:

'I hope, Glen, you are not spending all your money, but putting something by.'

'I am putting most of it into the business,' she answered.

'And that is all right, I suppose?'

'Oh yes,' she said easily; though, indeed, she knew as little about how the business was going, as of what she was spending.

Chapter IX

BOUND TO COME

'WELL, KELLY, I hope you approve of your portrait in the *Wasp*?'

Though still early in the forenoon, Mr Felton, who put the foregoing question, had evidently already partaken of what he called a 'pick-up,' and Barney accordingly scarcely knew how to take his inquiry.

'I have not seen it,' he answered.

'Ah! then you have a treat in store. There were half a dozen copies lying about the office, but they've all been carried off. Noll, just run round the corner and see if you can get one.'

'I wouldn't, Lance, if I was you,' expostulated Noll, resorting to his favourite formula; while Zack, with a saturnine grin, muttered it was 'too bad;' adding, upon his conscience, 'Lance was a good sort of fellow to help a lame dog over a style.'

'It's something not very complimentary then, I presume,' said Mr Kelly, who felt these various remarks did not augur a flattering likeness.

'Oh! that's just as you choose to take it,' answered Lance airily, 'but perhaps you won't be able to get a copy. I know the paper is selling as fast as it can be machined.'

'I'd better try to secure one then, before the proprietors stop printing,' suggested Barney ironically, for it was well known the sale of the *Wasp* was not equal to its merits.

'All right; I'm sure you'll be pleased,' was Mr Felton's comforting remark, as he beheld Mr Kelly depart. 'He'll not let grass grow under his feet, I warrant,' added the publisher, speaking to his partner and the ever-present Noll, whereupon the three laughed in concert.

'I wish there had been a copy here,' said Mr Laplash; 'I'd have given a sovereign to see his face when he saw the "young man in his native bogs".'

"Oh! the wife's the thing,' exclaimed Mr Felton.

'It is a shame, though,' remarked Noll; 'I don't think such personal matters should be permitted.'

'Why, hang it, man!' cried Lance, 'The *Wasp*'s no more personal than the *Dragon*. What are you dreaming about?'

Meanwhile Barney was speeding along the Strand to get a copy of the paper in which he guessed he was to form the staple of amusement for that week, and as he went he anathematised the whole race of authors, editors, publishers, ay, and even readers. Hitherto matters had gone with him so smoothly! His paper was the great success of the period. Since the *Saturday Review* nothing had appeared which took the public so utterly by storm. 'Kill and spare not' might have been his motto. Wherever there was sin, wherever there was folly, wherever there was even amiable weakness, he went down and slew. About him he had gathered a small but brilliant staff of unknown writers –writers indeed so utterly unknown that they were not merely unfamiliar to the world, but would have been strange to each other had the men happened to meet.

From the early and best days of the *Saturday* Mr Kelly had taken a leaf. The outsiders, the dark horses, he brought in to win. The *Dragon* represented, indeed, a new Cave of Adullam: for 'everyone [with brains] who was in distress, and everyone that was in debt, and everyone that was discontented, gathered themselves unto him, and he was a captain over them.'

Only consider the possible result – capital to pay – a mind to direct – the element of secrecy! From chambers, the occupants of which had never been gladdened with a brief; from parsonages preferment seemed to shun; from men who only looked at the great world afar off, in whose mirrors were not stuck the cards of milord and milady; from 'medical practitioners,' who had sufficient brains to question the wisdom of the great guns of the profession, and could hit off neatly all the humbug of the craft – Barney gathered together his weekly instalments, heretofore without a word being said in his disparagement; but now – good heavens! now what had come? As he rushed on his career he saw at a news vendor's a copy of the *Wasp* prominently displayed.

He went in and bought it. One glance was enough. His enemy had found him. His turn had come, and alas! Mr Bernard Kelly could not face ridicule and criticism with the unmoved front displayed by *Heron's Nest*. To quote Mr Lance Felton, she 'had not winked an eyelid' over the most adverse criticism; but she – she – what was anything Mrs Lacere ever faced in comparison with this awful thing Mr

Kelly carried in his pocket as he ascended the editorial stairs in Paternoster Row?

Mr Kelly's paper was far too strong and too respectable to be illustrated. The *Wasp* was so disreputable that it felt pen and ink weak unless aided by pencil. Conjoined, literature and art might have done anything, had not the manager, moved one night by some singular freak, gone off with everything he could lay hands on, except his wife. He took all the cash, though he did not take her. When he departed, many thousand pounds departed too. Really, the whole affair was touching. To quote Mr Donagh:

'The miscreant proved himself a ruffian of the deepest dye.'

But this catastrophe happened long after the appearance of that awful representation of Barney's career. There he was first in his 'native bogs' – finally in the editorial chair. He saw himself turned out of Sulby Park with fifty pounds in his pocket – arriving, carpet-bag in hand, at the gate of Mat Donagh's house, or, as the letterpress in old English letters described the scene:

'Ye goode yonge mann is receyved by hys frend.'

The brown coat, uncut hair, generally unkempt appearance of Mr Bernard Kelly's earliest London days were reproduced to a nicety. No need of any wizard to tell Barney who had supplied the materials for these sketches. There was but one man in the whole of the metropolis competent to instruct an artist as to the former *personnel* of the now successful editor – Matthew Donagh. He had kept his pebble ready in the sling all these years, and now he slang it with such unerring aim that Barney, social giant though he might be, felt the stone enter his forehead, and strike his pride and vanity to the earth.

At that moment there was murder in Mr Kelly's heart. Had the irrepressible Mat stood before him in the flesh, he could have killed him with pleasure – ay, and have faced the certainty of hanging afterwards.

There was no part of his career in which that wretched print failed to hold him up to ridicule. Receiving his rejected addresses from the hands of supercilious clerks; standing disconsolate in St James's Park; 'liquoring up' with the younger Dawtons; acting with the father of that clever family in *How's Maria?* – the veteran wearing an impossible wig, the traditional hessians, a white waistcoat, and a swallow-tailed coat – no single incident he could have wished forgotten but was recalled to memory. And, worst and cruellest of all, his wife was pressed into the service, and in one deliciously airy illustration was depicted as seated on a sack stuffed full of bank-notes; while Barney, standing before her with hand pressed to his heart watched out of the corner of one eye a group of young girls vanishing in the background, some crying, some laughing as they left him alone with an old hag who bore a terrible likeness to the widow of Robert Underwood, groom.

In the very last scene he was depicted in the editorial chair, haughtily waving away would-be contributors.

He laid down the paper. He could have wept with rage and mortification. He had known no mercy; he had smote hip and thigh. He had spared no man, he had been tender to no woman. Success only rendered him pitiless; and now his enemy had found and taken him by the beard and thrust a spear under his fifth rib, and inflicted a wound which, if not unto death, would never, he knew, heal while life lasted.

Yes; he had better have made terms with Mat.

'Politeness,' observed that gentleman to him on the occasion of their last interview – when Mr Donagh offered his services in the way of 'conciliating advertisers for a mere nominal sum' – 'costs little, and may, upon the whole, be regarded as a remarkably good investment. You, Bernard Kelly, Esquire – ha! it really makes one laugh when one recalls the bogtrotting Barney, of Callinacoan – have been pleased to despise the proffered services of a man who, at least, never forfeited his self-esteem by catering for the lowest tastes of the lowest public and marrying an old woman for the sake of lucre. You have also – as if Matthew Donagh, the descendant of Irish kings, were a dog! – flung me a twenty-pound note in settlement of all claims upon you. I take your twenty-pound note, sir, in settlement; but there is a debt I owe you which shall be paid, never fear. "I wait," is my motto; and I can wait. The doomed hour may be deferred, but it will strike; when it does, remember Matthew Donagh.'

Yes, he had waited, and the hour was striking even then. There was nothing clumsy in the blow; it went straight home. The sketches and the letterpress must have been the work of time and of cool deliberation. Barney writhed as he thought of the shrieks of laughter amidst which the narrative of 'Ye Goode Yonge Mann's Progress toe Successe' must have been written, and the way in which his wife's peculiarities were noted, possibly at some party where she thought she was exciting admiration.

If tearing his hair out by the roots could have done him any good, he would have torn it; if thrashing Donagh within an inch of his life could have remedied the evil, Mat had earned no commissions for many a month to come; if law, or money, or courage, or diplomacy could have availed to remedy the evil, Barney had not been heart-broken. But he was wise enouch to know his best chance lay in laughing the matter off; and it is not easy to laugh when a man's soul is wrung by ridicule, when he fails to see any fun in caricature, when he feels he has not on earth a real friend who will be sorry for his downfall.

Curiously enough, there recurred to him at that moment the image of Glenarva, as in her poor second-best attire she sat opposite to him in the railway carriage. He had not been generous to her – would she be delighted with this attack?

He did not think it. He had heard enough, at all events, of Mr Lacere to know he would feel indignant at the introduction of a woman's name in such a connection.

The blame of men like Messrs Felton and Laplash is the truest praise; and he felt sure that even if Glen, like most of her sex, lacked chivalry, she could not have been the wife of so true a man without at all events acquiring some of that lore which does not seem to benefit its possessor much here, but which, perhaps for that very reason, we may fain hope will prove of inestimable use hereafter.

'She could not help learning some good from her father and husband,' he considered; 'I wish I had not been so hard upon her, and yet she wanted a lesson.'

So had he, for that matter; but now it was given he did not feel grateful.

Supposing his wife saw the *Wasp*. Good heavens! She was so quick, that even without any friendly instruction she would understand the whole story at a glance. It was most unlikely she should chance to see the paper, but still, to guard against contingencies, Mr Kelly felt he had better at once take her out of town. Nevertheless, he hesitated; and, hesitating, he turned over the leaves of the *Wasp*.

Then, what was the first thing that met his eye, under the heading 'Literature'! A sweet likeness of Mrs Lacere, looking prettier than any human being had ever beheld her, handing in a manuscript, labelled with the name of the journal to which she was contributing. A minute previously his heart had felt softened towards *Heron's Nest*, but now, with a muttered curse, he closed the page, and feeling it better he should be seen out that day, walked westward.

'For those money-bags and the girls vanishing in the distance would play the very deuce,' he considered; as, indeed, when he got home he found they had played. Some devoted friend, not to be behind-hand when a good work was in progress, had kindly sent Mrs Kelly the *Wasp*, with the objectionable article marked; the consequence being an attack of hysterics, the doctor, retirement to her own room, and a scene with Barney, the details of which he never cared subsequently to recall.

Mr Matthew Donagh had waited to some purpose, but his laugh cost him first and last a larger sum than he could possibly have anticipated.

After all, revenge is not a cheap luxury, more particularly when a man who has to earn his living pits himself against a person pecuniarily independent of the world. There came a day when he wanted to 'borrow' five shillings from Barney, and did not succeed in the endeavour.

'You'd better have let him alone, Mat dear,' said Miss Cavan; 'ye know well enough there never was a Kelly yet but could sting like a nettle.'

It was about this time Mrs Lacere began to understand Mr Felton was in some difficulty. He had always been somewhat communicative to her about his troubles, and she now gathered, from the constant repetition of a remark to the effect that 'money was tight, deuced tight,' the publisher found pecuniary pressure uncomfortable. On his table he kept a basket of unpaid accounts, which seemed to grow fuller and fuller.

'I never look at one of them,' he said frankly, 'till I have the cash to pay, and then I just take the first that turns up or is asked for.'

'It is a great trouble examining and adding up bills,' sighed Glen, whose arithmetical acquirements were no greater than those usually possessed by her sex.

'It is such a trouble it would never pay me to do either one or the other,' retorted Lance. 'Time is far too precious to be wasted in totting up pence and halfpence.'

Mrs Lacere did not say anything, but she thought a great deal. Like most persons incapable of wrestling successfully with figures, she had immense faith in 'keeping accounts.'

'I wonder how in the world he manages his business,' she marvelled – a wonder which was not decreased by a subsequent statement of Mr Felton's to the effect that 'his bankbook told him how much money he received, and he knew his creditors would take precious good care to tell him how much he owed.'

Nevertheless, spite of the extreme simplicity of his bookkeeping arrangements, Lance was certainly beginning to find the shoe pinch, and, so far as she was able, Glen felt sorry for him.

Just about that period she often felt as though her brain refused to answer to the calls she made upon it – as though there were some closed door between her thoughts and the power which enabled her to give expression to them. She was not ill – oh no! not in the least. Nevertheless, she could not but be conscious now and then of a curious cloud which seemed to envelop her understanding. Words slipped away from memory; ideas, if not instantly written down, were difficult to reproduce; unless she took her mind firmly in hand, and shook it, she failed to arouse the faculty of attention. She suffered from a continual headache, not severe, but strange; if she tried to recall the events of yesterday, they seemed to loom upon her from a distance through a fog. How then was she to see that there was something amiss with her husband? Poring over her own work, which now occupied her about three times as long as it ought to have done, how could she be expected to take note of his work and his hours, when days full of labour were becoming blank to her?

All this time she looked well and seemed strong. No one, not even Mr Lacere, suspected there was anything wrong with her health.

Curiously enough, Mr Kelly was the first person who noticed how exceedingly strange Mrs Lacere was looking. At the special request of Mr Felton, she had driven over to a party, 'likely,' in Lance's phrase, 'to do her good.'

Afterwards, Glen could not have told for a certainty whether she entered the room in the ordinary way, or on her head. The lights seemed dim, the cloud grew darker, her disinclination to talk increased – it was an effort to her to speak the few words she uttered – the Society conversation appeared to her meaningless.

One great reviewer said he never recollected to have seen a bouquet so exquisitely arranged as that she carried, and, in a sort of dream, Glen remembered she had walked through the greenhouse, and culled and arranged the blossoms for herself. A noted editor asked if she could contribute some papers, and begged her to appoint a time for an interview; but afterwards she could not recollect what she said in answer, and knew if she had met him in the street she would have failed to recognise his features.

She heard great singers – singing as if they stood afar off; women and men she knew were all around her, yet they did not seem near. Suddenly there came upon her a yearning desire to get away from it all, to rid herself of the sound of voices; and pushing aside a curtain, she found herself in a little anteroom, which chanced at that moment to be quite empty. It was cooler there. Through a second door leading into the hall there came every now and then a rush of fresh night air, and with a sigh of relief, Glen dropped into an easy-chair beside the table, and tried to gather together her wandering wits.

'These long distances and hot rooms do not suit me,' she considered dreamily. 'I wish I had not come;' and in a feeble, purposeless sort of fashion she was wondering how she could best retire from the scene, when someone just at her elbow asked:

'Are you not well, Mrs Lacere?'

Lifting her eyes, she beheld Mr Kelly.

'Quite well, thank you, but tired.'

'Then why on earth don't you go home?'

'That is precisely what I am thinking,' she answered; and then, ceasing to fan herself, with a weary gesture she leaned her head back, while her glance roamed over the pattern of the carpet, as though it held the solution of the enigma.

Barney looked at her doubtfully.

'May I speak a few very plain words to you?' he asked.

'If you like.'

'Why do you drag about to these places? Why do you let Felton persuade you to accept invitations I am sure you would much rather refuse? You are killing your-self; and what is perhaps of more consequence, you are killing such genius as God gave you. In Heaven's name – when you find no pleasure in society, and it is impossible to look in your face and imagine you do – why don't you stay at home and write your books, or else rest body and mind, that you may write better hereafter?'

'I am sure I don't know,' she answered, a little surprised at the force and blunt-ness of his address. 'People say it is better not to shut one's self up, but to mix with the world.'

'People say!' he repeated contemptuously 'who are the people that talk such nonsense? Idle people, foolish people, rich people, strong people.'

'I come under the second category, I suppose,' she smiled.

'If I said I thought you were wise, I should be more polite than truthful,' he replied, smiling too. 'But seriously, Mrs Lacere, is it not a pity for you to allow yourself to be led so far out of the direct road by that mere abstraction "they say?" When you can't write any more, do you suppose Society will settle a fixed income

379

on you? When your health is broken, will it find a physician able to cure?'

'But why,' demanded Glen, recovering her spirits a little, and, under the surprise of this unexpected attack, rallying her scattered energies to do battle against the immaculate Barney, 'should visiting – and I now visit very little – unfit me for writing? Why should an hour or two of social intercourse ruin my health? Others go out night after night and day after day – why not I? Others find mixing with their fellows stimulate their energies and give them fresh ideas. What is there so exceptional in my organisation that where others lead I may not follow?'

'Have you a headache?' asked Barney, instead of replying to this series of questions. As she spoke he noticed she passed her hand across her brow, a habit which had latterly become involuntary.

'I have always a headache,' she answered pettishly; 'but that is of no consequence. Tell me why I alone should stay at home while all the rest of the world goes gadding?'

'I could give you some very good reasons, Mrs Lacere,' said Barney, 'but this is neither the time nor place for stating them. Let me instead get you something to eat; you look quite worn out.'

'Thank you; I do not want anything, except to get home. I wonder what the time is.'

'I dare say your coachman is somewhere about the house. Shall I tell him you wish to leave?'

'Oh, if you would!' exclaimed Glen. And the mist seemed to close around her once more, and the cloud to come nearer and nearer; for the short-lived excitement had died out, like a ray of winter sunshine, leaving all things darker than before.

'I will explain matters to our hostess,' said Barney, as he handed Mrs Lacere to her carriage, 'and we will resume our discussion on some future occasion.'

But it so chanced the discussion was never resumed. For a short time Glen fought bravely against the mist which stupefied and the cloud that blinded her; but there came at length a morning when she was forced to return to bed and stop there. Then after a few days she got up and set to work turning out copy once more. She could not go on, however; hand and head both refused their office.

It is but a step from Fame to Failure – as it is sometimes, according to medical testimony, but the 'sixteenth of an inch' from life to death.

The same hoardings, the same blank walls which had been placarded with the bills announcing in huge letters: 'New Novel, by the author of *Heron's Nest*,' now told all the world and his wife that 'in consequence of Mrs Lacere's dangerous illness her new serial *was suspended*.'

'I knew it must come,' said Mr Kelly to Mr Vassett; 'I felt as certain she would break down as I do that Felton will go smash.'

Chapter X

WHAT HAPPENED

MR FELTON WAS one of those persons concerning whom it is eminently unsafe to venture prophecies. While Glen was lying in enforced idleness looking with a great horror death straight in the face, and Mr Kelly in confidential talk with Mr Vassett expressing his conviction that the Burleigh Street bubble would soon burst, Lance, on his own account and quite independent of Mr Laplash, was negotiating for the purchase of one of the largest publishing businesses in London. His intentions were as simple as his bookkeeping. He meant to leave 'Zack' in Burleigh Street, and to take all his best authors with him. All 'trumpery pecuniary details' he left to the consideration of those who were going to find the wherewithal for the great experiment. Whether Mr Laplash was pleased or angry seemed to him a matter of indifference.

'If you think,' he said, 'I am going to be hampered in a big concern, as I have been in a little, with your petty notions, you are very much mistaken.'

'But you can't throw me over in a minute this way,' cried his partner, almost weeping.

'No; but I'll just get rid of you as soon as ever I can,' retorted Lance.

'Remember whose money it was started the firm.'

'Pooh!' said Mr Felton, 'what is the good of talking about that, when you know when we started we had but eight pounds ten between us?'

'And eight pounds five of that was mine.'

'And all the brains mine,' added Lance.

'Come, now, I wouldn't, if I were you, either of you,' suggested Mr Butterby, thinking the period had arrived when he might put in his oar with advantage. 'Least said about that, by either of you, soonest mended. I don't hold with bounce and lies and that sort of thing, but still there is no need to tell the whole of your affairs in the street. Don't fret yourself, Zack; if an equitable arrangement is come to, you'll be far safer and more comfortable here doing a quiet little profitable trade by yourself; and as for Lance, let him take his great swells and big authors, and much good may they do him!'

'There's one thing I'll not take, I'll swear!' exclaimed Lance, pale with passion – 'and that's you; and if I catch you hanging about the other office as you have been hanging about this, I'll give you in charge, that's all.'

'Only hark to him!' said Noll, with saintly composure. 'There's gratitude! Who'd think he owes everything he possesses on earth to me?'

'I owe nothing to you,' shouted Lance, in rejoinder, 'except a debt I'll take precious good care to pay you in meal or in malt. D— your impudence! Do you think I'm such a simpleton as not to know you thought to use me as a tool – that you imagined I was so hard up that I'd go touching my hat to you for the chance of earning a few shillings a week? You never meant me to get on – never. You'd have kept my nose to the grindstone for the term of my natural life, if you'd had your way. And where would you have been but for me, I'd like to know? Where would you have got your roomy house at Peckham, and that terrace up at Kentish Town, and the freehold cottages out Molesey way? Faith, if every rogue had his deserts, you'd be living rent free in a plainer and more substantial residence than Garden Villa, and have to put up with more frugal fare than you sit down to now.'

'I wouldn't. Lance,' said Mr Butterby, who had with blanched face kept turning his head round during the progress of this remarkable address to see if anyone entered the outer office, while Mr Laplash averted his countenance to hide the smile with which he could not help greeting Lance's utterances. 'Now I wouldn't really, if I were you.'

'If you don't quit that parrot-cry I'll brain you!' declared Mr Felton; and as he laid his hand on the inkstand he looked so exceedingly like carrying his threat into execution without waiting for further provocation, that 'more in sorrow than in anger,' Mr Butterby sauntered out of the office and into the street.

'If you can't keep him from drink he'll cut all our throats one of these days,' observed Noll to Laplash, when subsequently talking the interview over with him whereupon Mr Laplash, with a mighty oath, affirmed he didn't care whose throat Lance cut as long as he'd give him (Zack) a share in the new business.

'Now don't you take to swearing also,' remonstrated Mr Butterby; 'it's a wrong, and a foolish, and an – an unnecessary habit,' finished Noll, who, in addition to his other accomplishments, being an open-air preacher, sometimes indulged in a little redundance of expression.

'It may be,' said Mr Laplash, 'but I fancy if you'd much to do with Lance, you would find ordinary language quite incapable of conveying your feelings. To think, after how I've worked, that I should be pitched over in this fashion!' and he relieved his overcharged heart by uttering another malediction, which caused Noll to shake his sleek head in horror.

As Mr Felton knew money belonging to other people would have to pay for the privilege of 'securing' Mrs Lacere for the new business, it goes almost without saying that overtures were in due time made to Glen for a new book.

Still ill, still finding the completion of the novel already in hand a weary labour, Mr Felton's pet novelist did not greet the prospect of getting hard to work again with that delight he could have wished to see.

'Come,' he urged, 'you must not give way, you know. What will become of us all if you are laid on the shelf? You ought to have been guided by me, and not undertaken this serial; and I am beginning to think Kelly's right, and a quiet life is the thing to suit a woman who goes in for your line of writing. I don't mean to say this last thing is not very good, and has not taken, for if I did, I should be stating an untruth; but still it is not you. Now, sit down and write me a book like *Ash Tree* or *Due East*, and we'll not quarrel about terms.'

It had come to this. After all the trouble and turmoil and hurry, the mad haste to turn out copy, and the wild and expensive chase after fresh ideas and new pastures, she was asked to return to the modest plan and simple style which had won her early success, and out of the solid, if apparently unattractive materials of old, build up a story which, by its utter absence of all art, should again rivet the public, and inspire the eager interest and keen curiosity of old.

'Mr Felton might as well tell me to go back and be a girl again,' thought Glen; but she had either learnt enough wisdom not to contradict the publisher's fancy, or else felt too tired to argue the matter with him. So she agreed to do all she could to produce a satisfactory work, mentioning at the same time it was impossible for her to commence anything fresh till she got strong again.

'But now you've turned your corner you will soon be strong,' he said eagerly; 'and don't let yourself down and think you are worse than you are. Look at me. Bless you, if I was to begin to consider finger-aches and not feeling up to the mark, and the rest of it, I might never show in Burleigh Street at all. Get away for a few weeks. Take your writing with you. Why, down in some quiet place by the sea you ought to get a lot of inspiration. Margate, now – that's not very quiet, to be sure; but you needn't ever feel dull there. It's all nonsense your moping about home. Tell your maid to put up your things and start off – that's the plan; and if you want money, let Lacere come up to me. I dare say between us we'll manage enough to pay your lodging. Very likely I'll take a run down and see how you are getting on myself.'

With which cheering assurance Mr Felton took his leave.

In all her life there had never been a time when Mrs Lacere felt less inclined to 'go somewhere for a change.' She had lain still and looked at death; in the watches of the night she had reviewed her life, and found small satisfaction in the retrospect. This was her first pause in the race since that evening when she turned her steps toward Burleigh Street, and she was as reluctant now to enter the course again as she had been then to wend her way back to Mr Vassett to ask him for the manuscript of *Heron's Nest*.

What better was she for all the prizes she had won – all the money she had earned – all the people she had seen – all the flattery, all the praise which once seemed so sweet?

How much better – nay, rather, how much worse! If no one knew the fact, Glen was fully aware she had not done herself justice, that she owned higher capabilities than, so far as it now seemed, the world was ever likely to wot of.

The old, old story over again – acting in haste, repenting at leisure! What a good thing she might have made of life for herself and other people if she had only been wise, she thought, as night after night she lay watching with tired eyes for the grey dawn of another weary day; and now life seemed over. Even if she got better, she felt there was little worth living for. As Ned Beattie would have said plainly, she wanted something to cry for; and it was not long ere that something came. So far, events had moved but slowly; now they followed swift one on the heels of another.

'Don't you think it strange,' she said to her husband on a certain night, nearly three weeks after the day when she promised to write a book as nearly on the old pattern as she could, 'that Mr Felton does not send on the agreement! He seemed in such haste when he was here, and I never remember his being so long in what he calls "clinching" an affair before.'

'He has been ill,' answered Mr Lacere, after an almost imperceptible pause.

'Ill? When did you hear?'

'Today – this evening. Just before I left town.'

'What has been the matter?'

'I don't know.'

'Is he better?'

'Yes – no – the truth is, Glen –'

'What is the truth, dear? Why don't you go on? Is there any danger?' And then, without waiting for an answer, she cried out, 'He is dead!' and sat silent – stunned.

'Are you sure?' she inquired at last.

'Quite. I went down to Burleigh Street to inquire. Poor fellow! with all his faults, there was a great deal of good about him.'

'What a dreadful thing!' said Glen, still almost stupefied.

'I did not intend to tell you anything about it tonight,' said Mr Lacere.

'I am thankful you did,' she declared. 'It would have been terrible to hear me going on talking about the agreement when you know he could never send it. Do you remember how often he used to say he would not live long?'

'It is the unexpected which always happens,' commented Barney, when he heard the news. 'I certainly did not think this was what would occur,' and so in all manner of ways the changes were rung throughout London on Lance Felton's death. Even before the man was buried, the literary world seemed to proceed much on its way as usual. He did not appear to be missed by a certain set, as might have been expected. Save that he was not to be seen there, things in Burleigh Street went on apparently as heretofore. The postman delivered letters, which Mr Laplash opened; people paid money, which Mr Laplash banked; collectors called for books, and got them, just as though the busy brain which had built up so astonishing a business was not at rest. Noll lounged in and out as formerly. Except that Mr Laplash now sat in Lance's special armchair, and devoted himself to correspondence, and saw authors, and answered questions as one having authority, there was nothing to show the mainspring of the concern was broken, that Lancelot Felton would never again make a bargain, or crow over other publishers, or blow a trumpet about his 'big' authors, or thrust his subscription list under Mr Vassett's unwilling nose, or point to the long string of good names in the *Athenœum*, which had filled the souls of 'slow-going old coaches' with envy and dismay.

It had been a short life, but in reality not a merry one. The steam was always at high pressure; but perhaps nobody, save Mr Felton himself, knew the cargo of care he carried adown the stream with such apparent ease and jauntiness, and at such an express speed.

In a word, Lancelot Felton having, as his partner expressed the matter, died of 'drought' (there were those who said his sudden exit was due to quite an opposite cause), Mr Laplash remained, so far as pecuniary matters permitted, master of the position. He inaugurated his reign by serving writs on all those authors who were not 'up to time' with their manuscripts. 'Lance had made advances and received no equivalent,' so the new head of the firm stated, 'and he was determined to put things on a different footing' – which, indeed, he very soon did.

The process was simple, but effectual. He drove away almost every writer of reputation, and he found himself the possessor of a number of perhaps the worst manuscripts which were ever at one time showered in upon a publisher.

As it is not easy to procure good 'copy,' even if all the conditions for producing it are favourable, the quality turned out under pressure of a writ may be imagined.

Nevertheless, it was copy capable of being printed, with a good name on the title-page; and Mr Laplash, having thus 'got in his debts' and 'weeded' his lists, turned his attention to doing what he called a safe trade. He began this safe trade by cutting down authors' prices, and economising in advertising. When he published a work by a known writer, he trusted to the name of the writer selling the edition.

It was a suicidal policy for himself, and one which would have been death to authors had they stayed long enough with the Burleigh Street Solomon to be killed by this novel treatment; but, as a rule, they were sufficiently wise speedily to betake themselves elsewhere.

For a while Mr Laplash garnered golden grain. He reaped that which others had planted; his barns were full to overflowing; he felt jubilant; he extolled his own tactics, and regarded the wisdom of all the great publishers as folly.

But a day came when he perceived there was not much of a harvest ripening for him. Little seed had been cast into the ground since Lance Felton's death, and he could now count the stalks of wheat in his field, so few were they. Then he and 'Noll' laid their heads together, and initiated the plan since successfully followed by so many 'strictly conscientious' firms, of making amateurs pay for their whistle.

'Why shouldn't they?' said Mr Butterby. 'If a man wants to learn a trade, he has to pay a premium.'

Which was all very well, only in his zeal for his friend's interest Mr Butterby forgot that the wealth of Rothschild could not confer genius or even talent. And if he had remembered this, it would not have much mattered, since it was rather pecuniary profit to Mr Laplash than success to would-be authors which was desired.

Be very sure that in Burleigh Street the bitter pill was smothered in jam instead of being thrust nakedly before the sight in the honest practical way wherewith Mr Vassett still chills the enthusiasm of rising genius.

'If you want a brougham,' he observes, with a candour that is not cruel, though it may seem so, 'you have to pay for it. If you wish to appear in print, you must find the money. I fail to see sufficient merit in your manuscript to justify my spending capital upon it; and, indeed, to be quite candid, I should prefer you to take your novel elsewhere.'

Which was exactly what 'rising genius' did, though now, judging from the many, many failures in the book trade, 'lords and ladies, widows and orphans, clergymen and others,' are beginning to pause ere sending cheques or handing over their careful savings, their little all, to any Dick, Tom, or Harry who chooses to add the magic word 'publisher' after his name.

The glamour of success with which Mr Felton had invested his firm still enveloped Burleigh Street, and it proved no difficult matter to change the whole order of things, and get authors willing to pay for having their books brought out instead of being paid for writing them. Mr Laplash felt delighted.

'Ah!' he said to Mr Butterby, whom he liked to have hanging about his office, on the same principle that a devotee believes in the efficacy of any relic which once belonged to some sinful old saint, 'if poor Lance had only thought less of his authors and more of himself, he might have been living now, and a rich man, too.'

Mr Butterby shook his head, as if in grave and mournful assent; but he thought had Lance's brains been of no better quality than his partner's there would have been no business to talk of, and no authors worth mentioning.

'Felton had some appreciation of literature', observed one irate individual, in whose breast that invitation of 'Victoria by the grace of God' was still rankling, 'but this fellow is a mere tradesman. He looks on a book as a baker would on a roll.'

'No, he doesn't,' answered a friend, 'for a baker would like his roll to be of a good quality, and it is perfectly immaterial to Laplash what the book is, so long as it puts money in his pocket.'

Mr Felton's authors felt very sore indeed at the doings of the new potentate, and quoted in a bitter and satirical way the words of Rehoboam, and applied the retort of the Children of Israel to Mr Laplash, most of them at the same time leaving Burleigh Street.

But Mr Laplash did not care. He said he was very glad to get rid of them, that the firm had 'lost lots of money' over their books; and that for his part, from the first he entered an earnest though unavailing protest against the ridiculous sums paid for 'mere names.'

'Well, that was how Felton made the business, at any rate,' remarked Mr Kelly, who felt somewhat indignant at the sudden change of policy, and the mud so freely thrown on Lance's memory.

'Humph! a nice business,' grunted Mr Laplash.

'You ought not to disparage it, at any rate,' urged Barney. 'You had your share of the profits, no doubt.'

'There never were any profits.'

'Well, then, your share of the "debts,"' retorted the other.

Mr Laplash stared at him for a moment. Before turning on his heel he said shortly, and with a sort of snarl:

'I don't know what you mean.'

The sole partner was now a great man. People toadied and tried to propitiate him. He was asked out to dinner and to fashionable parties. If little Miss Green wanted to add to her income, she asked her dear aunt or cousin, Lady So-and-So, to show Mr Laplash some attention; and Mr Laplash, laughing at them all in his sleeve, was good enough to accept their attentions, and tell in his 'delightfully brusque way' the sums of money his firm had paid authors, and the 'great hit' such and such books had been. Then the family resources were tried, and little Miss Green paid down a given amount, and forthwith expected to make her fortune.

Anybody might have thought in those days literature was a lottery in which there were no blanks, so eagerly did people flock to take tickets for fame in Burleigh Street.

Intoxicated by the rush of moneyed amateurs knocking, with lordly cheques in their hands, at the door of his temple, Mr Laplash suffered himself to become captious and somewhat insolent to the unfortunate persons he 'employed' who expected money for 'their work'. It was necessary to keep a few good names on his lists in order to 'draw' amateurs, but he took care to 'teach them their true position' and 'take down their notions of their own importance'.

'Things ain't as they used to be,' he was wont to say. 'Authors will never get what they did again. There are such a deuce of a lot of you, the market's spoiled. A publisher can't bring out more than a certain number of books;' and then he would offer some ridiculous sum, finishing off with the civil remark:

'I never read one of you. I don't know whether your book is good or bad. I only know that you'll sell – that is all concerns me.'

In a moment of forgetfulness he said something of this sort to Mr Kelly, who answered, he thought authors had better turn their attention to some way of earning an honest penny.

'I am sure I wish most of them would,' replied Mr Laplash, lounging easily down the outer office after Barney: 'as for your matter, I am willing to give you what I said, though I don't know if I shall ever see my money back again.'

'You are very kind, I am sure', replied the author, in a white heat of rage, which quite escaped Mr Laplash's observation, as he proceeded to ask in a friendly way:

'How's your old woman?'

'*Sir!*' said Barney.

'How's your *young* woman, then?' persisted Mr Laplash, who regarded this mode of asking after a wife as a delightful pleasantry.

Mr Kelly did not answer. Without speaking a word, he strode out into the street, Mr Laplash staring after his retreating figure in amazement.

'You've gone and done it this time,' observed Mr Butterby. 'I told you before I wouldn't, if I was you.'

Next day a messenger arrived with Mr Kelly's compliments, and he should be obliged by the return of his manuscript. Now it happened that Mr Laplash did not want to quarrel with the great man, so 'Noll' was despatched as a dove of peace, bearing any number of olive-leaves with him. But Mr Kelly would have none of them.

'I blame myself greatly,' he said, 'for having ever endured for a moment the rude buffoonery of your office.'

'Not my office, if you please,' amended Mr Butterby.

'You found the capital to start it.'

'Certainly not.'

'Certainly yes; but not out of your own money,' retorted Barney.

'Your words are actionable, sir.'

'Commence an action, then.'

But Mr Butterby did not commence an action. He thought over matters, and decided for the future to deprive Burleigh Street of the pleasure of his society.

'I am not going to come here for a long time,' he declared.

'All right,' retorted Mr Laplash. 'I dare say I can manage my own affairs for myself.'

'Kelly said Lance was a very courtier in comparison to you.'

'Glad Lance's manners pleased His Highness.'

'Before I go I'll give you a bit of advice. Mind what you're about with Mrs Lacere. If she goes you'll never get such another horse in the Burleigh Street stable.'

'Much obliged; only she'll not go.'

'Oh! she won't, won't she?'

'No,' retorted Mr Laplash, 'and it is no business of yours why.'

Chapter XI

EVIL DAYS

IN COMMON WITH OTHER AUTHORS, more or less known than herself, Glen had, after Mr Felton's death, suffered a curtailment in her prices, which, after a time, began to affect her seriously.

At first Mr Laplash exhibited a considerable amount of diplomacy in his management.

When he came to look into affairs he found them, so he told her, in such a confounded mess he could not afford to give her within two hundred pounds of the amount named by his late partner.

She submitted to that reduction, so losing her first and best chance of resistance.

Then her husband was taken ill, and Mr Laplash said, 'she had been so long out of the market, her next book would take ever so much more advertising, and he really could not afford to give her above five hundred pounds.'

Glen said nothing, but she thought a great deal.

Mr Lacere had been very ill, consequently about the same time two facts began to dawn upon her mind – namely, that the 'big business' had gone, and that her own large income was going.

The great house down in the provinces, after biding its time, decided on sending one of its junior partners round the world to enlarge his mind. Concurrently with that enlargement all shipping orders ceased, and thenceforward not one single cheque worth having came to Mr Logan-Lacere.

Yet the large firm might have left him the small home and continental fish, to catch which he had advertised so long, angled so sedulously, and spent so much time and money. But no – Europe out of England, and England out of London, vanished simultaneously.

London was still left, but London alone could not possibly pay; further, at this crisis Mr Lacere's cousin's excellent business collapsed. Of course, Mr Lacere was once again involved in the failure of his relation, and after that the downfall of Mordaunt Logan-Lacere became a mere question of time.

It took about as many months to compass his destruction as it has taken minutes to exhibit the tactics of the great firm. There was the usual long-drawn-out torture, then the fierce fight, the mad attempt to stave off the inevitable.

After that, ruin, utter and complete, without a penny wherewith to commence a fresh fight; while everyone said, 'Oh! Mrs Lacere, able as you are to make a large income, you'll be so *much* better without business of any kind.'

Then, as if failure and bankruptcy meant a sort of jubilee, invitations poured in, and the Laceres, had they been made of the stuff out of which genteel paupers are moulded, might have lodged and boarded for a year free of cost. The world – their social world – was good to them beyond telling; the world – his business world – was cruel to Mr Logan-Lacere as Mr Laplash to Glen.

'Your wife's income must pay your debts,' said his creditors.

'You are not selling as you did. People are beginning to say you'll have to mind what you're about,' said Mr Laplash; so if ever there was a literary woman who paced the London pavements in a fine frenzy of despair, that woman was Glenarva Logan-Lacere.

Further, Mr Laplash's manners, never, even in Glen's most prosperous days, remarkable for respect or appreciation, now dropped into such easy familiarity, that Lance's 'crack author' felt at times almost beside herself with indignation. It would only have made matters worse to show she was offended further. Glen knew perfectly well her first serious quarrel with Mr Laplash would be their last. Till she should be prepared to leave him as a publisher, she bit back the words that often sprang to her lips, answering only by silence or some cutting retort, the full meaning of which Mr Laplash apparently did not wish to comprehend.

Sitting with his hat on (in which Mrs Lacere once asked him if he slept), this light among modern publishers would greet her with – 'How's Mordaunt? Got any work yet?' or, 'I can't speak to you today. Look in tomorrow;' or, 'You're a nice sort of young woman. Where's the rest of that manuscript?' or, 'I had your note, but it's of no use asking me for any money – we ain't got none here;' or, 'That last reprint of yours was a bad business for me, I wish it had been at the --- before I ever was such a fool as to take it;' and all the time while he was insulting her position, and depreciating her work, and grinding her down to the last penny, he was, as she found out afterwards, making a good income from her books, and finding her, as Mr Butterby truly said, 'the best steed in his stable.'

Which, from a literary point of view, was perhaps not saying much, for the Laplash stable was fast growing to be synonymous with a knacker's yard. To be quite fair, however, there was this much in Mr Laplash's favour – he had never liked Mrs Lacere or her books. So far as he possessed any literary taste whatever, it inclined to the 'penny dreadful' style of novel. He believed she had been totally overpaid in his partner's lifetime, and he felt it a true labour of love to recoup himself a portion of what she had over-received from the firm. Further, he did not know how he hurt her. Glen came of a race that could bear any amount of pain and make no sign, and she was not going to show him how his words cut into her heart, and the lash of his tongue touched the most sensitive part of her nature.

Burdened with the burdens of old, crushed to the earth with new burdens such as even a man might have found hard to carry, still Glenarva's soul would have rejoiced in her labour had one single appreciative word rewarded her endeavours.

Beyond anything, she was an honest worker. Not for the morning's meal or the day's bread could she have turned out a potboiler. Circumstances might be against her, the conditions of her life unfavourable for producing good copy, but the books she sent Mr Laplash were the best she had ever written. They were poorly paid; they were accepted with apparent reluctance; yet had any man offered her ten thousand pounds for her manuscript, she could have given him nothing better then.

In return, Mr Laplash flouted and disparaged her novels, sent barely half a dozen to the reviewers, advertised them at last scarce at all.

'He's killing your books,' said one who was behind the scenes.

Mr Laplash was doing worse. He was killing her powers. Taking such genius as she possessed by the throat, he had simply commenced to strangle it, and ere long would have done so, but that there came a time when matters between him and Glen arrived at a climax.

She had gone to Burleigh Street to ask for money – no uncommon petition, unhappily. On the occasion in question it was needed to avert impending legal proceedings, and Mrs Lacere was silly enough to tell Mr Laplash the fact. In total silence Mr Laplash heard all she had to say; then he answered that if she would come to his office on the next day at the same hour, he should be able to tell her what he could do.

When the next day came, Glen, on calling, found Mr Laplash absent. But he had left a note, which she tore open eagerly, expecting to find the desired cheque enclosed.

Instead of this, she drew out a large sheet of ruled paper, on which appeared something which purported to be a true account of the pecuniary result of her last book. In her long literary experience she had never received such a document before, but she knew enough of business to understand the figures which met her eyes. So much for printing so many copies – a very great number of copies – so much for paper, binding, advertising – the total cost amounting on the one side to a large sum.

On the other, so many copies sold to the trade at – per dozen, thirteen as twelve; so much to author; reviewers, five copies; *left in stock, five hundred copies* – the result being that Mr Laplash represented he was a loser to the extent of twenty-four pounds nine and tenpence halfpenny over the transaction.

As she folded up this extraordinary document, Glen noticed a half-sheet of note-paper, which had dropped from the envelope to the floor.

Feeling nothing more could amaze her, she lifted it, and read:

You will see from the enclosed that you are no such catch after all.

There and then the fortunate author would like to have done battle with Mr Laplash, but she knew enough of his habits to be aware he had gone away to avoid her, and did not mean to return to Burleigh Street that day.

'Tell Mr Laplash,' she said to the clerk, pausing for a moment in the outer office, 'that I shall come here tomorrow at three o'clock, and *wait till I see him*. Do not forget, if you please, to deliver my message.'

The young man was very earnest in his assurances that he would certainly do so.

Glen thought that as he spoke he was struggling to suppress a smile, but if he had laughed in her face she would not have cared.

She knew he had, under the direction of his chief, prepared that precious balance-sheet, and was perfectly aware Mr Laplash did not want to see her; and the tone of her voice was so full of this conviction, that, after he had given his principal Mrs Lacere's message, he added on his own account the information:

'You may as well see her, for she means to have the matter out.'

Accordingly, when next day Glen, true to her appointment, arrived, she was, with that charming absence of undue ceremony which prevailed at Burleigh Street, told, 'You'll find him inside.'

Inside 'she found him' seated, with his hat on, at the familiar table, apparently engrossed in writing a letter. There had been a time when she would have taken a chair without being invited to do so; but now she stood till she should compel his attention.

'Sit down, can't you?' he said at last, still busy with his writing.

Glen sat down, and waited, watching Mr Laplash, and losing herself in a perfect maze of speculation, till, suddenly throwing down his pen, and blotting off the sheet, and thrusting the letter into an envelope, he turned his head half round and said:

'Now, what is it?'

'I will wait till you are quite at leisure,' she suggested.

'I'm as much at leisure now as I'm ever likely to be,' he answered. 'You got my note yesterday?'

'Yes; that is what I have come to talk about.'

'You see just how the thing stands. I thought it better to show you the figures. What can't speak can't lie, you know.'

'I am not so sure of that,' she replied.

'Well, you can examine my books if you like. I can't say fairer than that, can I?'

'I don't want to examine your books,' said Glen. 'I may be very foolish, but I am not so foolish as to fail to know books can be kept to show anything. However, we need not go into that question. What I do wish to know is this. You say you have lost money by my last novel. How does it happen?'

'Why, you don't sell.'

'Why don't I sell?'

'Because, in the first place, you're not what you were.'

'My books are no worse, if that is what you mean; and in the second?'

'People have got sick of that sort of thing. They want something pleasant and genial. None of that cynicism and realism you're so fond of. I really think I might do a little good with a book of yours if you would turn your attention to the subjects novel-readers care about.'

'What do they care about?'

'Now, that just shows your deficiency. As an author, you ought to know. Love and beauty and children, and dress and jewels, and parties and pleasure, and everything coming right at the end, is the sort of novel there's a rush for at Mudie's. You think what I say over, and bring me a genial book with a good plot and a sympathetic heroine, and I'll see what I can do for you.'

Mr Laplash paused, and Glen kept silence for a moment. Then she said:

'And suppose I brought you a genial book with a good plot and a sympathetic heroine – not that at present I exactly understand what a sympathetic heroine is – how much could you offer me for such a triumph of art?'

'Come, don't sneer,' cried Mr Laplash; 'that's an awful fault of yours. What could I offer you? Well, you see how matters are. But I would try to give you half of what you had for your last.'

'And may I ask how you expect me to live?'

'Oh, that's your affair, not mine. You'll never live out of three-volume novels, that's very clear. You'll have to run your stories through the country newspapers; that's what they all do now – Collins, and Braddon, and the rest. And why not you? I've no objection. Then there are the magazines; so long as I've the book in time to publish three months before it finishes in serial form, you may do what you like with it. I'll not stand in your way.' With which generous declaration Mr Laplash took another sheet of paper, and would have commenced writing again, but that Glen stopped him.

'One moment, please,' she said; 'I will not detain you long. Do you recollect when I sold you the book, over which you say you have lost so much, I asked you to try and get me an engagement to run a serial through one of the magazines? There are at least three editors to whom you would have had but to speak to ensure its acceptance.'

'Now you mention it, I do remember your saying something of the kind,' answered Mr Laplash, wisely ignoring the last part of Glen's sentence.

'And when I spoke to you again, and reminded you of your promise – for you did promise – you said you had forgotten.'

'So I had – I have my own affairs to occupy my attention.'

'And the next thing I saw,' proceeded Glen, 'was that Lady Hilda Hicks and Miss Yarlow, and the author you have recently discovered "greater than Thackeray," "more genial than Dickens," were announced as appearing in each of the three magazines.'

'And the same chance was open to you; but you have no push, don't blame me.'

'Mr Laplash, I had not the same chance, and you know it. You can put just what you please into those magazines; as I heard a person say the other day, you are "hand-and-glove" with the proprietors. And as for the other magazines, you are perfectly well aware how I am situated, and how impossible it is for me, with illness in my home, either to wait for engagements or to be running about from office to office.'

'Well, that's no fault of mine. You had your chance. Why didn't you save your money when we were paying you those enormous sums? If you'd been wise you might have now capitalised enough to live on the interest for life.'

'If I had been wise,' retorted Glen, 'I should never have sold a book to your firm after *Heron's Nest*.'

'That's too good,' exclaimed Mr Laplash.

'Offers came to me then,' she went on, 'but I would not take advantage of them. I thought Mr Felton had acted generously by me, and that I would act fairly by him. The same feeling kept me with you; but it was a mistake. You have always been my enemy. God alone knows why, for I do not. But we will end the mistake now –'

'What's the use of all this talk?' he interrupted.

'I have not troubled you with much talk during the eleven years I have known this office, and I shall never trouble you with any talk again.'

'What are you going to do, then?' he asked.

'See if in London there is not a publisher who believes in me,' she answered boldly.

'I wish you luck,' he said. 'Now, look here. You have told me a lot of things today; in reply, I have only one remark to make to you. Novel-writing's not a gold mine, and, if it were, you're not the woman to dig out the gold. I can see very plainly what the result of your career will be. You'll have to apply to the Royal Literary Fund, and then you'll see whether you like their terms better than mine.'

'There is another alternative,' said Glen.

'What's that?'

'The parish,' she answered, 'the mercies of which I should prefer to working any longer for you.'

'Ah! you're angry now,' he said, as she rose; 'you'll be glad enough to come back in a day or two.'

'Shall I? Good evening, Mr Laplash.'

By this time he had fairly got the sheet of paper before him, and was writing away like a maniac.

She looked around the remembered office, and a thousand old associations laid their tender, softening hands upon her.

'I am going, Mr Laplash; good evening,' she repeated – even after what had passed she could not bear to part in malice.

He did not speak in reply; he did not look at the woman who had worked for his firm so hard, and out of whom he had made so much money; but he half lifted his head, and nodded farewell over his shoulder.

She stopped for a moment to speak to the clerk as she passed his desk, then, drawing down her veil, she went out into the gathering night, shaking the dust of Burleigh Street off her feet forever.

Of the months that followed, Glenarva never cared to speak. Safely it may be said, no woman who had climbed to the height where she once stood ever knew a similar experience.

They were months unillumined by success, in which, had she never written a line, she might have fared better. But seven years since she stood almost at the top of the literary tree, and for all the good that fame had done her, she had better have endured failure than scored success. She walked publishing London through – she toiled up flights and flights of stairs – she saw editors – she talked to the principals of great houses – and yet, but for the kindness of two men she had known in more prosperous days, during the course of those months her earnings would have been literally *nil*.

'I don't remember your name,' said one editor to her. 'What have you done?'

'*Ashtree Manor, Due East, Heron's Nest*,' answered Glen glibly enough, looking at her interlocutor by the light of his shaded lamp.

'*I never heard of one of them*,' he said. It was then the iron entered into Glenarva's soul. Rip Van Winkle himself was not so strange after twenty years' absence to the inhabitants of his village, as Glen to the new literary world of London. The children's children had, at least, heard of him; little more than a lustre, during most of which she was hard at work, sufficed to wipe all memory even of her name off public remembrance.

Given sickness in her home; poverty; persons dependent on her who had never even thought of trying to be useful, and an utter impossibility of procuring work – and how, it may be asked, did this once successful author manage to live?

Well, during that awful time she found friends, tradespeople, servants, and landlord different from the stereotyped examples depicted in books. Shoulder to shoulder, friends stood by her; tradesmen had faith, her servants love, the landlord patience. It was only Glen herself who sometimes failed, who thought, 'It is impossible I can ever fight through this;' and yet she did.

What Mr Felton said about her having no 'go' was utterly true. Mr Laplash's remark concerning her want of 'push' could not on the score of truth be quarrelled with; but she had one quality for which few gave her credit – dogged perseverance.

It was this which had carried her through the earlier part of her career; it was this which enabled her day after day to support fresh disappointment and cruel rebuff.

For even where her name was known she met merely with tolerance or scant civility. The days when she could sit down on a flight of stairs and cry were gone and past; but a worse bitterness than that which occasioned those tears now rankled in her heart.

'What have I done, or left undone,' she one day asked her husband, 'to be treated as the worst of impostors?'

'The evil comes from Burleigh Street,' he answered. 'But have patience, dear; the right must win in the end.'

'I do not know,' she said sadly; 'but I feel as if I had lost my position for ever.'

That was precisely what Mr Laplash trusted she would feel knowing; how she was situated, he hoped to starve her out. In his calculation, however, he made one great mistake. She would have preferred to starve to returning to the Burleigh Street servitude. More, she would have done menial work, or begged for those dependent on her, sooner than again take service under the Laplash banner.

'What's become of Mrs Lacere?' inquired Mr Kelly one evening, meeting Lady Hilda at a party. He saw she was heading the Burleigh Street list, and felt sure she must have some knowledge of the Laplash tactics.

'Mrs Lacere!' replied Lady Hilda. 'Oh! don't you know? She's quite used up. Can't write at all; her last books were awful failures. Didn't sell at all.'

'Indeed!' said Barney, interested.

'Yes, and she was dreadfully insolent to Mr Laplash, who acted most kindly to her. I couldn't have believed any woman could have been so ungrateful.'

'And to *such* a benefactor!' observed Barney.

'Yes, he kept her on even at a loss to himself; but at last she made herself so disagreeable he was obliged to get rid of her, and she and her husband now are in absolute want. Serve her right. I went over to see her – just to find out how things were, you know, and you wouldn't believe the impertinence with which she treated me. Said I was an emissary from the Laplash camp – come to spy out the land, and all that sort of thing.'

'And perhaps she was right, Lady Hilda,' hinted Barney; whereupon her ladyship made some remarks about Ireland and the Irish that subsequently did her no good.

'Now,' thought Mr Kelly, 'I'll just find out what the meaning of all this is; and if, as I shrewdly suspect, our friend has been trying to damn the woman, we'll see whether two people can't play at a game.'

He did not care for Mrs Lacere, but, hating Mr Laplash, he determined to wound him through her; and therefore, within a fortnight Burleigh Street and the world which had forgotten Glen were utterly astonished with a long article in the *Dragon* concerning her books.

'Why, here's the author I've been wanting,' cried an editor. 'Where on earth has my memory been!'

Before the day was out, he had called on Mrs Lacere and arranged with her for a serial.

'You'll do your best for me?' he said, as they shook hands at parting.

'I'll do the best I ever did for anyone in my life,' she answered, and she was faithful to her word.

'They are going to pay me in twelve equal instalments,' Glen said to her husband, whom she astonished with her news. 'So we can now take a little place out of town.'

That had for some time past been the dream of husband and wife. So far as he was concerned, he knew that in the busy haunts of men his place had long been filled up, and that the only chance of future work and usefulness lay down in the country; while for Glen, all she wanted was to get away from London for ever, to rest heart and brain and body in some remote region where she had not suffered and spent her strength for nought.

But to do this till the blessed certainty of regular work was ensured would have been utter madness. Even then she felt any residence they took could only be regarded as temporary.

'What we had better do, dear,' she said – for, alas! during that time of serious illness it had become necessary for her to take the helm – 'is to look out a house for the winter in some neighbourhood not too far from London you think you would like. Then when the spring comes we can perhaps find a place to suit us for a permanency.'

So said, so done. A small house was found and taken; just so many things were unpacked as they absolutely wanted; Mr Lacere set himself to get well; Glen bought some manuscript paper, and turned fiercely to work.

She had never been so happy before, never – not in her youngest days – not when hope reigned triumphant – not when fruition succeeded to hope. What though they were poor beyond relief? She had all her husband needed. What though the day's work seemed never ended? It was a work of love, into which Glenarva put her whole strength and soul and spirit. The hunger of her nature was at last satisfied. She had her husband to herself; she was all in all to him, in theory and in fact. Through devious and thorny paths God Almighty was leading her to the peace He alone can give, and at the same time teaching her the worth and truth of the great heart, the patience of which her fitful nature must so often have tried.

It was to outward appearance but a mean, poor house in which the Laceres lived, yet to Glenarva it seemed a palace.

With the outer door closed between themselves and the world and its troubles, husband and wife talked as they had never talked before during all their married life. Through her own suffering she began to understand the story of his; by reason of the strong compression she put on her feelings she at last comprehended the apparent reticence of a nature far nobler and grander than her own.

'Overweighted! undervalued! misunderstood! O God,' she used to think, 'what might my husband not have done with different surroundings!' and she would stand under the starlight with tears streaming down her cheeks, wrung from the divinest compassion a woman's heart can know. For at last she felt fully aware everything in her books the world thought great and true and useful was due to the husband who had never been able to make his mark. Without him she could have done nothing – nothing – and in return she had not half loved him as she ought.

There came a night when, casting herself on her knees, she told him something of what was in her mind.

'Why, my darling!' he said, in amazement, 'my dearest Glen, you are the only blessing I ever knew!'

'Do you mean that? Have I been a blessing?'

So then he told her; he recited his life; he touched on what he had done for others, and how he had been repaid.

'I think I had it in me to achieve something once,' he finished; 'but situated as I was, how could I do much? and besides –'

'Besides what, love?' she asked, twining her arms round him.

'I cannot lament any road which led me to you. Oh, Glen, how could I think any path stony, which in the end gave me such love as yours! You were right and I was wrong,' he added, after a moment; 'but what I did was all, as I thought, for the best. Now those for whom I sacrificed my best years leave me for you. They are right. My day to help anyone is over.'

It was the first cry of pain, loneliness and despair she had ever heard him utter – he, whose life had been spent for others – and she could not answer him for tears.

With her arms clasped round his neck – with her head buried in his bosom – she wept as she had not done since she lost her father. Still, even in sorrow there is infinite happiness, and all through that dreary winter Glenarva was most happy. Save for her husband's health, she did not know a care, except one which would occasionally obtrude:

'Suppose I died!'

This idea she kept for a long time to herself; but at last, when one day she was totally prostrate, she could not (womanlike) restrain its expression.

'Don't go out to meet trouble half-way,' said her husband. 'Have not means hitherto been given to us, and health to you?'

So she wrote on steadily, with a vigour, a determination, and a happy spirit of cheerfulness that it may be her labours had hitherto lacked. Throwing sentiment behind her, together with Mr Laplash's advice, she went on producing chapter after chapter of a book which charmed the public, and delighted those for whom she worked. At first, though greatly marvelling at the chapters she turned out, they only said they were satisfied; but that expression of opinion, when accompanied with regular cash payments, seemed sufficient praise to a woman who had lived for years in the depressing atmosphere of eternal grumbling. All Mr Laplash had found fault with was now accounted a virtue.

Reviewers soon discerned that Mrs Lacere did not profess to write for children and girls, but for men and women. Each month the *Dragon* inserted a long notice of her serial, a marked copy being duly and truly sent to Burleigh Street, as though it were supposed Mr Laplash, who was travelling fast the road that leads to Ruin, still published her works; but of all this Glen knew nothing.

At last she personally was out of all worlds, save that bounded by her small domestic horizon. Except for the daily papers, she knew nothing of how society was going on. The springing grass, the snowdrops peeping above the ground, the sobbing cry and rustling stir of the early springtime, were more to her than the latest literary review or the 'biggest' book on the New Year's lists.

She was happy – oh, how happy! God and herself only knew. If she could but become once more re-established in popular favour – and she thought she could – what a future lay before her – of fame, and peace, and love!

She valued fame merely for the sake of the only man, besides her father, she had ever cared for; she wished for money for nothing save to purchase him the poor luxuries he never even thought of desiring. For years after, Glen could not look at the shop-windows save with a sickening heart. She had wished for this, that, and the other to take to him; when her means sufficed she turned in and bought some article, trifling enough in value, yet such as wrung her very soul to see in the days to come. Self had then no existence for the once somewhat exacting woman. Save as regards work, she had forgotten the meaning of the word.

Yes, she was happy at last, most happy – spite of the mean house, and the sordid surroundings, and the daily labour for such little pay. Shall I leave her thus? No; it would be a most unfinished picture. Let us go on to the end with Glenarva Lacere.

There came a day when, in the pursuit of something connected with her work, walking across the park, she met Mr Kelly. Ever their acquaintance had been of the slightest – so slight, indeed, that feeling at once conscious of her own changed position, and the utter absence of style and fashion in her dress, she would have passed him by had Barney elected to be so treated.

'Why, Mrs Lacere,' he said, 'what an age it is since I have seen you!' and then without more to do he plunged head first into the Laplash question. Glen had not much to say likely to add to his knowledge; nevertheless, it sufficed.

'I suppose you have the ball at your foot again?'

'I am doing my best,' she answered humbly.

'And that best is very good,' he said. 'Indeed, I did not think you had it in you.'

She turned aside, and looked over the railings, for she could not answer him.

'You were very wise,' he went on, 'to leave Laplash. Now I know you will make your way.'

'I never could have made it to any purpose in Burleigh Street,' she laughed.

'No; we all made a mistake in leaving Mr Vassett,' he remarked; and then they walked on together a little way, talking as they went.

Barney made many particular inquiries concerning Mr Lacere, who, Glen said, was gaining strength rapidly. 'He must not try to live in town, though,' she added. 'He has found a place we think of taking – such a tiny dot of a house in the middle of a small farm. He is delighted at the idea of settling down there.' And then she went on to speak of the garden and the fruit trees, and what her husband proposed to do, and the stock he meant to keep; and Barney asked if some day in the summer he might run down and call – 'For I feel quite proud of you as a countrywoman,' he said, which pride must have been of remarkably recent date. But Glen did not think of that – indeed, it is never prudent to analyse compliments or motives too closely.

'Is there anything I can do for you?' he asked at parting.

'You have done a great deal for me,' she replied. 'I was always very fond of being praised; and the worst of an author's life is, one so seldom hears the applause.'

'Though one does the hissing,' said Barney. It was a very proud, happy woman who returned home that day to tell her husband all the pleasant things which had happened to her in town; and the evening's post brought a letter still more delightful than Mr Kelly's encouraging words. It came from her then editor, who stated he thought it but right to tell her the mark her serial was making. 'There were those,' he went on, 'who said, "Mrs Lacere is played out," "Her day is over." "Wait," I answered, "you don't know her staying-powers," and now they see I was right. I have not the slightest hesitation in saying you will do better work than you have ever turned out yet. You have made a gallant fight. Keep up your spirits a little longer. Money must follow fame.'

Oh, with what a light heart Glen rose the next morning to her work! She wrote nearly the whole day, only breaking off occasionally to listen to her husband's remarks about the new residence.

'If the agreement is signed tomorrow, can we move in a week?' he asked. 'I long to be there.'

'Tomorrow, if you like,' she laughed, for she had never known him so eager and anxious about anything before.

Then came the twilight, and the evening closed in and night drew on; and Glen, saying 'There is a passage in this book I want to read you,' sat down beside the table, and turned over the pages in order to find what she wanted.

As she was doing so she heard a slight noise, and looking up, in one moment started to her feet. 'You are not well!' she cried. Lord! what was this? She knew – she knew! Once again Fame had crossed the threshold hand-in-hand with Death!

Where had the hopes and the dreams, so bright and fair but a few minutes previously, departed? They were gone! withered and faded like gathered flowers – the glory of the morning light was shrouded in darkness. She was alone – alone – for evermore. Alone with her dead and God.

Chapter XII

CONCLUSION

THIRTY MONTHS HAD COME AND GONE since that night when Glenarva Lacere was left to make what she could of life alone. How those thirty months were passed it would have been impossible for her to tell, for she did not know herself. When we have fought with some great temptation, battled for our lives against death and disease, struggled to prevent an almost overwhelming grief, killing our reason or destroying our soul – who can analyse that process by which deliverance was compassed and salvation wrought?

All Mrs Lacere ever knew was that the time had somehow passed – that she had worked hard, that she had suffered horribly, and that she thanked God!

One August day in the year which came thirty months after that trouble which changed Glenarva and her life! Ned Beattie crossed Holborn in order to call on his old friend.

But recently arrived in England, his first care had been to ascertain her address and to write a few words of sympathy which touched Glen to her very soul. He had heard of her loss, he said, just on the eve of leaving San Francisco for Australia; he wanted to see her – he would go into Hampshire, where she was living, any day she liked to name.

In reply, she told him she was in London for a short time; and this was how it chanced he was crossing Holborn on his way to Queen Square. How should he find her, after the long, long years – after her struggle, her success, her trouble?

Would the Glen he had known be dead? How would she be dressed? How would she look? What would she say? How would she greet him? Since the morning when he lay on the beach at Ballyshane, with his head resting on her lap, he had been half over the world – made a large fortune; and she – she – He walked twice round the Square before he could make up his mind to knock at the door of the house where she was lodging; the tones of his own voice sounded strange to him as he inquired for Mrs Lacere. A minute after, he was upstairs and standing alone in a large drawingroom. Then, though he could not see her quite distinctly, he knew Glen had entered the apartment, that her hand lay clasped in his, that she was welcoming him back with tears; and the meeting, after long separation, which is sometimes so cruel and terrible, was over.

Now the mist had passed from before his eyes, and he could see her clearly, he did not think her so much changed. She was more like the Glen of his earlier remembrance than she had seemed when last they met. Ere a quarter of an hour was gone he felt as though he had never been away at all – as if they had but resumed the broken conversation of a previous day.

So, after he had crossed the actual mountains and oceans of earth, and she scaled heights of labour and passed through seas of trouble, they resumed the friendly intimacy of their youth, and spoke together freely on all subjects save one.

He tried to get her to speak of her husband, and failed.

As day succeeded to day, and he saw her constantly, she told him all about her home, her life, her books, her interests, her means, her friends, but so far as her sorrow was concerned, she might never have been wife or widow for all the mention she made of it.

'I wish she would talk about him,' thought Ned – but wishing was vain; and at the end of a month, during the course of which no day had passed without his seeing her, this old friend knew just as little of what was in her mind as the hour they first met. She was about returning home.

'And you must come and see my cottage,' she said. 'It is not really very far from London, you know.'

'Yes; you may be very sure I shall come,' he answered; and so they parted. He did not immediately avail himself of her invitation, but at last wrote to say he meant to run down on the following Wednesday, and take the express back to London in the evening. It was late on Thursday when another letter arrived from Ned:

'I hope he is not writing to put off his visit,' thought Glen: but as she read the first few lines the paper dropped from her hands, and with an exclamation of dismay she rose and paced the room. Then she picked up the letter again, and read it to the end.

'He imagined I should not have time to answer it before he came,' she said, going to her writing-table.

Dear, foolish Ned, [she began]

You know you do not want to marry me, and it is very certain I am not going to marry you or anyone else. I write at once, so that our holiday may not be spoiled by any fancied necessity on your part to mar your own life by trying to mend mine. My dear, kind, faithful, generous Ned, I am sorry you have forced me to say this.

Ever your attached old friend,
Glen.

She went over to the station to meet him the next day, and they walked through the woods and winding field-paths to her home. It was a fair, fair home – built on a slight eminence above the Wey, surrounded on three sides by dark, solemn pines; not the home she had once thought to inhabit with another, but a quiet, dreamy place where her bruised heart had found rest, and her tossed spirit peace. There had been a time when she could not bear to look on the face of nature, when the sunshine wrung her soul, and the budding leaves, and the springing grass, and the song of birds, and the ripple of water seemed all so many piercing swords; but that time was past, and her eyes now reflected the calm light of a better and happier world.

In her pleasant house the long French windows opened on to a terrace, beneath which turf, green and velvety, sloped gently to the river's brink. Will Ned Beattie, so long as he lives, ever forget that soft grass, that wealth of flowers, the white curtains swaying in the light breeze, the late roses twining round the pillars of the veranda, the clematis, the myrtles, and the fuchsias she had forced herself to plant and tend at a time when she might have watered them with her tears?

That time was gone, and Glen – his Glen also – Ned felt, as he stood looking upon her; but he loved this Glen better, who had no love to give him in return.

They rowed up the stream, coming back in time for early dinner; and then she showed him her little farmyard, and, side by side, they passed the limits of her small domain.

After that they sat on the grass close by the water, and talked of the old days departed, till Glen could almost feel the air of the hills fanning her forehead and see the waves breaking on the shore. It was a sad, tender afternoon for them both, though no cloud flecked the azure of the sky, and the September sun touched the shafts of the pines with golden light.

'Come in and have some tea, Ned,' she said at last.

'Not yet,' he answered. 'Glen, before I go I must speak to you. I got your note.'

'Yes.'

'And I can't live without you any longer. I don't know how I have lived so long, for I can remember no day since my boyhood in which I have not loved you.'

She looked at him with pitying tenderness as she answered steadily:

'There was but one man in the world for me, and I married him.'

'But, Glen, you are surely not going to live your life here, and alone? Why not be happy yourself, and make me so?'

'I could not make you happy, Ned; and for myself, I am content – utterly. If I could, I would not bring my dead back to life.'

'Oh! Glen – my Glen!'

She laid her hand upon his softly.

'We cannot choose our lot,' she said, 'and we are never happy till we feel it is appointed for us. Mine has been *most* happy.'

'And yet,' he said, with sudden bitterness, 'I remember you telling me once you were *most* unhappy. Do you think there is a word you ever spoke I forgot?'

'I *was* unhappy,' she answered; 'for I did not understand my husband then, or for many an after year. I do not know, indeed, that I ever did till I saw him in sickness and poverty supported by a faith which never failed him – bright with a thankful cheerfulness that adversity never destroyed. When I think of what a life his was – full of toil and trouble, disappointment and failure! He had nothing, Ned – nothing the world accounts of value.'

'He had you!' said Ned hoarsely.

'Yes, he had me,' she agreed dreamily; 'and I am thankful to remember that, though I must have tried that patient heart often, he loved me to the end.'

'You are talking nonsense, Glen!' exclaimed Ned. 'What more could a man desire than such a wife as you? Let me take you away from this lonely place and your morbid thoughts. I do not ask your love now. I only ask you to marry me. I will make you love me in time. I believe if your husband could speak to you now, he would bid you do what I want.'

'Let us end this,' she said sadly. 'I cannot bear much more. It breaks my heart to talk of him or myself. I shall never marry again. Rank could not tempt, or wealth buy, or genius dazzle, or love win me. These are my last words on the subject.'

There was that in her tone and in her expression which killed all hope. It was a dead and broken heart he had tried to warm into life. And Edward Beattie, after one long, steadfast look at the rippling river, rose and went with the woman he had loved so long and hopelessly into the house.

He dreamily accepted a cup of tea, and then, perhaps not sorry to find the minutes had crept on fast while they were talking, said he must be off; he had barely time to catch his train.

'Take the boat across the river,' she advised. 'You will save half a mile and more.'

For a moment he stood on the lawn, in which were beds gorgeous with autumn flowers – stood bareheaded, holding her hand in his.

'Goodbye – goodbye, dear Glen!' he said; and then, stooping, he kissed her for the first time since, boy and girl, they parted on board the Morecambe steamer.

She knew they would never meet again – that the words he had spoken must needs separate them as friends, and she stood, as his hand left hers, watching his retreating figure, feeling almost as though she were looking on one dead.

Without glancing towards her, he pulled across the river, sprang out, and fastened the boat securely; then strode along the field-path till he came to a stile, where his onward road dipped down among some trees.

There he stopped for a moment and looked back. Standing just as he had left her, he saw his brave, lonely Glen, who never for ever might be wife of his.

HE WILL ALWAYS THINK OF HER THUS. When he reads notices of her books, he remembers not a girl in her first youth, among a group of boys, ready to share their maddest sports; not a daughter seated beside a cultured gentleman, striving to read his thoughts; not a struggling woman trying to trace a pencil-mark on the tablets of time; not a wife whose very faults were loved by a husband who adored her; but simply the Glen he knew and would have married – Glen in her trailing black garments, with the sluggish river to her left hand and the darksome pine-woods to the right, with the sun westering behind the spot where she stood calmly waiting, with knowledge, but without fear, for the coming of that night which must preface the dawning of God's Eternal Day.

END OF VOLUME III